W9-BYZ-746

DREAM OF LOVE

Dream of Love

MICHAEL
PHILLIPS

Johnson County Public Library
444 Main Street
Paintsville, KY 41240

TYNDALE HOUSE PUBLISHERS, INC.
CAROL STREAM, ILLINOIS

Visit Tyndale's exciting Web site at www.tyndale.com

TYNDALE and Tyndale's quill logo are registered trademarks of Tyndale House Publishers, Inc.

Dream of Love

Copyright © 2008 by Michael Phillips. All rights reserved.

Cover photograph of battlefield © by Kenneth Garrett/Getty Images. All rights reserved.

Cover photograph of woman copyright © by Dougal Waters/Getty Images. All rights reserved.

Cover photograph of mansion copyright © 2004 by Joe Sohm. All rights reserved.

Interior photograph of battlefield copyright by John Aikins/Corbis. All rights reserved.

Author photograph by John Ward. All rights reserved.

Designed by Beth Sparkman

Scripture quotations are taken from the Holy Bible, King James Version.

This novel is a work of fiction. Names, characters, places, and incidents either are the product of the author's imagination or are used fictitiously. Any resemblance to actual events, locales, organizations, or persons, living or dead, is entirely coincidental and beyond the intent of either the author or the publisher.

Library of Congress Cataloging-in-Publication Data

Phillips, Michael R., date.
   Dreams of Love / Michael Phillips.
      p. cm.—(American dreams ; v. 3)
   ISBN-13: 978-1-4143-0178-5
   ISBN-10: 1-4143-0178-2
   ISBN-13: 978-0-8423-7780-5 (pbk.)
   ISBN-10: 0-8423-7780-8 (pbk.)
     1. Slavery—Fiction. 2. United States—History—Civil War, 1861-1865—Fiction. I. Title.
   PS3566.H492D75 2008
   813'.54—dc22   2007036781

Printed in the United States of America

14   13   12   11   10   09   08
7   6   5   4   3   2   1

Dedication

To those intrepid founders of what was eventually to become the United States of America, whose diverse spiritual roots stemmed from a common source—the desire to live practically the truths of gospel Christianity—and to those among them who dedicated their lives to the principle of freedom and equality between all men.

CONTENTS

The sense I had of the state of the churches brought a weight of distress upon me. The gold to me appeared dim, and the fine gold changed, and though this is the case too generally, yet the sense of it in these parts hath a particular manner borne heavy upon me. It appeared to me that through the prevailing of the spirit of this world the minds of many were brought to an inward desolation, and instead of the spirit of meekness, gentleness, and heavenly wisdom, which are the necessary companions of the true sheep of Christ, a spirit of fierceness and the love of dominion too generally prevailed. From small beginnings in error great buildings by degrees are raised, and from one age to another are more and more strengthened by the general concurrence of the people; and as men obtain reputation by their profession of the truth, their virtues are mentioned as arguments in favor of general error; and those of less note, to justify themselves, say, such and such good men did the like. By what other steps could the people of Judah arise to that height in wickedness as to give just ground for the Prophet Isaiah to declare, in the name of the Lord, "that none calleth for justice, nor any pleadeth for truth" . . .

The prospect of a way being open to the same degeneracy, in some parts of this newly settled land of America, in respect to our conduct towards the negroes, hath deeply bowed my mind . . . These are the people by whose labor the other inhabitants are in a great measure supported, and many of them in the luxuries of life. These are the people who have made no agreement to serve us, and who have not forfeited their liberty that we know of. These are the souls for whom Christ died, and for our conduct towards them we must answer before Him who is no respecter of persons. They who know the only true God, and Jesus Christ whom he hath sent, and are thus acquainted with the merciful, benevolent, gospel spirit, will therein perceive that the indignation of God is kindled against oppression and cruelty, and in beholding the great distress of so numerous a people will find cause for mourning.

JOHN WOOLMAN, C. 1760

Introduction

*P*robably the most frequent question posed to writers is: "Where do you get your ideas?"

As simple as the question seems, I find it a very difficult one. One cannot anticipate *when* or *how* an idea is going to come. Suddenly a lightbulb goes off somewhere in the brain and you think, "What if . . . ?" At least that's how it happens with me, wondering, "Where *is* the garden of Eden?" or, "What *would* a white girl and black girl do if they found themselves orphaned together during the Civil War?" or, "How *did* the first humans migrate to so remote a spot as Scotland, and why?"

The germ for American Dreams goes back many years. Judy and I have been intrigued by genealogy since we first met. Those preceding us kept sufficient records through the years that we were fortunate to know a number of details about both our families' heritages—native Cherokee in Judy's case, and English Quaker in mine. A fascinating potential connection between our two lines also existed whose roots extended back to Oklahoma. Judy's Cherokee ancestors came to the territory on the Trail of Tears. Some of those Indians eventually married whites, and many of those families of mixed blood remained in Indian Territory in Oklahoma, where Judy's grandmother was raised. My father, too, grew up in Oklahoma and used to tell stories of the *long* Cherokee names of his childhood Indian friends.

After we were married we took a trip to Oklahoma with our three sons, visiting both the little town of Vian where my father was raised, and also places in Craig County where Judy's ancestors had once lived. During that trip we realized just how close our two families had been. They had lived less than fifty miles apart back in a day, when, as the saying goes, everybody knew everybody.

As we stood in one of the several cemeteries we visited on that trip, poring over gravestones for familiar names from one of our two families, the lightbulb moment occurred: "What if some of our ancestors knew each other ? . . . What if we might even be distantly related!"

That possibility never left us. Eventually it developed into an idea for a book in which two girls would investigate their roots, and somehow discover their common ancestry.

But book ideas often go in directions you don't anticipate. Before that book was written, Katie and Mayme of *Shenandoah Sisters* came along and I couldn't help borrowing parts of the idea for their story. Yet in the back of our minds, Judy and I remained curious about the possibility of a tie between our two family lines.

The link, however, did not come in Oklahoma, nor through Judy's Cherokee roots, where we expected it.

I had known for years of Quaker connections in my ancestry. I had not been aware, however, that they extended back to the very founding years of the Society of Friends in England, nor that my Borton forebears were among the first Quaker immigrants to the American colonies and had come to escape persecution by English Puritans. Neither was I aware just how closely fused were the two names *Borton* and *Woolman* as two of the leading early Quaker families in New Jersey.

While traveling in Scotland several years ago with our friends Josanna Simpson and Julia and Grace Yacoubian and my sister Janet Stanberry, and—as was our frequent custom!—browsing in secondhand bookstores, Josanna spied on the shelves an old volume by Janet Whitney entitled *John Woolman, Quaker.* Not only did the discovery turn out to be a pearl of great price in illuminating the life of John Woolman, in its opening chapter I also read about the first landing on

American shores of my *own* Quaker great-great-great-great-great-great-great-great-grandfather John Borton. I had known of the name as an abstract fact all my life. Suddenly here he was, family and all. What an exciting discovery!

It had been my intent all along in this series to use Judy's and my Cherokee and Quaker lineages—weaving into the story what facts I could from our ancestries—as a springboard from which to tell a fictionalized early history of the United States, using the Civil War and the three interwoven races of this continent as backdrop.

Judy and I soon forgot trying to *connect* our two genealogies. I simply intended to use them independently to tell different aspects of the American story—as I did with hers in the previous volume, *Dream of Life,* where the focus was the "Old Books" of Cherokee history.

But now we discovered a fact that had escaped us earlier. The Ellis Harlan who married Cata'quin Kingfisher (Judy's great-great-great-great-grandfather and -grandmother), daughter of Nanye'hi Ward, was the son of a Quaker minister from Pennsylvania—just across and down the Delaware River from the first Borton homestead in New Jersey!

Our two ancestral families had emigrated from England just nine years apart and had landed within thirty miles of each other, both arriving in the formative years of two closely linked Quaker communities.

Our joint Quaker heritage provided the link we had been looking for!

Now obviously these particular names are of interest to Judy and me because they are *our* ancestors. They will not hold the same interest for you other than as characters in this series. I go into this background, not to bore you with personal anecdotes, but because something larger is at stake. Out of such specifics a more encompassing historical tapestry emerges. The story takes on grander scope, not because of these details, but because these people typify a *universal* story that has been played out a million times in the lives of millions of other men and women. In a very real sense, *our* ancestral background which I have woven into this story (an intermingling of different races, from different places and of different

religions, traveling and migrating from England to Pennsylvania
to North Carolina, then to Oklahoma and Ohio and Illinois, then
to Washington and Oregon and California, continuing to marry
and spread out and have sons and daughters and grandchildren and
great-grandchildren) is a story, in miniature, of this entire wonderful
country and how it was explored, peopled, settled, and populated.

All you who are reading have a similar story to tell! Anyone truly
can write "the great American novel." Each of us possesses a heritage
that could provide the raw material for a moving tale of brave and
interesting men and women and their personal histories.

The names and places and specifics would change. But at root it
would be the same story . . . a story of people who came to this land
of many nationalities and from distinct origins, who married and
intermarried and sent down roots, and had families . . . and who
gradually made this their homeland.

The drama of the courageous men and women who came before
us is a priceless heritage we all share. It underscores a truth woven
through the entire fabric of the Old Testament: Genealogy is intrinsic
to the history of God's people. I take it therefore to be something God
values—to know whence we came.

That is why American Dreams is a story of genealogies and roots
and *people*—because God values the ongoing life of the generations.
As Americans we share a unique bond of a fused and intermingled
unity of races that combine to make up our heritage.

There is another reason why focusing on *individual* men and
women is the best way to get at this *universal* story—individual people
can be remarkably courageous. The bravery of the people who came
before us is truly remarkable. Can you imagine setting sail on a treacherous journey of two months across a dangerous ocean in a ship the
size of a modest yacht of today, accepting the fact that you would not
bathe for two months or eat fresh food, knowing that a squall could
send you and your family to the bottom of the sea, or that smallpox
could break out onboard and you could do nothing about it? The
courage of our ancestors is astonishing.

And when they arrived, they would have no homes, no electricity, no running water, no food waiting for them, no shelter, no stores, no towns, no roads, no vehicles, no animals for either food or transportation, no means of contacting the world they had left behind. Isolation does not even begin to describe the aloneness our predecessors experienced. The scope of what it meant to start an entirely *new* life is beyond our imagination.

Through the years, this courage upon which our nation was founded manifested itself in a thousand ways—the courage to explore, continually to meet new challenges. And what of the courage of the slaves to endure their suffering until the day of their freedom, the courage of those who stood against the times and fought for that freedom.

The history of this land is filled with dark moments and scoundrels and contemptible men who sought their own gain. The unconscionable evil of religious persecutions, of hangings and witch burnings, the horrors of the slave trade and the evil perpetuated by the plantation owners of the South, are grievous sins against humanity for which the collective conscience of America will forever, to some degree, be continuing to atone in new ways.

Yet too, we are a nation of heroes. Bravery takes many forms. Not to be overlooked along with the courage to face physical fear and suffering is courage in eternal matters of spiritual import. It takes courage to face untruth and stand against the prevailing orthodoxies of one's time—be they social or political or doctrinal. Such heroes in the spiritual realm look to God as the Light of eternal truth. With their example before us, we can draw strength from the brave men and women of the Kingdom who have come before us. With them we can be bold to say to a timid and cautious and small-believing world, "Our God is a higher God. The Light of his truth shines out on a more lofty plane than you can at present perceive. But one day you will see it, for the Light of God's being will grow stronger and brighter to all eternity."

All this explains my emphasis on the individual lineages of the characters in the three books of American Dreams. Some of you may find yourselves thinking, "Why is he telling us the names of everyone's

parents and grandparents and great-grandparents? They have nothing
to do with the story." Without a doubt, no series of mine contains a
fraction of the *names* that are mentioned in this series. The reason is
simply to convey the importance of a great truth—we are a nation that
has emerged out of the lives and stories and bravery of our forebears,
millions of ancestors, most of whose names we do not even know, but
who transmitted to us their life, their dreams, their love.

We are a nation of *people*.

Cherity's search for her familial and ethnic roots, Seth's search to
discover truths long hidden and bring them to the light, Chigua's search
to reconnect with roots severed in childhood, Richmond and Carolyn's
discovery of spiritual roots and their connections to men and women
of God who went before . . . these all contribute to Everyman's story, a
story continually being written in each of our lives. Thus, the Quaker
contribution to this universal drama cannot be underestimated, and
serves as the climax to the series in this third book. The emphasis of
the early Quakers on the *Light* that lightens every man, the Light of the
world, points to an eternal truth. For the history of the universe is the
story of the gradual illumination of God's Light into every human heart.

We are indeed a melting pot of races and creeds and religions and
backgrounds. Yet somehow we have become a single nation. This is the
story American Dreams tells—how *three* races became *one* people.

I truly hope that you are reading this series, fictional though much
of it is, as your story too.

I would like to add one final word of acknowledgment and appreciation. This series, by its historical complexity, has required more
research than any project I have ever undertaken. That process was
made enormously more manageable with the help of my two wonderful research, brainstorming, and all-around assistants, my wife Judy—
as always!—along with our friend Josanna Simpson. And also thank
you to Rebecca Kraemer for her contribution. Thank you all!

Michael Phillips
Eureka, California

Crisis in England
1603–1689

The English sailing ship *Shield* under command of captain Daniel Taws had been at sea for eleven weeks when at long last it entered the wide mouth of Delaware Bay on the eastern coast of the northern of the two continents which for one hundred years had been known to the world as *America*.

The final leg of its long journey would take the *Shield* up the Delaware River another ninety miles to its final destination. Excitement among the ship's families was higher than it had been since the day of their departure.

A bitter cold front had accompanied them to the coast. The blue of a cloudless sky above was thinning and growing pale. After rounding Cape May into the shelter of the bay, for the first time since the coast of England had disappeared from sight behind them, they heard shipmaster Taws give the order to drop anchor.

Slowly the sun continued to set behind the thickly forested hills of the great land their eyes had longed to see for so long. Already the mercury had dipped below freezing. Candles and lanterns came to light throughout the ship as dusk deepened. It would be a cold but happy night on board.

Land ho! had been shouted from the crow's nest late that same morning some six hours before.

The ship instantly erupted into a beehive of activity . . . men, women, children all standing at the rails peering at the thin outline on the horizon, watching it grow by degrees larger and more defined. All afternoon women chattered excitedly amongst themselves. Children scurried about pretending to be Indians. Men clustered in groups handing spyglasses around for a closer look at the virgin land suddenly so close.

For two months the toll of the crossing had gradually wearied everyone aboard in both body and soul. The optimism and high hopes of departure had only lasted a week or two. Then the long loneliness had set in . . . along with the doubts . . . and the fears whether they would survive the crossing at all. Up and down in an endless succession of troughs and crests, rhythmically rocking from side to side, every creak and groan of the ship's timbers in the night, every crashing of wave against her hull, every whine of wind through her masts and rigging, reminded the *Shield*'s passengers of nature's power, in the midst of which they seemed suddenly so small and helpless. They also reminded the mothers among them that in the sixty years since the Dutch and English had been colonizing the northern portions of the New World, the bottom of the watery passageway between the two continents had become strewn with vessels that had not reached their destinations.

Many unknown graves lay below them. Not all survived the power of these waves and this wind.

They had set sail late in September. The chill of autumn had already begun in England. It was late to begin, but they could not wait another twelvemonth.

As the weeks passed, that chill gradually bit more deeply into their bones. The sky and the sea turned the same dreary gray. Waves whipped higher and higher sending salt spray crashing frighteningly up over the prow. Winds rose with increasing insistence. Two relentless storms battered them for days on end, whipping sails into rags and sending more than half the passengers retching to their beds. Yet the *Shield* bore bravely forward into winter's teeth, forward toward an uncertain future.

Yet suddenly today all the pent-up fears had evaporated. Two months of suppressed optimism had broken out in cheers and laughter and back slapping and congratulations at the sight of land stretching as far north and south as they could see in front of them. All afternoon the men spoke of felling trees for homes and about next spring's planting. The women and mothers were already taking stock of what provisions remained on board and planning what they would feed their families through the cold winter months ahead.

The year was 1678.

Most of the *Shield*'s passengers were of a growing religious sect in England called Quakers, come to the New World hoping to establish communities free from the persecutions they had suffered at the hands of the ruling authorities and religious establishments in their homeland.

"Captain Taws," said a nine-year-old boy to the man standing at the ship's wheel an hour or so after land had been sighted. Taws had made this journey many times before, but the first sighting of land always sent a thrill through him. Like his passengers he was in exuberant spirits. He glanced down on the lad with a kindly smile from his weather-beaten face.

"Yes, Master Borton, what is it?" he said.

"Will we land today, sir?"

"Not today, young John," replied the captain. "We will be lucky to get inside the bay by nightfall. There we will anchor until daybreak. The remainder of our journey will take us upriver, so we must sail only when we have the light of the sun to navigate by. The stars will do us no good now."

"Why, Captain?"

"The river is wide, son, but we must stay in the center and not run aground. It takes a man standing at this wheel who can see both shores to do that."

"When will we go ashore then, Captain?" asked young John Borton.

"We will weigh anchor at morning's first light tomorrow and sail into the river's mouth, hoping that the tide and currents are favorable. I do not think we will reach New Castle even tomorrow. But by the next day for certain you will again see the sight of a civilized town."

"Will we go ashore there, Captain?"

"Perhaps your father. But I think it best if you remain on board with your mother."

"I want to see Indians, Captain."

Taws laughed. "No doubt you will see as many as you wish in good time."

"When will we reach Burlington, Captain?"

"In three or four days, Master Borton. It is a good way upriver. You must be patient a little while longer. But you will see your new home soon enough."

Twenty or thirty feet away a man and woman stood at the ship's rail listening. The woman glanced at her husband and smiled.

"Thy son is anxious," she said.

"No more than thee and all the rest of us, each in our own way," replied the man.

They stood a moment gazing out at the sea in front of them. It was suddenly not nearly so fearsome now that the horizon was no longer endless.

"So, what think thee, Anne Kinton Borton?" said the man at length.

"That perhaps we shall see thy dream after all. . . . Oh, John, I can scarcely believe it—we have really made it to America!"

"Did thee ever doubt it, Anne?"

"It was a long voyage. There were times I was afraid."

Borton nodded. He understood. A man with a family is always more or less afraid.

"But our eyes can at last see the New Jersey coast," he said. "And as the captain said to John, tomorrow we shall sail upriver to our new home."

The movement of those who called themselves the Society of Friends in England was less than thirty years old when John Borton and his wife Anne, along with their six children, set sail with other families of like mind, including the Bortons' friend, aging William Woolman, a weaver, and his son John, fiancé to their own fourteen-year-old daughter Elizabeth. Their number had grown so rapidly and was now so widespread as to be causing major upheaval throughout England in an era of great civil and religious strife. Persecution and imprisonment had been inflicted on many Friends, including one of its newest converts, nobleman William Penn the younger. As the Society had at first drawn primarily from the working classes, Penn's conversion not only outraged his aristocratic father, it drew increasing national attention to the movement.

England in the seventeenth century found itself in the throes of social, religious, and political crisis. A battle had begun over control of the nation. For the present it was a battle between king and Parliament. But the struggle in the coming centuries would broaden in scope to become a contest between the entire aristocracy and the rising working and middle classes.

At this point, in the early days of the struggle, those involved in England's conflict came exclusively from the upper echelons of a society which in many respects was still feudal in nature. Outright serfdom was mostly a thing of the past, yet English society continued to be regulated by a strict hierarchy of class. All men may have worshiped the same God. But when they went to church, the nobles sat in their plush boxes, the working classes sat stiff-backed in theirs, and the peasants sat in rows at the back of the church or in the balcony where the nobles did not have to see them, mix with them, or perhaps more important on a hot summer Sunday, smell them. The Christian creed they shared was not a creed of equality.

As religious division was then rife in England, religion became the tool Parliament used to clip the wings of the monarchy. Such a change would have been unthinkable a century before, when Henry VIII's power was so unchallenged over state and church that he could lop off the head of Anne Boleyn on a whim without fear of reprisal. Now it was the heads of the kings themselves that were in jeopardy!

All wars and conflict between peoples and nations have their roots in contests over power and religion. The desire of one man, one sect, one people, or one nation, to dominate another in *rule* or *belief* represents the foundational source of human conflict.

Seventeenth-century England was engaged in a war within itself, a *civil* war, over religious authority and rule. While masquerading as a contest of true *belief*, at a more fundamental level it was a battle for *power*—for supremacy of church structure and allegiance, and therefore also of governmental supremacy. As the government controlled the church, the two could not be separated. The contest between king and Parliament for supremacy was equally a contest of *religious* sectarian dominance.

Had it been solely a contest over belief, one sect of Christians would not have burned those of another sect of fellow believers in Christ at the stake. But it was a war in which political rule and religious belief were fused into a single driving passion to dominate the nation. It was a battle for authority of ecclesiastical dominance. Which *church* doctrine and affiliation was supreme? Which church supported the king? Which supported Parliament? All opposing views, governmental and spiritual, must be rooted out and its adherents forced to submit . . . or pay with their lives. It was truly a Christian jihad. Yet it differed from its Arab counterpart that had dominated the religious struggle in the Middle East for a millennium in this: The English jihad of the seventeenth century was not waged against unbelieving infidels, but against its *own* fellow Christians of opposing parties and sects. They called themselves *Royalists* and *Parliamentarians*. The Royalists who supported the king were primarily made up of Catholics and traditional Anglicans. The Parliamentarians were made up mostly of Puritans, both Anglican and Presbyterian, as well as those from the new Protestant, or "Dissenting," sects.

Unquestionably those at the forefront of the battle truly believed in the *right* and *truth* of their cause. But in taking that belief to the further supposition that they must conquer and subdue by force those, as they saw it, of *false* and *untrue* belief, they left altogether the teaching of their Master. Something is dreadfully and eternally wrong when those who may perhaps to some degree possess truth are intent upon *forcing* and *compelling* fellow believers to their side, by whatever means possible, including killing them if they do not submit . . . all for the sake of Christian principle. This terrible evil of Christian rising up against Christian lay at the core of English politics in the seventeenth century, and it was a great evil. It was therefore a ruthless contest fueled by a lust for power, which used the tokens of Christian doctrine as weapons to do evil rather than as principles to bring light into a world darkened by sin.

The Reformation and its aftermath left England a confusing jumble of conflicting interests and church allegiances. The conflict was not only between Catholic and Protestant. The powerful Church of England was being split apart by Puritans, which eventually split into a half dozen or more offshoots. Out of the resulting tumultuous contest for supremacy, influence, and political control, grew what is called the English "civil war" between the years 1643 and 1689. Out of that environment of conflict, uncertainty, and religious strife, emerged a Christian people distinct in outlook from all the rest—the people who formed what they called The Society of Friends, but who came to be known simply as Quakers.

A Vision of Light
1647–1670

A boy named George Fox was born in England in 1624, son of a
weaver of the slowly rising working class, neither wealthy nor destitute. The Fox family were religious Puritans grown out of the Calvinist
tree of the continental Reformation. Young George was a thoughtful
boy, serious about spiritual things, and the desire grew within him to
live his beliefs more personally. His discontent with his apprenticeship
at shoemaking accompanied a discontent with the Puritanical world
of his upbringing. Nothing he heard in the church of his parents satisfied the longing in his heart for a more vibrant and practical Christian
faith. The Puritans may have spoken of purifying the church, but to
young George Fox it remained strict, dead, lifeless, and legalistic.

Where was a Christianity that practiced and preached and lived
by the daily living *reality* of the gospel of Jesus Christ? Or did such a
church exist at all?

When he was nineteen, only a year after the outbreak of civil war
between the king and Parliament, Fox left his home and apprenticeship and began traveling about England. His aim was to visit and
question priests and ministers of various churches and from many
congregations, hoping to find worthy individuals to guide him in
his spiritual search. He traveled up and down England, often in
great turmoil of mind, visiting churches and meetings and priests,
anywhere he heard there was to be a gathering of Christian people.

After three years, Fox came to the conclusion that *no* church possessed the answers, at least he found them from none of the priests of the High Church of England or preachers of Puritanism or Separatism with whom he had spoken. All he found was the same emphasis on ritual, church structure, inequality in the church boxes and benches, and legalistic adherence to what he considered dead formulas and doctrines and political alliances. Nowhere did he find men speaking of faith and obedience and practical living, only which side of the civil war they supported. Were they on the king's side or Parliament's side? The church in England, in *all* of its manifestations, had become so political at its core that nowhere could he find the principles of Scripture, only doctrines twisted to conform to one political outlook or another.

Nor did he find *sympathy* with his search. Instead, he was criticized for thinking there might be *more* to be found outside the church walls, a more that was not political at all, but deeply and personally *spiritual.* Something was missing.

Over and over again he watched as throngs of people poured into the churches of England from Sunday to Sunday—all its churches— and came out again. But were they any better off? Was their worship making them better people, better Christians? Were they becoming more loving and gracious and tolerant as a result of it? Were the teachings of their pastors and priests changing their lives? Did the people attend church because they loved God, or because church attendance was required by English law?

Throughout England, supposedly the most civilized and progressive country on earth, those claiming to be Christians were at war with one another . . . and *killing* one another. Sunday after Sunday, throngs continued to crowd England's churches, and pray for victory over their enemies . . . their *Christian* enemies.

For a time he began to despair of finding the truth. He made his way in great torment of spirit. He realized at length that he had to leave the pastors and priests altogether. He must depend on God alone to show him the light he sought.

And at last answers began to come:

The *Church* he had been seeking was not to be found in *any* of England's churches. The truth he hungered for did not reside in the Parliament or the monarchy, in King Charles I or in Oliver Cromwell, the Puritan commander of the Parliamentary army. The practical reality of gospel Christianity was an *individual* reality, not affiliation with an organizational entity, be it political or religious. In no one church, in no government, in no king, in no parliament was God to be found.

God dwelt in men and women, not in buildings or structures or priesthoods, not in organizations or hierarchies, not in robes or liturgies or kings or parliaments. God dwelt within human *hearts*! Within individual human hearts . . . within *his* heart.

Suddenly young George Fox realized that the answer had been right in front of him all along. He could go to God *alone*, in the depths of his own heart, and commune with him, and speak with him and pray to him and worship him, and receive answers and truth and light from him. He needed no king, no priest, no church, no parliament to stand between himself and God. Jesus had revealed God and he needed no other.

The Christian *Church* of Jesus was no organizational structure at all—it was made up of individual men and women, all equal, all sharing in the same priesthood of believers.

He wrote of his great discovery in his *Journal.* "As I had forsaken all the priests," he said, "so I left the separate preachers also, and those called the most experienced people; for I saw there was none among them all that could speak to my condition. And when all my hopes in them and in all men were gone, so that I had nothing outwardly to help me, nor could tell what to do, then, Oh then, I heard a voice which said, 'There is one, even Christ Jesus, that can speak to thy condition,' and when I heard it my heart did leap for joy."[1]

During the three years while he traveled and prayed and fasted and grew from nineteen to twenty-two, a slow change took place in young

George Fox. His uncertainties were gradually transformed into boldness. He began to feel rising up within himself a confidence to speak
concerning the truths that were being revealed to him.

Rather than merely asking questions of those he met, he stirred up
those with whom he spoke. He challenged his listeners to examine the
foundations of their Christian beliefs to see if more and different truth
might be present than they realized.

He continued to travel and speak wherever opportunity presented
itself, on street corners and in public squares, occasionally even boldly
interrupting church services. His message was a simple one: True
Christianity is not to be found in church at all. It is found within the
human heart. Each one must turn to God within himself, waiting
upon him in the silence of his or her own heart, where God will reveal
truth.

Gradually George Fox began to call this individually revealed truth
the Inner Light.

George Fox sought to live practically the new realities he was discovering. He stopped removing his hat to nobles and priests. If all men
and women were equal before God, why should he exalt one above
another because of birth and station? In his speech, for the same
reason, he discontinued using the more formal *you* in dialog with the
clergy and with aristocrats, in favor of the *thee* and *thou* that he used
with commoners. He took to simpler, plain dress so as not to seem to
exalt himself over those with less than he. And in his times of prayer,
he sometimes sat for long periods in silence, waiting for God's Spirit
to speak. The forms and rituals of England's churches became repel-
lant to him, as *distancing* rather than aiding people toward an intimate
experience with God in the quietness of their own hearts. Such actions
quickly began to make the religious and political authorities angry.
The fact that he spoke his mind made them angrier still.

George Fox continued to travel about, even though the country
was in upheaval. He was energetic and persuasive and forceful, both

of appearance and personality. In 1647, though still but twenty-three years of age, he began to attract a following. He also stirred up controversy. Those of the organized church, Puritans *and* traditionalists, took his convictions as an affront, saying that he denied truths that had been taught by the church for years.

In 1649, two years after the revelation of light had come to George Fox, King Charles I was tried for treason before the lower house of Parliament and executed in London. Oliver Cromwell, in virtual control of England, then took the unprecedented step of declaring an end to the English monarchy. The crown was abolished altogether. Cromwell, who claimed to believe in the equality of all men, had suddenly made himself the most equal of all. Now *he* ruled England in place of the king.

That same year, Fox was imprisoned in Nottingham for interrupting a sermon with an impassioned appeal to the congregation to be guided by the Holy Spirit alone. A year after that he was imprisoned in Derby as a blasphemer. It was there, after Fox told him to "tremble before the word of God," that Justice Gervase Bennett called Fox and his followers "Quakers."

But Fox continued to find a wide response to his unusual perspectives. Within a very few years, his following had become a movement. Meetings began to be held in the northeast of England, and soon others with him took to preaching Fox's principles up and down England wherever the situation suited it, in barns and homes or at market crosses in the center of towns. Fox himself became more mystical and inward in his spiritual orientation and began writing books and pamphlets to set down the principles of his beliefs. As his following grew, his writings increased his notoriety, and the controversy of his ideas still more.

The most well-known convert to George Fox's new brand of Christian faith, and the one which would have the most sweeping consequences across the Atlantic on the American continent, came in one of the

most respected of all England's families, that of Admiral Sir William
Penn. The conversion of the admiral's twenty-one-year-old son caused
all of London to take note of this rising new sect that had now reached
into the highest levels of English society.

Like Fox, William Penn the younger also began to write pamphlets
that detailed his beliefs and brought the movement still more into the
public eye. In *The Sandy Foundation Shaken*, his attack on what many
considered the orthodox views of Christianity, in particular the trinity,
were so strong that, even as the son of a nobleman, he was imprisoned
in the Tower of London for nine months.

Penn's writings from the Tower of London were forceful and unpol-
ished. Still relatively new to his Quaker beliefs, Penn used strong
language to attack what he considered the loose and unchristian lives
of much of England's clergy, not necessarily the best way to make
friends. But he matured and softened in the years that followed, and
continued to expand the themes begun in prison. These writings later
coalesced into what became the most important of his books, *No
Cross, No Crown*. In it he explained Quaker doctrines and practices—
particularly their refusal to remove their hats in respect to the nobility,
why they dressed simply, and why they addressed even those higher
on the social scale with the informal *thee* and *thou* rather than the
more formal term of respect *you* to which they were accustomed. His
book provided a thorough exposition of Quaker perspective on the
Christian faith. It was truly the first comprehensive book published of
Quaker belief, and laid a foundation for Quakerism for generations to
come. George Fox's *Journal* was in circulation by this time. And in *No
Cross, No Crown*, Penn illuminated Quakerism as an intellectually and
doctrinally sound Protestant movement that was here to stay.

While George Fox was a firebrand, William Penn was of gentler
temperament, a healer and uniter and conciliator. In spite of ongoing
persecutions and more imprisonments, his soft-spoken adherence to
his faith, and his education and the reputation of his family, gradually over the years won him the respect and admiration of most of
England's nobility. It became obvious to all that he *lived* by the prin-

ciples of his beliefs. No one had complaint against William Penn, and he bore his sufferings with dignity and grace. He became so highly respected, even as a member of a sect that was viewed as radical, that he spoke before Parliament on behalf of religious toleration, not only for Quakers but for all those of minority beliefs. Though the results were not immediate, his influence contributed to the Act of Toleration of 1689, which significantly reduced, though did not entirely eliminate, the religious persecution of earlier times.

William Penn gave Quakerism a gentler face. He spoke with reason, calm, simplicity, and intelligence. He did not stir things up with fiery pronouncements of judgment like Fox, but prevailed upon reason and common sense and goodwill. He tried to bring people together in the midst of spiritual differences. His skill translated this unifying spirit of toleration to the colonial governments he helped establish. William Penn, therefore, was instrumental in launching Quakerism forward into succeeding generations. Though he was twenty years younger, William Penn truly was a *cofounde*r with George Fox of the Quakerism that began to leave England's shores in the 1660s and 1670s, bound for new worlds where they could put down the roots of their new faith.

When his father died in 1670, William Penn found himself, at twenty-six years of age, the inheritor of what amounted to a fortune— £1,500 in annual income, and, more importantly, a claim upon the king of England for £16,000 which his father had loaned to Charles II during the war against the Dutch. It would be his shrewd request to the crown to repay this loan with land in America that would bring William Penn immortality as one of the most notable founding sons of the rising English colony across the Atlantic.

The persecutions borne by their people caused many Quakers to look toward the New World as a possible avenue whereby they might escape persecutions and live in peace. All through England they were being imprisoned, impoverished by fines, and their property confiscated. But *where* could such a place be found? Fox and Penn had spoken together about America but there was no free land available.

English King Charles II, on the throne after Oliver Cromwell's death, had granted to his brother James, Duke of York all the land in America between the Connecticut River and Delaware Bay. In 1664, the duke transferred ownership of these lands to Sir George Carteret and Lord John Berkeley, Baron of Stratton as a reward for their defense of the Channel Island Jersey on behalf of his brother, the king. This vast tract of land, loosely defined, had been known as New Amsterdam when under Dutch control. It was now given the name Nova Caesarea, or New Jersey. The new owners, Berkeley and Carteret immediately began making provisions to offer parcels to immigrants by a quit-rent system similar to that which had brought the earliest settlers to Virginia.

Two Quaker men, John Fenwicke and Edward Byllynge, instantly saw in the offer the opportunity to create a community free of oaths of allegiance to king, with no compulsory church and tithes and taxes, and no persecution. They jumped at Berkeley's offer and purchased his entire portion for the astonishingly small sum of one thousand pounds. Byllynge brought in William Penn as clerk and trustee for his share and gave Penn major administrative control in the future of the province. Penn's genius and foresight in democratic thinking immediately displayed itself. Under his leadership, an organization was formed to make colonization possible in the new province where Quakers would be free to practice the principles of equality, peace, and simplicity undisturbed. The company drew up a charter of government for the region called the Concessions and Agreements, and divided up the land into smaller parcels available for sale.

Suddenly the Quaker dream of available land in the New World was possible.

The Concessions and Agreements of the New Jersey colony, dated March 3, 1676, a monument to William Penn's statesmanship and foresight, and a true landmark in democracy, provided that every adult male should be eligible to vote without class or religious restriction, that they should elect representatives annually by ballot to an assembly with full power to make, change, and repeal laws, that trial by jury was to be unrestricted, and that complete freedom of conscience and absolute religious toleration were to be observed and enforced.

A public letter was distributed in England and the colonies with the Concessions and Agreements of the Proprietors, Freeholders, and Inhabitants of the Province of New Jersey in America. In this letter, foreshadowing the ideals of his great descendents in birthing democracy who would follow a century later, Penn wrote, "In the fear of the Lord and in true sense of his Divine Will we try here to lay foundations for after ages to understand their liberty as Christians and as men, that they may not be brought into bondage but by their own consent; for we put the power in the people."

In 1677, two hundred and thirty Quakers from London and Yorkshire sailed on the *Kent* to Salem and New Castle on the banks of the Delaware River. All purchasers of land had been required to sign the Concessions and Agreements before leaving England. Those among them who had purchased land from Byllynge higher up the river continued on by canoe and by Indian trail, where they founded a settlement which would become Burlington.

A year later, the *Shield* sailed, with the Bortons and Woolmans aboard to join them.

Pilgrims to a New World
1678–1720

*A*s the *Shield* made its way slowly up the Delaware River, gradually
the twenty-five-mile-wide bay in which they had anchored for their
first night in America narrowed. By the end of the day the mouth
of the Delaware had closed to within a mile or two of them on each
side. The frigid but crystal clear weather held and the next day, by
midmorning, the forested banks had come close enough to see clearly.

A sense of quiet solemnity descended over the ship as it glided ever
further inland up a river more gigantic than anything they had beheld
in their native England. They were at last penetrating into the strange
new continent. No longer was the Atlantic visible behind them.

The land was vast, silent, empty.

Yet . . . not altogether empty. Who could tell . . . Indians might
be watching them from amidst those very trees, most leafless now.
Despite all they had heard about the friendliness of the Delaware
tribes, they could not prevent a feeling of trepidation as they
progressed ever more deeply into the interior.

Nearly everyone on board had bought the land they hoped to tame
and settle sight unseen. They had put every penny they possessed into
the purchase, the ship passage, and the initial supplies they would
need. As they went, the men were therefore understandably nervous as
well as excited. This was gamble on which they had risked everything,
including the lives of their families.

William Woolman and John Borton stood silently at the rail taking in the sight. A man of about forty walked up behind them and took a place beside Borton.

"It is an awe-inspiring sight, is it not?" he said at length.

"It is indeed, Friend Harland," sighed Borton, glancing toward the newcomer, a man from Durham named Obadiah Harland. "William and I were just reflecting on what brought us here, and the hard work that lies ahead now that we have arrived."

"Hard but *happy* work," rejoined Harland. "We have been waiting for it a long time."

"What brought thee on such a difficult journey, Obadiah?" asked Woolman.

"Have not we all asked ourselves that question over and over since departing!" laughed Harland. "Of course there are a host of reasons. I want to live in peace. I am concerned for my family and hope that here my sons will be able to walk in simplicity and peace."

"Why Burlington?"

"I considered settling further north, for I have some acquaintances there," answered Harland. "But the Puritans care no more for religious freedom than does the king or Parliament. That they could *hang* fellow Christians for not believing as they do is beyond my comprehension. I pray with all my heart that things will be different here in New Jersey and in Penn's new colony."

"I believe they will," said Borton. "We Quakers take the *living* of Christianity more seriously than do the Puritans. For them, doctrine is everything. For us, *life* is everything. We will find a way to get along because we are ruled by the love of Christ."

"I hope thee is right. Several of my brothers are waiting to hear from me before making their own plans to come. They are contemplating property across the river."

Suddenly a shout went up and the three men turned.

"Look . . . it's a windmill!" cried someone on the other side of the ship. Their conversation abruptly halted, they joined others in running to the port side.

On the left in the distance the Dutch settlement of New Castle now came gradually into view. Though England and the Netherlands had been at war on and off for years, and the most recent conflict had ended a mere four years earlier, the Dutch sight was as manna in the wilderness for the weary travelers. They anchored in the middle, and took several small rowing boats of men ashore. They did not so much need supplies, though fresh water would be welcome, as they simply wanted to set foot again on dry land and greet others from their homeland.

But Captain Taws, who would remain aboard the *Shield*, urged a brief visit.

"Our destination is still more than a day away," he told them. "We must get under way before sunset and move at least another hour north before anchoring. Then, if we embark at first light, and ride the incoming tidal current, and as long as the wind continues from the south, we just may make Burlington by nightfall tomorrow. I am not eager for a delay, for I fear ice. I have been watching it accumulate in the shadows along the shoreline as we have progressed. And the river will continue to narrow."

The men nodded in agreement. They were more anxious than he to reach their destination. Many had family and friends who had come a year before and were waiting for them in the small Quaker settlement now only forty or forty-five miles further on.

"We will see what supplies are available here," replied John Borton, "and deliver the mail in our possession for New Castle and Salem, then return to the ship as quickly as possible."

In two hours, with little daylight remaining, the *Shield* weighed anchor and continued up the Delaware. At the wheel, Captain Taws waited until the last possible moment, when at last he knew his squinting eyes could see neither shoreline, then gave the order to drop sail and anchor for what everyone hoped would be their last night before reaching Burlington. As cold as it had been, this night was the coldest yet.

When John Borton and his future son-in-law John Woolman found

Captain Taws on the ship's deck in the gray of dawn the following morning, he was peering at the shore through his spyglass.

He lowered it as he heard their steps behind him, and turned.

"The ice has crept toward us in the night," he said. "But the center of the river is clear. It will not hamper us today. But it is time to rouse the men and weigh anchor and be off!"

It was a day of unparalleled excitement. About halfway through the day the river widened suddenly and bent sharply to the right as another smaller river poured into it. Then came almost a direct ninety-degree bend left and northward, and a gradual narrowing. By then all the passengers crowded the railings of the top deck, anxiously peering ahead for any sign of their destination.

Yet the hours continued to pass slowly. Gradually the sun arced lower and lower westward and the brilliant blue of the sky began to grow pale and they began to despair of reaching their destination before dark. But they had already passed the mouth of the creek the Indians called Rancocas, upstream on which lay both the Borton and Woolman purchased tracts of land. They were closer to Burlington Island than they knew.

At last, as the freezing dusk was closing down upon them, the island began to come faintly into view. Again a great cheer went up for Captain Taws and his crew.

They had arrived!

But as anxious as they were to set their feet on solid ground, it was clearly too late by the time the anchor had splashed into the river to lower the smaller boats now. They would have to spend one more night aboard the *Shield*.

It was hard to sleep, knowing that their fellow Quakers and friends and relatives were so close! They could see the lights of their homes from on deck! Had those on shore seen them arrive in the thickening dusk, or heard their cheering voices? Did the little settlement of Burlington know that the *Shield* had arrived?

There was no doubt at first morning's light that the word had spread. The December day dawned bright and sunny. To the shore to greet the passengers of the *Shield* flocked those who had come a year before.

But everyone was in for a surprise, especially the passengers of the *Shield* when they rose from their bunks and hurriedly dressed in the cold, and climbed up on deck. They were anxious to lower the small boats and go ashore.

But the blue green river had disappeared! It had turned white in the night. The *Shield* was locked fast in ice!

"Oh, no!" said Elizabeth Borton as she saw the sight. "What will we do, Mother?"

"I do not know, Elizabeth," replied her mother, who held three-year-old Susanna in her arms. "We must see what Captain Taws says."

"We will have to wait until it thaws," said their husband and father walking toward them with young John. "If the mercury remains below freezing all day, it will not break up for some time."

"Why do we not walk across it, Papa?" asked the nine-year-old boy. The rest of the Borton family, his older sisters Ann, Elizabeth, and Esther, his younger brother William all stood beside him.

"It is too thin to hold thee, John," replied his father. "Thee would be into the river and frozen to death in seconds."

"Come over. . . . What is thee waiting for?" cried a voice shouting from shore.

They looked to see a man among the gathering crowd of welcome waving his arms and beckoning them toward him.

"The ice!" shouted Taws.

"It will hold!" came the voice echoing back from shore.

And then, to prove his point, the man began walking toward them. Several others nearby joined him.

"Look, Papa!" cried young John Borton. "They are walking on the ice! Can I too, Papa? Can I please!"

Still shaking his head at the sight before him, John Borton thought a moment. Suddenly he turned to Captain Taws.

"Captain," he said, "how much would thee say our oak water barrels weigh? Is it equal to a man?"

"Empty or full, Borton? Empty, perhaps the equal of old Bill Woolman there. But he is a wiry man, and it would not be your equal."

"Then let us send a full barrel over the side! What use have we for water now? We have all the rivers and streams of New Jersey before us!"

A few questioning glances were exchanged, until they realized what Borton had suggested. All at once half a dozen of the men bolted together below deck. Within minutes they were struggling to hoist one of several remaining casks of water up the stairway. With a great banging and crashing, they managed it, then rolled the barrel to the side of the ship.

"Permission to throw one water barrel overboard, Captain?" said Borton.

"Granted!" laughed Taws.

"Up, men!" said Borton, lifting the side of one end.

"Give me an end of that, John," said young John Woolman, stepping in beside him.

Two other men set their hands under the rim of the other side, and up over the rails they lifted it.

"Mind my ship!" said Taws.

The four men heaved with all their might and released the cask overboard. For a second all was silence, then a great crash sounded of splintering wood. The barrel would never be of use again for anything but firewood. It lay shattered on the surface. But not so much as a crack was visible in the ice.

"That's good enough for me!" said John Borton. "Ladders overboard! Come, John," he said to his son. "We're going ashore!"

And so it was that within the hour a stream of men and women walking gingerly across the ice met their welcoming neighbors, some on the ice, some on shore, with hugs and excited introductions and greetings brought from England.

The Quaker community of Burlington, New Jersey had just doubled its population.[*]

---

[*] Though I have fictionalized the landing of the *Shield*, and drawn upon other sources as well, I am deeply indebted to Janet Whitney's marvelously written and engaging book, *John Woolman, Quaker*, George G. Harrap & Co, London, 1943, for its insightful perspectives on New Jersey's colonization by the Quakers. It is one of the most expertly written and readable biographies I have read and I heartily recommend it to anyone wishing a more in-depth treatment of John Woolman's life.

The next few days were busily spent unloading the *Shield*, aided enormously by the thick ice. It soon began to break up, however, as a thaw set in. Operations had to cease until smaller boats could navigate back and forth to shore with the goods and possessions that had made the long journey. Among the most important commodities on board were sufficient English bricks, used as ballast in the lower portions of the ship, to build a dozen or more houses the following spring. Other building materials and tools were also on hand, though there was no hurry to unload anything but necessities. The *Shield* would not return to England until the weather turned and it could be loaded with merchandise, primarily animal skins, to take back to England. Most of their things would be safer kept on board until spring than anywhere else.

The Bortons and Woolmans and the others, staying in the homes of those who had arrived the previous year, survived the winter. The men were of course anxious to survey the lands they had purchased. As soon as the ship was unloaded, and as the weather permitted, they explored their environs and began to cut trees and plan where to build their houses. They would not be able to do a great deal before spring, when the work of clearing and planting would get under way in earnest. But these were not men to sit idly by while time passed. Unless it was snowing a blizzard or blowing a hurricane or raining a torrent, they were hard at work.

The Woolmans and Bortons had together, with William Petty, purchased a large joint tract on Rancocas Creek of some 350 acres. In establishing their homesteads they were a big help to one another. The eight Bortons possessed the advantages women bring to a household, cooking, mending, and the simple women's touch added to a rough life. The Woolman father and son contributed the strength of two men to the informal partnership. But it remained for another five years to pass before John Woolman and Elizabeth Borton were married.

John Borton and William and John Woolman cleared the land for
their plantations on Rancocas Creek and built sizeable brick houses
from the bricks carried in the hold of the *Shield*, and planted crops,
and prospered. The Borton and Woolman names were for generations
respected leaders of the colonial Quaker "Meetings" and passed down
thriving estates to their heirs. Both family names were known among
American Quakers not merely for decades, but for centuries.[2] Most
of their men were ministers and many also served as representatives to
the colonial government.

The Quaker community in Burlington thrived and grew. More
ships arrived bringing more settlers, and the banks of the Delaware
sprouted communities and towns. Venison, fowl, and fish were plentiful, as was wood for construction and warmth.

The Indians along the Delaware were friendly and fascinated by the
courteous white Quaker settlers, in whose eyes they appeared super-
human in their capabilities and knowledge and power to transform a
wilderness. The Indians proudly taught them the ways of the forests
and weather and instructed them in what crops to plant in the spring,
introducing yet another group of Europeans for the first time to corn.

The newcomers did not take long to acclimate themselves to their
new surroundings. In awe the natives watched as first houses then
whole towns were raised before their eyes. Wagons and plows, iron
implements and bronze, hammers and saws, jewelry of gold and
silver, forges, mills, enormous boats, windmills, clothes, looms . . . the
sights and skills they witnessed were stupendously unlike anything in
their ken. Towns and communities became almost immediately self-
sustaining and grew quickly. Truly these people had the skills and gifts
and ingenuity and knowledge and inventiveness of gods in the eyes of
the Indians, for whom even the wheel was at first a simple yet by them
an undiscovered mystery.

George Harland of Durham, England, who had recently fled to
Ireland to avoid persecution, sailed with his wife Elizabeth Duck
and their first four children, along with George's unmarried brother

Michael, in 1687. They settled near New Castle, then moved higher up the river near Brandywine Creek, and were leaders in the new government of Pennsylvania. They dropped the final letter of their name and were henceforth known as *Harlan*. The grandson of George and Elizabeth, Ezekiel Harlan, became a Quaker minister of the Chester County Meeting. Among others who came during this influx of Quakers were those of the name *Mueller* from Germany, *Brannon* from Ireland, and the name *Davidson* from England, whose descendents would migrate south into Virginia.

A son, Samuel, was born to John and Elizabeth Borton Woolman, and in time a son would also be born to him, the most famous son to bear the proud family name. The Bortons and Harlans and Davidsons also increased and married and gave the life and energy of their seed to a continent which they would help subdue.

William Penn's father died in 1670. Ten years later, after the New Jersey "experiment" was off to a strong start, Penn requested of the king, in exchange for his father's debt, a tract of land in America west of the New Jersey colony.

The request was granted.

It was an *enormous* expanse of land, the largest of its kind in the New World, measuring approximately 160 miles by an incredible 300 miles westward. Penn suggested the name *Sylvania* (Latin: *woods*) for the land, but, against Penn's objections, the king added the name *Penn*, in honor of Admiral Penn, William Penn's father.

Suddenly a second, and far larger Quaker colony in the New World was born.

William Penn immediately began planning to make the land available for colonization, primarily to Quakers, who were now flocking to the New World in droves, but to anyone willing to live under the terms and conditions he envisioned. He drew up a charter of liberties along similar lines as that which now governed New Jersey. Truly, William Penn was the father of what was to become American democracy. His writings and the two charters he had drawn up for Quaker New Jersey and Pennsylvania were later studied by Benjamin Franklin, the Quaker Thomas Paine, and others.

The colony of Pennsylvania was well under way, and a vision for the city of Philadelphia ("Brotherly Love"), laid out and planned by the time Penn himself was able to set sail and lay eyes on his new colony for the first time in 1682. His arrival in the colonies was eagerly anticipated by everyone who owed so much to this singular man and his vision of peaceful life and peaceful coexistence between peoples in America. As the *Welcome* sailed up the Delaware River, the shores were lined with settlers and half-naked Indians all anxious to see the man about whom they had heard so much.

Shortly after Penn's arrival, the elected assembly of Pennsylvania met at once and passed what was called the "Great Law of Pennsylvania," which established that Pennsylvania was to be a Christian state built on Quaker ideals.

William Penn brought Christian values into every aspect of his governance of the colony. One of his first acts was to befriend and make treaties with the Indians of his territory. A great conference was arranged with the Indians of the Delaware valley, at which Penn accorded their leaders every respect. Out of the conference came what is called the Great Treaty, one of the notable high points in European and Indian relations, a treaty which was honored for half a century and for which Penn became esteemed and loved by all the Indian tribes of the region. Over the next few years, Penn paid them generously for their lands, feeling that, though the king of England had granted him Pennsylvania, the land really belonged to the Indians. He could not take what they did not consent to sell. A tall and athletic man, he traveled among them, learned their languages, joined in their sports, always paid them fairly, and in all ways won their undying loyalty.

By 1700, Quakers mostly controlled Delaware, New Jersey, and Pennsylvania and were politically powerful in most of the other English colonies as well. Shiploads of new settlers were arriving, not now just a ship or two a year, but dozens of ships leaving England together and traveling in convoy to North America. Ahead of his contemporaries in so many ways, and seeing where such rapid growth must lead in the end, William Penn wrote and urged for a union of all the English colonies in America.

The ideal of religious freedom, however, was not practiced throughout the colonies with the same reality as it was by the Quakers. Even prior to the Concessions and Agreements, a handful of Quakers had immigrated to Boston, where persecution had followed them from England. Four peace-loving Quakers were hanged by fellow believing Puritans, the rest deported, and Quakers banned completely from the Massachusetts colony.

Yet no matter what the ideals upon which any enterprise is founded, growth invariably produces stress and change and inevitable conflict. As the country continued to grow, immigrants continued to flood in. Not all were Quakers. Not all were spiritually minded. The new land also drew the greedy and opportunistic.

And as farms and plantations and commerce widened, a trade in slaves slowly began to develop and expand which would become the evil bane of a land founded on the basis of religious "freedom" and equality.

Slavery of blacks and the cruel mistreatment of Indian tribes were cancers growing beneath the surface of the new nation that would ultimately test the strength of its spiritual roots.

A Nation's Conscience in Simple Garb
1720–1772

The mutual great-grandson of old William Woolman and of John and Anne Borton, who had come to Burlington together on the *Shield*, was born in 1720 at the Woolman homestead on Rancocas Creek to Samuel Woolman and his wife Elizabeth Burr. In the years since that landing, Burlington on the river had grown from a fledgling settlement to a thriving town. The child was named John after his Woolman grandfather and Borton great-grandfather.

Philadelphia, just downriver, was no longer a mere dream in William Penn's brain but already one of the largest cities in the colonies. All around Burlington County, New Jersey, other towns had sprung up among the Quaker settlements, towns such as Mount Holly a little further upstream from the Woolman Homestead, and Moorestown, which lay east about halfway between Mount Holly and Cooper's Ferry. Roads connected them all, and linked Philadelphia to New York, and, further north, to Boston. The colonies were fairly bursting with life and activity and business and growth. More immigrants arrived from England every year.

The Quaker immigrants to the New World had indeed found in New Jersey and Pennsylvania and Delaware what they had come seeking—as near an idyllic life as could be imagined. And they thrived in every way—families and communities grew without care of want or crime or greed. They prospered, financially and spiritually. The land was good to them and they treated it, and one another, with kindness and respect. Life and family and values were simple, but full of the rewards of simplicity and hard work. More than one Quaker writing of the period could not keep from comparing this world to Eden.[3]

The boy John Woolman grew up in this environment where family, church "Meeting" and school with other children of the community provided the framework for the values of Quaker life to be passed on from generation to generation.

Though Quaker Meetings were established on the principle of silence, and each man or woman's inner dialogue with God, the Quakers were nonetheless a remarkably *social* people. It was, in every sense, a society and community of *friends*. And its organization of mandatory Meetings—weekly local meetings, monthly county meetings, half-year and yearly regional meetings—insured constant social exchange throughout the entire Quaker community of Pennsylvania and New Jersey and beyond. Add to this that it had became a prosperous community, with many well-to-do families with large homes, and that the average family had eight or ten children, sometimes more, and with Philadelphia growing as a vibrant, thriving, bustling city . . . a vision emerges of an exciting time to be young with all of life and its multitude of opportunities spread out like a feast.

Quaker society at this time was not puritanical and stuffy. The simplicity of Quaker values had not translated into Spartanism. Though dancing was forbidden, alcohol and laughter and frivolity were not. It was a gay atmosphere of travel, cultured etiquette, refinement, and social grace in the best houses of Philadelphia society. In this environment, young John Woolman came to be known as an engaging, witty, personable young man.

Gradually, however, between his sixteenth and eighteenth year, an awareness of the emptiness of what he called the "vanities" of such a life began to waken in the soul of John Woolman.

For two or three years, he lived what might be called a double life, drifting in and out of what he calls a life of "folly," periodically convicted by God to give it up, yet unable and not altogether willing to stop.

It is impossible to say whether in these years he was influenced by the preaching and teaching of Jonathan Edwards, John Wesley, and George Whitefield and the Great Awakening then beginning in the colonies among the Puritans. As time went on, he must certainly have been aware of the huge crowds gathering in Philadelphia to hear Whitefield's preaching of the eternal burning fires of hell, and of the scorching fiery brimstone ready to overtake those who did not repent. It was a message that had swept England up in its wake and was now raging through the colonies, a new rousing into dramatic and emotional flame of English Puritanism, which would in time become known as *Evangelicalism.*

Yet the force and explosiveness of this movement seemed largely to pass by the Quakers. It was not fear of hell that tormented young John Woolman's soul. The spiritual yearnings within him were entirely positive. The desire of his heart was to know God, love God, be close to God, and to live a life pleasing to God.

Gradually young Woolman became convinced that he must leave the frivolous activities and pastimes of his Quaker friends. Slowly he began to withdraw from their company and keep more to himself.

As the change deepened, he began to discover the communion with God and the peace of soul he desired. While continuing to attend meetings, most of his leisure time he now spent at home, reading on Sunday afternoons and at night by the fire. The devotional writings of Francois de Fénelon and Thomas à Kempis's *The Imitation of Christ,* as well as Diderot's Encyclopedia, were all favorites in the Woolman home.

Having no particular ambitions, and feeling that he was to be single for a time, John remained at home working for his father on the family farm, and at the family craft of weaving, which had been the occupation of both his father and grandfather. At twenty-one, however, after a particularly hard winter, he came to the conclusion that he was perhaps not fit to endure the work for a lifetime as his stronger father had. Woolman thus began to consider other options that might be available for making a living.

About this time a man in the village of Mount Holly offered the twenty-one-year-old a job tending his baking and merchandise shop, and keeping his books. Woolman told his father of the offer. The two discussed it for several days, and at last mutually agreed that John should accept it.

The move to Mount Holly for his new career in the world of business was only a move of five miles, but it was a major change. For the first time in his life young John Woolman would be living alone, and would be entirely self-supporting. Having for several years kept to himself during his leisure time, he suddenly found himself among people again, possibly facing temptations toward his former life.

Though *silence* lay as a spiritual cornerstone for the Society of Friends, its counterpart *solitude* was not so widely practiced or sought as a doorway into wisdom. Everything about Quakerism was built around the social fabric of a "church" structure none the less that the word *Meeting* was employed in its stead. As *individual* as had been its roots, the *structure* was no less that of an organized church than that which George Fox had so unceremoniously rejected.

In his move from the family home and farm to the small lodging above his employer's shop in town, John Woolman discovered the balance, so rarely sought, and even more rarely found and practiced, between interaction with his fellow man and that solitude away from man so necessary to spiritual life and so exemplified in the life of Jesus. His daily dose of solitude balanced with work in the shop to feed and nurture the growing spiritual plant within him. The roots had been sent down during his years at home. Now the tree began to flourish and grow strong.

Thus, the years of his early twenties, as he tended his employer's shop, and as he grew and read and studied in the quietness of the lonely evenings, the good soil of John Woolman's Quaker upbringing bore fruit, thirty, sixty, and a hundredfold.

It did not take long before both Woolman and his employer discovered that the young man possessed an affinity for business, and enjoyed it. He liked his customers and they liked him. He was honest, had a head for books and numbers, was pleasing in manner, affable, enjoyed the flow of village life as relatives, family, friends, and strangers came and went, exchanging news, buying, asking advice, and passing the time of day. At the same time, the life of a shopkeeper was not without challenges.

"At home I had lived retired," Woolman wrote in his *Journal*, "and now having a prospect of being much in the way of company, I felt frequent and fervent cries in my heart to God . . . that he would preserve me from all taint and corruption; that, in this more public employment, I might serve him . . . in that humility and self-denial which I had in a small degree exercised in a more private life.

"By day I was much amongst people, and had many trials to go through; but in the evenings I was mostly alone, and I may with thankfulness acknowledge, that in those times . . . I felt my strength renewed."*

In addition to the business of the shop, Woolman found that he had an aptitude for much else besides. He had been studying at home, as he says in his Journal, to "improve himself" beyond what he had received in"schooling pretty well for a planter." His father had taught him much beyond farming—weaving, the rudiments of law and accounting. From his friend Josiah White he learned much in the way of amateur medicine—natural remedies, and herbs and potions gleaned from local Indians. His wide range of expertise began to manifest itself in requests for help in writing various accounting and legal documents, and occasionally even being sought for medical advice and treatment. His visits home now produced talks with Samuel Woolman that were the mature discussions between man and man. The love and mutual respect between father and son blossomed,

---

* John Woolman's *Journal*, Chapter 1

as young John continued to look to his father, as he had in the matter of the job, as his chief adviser and counselor.

⁓

Being in the shop provided fertile breeding ground for ideas and growth and new spiritual dilemmas. Woolman soon began thinking more about higher concerns of society and the plight of his fellow man. Gradually the condition of the Negro began to concern him, though it was not the first "social ill" about which he took courage to speak.

The silence of the Quaker meeting service, distinctive in Christianity, was based on the principle of hearing rightly what the Spirit of God was saying, then, if so led, speaking it forth for the collective good. Anyone was free to speak—man, woman, boy, or girl—but such speech must only be led by the Spirit and prompted by "Divine opening." A lesson which never left him came from an experience about this time when young John Woolman rose to speak in a Meeting. But then, as he described it, "not keeping close to the Divine opening, I said more than was required of me."

The blunder, as he considered it, tormented him for weeks, until gradually, through much prayer, peace of spirit gradually returned. About six weeks after the first incident, again he felt "the spring of Divine love opened, and a concern to speak," and once more he said a few words in a meeting. This time, however, he felt peace afterward, sensing that he had said just what God wanted him to and no more.

The two incidents proved pivotal in John Woolman's life. As a young man now of about twenty-three, increasingly he felt a call to speak to some need that he felt ought to be addressed. Along with this came a corresponding check to speak carefully, after much prayer, making sure his own house was in order before attempting to set straight anyone else's. After the two meetings, in his *Journal* Woolman wrote: "Being thus humbled and disciplined . . . my understanding became more strengthened to distinguish the pure spirit which inwardly moves upon the heart, and which taught me to wait in silence sometimes many weeks together, until I felt that rise which prepares the creature to stand like a trumpet, through which the Lord speaks to his flock." The principle would be one to guide him for the rest of his life.

Soft-spoken as he tried to remain, there were those in Burlington and Mount Holly who began to notice the gifts of young John Woolman's speech and countenance. Talk began to circulate concerning his selection to what was called "ministry."

There being no paid professional clergy within the Society of Friends, all were equally free to speak and contribute at meetings. Out of the laity were chosen those called "ministers"—men and women, from age fifteen onward who were recognized to possess insight and the ability to share their wisdom. The Ministers and Elders were the recognized leaders of each Meeting, and often traveled about together, visiting other Meetings and congregations. Such travels also provided opportunity for the elders among this invisible Quaker priesthood to train the younger ministers who would gradually assume leadership after them. Traveling about between Quaker meetings provided a spiritual apprenticeship and training ground.

In the Burlington Monthly Meeting of 1743, twenty-three-year-old John Woolman, among others, was recommended as a minister. It was a new role that he took seriously.

Of this gradual change in his outlook toward a more public and outspoken ministry, he wrote, "From an inward purifying, and steadfast abiding under it springs a lively operative desire for the good of others. All the faithful are not called to the public ministry; but whoever are, are called to minister of that which they have tasted and handled spiritually. The outward modes of worship are various; but whenever any are true ministers of Jesus Christ, it is from the operation of his Spirit upon their hearts, first purifying them, and thus giving them a just sense of the conditions of others. This truth was early fixed in my mind, and I was taught to watch the pure opening, and to take heed lest, while I was

standing to speak, my own will should get uppermost, and cause me to
utter words from worldly wisdom, and depart from the channel of the
true gospel ministry.'"*

One of his first opportunities to "speak out" came close to home
and was not in a Meeting at all. His employer's shop sat next to
a tavern, and since his coming to Mount Holly John had been
struck with the rowdiness of its inns and public houses, especially at
Christmas. He therefore went to the owner of the tavern and spoke
to him, simply and gently, with none of the fervor of judgment and
denunciation so common among religious zealots, suggesting that he
might temper the quantities served to some of his potentially wild and
rowdy guests.

And because he did not flash the fiery eye and point the angry
finger of judgment the gentle manner of John Woolman won friends
even among those whose consciences he sought to awaken. The owner
of the tavern treated him with all the more respect after his visit.

It was not against drink or riotous living or "folly," however, that
John Woolman's soft-spoken yet persistent voice would come to be
recognized as prophetic in his new land, but against the mushrooming
practice of slavery so linked to seafaring colonial expansion. Slavery
did not exist in England. The very idea of it would have been repug-
nant. Yet somehow those same English, transplanted to the American
colonies, gradually accustomed themselves to the notion of slavery
without the accompanying outrage it would have occasioned in their
own homeland.

Though from the beginning, slavery was not widespread among
Quakers, it was yet present in the Society and was a source of concern.
George Fox had written a pamphlet, "To Friends Beyond the Sea that
Have Blacks and Indian Slaves," reminding them of the mercifulness
of Christ and the necessity of displaying kindness "to every capti-
vated creature under the whole heaven." And in the very first years of

---

*   John Woolman's *Journal*, Chapter 1

Quakers settling near Philadelphia, at a monthly Meeting a discussion took place over the question, *Was it possible for slavery to fulfill the Golden Rule?*

Slavery grew out of indentured servitude, which, in the beginning, provided a legitimate means for an individual without resources to establish a new life in America.

The bound or indentured servant was thus an integral aspect of life in the colonies, and the line between indenture and outright slavery was often a murky one. If a man ran away before his agreed-upon time was up, and if apprehended, he was subject to a flogging at the public whipping post in the center of town. Newspapers regularly ran advertisements for runaways. John's uncle Burr had advertised in the *Pennsylvania Gazette* when John was nineteen: "Run away on the 12th inst from Mount Holly Iron Works in Burlington County, a Servant Man named Cornelius Kelly, about 21 Years of Age, tall & slim, thin face, short brown Hair . . . Had on when he went away a Felt Hat, a new brownish colored Coat much too big for him."

Gradually, however, as the commerce of the colonies expanded, especially in the southern colonies, and as trade in slaves from Africa became more and more a lucrative commercial enterprise, conditions of slaves in the colonies deteriorated.

Nor was there universal condemnation of slavery among Quakers. Indeed, some Quakers bought slaves in order to give them a better life. Yet on the whole there existed a general discomfort on the matter that kept the collective Quaker conscience stirred.

Many owned slaves in Mount Holly. Negroes were a familiar sight going about their errands. John Woolman's employer kept a Negro woman in the home as a slave and part of the household. Yet from early in his life, John was distressed about slavery. His objection was not primarily based on the *treatment* of slaves among Quakers, for in general Quakers were kind to their slaves as befitted their beliefs. He considered slavery itself wrong, and felt that it was spiritually damaging to slave owners themselves as well as oppressive and degrading to those trapped in slavery. His concern was equal for slave and owner.

Then arose a crisis that would change John Woolman's life. He was doing bookkeeping and legal business for his employer. His father had trained him to draw up wills and deeds and to carry out other duties of an attorney. One day his employer appeared in the shop with his slave woman beside him whom he was selling. He asked, almost casually as a matter of course, that John make out a bill of sale for the transaction. The woman was to be purchased by a Quaker of good standing in town.

Inwardly John recoiled. The prospect of writing out a bill of sale for a fellow human being repulsed him. But after brief deliberation, and as the buyer was an elderly Quaker known to him, he wrote out the document. His conscience was not easy about it, however, and the next time he was asked by another in his Meeting to write up a similar document, he declined.

"My employer," he wrote, "having a negro woman, sold her, and desired me to write a bill of sale, the man being waiting who bought her. The thing was sudden; and though I felt uneasy at the thoughts of writing an instrument of slavery for one of my fellow-creatures, yet I remembered that I was hired by the year, that it was my master who directed me to do it, and that it was an elderly man, a member of our Society, who bought her; so through weakness I gave way, and wrote it; but at the executing of it I was so afflicted in my mind, that I said before my master and the Friend that I believed slave-keeping to be a practice inconsistent with the Christian religion. This, in some degree, abated my uneasiness; yet as often as I reflected seriously upon it I thought I should have been clearer if I had desired to be excused from it, as a thing against my conscience; for such it was. Some time after this a young man of our Society spoke to me to write a conveyance of a slave to him, he having lately taken a negro into his house. I told him I was not easy to write it; for, though many of our meeting and in other places kept slaves, I still believed the practice was not right, and desired to be excused from the writing. I spoke to him in good-will; and he told me that keeping slaves was not altogether agreeable to his mind; but that the slave being a gift made to his wife he had accepted her."[*]

The two incidents crystallized John's position. Quickly now the conviction took shape and settled into what would become the predominant focus of his "public ministry."

By John Woolman's day, the name George Fox was legendary among Quakers. Many Quaker ministers followed his example, in the tradition of the spiritual pilgrimage of old, guided by a common "leading" from the Light Within, of traveling about, meeting people, attending meetings, writing journals, listening, speaking when led, and thus finding the way, alone with God, into deeper and more personal faith. Usually they traveled in pairs, one of the two having felt the "burden of concern," and the other accompanying him as a companion.

Shortly after the incident of the bill of sale, Woolman was asked to accompany one of the elder Quakers of the area, on a short journey around New Jersey. Woolman agreed, mostly remaining silent at the meetings and learning what he called "some profitable lessons."

Returning from the brief travels, he settled again into the business of his employer's shop. Other business offers came his way but he turned them down. He decided instead to learn the tailor's trade as a simpler profession "so to pass my time," he writes, "that nothing might hinder me from the most steady attention to the voice of the true shepherd." He was henceforth known in town as "the shopkeeper" or "the tailor." Gradually he shifted his emphasis to tailoring during what time he had available and to the extent his shopkeeping duties would allow.

After some time his employer's wife died and his employer retired and closed his shop. John Woolman thus set off on four lengthy journeys through New Jersey, Pennsylvania, Maryland, Virginia, and North Carolina and north through New York and Long Island to New England. As he went, especially in the South, the evil of slavery grew

---

[*]   John Woolman's *Journal*, Chapter 1

steadily stronger upon his mind. He saw the slave markets in nearby
Perth Amboy and Cooper's Ferry through newly horrified eyes. Even
as a boy he had seen the slave ships sailing up the Delaware as had
his ancestors, and their stench could be smelled even from the shore.
But among those slaves who were fortunate enough to be sold in the
North to be trained as house slaves or coachmen or grooms or garden-
ers or stablemen, life was not too bad. They were treated well enough,
even loved, by their owners. But settling all the more deeply into the
marrow of John Woolman's being was the fundamental question: *Was
it right?*

As he and his companions traveled south and witnessed field slavery
for the first time, the vastness of the cancer became far more personally real to him. When opportunity presented itself, John gently
attempted to bring the matter of slavery to the forefront of discussion
with those he visited. Whenever he had, in his opinion, been served
in any way by a slave, upon departure he left a small payment in the
hands of his or her owner to be given them with his gratitude.

As they moved south into the region of the Quaker Virginia Yearly
Meeting, Woolman and his companions beheld a scene unfamiliar to
their New Jersey eyes—Negroes at work in long rows of "the bewitch-
ing Vegetable Tobacco," the men in red cotton trousers and battered
broad hats, the women in faded dresses with white kerchiefs wound as
turbans round their heads. A white overseer, whose job it was all day
to prevent idleness, leaned against a tree in the shade. Close of day
was approaching as they rode in, and cheerfulness was evident in the
expression of the workers. Fatigue was forgotten in anticipation of the
happy evening close at hand.

Observing it all, John Woolman perceived no outward sign of unhap-
piness. The sweating black faces wore good-natured smiles. If now and
then a groan sounded, it disappeared the moment the welcome whistle
sounded and husbands and wives rejoined each other for the happy trek
homeward. But the bare legs and feet scuffling along the dusty road
were thin and covered with sores.

Later as he attended to his horse in the stable, Woolman looked out behind the stable to the row of Negro cabins behind the house. The slaves who dwelt in the tiny village were grinding corn and preparing the evening meal. At first glance it was a scene of cheerful bustle. A voice was raised in song. Children who had been left behind all day in the care of an old granny scampered about at the feet of their mothers.

Woolman observed it all through the lens of one who had himself grown up on a farm and had worked long days in the fields on his father's plantation. He knew both the joys and hardships of the farming life.

"Do these people," he asked his host later in the evening, "have to grind their own corn after they come in before they can get anything to eat?"

"Of course," replied the man.

Woolman nodded but said no more. He was thinking.

It being Saturday, the next day was the first day of the week. At the Meeting, though a number of planter families gathered, Woolman noted that no Negroes were present.

After the meeting, as he spoke informally with the men, he asked if their slaves ever came to Meeting. The men glanced about at one another. A few shook their heads.

"Do they then hold any kind of church meeting of their own?" he asked.

Again the answer was in the negative.

"What then is done for their religious enlightenment?" John persisted.

"By us, does thee mean?" asked one of the men.

"Yes, by thee who are responsible for their welfare."

"Nothing, I suppose," shrugged another man.

"Are they then, in fact, left to live like animals?" rejoined Woolman. "How does this affect their whole moral sense? What standards do they have of duty, honesty, right, or wrong? If they are not instructed in these things, how can they know them? And what about their marriages? If they never go to any church, who marries them, and when, and how?"

The men had no answers to give. Their visitor pressed no further.
He had sensed his own traveling companion squirming as well from
his pointed questions. It was time to let his words settle.

In such out-of-the-way plantations as these conversation was at a
premium. Any discussion was welcome. Day after day passed monoto-
nously with no mail, no newspapers. The hospitable, well-meaning,
and unsuspecting hosts where the men from New Jersey stayed as they
proceeded south were delighted to have visitors. They were fascinated,
too, by John Woolman—so easy a talker, so open and friendly, so well-
informed about events and stirrings in the outer world. Yet they found
themselves getting more than they bargained for. In this graceful
young man they found that they were entertaining a thief who robbed
them of their complacency. Yet his manners were such that they
took his questions and occasional probing remarks without offense,
with usually a memory left after his departure of a conversation that
searched the soul.

Woolman's method of exploring any thorny issue was by conversation. There was always give and take. Woolman was an inquirer, not a
lecturer. He wished to learn about the slave system, and was anxious to
have the owner state his case. He listened earnestly to all that was said.
But invariably he brought the subject eventually around into the light
of what seemed to the planters an impractical, and perhaps youthful,
idealism. Chatting informally with his host—whether on horseback,
or strolling about the plantation, or seated by candlelight after the
evening meal—Woolman slowly and modestly unfolded his remarkable ideas to the planter.

John Woolman's acute perception made it impossible for him to
observe slavery in a pained and discreet silence. Every comfort around
him in a plantation house came as the direct result of the profit from
the slave. Once you looked in that direction you could see nothing
else. The slave grew the tobacco, and it was exchanged for the ornate
furniture, the woven carpet, the glass and silver, the lady's dress, the
planter's fine pair of boots, the book of poems or sermons—and the

ever-present jug of rum. He could not take the existence of such
things for granted.

"Two things were remarkable to me in this journey," he later wrote:
"first, in regard to my entertainment. When I ate, drank, and lodged
free-cost with people who lived in ease on the hard labor of their slaves
I felt uneasy; and as my mind was inward to the Lord, I found this
uneasiness return upon me, at times, through the whole visit. Where
the masters bore a good share of the burden, and lived frugally, so
that their servants were well provided for, and their labor moderate,
I felt more easy; but where they lived in a costly way, and laid heavy
burdens on their slaves, my exercise was often great, and I frequently
had conversation with them in private concerning it. Secondly, this
trade of importing slaves from their native country being much
encouraged amongst them, and the white people and their children
so generally living without much labor, was frequently the subject
of my serious thoughts. I saw in these southern provinces so many
vices and corruptions, increased by this trade and this way of life, that
it appeared to me as a dark gloominess hanging over the land, and
though now many willingly run into it, yet in future the consequence
will be grievous to posterity. I express it as it hath appeared to me, not
once, nor twice, but as a matter fixed on my mind."[*]

In this first impact upon him of the Southern slave system, seeing it
up close for the first time, Woolman's initial impression was not one of
abject cruelty. How different Woolman's impressions were from George
Whitefield's about the same time. After a similar sojourn, Whitefield
wrote a letter to the inhabitants of Maryland, Virginia, and North and
South Carolina, in which he enumerated the "miseries of the poor
negroes." A plantation owner, conscience-stricken by Whitefield's fervor,
might easily rectify such conditions by feeding his slaves more and beating them less. Whitefield spoke to surface conditions. He did not probe
uncomfortably deep. When it came to the principle of slavery itself he
did not condemn it outright.

---

[*]   John Woolman's *Journal*, Chapter 2

It was Woolman, more than a hundred years before the name Abraham Lincoln was known, who went straight to the root.

Rather than immediately decry the plight of the Negro slave, Woolman had the insight equally to observe the harm done to white owners of slaves. In his first glimpse of the tobacco fields Woolman had not been struck by the miseries of the slaves so much as by the lethargy of the overseer.

He looked deeper than the labor itself, to the will behind the labor. The overseer had to supply all the driving power, all the motive, for his workers . . . all the *will*. The laborers had no ambition, no initiative, no interest in the work. Their only desire was to do as little as possible. The overseer's task was to coax, praise, scold, persuade: to set *his* will behind *their* inertia and somehow get the necessary minimum of work accomplished. It was not surprising that, like the schoolmaster, he often took the whip in hand. And once the incentive of physical pain was resorted to, with unlimited power and no one to interfere, it could lead to the most horrifying of excesses.

Such excesses, however, were not universal. On this journey Woolman mentions none. The easygoing planters of Virginia and Maryland did not expect or require a maximum efficiency from their slaves. Many of them inspired their slaves by working themselves, at least in the way of personal oversight. This was better, said Woolman. But it was simply a poor system, harmful to everyone—to the plantation owner, to the slaves, to the economy of the South, and to the whole white population. Slavery was bad for everybody.

Woolman's conclusion went straight to the heart of the matter and laid axe to the trunk: *And as for a Christian,* he said, *is there any Christian way to treat a slave except to set him free?*

"When we remember," Woolman later wrote, "that all nations are of one blood, that in this world we are but sojourners . . . and that the All wise Being is Judge and Lord over us all, it seems to raise an idea of a general Brotherhood . . .

"To consider mankind otherwise than brethren, to think favors are peculiar to one nation and exclude others, plainly supposes a darkness in the understanding. For, as God's love is universal, so where the mind is sufficiently influenced by it, it begets a Likeness of itself, and the heart is enlarged toward all men.

"When self-love presides in our minds, our opinions are biased in our own favor . . .

"To humbly apply to God for wisdom that we may thereby be enabled to see things as they are and ought to be, is very needful. Hereby high thoughts will be laid aside, and all men treated as becometh the sons of one Father, agreeable to the doctrine of Christ Jesus."

When John Woolman returned to Burlington County after three months in the South, he rode up to his father's house, greeted by younger brothers and sisters and mother and father all anxious to hear of his journey. When supper was over, they gathered on the grass outside in the warm August evening to hear everything he had to tell them. It was so serene and peaceful there.

But John Woolman's mind and heart were full of slavery, and his firsthand witness of conditions in the colonies south of New Jersey and Pennsylvania.[*]

When the idea first came to John Woolman that he might influence his fellow Quakers by the power of the pen is unknown. But at some point after these first journeys south, in his late twenties, he began to write down some of his thoughts concerning slavery, sharing his work at every stage with his father. Apparently he did not intend at first to publish what he was writing. Still strong within him was the sense of spiritual conviction as a private matter. Yet as he and his father discussed the matter, his work on the writing was sufficiently serious that he sought his father's advice concerning it. And after reading his thoughts, the father pressed the son to publish his work.

---

[*]   This fictionalization of Woolman's southern journey is adapted from Janet Whitney's wonderful account in *John Woolman, Quaker,* pages 110-115. I have occasionally used her words and would here credit her not only with perception and insight in her handling of this phase of Woolman's life, but with her masterful writing craft upon which I could never hope to improve. The brilliant analogy of John Woolman as "thief of complacency" is hers. Her account brings John Woolman the man alive as no other account I have read.

The younger Woolman, however, was reluctant. His efforts till now had remained personal and conversational—one on one. At the time he was thinking of other things as well, namely his future. He purchased the premises of his former employer and opened his own shop, and a year later married Sarah Ellis. The two moved into Woolman's newly purchased house on eleven acres just outside Mount Holly, and a year later a daughter was born to them.

His relationship with his father remained one of the strengthening foundation stones in John Woolman's life. He and Sarah often rode over to the home farm, and Samuel Woolman, still strong at sixty, would ride into Mount Holly to spend the evening with his son and new daughter-in-law and to discuss slavery, business, farming, war— which had now come to the colonies—and to read John's manuscripts. Sarah was a sympathetic listener. But it was Samuel Woolman who provided the steadying rudder for his son's thoughts, and was the most valued and candid critic on his writings.

John's father died in 1750. On his deathbed Samuel Woolman asked his son again whether he intended to publish the small book on slavery. "I have all along," his father told him, "been deeply affected with the oppression of poor Negroes, and now at last my concern for them is as great as ever."

At the death of his father, John Woolman at thirty stood as the head of his family as the eldest son, and was by now widely recognized by the men of Burlington Meeting as one of their leading spokes-men. Slavery continued to gnaw at him as a scourge on humanity's conscience. But his slavery manuscript remained unpublished for another three years. Others would launch crusades, Whitefield and Wesley and Wilberforce, as had George Fox before them. But John Woolman waited.

Several years later, at last he decided to speak publicly. He had been refining and polishing and honing his manuscript for six years. Finally he submitted it to the Ministers and Elders of his meeting. With their approval, *Some Considerations on the Keeping of Negroes* was published in 1754 and sent to every Quaker Yearly Meeting throughout the colonies. Though circulated at first through the network of the Quaker community, Woolman nowhere mentions the Society of Friends specifically. He addresses his work "To the Professors of Christianity of Every Denomination," meaning all those who *professed* the Christian faith.

The reaction was instantaneous. No other document opposing slavery had ever been so widely distributed. Its message, as was said, sounded through the Society of Friends "like a trumpet blast" and roused Quakers everywhere to the controversy. Suddenly the simple tailor of Mount Holly was a figure of renown.

Even with a "reputation" now following him, as a man devoted to simplicity in his life, John Woolman sought to live his convictions practically. If too much business began coming to him, he sent customers to other shops. If a woman was debating between choices of cloth, he would encourage her toward the simplest and least expensive. Mostly his was a simplicity of outlook, an *inward* simplicity rather than what might have been visible externally. Balance regulated all—balance between outward concerns and inner convictions, between keeping silent and speaking out, balance between business profit and a life of frugality. In Woolman's view, his first duty was to live a consistent life within himself.

Very early in his *Journal,* Woolman wrote what would be a guiding principle throughout his every business venture large and small: "Being clearly convinced in my judgment that to place my whole trust in God was best for me, I felt . . . that in all things I might act on an inward principle of virtue, and pursue worldly business no further than as truth opened my way."

He amplified on this principle, saying, "My mind, through the power of truth, was in good degree weaned from the desire of outward greatness, and I was learning to be content with real conveniences, that were not costly, so that a way of life free from much entanglement appeared best for me, though the income might be small. I had several offers of business that appeared profitable, but I did not see my way clear to accept of them, believing they would be attended with more outward care and cumber than was required of me to engage in. I saw that an humble man, with the blessing of the Lord, might live on a little, and that where the heart was set on greatness, success in business did not satisfy the craving; but that commonly with an increase of wealth the desire of wealth increased. There was a care on my mind so to pass my time that nothing might hinder me from the most steady attention to the voice of the true Shepherd.""

And now, many years later, that same principle continued to guide him.

Yet his determination to live by his scruples, never to tell a lie, never to overcharge or sell goods or services that were unneeded, did not dim his sense of humor, his wit, his keen intellect and business sense. He remained the man his friends and relatives were most likely to go to for perspective, for advice, for insight concerning any dilemma. All his life he was engaging, charming, full of grace and selflessness. He was simply a man doing his best to live a humble, consistent, and balanced life.

Woolman's intent was for his shop to serve as an adjunct to his tailoring trade. Making clothes for his neighbors and friends seems to have been his first love. He had merely intended to sell linens, buttons, and the other necessary trimmings. For in addition to the tailoring of garments, Woolman now desired to devote more time to writing.

But the demand for much else gradually led to a shop with a great variety of merchandise, from tea and thread to rum and coffee and butter and molasses, dishes and utensils, chocolate and candy, gloves, even a small stock of lumber. The shop prospered in spite of his efforts to keep it on a small scale.

As slaves were used on indigo plantations so fundamental to the making of dyes, sometime later he began to wear undyed clothing. Though he loathed calling attention to externals, he felt he must modify his dress to be consistent with his convictions. His appearance mostly in white or natural-colored clothing was unique and recogniz-

---

*   John Woolman's *Journal*, Chapter 1

able around Mount Holly. He was always asking God to illuminate some additional area of his life that needed to come under Divine scrutiny. He was never *satisfied* with himself. In his fiftieth year he gave up the use of rum. He had never regarded alcohol as such as evil. He spoke, rather, against excess and misuse. And when he finally gave up rum, he gave up sugar and molasses at the same time—he had recently learned about the cruel conditions of the slaves in the West Indies where all three were mostly produced.

In three chief areas he felt the simple life was undermined in the life of many Christians: love of money, haste and urgency, and spiritual compromise. "In the love of money and in the wisdom of this world," he wrote, "business is proposed, then in the urgency of affairs pushed forward, and the mind cannot in this state discern the good and perfect will of God."

Woolman's empathy toward the plight of the American Negro was mirrored in his love and concern for the native Indian tribes of America, leading him to undertake a difficult and dangerous journey among them in 1762, even though the French and Indian War was still in progress.

At a meeting in Philadelphia he found himself in conversation with a Quaker minister by the name of Ezekiel Harlan from Chester about whom he had heard news that intrigued him.

"Tell me, Friend Harlan," Woolman asked, "is what I hear of thy brother true, that he has taken an Indian maiden for a wife?"

"It is true, John," replied Harlan. "He was traveling in the Carolinas with some of our brethren and chanced to meet her in the western woodlands. She is said to be the daughter of one of the famous women of the Cherokee. She had been twice widowed when Ellis met her, though had no children."

"What is the girl's name?"

"Cata'quin Kingfisher."

"An Indian name indeed!" smiled Woolman. "And your son remains there?"

"He is happy living with the Cherokee. He says they are the most

civilized people he has ever met, outside Quakers, that is. They now
have four children, but we expect more."

"I would dearly like to meet thy brother . . . and his wife," said
Woolman. "I am considering a journey among the Indians myself
very soon."

Of his decision to make more personal acquaintance with Indians,
Woolman wrote, "Having for many years felt love in my heart towards
the natives of this land who dwell far back in the wilderness, whose
ancestors were formerly the owners and possessors of the land where
we dwell, and who for a small consideration assigned their inheritance
to us, and being in Philadelphia . . . on a visit to some Friends who
had slaves, I fell in company with some of those natives who lived
on the east branch of the river Susquehanna at an Indian town called
Wehaloosing, two hundred miles from Philadelphia. In conversation with them by an interpreter, as also by observations on their
countenances and conduct, I believed some of them were measurably
acquainted with that Divine power which subjects the rough forward
will. . . . Love was the first motion and thence a concern arose to
spend some time with the Indians that I might feel and understand
their life and the spirit they live in, if haply I might receive some
instruction from them, or they might be in any degree helped forward
by my following the leadings of truth among them."[*]

The following June, with Indian guides arranged for, he set out into
the Pennsylvania wilderness on a journey that proved as dangerous as
it was eventful.

Returning home, he continued to work on his *Journal* and write
on an increasing variety of topics of concern to his Quaker brethren
in increasingly turbulent times. A second installment of *On Keeping
Negroes* was published by Benjamin Franklin in Philadelphia.

John Woolman continued to speak out against slavery and traveled
more and more. As the country moved toward conflict and eventual
war with England over independence, John Woolman planned a trip
back to the homeland of his ancestors. He sailed at the end of April

---

[*] John Woolman's *Journal*, Chapter 8

1772, steerage class, arrived in London in June, and visited Quaker Meetings throughout England, walking almost the length of the country up into Northumbria, and partway back.

He contracted smallpox and died at York in late September. He was fifty-two.

John Woolman's *Journal* was first published two years later, only two years before the outbreak of the American Revolution. It was published in dozens of editions in the years since, and became a spiritual classic, equal in influence to the *Journal* of George Fox and William Penn's *No Cross, No Crown* among Quaker writings. It is certain that most, if not all, of the founders of the fledgling nation surely knew of and were to some degree influenced by the writings of John Woolman.

During his lifetime, Woolman did not succeed in eliminating slavery within the Society of Friends. But his efforts changed many Quaker viewpoints, and within twenty years of his death, the Society of Friends eventually banned slavery among their people, and in 1790 petitioned the newly formed Congress of the United States for the abolition of slavery.

The tailor of Mount Holly lived on through his writings, and devout men and women were still reading them a century later.

Freedom and Bondage
1852

$\mathcal{A}$ tall, strong, muscular Negro man, sweat pouring from his face, bare chest, and shoulders, glanced up to see his employer, a white man wearing blue trousers, plain linen shirt, and a wide-brimmed black hat, walking toward him. The black man relaxed his right hand from its clutch on a heavy iron hammer, and with the tong in his left thrust the horseshoe he had been shaping under merciless blows steaming into a rusty water tub in front of the forge.

"How is the new gate coming, Aaron?" said the white man as he approached.

"Be finished today or tomorrow, Mr. Borton," replied the blacksmith. "I'm just getting this shoe on Mr. Pemberton's horse from that one he threw yesterday, then I'll be back to the gate."

"Fine, then. No hurry, though I would like thee to have it completed before I leave for Yearly Meeting in Philadelphia."

"When will that be, Mr. Borton?"

"Next week."

"We'll have it up by then, so long as thee and Mr. Pemberton can give me a hand with setting it in place."

"Of course. Let me know when thee is ready for our help."

John Borton and Aaron Steddings had known one another since boyhood. They had played with other Quaker boys, white and black, on the banks of Rancocas Creek, and rafted and fished on the mighty

Delaware that Borton's ancestors had sailed up for the first time 170 years before. Now they were men who worked alongside one another in mutual consideration and respect without regard for their difference of race.

New Jersey was a Northern state where, since 1804, slavery, though not technically abolished, had been in steady decline. The roots of Burlington County were so strongly Quaker that slavery had never been widespread here, and the Quakers from this region had altogether given up slavery two and three generations earlier.

The fact that this particular black man worked for this particular white man had nothing to do with the color of their skin. The arrangement was purely economic. John Borton was one of the leading men of Mount Holly, a farmer and businessman with sizeable holdings, not unlike many descendents of those first Quaker settlers. They had thrived in the new land to which they had come, and their descendents has prospered after them. Aaron Steddings was a laborer, without the inherited means of his employer. His grandfather had come as an indentured servant to this region and had worked faithfully for his freedom. Aaron worked with his hands at the smithy's trade and was grateful to have a good job wherewith to feed wife and children, and, perhaps in time, as was the American way with free and hardworking men and women, to better his lot. He had his eye on a five-acre parcel one of the men of their Meeting planned to sell, and dreamed of someday building a house with his own hands that he could pass on to his son.

Both men attended the same Quaker Meeting. Spiritually they were brothers in Christ.

They were distinct from other residents of Mount Holly, New Jersey, however, in this. Both descended from well-known families of history in the region.

John Borton still bore the respected name of his legendary great-great-great-grandfather who had come ashore across the ice that first day in 1678 after the arrival of the second shipload of Quakers to the New World from England. The Bortons had been here ever since, and the name had spread throughout the colonies. Even as the original homestead of 110 acres had gradually shrunk between sons and grandsons and great-grandsons, new land had been purchased and sons and grandsons and daughters and granddaughters of large families had married and taken their Quaker roots up and down the Atlantic seaboard and west to Ohio and Indiana. John and Anne's inquisitive son, who had crossed the wide Atlantic at nine, lost two wives and with his third moved to join Quakers in William Penn's Pennsylvania. His son Obadiah, a widely respected Quaker minister, married Susanna Butcher, of English name as longstanding as her husband's and whose family had also immigrated to Burlington County. Their son John married Hannah Haines. Their son John became a Quaker minister, whose son John married Ketturah Haines, and upon her death Martha Woolman, possessor of an equally prestigious pedigree as great-great-great-granddaughter of old William Woolman who followed John Borton ashore from the *Shield*. The present John Borton was therefore the fifth *John Borton* in six generations to carry on the proud family name from Aynho, Northhamptonshire, England.

Though he could not trace his ancestry back to his native land of Africa as could the Borton, Woolman, Harlan, and Davidson names to their native England, Aaron Steddings' *spiritual* pedigree was no less significant in the annals of Quaker influence in the history of this nation called the United States of America. It was a spiritual pedigree linked to the Woolman name of Borton's wife Martha.

In the early 1750s, almost a century before when Mount Holly had been much smaller than today, one of its prominent farmers was thrown from his horse and, though no bones were broken, a serious bruise on his thigh resulted. The bruise worsened, swelled, the whole leg became inflamed, and the man began to fear for his life. With his wife's help, for by now he could hardly walk, he paid a visit to his neighbor, a literate man of unusual talents who had a tailor's shop in the village, who knew medicine, and to whom many in the neighborhood also went for legal assistance.

Assisted by his wife, the farmer limped into John Woolman's establishment, obviously in great pain, and requested Woolman to bleed
the wound. The tailor of Mount Holly led them into the back where
he had his office, equipment, and supplies, but after the treatment, his
pain and distress seemed as great as ever.

"I also wonder, if you do not mind, John," said the farmer, grimac-
ing in pain, "if I could prevail upon you to write my will."

"Of course," replied Woolman. He immediately rose, got pen and
ink and paper, then sat down again and began to take notes as the
man specified the disposition of his property, which was not extensive.

"I also have a young Negro slave girl," he said. "Her name is Betsy
Ferris. She is to become the property of my son William."

Woolman completed his notes, and, with a few instructions about
his leg, the man returned home and took to his bed.

Woolman called at the farm several days later. He was shown to the
man's bedside.

"I am sorry thy troubles have not abated," he said. "But I have
prepared thy will and hope that will help set thy mind at ease."

"Ah, good . . . sit down," said the farmer. "Read it to me,
Woolman."

The tailor took a chair and proceeded to read the will he had drawn
up. At length he came to the point where his conscience had required
him to cease.

"I am deeply sorry," he said, "but further than this I have not written. In the matter of thy slave girl, I am unable as a matter of principle
to write any legal instrument by which my fellow creatures are made
slaves of any other. I know such was thy wish, but it is something I
cannot do. I will charge thee nothing for what I have prepared."

"I have heard of your scruples over such matters, Woolman,"
smiled the man. "I cannot say I am surprised. I know the story of old
Alexander Hawkins' will and your refusal to dictate in writing the
disposition of his slaves to his son. The whole town knows of it."

A lengthy talk on the subject of slaves followed.

"Well, Woolman," said the man at last, "I cannot tell whether you are stubborn or a simpleton, but no one will accuse you of not being a man of conscience. And if old Alexander Hawkins can free his slaves and still count you his friend, I suppose I can too. So finalize the will as it stands, and I shall sign it. Along with it prepare a writ of release for Betsy. She shall be a free Negro and your conscience shall be at liberty, and I shall die having at least done one good turn from my sickbed."[*]

Betsy Ferris continued to work in the employ, now for pay, of her former master, who recovered from his injury. In the next twenty years, as Woolman's influence grew throughout the Quaker community from Virginia to Boston, most Quakers eventually set their slaves free, such that in Burlington County hundreds of free Negroes lived and worked alongside their white neighbors.

Betsy Ferris married Jacob Hern. Their daughter Elsa married Elijah Steddings, indentured servant who eventually won his freedom. Their son David married Samantha Jenkins. To them in 1801 was born a son Aaron, now a third generation free Negro of Mount Holly, New Jersey. Aaron Steddings married Zaphorah Enderts, and to them were born two daughters, Mary and Deanna, and a son Moses, and now Zaphorah was three months on her way with a fourth child.

In truth, the life of Aaron Steddings was therefore fruit grown from the Quaker tree of equality between man and woman.

"What wouldst thou think, Aaron," said Borton after the two had chatted for several minutes concerning the construction of the new gate, "after I return from Philadelphia, of making a trip to Virginia for me?"

"Virginia—that is a long way, Mr. Borton. That is south of Delaware, is it not?"

"That's right. It would be a journey of perhaps two hundred miles."

"I would dislike leaving Zaphorah and the young ones for that long."

---

[*]   Though here amplified and fictionalized, this account is taken from John Woolman's *Journal*, ch. 3.

"What if I was to say thee could take them along?"

"That would be an even longer trip to take with a wife and with children!" grinned Steddings.

Borton laughed. "Thee has indeed spoken truly!" he said. "But it would be a great favor to me, Aaron," he added seriously. "My sister's husband has recently died and she is unable to get the work of the farm done. She has but two hired men, both free Negroes like thee. But she needs a man to instruct them. The work is falling badly behind. Pemberton and I need to be here for the same reason, for our harvest. We have told her about thee and that we trust thee entirely. That is of course if thy wife's condition will permit it. I understand she is with child."

"Yes, sir. And she is feeling well, but . . . there are still slaves in Virginia, aren't there?" asked Steddings.

"Slavery still exists, if that is what thee means. Our sister, of course, has no slaves."

"It would cause me some uneasiness to travel where there are slaves. White folks down there, they are not like white folks here."

"I understand. But Virginia is one of the more tolerant Southern states. It probably has more free Negroes than any other. I am certain thee will encounter no difficulty. But as a precaution, I will prepare documents that will attest to thy freedom if thee is questioned. They will say that thee works for me."

Steddings nodded thoughtfully. Borton went on to further outline his request.

"How will we find our way all that distance?"

"I will give thee a map of the Great Road, as well as how to find our friends along the way. My sister will pay thee well," he said. "Thee will have a comfortable place to stay for thy family, and all thy food and whatever thou needs will be provided. Thy wife should be as comfortable as she is here."

"What about the house here in Mount Holly, Mr. Borton?" asked Steddings. "We have our bills to pay."

"I will see to thy rent with Mr. Burr while thee is away," replied

Borton. "Thee will owe me nothing in return. It will be a way of expressing my gratitude for this favor. I know thee has wanted to set enough aside to purchase that five acres from Brother Buffington. Thee might earn enough from this harvest for a first payment. My sister does not want for money. She will be most grateful for thy help."

Steddings took in the information with obvious interest. This did change things.

"I do not mean to twist thy arm, Aaron. The decision is thy own to make. Thee and Zaphorah pray the matter over and see what the Lord would have thee do."

"I thank thee, Mr. Borton," said Steddings. "Thee has always been very kind to us. We will be quiet before the Lord and see what the Light has to say."

The white man turned and walked back in the direction of the plantation house, while the blacksmith returned to his forge and horseshoe.

Three weeks after his conversation with his employer, Aaron Steddings led a large covered road-carriage pulled by two horses from the Borton farm through gently rolling farmland of eastern Virginia. Steddings and his family had been on the road for six days, staying at homes of Quaker families on their route, to whom letters of introduction had been sent ahead by John and Martha Borton.

They had crossed the mighty Delaware at Philadelphia, then had followed the Great Wagon Road south through Baltimore. They had marveled at the cities, the likes of which they had never seen, and were grateful for the homes of Friends as a refuge from the teeming noise and bustle and activity. Their journey had now brought them halfway between Washington and Richmond.

As they progressed south through Maryland, and now Virginia, they passed many fields full of Negro laborers, some readying for and some already in full harvest of their crops of wheat, cotton, and tobacco, occasionally with melancholy songs of bondage drifting toward them. They were seeing the widespread reality of slavery for the first time with their own eyes. Aaron and Zaphorah became subdued as they went. The sight was sobering. These were their own people, their own race with whom they shared a common African heritage. And they could not help feeling a pang as now and then a weary laborer from the fields glanced up and cast upon them a longing, questioning, forlorn gaze as they went slowly by.

They also encountered more and more unfriendly stares from those they passed on the road. The sight of Negroes traveling alone seemed offensive in the eyes of whites. But the fact that they were moving south rather than north kept anyone from asking too many questions.

At the Quaker homes where the Bortons had arranged for them to stay, however, they were warmly received as if they were part of the family, as indeed they were. On account of the letters sent out, they were welcomed as emissaries from the two legendary Quaker families they represented, reminding their hosts nostalgically of a golden age in Quaker history when ministers such as John Woolman traveled up and down the country visiting in homes and, one person at a time, changed the attitude of many in the country toward slavery. In the circles in which they were traveling, the name *Woolman* was of a stature equal to, if not greater than, those of Franklin, Washington, Adams, Madison, and Jefferson. Even after his untimely passing from smallpox, the tailor of Mount Holly spoke as an invisible conscience to the fledgling nation.*

Thus the arrival of Aaron and Zaphorah Steddings and their three children each night at a new Quaker home or farmhouse was imbued with greater significance than it might have been had the letter of introduction not come from scions of the Borton and Woolman lines. And the fact that they were *Negro* Quakers, a uniqueness of its own, added to the charm of their speech and the fascination of the visit. Zaphorah was well spoken, and their children respectful and delightful. The family could not help enchanting most of their hosts.

---

* Though the scenes of the story, and the persons of Aaron and Zaphorah Steddings and their family, are all fictionalized, John and Martha Woolman, and their ancestry, are factual.

Quakerism had changed over the years. Gradually, as they had prospered and integrated into the society of the English colonies and later of the growing nation, Quakers became in general patriotic and lawful citizens. As much of colonial government, especially the laws of Pennsylvania and New Jersey, had been founded on the basis of Quaker principles, the need for civil disobedience on the part of religious individuals had not been widely felt as it had been earlier in England.

But as the problem of slavery intensified in the decades of the nineteenth century, a split began to be felt within the Society of Friends, brought into sharp focus in 1793 by the Fugitive Slave Law.* Though Quakers were opposed to slavery as an institution, this law presented them with a difficult quandary—whether or not to *obey* the law of the land and return runaways to their owners, or to government officials and bounty hunters, or whether, like their English forebears, to *defy* the nation's laws on a principle of conscience. It was a moment in their history when Quakers had to put their beliefs to the test.

Many Quakers were prosperous businessmen, farmers, and plantation owners. They understood the principle of ownership. Some felt that not to return a slave to its owner was equal to robbery, preventing a man regaining what he owned. Those on the opposite side of the argument insisted that slave owners had no right to what was in truth stolen property in the first place. The slave had been stolen from his homeland. His freedom had been stolen from him . . . everything he possessed as a human being—family, dignity, ancestry—had been stolen *from him.* What right, then, did a plantation owner have to claim that he "owned" such a man from whom all human dignity had been stripped?

So the arguments went. Some Quakers insisted that they had an obligation to obey the government in support of the Fugitive Slave Law. Many others believed that they must help runaways to get north where they would have a better chance of being free. By the middle of the nineteenth century, most Quakers agreed that slavery was wrong.

---

* A second Fugitive Slave Law, which figured even more prominently into the activities of the Underground Railroad as the Civil War approached, was passed in 1850.

But would they or would they not place that conviction against slavery on the line when it came to *helping* runaways?

The dispute was heated. Men and women were read out of Meetings for helping runaways. Some entire Meetings were read out of their larger regional Meetings for their policy of aiding runaways.

As more and more slaves escaped and fled north, more and more Quakers did choose to help them. The term "Underground Railroad" first came into widespread use in connection with Indiana Quaker Levi Coffin, later called the President of the Underground Railroad, who helped more than three thousand runaways escape.

By the 1830s and 1840s it had become extremely dangerous to participate in the illegal activity of helping fugitive slaves, with hostile neighbors or accidental visitors reporting suspicious activity. Yet throughout the states, more and more Quakers ran the risk of detection, even imprisonment. The homes and farms and plantations of such brave men and women secretly became known as safe havens for runaways.

Quietly the word about such places of refuge spread.

The Steddings arrived at the Virginia home of William and Hannah White, a day's ride south of Richmond. The sun was just setting. After unhitching the team and seeing to the horses, they were shown to the water pump to wash, and then straight into the house for supper.

"So, thee is from Mount Holly," said Mrs. White as she set down a steaming platter of meat on the table in front of their guests.

"Yes, Mrs. White," replied Aaron.

"And thee works for John Borton?"

"Yes, ma'am. He is a good and fair man."

"He speaks well of thee also, brother Steddings," said William White from the head of the table as his wife continued to set plates and platters of vegetables before them. At last she sat down beside her husband.

They all bowed their heads. "We thank thee, God," prayed White, "for thy bounty which we are about to receive, and we pray thy blessing upon our lives for thy service. Amen.

"So tell me, friend Steddings," said White as they proceeded to serve onto their plates the bounty they had received, "has thee read the *Journal?*"

"To be honest with thee, Mr. White, I do not read very well. I have not been to school. But most folks in the Meeting, they are proud of old Mr. Woolman, all right."

"Aaron's great-great-grandmother's in Mister Woolman's book," said Zaphorah proudly.

"Is that a fact!" said White with interest.

"She was one of the slaves he wouldn't write a will about that was later set free."

"I am familiar with the account," said White. "That is interesting indeed! You are almost a celebrity then, Mr. Steddings!"

"Hardly that!" laughed Aaron. "I am just a man who is trying to live by the Book and keep my family happy."

"Is Mr. Woolman's shop still in Mount Holly?" asked Hannah White.

"Yes, ma'am, it is," replied Aaron. "I think one of his people owns it now, though she is not called Woolman."

"It must be wonderful living so close to where events in the *Journal* actually took place."

"I reckon so, Mrs. White. And I think most folks in the Mount Holly Meeting, like I say, are proud of it because there are still a heap of Woolmans around that area. Woolman and Borton and Haines and Burr and the rest of the names from those first days—they are all still around Burlington and proud of their heritage. But there are lots of folks that are not Friends too, and they don't know or care much about what went on a hundred years ago. They are busy with their own lives, I reckon. Folks forget quickly."

"Does thee read, Zaphorah?" asked Mrs. White, turning to Aaron's wife.

"A little, Mrs. White," she replied. "But not well. But my girls, they are learning to read very well, is thee not, Mary?"

"Yes, Mama," replied the seven-year-old.

"I hope thee will not mind sharing the guesthouse with another family," said Mrs. White. "We have—"

She paused, suddenly reluctant to finish what had been on the tip of her tongue. She glanced toward her husband.

"We had unexpected guests arrive yesterday," he said.

"We do not mind, do we, Zaphorah?" said Aaron. "We are just grateful for a roof over our heads. If thee hasn't room, we can sleep almost—"

"It is not that at all, brother Steddings," interrupted their host. "Thee and thy family are most welcome, especially at the request of John Borton himself. Tell me . . . what does thee know about the railroad?"

"There is a train that goes to Philadelphia," replied Aaron, "but I have never been on it."

"I meant a different kind of . . . ," began White. "Well, never mind. I do not suppose it matters. It is just that the only extra beds we have are out in the guesthouse, and there is another family spending a few nights with us too."

"We are happy and grateful for wherever thee has to put us, Mr. White. We are just simple folk and not overly particular."

As supper concluded, Mrs. White could not help noticing that the younger Steddings girl had not eaten much from her plate.

"Is thy daughter not hungry?" she asked.

"Deanna has not felt herself today," replied Zaphorah.

"Is thee ill, child?" asked Mrs. White with a smile.

The six-year-old girl shrugged and glanced down.

"Perhaps, William," said Mrs. White, rising from the table, "we should show them their beds."

⁓

William White led Aaron Steddings outside, followed by his family, across the yard, and into a smaller detached guesthouse that had at one time, many years before, been used as the small farm's slave quarters. The main house was unusually small and the guesthouse, though mostly one large room, was nearly the same size. As they entered, by the light of two lanterns burning inside, they saw three adults—two men and a woman—and three or four children, all black, seated on wooden chairs and lying on bunks across the room. An empty food tray and a pitcher of water and cups sat on a small wooden table.

"I am afraid it will be a little crowded," said White. "I am sorry, but there should be enough bunks for everyone."

He left them and the Steddings family sat down together on two of the empty beds. One of the women came toward them.

"I's Elvira," she said. "Y'all jes' git here?"

Zaphorah looked up and smiled. "Yes," she said. "We are the Steddings. This is my husband Aaron, and I am Zaphorah."

"Pleased ter make yo' 'quaintence," said the woman. "Where's y'all boun'?"

"Where is it, Aaron?" said Zaphorah, glancing toward Aaron.

"Down in southern Virginia, a place called Stony Creek."

"You's trablin' souf!" the woman exclaimed.

Aaron nodded.

"Why you wants ter do sumfin' like dat?"

"I have work there."

One of the other men who had been listening, now sauntered over to join the conversation.

"You's gots ter git norf, man," he said. "Dat's where all us be tryin' ter git—norf. Dat's where freedom be. You go souf, you's git caught! What kind er work you talkin' 'bout anyway?"

"Just work, a man's honest work."

"You talkin' 'bout *paid* work?"

"What other kind is there?"

"Dere's nigger work, dat's what kin'! Dere's paid work an' dere's nigger work. An' paid work—dat's da talk er a free man."

"We are free," said Aaron.

"Laws almighty—you's *free* niggers!" exclaimed the woman called Elvira. "What's you doin' dis far in da Souf?"

"I am going down to help with the harvest, to help a lady—she is the sister of a man I work for."

"An what's you gwine do den, when you's done?" asked the man.

"Go back home. We are from up Philadelphia way. But what is thee doing here?"

"We's runaways. We's tryin' ter git norf ter freedom."

"Runaways!" exclaimed Zaphorah. "Are Mr. and Mrs. White part of it . . . they are helping thee?"

"Dat dey is. Dat's why we's here. Dese kin' er religious folks, dey gib us a place ter stay an' den sen' us on ter da nex' station, on what dey call the Underground Railroad."

Just then Hannah White walked in. She walked over and picked up the tray of supper things.

"Is there anything else you need?" she asked.

"We's jes' fine, Missus," said Elvira.

Mrs. White smiled and walked toward the door, then paused. "Zaphorah," she said, "might I speak with thee?"

Zaphorah rose and followed the farmer's wife outside.

"With thy young one ill," said Mrs. White, "perhaps thee would be more comfortable in the house. We have but a small extra room with one bed. Why dost not thy daughter and thee come and sleep inside."

"That is kind of thee, Mrs. White. I shall go ask what Aaron thinks."

An hour later, Hannah White softly entered the room where she had put Zaphorah and Deanna Steddings.

"How is she?" she asked.

"She has just fallen asleep," replied Zaphorah. "I have sung her all the lullabies I could remember."

"It must be difficult traveling so far with young children," she said, pulling a chair toward the bed and sitting down.

"It has not been too bad," said Zaphorah where she sat on the bedside. "The Bortons gave us a comfortable carriage to ride down here in. We have enjoyed our time together, and meeting such a lot of nice people. It was fine until Deanna took sick today. But we will be to Mr. Borton's sister's in another two days."

"How long will thee stay?"

"Until Aaron gets her harvest in. She lost her husband and Mr. Borton asked us to come down and help her. We have better lives than those poor slaves we see in the fields everywhere. And those people out in thy guesthouse, they said they are runaways. Are thee and Mr. White really helping them escape?"

Hannah White smiled, then nodded.

"How could we turn them away?" she said.

"But isn't it dangerous?"

"Yes . . . yes, Zaphorah, it is. But what does being a Friend mean if it does not mean being a friend to those in need?"

"Like Mr. Borton to his sister. I know what thee means. That's how everyone in Mount Holly is, always helping one another."

"I am happy to think that Mr. Woolman's influence lives on in such a way."

"But how do people know to come to thee?" asked Zaphorah.

"It all began with our neighbor about four years ago," said Hannah. A sad look crossed her face. "He had been helping runaways for some time, though William and I knew nothing about it. I don't know how it began. We were neighbors and friends and he was in our Meeting. But not everyone in the Meeting believes it is right to help runaways and he kept his activity to himself.

"Then there was a day when Isaac came to us—he was our neighbor. He was what is called a conductor on the secret slave railroad."

"Is that . . . the *Underground Railroad*?" said Zaphorah.

"That's what many people call it," replied Hannah. "Isaac came to us one afternoon. We could see something serious was on his mind. That's when he told us what he had been doing. He said that he was being watched, that he was afraid he had been found out. There was a bounty hunter watching him, a terrible man, he said, mean and ruthless, who had descriptions of several runaways he had followed to his place. Isaac said that he had hidden them in the woods, he didn't say where, and he asked us to take them in and keep them overnight until he could come for them and send them on their way."

"What did you do?" asked Zaphorah.

"I said no," replied Hannah. "It was against the law. The thought of it frightened me. Isaac pulled out a clipping from a newspaper and handed it to me. I read it and I can still recall the words: *Four slaves, escaped from Buford Streek farm, southeast Virginia: Teen boy gingerbread color, mother tan to yellow with wide nose, two men—one dark black half bald and thin, the other dun color, short and fat.* The very words disgusted me. It sounded like they were describing cattle. I was so offended I never forgot. Then William rose and left the room, and I knew where he was going. He was going out to the barn to be alone, and to be quiet and still, and to see what the Spirit would say to him. I served Isaac a cup of tea and we chatted awhile, then William came back into the house. He nodded to Isaac and told him to bring the Negroes and we would hide them.

"Isaac left and came back about dusk with the four slaves. We put them in the barn and gave them something to eat. Isaac left again. He said he was going to lead the bounty hunters on a wild goose chase and hope to get them good and far away from both our places. He was supposed to be back the next morning but he never came. Finally William rode over to his farm and discovered Isaac in his bed, several bones broken and unconscious. One of his workers had found him about a mile from the house, beaten to within an inch of his life. He had managed to get him home and had sent for the doctor."

Hannah paused and glanced down. It was silent a minute, then she drew in a deep breath.

"Isaac died three days later," she said softly.

Zaphorah's hand went to her mouth with a sharp gasp.

"And that is how it began," Hannah went on. "We had no idea where the four slaves were supposed to go, and now we were afraid that the bounty hunters would find out about us too. But by and by we managed to learn a few names of others in the Meeting in the next county who were helping. We took the runaways to them. Before long William had taken Isaac's place as a conductor and people kept coming to us.*

"I will never forget one young woman. She was so light I thought she was white. She had no Negro features at all, yet was a slave and a fugitive."

"But why?" asked Zaphorah.

"Her father was the owner of a plantation, and he regularly bedded all his slave women who had no husbands of their own. It was the cheapest and easiest way to get free slaves. Those he didn't need, he sold without regard to the fact that they were all his own children. If one of his own daughters reached childbearing age, he would do the same with her. The girl who came to us was the daughter of her owner and had inherited his fair skin and looks. I was deeply angered by the manner of atrocities I heard of."

Zaphorah shook her head in disbelief. She had never encountered such things before. Until this moment she had not fully realized how sheltered had been her life in Mount Holly.

The two women talked for another hour about many things. By then the evening was well advanced. Hannah leaned forward and embraced the black mother.

"Sleep well, Zaphorah," she said, "and thy dear little one."

She rose, patted sleeping Deanna where she lay beneath the blanket, and withdrew.

Meanwhile, outside in the guesthouse Aaron was engaged in conversation with Elvira's brother and husband as Mary and young Moses slept.

"How did thee know to come here when thee escaped?" asked Aaron.

---

* A similar account is told in the classic, *Friendly Persuasion* by Jessamyn West, from which I have adapted Hannah White's story.

"Hit's all arranged," said Elvira's brother Nathan. "Da conductor jes' tell you where ter go."

"What does thee mean, the *conductor?*" said Aaron.

"Dey's who leads you from stashun ter stashun. Ain't you heard ob da Undergrou' Railroad?"

"I do not think I have, at least not what thee is talking about."

"Da railroad's how we gits ter da norf."

"These conductors thee speaks of," said Aaron, "are they white or black?"

"Dey kin be either. We's had w'ite conductors an' black ones. Even sum dat are slaves derselves."

"They men or women?"

"Bof."

"But how does thee know where to go?"

"Word gits aroun', secrets spread from place ter place, where ter meet a conductor, where dere's hidin' places, where dere's a stashun. But you's gotta know da roads an' know which way you's boun', an' you gots ter be able ter talk an' act like you is free. . . . Why duz you talk like dese w'ite folks, wiff dat *thee* an' *thou?*"

"We're Friends," said Aaron, "what most folks call Quakers."

"Den *you* cud talk like a w'ite man effen you had to!" laughed Nathan. "You already duz."

"An' you gots ter stay out er sight an' go at night," said the other man called Ezra. "Only at night."

"An' dere's always w'ites out huntin' you down wiff dogs an' dey's got papers sayin' who you is an' lookin' fo' you, an' effen you gits caught, you's git terrible whupped er sold er worse. Dere wuz one man got his toes all chopped off wiff an axe when his master got him back."

"But how did thee get away from where thee were slaves?" asked Aaron.

"Any way you kin," replied Nathan. "Sneak away at night, steal a horse, disguise yo'self wiff wigs an' powder ter look like a w'ite man, bleach yo' skin an' hair . . . any way you kin. You gots ter outwit da master, an' outwit his nigger dogs, any way you kin . . . hide under a wagonload er hay an' feed . . . dere wuz sum I heard 'bout who even hid in a wagon full er manure!"

"You gots ter be watchin'," said Ezra. "Always watchin' . . . watchin' ter learn habits an' ways, what da master does an' when he does it an' where he goes. Dat's how yo' opportunity comes . . . from watchin' an' thinkin' an' waitin'. You gots ter wait till da right time, 'cause you only gits one chance, so it's gotter be jes' right."

"What we done," said Nathan, chuckling aloud, "wuz we pretended ter be goin' ter a funeral. We wuz helped by a w'ite man pretendin' ter be comin' roun' inspectin' plantashuns fo' sumthin', I don' know what. But he wuz a w'ite man dat hated slavery an' he wuz determined ter help slaves escape, though he said he'd been in jail a few times already fo' it. So he'd git da trust ob da master, but den at night he sneaks down ter da slave village an' he tol' us ter be dressed up an' ready ter atten' a funeral da nex' day. We wondered who wuz dead, but on dose plantashuns dere wuz always sumbody dyin' so we didn't ax no questions. I don' know what he dun tol' master, but nex' day he let us go into town, dere wuz twelve ob us, an' we wuz carryin' a coffin all slow like, an' we walked through town wiff da women pretendin ter cry, an' when we wuz through town, we dropped dat empty coffin an' we run fo' da trees lickety split, an' dere was dat w'ite man waitin' fo' us wiff fo' blacks like us, an' dey took us an' hid us dat day, and dat night dose black conductors took us ter stashuns roun' 'bout, an' we been travlin' on dat railroad eber since."

Aaron sat spellbound as he continued to listen to tales about the Underground Railroad. He had never heard the likes of such things before, little realizing how vital the memory of what he heard this night would one day prove in his own life.

The Steddings set out from the White farm the following morning.

About midday, singing hymns as they went, suddenly Aaron heard riders ahead. An evil premonition swept through him.

"Quiet, all of thee," he said.

"What is the matter, Papa?" asked five-year-old Moses.

"I hope nothing, Son," replied Aaron. "I just don't want us making a racket, that is all."

Several seconds later three men came riding toward them. Seeing a carriage full of blacks, they pulled up, looking them over. Slowly they spread out around them, blocking their way as Aaron reined in.

"Hey, you nigger boy," called out the lead rider. "Where's you going?"

"Down to southern Virginia, sir?" replied Aaron. The two girls inched closer to Zaphorah. But Moses was too young to be afraid.

"That's a mighty fine looking carriage," said the rider. "How's a boy like you afford an expensive carriage like that?"

"It belongs to my boss, sir."

"Your boss! You mean your master, don't you, boy?"

"No, sir. My boss."

"I think you're lying!" the man shot back. "You stole it, nigger boy! Who'd you steal it from?"

"Nobody, sir. I'm telling thee the truth, that—"

"*Thee!* Don't get high and mighty with me, boy!" he said angrily. "What's that kind of talk? You trying to make me look stupid?"

"No, sir. I wouldn't do that."

"Then why you talking uppity like a white man?"

"I'm sorry, sir. I didn't mean to do that."

"Mister," said Moses, "why is thee talking to my daddy like that?"

"Why, fancy this, boys," said the leader, turning around to his cronies. "We got us an uppity little nigger kid just like his daddy! I think we need to teach these niggers a lesson in manners!"

"Hey, Rube," now said one of the others, "what you figure a big, strong nigger like this'd fetch?"

"Good money, that's for sure! I hear big field hands fetch a thousand, sometimes two."

"We'd be rich! How much is that each, Rube—five or six hundred?"

"And that woman of his is mighty handsome," said the third rider. "Some rich white man'd give plenty for something like that to keep him company at night!"

"All right, you nigger boy," said the one called Rube, "get down from there."

"I have papers," said Aaron, his voice quivering a little but trying to remain calm.

"The boy says he's got papers, Rube. What we gonna do about that?"

"I reckon we better see 'em. Show me your papers, boy," said Rube, dismounting.

Aaron climbed down, pulled the paper from John Borton out of the pocket of his coat, and handed it to the man. The man glanced it over, then ripped it in pieces and tossed it to the ground.

"Those are New Jersey papers, nigger boy!" he laughed derisively. "They ain't no good here. You may be free up there, but this here's Virginia. Here you're a slave! Now you get up on my horse there," he said, "and follow my friends there."

He jumped up and sat down in the carriage beside Zaphorah, who was terrified, and grabbed the reins. "I'll just take care of your team and the carriage and this little woman of yours."

He flicked the reins. "Gid-up!" he shouted. "Let's go, boys!" he cried. "We'll take 'em over to my place and then decide what to do from there."

The letter that arrived at the Borton farm three weeks later caused instant anxiety. Martha saw the look of concern on her husband's face as he read.

"It's from Sarah," said John finally, glancing up. "She says that Aaron and Zaphorah never arrived."

"What!" exclaimed Martha. "How can that be?"

"I don't know. They aren't there. She has not seen nor heard from them."

"What could have happened?"

"I cannot imagine," said John. "But if they never got to Sarah's—"

Borton let out a sigh and shook his head. "It's not good . . . not good at all."

Again he paused, thinking quickly.

"I know the fields are almost ready," he said after a few seconds, "but I see nothing else for it but to go to Virginia."

"What will thee do?" asked Martha.

"I do not know," replied John. "Try to retrace their steps . . . that's all I can do. We knew where they were supposed to stay as they went. I don't know what else to do but to follow the same route and see if I can find out what happened, or at least where they were last seen."

Prologue Notes

A Vision of Light

1. "About the beginning of the year 1647 I was moved of the Lord to go into Derbyshire, where I met with some friendly people and had many discourses with them, Then, passing into the Peak country, I met with some more friendly people, and with some in empty high notions. Travelling through some parts of Leicestershire, and into Nottinghamshire, I met with a tender people. . . . With these I had some meetings and discourses; but my troubles continued, and I was often under great temptations.

"I fasted much, walked abroad in solitary places many days, and often took my Bible, and sat in hollow trees and lonesome places till night came on; and frequently in the night walked mournfully about by myself; for I was a man of sorrows in the time of the first workings of the Lord in me . . . I kept much as a stranger, seeking heavenly wisdom and getting knowledge from the Lord, and was brought off from outward things to rely on the Lord alone. . . .

"Now, after I had received that opening from the Lord, that to be bred at Oxford or Cambridge was not sufficient to fit a man to be a minister of Christ, I regarded the priests less, and looked more after the Dissenting people. Among them I saw there was some tenderness; and many of them came afterwards to be convinced, for they had some openings.

"But as I had forsaken the priests, so I left the separate preachers also, and those esteemed the most experienced people; for I saw there was none among them all that could speak to my condition. When all my hopes in them and in all men were gone, so that I had nothing outwardly to help me, nor could tell what to do, then, oh, then, I heard a voice which said, 'There is one, even Christ Jesus, that can speak to thy condition' and when I heard it, my heart did leap for joy.

"Then the Lord let me see why there was none upon the earth that could speak to my condition, namely, that I might give Him all the glory. . . .

"My desire after the Lord grew stronger, and zeal in the pure knowledge of God, and of Christ alone, without the help of any man, book, or writing. For though I read the Scriptures that spoke of Christ and of God, yet I knew Him not, but by revelation, as He who hath the key did open, and as the Father of Life drew me to His Son by His Spirit. . . .

"I was afraid of all company. . . . I had not fellowship with any people, priests or professors, or any sort of separated people, but with Christ, who hath the key, and opened the door of Light and Life unto me. I was afraid of all carnal talk and talkers, for I could see nothing but corruption, and the life lay under the burden of corruption. . . .

"One day, when I had been walking solitarily abroad, and was come home, I was taken up in the love of God, so that I could not but admire the greatness of His love; and while I was in that condition, it was opened unto me by the eternal light and power, and I therein clearly saw that all was done and to be done in and by Christ . . . The Lord opened me, that I saw all through these troubles and temptations. My living faith was raised, that I saw all was done by Christ the life, and my belief was in Him." [*The Journal of George Fox*, Chapter 1, "Boyhood."]

Pilgrims to a New World

2. "Here was the great Delaware, a river such as the white settlers had never seen, even as high as Burlington running nearly a mile wide, and plenty more of it unexploited beyond that. Dwellers by the Thames and the Severn, the Trent and the Usk and the Ouse, the Derwent and the Clyde, were intoxicated by the sheer size of this mighty flow. . . . In many old records . . . can be read the exhilaration of the Englishmen when set down in the flower of manhood upon the richly yielding land. The unbreathed air of the wilderness was so stimulating and sweet; above all the unstinted sunshine lifted the heart. These colonists had been sturdily bred in the more northern climate and under the prevailing grey skies of England; they were almost over stimulated by the daily acceleration—the mental and physical speeding up—of ultra-violet rays, the dazzling sky of cloudless blue. They performed prodigies. The forests rang, first with the dull blows of their axes, then with the music of their saws and the sharp rhythms of their hammers. The ships that brought them were well stocked. It is a continual marvel in retrospect how much those little ships could carry. The houses that rose in the cleared land along the Delaware were many of them built of brick, and every brick for those first houses was brought across the wide

Atlantic—ballast in the deep keel of the top-heavy ships." [From *John Woolman, Quaker* by Janet Whitney. London: George G. Harrap & Co., 1943, pp. 23–25.]

The Tailor of Mount Holly

3. "The aim of the planters . . . was not to make each plantation completely self-supporting, but to move towards differentiation and specialization, as in the home country. Sawmills and flour-mills were early established; professional shoemakers went round from house to house, staying long enough at each to equip each member of the household with shoes by mending and making; carpenters and furniture makers brought their skill to add to the rougher efforts of the householder; brick kilns produced bricks of native clay, regulated by law and inspected as to uniformity of quality and size; and weaving itself was not for the most part done by the woman in the home, but by professional weavers, trained masters of their craft.

"One reason for the rapid prosperity of the Quaker colonies was the fact that the majority of the men of substance who came over to them were master craftsmen, not like the Virginians, aristocrats unpracticed in anything but land and horses, or, like the first men on the Hudson and Delaware, merely traders wishing to buy furs cheap and sell them dear. The New Jersey planters used their farms as a direct source of food and places in which to breed sheep and cows for their meat, wool, and leather, but they expected their craft to be their chief source of money revenue. Many of them wished to grow rich, but none expected to grow rich at farming. The mill, the dye vat, the loom, the smithy, formed the foundation of many a sound fortune, while the plantation provided immediate necessities and made a frame for the kind of ample, stable, honourable life the colonists wished to live." [From *John Woolman, Quaker* by Janet Whitney. London: George G. Harrap & Co., 1943, pp. 23-25.]

PART ONE

A Nation Divided

Spring, 1862

One

The year was 1862 and the war between the North and the South was a year old.

After a sluggish start in the spring and summer months of 1861, the Confederate army had won the first major decisive battle of the war at Manassas Junction in northern Virginia, repulsing a major Union offensive that had been intended to launch Union forces all the way to the Confederate capital of Richmond and put a quick end to the war.

The people of the North were shocked. Suddenly fear replaced optimism throughout the Northern states. This was not going to be as easy as most had assumed. The will to win throughout the South was strong, and their army more determined than Northerners had imagined.

Civil war was nothing new in the world. But that in the United States of America—built on Christian principles of liberty, equality, fairness, and reason—the sons of the North and the sons of the South should take up guns and now be engaged in a great effort to kill one another, could only be seen as an enormous national disgrace.

Perhaps war is a necessary purging fire for all nations, even democracies, at various junctures of their histories, even as the eternal cleansing fire will sweep the universe clean of sin that ultimate righteousness might shine out like the sun. Whether this present conflict between the army of the Union led by President Abraham Lincoln and the army of the Confederacy led by Jefferson Davis, would effect such a cleansing to the ultimate good of the now-divided country, or would tear this great experiment in democracy apart into a fragmentary shadow of its lofty ideal . . . it was too early to tell.

But such high matters of eternal consequence did not occupy the thoughts of the soldiers carrying out the orders of their commanders. Though there was lofty talk about preserving the Union or defending states' rights, most had joined up in support of a cause they believed in—in its simplest terms, either to preserve slavery or to eliminate it. The heat of battle, however, quickly reduces ideals to practicalities. And the most practical of all practicalities was kill or be killed.

The Confederate army was aided enormously in the early stages by an ingenious Confederate spy ring that infiltrated the highest levels of government. Its foremost operatives were not what the unsuspecting officers in charge of Union troop movements would have recognized right in front of their noses. What made the ring so cunning was that its recruits were mostly beautiful women of high society, who used their feminine wiles to lure information out of unsuspecting officials —information passed south which eventually came into the hands of the generals of the Confederacy.

Recruited by former army officer and now Confederate colonel Thomas Jordon, Washington widow Rose O'Neal Greenhow was, even by the outbreak of the war, one of the most important figures in this secret war. Of Southern birth and loyalties, the beautiful Mrs. Greenhow was still young and admired in Washington social circles by one and all. She was friend to senators, generals, and former presidents and particularly admired by Senator Henry Wilson of Massachusetts, chairman of the Senate Military Affairs Committee. Through her friend Bettie Duval, Greenhow smuggled information extracted from Wilson about Union troop movements near Manassas Junction, Virginia. The information was smuggled to General Beauregard who used it to turn the first great battle of the war into a Confederate victory.

On the heels of such success, the Confederate spy network in Washington D.C. and in all the North continued to expand.

⟝⟞

Throughout the remainder of 1861, as a result of the victory at Manassas Junction, optimism in the South was unbounded. Talk ran rampant of an invasion of Washington D.C. and a quick Confederate victory.

But there was no invasion of the Northern capital. Confederate forces pulled back. The rest of the year passed uneventfully. Only four minor skirmishes took place all year. Both sides were bolstering their armies, and making plans for the real fighting they knew was coming.

And it came with a vengeance. In the second month of 1862, Southern invincibility was dealt a stinging blow with the Confederacy's introduction to a man they would come to know all too well by the name of Ulysses S. Grant. In Tennessee, Union gunboats captured Fort Henry on the Tennessee River as Grant's troops captured Fort Donelson on the Cumberland. Both rivers were suddenly in Union hands, making possible Union offenses deep into the South. Over 17,000 casualties shocked the nation on both sides—four times the casualties at Manassas. It would not only be a longer war than anticipated, it would be bloodier.

But the worst of early 1862 lay ahead for Confederate troops. It came south of Fort Donelson at Shiloh, Tennessee, in April. Again the struggle was for control of the vital Tennessee River and nearby railroad lines. The battle pitted two giants head to head, again Grant of the Union against General Beauregard of the Confederacy.

Thomas Davidson had fought in the battle of Manassas Junction. He had emptied his rifle many times throughout the day but didn't think he had shot anyone. At least he hoped not. But for the first time in his life he had seen men die—up close, bleeding, arms and legs blown off . . . men screaming and crying out for the mercy of death.

The experience had sobered him. Though the war was barely begun, he lay awake nights for the next month, the horrifying sounds of death in his ears, asking what he was doing there. He was scarcely more than a boy, eighteen when he joined in April, nineteen now. But never had he felt so alone and afraid.

Most of the men of his regiment were just like him, some older, some younger. They all pretended to be tough and courageous. But inside they were boys. Thomas wondered if they were afraid too. Most didn't act like it. Some almost seemed to enjoy the shooting and destruction. What did they think about at night, he wondered. Did they remember the faces of the men they'd shot?

The initial horror gradually faded throughout the year. Thomas did not again fire his gun in battle. But having been assigned to General Beauregard's army, he followed the general west into Tennessee and was part of his 40,000-man army that gathered at Corinth on the Tennessee River in April of the following year. Reports had reached them about the movement of Grant's army upriver toward them. It was their job to stop him.

Finally General Beauregard gave the order. Grant had disembarked his troops at Pittsburgh Landing. They would advance to meet him and beat his army back before reinforcements arrived. Thomas knew serious fighting was coming and tried to prepare himself for it. But inside he wondered if he would live through it.

The fighting that took place on April 6 near Shiloh Church two miles from the landing was senseless, savage, and confused. It was the first real action many of the young men on both sides had seen. Their enthusiasm without an effective battle plan only increased the panic and disorder. Neither side could successfully maneuver their troops. Many boys not yet twenty years of age killed for the first time that day. Just as many died. When darkness closed in and the day's fighting ceased, nothing had been achieved, other than that thousands of American youth lay dead on the fields and in the woods.

Dirty, hungry, exhausted, and afraid, Thomas Davidson lay down on his bedroll that night, terrible images from the day rushing back upon him. Manassas had been a Sunday picnic compared to what he had witnessed today.

The camp was silent except for the snoring here and there. But how could anyone sleep after an experience like that? He knew Grant's army was encamped over the ridge less than a mile away. Tomorrow they would all be trying to kill each other again. Yet here they lay, so close . . . quiet . . . sleepless . . . probably many like him trying to remember how to pray and wishing they were home. Yet tomorrow they would again load their guns and aim them at each other. How stupid and senseless it all seemed!

He knew Cameron Beaumont had also been assigned to General Beauregard's army. Though he was in a different unit, he had seen him a few times on the march west through the summer and fall. To have a friend in the midst of all this might make it a little more tolerable. But Cameron had looked at him as if they hardly knew each other. He had always seen Cameron as a little kid, though he was only one year younger. He was certainly grown up now—hard and cold and mean looking.

Thomas wondered about the others from Dove's Landing. Were any of them here at Shiloh too?

Thomas's thoughts drifted toward home, and his father and mother. Unconsciously he wiped at his eyes. He couldn't allow himself to think about home! Not here, not now. It was too painful, the memories too confusing.

Whether what could actually be called sleep ever came to him that night, Thomas wasn't sure. He drifted and dozed and dreamed in and out of semiconsciousness, all the time realizing that morning would come eventually.

Thomas found himself suddenly awakened sometime around five o'clock in the morning to the explosions of cannon and gunfire. He hadn't realized he had fallen asleep, but he was awake now!

Grant had attacked their weakened position before anyone had expected it. Everyone was yelling and running and Captain Young was shouting orders. Chaos spread through the camp as they scurried for cover, grabbing rifles and boots in a disordered attempt to protect themselves and fight back.

The blue haze of cannon smoke filled the gray dawn. It was impossible to see anything. A deafening explosion shattered one of the supply wagons only thirty feet away. Thomas jumped up, grabbed his rifle again, and rushed away, heedless of direction. He sprinted blindly for the cover of a small thicket of trees, not sure whether the enemy was ahead or behind. It seemed they were everywhere!

Thomas stopped and tried to think. Gunfire and the explosion of Grant's cannons sounded from every direction. For all he could tell he was surrounded.

He had to get back . . . he had to find Captain Young and the others!

He crept toward the edge of the woods. It was too hazy to see clearly. He must have turned himself around. He turned and ran through the woods in the opposite direction.

From among the trees in front of him came now another figure running toward him.

Thomas stopped in his tracks. But the soldier in Union blue did not see him until they nearly collided into each other.

He came to a stop. Both were staring straight into the other's eyes. Opposite him Thomas saw a boy who could not have been more than fifteen, trembling in terror.

For two or three seconds they stood staring no more than five feet apart.

All at once the boy raised his rifle and aimed it at Thomas's face. Without thinking, Thomas swung the butt of his gun and knocked it away just as the boy pulled the trigger and a shot exploded. The rifle shattered to the ground and, clutching his own, Thomas ran past him and disappeared, trembling from head to foot at how close he had come to being shot.

What was the stupid kid thinking! He wasn't going to hurt him.

By the time Thomas found his unit, the first wave of the assault was dying down. Their troops were managing to reorganize and Captain Young now led them in a wide arc nearer the river to connect with the main bulk of Beauregard's army that had been scattered by Grant's attack.

Sporadic fighting continued the rest of the morning. Shortly after noon, suddenly again came cannon and gunfire from their left flank.

But this time Beauregard's officers were ready for it. Quickly through the ranks they ordered a counteroffensive.

"Attack, men!" cried Captain Young. "This time we'll beat them back!"

Charging on foot over open terrain, several units of Beauregard's force charged together, firing blindly as they went. Thomas could not even see the enemy ahead, though hundreds of tiny flashes, gunfire and explosions of cannon, indicated clearly enough that the Union force was in front of them and returning their fire.

Beside him he heard a cry. He turned as one of his comrades fell.

Thomas kept on, firing occasionally, stopping to reload, and continuing on. He saw a blur of blue a hundred yards ahead . . . thousands of Union soldiers were bearing straight for them!

The two armies met. Suddenly all became a chaos of yelling and close fighting and screaming and clashing of swords and bayonets. The air was thick with choking smoke. Thomas kept running. All at once he stumbled. His rifle flew from his hands and he fell facedown, splattering mud over the front of his uniform.

Struggling to pick himself up, he looked back. A few feet away lay the motionless form of a Union soldier lying facedown on the ground where he had tripped over him. He knew instantly that he was dead.

Thomas crept toward the body on hands and knees. Slowly he rolled him onto his back.

He gasped and his stomach went to his throat. It was the boy he had seen in the woods! The whites of his eyes were wide even in death, for the bullet that had found his heart only a minute or two before had killed him instantly. His chest was dripping in blood, still warm and wet.

Thomas turned away, lurched two or three times, then vomited violently.

When he came to himself he was running . . . in what direction he had no idea . . . he had to get away . . . as far from it all as possible . . . away from the horror . . . away from the killing . . . away from the death.

He did not know that Beauregard had given the order to retreat, and that the rest of his company was running with him away from the scene of the battle.

Gradually his senses began to return. He had no gun in his hand. His eyes were wet and he knew he had been crying.

Suddenly he heard his name.

"Tom . . . Thomas, is that you?" called the voice again.

He stopped and glanced around.

"Thomas . . . over here . . . help me! I'm shot."

Thomas ran toward the sound. Everywhere around him was pandemonium. Shots were still being fired. The Union soldiers were chasing them as they ran, killing as many as they could before they could get away.

Lying on the ground a little way ahead he saw the form of a soldier dressed in the Confederate gray.

"Cam!" he cried, running forward and stooping down. "What happened? Are you . . . how bad is it?"

"Help me, Tom," said Cameron in desperation. "It's my leg . . . I can't walk. I'm wounded in the leg. They'll kill me if they find me lying here. They're all crazy . . . help me, Tom—please!"

Thomas slid his hands under Cameron's knees and shoulders and scooped him off the ground. With a great effort he stood, glanced around to get his bearings, then hurried off in the direction of the retreat as rapidly as he was able.

The Union victory at Shiloh, though not decisive, placed most of west and central Tennessee under Union control.

Two

A muscular dark Negro man slowly slid the end of the pitchfork in his hands beneath the muck of manure and straw in the stable yard, scooped out a dripping forkful, and splattered it onto the handcart beside him.

His owner had realized within days of purchasing the man more than a decade ago for, as he thought, the bargain price of sixteen hundred dollars, that he'd been swindled. By looks the man was everything he had been looking for, but Locke discovered soon enough that he was worthless as a field hand. Where he had been before now, he had no idea, but one thing was certain, he had never picked cotton.

But he could shoe a horse better than anyone he had ever seen, white or black, and he knew his way around machinery and wagons and horses and knew every farm implement he had and how to better most of them with some little addition or other. So gradually he had put him to work in his stables and equipment barn, and he had kept his wagons and harnesses and wheels and other farm machines in good repair. He had always intended to sell the fellow again and try to get his money back by passing him on to some other unsuspecting plantation owner he could trick like he'd been tricked. But he hadn't gotten around to it yet. In the meantime, the fellow was useful.

As he cleaned out the horse and cattle stalls before making his way to the pigpens, the black man paused briefly, listening carefully and glancing about, then looked toward the big house where his master and his son and men were now eating their breakfast.

Satisfied that no one was about, he set aside the fork, took the shovel that was leaning against a nearby wall, and hurried into the adjoining stable which he had finished cleaning only moments before.

Working quickly now, he bent down and began clearing away the dirt and straw and dried manure from one corner of the floor at the point where two walls of the corral came together. He shoved it into a pile to one side until the shovel in his hand scraped wood. A few seconds later he uncovered two pieces of board a foot wide and approximately three feet in length that had been buried about three inches below the surface. He grabbed them, lifted them, and tossed them aside.

Beneath where the boards lay was now revealed a hole in the earth, dug straight down in a perfect rectangle four inches shorter in dimensions in both directions than the boards that had covered it. The man stepped down into the hole—careful not to disturb its edges which must continue to support the boards when he replaced them, even with a horse standing on top—to a depth of some two feet. Working with the shovel, he whacked and loosened the compacted dirt at the bottom of the hole, then dug out a scoop of the earth in the shovel.

Gingerly he stepped out, again careful of the all-important edges. It was gradually becoming more and more difficult to step in and out as the hole deepened. He would eventually have to devise some other means to get the dirt out, possibly with a makeshift ladder of some kind. But that time was not yet.

With careful step so as not to spill any of the telltale dirt in his shovel, he hurried outside, glancing about again, and sprinkled the dirt over the top of the pile of manure in the cart.

Working rapidly now, he hurried back into the stable and gently set the two boards back in place over the hole, making sure as always that they were tight and with no hint of wobble. He covered them back over with the dirt he had earlier removed, adding a fine sprinkling of fresh straw, and stepped about over it to make sure no movement or soft depression in the dirt nor dull echo of sound gave away the hole beneath. Satisfied, he quickly hurried back outside, wiped the shovel clean and set it back in place, careful at every stage to leave no trace of his activity, and set about to continue cleaning the rest of the stalls. He was just in time to see the master's overseer walking toward him.

Hastily he scooped up a fork of manure, splattered it onto the cart, and mixed it about briefly with the prongs of the fork to hide the dirt he had just added to the mix.

The whole thing took less than five minutes a day, on the days he could manage it—which was not nearly every day. At first he had been too anxious and excited over his plan and had tried to remove too much dirt at a time. He had tossed his first few shovelsful about the yard, but then quickly realized that if he continued to do so it would be noticed. The vegetable garden was too far from the stables to use to conceal the dirt, ideal though it would have been.

He had to go slow, and be very, very careful. Finally he settled upon what became his routine whenever he was left alone in the stables—to remove but one scoop of dirt a day, sprinkling it in with the manure from the stalls—the last place anyone would want to inspect. Once the cart was dumped, as long as he left no traces inside the stall, no evidence remained that anyone would ever find. He just had to remind himself that, even one little bit at a time, the dirt added up. A shovel a day . . . even a scoop every three days . . . and he would be able to dig a huge hole in a year. He *must* be patient!

Everything within him cried out to work faster. But his great enemy was haste. Impatience would only lead to detection. Every day in this bondage was an evil trial to his spirit, even more grievous when he had to watch his family suffer. But the Israelites were four hundred years in their bondage before the arrival of the hour of their deliverance. He could be patient if in the end the dream he sought was realized.

One shovel a day, day after day, would move a mountain. He did not need to move a mountain, only excavate a tiny cave to freedom.

"Aren't you through with that mess yet?" said the overseer as he approached.

"I'm nearly done, Mr. Roper, sir."

"Well get on with it and saddle my mare and Mr. Locke's roan."

"Yes, sir, Mr. Roper."

"We'll be back in five minutes. Have the horses ready."

Exactly how much time had passed since he had started his daring excavation, or how many days he had worked and how many shovels of earth he had removed, he could not have said. Time was a different commodity for a slave than for free men and women. When your time belongs to another, when your whole being belongs to another, time loses its value. Days fade into weeks, weeks into months, months into years of endless drudgery and meaninglessness.

Seasons came. It grew hot. The sixteen-hour days of labor in the harvest fields slowly passed and gave way to the short cold days of winter. All was a blur of tedium and labor and inhumanity of man unto man.

The only measurement of time that mattered was the passage of years he observed on the faces of his four precious young ones. From children they had grown into youths in the bondage of their affliction. He knew his son no longer even remembered the days of his freedom, and it smote the father's heart to realize that the boy thought of himself as a *slave*. And his little girl Suzane *was* a slave. She had been born into this evil.

His oldest daughters remembered. For that he was grateful, though the memory of freedom only made the indignity of their suffering all the more painful.

He listened. He paid attention. He knew when the war had begun. Indeed, he knew far more about the world beyond the plantation than his master gave him credit for. Quickly he had learned to curb his tongue, to speak softly and walk slowly. To be taken for a simpleton was refuge from the dangerous charge of being uppity, and from the whip which always followed the accusation.

It was not the passage of years on the face of his son that caused him the most anxiety, or that had prompted his daring, foolhardy, reckless plan. Rather it was the changes in his two older daughters that were obvious to anyone with two eyes.

At seventeen and eighteen, they were rapidly turning into young women. And that fact, as natural as it might have been, frightened him. It was only a matter of time before their master would have "plans" for them. Marriage to a good young man who cared for one of his girls, even a slave boy . . . he would be happy enough for that. But to see one of his daughters raped by a white man, especially the master or his son, merely to produce a slave baby . . . he would give his life to prevent that. They were lucky it hadn't happened already.

For just such a purpose had he begun his once-a-day secret ritual beneath the stall of his master's favorite and fastest horse.

And still the days passed, and invisible sprinkles of dirt continued to add to the manure of cows and horses and pigs spread about the fields.

Nor did he ever forget the words of a runaway slave by the name of Ezra whose path had once crossed his: You gots ter be watchin'. Always watchin' . . . watchin' ter learn what da master does an' when he does it an' where he goes. Dat's how yo' opportunity comes . . . from watchin' an' thinkin' an' waitin'. You gots ter wait till da right time . . . you only gits one chance . . . it's gotter be jes' right.

So he continued to wait, to watch, to think . . . and he continued to dig.

Three

The lone rider scaling the high plateau of north-central Virginia had ridden this familiar path at least a hundred times in her memory in the months since the outbreak of the war. But Cherity Waters had not come here since the day she and Seth had ridden up together for the last time the day before his departure. It hadn't seemed right to come alone—not after that day, not after the things they had said to one another.

But it was now early spring. The leaves were again budding out on the trees after the long lonely winter. A new warmth was in the air. Yet Cherity's heart was heavy today. Moments still came when her father's death a year ago overwhelmed her anew and she needed to cry. Today she wanted to share her tears with Seth. The only place she could do that was on Harper's Peak.

Carolyn Davidson was strolling through the beloved Greenwood gardens. Her thoughts, too, were quiet and melancholy. Like Cherity, she was thinking of those who were no longer here.

The gardens were not the same these days with both her sons gone. It seemed such a short time ago when Seth and Thomas had romped through these paths yelling and chasing each other as playful little boys. But they were boys no longer. She now had both a Confederate and a Union soldier to worry about, as well as a Union photographer. She had Cynthia here with her, of course, and that helped. It did not lessen the anxiety, but it gave her one more person to share it with.

The memories of days gone by brought the nostalgically sad smile of a mother's heart to Carolyn's lips. She could almost hear their shouts and laughter. What happy times those had been! As they had grown up alongside the black slave children, their games and adventures, with Nancy and Malachi Shaw's two boys and Phoebe, had widened to encompass the entire countryside around Greenwood. Horse rides . . . forts in the loft made of bales of straw . . . swimming in the river . . . the wonderful laughter of childhood innocence . . . they were all now but haunting, silent memories.

How quickly the years flew by. Now Malachi was dead and both her sons and her daughter's husband were involved in a terrible war.

She could not help it. Carolyn's mother heart was afraid.

Meanwhile, Richmond Davidson was just returning from Greenwood's former slave village where another three blacks had arrived that morning in their journey north toward what they hoped would be freedom.

Much had changed at Greenwood. His sons were gone. Malachi was gone. The nation was at war. Gradually his workforce was diminishing. One by one his hired Negro laborers were deciding to seek their fortunes elsewhere, mostly in the North, either to fight for the Union army or seek employment or join family and friends. How they would be able to plant and harvest next year's crops, Richmond did not know.

One thing that hadn't changed was the steady influx of passengers on the enigmatically styled Underground Railroad, that complex invisible network of conductors and stations by which runaway slaves made their way undetected out of the South to freedom in the North. Richmond and his wife had been drawn into the network some years before more by accident than design. But once the desperate travelers had begun to come, and word had spread that Greenwood was a "station" where runaways could find refuge, there was no stopping it. The original ones and twos became a flood. Eventually he and Seth and Thomas had built a weathervane in the shape of a horse's head to serve as a secret sentinel to travelers on the clandestine railroad that here was a safe haven where they could pause in their travels for an hour, for a day, for a week. The sign of the weathervane had not been so much to attract fugitives as to protect them from the dangers of the nearby Beaumont estate, where runaways were anything but welcome. Though Denton Beaumont and his treacherous sons were no longer in Dove's Landing, Oakbriar remained a threat.

New arrivals now sometimes arrived nightly, creating such a strain on space and time and available food that it was all they could do to keep pace with it. Moving the travelers along toward the border a hundred miles north also presented an ever-increasing challenge with so many troops from both armies moving about in northern Virginia. Though the outbreak of war had reduced the number of bounty hunters in search of runaway slaves, their danger from rebel soldiers, who hated blacks along with Abraham Lincoln for, as they saw it, starting the war, was greater than ever. Greenwood's resources were diminishing, yet the demands upon those resources were greater than ever.

As Richmond approached the house, a black man came toward him from around one side.

"Ah, Sydney!" he said warmly.

Richmond Davidson would have been overwhelmed by the flood of black refugees moving through Greenwood, especially without Malachi, had it not been for the untiring help of Sydney LeFleure and his Cherokee wife Chigua. They had themselves passed through Greenwood, with their four children, in their own escape to the North. Sydney had later returned to help in the cause. His appearance was timely, for with a shrinking workforce of hired black labor, as well as the multiplying demands placed upon them by the steady influx of fugitives, Richmond was finding it increasingly difficult to keep up with the necessary work of the plantation. Fences and roofs were falling into disrepair. They were unable to cultivate as much acreage as before. Gradually the most outlying of fields that Grantham Davidson, and Albert Davidson before him, had claimed from the wilds and had cultivated with wheat, tobacco, sweet corn, and potatoes were falling fallow and filling with weeds and wild grasses.

Nearly every able Negro of working age who passed through Greenwood found himself closeted with their benefactor being offered paying work, in addition to room and board, to stay on at Greenwood as a hired hand. But having come so far, and now being so near the North and their dream of freedom, most could not be talked into ending their flight only a hundred miles from the Pennsylvania border. Sydney's appearance proved a boon to Greenwood's declining fortunes. His knowledge of farming and planting and harvesting was invaluable. Desperate to find a replacement for Malachi Shaw, Richmond offered Sydney the position as Greenwood's foreman, which the former Jamaican happily accepted. He would have taken the job even without pay. Yet Richmond's lucrative offer made it possible for him to begin setting aside the means one day to establish a home and small farm of his own, and he was humbly grateful for Richmond's generosity. At great danger to themselves, Chigua and Sydney's family returned to Virginia to join him. Sydney and Richmond had upgraded and added a room to the largest of the former slave houses as a home for Sydney and Chigua and their four children. For the present Greenwood was their home, and Richmond and Sydney had become great friends.

"Good morning, Richmond!" replied Sydney with his characteristic French accent, walking forward with a broad smile. "What would you like me to do today?"

"We have the Jackson family and the three Hobarts ready to take across to our good neighbor Brannon," replied Richmond. "One or the other of us should probably handle that ourselves. What kind of progress did you make with the ploughing yesterday?"

Sydney sighed. "Not as much as I had hoped," he said. "I started the day with twelve men, but by the afternoon was down to six. They don't want to work, Richmond. They are so infected with the idea of gaining their freedom that even wages mean little to them. They think the North is a land flowing with milk and honey, as if money and jobs and wealth will be heaped upon them the moment they cross the border."

Sydney paused, shaking his head in frustration. "I try to tell them otherwise," he went on. "I tell them that I have been there myself, that my family and I made it to that great promised land and found it very difficult. I tell them that jobs are scarce, that even in the North there is no red carpet rolled out for refugee blacks, that the best jobs go to whites. I tell them why I returned to Greenwood. I tell them that they will not readily find the like of your generosity even in the North. But they are not to be dissuaded. With their stomachs full of a single warm meal, yet without a penny to their names, they are full of optimism that all the opportunities of the North lie open to them."

"I don't suppose it does much good to dash that optimism," said Richmond. "Most of them have journeyed this far with only hope to sustain them."

"Hope will not feed their families."

"True enough, Sydney. But they will have to learn to face the realities of life after slavery, each in his own way."

Again Sydney sighed. "I don't know, Richmond," he said. "I feel like I am swimming upstream. I had hoped to finish that field so that we could plant the wheat next week, and then get to that stretch of fence the cattle tromped through as well. But I just didn't have the men."

"We will get by, even if we must plant less acreage this spring," said Richmond. "Perhaps you and I can go get that fence put back together ourselves this afternoon. We will take the two Shaw boys with us."

As Cherity approached Harper's Peak, her thoughts continued to dwell on the two most important men in her life, Seth Davidson, whom, she now realized, she loved with the full love of a woman's heart, and her own father, the man she had always known by his Americanized name,

James Waters. She had lost them both almost at the same time—Seth, though she knew she would see him again, to the war, and her father, whom she would not see until the next life, to the God and Creator whom she now knew as her Father and his.

Cherity was still new enough to Greenwood that she was unaware of many of the dangers of their work with the Underground Railroad. She had heard many stories, but had not herself witnessed much about which she had heard. Nor had they told her the worst of it—about the killings and beatings and hangings that had taken place in their own community, and of the constant threat that existed not merely to blacks themselves, but also to Richmond and Carolyn and their family.

In her natural optimism, therefore, Cherity did not worry about her safety in the environs of Dove's Landing, nor take any unusual precautions when she was out alone. And on this particular day as she rode, she had no inkling that she was being watched. Even if she had, she would not have been concerned about it. Despite her diminutive size, she had always been a girl capable of taking care of herself. She was plucky enough to think herself equal to any situation.

The huge black man who had seen her from some distance, and who had now been following her movements for ten or fifteen minutes, did not have an eye for young white women any more than the young blacks of his own race. His lust was color-blind. He had come close to getting himself killed over Veronica Beaumont, but there was no danger of that now. If this girl whom he had seen once or twice in town came from the Davidson place, he had to fear no more repercussions than had resulted from his involvement with Phoebe Shaw.

But he was on foot and she on a horse, and, though she was moving slowly, when she turned and started down the far slope of the ridge, he lost her from view. He followed another ten minutes, failed to get sight of her again, and at length returned to Oakbriar.

Making her way down from Harper's Peak by a different path than her ascent, consciously or unconsciously Cherity found herself following the same route that she and Seth had taken when they had first ridden here together. Before long she approached the old Brown farmhouse, by now familiar to her yet at the same time as mysterious a place as when she had first laid eyes on it. She had been here numerous times since then with Seth, with Carolyn and the black women, and several times with Carolyn or Richmond or Nancy Shaw to retrieve runaway slaves hiding out in the woods or in one of the caves that had become known among fugitives. But she had not come here alone.

As she approached the Brown house on this day, dismounting and walking slowly toward the porch and front door, peculiar sensations stirred within her similar to what she had felt at first sight of the place years before.

She knew the stories of mysterious Mr. Brown well enough by now. But though she did not know of her own Cherokee roots, she nevertheless *felt* the compelling pull of her native heritage every time she drew near this place. She did not yet know why she felt such things, yet they drew her.

The woods and hills grew still with what seemed a preternatural silence. Cherity climbed the steps and walked inside the home that had once belonged to the enigmatic Mr. Brown. Nothing had changed. Yet her whole being tingled with expectation. Slowly she walked about, as if hoping to lure from the very walls the secrets they contained. And they did contain secrets, for these walls had been silent witness to two conversations on two different nights many years before which to know would unlock more mysteries than Cherity had any idea even existed. The one had been a night when four of Brown's Cherokee brothers had come to see him stealthily in the night and they had discussed the future of their people and the protection of their heritage. The second had been a meeting between Brown and Richmond Davidson's father concerning the protection of that heritage and the disposition of Brown's house and land.

But the walls remained silent. Cherity would not learn its secrets on this day. What she would in time discover about her heritage would be divulged by other means.

As she left the house five or ten minutes later, a movement in the woods caught her eye.

She took several steps toward it. Slowly a lanky black man stepped out from behind the trunk of a thick pine.

"Who are you?" asked Cherity.

"Please, missus," he said, taking off his soiled hat and crumpling it nervously between both hands, "I's jes' a hungry trab'ler lookin' fo' shelter, ma'am."

"How do you come to be here?" asked Cherity, slowly approaching.

"Dey tol' us dere be a place roun' 'bout here what's kindly disposed ter folks seekin' freedom. Dey tol' us 'bout a cave where effen a body waits long enuf sumbody'll cum ter help an' dat's where we been."

As Cherity walked toward the tree, her eyes were momentarily diverted to something odd on its trunk. A portion of the bark had been torn or cut away down to the surface of the sapwood, and a peculiar set of lines and circles had been carved into the surface of the wood. It was obviously man-made, though not recent, for the subsequent growth of the surrounding bark had all but obliterated it. At first glance, she took it to be some youngster's initials carved long ago, maybe even Seth's, she thought. But as she continued to stare at it, she saw nothing resembling an *S* or a *D* or any letter of the alphabet for that matter.

A shuffle of the man's feet brought her out of her brief reverie. She glanced back toward him.

"How many of you are there?" she asked

"Four, ma'am," said the man.

"And what if I'm not someone who is friendly to runaways? Aren't you speaking rather freely with a stranger? What if I am a bounty hunter?"

A wide grin of humor spread across the man's lips revealing a wide set of pure white teeth.

"I reckon you jes' had da look ob sumone I figgered I cud trust, ma'am. I reckon you looked like a frien'."

"Well then, why don't you take me to the rest of your people," said

Cherity. "And I will see what we can do to find them some better quarters than a cold damp cave."

That evening at dusk, one of the Greenwood wagons, filled with seven blacks and with Sydney LeFleure at the reins moved slowly away from the precincts of the plantation toward the isolated hill region to the east. Their journey would take them half the night. By morning the travelers would be safely in the hands of the Davidson's Quaker neighbor, who would see to the next stage of their long trek.

Yet there was no respite for the weary hands of ministry, for these seven had already been replaced by the four brought down the hill from the cave by Cherity—two men and their wives, one who was so exhausted by the journey from Florida that she seemed nearly unable to take another step.

Richmond came into the house that evening at about eight o'clock and sat down wearily in the parlor where Carolyn was waiting for him.

"Are they all settled?" she asked, pouring him a cup of tea from the pot on the sideboard.

"As well as can be expected," sighed Richmond. "Honestly, I don't see how these people do it. They want freedom so desperately. We take it for granted, yet they are willing to risk their lives for it. One cannot but admire their courage. But one of the women is tired and weak. She needs a long rest."

"When will Sydney be back?"

"In the morning sometime," replied Richmond, taking a drink from his cup and lapsing into thought.

"Where will it end, Richmond?" asked Carolyn at length. "Will this war solve anything?"

"I don't know. There is talk that Lincoln may free the slaves by executive order. Jeffrey's last letter to Cynthia spoke of the Union troops expecting a major push by the Confederacy as a result."

"Do you think that will change anything down here?"

"I doubt it. The Southern states will recognize nothing he does anyway. And as Jeffrey thought, it will only increase anger against the president. So it seems the blacks will continue to come."

"Which president?" asked Carolyn. "I presume you mean Mr. Lincoln."

"We may be Virginians, Carolyn, but first of all I am an American loyal to our country—our *whole* country. Yes, Abraham Lincoln is my president. I cannot recognize a government founded on rebellion."

"Our whole nation was founded on rebellion against British rule."

Richmond nodded. "That is true, of course," he said. "I confess I struggle with that concept from time to time. But that was a rebellion of our nation's founders three generations ago and for which we living today cannot be answerable. What would have been my stand had I been living at the time, I cannot say. But this present rebellion is one for which we alive today *are* answerable. I therefore cannot endorse it."

"How long will Greenwood be able to keep up with those who come?" asked Carolyn. "We are already stretched to the limit."

Richmond nodded. "I miss the boys more than ever," he said. "Sometimes the work is overwhelming. I despair of catching up. I'm not as young as I once was, Carolyn."

"What are you talking about? You are still remarkably fit, Richmond."

"That may be. But I confess I am tired—physically and emotionally. I feel like my spiritual reservoirs are running dry."

"I suppose I know what you mean. As much as I love dear Cherity, and as great a comfort as it is to have Cynthia with us, sometimes I find it hard to smile. I miss the boys so much."

Carolyn paused and thought a moment.

"Cynthia seemed ready to be grown up. Maybe I should say I was ready for her to grow up. But I wasn't ready to let go of the boys yet. It came too suddenly."

"I think that is it exactly," said Richmond. "The change came too suddenly. I miss them with all my heart."

"As hard as it is sometimes, I know we can't stop living just because they are gone. Nancy has to keep living without Malachi. We have people who depend on us and work that God has given us to do."

"You are right, of course," nodded Richmond. "I have to keep reminding myself that Seth and Thomas are men now. That's hard to accept. Not recognizing that they are men—that's not the hard part. It's having them gone that is hard. I anticipated this time of life for years. I wanted to share in it with them. I hoped to be a father to them in their young manhood—a father of their manhood rather than their boyhood. That was one of the most exciting challenges I had been looking forward to. Then suddenly the moment they reached that wonderful age of maturity, they have been taken from us. Perhaps it is selfish of me, but I feel deprived, almost cheated in a way—not cheated by God or them, just by the circumstances of life—to have something I had been praying for and preparing for all their lives taken away. I don't know if I will ever be in a position to be in active, daily, working relationship with them again. I hoped to work side by side with them at work that God had given us to do *together*. What a joy it would have been to be engaged in meaningful work and ministry with grown sons."

He smiled. "But perhaps that was my vision not theirs. I don't know if they want such a thing even if they do come back. Young people don't always share the same outlook on relationship with their parents that parents do."

Carolyn nodded thoughtfully.

"Maybe that is the hardest part of all," Richmond went on, "especially with Thomas, knowing that even if he were here, he would want to be independent from me. It is a knife in my heart every day . . . but you are right, dear wife—life has to go on. And we do have the blessing of being able to enjoy such a relationship with Cynthia."

He paused and a thoughtful look came over his face. "I wonder how things are getting on over at Oakbriar," he said. "The war must be changing things for them too. I haven't seen Denton since the attack on Fort Sumter."

"Has he been in Dove's Landing?"

"He must have come back when Congress wasn't in session. To be honest," said Richmond, "I've almost been afraid to see him again.

With all the threats that were made, with Wyatt and that other fellow, and with everything that's been going on here . . . it's been a relief not to see any of them."

"I admit I don't miss Wyatt either," reflected Carolyn. "What evil got into that poor boy! Do you ever see Leon?"

"Occasionally in town. He doesn't say much. Although that reminds me, I meant to tell you . . . he said that Lady Daphne is back."

"Oh, I'll have to go over for a visit."

"I'm sure she would appreciate it."

Four

Vincent Locke was a virile twenty-four-year-old Southern boy who had never in his life been deprived of anything he wanted. He knew his father's plantation would be his one day and he did everything in his power to enhance his future investment. He knew his father had sired probably twenty or thirty slaves in his day, and was probably not through yet. He saw it as his duty to carry on the family tradition. While most young men his age were off fighting the Yankees, he deemed it his higher duty to stay at home to keep the plantation prospering . . . and growing.

The expression on Vincent Locke's face when he eyed Mary Steddings had not been lost on her father Aaron. Even after eleven years as a slave, he still thought like a free man. The outrage he felt at seeing a man look that way at his daughter was nothing he could control. He might tell himself that he was a slave now and could do nothing about it. He might remind himself of his Quaker principles of peace and nonviolence. He might tell himself any number of things. But the indignation of a father protective of his daughter's purity rose stronger within his breast than any arguments that could be brought against it.

He hoped and prayed that the master's son would lose interest and that nothing would come of it. But in the meantime, he worked harder than ever on his secret plan. He began to stash a few supplies—water, candles, matches, dried meat—and stabilized the walls with boards as he widened them out as he went lower. And at every opportunity he continued to dig, now, when he *knew* it was safe, risking even four or five scoops of dirt at a time. He also began experimenting with methods for covering the hole back up from the inside—the two most important aspects of his plan of all—and for supplying air to the hole once it was covered over with the boards and dirt.

For air, nature itself solved the difficulty. One day, pulling back the boards, he noticed a pile of loose dirt at the bottom, above which, about six inches up on the wall, was the perfectly round bore of a mole tunnel. After falling into his excavation, the mole had apparently dug down into the floor and made his way back into his network. But after licking his finger and holding it up to the hole in the side wall, Aaron detected a faint movement of air. If he could find where the maze of tunnels came up outside, and make sure the hole to the outside was kept clear, he would have a passageway for air to enter the cave that would be completely undetectable.

Master Locke and his son left the plantation for a week. Aaron had to be just as careful about Mr. Roper, but with father and son gone, the overseer was longer in the fields and he was left alone for longer stretches of time. He was emboldened to dig furiously, widening the bottom of the cave, now five feet deep, to a width of about four feet square. He only hoped the depth along with the bolstering vertical planks he had put in place would prevent a collapse. He added more water, an empty bucket for refuse, another candle or two, and what matches he could scrape together.

Once everything was in readiness, he thought, it would be best to wait no longer, especially with the master gone. He was just thinking through all the final preparations when out in the yard he heard the dogs barking and the sound of horses. His heart fell as he glanced outside and saw Master Locke and his son riding in.

He closed his eyes and sighed. He had waited too long.

It didn't take long for the worst he had feared to come upon them. Two days later, from where he was at work rebuilding a wheel for one of the wagons, he heard a faint scream from the direction of the slave village. Though she had been out in the cotton fields with the others all morning, instinctively he knew it had come from Mary.

Aaron dropped the iron he had been bending into shape and ran from the building. He was just in time to see his daughter being dragged by the wrist toward their small cabin.

He glanced about. Neither Master Locke nor Mr. Roper were anywhere to be seen. Without considering the consequences, Aaron broke into a run.

Reaching the slave village, he burst through the door and saw Mary crouching in terror where the master's son had shoved her onto one of the beds. Vincent Locke already had half his clothes off and was just bending over her. At the sound of footsteps, he spun his head around.

"Papa!" Mary cried out.

"What are you doing here, Steddings?" said the master's son. "Get back to work!"

The words had hardly left his mouth when the strong grip of the black man's hand grasped his shoulder and pulled him forcefully away.

"Steddings, how dare you lay a hand on me!" he cried, jumping to his feet and turning to face the father. "This is none of your concern. Now get out of here—this girl and me has business, and it ain't yours. If you get out of here now, I'll ignore what you just did."

"She's my girl, that makes it my business," rejoined Aaron heatedly. "And you aren't going to lay a hand on her."

"Who's going to stop me!" laughed young Locke with derision.

"If I have to, I reckon I will," said Aaron.

"You try and you know what'll happen. Don't be a fool, Steddings. You know how these things are. She's marrying age."

"That may be, but she is not going to marry the likes of you."

Vincent Locke laughed again at the impudence of a slave to challenge his right to do anything he wanted. "Have it your way, then," he said. "If you want to watch, then stick around. But you can't say I didn't warn you."

He turned back to where Mary half knelt on the floor. "Get your dress off, girl!" he said. "I ain't got all day." He grabbed her wrist and started for the bed.

But again the strong grip of a blacksmith's hand yanked him from her. Locke spun around again, and now his eyes were filled with fury. The fool slave had pushed him too far. He jumped up and ran toward Aaron with fists clenched intending to beat him senseless and then have his way with his daughter. He charged wildly, not expecting the man to fight back. Every slave knew the penalty for striking a white man. He did not expect even Aaron Stedddings to be that big a fool.

But the black man was quick on his feet and Locke's first blow missed his head by three inches. He swung again but again hit only air.

"Go back out to the field, Mary!" said Aaron. "He won't hurt thee now."

"But Papa—" she cried, realizing that his danger was now greater than hers.

"Go, Mary!" he said. "There is nothing thee can do for me here. It is between me and this boy."

Infuriated yet the more to hear Aaron Steddings giving orders, Vincent Locke flew at Mary's father like an enraged tiger. He rammed into his midsection and sent Aaron stumbling back against the wall. With a momentary advantage, Locke drew back his fist and sent a mighty blow toward Aaron's face. But Aaron recovered himself and jerked his head sideways. Locke's closed fist crashed into the wall.

He cried out in pain and attacked with all the more fury. This time his fist found its mark and struck Aaron viciously across the face. At last Aaron Steddings' Quaker creed left him altogether. The next moment Vincent Locke lay sprawled on the floor, blood oozing from his nose.

"Now get back out there, Mary!" said Aaron to his daughter who stood staring on the scene in shock. "He won't try anything more today."

Without a word, Mary fled back to where the slaves were working, too terrified even to tell her mother what had happened. Aaron dragged Vincent Locke out of the cabin, tossed his shirt onto his bare chest, and left him lying on the dirt, then returned to his wagon wheel.

Vincent Locke had his own reasons for not wanting the full details of the incident to get around the plantation, much less spread to town. He was vague in his explanation to his father, which fact probably kept Aaron Steddings alive, for a day or two longer. It did not, however, keep him from a merciless whipping at the hand of young Locke, which, with Aaron tied to a post, he had been able to carry out without opposition. When his fury was abated and the cords binding his victim's hands cut, Aaron slumped to the ground all but unconscious. Locke walked slowly away as the rest of the plantation's slaves, who had been forced to watch, stood in silence, Zaphorah Steddings weeping in horror at the sight. Finally a few of them came forward and picked up Aaron's battered bleeding body and carried him home.

He was alive. But as consciousness slowly returned Aaron Steddings knew it would only be a matter of time before Vincent Locke sought more revenge than a whipping. If Master Locke decided to punish him further, he would probably sell him. A strong slave was worth good money. That alone was reason to delay no longer. But Vincent Locke would not care about the money. He would not rest until he saw Aaron Steddings hanging by the neck from a tree.

It was all Aaron could do to move an inch where he lay on his pad that night. He had had a few whippings since that day he and his family had been captured by three white Virginia boys and sold to North Carolina plantation owner Sutton Locke. But never one like this. Most of the skin from his back was gone. His entire body quivered and trembled with pain.

But he could not afford to wait . . . not even another day. After making sure he could do nothing to stop him, Vincent Locke would try to bed Mary again, probably tomorrow.

He waited until he judged it an hour or two after midnight, then gently roused his wife.

"What is it, Aaron?" whispered Zaphorah. "Have you been able to sleep?"

"There's time for sleep later," said Aaron. "We're leaving."

"What . . . where?"

"We're going, Zaphorah. We must go . . . tonight."

"But, Aaron—"

"That boy is going to take Mary again, and I won't be able to stop him. We have to go. Get the girls . . . I'll wake Moses. They can't make a peep. We have to be so still the dogs don't even hear us."

"But, Aaron, your—"

"It has got to be tonight, Zaphorah. There is no other time. Now get up, wake the girls. Get them dressed. Get coats for everybody, and a couple of blankets. We can't take anything else."

Still bewildered, for neither she nor any of the four children knew of Aaron's plan, Zaphorah rose and dressed quietly in the dark.

Twenty minutes later, Aaron Steddings, his body screaming in pain with every step, led his wife and sleepy, bewildered daughters and son—Mary eighteen, Deanna seventeen, Moses sixteen, and Suzane ten—away from the slave village and toward the big house, barns, and stables. They made their way slowly, step by careful step, in single file behind him. Had there been a moon, in their dark clothing and black skin, they might still have been almost invisible. But there was no moon. And Aaron had rehearsed this treacherous journey of three hundred yards so many times in the past year—mentally planning out the steps during his daily work—that he could have led his family safely to their strange destination with his eyes closed.

His chief worry had always been the dogs. And the horses, too, if they became skittish. But he had spent the year befriending Dawn Sky, as Master Locke called his light orange mare, and Midnight, his pure black stallion, with bits of fruit and sugar, getting them accustomed to his voice and smell. He hoped that his approach in the middle of a dark night would not startle them.

The dogs were the difficulty. He was not concerned about smell from this distance. But one tiny misstep, one faint sound in the night, and the dogs would have the whole place awake.

Step after slow step they walked . . . slowly . . . slowly. The others were wide enough awake in the chily night air now to realize the danger well enough. They still did not know what they were doing. But trust in their father, and a spirit of daring and adventure was sufficient motivation for the moment.

They reached the stables. Aaron paused, and turned.

"We have to keep on our toes," he whispered so softly that Zaphorah bringing up the rear could hardly hear him. "Not a word . . . not a sound. Just keep at my back. We're going inside now."

Carefully he swung back the door. He had in the past year had occasion to make sure its hinges remained well oiled.

Once inside, Aaron led the five nervous fugitives across the dirt floor toward the stall which had been the scene of his clandestine activities.

"Wait here," he whispered. "I'll be back in a minute or two."

He tiptoed toward Pale Dawn's stall and began to whisper softly. He opened the rail gate, inching toward her, patting her nose and offering her the bits of apple he had managed to put in his pocket earlier. She snorted softly and took the treats as he slipped a rope around her neck. Continuing to speak, he led her out of the stall and tied the rope to a post. The horse sensed the presence of others in the blackness and began to fidget. Aaron stood beside her, patting and stroking her and whispering gently until she calmed. He found his tool where he had left it earlier that morning, and returned to the stall.

In pitch blackness, working quickly now, he probed with the tip of the shovel until he found the spot, then hurriedly scraped the dirt back as he had hundreds of times . . . then set the boards aside. He climbed down into the cavern he had excavated and fumbled for a candle and match. Within seconds light flickered and lit up the tiny cave. He set the supplies he had placed on the floor to one side, then scrambled back up his makeshift ladder and hurried to where the others waited.

"Papa, what—," began Moses.

"Shush, Son!" said Aaron in an importune whisper. "Not yet. Come . . . come with me!"

He led them into Pale Dawn's stall. The sight that met her eyes brought a gasp of astonishment to Zaphorah's lips. But she tried to remain calm, for the sake of the children, only casting upon Aaron a wide-eyed look that said, "What are we doing?"

"Climb down, Moses," whispered Aaron. "Thee must lead the way, Son. Mary . . . Deanna . . . Suzane, follow thy brother. There isn't going to be much room. We'll have to snuggle close."

"But why, Papa?" said Moses, unable to contain his curiosity any longer. "What are we doing?"

"We're fixing to make a run for it, Son," replied Aaron. "But hurry. We have got to get down there before the dogs hear us!"

That was all Moses needed. He had grown up terrified of the master's nigger dogs.

A minute later Zaphorah and the four children sat huddled at the bottom of the cave. Aaron struggled up the ladder one last time. Now came the most daring and uncertain part of his plan. If this failed, everything failed. He had to get Pale Dawn back into her stall, the gate closed, and the boards back in place with dirt over them . . . and himself down with the others, without terrifying the horse. He did not know if it would work. But freedom was worth the risk.

With care he cleared back the edges of the hole where the two boards had to sit snugly on solid earth. Resting them on either side beside the hole, he piled three or four inches of dirt on top of them.

"Zaphorah," he said down the hole, "blow out the candle."

She did so. All went black again.

Now came the most treacherous part of all, keeping Pale Dawn from becoming agitated and get her into the closed stall and himself into the hole. Slowly he went to the mare's side, untied her from the post, whispering gently. He stood beside her, stroking her nose for several seconds until the smell of the extinguished candle was gone.

"All right, girl," he said, "we're going back into thy stall and everything's going to be fine. Thee must stay at the front for a time, that's all."

Slowly and carefully he led her back inside, keeping away from the hole at the far corner, swinging the gate closed behind them, keeping her to one side. When he judged it safe, he slipped the rope off her neck, then stepped away.

"Thee must stay right there, girl . . . don't move."

Quickly he backed away, felt for the hole, and scrambled down. With his feet on the bottom and head and shoulders at ground level, he reached behind him and pulled the first board over half the hole and set it in position. Reaching up he covered it with straw. Then covering the last board with straw, he crouched low and pulled the second from the other side over his head to meet the first. With a soft thud he felt it lodge into place. The air suddenly became close and still and heavy. They were closed in.

Aaron sighed in relief, then crouched to his knees, fumbled for his supplies, and a moment later the flame of a match exploded into light.

"Everybody safe?" he said as he lit a candle and glanced around to take stock of his family huddled together beside him. "I knew it would be small, but this is more crowded then I figured! I know it isn't too comfortable, but we have to sit here a spell and try to get some sleep."

"Aaron, what are we going to do?" said Zaphorah, at last voicing her fears at her husband's plan which she did not understand in the least. "They'll find us. We can't stay here."

"Well, they may find us," said Aaron. "If they do, I suppose they will hang me. But I don't think we had much time left together anyway. That Locke boy had evil in his eye. And I'm thinking maybe they won't find us. I'm hoping that mare will move around the rest of the night and stir the dirt around those boards. We just have to hope she doesn't cave it in on us. And I'm thinking this is the one place they *won't* be looking for us. They won't imagine that we would stick around—they'll be searching all day tomorrow high and low for us out in the woods and round about."

"But why are we staying here, Papa?" said Moses. "What are we going to do? If we are going to escape, why don't we just go now?"

"If we tried to run now, Mister Locke's dogs would find us before we got a mile away."

"Then Aaron—what *are* we going to do?" asked Zaphorah again.

"We're going to wait right here and try to sleep. I know it's tight. But we have water and a little food, and a bucket for our necessaries if we can't hold it. It's going to be a mite unpleasant and won't smell very good, but it won't be for long."

"And what then, Papa?" asked Deanna.

"Tomorrow night, after they have searched all day long and have run the dogs miles and miles, after those dogs are tuckered out and they and the horses have been everywhere round about stirring things up and mixing up all the smells so their noses don't know what to think, that's when we will go. And when they figure we are long gone somewhere, then when everybody is sound asleep and thinking we're miles away, we'll make our run for freedom."

"But why won't they catch us tomorrow, Papa?" asked Mary.

"Because we're going to fly out of here on the backs of Mister Locke's horses. And I don't want to go till the dogs are so tired they have no running left in their legs. When they get tuckered out, dogs are about the laziest animal there is. And that's what I want chasing us . . . lazy, tired dogs. So we are just going to have to sit here together till tomorrow night."

At last it was quiet in the cramped little cave.

"I can't breathe too good, Papa," said Suzane.

Aaron glanced about.

"Scoot over this way, Suzane," he said.

Behind her on the dirt wall, he knelt forward and held the candle up to the mole tunnel. The flame flickered and bent slightly.

"There, thou sees," he said. "Hold thy nose up to that hole. It goes all the way outside. Moles have to breathe too, and some mole made us a breathing tunnel!"

"How is thy back?" asked Zaphorah, inching next to her husband.

"It is not too good," said Aaron, putting his arm around her. "All right, everybody, we must try to sleep. We are safe, and we are together—that's all that matters. Now we need to blow that light out. We can't make too much smoke in here or none of us will be able to breathe!"

Aaron blew out the candle, and they were left in deeper darkness than any of them had ever been in before.

"We thank thee, Lord," Aaron prayed aloud, "for protecting us and watching over us all these years of bondage in this Egypt. And we ask thee to protect us tomorrow, and guide us even in the darkness by thy Light. We commit our way unto thee, and we ask thee to help us get back home again. Amen."

"Amen," whispered Zaphorah. It was comforting to hear her husband pray in the old way.

Four more soft *Amens* sounded in the blackness.

It was silent again for several minutes. Gradually the breathing of the four children grew rhythmic with the sound of approaching sleep as they sat leaning against one another.

Softly Zaphorah began to sing.

Amazing grace! how sweet the sound . . .

Softly the others joined her one by one.

That saved a wretch like me!
I once was lost but now am found,
Was blind but now I see.

"I like the sound of that," said Deanna sleepily. "I know we aren't free yet, but just thinking about it makes me happy."

In their tiny cramped hideaway, the six Steddings knew nothing of the commotion caused by their disappearance the following morning. Both Lockes were white hot with threats, though the father's anger was equally directed at his son for having precipitated the series of events. Vincent Locke secretly vowed not only that Aaron Steddings would not make good his escape, but that he would not live to tell about it.

But all the resources available to them, including dreadful threats and interrogations of the other slaves, turned up no sign of Aaron Stedddings and his family. They had simply disappeared in the night, leaving neither clue nor scent behind them. The dogs' apparent interest in the stables was explained by the fact that Aaron worked there every day. And with so many animal smells about, all the dogs could do was run around in circles barking at the pigs and horses and each other.

A daylong search of the fields and pastures and woods in every direction turned up not a trace. As Aaron had predicted, the dogs were sound asleep before the crickets came out that evening, their mouths open and their tongues lying on the dirt in exhaustion.

"How will we know when it's night outside, Papa?" asked Suzane for perhaps the tenth time that day, which had been one long underground night for them.

"That I don't know," replied Aaron. "I reckon we'll have to listen as best we can, at that mole tunnel and maybe we'll be able to hear above us like we can hear Pale Dawn's hooves shuffling about."

"I can't hear anything, Papa," said Mary.

"We'll have to be still and try. But if we can't, then I'll have to lift up the boards and sneak a look."

At last Aaron, too, became impatient. Misjudging the time by several hours, his first attempt at lifting one of the boards a crack was met by the sounds of men's voices somewhere. Quickly he lowered it again. Thankfully the mare hadn't taken notice of the movement at her feet.

He tried again several hours later. This time he heard crickets. Night had fallen.

"It's time to go," he said. "Be still and quiet till I get the horse out of the way."

"I'm afraid, Papa," said Suzane. "I don't want to get whipped."

"Thee won't get whipped, little girl," said Aaron. "We are going to get away from here and never be slaves again."

Aaron stood, to the height he was able, and lifted the board above him slowly and carefully a few more inches. As he did he began talking quietly to the mare. He knew it was dangerous. She would not expect him to come from beneath her. He could not risk a candle. The smell of a flame would incite her.

When he had a crack open to the stall above he listened to see if he could tell where the horse was. She had heard him and was shuffling about. He saw the dim outline of her shape. Thankfully she was not directly above him.

"That's all right, girl," he whispered. "It's thy old friend Aaron. Just stay calm and easy."

He continued to speak quietly until she calmed. As softly as he could he lifted the first board up and set it aside, then the other. Dirt from the edges fell down on his head and face as he then quickly climbed up and stood.

Pale Dawn whinnied briefly. The movement had startled her. But instantly Aaron was at her side, stroking her nose and speaking softly. With one hand he felt for the gate, opened it, reached for the rope where he had left it, slipped it over her neck, and carefully led her out of the stall.

"All right, come up . . . it's safe," he whispered down into the cave. "Light a candle, Zaphorah. Everybody stay quiet. I don't know what time it is. They may still be up in the big house, but if not it's time to go. Bring the blankets and put on thy coats."

Happy at last to stand and stretch their legs, Mary, Deanna, Moses, Suzane, and Zaphorah climbed one by one up the ladder. Aaron now led Midnight also out of his stall.

Two minutes later, Zaphora, Mary, Deanna, and Suzane were on the backs of two horses. Aaron and Moses led them outside, slowly and as quietly as Aaron was able, then he returned by the light of the candle where Zaphorah had set it. He opened the stalls of the rest of the horses and did his best to coax them outside. By now the horses were jittery.

A lone bark sounded from the far side of the house.

"Aaron!" exclaimed Zaphorah.

"Moses," he said, "see if thee can find a rope in there and get it over the head of that gray one there. I've seen Mister Roper on him. I reckon he's fast enough. Hurry."

In another two minutes Moses was on its back. Aaron lifted Deanna from behind Mary on Midnight and set her behind Moses.

"Hang on to thy brother, girl!"

Another two or three dogs started barking.

A light in the house went on behind them.

"Papa, they hear us!" cried Deanna.

Aaron hurried back inside, blew out the candle, then jumped up onto Midnight's back and reached around Mary's waist for the rope.

"Hold on, everybody, we don't want anyone falling off! Thee's got thy rope, Zaphorah . . . Moses?"

They clomped out of the stable into the yard. Still hoping not to be heard, Aaron led them at a slow walk toward the main road. By now the horses were snorting and whinnying, their hooves echoing on the hard-packed dirt.

"Hey . . . what's going on out there—hey . . . Vincent, get up and get outside!" they heard Sutton Locke cry. "They're after the horses!"

"Let's go," cried Aaron.

Aaron kicked at the stallion's flanks. Within moments they were galloping away in the night. By the time more lanterns began flickering from several windows of the main house, they were two hundred yards away and flying along the road, with most of the other horses galloping after them.

Five

*C*ecil Hirsch was a man who believed in fate. One could not count on Lady Luck making an appearance at the opportune moment. But when she did, the prudent man acted without delay.

What were the chances, he said to himself, walking along a street in the Union's war-tense capital of Washington, where he himself had only planned to be for a day, that he would see one face out of all the faces in the world? Especially one who was not even supposed to be in the country from the last he had heard?

But it was her . . . he was sure of it!

Hers was not a face he would mistake, no matter how many changes had taken place upon it. She was even more beautiful than he remembered. Stunning was the only word for it. And yet with a certain hint of care and weariness about the eyes—useful qualities for the man who knew how to exploit them.

What was she doing here? he wondered. Not that it mattered. She was here, and suddenly his brain spun with possibilities.

Best of all, she had not seen him. It would give him time to make a few inquiries . . . and plan his next move with care.

Aaron Steddings rode his family as hard as he dared for an hour.

A half moon breaking through the clouds gave them enough light

to keep their mounts on the road. The other horses from the plantation followed for a mile or so and then one by one turned back. But
by the time the master and his son were able to get a couple of horses
in from the pasture and saddled, Aaron thought they would be far
enough away that they would not be able to pick up their trail. None
of the dogs, in their condition, would last a fraction of this distance.

Their chief worry was getting too close to other plantations. They
would be recognized as runaways in an instant. And the three horses,
while giving them an advantage of speed, were also visible, noisy, and
impossible to hide.

Traveling on horseback also made nighttime travel more difficult.
To have a chance Aaron knew they somehow had to make contact
with the Underground Railroad network.

When he judged dawn perhaps an hour away, Aaron began looking for a place to get off the road where they could hide out, rest, and
sleep for the coming day. He had changed directions several times as
they came to crossings, hoping that in every case they kept moving
further from the Locke plantation. He had always had a pretty good
sense of direction. He would try to get better bearings after the sun
came up.

The others were exhausted, frightened, and probably more than a
little bewildered about their sudden escape. He didn't want them falling off their horses in the darkness! He had been preparing for this
night for a year in secret. It was hardly any wonder they were confused
and tired. They needed a rest.

Gradually he slowed the pace and scanned both sides of the road in
the dark. After crossing a bridge over a small stream, seemingly where
no farmhouses were around, he led the way off the road. They continued a short distance along the stream, then stopped. Aaron dismounted and helped the others to the ground.

"We'll stop here awhile," he said. "We can drink and clean up and
we'll have a little something to eat, though all we have is more dried
meat."

After he had watered the horses in the stream and tied them so they could graze in the nearby grass, Aaron sat down beside his wife. The four children were already dozing off.

"Before thee is all asleep, I want to talk to thee and tell thee what we're trying to do," he said. "I know this has taken thee by surprise, but I wasn't going to let anything happen to Mary. I'm sorry I didn't say anything sooner, but I thought it best nobody know so that nobody would let a word slip. I considered it safer if thee didn't know. I have planned for a long time how we could get back home. But we had to wait till the right time, and I figured when that Locke boy did what he did, well this was it. So here we are."

"Does thee think we will get home, Papa?" asked Mary. Being the oldest it was natural for her to lapse into the familiar talk.

"I don't know. But if we don't try, we never will. Who knows how long this war will last or what will become of us when it's over. But thee two girls were bound to get put with a man soon. Maybe we already waited too long. Maybe I should have tried for us to escape a long time ago. But I was afraid of something happening to thee, and I thought as long as we were together and safe and healthy, well that was still a lot to be thankful for. A lot of slaves don't have a family like we do. We have been fortunate and the Lord's been good to us. But it looked to me like times were going to change. And I listened all this time, picking up little bits here and there. I think I have an idea which direction runaways find that railroad. I hope and pray I've done the right thing. I'd never forgive myself if anything happened to any of thee. I'm sorry for getting thee into this mess in the first place—"

"Oh, Papa, it wasn't thy fault!" said Mary. "Thee has been the best papa ever. And the way thee saved me from that terrible boy, made me so proud of thee. Thou should have seen him, Moses. He knocked him right unconscious."

"Aaron . . . ?" said Zaphorah.

"I'm afraid I lost track of the Testimony of Peace for a minute or two," said Aaron. "But when I saw what he was doing, I couldn't help it."

"Well, I'm proud of thee, Papa," said Mary, "and very thankful for what thee did."

"Now this is going to be dangerous," Aaron went on. "There are still lots of bad things that can happen, and they'll be looking for us, so . . . if we should get separated, I'm telling thee find other slaves . . . try to get with other runaways and get to a Quaker safe house. Tell them thee are Friends too. Tell them thee lives in Mount Holly, New Jersey. Suzane, thee is too young to know what it's like there, but that's where we are going. Remember that name—Mount Holly. It's in New Jersey. That's our home. So ask thee of Quaker folks to help thee get there. All Quaker folk know where Mount Holly is. It's a famous Quaker town."

"Why you and Mary talking funny, Papa?" asked ten-year-old Suzane.

"Because that's how Friends talk, and we're free now. We don't have to pretend to be slaves any more."

"I'd almost forgotten," said Mary dreamily. "It sounds so nice to hear thee talking like Friends again, Papa."

"All right, now," said Aaron, "let's all try to get some sleep."

The four children were all fast asleep as dawn began to break. Aaron and Zaphorah dozed together, Zaphorah leaning against her husband's chest with his arm around her. As Zaphorah came to herself she knew Aaron was awake

"What Mary said before," she said, "—that goes for me too . . . for us all. I'm so proud of thee. Thee always tried to take the best care of us thee could."

"I didn't feel I did much of a job of it," said Aaron. "Now that we're away, I wish I had tried to escape before."

"Thee couldn't help what happened. We were slaves. It was dangerous. Thee kept us together, and we still are together. Now thee has gotten us away from there. But, Aaron," added Zaphorah, "how will we know where to go?"

Aaron reached into his pocket and pulled out a small piece of paper that had been folded many times. "This is the map that Mr. Borton gave me when we set out for his sister's," he said. "I kept it hidden all this time, just waiting for this day. I knew someday we would have our chance. I waited for the right time. I think I know where we are, and where his sister was. We'll try to get to her place, even if we are ten or eleven years too late."

"Won't they come after us?"

"I reckon they will. But we're going to keep moving and they won't know which way we went. Of course we need to watch out for bounty hunters and suspicious white folk, and we should move only at night. But if we can follow this map, I don't think Virginia's that far."

The Steddings family had been clomping along slowly for two or three hours since darkness had fallen. They had been away from the Locke plantation for three days and Aaron estimated they had covered eighteen or twenty miles. They had not moved fast but had made steady progress northward. They had not, as he had hoped, seen other runaways or so much as a hint of Underground Railroad activity.

They were also getting *very* hungry. The dried meat was gone. It was too early for apples. All he had managed to find was a planted field of potatoes. But raw potatoes didn't do much to satisfy four vigorous growing young people. Tomorrow, while they slept, Aaron had decided to try to get close enough to a farm somewhere and make contact with its slaves in hopes of getting some food for his family. It would be dangerous walking about in broad daylight. But he couldn't let them get so weak they were unable to travel. And perhaps too, he could ask if anyone knew of underground stations in the vicinity.

Aaron continued to reflect on his plans for the following day.

Suddenly lights flashed in front of them. Burning torches lit up the road. Four or five white men he did not recognize stood barring their path thirty or forty feet ahead.

The horses whinnied and reared briefly. Aaron reined back and pulled them to a stop as they pawed and moved about nervously.

"All right, it's all over now," said one of the men, walking toward them with a great burning torch. "You've had your little fun, but you're not going any further. We heard there was some runaways coming our way, and since I'm a little shorthanded on account of the war, I figured you'd do me right nice. Now get down off them horses."

But Aaron Steddings had not come this far to give away his new freedom as easily as that. He did not even pause to think.

"Follow me!" he cried, turning back toward the others. He kicked his heels into Midnight's sides and galloped off the road. "Hold on to me, Suzane!"

Zaphorah followed, Mary clinging to her waist for dear life.

"Hey, nigger boy—come back here!" yelled the man after him. "You can't get away—we'll track you down if you try to run!"

But Aaron was already gone and Zaphorah and Mary right behind him.

Bringing up the rear, Moses kicked at Pale Dawn, urging her after his father and mother. But seeing the first horses gallop into the darkness, the man ran forward to stop him.

The mare reared high in terror from the flame of his torch. Momentarily losing his balance, Moses leaned up onto her neck desperately clinging to the halter. Behind him Deanna shrieked and slipped. But the man was yelling and the horse whinnying and Moses did not hear her.

Moses righted himself as Deanna slid off the mare's back and fell to the ground, then whipped and kicked Pale Dawn forward into a gallop. Moses flew past the man, knocking him to the ground, and disappeared after the others in the night.

Aaron slowed the moment he was out of danger to wait. Seeing the outlines of the other two horses coming up behind him in the darkness, he did not pause to look more carefully. He quickly led off again, and they rode hard through trees and then open pastureland for perhaps another ten minutes. The terrain was uneven and they bounced and jostled about hardly able to keep their seats. Finally Aaron reined in to regroup and make sure the men were not following them. As they slowed and he stopped bouncing about, suddenly Moses realized he was alone on Pale Dawn's back.

"Deanna's gone!" he cried.

"What . . . where is she?" said Aaron in alarm, leading Midnight over to his side to see for himself.

"I don't know," said Moses in a panic. "She must have fallen off!"

"When . . . what happened?"

"I don't know—the horse reared."

"Where, Son . . . where could she be?"

" I almost got thrown off too. One of those men rushed at us. He was trying to grab me and I just kicked and tried to get away. I didn't know she wasn't behind me. I'm sorry, Papa!"

"Thee didn't know, Son," sighed Aaron. He paused to think. "All right . . . I'll go back and look for her. Wait right here."

"Oh, Aaron . . . no—please," implored Zaphorah. "What if something happens? Why don't we all go?"

"We can't risk that—not with those men."

"But, Aaron . . . what if we get separated!"

"We can't leave her back there, and I don't want the rest of thee in more danger. I'll go back and find her. If something happens, remember what I said. We all will get home, one way or another. Zaphorah, thee must take care of these three and thyself."

"Aaron . . . please!"

"Just wait here."

"But how will thee find thy way back in the dark?"

"I'll find it. Wait here and get some sleep. If we have to we'll sleep here tomorrow. Don't leave this place. But if I'm not back by tomorrow night, then thee's got to move on."

"Oh, Aaron . . . I can't do it alone!"

"If thee has to thee can. Don't worry . . . I'll be back."

Aaron disappeared into the darkness, leaving mother and two daughters and son alone.

⌒⌒

Midway through the morning a terrified Zaphorah Steddings heard the sound of a single horse coming toward them.

"Moses!" she whispered. "Somebody's coming!"

"Get down . . . Mary, Suzane, lie down," said Moses, running to his sisters.

"What about the horses?" said Zaphorah after him.

"We can't worry about them now."

They crouched low and waited. Slowly the sound came closer and closer.

"It's Papa!" cried Suzane.

They all jumped up and ran to meet him. But their excitement was brief. The eager smiles on their faces disappeared the moment they saw the expression on Aaron's face.

He was alone.

"There is no sign of her," he said, shaking his head dejectedly. "I found the place where those men surprised us, and saw the signs of the horses and scuffling about. But Deanna wasn't anywhere to be found. They must have got her."

"Oh, Aaron!" exclaimed Zaphorah, bursting into tears as he climbed down. "What are we going to do?"

"I don't know . . . we need to think."

Aaron went to the nearby stream, and knelt down and washed his face and hands, took a long drink, then came back and sat down. The others gathered around in silence.

Finally Aaron spoke. "I think there's only two things we can do," he said. "I figure either I go back looking for Deanna myself, that way if anyone else is caught, it's only me, while the rest of thee goes on and tries to get to that Underground Railroad . . . or else we all keep on together. I don't see what else we can do."

"Oh, Aaron," said Zaphorah, her tears flowing again. "How can we possibly go on? Wouldn't it be better for us to stay together even if we do get caught?"

"Thee wants to be a slave again?"

"No, but if we're together—"

"But we wouldn't all be together. If those men got her, and we go trying to get her back, they'll just capture us all. Maybe somebody gets hurt. Then they're likely to split us up anyway."

Zaphorah sat weeping. Aaron reached his arm around her and pulled her to him. She burst into tearful sobs. Moses sat silent, filled with remorse and guilt that he had ridden off and left his sister behind.

"Look, Son," said Aaron, "what happened wasn't thy fault. If thee'd gone back, thee would have been caught too."

"Then maybe I could have helped her," said Moses glumly.

"Thee doesn't know that," said Aaron. "We must suppose what's happened is for a reason. Maybe thee is still with us for that reason, whatever it is."

A long silence followed.

"We need to go," said Aaron at length. "Otherwise those men could come looking for us too. We have got to commit Deanna to the Lord, and then move on. There is nothing else to do."

Six

The years of the 1850s had been relatively calm for the Cherokee nation. Rivalry between the Ross and Ridge groups settled into a peaceful, though mistrusting, alliance on the Tribal Council, enforced by a federal treaty imposed upon the two groups to put an end to the early years of violence in the West. Watie became speaker of the Cherokee National Council. But though they now had to work together, he always blamed Ross and his followers for the murder of his brother, cousin, and uncle. And with the first sounds of cannon fire against Fort Sumter in 1861, the fifteen-year truce among Cherokee factions broke asunder.

The many and conflicting motivations that led the states of the North and the South into war cannot compare to the hundredfold complexities to engulf the Cherokee. What began as "the white man's war" soon led to bloody feuds in the Indian Territory of Oklahoma. Ancient animosities were stirred up, and vendettas long nourished in secret broke out afresh at the scent of blood in the air.

Confederate and Union emissaries issued rival promises to any Indian tribe who would join their side, as well as threats against those that would not. The result was that, as brothers of white fought against one another, so too did those of so-called red skin take up bow and arrow, spear and tomahawk, against their own native mothers' sons.

The smoldering feud between Chief John Ross and his long-standing opponent, Stand Watie, survivor of the 1839 massacre of his kinsmen, sparked into new flame almost the moment the war broke out. No longer was their dispute over the sale of Cherokee land in the east. Now the two men fought for control of the Cherokee nation as the Union and Confederacy went to war.

Chief Ross hoped at first to keep the Cherokee united and neutral and thus prevent the war from invading Indian Territory altogether. But Stand Watie—by then a wealthy plantation owner who had amassed much of his wealth from the slave system—adopted the Confederate cause. Tensions immediately mounted between the two sides, and the old Cherokee feud was on again at full boil.

Watie used the opportunity to capture the attention of his fellow Cherokee, urging every man who called himself a warrior to join him on the Confederate side. His message found receptive ears. By the time cannons were heard in the states bordering their lands, Watie had rallied a sizeable company of full blood, half blood, and mixed blood warriors under his leadership in support of the Confederacy.

Cecil Hirsch had been wrangling himself invitations, or getting into social events to which he had *not* been invited, for so many years in so many different kinds of situations, that he scarcely now even looked upon it as a challenge. It was, therefore, less than a week after she had been seen in the street that Veronica heard a familiar voice above the low chitchat of a diplomatic gathering in the Georgetown home of a high-up general in the Union army whose name she had already forgotten.

"Is it . . . I cannot believe my eyes—it is Miss Beaumont . . . Veronica Beaumont!"

She turned to see the equally familiar figure of Cecil Hirsch, smiling broadly and walking toward her.

"Ah, excuse me," said Hirsch, "I am forgetting myself—you are married now, what is it . . . Mrs.—?"

"Yes, Mrs. Fitzpatrick," said Veronica, flushing with perhaps a little too much pleasure at the sudden reacquaintance as she took Hirsch's offered hand and allowed him to kiss her own. "My husband Richard is the son of the ambassador to Luxembourg where we were living until recently. He worked at the consulate."

Hirsch nodded. "I believe I read something about the wedding and your plans," he said. "You always were one to be at the center of activity," he added with a hint of his old mischievous smile. "I am not surprised to see you back in the capital. Being so far from the hub of things does not suit you, Mrs. Fitzpatrick." Again came the smile.

"I have to admit that Luxembourg was a bit of a bore," rejoined Veronica.

"What—Europe a bore?"

"I thought it would be exciting. But I didn't know a soul. . . . I had no social life."

"And now you are back. How long have you been here?"

"Only a few weeks. When I first learned we would be returning, I was thrilled. But everything is so changed with this nuisance of a war. Many of my old acquaintances are gone or moved. Or *changed* . . . people are so different now! Even my parents are gone. Everything's turned upside-down. I hate it. It's just as boring here as it was over there."

"Perhaps I can help with that," said Hirsch, smiling yet again in a way Veronica understood well enough.

"Shame on you, Mr. Hirsch! I do believe you are trying to corrupt me. I am a married woman, after all."

"I meant nothing like that, I assure you!" laughed Hirsch. "I was only thinking that you—and your husband of course—might find some of my business ventures more exciting, even more lucrative than government work. Your husband *is* still with the government?"

"Oh, I don't even know anymore," sighed Veronica. "He won't tell me a thing. All I know is that after the war started there were all kinds of letters going back and forth between Richard and his father and Washington. Then somebody connected with the government told

Richard they wanted him to come back and I was glad at first, but now I don't know what's going to happen."

Hirsch listened with more interest than he allowed himself to divulge.

"And what about your father and mother?" he asked in a casual tone.

"They're the lucky ones!" said Veronica. "They were able to go back to Virginia. As soon as the war started and there was all that confusion with the Confederacy starting up—I could hardly understand what was going on, and we were still in Luxembourg at the time—everything was so mixed up! Mother and Father left Washington with all the Southern congressmen. Now Daddy's in the new Southern senate in Richmond and here I am all by myself in the North."

"Is your husband a loyal unionist?"

"I don't know. . . . I suppose."

"That places you in an awkward position—your family in the South, your husband working for the Union."

"I don't really know what to think—it's all so confusing. I thought moving to Washington would be different than this. I wish this stupid war would just get over and everything would go back to how it was."

"Why did your husband come back from Europe? You say he is still working for the government?"

"I think so."

"In what capacity?"

"I don't know—I think it has something to do with how smart he is and his connections with the European countries because of his father. What's the word . . . ? There's a funny word . . . I think it starts with *l*."

"Liaison?"

"That's it!" said Veronica. "They wanted him to be an intelligent liaison."

Hirsch could not help smiling. "Would it perhaps be an *intelligence* liaison?" he said.

"Yes, I think that's it—whatever that means! Oh, here comes Richard now. You can ask him yourself."

Richard Fitzpatrick walked toward them drink in hand. "Hello, darling," he said, kissing Veronica lightly on the cheek.

"Richard," she said, "I want you to meet an old . . . uh, friend of our family—Cecil Hirsch. Mr. Hirsch, this is my husband, Richard Fitzpatrick."

"It is good to meet you, Mr. Hirsch," said Richard as the two shook hands.

"And you, Fitzpatrick," rejoined Hirsch. "You are a lucky man— this is quite a young lady you managed to snag!"

"I was never quite sure who snagged whom!"

Hirsch laughed. "I know what you mean! She is a sly one all right!"

"Veronica," said Fitzpatrick, "if you don't mind . . . there are people I would like you to meet."

Veronica smiled and nodded. As the two moved off through the crowd, she cast one last brief glance over her shoulder where Cecil Hirsch was still watching them. Their eyes met for but an instant.

The expression on her face told him all he needed to know.

PART TWO

REUNIONS AND LOSSES
May-December, 1862

Seven

*A*t the southern Virginia farm of William and Hannah White, after John Borton's frantic visit in 1851 to find some trace of what had happened to his friends, the Whites had asked every runaway to come through if there was any word anywhere about a family called Steddings. None of their inquiries produced anything more than Borton's desperate search between his sister's farm and theirs. No trace of the carriage was ever found, nor any hint of the family.

Eventually, disconsolate, and after doing what he could for his sister, Borton had no choice but to return home, fearing the worst.

William and Hannah continued to inquire for news. But after years without word, gradually they gave up hope.

Once the war began, fugitive activity in Virginia increased dramatically. Though the White farm itself was in no danger, most of the underground routes they had previously used went too close to Richmond, an area now overwhelmed by troop activity. They could not use their former avenues of escape without adding to the danger. With Confederate troops everywhere not sympathetic to runaways, they had to be more careful than ever. Most of those who came to them now, they sent north and then west into the foothills of the Alleghany mountains, and ultimately toward Maryland and then Pennsylvania.

When Hannah White opened the door in the summer of 1862, her eyes shot wide in disbelief. She wasn't sure for a moment if her brain was playing tricks on her, but the moment Zaphorah spoke she knew the family she had been praying for all these years had at last returned.

"Hello, Mrs. White," said Zaphorah, "it's us—we finally came back."

"Oh . . . oh!!" exclaimed Hannah, then rushed through the open door and nearly swallowed Zaphorah in her arms. As the white woman and black woman embraced, both wept freely.

"And thy young ones are all grown up!" exclaimed Hannah, stepping back and glancing behind where the others stood.

Hearing his wife's cries of joy, William White approached from inside the house.

"William, look—it is the Steddings!"

"Well, well!" he said, striding forward with a great smile, "welcome again!"

He reached his hand toward Aaron, who took it and shook it vigorously.

"Thank thee, Mr. White," said Aaron. "It's good to be back. It's been a long hard road."

"We want to hear everything. . . . Come in, come in!" said Hannah.

A cloud settled over the happy reunion soon enough. Seeing the two girls and not realizing at first that young Suzane had not been with them during their earlier visit, Hannah White was devastated as Zaphorah told her what had happened and that Deanna, whom Hannah remembered as a child, was not with them. Meanwhile, Aaron and William walked together outside. The normally placid William White was livid at the story he had just heard of the capture eleven years earlier of Aaron's family less than twenty miles from his own home.

"I should have suspected it," he said. "There had been reports about young Eliott Tyson capturing runaways and carting them off to North Carolina and selling them. I never put it together, but I have no doubt it was him. Nothing we can do about it now," he added with a sigh, "but . . ." He shook his head in frustration.

"I have another favor to ask of thee, Mr. White," said Aaron as they walked. "Thee has already done more then I can expect for—"

"Don't mention it, brother Steddings," said White. "We've hardly done enough. Thee has but to name it and I will do whatever I can."

"I have not told Zaphorah yet," said Aaron, "All the way back here, I have revolved a plan in my mind, and it's this—now that they're safe, I have to go back and see if I can find our daughter. I'm hoping thee won't mind keeping my family for a spell."

"Of course. We will be happy to. But is it safe for thee to return south?"

"I don't suppose it is. But I can't just leave her there. I must do what I can to find her."

"What will thee do if thee does find her?"

"I don't know. I'm thinking that maybe I'll have to offer myself in her place, tell whoever's got her that they can have me if they'll let her go."

"A dangerous proposal, Friend Aaron."

"It is no less than what our Savior did for us. Can a father do less for his son or daughter?"

Aaron's words sobered William White. This was a man of uncommon character whom God had brought across his path.

"Then I shall go with thee," he said at length. "Thee will be safer with a white man who can vouch that thou art free. And if thy plan succeeds and we find her, then she will be safe with me and I will bring her back here with me. Yet perhaps a better plan would be for me to purchase her freedom and we will all come back here together."

"I would be more grateful than I can say for thy help," nodded Aaron.

Paralyzed at the very thought of losing her husband again to slavery, yet moved beyond words at William White's willing eagerness to help, it was with a full heart and many tears that Zaphorah said good-bye to the men two mornings later.

"Moses," said Aaron, "with Mr. White gone, thee will be the man around here for a spell. So do whatever Mrs. White needs and tells thee."

"I will, Papa."

"But be careful of white men and bounty hunters. Don't forget that we are still in the South and there's still danger. We're still runaways. So always keep an eye out for trouble. We've come too far to get dragged back again."

A few more hugs and handshakes and tears followed.

Then William and Aaron set off on two of William White's horses, leaving the two Quaker women, one white, one black, and the three young people, alone together at the White farm, their hearts hopeful . . . yet also afraid.

Eight

The first time Chigua LeFleure had visited the strange old house on the ridge above Greenwood with Cherity and Carolyn and the black women from the plantation, she felt the unmistakable sensation that she had stepped into the presence of the ancient spirit of her Cherokee past. It was not a past she often thought about. She had been kidnapped from the Trail of Tears at nine, and the memories of her childhood before that were dim. But the old Brown house brought that distant past back again like no other sight ever had.

She had heard a few vagaries about Mr. Brown. She knew that it had been many years since he had disappeared from the region. Yet the moment she stepped across the threshold of his former home, she almost felt he was there with her.

Her eyes had immediately gone to the stretched and dried leather skin hanging over the fireplace. Though the markings were faded with time, she at once recognized the symbols of the Cherokee language, though did not so quickly discern the images beneath the writing. That night, back in bed in the Davidsons' home, with Sydney asleep at her side, she could not get the old faded painting out of her mind.

She had not stopped thinking about it ever since. And after she and her family returned to make Greenwood their home, one of the first things she had done was go to Richmond and Carolyn with a request.

"Would you mind if I cleaned and tried to restore the deerskin painting above the fireplace at the Brown house?" Chigua asked.

Richmond and Carolyn looked at one another with questioning expressions.

"You remember, Richmond," said Carolyn. "It is hanging on the wall over the mantel. It is faded so badly that you can hardly make out the drawings and symbols. It's been there since the first time I saw the place."

Richmond nodded. He remembered it now.

"What can you do with it?" he asked.

"Clean it first," replied Chigua. "Skin painting is an ancient art among the Cherokee. My grandmother was highly skilled at it and taught me when I was young. I would like to study the painting to see if I can interpret the figures and perhaps paint over the most faded of them to bring out their original colors. The writing at the top is in the Cherokee alphabet, though I have forgotten much of what I once knew. I could not read it when I saw it—when I was with you, Carolyn. But I hope it will come back to me if I study it."

"I certainly have no objection," said Richmond. "I would love to know what the painting means—that is, if it has a meaning."

"I am certain it does," said Chigua. "All skin paintings have meaning."

"Then why don't we bring it down here and have you get to work on it? It will be exciting to see what you discover."

They went to the Brown house the very next day, and carefully removed the skin from the wall. Chigua rolled it up with extreme care, and they slowly returned with it to Greenwood. The painting was laid out flat on a table in one of the upstairs bedrooms where the light was good and where Chigua could carry out her work. She began immediately. A feather dusting and gentle brushing with a soft-hair brush removed enough of the film of accumulated years so that the three sets of images on the skin began to reveal themselves with greater clarity.

Chigua carefully sat, gently brushing and blowing the hardened skin as Carolyn and Richmond and Cherity and Sydney stood around the table watching with keen interest.

"This writing on top," Chigua said, pointing to the three lines of strange symbols, "is written in the Cherokeee alphabet. I cannot make it all out yet. . . . I think this word," she said, pointing, "is the number seven, and there it is repeated. You can see that many of the letters are common to English. But it has been long since I have spoken the old Cherokee tongue."

"What are these?" asked Cherity, pointing to a series of forms or figures below the writing. "They almost look like trees decorated with feathers instead of leaves. That one on the end looks like it was painted in red, all the others—let's see . . . there are six of them—they are all white."

"I don't know what they represent," said Chigua.

"And then below them . . . those round things."

"Yes, I've been curious about—"

All at once Chigua gasped.

The others glanced toward her and saw that her face had gone pale and her eyes were wide.

"What is it?" said Cherity excitedly.

"I think it's . . . it's the rings," said Chigua.

"What rings?" Even as she said the words, Cherity felt tingles of mystery pulsing through her.

"The seven Cherokee rings that were presented to our great chief and his comrades by the king of England. They are legendary among the Cherokee."

Briefly Chigua went on to recount the story of the visit of the seven Cherokee youths to the court of King George in the eighteenth century.

"Where are they now?" asked Carolyn.

The room fell silent. All eyes rested upon Chigua.

Without speaking, she stood and left the room. Only Sydney knew what was coming. Chigua went to the small house that had become theirs since their return to Greenwood. When she returned, her hand clutched an object which she set down on the table before them. It was a solid gold signet ring.

Sounds of astonishment went around the group.

"Is it really one of the seven?" asked Cherity. "It actually came . . . from the king of England!"

Chigua nodded solemnly. "This ring once belonged to our great peace chief of the white feather Attacullaculla. It came to me through my great-grandmother, the *Ghigua*, Nanye'hi Ward, for whom I was named."

"Where are the other six?" asked Cherity.

"I do not know. I was only nine when my half sister and I were kidnapped by Seminoles. How I kept them from finding it is a miracle. But I managed to hide it until I met Sydney, and then he kept it for me all the years we were slaves. Somehow we were able to preserve it."

"So you are related to Cherokee royalty . . . to a Cherokee king!" said Carolyn excitedly.

Chigua smiled a little sadly. "Well, to a chief," she said. "But what does it mean to be related to the leader of a conquered and displaced people? Even our proud heritage cannot remove the pain from the heart of the Cherokee—the pain of being taken from our homeland. One of my early memories is of my grandfather, when I was but a child as we prepared to set off to Oklahoma, telling me the history of our people. He knew the legend of the rings too. But he said the days of peace and prosperity would never return to our people. His words saddened my heart even then."

"What was the legend of the rings?" asked Cherity.

"When my mother's sister gave me this ring," said Chigua, looking at the gold band on her finger, "she told me what her mother had said to her, words passed down from the Ghigua. She said, 'When you wear this ring, beloved daughter, you are wearing a symbol of the unity and peace and trust that once existed between our pale-skinned brothers and the Ancient People. It is a sacred trust given to you, as the Great Chief Attacullaculla once gave it to the Beloved Woman, Nanye'hi.' I think my aunt hoped our people might find peace in the Oklahoma Territory."

"What about your other relatives?" asked Cherity.

Chigua shook her head.

"I know nothing of what happened to them. A few of my aunts and uncles married whites and did not have to leave North Carolina. But my grandfather was a full-blooded Cherokee and proud of it. He had practically raised me and my half sister and I adored him. He was the one who told me to guard this ring with my life, for I came from the royal line of Chief Attacullaculla and Nanye'hi Ward, the Beloved Woman of the Cherokee. During all those weeks and months before the soldiers herded us away from North Carolina, the men and women of our tribe hid the Cherokee gold in the caves of North Carolina. And then the time came and we were rounded up and taken away."

"That is such a remarkable and at the same time terrible story!" said Carolyn. "How can people be so cruel to their fellow man?"

"It was always my feeling that our Mr. Brown was one of those who left North Carolina before the worst of the trouble came upon the Cherokee," said Richmond. "But I was away when he left."

"I wish I could have met him," said Chigua. "Surely he could tell me much about our people that I never knew."

"I am amazed and honored to discover that we have a Cherokee daughter of chiefs with us!" said Richmond. "Now it is clear why you wanted to restore this painting of Mr. Brown's."

"It is my own history," nodded Chigua. "I did not know it at first, though I felt that something special must be here."

In the following days, Chigua continued to pore over the old skin painting, studying its every detail and experimenting with paints of white and black and red—made from certain berries and bits of crushed bark and leaves soaked in water—to get just the right shades with which to touch up the most badly faded portions of the images on the leather.

At length a day came when Carolyn and Cynthia and Cherity heard a shriek from Chigua's workroom. They dropped what they were doing and ran to her. They found Chigua standing staring at the painting with excitement.

"I've finally managed to translate the writing!" she exclaimed.

"What does it say?" asked Cherity, staring down at the table where the skin lay spread out before them.

"Look at these words on top," said Chigua. "They say, 'Seven rings for seven chiefs—the chiefs of the Cherokee—they of the white feather and he of the red feather, the white chiefs of peace, the red chief of war.' And these," Chigua went on, pointing below them, "I believe these seven figures that look like trees decorated with feathers represent the seven chiefs. See, six are standing painted in white, and the one red tree is fallen and lying sideways, showing the folly of war. And then below them are the rings."

"But there are only six," said Cherity.

Chigua nodded. "I do not know why that is so . . . unless one of them was lost."

The three women were silent.

"And what is that?" asked Cherity pointing to two small triangular diagrams of lines and dots on the bottom at both corners of the skin.

"That I am not sure of," answered Chigua. "It looks to me like some symbols I faintly remember seeing my grandfather make before we left North Carolina. He was out many nights with others of our men, taking the tribe's gold to hiding places in the mountains. They marked the locations, I think, with symbols and markings similar to these, though I have no idea what they mean."

As Cherity listened, her brain was spinning. She had seen a symbol just like these before!

Nine

$\mathcal{A}$s different as he now was from his onetime childhood friend, Denton Beaumont's thoughts had recently been moving in channels remarkably similar to those of Richmond Davidson. Like his neighbor, he too had been receiving disturbing reports from his overseer Leon Riggs that the work of the plantation was falling behind. And without his son Wyatt at home to help keep both Riggs and the slaves in line, his options were severely limited.

Abraham Lincoln and his talk of freedom had poisoned the minds of slaves everywhere. Every month Riggs reported another one or two escaped and gone. Even the presence of the behemoth Elias Slade could not stop them. He no longer had the manpower to chase them down as he once did. And Riggs and Slade could not alone plant and harvest all their fields. If many more slaves left, Denton Beaumont could find himself in desperate financial straits.

But what could he do from the city of Richmond? Here in the Confederate capital he sometimes felt powerless. The distance home was not so very great, though further than it had been from Washington. But his responsibilities in the new Congress demanded his presence. Or at least so he tried to convince himself. The fact was, until this war was over they weren't really doing much of anything. He would not say that to Jeff Davis's face, of course. They all pretended to be running a new country, the Confederate States of America. But it was the generals who were really in charge. Without the army there was no country. Unless Lee and Beauregard and the others defeated McClellan and Grant and the rest of Lincoln's brood, there would be no more Confederate States of America and he would never serve in politics again. And if they were defeated, it would mean an end to slavery and the Southern way of life . . . and probably an end to Oakbriar as well.

Beaumont sighed and sipped at the glass of Scotch in his hand. For the first time a few shadows of doubt began to cross his mind that perhaps he had bet on the wrong horse, and that perhaps the Confederate experiment was not destined for the rosy future they had all anticipated.

He needed to get out of the city. He had chided his wife for wanting to return to Oakbriar three weeks ago. Maybe she had been right after all.

When Denton Beaumont stepped off the train onto the platform of the Dove's Landing station and glanced around, he felt none of the triumphant sense of the return of the conquering hero that he once had. People were coming and going. Most took no notice of him. A few nods and greetings followed him out to the street, but he did not recognize half the people milling about the station.

The town was changing. Troops from both sides had come through the area. All the fighting in northern and central Virginia had taken its toll. There were also a few soldiers about, some wounded and returning home to recuperate, others taking trains to join their units. But he knew none of them. The buildings and boardwalks and fences and watering troughs and hitching rails of Dove's Landing looked old and tired and run-down. Here and there he saw a broken window. More than one storefront was newly vacant.

He looked about, saw Jarvis—more white-haired than the last time he had been here—standing beside a waiting carriage. Beaumont strode toward him.

"Good day to you, Massa Bowmont," said the black man.

"And to you, Jarvis," nodded Beaumont. He climbed up and sat down on the seat with a sigh. "Get me home."

As the carriage bearing the owner of the once proud plantation clattered toward the great house of Oakbriar, its occupant gazed about with none of the feeling of exhilaration he once would have felt at such a moment. Instead a feeling of uncharacteristic depression came upon him. He saw no evidence of activity and life. All was too still, too quiet.

As he entered the house a few minutes later, the feeling of desolation grew. Wyatt was gone, Cameron was gone, Veronica was gone. The house seemed empty.

"Oh, Denton, you're back!" came the high-pitched voice of his wife from somewhere, followed a moment later by the breezy sound of her dress sweeping into the room.

Inwardly Beaumont sighed, gave Lady Daphne a perfunctory kiss on the cheek, then went in search of Leon Riggs.

⟡

"I don't know, Mr. Beaumont," Leon Riggs said as the two men wheeled their mounts around and cantered westward from the stables toward the field where his crew was at work, "they was always a lazy lot, but it seems these days I can't get nothing out of them. They take their whippings in silence, but don't work no faster with their backs bleeding than without it."

"You told me there have been several escapes. . . . Any more in the last month?"

"Nope—me and Slade's been watching them real close."

"What about McCann? He was always the best tracker we had. Why didn't you send him and the dogs after the runaways?"

"We did, Mr. Beaumont. But the other darkies, they'd mess up the dogs' noses by sticking their own shirts in their face and after a while the dogs is just running around in circles."

"Then send McCann and the hounds after them by himself."

"He done quit, Mr. Beaumont."

"What! Where's he gone?"

"Over to the McClellan place, Mr. Beaumont. Mr. McClellan offered him more money."

Beaumont cursed under his breath.

"Well, no matter," said Beaumont, his hand fingering the leather whip at his side. "I'll put a stop to this laziness and these escapes once and for all."

"Whipping them don't do no good no more," said Riggs. "They just look at you and smile."

"They won't smile when they see me with the whip in my hand!" growled Beaumont, his annoyance with his overseer mounting by the minute.

"I tell you, Mr. Beaumont, things is changed. That's why I let up with the whip. Seemed like after every whipping, the next day another one was missing and they was all silent as statues—wouldn't say a word. The more I cracked down, the more escapes there was. I didn't know what else to do."

"You're too soft, Riggs. I've always told you—darkies understand nothing but the whip."

"Things has changed, Mr. Beaumont," repeated Riggs. "It just ain't like it used to be."

They rode on in silence until they came to a ten-acre field, half ploughed, where some twenty-five male slaves were working, though not fast enough to please their owner. They reined in from fifty yards away and Denton Beaumont surveyed the scene before him. The giant Elias Slade, his one free paid Negro, stood leaning on a shovel. Several groups of blacks scattered about the field wrestled haphazardly with horses, ploughs, and reins to upturn the dirt and cut furrows from one side to the other.

"How long have you been at it here?" asked Beaumont.

"Four days, Mr. Beaumont," answered Riggs.

"Four days!" exploded Beaumont. "We used to plough this ten acres in three. . . . And look at them—they aren't even halfway through!"

He dug his heels into his mount and galloped ahead of Riggs. By the time the workers glanced up at his approach, the whip in his hand was already raised above his head.

And he was anxious to use it.

When Sydney LeFleure, returning from another delivery of passengers to the neighboring station of their journey, encountered the lone black man wandering apparently aimlessly along the dirt wagon track east of Greenwood, he took him for yet one more fugitive runaway from somewhere in the South. He reined in and climbed down as the man staggered in front of his team, then fell to the ground.

Sydney hurried to him. The man lay on his stomach and the moment Sydney reached him he knew him to be no ordinary runaway. The back of his shirt was shredded and torn and caked with dried blood. Sydney knew the signs of the whip well enough. His back bore the scars from many such whippings during his own years of exile. But there was one difference between his and this man's scars. One look was enough to see that these wounds were fresh.

Sydney stooped down and rolled him onto his side, then eased his arms under his shoulders and knees and picked him up in his arms, carried him unconscious to the wagon, then jumped back onto the seat and urged the two horses home with as much speed as he dared.

Ten

The next time Cecil Hirsch saw Veronica, the meeting was obviously no accident. He knew it, and she knew it. By then Hirsch was well acquainted with the house where she and her husband lived, with their movements and activities, and knew more about Richard Fitzpatrick's new governmental responsibilities than Veronica did. He also knew that Fitzpatrick had just left for New York, would be gone several days, that Veronica had begged to go with him, and that she was more than a little put out that he had declined to allow it. The setup, in Cecil Hirsch's opinion, could not have suited his purposes better.

The day after Fitzpatrick's departure, at about the time it was Veronica's custom to go into the city or to meet one or another of the wives whose acquaintance she had recently made, Cecil Hirsch rode up in front of the Fitzpatrick home in a handsomely appointed carriage. There he reined in to wait at the side of the street until the lady of the house should make her appearance. The smile of pleasurable surprise that came over her face when she saw him was all the confirmation he needed that his timing had been perfect.

"Cecil . . . what in the world are you doing here?" said Veronica, walking out to the street.

"Merely passing by," he returned with a smile of feigned innocence.

"Passing by!" she laughed. "Now I know you are lying to me."

"You are right. The truth, then . . . I came to offer you the services of my humble carriage. I hoped my stimulating company might be more interesting than a ride into the city beside your own dull fellow. You told me last time we met that you were bored, and I told you that I would do what I could to help remedy that situation. So here I am— offering you a ride guaranteed to put interest back into your life!"

He jumped to the ground, gestured to the waiting carriage, then offered his hand.

Veronica smiled, as if in hopeless resignation, though inwardly she could not have been more pleased once again to be in the position of having a man, to all appearances, trying to win her over, then slowly nodded her consent.

Cecil helped her onto the leather padded seat. He climbed up beside her, swatted the horse's back with the reins, and they bounded into motion.

"I had the feeling I would probably see you again," said Veronica.

Hirsch could not help smiling. From the day he had first laid eyes on Veronica Beaumont he had known that they were kindred souls who thought alike. They still were.

"Are you disappointed?" he asked.

Veronica smiled a moment before answering. "No, not disappointed or I wouldn't have come with you. Let's just say I am wary, asking myself what you are up to."

Hirsch roared with laughter.

"I am up to nothing," he said, still chuckling through the lie, "I just wanted the chance to see an old friend and have a good time in the city for a day. True, I thought it best, for your sake—call it propriety—that we renew our acquaintance when you were, shall we say, alone. I merely thought you might enjoy some shopping, perhaps lunch at Garabaldi's."

"Garabaldi's—I have never eaten there. I hear it is quite exclusive. Will we be able to get in?"

"I am a friend of the manager's. We will get in, I assure you. But before that, I want to take you to Madame Rochelle's—"

"The Paris dressmaker!"

"You know of her."

"Who doesn't! But on Richard's salary, I could never even think of being able to afford anything of hers."

"I resolved when we met a few weeks ago that I would do what I could to alleviate what you described as the boredom of your life. A new dress by Madame Rochelle seems the perfect place to begin. You will be the talk of the capital!"

"Oh, Cecil! I cannot even imagine it! But how can *you* afford it?"

"The war has been good to me. Just set your mind at ease and know that I *can* afford it."

"I can't believe you would do that for me!" said Veronica excitedly. "Just imagine—a Madame Rochelle original! But what will I tell Richard?"

"Whatever you like. Tell him the truth, that you ran into me again and that I bought you a dress as a wedding gift."

"Oh, yes . . . yes, of course . . . that's perfect—a wedding gift. He would believe that. And why not . . . you and I are, just like you said, old friends."

"Of course," smiled Hirsch. "There is nothing untoward in it at all."

By the time Cecil and Veronica sat down in a booth at Garabaldi's three hours later, the fittings completed for what would easily be the most expensive dress she had ever owned, Veronica was positively exuberant with pleasure such as she had not felt for a long time. She was not meant to be a sit-at-home wife. She needed to be out where things were going on, and with herself in the middle of them. And with a dress, two hats, and three new pairs of gloves to be delivered to her doorstep by the most renowned dressmaker south of New York City, she had begun to feel like her old self again.

"Well, what shall it be, Veronica, my dear," said Hirsch, glancing over the menu. "Ah, Pierre," he said as a white-clad waiter approached.

"Hello, Monsieur Hirsch," said the man in a thick French accent, "it is a pleasure to see you again. Mr. Garabaldi asks me to convey his regards, and hopes that you will accept this bottle of wine with his compliments."

"That is very good of him, Pierre," nodded Hirsch, taking the bottle and setting it on the table beside him.

"Will you be having your usual, Monsieur?"

"I think perhaps a change is in order, Pierre," said Hirsch thoughtfully. "I think . . . hmm, let me see, I think we will have the *nonnettes de poulet* and *ris de veau à la financière,* and also bring us another bottle . . . say, the Rothschild '56."

"Very good, Monsieur Hirsch," said the waiter. "Mr. Garabaldi also asked me to convey his wish to speak briefly with you after your meal, on a matter, he says, of the utmost importance."

"Of course, Pierre," nodded Hirsch.

The waiter left, then returned a minute or two later with the second bottle of wine. He poured out two glasses, and again disappeared.

"How do you know all these people?" said Veronica in a low voice. "One would think you were Mr. Lincoln or someone just as important!"

Hirsch laughed good-humoredly. "I told you that the war has been good to me. I make no secret of that fact."

"It all seems very mysterious."

"Just business, Veronica—simple business. As I said that other day we met, I see nothing wrong in sharing my good fortune . . . with old friends."

He lifted his glass meaningfully in Veronica's direction, then took a sip.

"I remember you saying no such thing," rejoined Veronica playfully, also drinking from her glass.

"Well, I said something that amounted to the same thing. At least that's what I meant."

Veronica glanced across the table and eyed Hirsch carefully. If she thought she would be able to read his thoughts she was badly mistaken. He was every bit her equal in the same way that she was his. Both were possessed of a lifetime of practice in divulging only what they wanted to divulge. In this case, Veronica had more than met her match. The fact that she did not realize it increased her danger tenfold.

When the two had finished their meal, Hirsch rose and helped Veronica, slightly light-headed from the wine, to her feet. He offered her an arm to steady her legs, then picked up the unopened gift bottle with his other hand. Instead of moving toward the door, he led her to the back of the restaurant, through a short corridor, then stopped at a closed door, knocked, opened it, and walked inside.

"Ah, my good friend Hirsch," said a portly man seated behind a desk. "Good of you to come by."

"Hello, Garabaldi," said Cecil. "Please meet Mrs. Veronica Fitzpatrick."

"Charmed, I am sure, Mrs. Fitzpatrick," said Garabaldi, rising and nodding toward Veronica. "Listen, Hirsch," he went on, "I hoped I might ask a favor. I have an important letter here that I need to get to Congressman Wyler, in Richmond." His hand fell on a sealed envelope on his desk which he tapped a couple of times. "Unfortunately I am unable to leave the city just now. I thought perhaps with your travels, that . . . that you might be going down that way."

"Richmond . . . that's in the Confederacy," said Hirsch, as if the idea of crossing into Virginia were too dangerous to consider.

Garabaldi nodded. "Of course, that is the difficulty," he said. "Wyler and I are old friends, but with this cursed war, him now being in the *Confederate* Congress . . . communication with him is difficult. I cannot simply use the mail, you see . . . people might get the wrong idea. And with the war, the mail is, as I am sure you know, so undependable. His wife is ill, you see . . ."

His voice trailed off, leaving the sentence unfinished.

"If only I could," said Hirsch. "But I have no plans taking me down that way." He glanced with an expression of helplessness briefly at Veronica, then back to the restaurant owner.

"Hmm . . . that does make it rather difficult. I would go myself, but I am shorthanded here at the minute and I cannot leave. I would pay for your railroad ticket."

"I don't know . . ." hesitated Hirsch, shrugging and again glancing toward Veronica.

Suddenly Veronica's face brightened. "Why don't I take it for you, Mr. Garabaldi?" she said. "I would love to go down to Richmond for a day or two."

"You . . . why would you be traveling to Richmond?" asked Garabaldi.

"Because I am from Virginia. It would be a good opportunity to see my parents again. My father is a Confederate senator."

"You don't say! What a coincidence. Why that is a capital idea. You are certain you don't mind?"

"Not at all. I would enjoy the trip."

"It would certainly be a big help to me. I would be most indebted to you, Mrs. Fitzpatrick. But you would have to guard this envelope carefully. I would suggest you place it among your personal things so that it will be seen by no one."

"I will have to give it to my father to give to your friend—he will see it."

"Hmm . . . yes, I see what you mean. To be honest, Mrs. Fitzpatrick, I think I would prefer you deliver it yourself . . . in person—that is if you don't mind. It is a personal matter. The fewer people who know of it the better."

"All right. But how will I know where to find this Mr. Wyler?"

"Come back and see me tomorrow, here, in my private office, and we will arrange everything. I will give you a train ticket, and a little extra for your trouble, and tell you everything you need to know."

After a few more pleasantries, they left the office.

"He seems like a nice man," said Veronica as they walked out of the restaurant.

"It is kind of you to offer to help him," said Hirsch. "I know it means a great deal to him. And to me as well—he is a good friend. I was only sorry I could not oblige him myself."

"It is the least I can do. You have been so kind to me, and he is your friend, after all."

"And your friend now as well. I could tell that he took a liking to you."

Eleven

Richmond and Carolyn made every attempt to talk personally with each visitor to Greenwood, no matter how brief their stay. Some they got to know well. Others remained only long enough for a handshake, a meal, a night's sleep, and a hearty "Godspeed" as they continued on their journey. The moment Sydney arrived with their most recent boarder, however, they knew they must hear the man's story in detail. Richmond suspected the cause of his condition well enough.

When he was informed that the man had regained consciousness, he walked down the steep stairs of the basement of the main house where they had taken him to wash him, clean and treat his wounds, and put him to bed until he was in condition to begin eating and drinking. He found him just coming awake, with Carolyn seated at his side trying to get a few sips of water into his mouth. Richmond sat down on the other side of the bed.

"Hello, my friend," he said. "I don't know if my wife has told you where you are. One of our people found you out in the hills and brought you here. We were more than a little worried about you, but I am glad to see you coming back around. My name is Richmond Davidson and this angel beside you is my wife Carolyn."

"I knows who you is well enuf, Massa Davidson," said the man in a weak voice. "Everybody roun' dese parts knows who da two ob you is."

"Well, then you must know that I am nobody's master."

"Yes, sir."

"So you live nearby?" asked Richmond.

"I's from Oakbriar, Mister Davidson. I's one ob Massa Beaumont's slaves."

"What is your name?"

"Jimmy . . . Jimmy Grubs."

"Did Mr. Riggs do this to you?"

"No, Mister Davidson. He wudn't neber do dis, though I ain't sayin' he don' know how ter use a whip well enuf."

"Who, then?"

"Massa Beaumont, sir."

"What happened?"

"He cum home an' he was angrier den I'd eber seen him an' he jes' lit inter us like a wild man."

"Why did he do that?"

"I reckon he didn't figger we wuz workin' hard enuf. Dat's why I ran away, me an' two others. Dere's lots er talk er freedom dese days an' we figgered we didn't hab ter take dat kind er thing from nobody, eben our massa."

"How did you get away without being seen?"

"We waited till the middle of the night when Elias Slade wuz asleep an' we run from da cabin, but I los' my way. I wuz feared ob da dogs, so I kep' runnin' an' runnin' till I cudn't no more. I think I fell down, an' den all at once I woke up an' I wuz here."

"Well you will be safe and well taken care of as long as you are with us," said Richmond. "So drink and eat and get your strength back and then we shall decide what is to be done."

"Thank you, Mister Davidson. You an' da missus is real kind ter our kind er folks."

Richmond rose, casting upon Carolyn a look of concern which said what they were both thinking—that they had been in this situation before.

"Would you tell Moses that Mr. Grubs is awake," said Carolyn as her husband walked toward the stairs, "and ask him to bring down some bread and soup?"

When Chigua completed the restoration of the Cherokee skin painting, she said she would like to take it back to the Brown house alone.

"I don't know why exactly," she said. "Working on it, seeing the old
writing, seeing these images of the ring and the symbols of the chiefs
. . . it has reminded me again of my heritage and made me realize
what a treasure that heritage is. The heritage of being a Cherokee isn't
about the gold that was hidden that may never be found, it is about
having Cherokee blood flowing in one's veins. That is a heritage *more*
priceless than gold. And knowing that your Mr. Brown was one of
my own people . . . I don't know, I would like to be alone up there to
commune with the spirit of my ancestors and their legacy."

"Of course, Chigua dear," said Carolyn. "We think that would be
wonderful."

Before Richmond had resolved how to handle the newest situation
that threatened to draw him again into conflict with his onetime
friend, he received an even greater surprise than the appearance of
Jimmy Grubs.

Three days later, shortly after noon, Denton Beaumont rode
slowly up the long drive into Greenwood. He was uncharacteristically
thoughtful as he came, glancing this way and that at the condition of
the Davidson plantation in comparison with his own.

His pensive mood was not reflected inside the house when his
approach had been announced. That he was alone and without a
posse of bounty hunters was a relief. But his unexpected appearance
nevertheless took everyone by surprise and sent Carolyn and Cherity
scurrying about the house to hide evidence of their runaway guests,
while Richmond sent Sydney to the black village to do the same.

What had prompted the visit, even Denton Beaumont himself
could not have said exactly. Was it a subconscious longing for what he
perceived as the simplicity of former times, or perhaps the curiosity to

know whether things at Greenwood were as precarious as they suddenly seemed at Oakbriar? Might it even have been something deep within him reaching out to that which he had not had for a long time . . . a friend?

He had ridden back to the house three days ago, after whipping several of his slaves to within an inch or two of consciousness, sweating and breathing heavily as his fury subsided, and realizing something he had not realized very many times in his life, that he had gone too far.

Whether a man such as Denton Beaumont was capable of feeling what is commonly called remorse, he was feeling nothing like it after the whipping. He was only recognizing in some dim way that a merciless lashing was unlikely to get work done any faster or more efficiently. Part of him was still angry at Leon Riggs and Abraham Lincoln and all his slaves and the entire changing way of life that had infected people everywhere. But along with such thoughts, on the next day, hearing that three of the slaves he had beaten had escaped in the night under the imbecile Elias Slade's fat snoring nose, and with nothing apparently that he could do about it, there began to awaken in his brain the hint of a stunning realization—if he kept it up, he could well lose them all and be on his way to bankruptcy.

What was he going to do, go chase after them himself? Where was a man like Malone Murdoch when you needed him? Denton Beaumont felt powerless.

It was not a pleasant sensation.

His reflective mood throughout the day, after losing his temper briefly at Riggs when he told him of the escapes, stemmed from no compunction at having done wrong, only from the practical realization that maybe a gentler hand was required. Things were more straightforward in the old days. Everyone knew where they stood and what was expected of them. But if he could not stem the changes that new times were forcing upon him, gradually—and not without his annoyance flaring up—he saw that it behooved him to do what he must to ensure Oakbriar's continued prosperity, even if it meant having to hang up his whip until this war was over and things returned to normal.

Sometime during the day, as he reviewed the records of the previous harvest and continued his inspection of his property, he found himself wondering how things were going for his neighbor. Rumors had abounded about Greenwood ever since Richmond and Carolyn Davidson had freed their slaves six years ago and begun paying them wages. Tales had them prospering one moment and on the verge of financial collapse the next. There were also rumors—which he had always believed—that runaways were occasionally hidden at Greenwood on their way to the North. Richmond had always come in for a greater share of blame, in his mind, for the problem of escaping slaves than anyone but Abraham Lincoln. But now suddenly Beaumont found himself curious to know more, and for very practical reasons. In his heart of hearts, he was worried about Oakbriar and his own future. Was it possible that Richmond, fool that he still considered him, had seen the handwriting on the wall and—it galled him even to admit the possibility!—had stumbled on a revolutionary way to turn a profit and prevent his Negro workforce from slipping through his fingers?

Beaumont looked around as he rode into Greenwood, taking everything in with newly interested eyes. There were a few blacks about in the distance, one walking in a hurry past the barn toward the slave village. The horses in the near pasture appeared well taken care of, as did the house. He saw two Negro women hanging laundry on a line and a couple of black children playing nearby. Everything appeared normal, just as he might have expected. At the moment, nothing could have been further from Denton Beaumont's mind than that one of his own escaped slaves was recovering in a bed in the basement of Richmond Davidson's plantation house.

"Hello, Richmond," said Beaumont, dismounting as his neighbor came out the door and walked down the steps toward him.

"Denton!" said Richmond with a genuine smile of warmth and an outstretched hand. "It is good to see you again. It has been far too long."

Even as he shook his friend's hand, Richmond detected a change, an expression in Beaumont's eyes that he could not account for. Beaumont continued to look about, taking in the appearance of barn and stables and fields.

"Things appear to be going well for you," he said.

"We have no complaints," replied Richmond, leading his neighbor slowly away from the house. "That is not to say there aren't challenges. These are difficult times for everyone. Not having my sons to help out adds to the burden of trying to get the work done—something I am sure you are aware of yourself."

Beaumont nodded thoughtfully. "But you have plenty of laborers?" he said in a probing tone.

"Not as many as I would like," said Richmond. "My workforce is down in the last year or two and I am having a difficult time finding men to work."

"Even with your policy of . . . ah, paying them wages like white workers?"

"A good number of my people have left, Denton. When we gave them their freedom, even with the offer of paid wages, quite a few decided to go north. And we must respect that decision. We gave them their freedom with no strings attached."

"What do they hope to find there?"

"I think mostly an environment where they do not have to be afraid of reprisals against them. As great a thing as freedom is for a black man or woman, this is still the South. Now we are even a different country and at war with the North. They know they will never really be free as long as slavery remains the accepted norm here. They want to live where all men and women are free no matter what the color of their skin. They know the only place where that is possible, at least right now, is in the North. So yes, we are struggling with a diminished workforce. Every year we are able to plant less acreage."

"That darkie I saw over by the barn as I was riding up," said Beaumont, "—a light-skinned black man . . . I don't recognize him as one of yours, but it seems I have seen him before. Wasn't he the fellow who spoke with me on the train, the man with the peculiar accent—though I must say he was well spoken and seemed intelligent enough."

"Yes—Sydney LeFleure . . . he is a French Jamaican Negro."

"I understood him to be on his way to Pennsylvania."

"He was. But he came back."

"Why?"

"I offered him a job. He is my foreman now—a very resourceful and, as you say, intelligent man."

"Why did you offer the job to . . . a Negro?"

"The color of a man's skin has no bearing on his capabilities. Malachi Shaw was my foreman before your man Elias Slade killed him."

Beaumont glanced over at Richmond as they walked, thinking at first that his words were meant as an accusation. But Richmond's expression revealed nothing other than that he had been merely stating a well-known fact.

"Do you really think Slade was responsible?" he said. "That's not the way I heard it."

"What exactly did you hear?" asked Richmond.

"That Slade was nowhere around at the time. His involvement was never proven."

"Denton, good heavens! My own son was an eyewitness. I know you and he had difficulties over the situation with Veronica—for which I regret my own negligence in allowing it to go on as long as it did. But knowing my son, do you honestly take the word of Elias Slade over Seth's? Surely you know that Seth would never tell a lie."

Beaumont said nothing. It was a strong declaration for a father to make about a son, and exactly as Richmond said, he knew it to be true. He only wished he could have said the same about either of his two sons, or his daughter too for that matter. They walked on a minute in silence.

"If what you say about Slade is true," said Beaumont at length, "why did you take no action?"

"What would it have accomplished?" rejoined Richmond. "Malachi was dead. Who would have done anything about it? You . . . Wyatt? What authority in this state would have cared enough about the death of a black man to go against what you said? Let's face it, Denton, you were not kindly disposed toward us at the time. You just said yourself that you considered Slade innocent."

"Well . . . perhaps I was wrong."

"Even so, what could have been done? One black man killing another . . . realistically, Denton, we do not live in a time or place where the same justice exists for white and black."

"And you are content even now to let the matter remain, as you see it, unresolved?"

"Of course not. But nothing will bring Malachi back. And with a war on, there is even less chance that Elias Slade would be brought to justice. My only hope is that the day will come when you will send him away so that he will be a threat to none of us any longer, and then perhaps that you will issue a warrant for his arrest."

"I don't understand you, Richmond. You said yourself that such action would do no good."

"My only thought, with an active warrant circulating, his appearance being uniquely identifiable, is that others might be warned of the danger he poses. It is difficult for a man like Elias Slade to hide. A warrant following him around might save others from further evil at his hand."

"Hmm . . . I suppose I see your point. Still, it strikes me as an unusually calm response to something so serious as a charge of murder."

"I cannot change the world," said Richmond, "or Virginia . . . nor even Dove's Landing. But at least I can change Greenwood."

"*Change* it . . . I'm not sure I follow you. Change it . . . how?"

"For *good*, Denton. To bring good to our world in whatever ways God gives each of us to live out his goodness among our fellow men. It is what we are put on earth for—to do good, to learn to *be* good, and to grow into goodness of character that reflects the goodness of God in human life."

"If you say so, Richmond," said Beaumont in a patronizing tone. "But I hardly see what any of that has to do with Elias Slade."

"We each must make a difference for good, for betterment, for change, for justice, wherever we can. I take that to mean in our own corners of the world, not necessarily in the whole world. I cannot live out my convictions anywhere but in my own life. That's why I freed our slaves and why I now pay our blacks wages—both those who have been with us for years and new blacks that come who want to work. I try to treat anyone who comes to Greenwood fairly and with compassion, white and black alike. It won't bring Malachi back, or bring justice to Elias Slade. God will have to see to that, just like he will have to see to the ultimate salvation of mankind. But it does allow me to sleep at night with a clear conscience."

His neighbor's words, rather than strike root in the hardened soil of his own conscience, sent Denton Beaumont's thoughts in a new direction.

"*Do* you have new Negroes coming regularly looking for work?" he asked, arching one eyebrow as he looked at Richmond.

Richmond realized that he had inadvertently said more than he intended. But this was no moment for duplicity.

"Actually, yes . . . surprisingly we do," he replied.

"That's odd because we never see *anyone* wanting work. Where do they come from, these people who come to you?"

"I don't know, nor do I ask. If a man asks for my help, to the extent I am able, I try to give it."

"But they may be runaways, fugitives from the law."

"They may be. But fugitives from a bad law that is in its death throes even now."

"But in helping them, Richmond, you break the law yourself. You could be arrested."

"In one way, of course, you are right. It is one of the great dilemmas of our time—balancing man's law with God's higher law. I make no claim to know how to do so perfectly. Still, I must follow my conscience as it gives me light. And as I say, most of those who come move on anyway and I never know much about their personal circumstances. I offer work to the able-bodied among them, but few take me up on it."

"So what they say is true . . . that Greenwood is a haven for runaways?"

"I don't know what they say, Denton. Look around—what do you see? You see what Greenwood has always been, a plantation trying to make ends meet and having a difficult time of it during wartime. If people come along—white or black—whom the war has displaced and who are moving about and seeking a better life elsewhere, I will not turn them away."

"Well," said Beaumont with a forced laugh, "I can use a few more hands. You could send some of them my way . . . I might even be willing to match your wages."

"*You* . . . hire free Negroes, or even those who might be runaways?" rejoined Richmond.

"You said yourself that times are changing. Once the war is over, things will return to normal. I hope by then you may have come to your senses and see the folly of these absurd ideas of equality. The races will never be equal, Richmond. They were never intended to be. But until then, I will do what I must to get the work done and the crops in."

"Has it ever occurred to you," asked Richmond, "that things may *never* return to the way they were . . . that slavery in this country may soon be a thing of the past?"

"You mean, that the Union may win and Abraham Lincoln have his way over a subdued and compliant South? It will never happen, Richmond. Our cause is right and our army strong."

"Perhaps. But it never hurts to prepare for the unexpected. The Confederate army has taken several drubbings at Grant's hand these last six months. The day may come, Denton, when you will have no choice but to pay your blacks as free, hired, wage-earning workers."

"I will sell Oakbriar before allowing it to come to that."

"Sell . . . I thought you wanted to expand."

"What do you mean?"

"The Brown land . . . are you not still interested in purchasing it?"

"Why, have you changed your mind about selling?"

"No. I was merely curious about your plans."

"My plans are none of your—" Beaumont snapped irritably, then stopped himself. "I am sorry, Richmond—I meant nothing by it," he added. "It is just the pressure of the times."

"I understand."

"I had three more slaves disappear the night before last," Beaumont went on. "I must confess, it has put me on edge. You haven't . . . ah, seen or heard anything that might help me learn which way they went?"

"Actually, Denton," replied Richmond slowly, realizing that he might be walking into relational quagmire, "one of your men, a Mr. Grubs, is here with us."

"What! Why wasn't I informed?"

"It only just happened. I hadn't had the chance to tell you yet. My Mr. LeFleure found him out in the woods and brought him home."

"You should have returned him to me immediately."

"Sydney did not know where he was from. Nor did I at first. He was unconscious and in pretty bad shape."

"Well you know where he is from now. He is a runaway. I will take him with me."

"I am sorry, Denton," said Richmond. "I am afraid I must insist that he remain with us a while longer."

"You said you never turn down anyone's request. Now I want your help, and I want the man back."

"It is a little different, Denton. You don't want my help except to get your own way. To comply with your request would be to break God's higher law of goodness toward Mr. Grubs. I don't think I need to tell you that he has been whipped badly. Some of his wounds are deep. He needs time to heal."

At last Denton Beaumont's composure cracked.

"Who are you to preach to me, Richmond!" he said angrily. "You

and your ridiculous notions about God and right. I'll lay odds you've
whipped a black back or two in your time! Greenwood wasn't always
a monastery for interfering clerics! Your father and brother were no
priests, that's for sure. I can tell you that firsthand. I've seen your
brother so drunk he couldn't stand! Put that little tidbit of family
history in your Bible. So don't lecture me with your high-and-mighty
words. I know you too well, Richmond. And if Jimmy Grubs is not
returned in two days, I will not follow your example in the matter
of Slade, but will issue a warrant against *you* as a thief. Don't think I
won't, Richmond. I am still a very powerful man. I can make a great
deal of trouble for you."

He turned and stormed back to his horse where it was tied in front
of the house, mounted, and galloped away more rapidly and in a far
more agitated mood than that in which he had come.

As Denton Beaumont rode away from Greenwood, his mind was
racing in a dozen directions at once. He was too angry to place
his thoughts in coherent order. Yet gradually as he went he found
his brain drifting into a neglected but familiar path. Talk of the
Brown land reminded him of his unfinished business with his and
Richmond's mutual neighbor . . . or, if not their neighbor himself,
with his land, and with what he had always been convinced the
mysterious Brown had left behind.

He chastised himself momentarily for blurting out the reminder
of Clifford Davidson. But he had divulged nothing. The incident
sparked the idea, however, that there might be another way to meet
his present difficulties than with additional workers. He had not been
successful before, but one never knew when persistence might pay off
and yield its long-hidden rewards.

Halfway to Dove's Landing, Beaumont wheeled his mount off the
main road and galloped along a narrower wagon track, mostly now
overgrown, toward the high ridge of land that separated his plantation
of Oakbriar from Greenwood.

Ten minutes later, he slowed and continued on toward the house, for years now unoccupied, which he was certain contained secrets which, if he could just find them, would make him a wealthy man . . . with no more need for laborers or workers or overseers of any kind, white or black, slave or free.

He reined and sat for a minute or two on his horse's back. Everything was quiet. To all sound and appearance, not another soul was anywhere within miles. After the turbulent upheaval of his recent mental activity, he found himself sitting almost trancelike, staring at the wood house and its stone chimney and the overgrown grass and shrubbery around it.

What had Brown been thinking just before his mysterious disappearance? If he could just get inside the man's head. But how could a white man probe the mind of an Indian? They thought differently than other people.

If only his own mind had been more lucid at the time, he told himself for the thousandth time. But the only words and images he was able to call upon were hazy and distorted and weirdly overlaid with dreamy fantasies which made no sense whatever. Of only one thing he was certain—and he had remained certain of it ever since the night of Brown's strange visitors.

He knew they had spoken of *gold*.

His memory of that single fact was no dream. And to find where Brown had hidden it had taken hold of his youthful passion and possessed him. He had nearly given up the search in recent years. But it *had* to be here. And he needed to find it now more than ever.

Beaumont dismounted and walked toward the house.

Some time earlier Chigua had walked rather than ridden up to the Brown house. She had just put the restored skin back up over the mantelpiece when she heard the approach of a rider outside.

With the instinctive stealth of her race, she crept to the window, and after a quick peep, though she did not recognize the man sitting on his horse in front of the house, she hurried noiselessly to hide.

Denton Beaumont entered the house almost on tiptoe. The quiet spirit of antiquity had infected him while outside. Even the greed in his heart, which was his only reason for being here, could not prevent the mystery of an ancient people having a profound effect on him.

He glanced about. The house was empty and quiet, yet . . . something odd was in the air. He felt . . . was it a *presence*?

For the briefest moment, even self-assured Denton Beaumont shuddered from the spooky sense of not being alone. If Brown was dead, which he more than half suspected, had his ghost come back to haunt the place?

Or was it the ghost of *another* . . . come back to accuse him for the dark secret he shared with no other.

He turned and spun about, almost as if expecting to see someone standing staring at him.

Quickly he chastised himself for being afraid of his own shadow. He shook himself out of the uncomfortable reverie that had come over him, and began to walk about. It was uncanny, he thought again, how well-kept the place was. There were no signs of decay or mildew or mice or rats or cobwebs or dirt.

But why shouldn't it be kept up? Richmond owned it now, though the reminder galled him. He was probably keeping it tidy in hopes that Brown would come back to claim it. It was how Richmond thought—loyal to a fault with his ridiculous notions.

Another brief shiver coursed through him. Unconsciously Beaumont moved in the direction of the fireplace, though it had not been used in years, as if somehow heat might be radiating from it. As he approached it, however, his eyes were diverted by the colorful painting, apparently on an animal skin of some kind, hanging above it.

How could he have never noticed it before!

Surely it had been here for years. Yet suddenly on this day the images painted across the pale skin leapt vividly out at him as if he were laying eyes on it for the first time.

He walked closer, eyes squinting in the subdued light of the room. He took in the strange words at the top of the skin, though they conveyed nothing to his brain, then let his eyes drift down to the white and red trees, and then to what were apparently six gold circles beneath them. Finally his gaze came to rest, first at the one lower corner, then the other.

Suddenly his eyes shot open and he stood staring with mouth gaping open. He knew those odd-looking symbols of dots and lines. He had seen them before!

It was the clue he had been waiting for!

He turned and raced from the house in a frenzy of excitement. He had to get back up here without delay.

From the next room, Chigua heard the footsteps running across the floor followed by the slamming of the door. She waited until they were followed by the retreating sound of galloping hooves down the hill, then slowly crept from her hiding place and hurried back to Greenwood.

When Denton Beaumont arrived back at Oakbriar, intent on racing straight back to the Brown place with the paper he hoped would finally unravel the mystery and lead him to what he was now convinced were the untold Indian riches that Brown had hidden years ago, he was met by his wife with the unwelcome news that during his absence an urgent telegram had arrived. He took it from her and read it hastily.

He was to return to Richmond immediately. A Union force 100,000 men strong under General McClellan was sailing down the Potomac and was anticipated to march on Richmond from the west. They were expected to assault the city by the middle of June. An emergency session had been called to discuss strategy for evacuation of the government if it came to that.

Inwardly cursing his foul luck, Beaumont crumpled the paper in his fist and went upstairs to his study. He had to think.

Twelve

$\mathcal{U}$pon her arrival in Richmond, Veronica went immediately to meet Congressman Wyler at his office, which was down the hall from her father's. Holding the letter from Garabaldi, she was shown inside.

"Hello, Mr. Wyler," she said. "I am Veronica Fitzpatrick. Mr. Garabaldi in Washington asked me to deliver this to you."

She handed him the envelope. Wyler took it, looking puzzled.

"Thank you," he said. "I, uh . . . did not expect, that is . . . how do you come to be associated with Garabaldi?"

"I only just met him," replied Veronica. "But as my parents live in Richmond, I told him I would bring it to you. My father is Senator Beaumont."

"Ah, Beaumont . . . you are his daughter—I have heard him mention you. I see . . . I see."

"How is your wife, Mr. Wyler?"

"My wife?"

"He said your wife was ill."

"Oh, my wife . . . yes, much better, thank you. Yes . . . quite—she is doing better. Well, thank you very much, Miss Beaumont—"

"It is Mrs. Fitzpatrick, now, Mr. Wyler. I am married."

"Yes, of course . . . Mrs. Fitzpatrick. As I say, thank you very much. When do you return to Washington?"

"In two or three days."

"I wonder if you would be so good as to take a bottle of wine back to Mr. Garabaldi, with my compliments?"

"Of course."

"I have it here in a drawer of my desk."

He pulled out a drawer and took out a bottle of wine and handed it to her.

"You are certain you do not mind?"

"Not at all."

Veronica left the office a minute or two later and, following Wyler's directions, walked down the corridor and into her father's office.

"Hi, Daddy!" she said beaming.

"Veronica!" exclaimed Denton Beaumont, standing and hurrying around his desk and embracing her. "What are you doing here?"

Veronica thought it best not to mention that Richard did not know she was in Richmond, and that the man behind the whole arrangement was none other than Cecil Hirsch, whom she knew her father would remember, and probably not altogether fondly.

Riding beside William White, a disheartened Aaron Steddings was not looking forward to what he knew was coming as they approached the White farm. He knew that as much as Zaphorah might be anxious to see him again after a month, the one thing she would most be looking for was whether Deanna was with them.

Moses saw them from a distance and ran inside with the news that the two men had returned. Moments later, Zaphorah hurried out, with Mary and Hannah and Suzane on her heels. She ran down the porch and toward the two approaching horses, but came to a stop and already stood weeping in grief by the time Aaron was able to dismount and take her in his arms.

"We looked everywhere," he said softly. "We went to every plantation for a hundred miles. Mr. White spoke to every farmer we could find and offered good money for information. But nobody had seen anything of her. Whoever that was who took her must have sold her somewhere else."

"Oh, Aaron . . . what are we going to do!"

"I don't know what we can do but either go back and keep looking, or go ahead and get back on that railroad and get home."

"But how can we go on without her?" sobbed Zaphorah.

"We have to hope she finds her own way there eventually."

Aaron had had time to accustom himself to not being able to find their daughter. But Zaphorah's month of hope was shattered in a moment, and it turned into the heartwrenching grief of a mother's greatest loss. It was some days before they could begin to think seriously about moving on.

Finally the time came, however, and they were ready. Aaron still had the old and faded map that had guided their movements thus far. Of far more help, however, were William White's instructions. He had been a stationmaster long enough that he knew exactly where to tell them to go. Many of the old methods had changed since the war, he said. They would need no conductor. If they traveled at night, in two days they would be well able to find their way to the next station, and there receive reliable instructions to the next.

But they had to watch out for Confederate troops. That had become the most worrisome unknown. There were more renegade and runaway soldiers roaming about all the time. They were probably more dangerous than the bounty hunters had been before.

They could take their three horses, if they wanted, William added. However, he recommended travel by foot, though slower, as safer. He would pay them fifty dollars apiece for the three.

The offer reminded Aaron that they were not his horses at all and that, besides being runaways, technically they were also horse thieves. He therefore left the three horses with William White with the request to have them returned to the Locke plantation in whatever manner White deemed most prudent that would not bring danger to themselves.

With a few final instructions, many handshakes and hugs and Godspeeds, the family of Aaron Steddings, now numbering five, again found themselves alone . . . and on their way north.

Thirteen

$\mathcal{A}$ young man of sun-weathered skin, some would have called it red, but which in reality was a deep bronze, stole quietly into the village of Wauhillou in the Cherokee Indian Territory of Oklahoma. He did not particularly care if he was seen, but secrecy by now was so deeply part of his nature that it was almost by instinct that he kept to the shadows. He lifted the flap that covered the doorway into the small rundown house he called home and quietly stole inside.

He had been born a year before the infamous removal known as the Trail of Tears. He and his father and mother had been among the lucky ones to survive it. Thousands hadn't. Through the bitter reminiscences of his father he had learned whom to blame for the tragedy even more than Andrew Jackson—those among their own who had betrayed their people.

He had just been gone for two days, north into Kansas and the plains where his acquaintances and comrades among the Sioux, the Chiricahua, the Kiowa, and the Pawnee were now being driven from their lands as his own people had been driven from Georgia, North Carolina, and Tennessee three decades earlier. He knew the tales from the old times. A warrior's spirit had resided in his bosom since earliest boyhood, implanted by his father, along with a hatred for the white man who was consuming Indian land inch by inch in a relentless march westward. Within his heart had awakened the fervor of old

chief of the red feather Oconostota and Dragging Canoe. And now
the new plight of his northern plains native cousins gave opportunity
for that hatred to vent itself in the spilling of white blood.

Even before his twentieth birthday, unknown to those of his own
village, he had been involved in several wagon-train massacres in Sioux
territory. And with a half dozen Kiowa youths whose brains were
soaked with alcohol they had stolen from the trading post, he had
helped set fire to a settler's farmhouse in southeast Kansas and killed
the entire family. He had a memory for vengeance which he nurtured
in private ways—a vengeance fueled by reminders of Cherokee betrayal from long before.

He came from a family of Cherokee hard-liners. His father and
grandfather before him had resisted with all their might against the
gradual infusion of white culture into their Indian heritage. Prowling
Bear, his father, had been one of those invited to the secret council of
Cherokee leaders in June of 1839 in Takotoka in which the leaders
of the Treaty Group—Major and John Ridge, and Buck and Stand
Watie—were condemned to death for making a treaty with the U.S.
government and selling Cherokee lands in Georgia, North Carolina,
and Tennessee. They had violated tribal law, and the decree of the
council vowed vengeance.

Prowling Bear along with several others had volunteered for the
Elias Boudinot assassination at Park Hill on the following morning.
How many times had he repeated the story to his growing son, with
pride in his voice and fire in his eyes, how as his comrades distracted
the man born as Buck Watie he had crept behind him and then, with
a vicious downward slice, how he had split Boudinot's skull in a single
blow and watched him crumple dead at his feet.

Visions of splattering blood and wild war cries of revenge still rang
in Black Wolf's head after all these years, along with his father's words,
"We killed three of them that day, though the traitor Watie fled like a
coward. But the hour of retribution will fall on him in time. He will
not escape the justice of blood. Neither he nor all those who betrayed
our people."

Again Cherity Waters set out for a ride up the ridge.

On her mind as she went, however, were neither Seth nor her father as on her ride of a month or two earlier. On this day, Mr. Brown and his secrets occupied her thoughts.

A brief errand took her first into Dove's Landing. Leaving the town to scale the ascent to the Brown tract, she had no idea that a second horse had picked up her trail and was following behind her.

Cherity rode to the house, dismounted, and walked inside. She went straight to the fireplace. There she stood studying the patterns at the bottom of the skin that Chigua had replaced over the mantel. A minute later, with its images fixed in her mind, she returned outside. Leaving her horse tied at the house, she walked across the open field to the edge of a small wood where she had encountered the runaways. In front of her stood the large pine just as she remembered it. And there was the curious carving she had seen.

She walked toward the tree just as she had on that earlier day. Her thoughts were consumed with what the design—appearing in both places, on the tree and the skin—could possibly mean. If it was indeed a Cherokee image, who but Brown himself could have made it?

And why? For whom was it intended? As a sign . . . of what?

She stopped in front of the pine. Slowly she reached out and ran her fingers over the lines and dots, gnarled and bumpy with time.

A thrill of excitement surged through her. It was exactly the same pattern as that on the skin!

What could it mean!

A sound and a movement startled her.

Cherity turned. Twenty feet away among the trees stood the most enormous black man she had ever seen.

He looked too well fed for a runaway. *Much* too well fed. And she wasn't sure she liked that gleam in his eye.

"What . . . is there something you want?" she asked hesitantly.

The man took several steps forward, a cunning smile forming on his lips.

"Do you need help?" asked Cherity, still not fully aware of her danger. Yet she could not prevent a tremor creeping into her tone.

Still the man did not speak but walked straight toward her. Unconsciously Cherity stepped back. The movement triggered the man's predatory instinct. He lunged forward with the stride of a giant. His hand shot out with the lightning strike of an uncoiling snake and his fingers closed on Cherity's tiny wrist.

She screamed, both in fright and pain, and yanked away her arm. Her strength was far greater than he had anticipated in one so small. Before he knew it, Elias Slade stood watching his quarry sprint away from him. Surprised by the girl's pluck, yet enlivened all the more by the challenge to conquer this little vixen, he broke into a run and lumbered after her.

But even with legs half as long, Cherity in her blue dungarees could have outrun him in a dead sprint. She was in the saddle before he had covered three quarters of the distance. She spun her horse's head around and dug in her heels.

There was Slade charging straight for her.

As her mount burst into motion, Cherity's hand went to the whip tied to the saddle. Though she rarely used it, and never on a horse's back, it proved an effective weapon to ward off a startled Elias Slade. Her quick blows slowed him enough to prevent him grabbing her leg and twisting her out of the saddle.

As the leather came crashing down over his shoulders and head, Slade swore angrily and fought against it, grappling frantically to lay hold of the leather cord. Finally he managed to yank it from Cherity's hand. As she released the handle, Slade stumbled momentarily backward. Seizing her brief advantage, Cherity kicked and shouted wildly and flew off down the hill.

Slade recovered quickly, but found himself left watching four retreating hooves sending up great clods of earth as horse and rider disappeared along the trail among the trees. A great roar of impotent fury echoed after them.

His voice slowly died away and Elias Slade stood alone, vowing that whoever the girl was, he would subdue her and have his way with her in the end.

⟶

Somewhat calmed, but perspiring and breathing hard, Cherity galloped into Greenwood in a flurry of hooves and dust and jumped to the ground. Alexander was just coming from the barn. He stopped and looked up in surprise.

Cherity tossed him the reins, said she would be back in a few minutes, and ran toward the house. She found Richmond in his wood shop at the back of the house.

He glanced up from the board being planed beneath his hand as she burst in.

"Cherity!" he exclaimed. "You look like you've . . . well, not seen a ghost exactly, but seen something that frightened you."

"I went for a ride . . . I was up on the ridge near Mr. Brown's house," Cherity began, then paused to take several deep breaths. Gradually she began to breathe more easily.

"There was a man out there . . . a black man," she added.

"Another runaway?"

"I am sure he wasn't. He was alone and didn't look like he had been traveling."

"What happened?"

"He tried to get me, Mr. Davidson. He grabbed me. The look in his eyes . . . it was terrible. I shudder to think what might have happened if I hadn't gotten away."

"What did he look like?"

"He was the biggest man I have ever seen. He was twice my size. My head didn't come higher than his chest. He had big eyes that looked at me with an expression that I . . . I don't know what to call it but mean . . . menacing . . . frightening."

"Elias Slade!" sighed Richmond. "It couldn't be anyone else."

"I don't know why I didn't run away the instant I saw him. But right at first I thought maybe he was someone who needed help."

"But you did get away—that is the important thing."

"What should I do, Mr. Davidson? I don't want to be afraid every time I go out for a ride."

"We shall have to give the matter some careful thought."

"Who is he, Mr. Davidson?"

"A freedman," replied Richmond. "He works at Oakbriar. Seth tangled with him once and it cost him a broken arm and several broken ribs. It was rather terrifying. He could have been killed."

"My goodness!"

"He is a very dangerous man. He is also the man who killed Nancy's husband. So my very strong advice—no, it is more than mere advice . . . if you ever see him again, you must never let him near you."

Richmond paused and thought a moment. He set down the tool in his hand and walked to a cabinet on the other side of the workroom. He opened the door and reached inside. He returned a moment later with a small pistol in his hand.

"Mr. Davidson . . . what is that?" exclaimed Cherity. "I didn't know you had a handgun."

"I only keep it here in case of an emergency," Richmond said. "I am going to give it to you to take with you when you go riding out in the hills. I want you to take it from now on, even if you are not alone, or if you and Cynthia go for a ride together. I think I may have a belt and holster somewhere in the house, though we will probably have to add a few more holes for the buckle to make it fit."

"I don't know how to use a gun!" said Cherity.

"I will teach you."

"But I could never shoot anyone."

"I don't want you to shoot anyone. I only want you to know how to use it if you have to, at least well enough to scare Elias Slade if he tries anything again. I told you, he is extremely dangerous. But as long as Denton Beaumont continues to keep him on at Oakbriar, we have to be wary. He prowls the hills and is often on our land too. We have to take precautions."

He paused and a smile came to his lips.

"I would like to ask you not to go out riding alone," he said slowly. "But I think I know you well enough by now to realize that I had better not press my luck."

"If you did tell me not to," smiled Cherity, "I would try to obey. But I hope you won't. I will promise to be more careful."

Cynthia Verdon was startled two afternoons later to hear the sound of gunfire suddenly exploding from behind the house. It sounded close!

She ran to the window of her room. Some distance out near the wood to the west stood Cherity holding a pistol with Richmond at her side giving her instructions on its use.

Cynthia ran from her room, downstairs, and outside.

"What is going on!" she asked as she hurried toward them.

"The first time I met Cherity," replied Richmond, glancing toward his daughter as she approached, "she was a great fan of the Wild West."

"I always dreamed of being a cowgirl," laughed Cherity.

"So now I am making a gunslinger of her," said Richmond. He quickly became serious. "Actually, Cynthia," he went on, "there was a little trouble with a fellow from Oakbriar. I asked Cherity to carry this gun when she rides. So I am showing her how to use it and giving her a little target practice. . . . There you go, Cherity," he said, "see what you can do with those bottles lined up there."

Cherity held the gun up, extended her arm, squinted one eye along the barrel and pulled the trigger. A shot fired as the gun popped upward in her grasp, but no sound of glass breaking followed.

"Try again," said Richmond.

Again Cherity fired . . . then again, and a fourth time. All the bottles remained undisturbed.

"I can't do it!" moaned Cherity.

"Practice, Cherity . . . everything comes with practice," said

Richmond. "Keep at it. I will leave you this box of shells. I've shown you how to reload. Shoot another three or four rounds until your hand and arm get tired."

He and Cynthia turned and walked back toward the house together.

"Is it safe?" Cynthia asked when they were a little way off. "I mean . . . is she—"

"She will be fine," said Richmond.

Another shot sounded behind them, followed by a squeal of excitement.

"I hit one, Mr. Davidson!" exclaimed Cherity as he glanced back.

"Good for you!" he said over his shoulder, then turned back to Cynthia. "You see," he said. "My worry isn't Cherity. She will be careful enough. My worry is Elias Slade."

When Veronica Fitzpatrick arrived back in Washington, she immediately went again to Garabaldi's and asked to see the restaurant owner, who was out visiting with the luncheon crowd.

He received her warmly, took her back again to his private office, and received the bottle of wine from Wyler with gratitude. The two chatted for five or ten minutes, the restaurant owner showing particular interest in Veronica's father and his connections throughout Virginia and the South, about which Veronica shared freely. The visit concluded with his expressed hope that they would meet again.

Veronica all but forgot Cecil Hirsch when summer came and then another two months went by and she saw nothing more of him. She heard, of course, how General Robert E. Lee had beaten back McClellan's troops from Richmond and sent them back toward the coast in wholesale retreat. But she little dreamed the role she had played in the Confederate victory by the information Wyler had managed to get to Lee about McClellan's plans.

Veronica had just begun again to rue the boredom of her life when a messenger appeared at her door midway through the morning. The handwritten note was brief:

Mrs. Fitzpatrick,
I wonder if you would do the honor of coming to see me as soon as
possible. I am afraid I have another favor to ask. I would be forever
in your debt if you would consider helping me once again.

G. Garabaldi.

Puzzled but intrigued, Veronica set out for the restaurant ten
minutes later.

When she arrived, Garabaldi sat down behind his desk, his expression serious.

"My predicament is this," he said. "I again find myself in the position of needing to get an extremely delicate letter to my friend Wyler.
Time is somewhat pressing—actually, *extremely* pressing. If you would
consent to delivering it, as you did before, I would pay you two
hundred dollars for your trouble."

"Two hundred dollars!" exclaimed Veronica. "Goodness, Mr.
Garabaldi—that's more than my husband makes in a month! What
could possibly be so important as that about a letter?"

"Unfortunately, that I am not at liberty to say. Of course, if you are
too busy . . ."

"No, it's not that."

"I could get someone else. I simply thought, as you seemed to enjoy
the trip before, that I—"

"Yes . . . I did. And thank you, Mr. Garabaldi . . . I am glad that
you thought of me. I will do it."

Veronica left Garabaldi's in a more subdued mood than she had
entered. It was not that she minded secrets, even having secrets from
her own husband. She had always thrived on secrets. But now she
realized that Mr. Garabaldi possessed secrets *he* was keeping from *her.*
That wasn't quite such a comfortable a position to be in. When it
came to secrets, Veronica was accustomed to holding all the cards.

The two hundred dollars, however, was sufficient inducement to
encourage her to overlook the fact that she didn't really have any idea
what she was getting herself involved in.

Fourteen

The troops came to Greenwood almost without warning. It was toward the end of the first week of September, 1862.

The first premonition anyone had that suddenly the war was about to intrude more closely was the sound of distant thunder coming from somewhere east of Dove's Landing. The faint dust cloud rising from the same direction indicated the movement of troops and what were obviously hundreds of horses. But as he watched and listened in the field with a small crew of workers, Sydney LeFleure had no way to judge whether the soldiers on those horses wore the Union blue or the Confederate gray.

Ten minutes later, suddenly a small detachment of six Union soldiers galloped out of the woods and across the planted field toward him. Sydney stood and relaxed the hoe in his hand, and waited.

The men rode straight toward him and reined in. One of the six urged his horse a few steps forward.

"Who's in charge here?" he asked.

"I am," replied Sydney, stepping away from the group.

"Where is your overseer?" said the man, glancing about at Sydney's laborers, about a dozen men and a handful of women, all Negroes with hoes in their hands where they stood between the rows of ripening tobacco.

"I am the foreman of the Davidson plantation," said Sydney.

Obviously surprised both by Sydney's self assurance, and his impeccable Jamaican accent, the man continued to look about at the rest. "You are in charge of these slaves?" he said.

"We are all free wage earners," replied Sydney. "There are no slaves on the Davidson plantation. And yes, I am in charge."

"Well, we appear to have stumbled into an interesting situation. I would like to meet your owner."

"We are about a mile from the house."

"Then if you don't mind, would you take me to him? Do you have a horse?"

"Yes, sir—over by the wagon," said Sydney, gesturing toward the wagon in the distance that had brought them to the field.

Richmond was on the roof of one of the black cabins with Isaac and Aaron Shaw repairing a few loose boards when Sydney's wagon clattered into the midst of the collection of houses. Richmond looked up at Sydney's approach, and saw six riders in blue following him. He set down his hammer and waited.

"Richmond," said Sydney, reining in and looking up to where Richmond sat on the roof, "these men are from the army. . . . They asked to meet you. This is my boss," he added to the man on the horse behind him, "Richmond Davidson."

The man rode forward and looked up to Richmond sitting on the roof.

"Mr. Davidson," he said, "I am Colonel Garner, second in command to General Irvin McDowell of the United States Army."

"I am pleased to meet you, Colonel," said Richmond. "What can I do for you?"

"The general has asked me to find a suitable location to garrison his men for several days. I would like to inspect your house to see if it would serve as temporary headquarters for the general and his staff. Your man here said you have no slaves?"

"That is right," replied Richmond, his brain spinning at this sudden development. Twelve fugitives had arrived within the last forty-eight hours and the plantation was bursting at the seams with Negroes! He crept across the roof and began slowly climbing down the ladder, his mind working quickly.

"Sydney," he said, moving slowly and deliberately, "would you please run up to the house and tell Carolyn that I am bringing some men up?"

Grasping his meaning well enough, Sydney jumped to the ground and dashed toward the house. Richmond reached the ground and began walking, still slowly, in the same direction. The six soldiers followed. By the time they reached the house, Sydney, Carolyn, Chigua, Cynthia, and Cherity had managed to get all their guests out of sight.

⌒⌒

During the time between Colonel Garner's leaving them half an hour later and the general's appearance two hours after that, they managed to frantically relocate everyone to the black village, which was now bulging far beyond its capacity. At the same time they made hasty preparations to move as many of the runaways as possible with all due haste along the nighttime railroad to the North.

The days following General McDowell's arrival at Greenwood were more hectic than any since the start of the war. Though they feared no reprisals from discovery of Greenwood's clandestine fugitive-hiding activities, they saw no good that could come from it. Though they assumed Union soldiers would be sympathetic toward the effort, they knew too that word of it could far too easily spread and become widely known, and ultimately endanger them and whatever runaways might be here. That McDowell's staff was pleasantly surprised at the gracious treatment they received from the Southern Davidsons, kept too many probing questions from surfacing.

Anticipating the need to use the brute authority of their obvious military advantage to enforce their right to commandeer what they assumed to be an enemy plantation, General McDowell and his senior staff came brusquely into Greenwood as they had on a number of previous similar occasions expecting everyone about the place to make things difficult for them. They were hardly prepared to be welcomed with tea and coffee and sandwiches and cake set out in the parlor for them.

"I must say, Mrs . . . .uh, Davidson," said the general, "this is very gracious of you, hardly what we are used to."

"God seems to have blessed us with an unusual number of . . . guests recently," said Carolyn as she poured the general a cup of coffee, "—mostly entirely unexpected. We try to make everyone who comes to Greenwood welcome—whatever the color of their skin or their reason for being here."

"Would that also include the color of their uniform?"

"Of course—though you are the first Union soldiers we have seen."

"Well we certainly appreciate your Southern hospitality. But surely you must be personally loyal to the Confederacy?"

"We try to be loyal to America," rejoined Carolyn. "One of our sons is in the Confederate army. Our other son is a photographer attached to the Union army. And our son-in-law is a lieutenant in the navy, also for the Union."

"That must make it very difficult for you."

"It is difficult to be a mother in wartime. But I am glad to have my daughter with me."

"Her husband, you say, is a Union officer?"

"That's right."

"What is his name?"

"Jeffrey Robert Verdon . . . Lieutenant Verdon."

"I would like to meet your daughter and find out where her husband is assigned."

Just then Richmond entered with a few more of McDowell's men whose horses he had been helping them attend to.

"Your wife outdoes herself with hospitality, Mr. Davidson," said McDowell.

"She outdoes herself in all ways, General. I am the most blessed and fortunate of men."

General McDowell would not have the opportunity to meet Cynthia just yet. As her parents were sitting down with his men for tea and coffee, she and Cherity and Chigua were frantically trying to find beds or cots or corners for everyone in the cottages of the black village, and keep the children inside and out of sight.

Sydney found Cherity seated in one of the houses with three black youngsters scrambling alternately in and out of her lap as she tried to keep them still long enough to finish a story.

"Richmond managed to sneak in a quick word with me," he said. "He told me to ask you to ride over to the Brannons, tell them what has happened, and ask—"

"Sarah . . . goodness!" exclaimed Cherity to the girl squirming in her lap. "Try to be still just a minute more. I'm sorry, Sydney, what were you saying?"

"Richmond wants you to tell the Brannons what is going on here and ask if they can take our overflow as soon as possible. He wants me to try to get a group organized and out of here tonight if I can."

"It's half a day's ride there and back," said Cherity.

"That's why he's sending you," smiled Sydney. "He says you're the fastest rider for miles around."

"You know what they say about flattery, Sydney!"

"He really did say so," laughed Sydney.

"But it's already midafternoon."

"He said for you to spend the night with the Brannons and get on your way back here at first light. But," Sydney added, "he said to take the pistol with you, and to take the long road around south from here until you reach the road west."

"Well, you heard Mr. LeFleure," said Cherity to the three children. "As soon as I finish the story I have to go."

"Please, Miz Waters," pleaded the little girl, "jes' one more!"

Cherity laughed. "Maybe one more short one. Then I must go and you will need to stay here with Mr. and Mrs. LeFleure and be as quiet as you can."

"Oh, one more thing," said Sydney, turning back from the doorway. "Some of the soldiers are busy about the barn and workshop. So we won't be able to use the loft like we sometimes do. Richmond just said to watch yourself around them. Most of them are young men who have been away from home a long time, if you know what I mean. You are a very pretty young lady."

"Thank you, Sydney," nodded Cherity with a smile. "I will be careful."

The comfort and hospitality at Greenwood proved such that McDowell's staff stayed on longer than expected. With his army encamped comfortably and safely on the high flat meadow below Harper's Peak, and each of McDowell's officers with a room of his own on Greenwood's expansive second floor, and being served meals and treated to every kindness as if they had stumbled into a luxury hotel, none was anxious to leave.

McDowell found his lengthy talks with Richmond invigorating and challenging. He also had the chance to observe much about the place, and though he did not suspect the true reason why so many Negroes were coming and going and why the place was such a beehive of activity, he was able to see clearly enough the underlying foundation of Greenwood's pulse of life—that people of all racial backgrounds were living and working together in harmony. They all seemed to like and respect one another! He had never witnessed anything like it.

What was this place? he wondered. Who was this man called David's son? And why did he treat his enemies and those less fortunate than himself with such kindness? Whence sprung this remarkable fountain of life?

Before two days were out he realized he could not keep what was going on here to himself.

One of McDowell's men who was not able to enjoy as lengthy a stay as he might have liked was the first man Sydney had met. Before daylight on the third day, with a small escort chosen specifically for speed, Colonel Garner was on his way back through Confederate lines to Washington.

Abraham Lincoln perused the brief letter a second time, then glanced up at the uniformed officer who had delivered it personally from one of the president's most trusted generals.

"So General McDowell seems to think I ought to meet a certain plantation owner in Virginia," he said. "Tell me, Colonel, have you met the man?"

"I have, Mr. President," replied Garner.

"Do you share the general's sentiments?" asked Lincoln.

"I do, Mr. President. He will shatter the common image we in the North have been led to expect concerning Southern plantation owners. Just how unusual he is you will have to determine for yourself. Speaking for myself, I find him one of the most remarkable men I have ever met."

"That is saying a great deal, Colonel."

"Indeed it is, sir."

"How does the general propose to get me there?" smiled Lincoln wryly. "If McClellan cannot enter Richmond with a hundred thousand men, does he suppose they will let me through alone?"

"Begging the president's pardon," rejoined Garner, "but General McClellan was something less than forceful against Lee's inferior army."

"I do not need to be reminded of the general's temerity, Colonel. He is single-handedly making me old before my time. I would relieve him of command if I thought it would not demoralize the troops. Unfortunately his men love him."

"Perhaps his failed assault on Richmond may yet prove useful," said Garner.

"How so?" asked Lincoln.

"Returning to your question, Mr. President," said Garner, "General

McDowell suggested that I propose the following, that you travel south along the east of the Potomac with a small secret escort, then cross the river east of Fredericksburg where we still have many vessels returned from Richmond. We still control the river, Mr. President. You could be spirited across and moved south of Fredericksburg inland toward Columbiasville and to the Davidson plantation almost invisibly. There are almost no Confederate troops between the Potomac and Columbiasville."

"A daring plan. If I were captured, it could cost us the war."

"General McDowell does not think the danger so great as that. Nor do I, Mr. President. It is the route I took to get here and I saw scarcely a hint of troop activity and covered the distance in two days."

"And General McDowell thinks I would benefit from meeting this man."

"Very much, sir."

Carolyn Davidson awoke suddenly. It was the middle of the night.

"Richmond . . . Richmond, did you hear that?" she whispered.

Again came the sound that had awoken her. Someone was knocking on their bedroom door!

Richmond came to himself and sat up in bed. The knock sounded again.

"Mr. Davidson . . . please, sir . . . Mr. Davidson—wake up, sir. It is Colonel Garner."

Richmond shook his head again to clear out the remnants of sleep, then stood, turned up the lantern, threw his robe about him, and went to the door.

There stood Colonel Garner, whom they had not seen for several days, in full uniform, lantern in hand.

"I am sorry to disturb you, sir," he said. "Would you and your wife please dress quickly and then accompany me downstairs?"

Richmond closed the door and looked at Carolyn.

"You heard?"

"Yes," said Carolyn. "What is it all about?"

"I haven't the remotest idea. But I think we had better do as he says."

A few minutes later they appeared at the door.

"Before I take you downstairs," said Colonel Garner, "you must give me your solemn promise never to divulge what you are about to see. Too much danger for too many people could result if word of it leaks out. No one must ever know."

"As far as my conscience allows it," said Richmond, "you have my word."

Carolyn, too, nodded her assent.

"Knowing what manner of man and woman you are, and what a pledge of conscience means to you, I will take that as sufficient. Come with me."

The colonel led the way along the corridor and down the stairs to their own parlor where they were surprised to find two or three lanterns burning and several men inside. The moment they walked into the room a gasp of astonishment burst from Carolyn's lips.

"Ah, here are our hosts now," said McDowell, walking toward them. "I apologize for the secrecy and further inconvenience to you after all your kindnesses, but it really could not be helped. Mr. and Mrs. Davidson, may I present to you the president of the United States, Abraham Lincoln."

Unknown to Colonel Garner or General McDowell or any of their men, even as their highly secret entourage had pulled up to the front door of the plantation house, half a mile away, Sydney and Chigua LeFleure had just embarked on an equally secretive mission about which no president nor general would ever know.

A second group of fugitives were silently on their way to meet their next conductor east of Dove's Landing, having no idea that the tall white man every Negro in the South considered the savior of their race was little more than a stone's throw away.

It was an hour or so after a late breakfast on the following morning when at last the meeting for which the president had traveled deep into the heart of the Confederacy got under way. The door of the Greenwood sitting room closed. Richmond Davidson and Abraham Lincoln were at last left alone.

"I am sorry for this inconvenience to you and your family," said Lincoln.

"Think nothing of it, Mr. President."

"So . . . I have been informed that you voluntarily freed your slaves."

"That is correct."

"Then tell me, Mr. Davidson, why did you do it?"

"Because it seemed to me the right thing to do, Mr. President. It seemed the right thing to do as a Christian."

"You profess to be a Christian?"

"I do, Mr. President."

"As do millions on both sides of this conflict—each summoning God to their defense."

"It grieves me to see it, Mr. President. All through the South, for years, I have listened to the invoking of God on behalf of the scourge of slavery. It sickens me. Of course, as they say, the Bible does not strictly *forbid* slavery. But that hardly makes it right."

"You certainly do not speak like a loyal Southerner," said Lincoln dryly. "My men warned me that you were a free thinker."

"As I told my wife recently, I am a loyal American first, then a loyal Virginian. Well, that is not exactly true . . . I am a loyal *Christian* first, then a loyal American."

"So if I as your president ordered you to do something that went against your faith as you perceived it, you would not obey me?"

"I am afraid that is correct, Mr. President. I have been reading a great deal about the Quakers recently. I find a kinship in my heart to some of their great men and their ideas. Conscientious disobedience is one of their founding principles."

"Ah, yes . . . their man John Woolman. I have been reading portions of his *Journal* lately myself as I struggle with what to do concerning slavery."

"He was a remarkable man," said Richmond.

"I admire him greatly," rejoined Lincoln. "Woolman spoke of slavery and its evils a hundred years ago. Would that the country had listened then," he sighed. "He was certainly a man of principle, as I perceive you are."

"I hope I am, Mr. President. But only God holds the key to my conscience. I hope you are not offended."

"On the contrary," smiled Lincoln. "In fact, I am glad to hear it. It makes me know you to be a man I can trust."

"I am not sure I understand you, Mr. President."

A long and thoughtful silence followed.

"I have a great decision to make with regard to slavery," said Lincoln at length. "I must seek the counsel of trustworthy men, on both sides. That is no doubt why my men insisted on my coming to see you. As you might imagine, I have few opportunities to speak with Southerners these days! But I have to make a decision that is best for the entire nation, and its future."

Lincoln paused thoughtfully. It was silent for several seconds.

"I recently received a letter from Horace Greeley," he went on, "an open letter that was printed publicly. In it he said that slavery is everywhere the inciting cause of the treason behind this war. He urged me to do away with it completely. I cannot say I disagree with him. I think I agree with our Quaker friend Woolman that slavery at its root is intrinsically evil. Yet I am the president of a political country. I must make decisions on the basis of the good of the nation. My answer to Greeley, which you may have read, if it was printed in the papers down here, is that my paramount object in this struggle is to save the Union. It is not primarily to save or destroy slavery. If I could save the Union *without* freeing any slaves, I would do it. If I could save it by freeing *all* the slaves, I would do it. If I could even save the Union by freeing some and not others, I would do that also. We *must* preserve this nation. But now that the South has taken us into this conflict, the question of how to do so is very difficult."

He paused and took a long breath. When he continued, it was in a different vein.

"I am therefore interested in the effect freeing slaves had on your plantation," said Lincoln. "Tell me, how long ago was it when all this took place?"

"Six years."

"And your plantation has continued to prosper?"

"The war has made finding workers difficult," replied Richmond. "Times are hard right now and I confess that we are falling behind with certain financial obligations. But prior to the war . . . yes, we were doing quite well."

"You must have suffered some serious opposition?"

Richmond smiled and nodded.

"At one time some of my Virginia colleagues wanted me to run for Congress," he said. "Needless to say, their enthusiasm declined sharply after our decision."

"By that you mean you and your wife? She was in agreement with you?"

"Completely."

"Would you mind telling me how your decision came about?"

"Not at all."

"I am especially intrigued with what mental processes you went through to arrive at the course of action you chose and what have been the long-term effects, both pro and con."

"Well for us, Mr. President, it was a decision of prayer, based on what we felt was our personal responsibility. Unlike yourself, we had nothing else to consider. We did not have an entire nation to worry about. I do not envy you."

Lincoln sighed. "It is daunting," he said. "But I came to hear your story not bemoan my own troubles."

Richmond went on to explain how he had spoken with their slaves and given them money to go north or stay and start new lives as free wage earners. He then recounted how things had gone at Greenwood since, not, however, dwelling on their recent activities with the Underground Railroad.

"Thank you for illuminating your story to me," said Lincoln. "I must say I have never heard the like before. Even more than that I must say thank you for the courage your action obviously took. That is what this country needs, more men and women to take their spiritual convictions seriously. Men are eager to take any conviction seriously—slavery, states' rights—except *spiritual* convictions. But we are a nation of Christian roots. All too often, however, it seems that politics rule men's opinions and decisions more than the spiritual priorities of this nation's foundations. If it continues, I shudder to think where it will lead—"

Suddenly the door crashed open and a little black girl of seven or eight burst in. She scampered across the floor toward the two men seated on the far side of the room. Richmond Davidson's first instinct was to shoo her away before she divulged the very thing they had been trying so hard to conceal. But almost immediately he realized the incongruity of doing so in light of everything they had just been speaking of. Was this little girl any less worthy or precious in God's eyes than even the president of the United States?

She ran straight toward him and he opened his arms to receive her.

"Hello, Sarah," he said. "What are you doing here?"

"I wuz playin' wiff Miz Waters," replied the rambunctious girl, "but I ran away an' hid from her. She's neber fin' me here! What is *you* doin', Mister Dab'son?"

"This gentleman and I were having a talk."

"Oh . . ." said the girl, drawing the word out slowly as she turned around. Now first she realized that Richmond was not alone. But one thing young Sarah was not was shy. She walked straight toward the Davidsons' esteemed guest where he sat on the couch. She stopped in front of him and gazed up into his dark rugged face.

"I'm Sarah," she said.

"I heard that that was your name," said the president in a deep baritone. "Do you and your parents live here and work for the Davidsons?"

"No, we's jes' stayin' her till we can git norf," replied Sarah. "We's slaves but we run away an' we's hidin' from da men dat do bad things ter slaves like us."

Unexpectedly Sarah now jumped onto the couch and climbed into the president's lap. Taken by surprise, slowly Lincoln's arm reached around her. Sarah leaned back against his chest, then arched her neck around so that she could see the president's face.

"Duz you help slave folks like Mister Dab'son?" she asked.

"I don't have the chance to meet very many slaves," he replied.

"Why not?"

"Because I live in the North. There are no slaves there. I am visiting Mr. Davidson too."

"When we gits ter da Norf, we won't be slaves no mo' either. Den we's be free cuz dere's a man named Abraham dere dat's jes' like dat Abraham or Moses or sumbody in da Bible, dat's what my mama seyz, an' he don't let nobody hurt no black folks, even effen dey be runaways. So we's goin' ter da Norf. Dat's where freedom is. Dat's where Abraham is. What's yo' name, Mister?"

Richmond glanced over and saw tears rising in the president's eyes.

"What's the matter, Mister?" said Sarah. "You look sad."

Lincoln smiled, reaching one hand up to wipe at his eyes. "No, Sarah," he said. "Actually, I think I am very happy . . . happy to talk to you."

"Well, good-bye, Mister," said Sarah, scrambling down to the floor. "Good-bye, Mister Dab'son. I's go fin' Miz Waters now so we kin play sum more."

As quickly as she had appeared, she hurried out the door and was gone. It remained silent for some time between the two men.

"Let me tell you something, Richmond," said Lincoln at length. "I hope you do not mind if I address you with such familiarity."

"Of course not."

"You have been so kind to my men, and myself, that a *Mister* hardly sounds right on my lips. But what I wanted to tell you is that I have a dream, a dream of equality and freedom for all Americans. I doubt that I shall live to see it. But some dreams must wait. Yet they are worth fighting for, even if we do not see all that will become of them one day. I call it my American Dream."

"I think it is a worthy dream, Mr. President. And perhaps you and I shall live long enough to see more of it than we think. When little Sarah climbed into your lap just now, I think I saw some of your dream being fulfilled before my eyes."

That same evening at dusk, Abraham Lincoln disappeared into the night to begin his secretive journey back to the safety of the Union, leaving Richmond and Carolyn Davidson to wonder whether they had imagined the whole thing.

The battles of mid-1862 might well have ended the war. Though Robert E. Lee was outnumbered in his defense of Richmond against McClellan's superior numbers, McClellan's chronic hesitation, a defect Lincoln had already noticed, failed to seize the advantage. His golden opportunity to take the Confederate capital was lost and he was compelled to retreat.

Lee's strategic victory led to a second Confederate victory in as many years at Manassas Junction, and Lee marched his army north in an attempt to invade the North through Pennsylvania and to take the federal rail center at Harrisburg. Had he succeeded, the northern border would have been breached and Lee might have had a clear march to Philadelphia, even New York.

After his waffling and indecision throughout the seven-day assault on Richmond, which ended in failure, Lincoln relieved McClellan of command of the Potomac army. But now, only a month later, he was compelled to send General Pope west to deal with an uprising of the Sioux. Lee was moving north, and with no one else close at hand, Lincoln reluctantly had little choice but to put the incompetent General George McClellan back in command of the Grand Army of the Potomac. It was a decision the president would bitterly regret.

McClellan pursued Lee north through Virginia to try to ward off the invasion of Pennsylvania. The two armies met at Sharpsburg, Maryland on September 16, facing one another across the little creek called Antietam.

But even an incompetent general, if he has vastly superior troops, ought to be able to win a decisive victory. And McClellan had more than twice Lee's number. He also had something else—he knew Lee's battle strategy ahead of time. Three days earlier, in a deserted Confederate camp en route to Sharpsburg, a Union corporal had discovered three cigars wrapped in a piece of paper. That paper was a copy of Lee's orders and battle plan.

Yet with such a great advantage on his side, McClellan did not seize his strategic superiority and attack. He waited and waited, allowing Lee to deploy his troops to the best advantage. When the fighting finally began, though the sheer numbers made a Union victory inevitable, McClellan's timid responses to Lee's moves, and his constant hesitation to hurl the might of his army forward against Lee, allowed the Confederate army to remain defeated but not broken.

September 17 was the bloodiest single day thus far in the history of the nation. After three days there were more than 23,000 dead and wounded. Finally Lee fell back in retreat.

With the Confederate invasion of the North stopped, McClellan might have ended the war then and there and become a national hero. His advantage was so great that, by pursuing Lee, the Confederacy could have been crushed in a single blow.

But he did not act.

Lincoln wired him with specific orders: "Destroy the rebel army if possible."

But McClellan did not respond, and Lee and his army slipped quietly away into the Virginia hills.

In the days after the battle, while George McClellan rested his troops and did nothing, President Abraham Lincoln, on the other hand, acted decisively with the single act, among a multitude, for which he would be best known by history, and either loved or hated by his contemporaries. Taking the Union victory at Antietam as a sign from God, Lincoln seized the opportunity he had been waiting for.

He released a proclamation which read:

> *On the first day of January, in the year of our Lord one thousand eight hundred and sixty three, all persons held as slaves within any State, or designated part of a State, the people whereof shall then be in rebellion against the United States, shall be then, thenceforth, and forever free.*

Jefferson Davis called it the "most execrable measure recorded in the history of guilty man."

Another week passed and still McClellan sat at Sharpsburg.

Frustrated almost beyond belief with McClellan's inaction, two weeks after the battle and a week after his Emancipation Proclamation, on the first of October, Lincoln himself traveled to Sharpsburg. In the two weeks since the battle, McClellan was still encamped at the site of the battle. The president and the general met in McClellan's tent and Lincoln made his will clear—McClellan was to pursue Lee's army with the objective of destroying it.

Thinking he had been clearly understood, Lincoln returned to Washington only to receive telegrams from McClellan explaining why he felt it imprudent to move. Lincoln wired back peremptorily *ordering* him to advance.

Yet nearly another month passed before McClellan began reluctantly to pursue Lee. By then Lee's army was back across the Blue Ridge Mountains and safely out of McClellan's reach.

At long last, in November of 1862, Lincoln relieved General George McClellan of command for good.

Abraham Lincoln's unpopularity, even in the North, resulted in a drubbing in the midterm elections of November. Many of his own Republicans, disappointed that the Emancipation Proclamation did not go further, and frustrated by Lincoln's conduct of the war, did not campaign aggressively for the president and their party. On the other side, the Democrats accused Lincoln and his administration of incompetence and abuse of power, and won both houses of Congress easily.

Rumors began to circulate that Lincoln would resign and that General McClellan would return to Washington and somehow be given command in Lincoln's place, not merely of the Army of the Potomac, but of the entire Union.

After McClellan's dismissal, the new commander of the Union Army of the Potomac, General Ambrose Burnside led McClellan's former, and now grumbling, army, upset at his firing, south, intending another assault on Richmond, this time from the north.

But by early December, Robert Lee's forces were again ready for battle. Now Stonewall Jackson had joined him from the Shenandoah and they marched east and intercepted Burnside's army as he was attempting to seize Fredericksburg.

The war now came closer to Greenwood than at any previous time. In the distance, in the early days of December, could be heard to the north the sounds of Lee's and Jackson's armies moving toward Fredericksburg.

Winter set in early that December of 1862. It rained and rained and in the second week a great snowfall covered all of Dove's Landing.

Yet unknown to anyone at Greenwood, the people of Fredericksburg only forty or fifty miles away had been ordered to evacuate the city under the Union siege. Thousands of civilians were left without homes in the freezing weather.

When the battle began in earnest, Burnside proved no more able or decisive than McClellan, and days of fighting resulted in what could only be described as a slaughter of the Union army.

1862 ended with Confederate troops under Robert E. Lee again supreme in the East. The year had cost America 268,000 casualties, over a quarter of a million young American men killed and wounded . . . in a single year.

PART THREE

CONFUSED LOYALTIES
1863

Fifteen

Through the winter of 1862–63, no one on either side could see where the war would end. All optimism for quick victory was gone. The winter was long and cold. Homesickness, disease, and desertions ran rampant. Many of the boys on both sides, joining up in the heat of emotion, had begun to wonder what they were risking their lives for.

The strain as the war entered its third year was showing more decidedly in the Confederacy. After the Union's near disastrous string of blunders, near misses, and outright defeats in the East, 1863 was the year in which the tide slowly began to shift. The huge advantage of the North in manpower and rail power and manufacturing power, alongside the South's fewer men, fewer trains, and an economy based on agriculture, was beginning to tell.

Another major Confederate victory, even in the face of superior Union forces, repelling yet one more advance against Richmond, came in the first week of May at Chancellorsville near Fredericksburg, again under the command of Robert Lee. It seemed the Union army could accomplish nothing in the East, especially against Lee.

Yet Grant continued to make up for it in the West. After his string of victories the previous year he now laid siege a second time to Vicksburg, the South's "invincible city" on the lower Mississippi, in the late spring and early summer.

Lee controlled the East. Grant controlled the West.

Richmond Davidson had been reading in the *Journal* of renowned
Quaker John Woolman that he had discovered shortly before the
outbreak of the war. Though his devotional reading was broad and
varied, during the past year it was often to the writings of Woolman
that he returned as a spiritual touchstone in his attempt to blend into
his faith practicality, the unity of Christian brotherhood, daily obedience, common sense, and doctrinal integrity.

He and Carolyn were riding back from Dove's Landing one afternoon when Richmond's prayers from that morning came up in their
conversation.

"I could not help being struck as I read," said Richmond, "with the
affinity that exists between how the Lord has led us in our outlook and
priorities, and old John Woolman. He so often puts into words, even
if the style is a little outmoded, exactly what I feel. It is not only in
the matter of slavery, but in matters of business and personal relationships, in the balance between money and possessions and spirituality.
I now begin to see why I feel a spiritual camaraderie with many of the
Quakers we meet—Brannon and Mueller and others."

"Perhaps you should convert," suggested Carolyn. "Perhaps we
should all become Quakers."

Richmond laughed. "I do not think the extenal brand of church or
affiliation is so important," he said. "It is Woolman's outlook on life
that I admire and would hope in some small way to emulate."

"He was indeed a remarkable man," said Carolyn.

"Of all the sects that contributed to the founding of the country,
from the Puritans to the Baptists to the Moravians and Brethren,
the Quakers really seemed, at least in those formative years, to get it
right. They were so nonsectarian, so principled, so open, and such
rounded and balanced individuals—at least, knowing no more than
I do, so it strikes me."

"There were certainly no stories of Quakers burning people at the
stake!"

"It would have been helpful had we known of Woolman's writings when we were struggling with our own decision about what to do with our slaves years ago."

"Perhaps the Lord wanted us to make that decision entirely within ourselves."

As they drew up in the buggy in front of the house they found Nancy Shaw approaching from her house.

"Another family jes' arrived," she said as they stepped out and to the ground. "Dey seem like real nice folks. Dey talk like w'ite folks. Dey came right ter da big house but I took 'em down ter my place an' fixed 'em sumfin' ter eat."

"Thank you, Nancy," smiled Carolyn. "That was kind of you. We will put our things away and be right down."

Ten minutes later Richmond and Carolyn walked into the Shaw house. The newcomers were seated around Nancy's table. One of the family, a young black boy, was clearly taken with Nancy's two older sons. And what they took to be his sister was stealing an occasional glance in the direction of the Shaw boys as well.

"Here are da Dab'sons I wuz tellin' you about," said Nancy.

A lanky black man rose from the table and offered his hand to Richmond.

"I'm pleased to meet thee, Mr. Davidson," he said. "I am Aaron Steddings, and this is my wife Zaphorah and our three children, Mary, Moses, and Suzane."

"I am happy to meet you too, Mr. Steddings," said Richmond, shaking his hand warmly. "Please meet my wife Carolyn, and consider yourselves welcome here at Greenwood for as long as you need to stay."

"I thank thee, Mister Davidson."

"Well, we shall let you finish up here," said Richmond. "We will have the chance to visit a little later. Nancy," he added, "when they are through, would you please bring them up to the house."

$\backsim$

Carolyn put their new guests in two of the second-floor rooms of the main house.

It did not take long in conversation later that day for Richmond to realize that they had opened their home for the first time to a Quaker family who had found it necessary to escape slavery on the very Underground Railroad their fellow Friends had begun.

But it was not until some time later, as they discussed their plans and where they were bound that they were in for their greatest surprise.

"I don't suppose thee would have heard of it," said Aaron, "but we are from a little town in New Jersey just on the other side of the Delaware River. It is called Mount Holly."

"Mount Holly!" exclaimed Richmond. "You don't say!"

"Thee has heard of it?" asked Zaphorah in surprise.

Richmond jumped from his chair and strode across the room, where he picked up a small volume next to his reading chair. He returned and handed it to Aaron Steddings.

"It is one of my most prized books," he said. "I'm afraid in the last year my copy of Woolman's *Journal* has become as thumb worn as my Bible! I am a great admirer of your humble tailor."

"Then let me read you a passage from it," said Zaphorah with a smile, "and tell you a little story."

She took the book, found the passage in which Woolman had been instrumental in the freeing of Betsy Ferris, and read it aloud to them. When she had finished, Zaphorah put the book aside.

"That black lady happens to have been Aaron's great-grandmother," she said.

Now did Richmond Davidson's astonishment mount to yet greater heights!

"But this is incredible!" he exclaimed. "I was just reading that section again yesterday! And suddenly here you are with us. The legacy of John Woolman himself has stepped off the pages into our own lives!"

Aaron laughed. "Well, I am not the kind of spiritual man he was," he said. "I am just a simple man trying to take care of my family and live by the Book as best I can."

"I can hardly think of a more fitting description of Woolman himself."

They continued to talk and share late into the evening, as freely and spontaneously as had they known one another for years.

When Richmond and Carolyn returned together to their room, few words passed between them. Both had been moved by the events of the day. These were no ordinary runaways whom the Lord had brought them. More than ever before they saw his guiding hand in this present circumstance in their lives. Both sensed that in Aaron and Zaphorah Steddings they had discovered true friends of the Spirit.

Nothing would have suited Richmond and Carolyn Davidson better than for Aaron and Zaphorah Steddings to have remained with them at Greenwood indefinitely. There was so much Richmond wanted to ask Aaron, so much about his Quaker faith, as well as life in Mount Holly, one of the very foundations of Quakerism in this country, that he was hungry to learn.

And in Zaphorah, Carolyn found one to share with on a level of the Spirit that she had never before shared with anyone but Richmond. As dearly as she loved Nancy Shaw, the cultural divide between herself and one who had spent most of her life as a slave, was simply too great to bridge completely. The distinction between them, mostly in Nancy's mind rather than Carolyn's, would always be present. In Zaphorah, however, though her skin was black and Carolyn's white, Carolyn yet discovered a oneness of spiritual outlook, a depth of thought, and a breadth of awareness about life and the world that Nancy, as a simpler woman, could not share with her in the same way.

They spoke about children, about husbands, about the differences in a woman's responses to matters of faith from a man's. They spoke of intimacies, of secret longings, of disappointments, of hopes, of fears. They laughed together, they prayed together, and they cried as Zaphorah poured out her grief over their lost daughter. And they held one another as only two women can whose hearts have been knitted together as one.

As the time drew closer when Carolyn knew they must leave them, her heart quieted and she grew sad. She had not recognized within herself the need, or even the desire for a woman-friend of the heart. Richmond had always been everything for her. She had been satisfied and content. Now that such a friend had been given her, she did not want to let her go.

Yet she would treasure the memories of her long walks and talks late into the night with Zaphorah, and would know that wherever life took them God had kindled a love in their hearts for one another that would last a lifetime.

It was clear, however, that the Steddings' situation was unlike that of Sydney and Chigua when they had first come to Greenwood. Aaron and Zaphorah had a place they had come from and friends they were anxious to see again. They had been away too long.

They just wanted to get *home*!

The predawn wagon ride from Greenwood over the hills west into the neighboring county was unlike the many former such trips that had been taken by Richmond or Seth or Malachi Shaw with a delivery of runaways for the next station. On this occasion, both Richmond and Carolyn accompanied their guests to see them safely into the hands of their Quaker neighbor Brannon.

Though the times were dangerous, with Lee's army moving north and reports of Union troops not far to the west, they arrived without incident.

Brannon met them with some surprise, not having been informed in advance of their coming.

"Ah, friend Brannon!" said Richmond, getting down from the wagon and shaking the Quaker farmer's hand warmly. "We have brought you some weary travelers who are more than mere refugees from the South, but rather true friends indeed. They have a story to tell that I am confident will interest you greatly. It is our hope that you will be able to get them safely to their destination."

"Where is this destination?" asked Brannon.

"A small town in New Jersey," replied Richmond with a twinkle in his eye. "It is called Mount Holly."

Brannon's eyes widened in astonishment. He glanced toward the wagon where Aaron was just stepping down, followed by Carolyn and Zaphorah.

"Let me introduce to you Aaron Steddings," said Richmond, beckoning Aaron forward, "and his dear wife Zaphorah. We will leave them to tell you their story themselves."

When Cecil Hirsch called at the Fitzpatrick home in early 1863 to invite Veronica to lunch, Veronica's reaction was mixed, and more confused than she could herself account for. When she opened the door and saw him standing there, her heart leapt momentarily with pleasure. At the same instant, however, a sarcastic remark rose to her lips such as she might a few years earlier have given Seth Davidson for not coming to see her often enough, or failing to notice the new hat she was wearing.

Cecil observed the brief internal battle with amusement. His design was to keep Veronica, to a certain extent, off balance, and he realized he was succeeding. He just had to be careful not to make her *too* angry. That would serve no one's interests, least of all his.

"My apologies for not seeing you in so long!" he said effusively. "I have been away a good deal, but am here to make amends and humbly request you to join me for lunch at the Ritz."

He took off his hat and made a slight bow.

The annoyance died on Veronica's lips. How could she be angry with a smile like Cecil's? And she remembered the dress from Madame Rochelle's.

"Garabaldi tells me you have been helping him out regularly," said Hirsch after they had ordered. "I am glad it is working out well for you—that is, I assume it is."

"I suppose so," said Veronica. "He pays me well to go to Richmond for him—too well, actually."

"You once asked how I was able to make so much money during a war. Now you know. There are people willing to pay for things, for information, for delivering letters for them, willing to pay to do things they do not want to do themselves. I told you the war had been good to me and I saw no reason not to let you in on my good fortune. My advice is, enjoy it and don't ask too many questions. But tell me about Richard's work. What is he doing these days?"

"Oh, I don't know. He doesn't tell me anything."

"I understand he is now on the staff of the Senate Military Affairs Committee."

"Then you know more about his job than I do!" laughed Veronica.

"I can understand his keeping his activities secret. After all, your father is in the Confederate Congress."

"What is that supposed to mean?"

"Just that he has to be careful not to share military secrets with you that could fall into the wrong hands."

"You mean that I might tell my father?"

"Maybe not even intentionally . . . sometimes things just slip out."

"That's not why Richard keeps his activities to himself . . . at least I don't think so."

"Where *would* your loyalties lie if you had to choose between your husband and your father?"

"What kind of a question is that?"

"I mean if you had information from something your father let slip that might help, say, the Union army, would you tell Richard about it?"

"I don't know—I've never thought about it. Let's just hope it never happens. They would pay no attention to what I said anyway. Nobody cares what a woman thinks."

"Don't be too sure. What would you say if I asked you to try to secretly find out something from Richard that I needed to know—would you do it?"

Veronica looked at Cecil with an odd expression, not quite sure whether to take him seriously.

"I . . . I don't know," she said slowly. "I hope you wouldn't."

"But if I did."

"I don't know . . . I suppose it would depend on what it was, on whether it put anyone in danger, or whether anyone would get hurt. I would never do anything to put Richard in danger. Whatever you may think, Cecil, I do love him."

"I am glad to hear that. I would feel sorry for you if you didn't."

"Do you feel sorry for me?"

"Not you, Veronica. You always manage to land on your feet." Hirsch sipped at his coffee and grew slowly more thoughtful.

"I understand your husband is leaving for Europe in two weeks," he said at length, "to brief our English allies on the war effort."

"How did you know that?"

"I have my sources," smiled Cecil. "I once told you information is the most prized commodity in the world."

"That is something else I do not remember your saying! Cecil Hirsch, I declare you make up half the things you tell me!"

Hirsch roared with delight. "Well maybe I didn't use those exact words. But I said something like it. Whether I said it or not, information is the commodity that makes people rich. And that is why I make it a point to know as much about the people in this town as I can. The reason I mentioned your husband's trip is that I thought perhaps while he is gone you would like to accompany me to Chattanooga, and then north to Chicago."

Veronica stared back across the table expressionless, her mouth almost hanging open.

"What do you mean?" she asked.

"I must see some people in Chattanooga. After that I am going to Chicago for a few days before returning to Washington. I thought perhaps you would like to go with me."

Slowly Veronica shook her head and smiled. "You are always full of surprises!" she said. "But I must say this takes the cake. How am I supposed to reply to a proposal like that!"

"Say yes, of course," smiled Hirsch.

Richard Fitzpatrick could not help noticing that his wife was quieter than usual and seemed moody and out of sorts as the time for his departure for England drew near. He had never seen Veronica like this. The only thing that was different was her sudden interest in his work, asking him questions about who he was going to see in England and what he was going to tell them. She had wanted to help him pack his bags and kept looking at the papers in his briefcase even though they concerned things she could not possibly understand. By the day his ship sailed, it was almost a relief to be away from her.

As for Veronica, with Richard gone and the house empty, suddenly the enormity of her impending decision loomed all the more heavily upon her. She was both excited and afraid. What if she was seen by someone who knew Richard? What if word got around about her involvement with Cecil Hirsch?

Was this one of those moments when a small decision would alter the course of her whole future?

Was it a *small* decision?

True, there was the morality of the thing to be considered. She would simply insist on separate rooms. Cecil would agree or she wouldn't go with him. She didn't want to complicate her life sexually, only to put some adventure back into it.

Whether it was because of her anxiety about being seen with him, or for the purpose of keeping their trip secret for reasons of his own, Cecil sat alone on the train, and allowed Veronica to do likewise, until the second day of their journey to Chattanooga. By then they were far enough into the South that there was little risk of meeting anyone from Washington D.C. Also by then Veronica's nervousness over the impropriety of the thing had begun to diminish. She began to enjoy the adventure.

Signs of the war were unmistakable and all about them. The train

had more soldiers than civilians, many of them wounded, with arms
in slings or hobbling on crutches. In Washington she had been able to
keep the war at a distance. Suddenly they were riding straight into the
middle of it. She saw the fear and weariness on the faces of the young
boys in uniform and thought of her own two brothers, Wyatt and
Cameron. The sights were not pleasant.

Cecil seemed unaffected by it all. But as they went, Veronica grew
quiet and thoughtful. It was a new sensation. But along with disgust, a
distant cousin to compassion rose in her heart for the wounded. It was
a cousin, however, whose acquaintance she had not before made—she
was uncomfortable in its presence.

By the time they reached Chattanooga, soldiers were everywhere.
The city was quiet and depressing as they rode in a rented buggy to
their hotel. Veronica had expected a gay, lively, sparkling Southern
city. Where had everyone gone?

They reached their hotel and Cecil said he had to go out.

"But we just got here, Cecil," said Veronica. "I don't want to be left
alone."

"I won't be long. As soon as I get back, we'll go out for dinner."

He turned and left Veronica alone in her room.

On an impulse, after a moment or two, Veronica decided to follow
him. There were so many mysteries about Cecil Hirsch. There had
been from the first day she had met him. Why shouldn't she try to
learn more?

Replacing her hat with a scarf pulled down over her head to her
chin, she hurried downstairs and left the hotel, glanced up and down
the street, and saw Cecil's back in the distance. She hurried after him,
as much as possible keeping close to the shadows of the buildings.

He walked some distance, reached the river, then turned and
made his way along the waterfront. There were few people about and
Veronica was nervous that he would turn back. But she kept on.

After about ten minutes, Cecil stopped. A man wearing a thick
overcoat and broad hat approached him. Veronica crept closer then
stopped, hiding behind a brick warehouse, and peered around the

edge of the wall. They talked for a few minutes, then Cecil handed the man a packet. They shook hands. The man turned, walked toward the river, got into a small boat, and began rowing across.

Realizing they were through with their business, Veronica turned, ran along the side of the building, and tried to regain her bearings. She hurried back to the hotel, just barely reaching it in time to remove the scarf and sit down and try to relax and seem bored. Two minutes later Cecil's knock came on the door.

"Where did you go?" she asked, doing her best to hide the fact that she was still out of breath herself.

"Oh, just downstairs to the lobby," he replied. "I had to see someone."

"I thought you were going into the city somewhere."

"No, just downstairs. But now you and I can go out. Do you feel like some dinner?"

"It's not . . . dangerous, is it? I mean—are there any Union soldiers about? Do you think there could be any fighting?"

"No, nothing to worry about!" laughed Cecil. "Where is the brave spirit of the Beaumonts?"

"I thought the Union army was nearby."

"I think there might be a regiment across the river somewhere, but I assure you it's nothing to worry about. This is a strategic city and there is little doubt the Union will make an attempt on it eventually. But it won't be in the next few days. Most of the action is south of here at Chickamauga where the armies have been facing off for months. But that's eight or ten miles away."

"Ten miles! There's fighting that close?"

"They're not fighting, my dear," laughed Cecil. "At least not yet. That's just where they are."

"That sounds close!"

"Not to worry, I tell you. What's come over you, Veronica? You're more jittery than I've ever seen you."

"Oh, nothing . . . it's just . . . different here." Veronica forced a laugh. "Maybe I *am* a little nervous," she added.

The next two days were not what Veronica had expected. There was little to do and she kept mostly to the hotel. Cecil met a few people, introduced her to some of them but spoke in low cryptic tones to others, making it clear he did not want her to hear the gist of the conversation.

As they were returning one evening to the hotel, Cecil glanced back over his shoulder.

"What is it?" asked Veronica. "You've been acting funny all day. Now it's *you* who are nervous."

Cecil laughed. "Nothing to worry about, I've just had the feeling someone is watching us and I don't like it."

"You've been meeting strange people ever since we arrived," laughed Veronica. "It's probably one of your mystery people who wants to talk to you!"

Cecil looked at her with an odd expression.

"What do you mean . . . my mystery people?"

"You know—you're always talking with people like everything's so secretive."

Cecil nodded but said nothing more. He did not seem pleased by her comment.

They left Chattanooga the following morning, taking the train to Nashville, then Louisville, and north to Indianapolis, and finally Chicago.

The moment they were out of the South, everything changed. In the cities of the North life seemed normal again. Within no time Veronica forgot her fears and hesitations in the glamour of the great Midwestern city. Every day they went shopping and sightseeing. Every night they went to the finest restaurants. Cecil was in rare form as a host and man about town. They went dancing, he bought her gifts. Was he, thought Veronica, made of money?

How would she explain to Richard all these new dresses and hats, gloves and shoes?

Even in Europe, Richard had never shown Veronica such a time as she had in Chicago with Cecil Hirsch. By the time they returned to Washington, she was more under his spell than she would have thought possible.

Sixteen

*I*t was with great relief in their hearts that the family of Aaron Steddings crossed the border from Maryland into Penn's Woods. Tears rose in Zaphorah's eyes to know they were out of the South and the Confederacy. They were tears that spoke many things, and they rode for some way in thoughtful silence.

With the help of many new Quaker friends, they arrived in Philadelphia a week after leaving Greenwood. There they caught a train to Burlington, where they rented a buggy for the final several miles of the journey.

Their keen sense of anticipation rose with every mile of the way that led them along Rancocas Creek, past the original homestead of John Woolman and his father William, from whom by now more than a thousand Woolman descendents had sprung. Just beyond it, they turned into the long road leading to the several homes that had been built through the years on the original Borton land, one of which was now occupied by Aaron's former employer John Borton and his brother Pemberton.

They heard the *clank, clank, clank* of hammer on anvil as they rode toward the house.

John Borton himself, gray and showing the signs of his sixty-eight years, was out in the blacksmith's shop that had been Aaron's domain twelve years before. Hearing the sound of an approaching buggy, the pounding stopped and Borton walked out, hammer in hand. A buggy was just reining in.

He squinted in the sunlight. A man and a woman were getting down, both black. Three black children were with them.

He walked slowly away from the shop . . . the fellow was running toward him . . . what was that great smile on the man's—

Suddenly Borton's face went pale. The hammer fell from his hands and landed with a thud on the ground.

He stood in disbelief, tears streaming down his face as he beheld the friend approaching whom he had never expected to see again.

"Aaron Steddings!" he breathed in a voice not much more than a whisper as the two shook hands. "My dear friend! How . . . but . . . the Lord be praised! Thee has come home!"

Aaron stood before him beaming, his own face also wet in unashamed joy.

"And thy beautiful wife!" Borton went on, seeing Zaphorah walking up behind Aaron, ". . . and thy young ones, now all grown into fine young men and women! Will thee not all come in . . . we shall have something cold to drink. I . . . I am simply overwhelmed . . . I do not know what to say. I am eager to hear everything!"

"And thy wife?" asked Zaphorah. "She is well?"

Borton drew in a deep sigh.

"I am sorry to have to tell thee," he replied. "But I lost my dear Martha only a year or two after thy disappearance."

"Oh, the dear lady!" said Zaphorah. "I am so sorry for thy loss."

Seventeen

*B*oth the Union and the Confederacy were about to face their greatest challenge of the war. In a single week of July, two massive battles, one in the East, one in the West, changed everything.

In the summer of 1863, the Confederacy again attempted an invasion of the North under General Lee. This time Lee's army crossed the Pennsylvania border, and moved into Union territory. It finally seemed that no one was capable of stopping Robert E. Lee.

Only when its own soil was threatened, as at Antietam, did Union forces rise to the occasion. Now came another such encounter. The Confederate army was met in late June by a huge federal force under the command of General George Meade at the small town of Gettysburg. The very name would forever after be linked with the most terrible battle ever fought on American soil. Once again the Union army stiffened and rose to repulse an invasion. When it was over, after three days of fighting, over 50,000 young American men were dead or wounded. The wagons full of the casualties of the defeated rebel army stretched seventeen miles as they made their way back south.

But Gettysburg was not the Union's only victory that week. The war turned on two fronts simultaneously.

In the West, on July 4th, the day after the final shots had been heard at Gettysburg, after a forty-eight day siege, Confederate Commander

John Pemberton, a Pennsylvanian, at last surrendered 30,000 Confederate troops to Ulysses Grant at Vicksburg.

The Union now controlled the Mississippi all the way to New Orleans and the Gulf.

In one week, the entire course of the war had shifted. Lincoln wrote to a friend, "Victory does not appear so distant as it did."

Yet again, in spite of the victory at Gettysburg, Lincoln's eastern generals disappointed him. As before, a decisive opportunity to crush Lee's retreating army and possibly end the war was lost by a tentative Meade. The fighting as a result would drag on for another two years.

After his defeat at Gettysburg, Lee wrote to Jefferson Davis offering to resign. "I generally feel a begrowing failure of my bodily strength," he said. "I anxiously urge the matter upon Your Excellency from my belief that a younger and abler man than myself can readily be obtained."

But to find a better commander than Robert Lee, Davis said in reply, was "an impossibility." Lee's offer was not accepted.

With their guns silent and their cannons stilled, the armies moved on from the catastrophic scene of battle, leaving just over two thousand residents of Gettysburg to care for and bury the 25,000 that were left with them. A woman wrote, "Wounded men were brought into our houses and laid side-by-side in our halls and first-story rooms. Carpets were so saturated with blood as to be unfit for further use. Walls were bloodstained, as well as books that were used as pillows." And on the hills and in the fields surrounding the town, dead lay everywhere by the thousands, corpses putrefying under the summer sun.

In the West, meanwhile, now that Grant had secured the Mississippi, the Union looked toward the strategic city of Chattanooga, on a bend of the Tennessee River where two important railroad lines joined, guarding the routes to the eastern Confederacy and Georgia, as its next objective.

But standing in the way were the Confederate forces at Chickamauga Creek just across the border in Georgia.

The battle at Chickamauga in the third week of September in defense of Chattanooga brought one of the rare instances in the war when Confederate troops outnumbered those from the Union. A six-month standoff between the two armies at last erupted when Confederate forces pummeled the Union.

The fighting raged furiously for two days.

Thomas Davidson was now fighting with Captain Young's regiment under the command of the general most of his troops considered a tyrant, General Braxton Bragg. Cameron Beaumont had been promoted to sergeant and was now also assigned to Captain Young's command. But though they all hated him, Bragg's Confederate troops had the better of it.

Thomas's regiment found itself in the thick of the afternoon's charge. The air was thick with the gray smoke of cannon explosions. All about was yelling and shouting and running as the commanders shouted orders in a chaos of confused smoke and mud and blood.

By late afternoon the badly routed Union army was fleeing in full retreat, staggering back toward the city.

But, their victory assured, Bragg called off the charge. He was reluctant to pursue Rosecrans across the creek. Young and the other officers were furious. Had Bragg ordered a full assault on Chattanooga, they might crush the entire Union army in Tennessee!

It was a massive defeat for the Union, and included the death of Mary Todd Lincoln's brother-in-law. Yet even in defeat, Union troops occupied Chattanooga, and Bragg's hesitancy made it not so severe a defeat as it might have been. And federal reinforcements were on the way to attempt to turn the defeat into a victory.

They were led by Ulysses S. Grant.

That night as he lay on his bedroll, Thomas Davidson lay awake unable to sleep.

The day had been a savage one. Even in what everyone was calling a victory, dead had fallen all around him. He was hungry and tired and homesick. Even going into battle, their rations of meat were too skimpy to keep a rat alive. Sometimes Thomas wondered if that's what they were eating!

One by one incidents from the day replayed themselves in his brain . . . the shrieking . . . the smell of gunpowder . . . bodies lying everywhere . . . wounded crying for help . . . running . . . stumbling sometimes over but half a broken body.

Late in the day, before Bragg had called them off, his regiment had been in pursuit of a dozen or more Union soldiers who had dropped their guns and were fleeing for their lives.

"Don't let a single mother's son of them escape!" shouted Young. "After them, men . . . the cowards are on the run!"

Shots sounded on all sides. One by one, fifty yards ahead, the young men in blue continued to fall. Unable to keep up, Thomas saw one gradually slow.

Beside him an explosion sounded from Travis Durkin's gun. Thomas saw a splotch of red explode over the blue uniform, and the man toppled to the ground.

Durkin ran up and looked down, and shot him again, this time in the head. He turned to where Thomas watched in shock. A look of disdain spread over Durkin's face.

"What's the matter?" he said. "Why didn't you shoot him? You were closer than I was."

But the others were continuing in pursuit and Thomas ran on to join them.

Max Cardiff had just emptied his gun and stopped to reload. "Travis, get that guy on the right," he cried. "Look, he's still got his gun—get him before he fires!"

Durkin slowed, raised his rifle, and fired.

"I missed!" he yelled, swearing loudly. "Get him, Davidson—that's an order. Shoot him!"

Thomas hesitated.

"Come on, you sissy, fire!" shouted Durkin again. "I'll have you up on charges if you don't empty that gun of yours!"

Gunfire was exploding all around him. Thomas raised his gun and aimed high, then pulled the trigger. The next instant he saw the blue form stumble and fall forty yards ahead.

A silent pang of horror overwhelmed him. Thomas shut his eyes and tried to shake the image from his mind. But he could not keep away the tears of agony and grief. Had he actually *killed* a man today? The thought was too horrible to dwell on.

Shots had been coming from everywhere, he tried to tell himself.

"Oh, God!" he thought. "Let it have been somebody else!"

Why did he join this army? he agonized with himself for the hundredth time. He didn't believe in this war. He didn't believe in slavery! He thought of the Shaw boys. They had been his and Seth's best friends.

As much as he had tried to tell himself that his father was crazy for what he had done, he realized now that his father had been right— slavery was wrong, this war was wrong, killing was wrong!

"I'm sorry, God. . . . Help me get out of this awful war! Help me, God . . . please help me!"

Thomas turned over, buried his face in his dirty blanket, until, mercifully, sleep finally overtook him.

⟨⁓⟩

They recovered from the battle, buried their dead, and got their wounded into field hospitals and nearby homes.

Reports confirmed that Grant was on his way north, some said with as many as 17,000 reinforcements.

Scouting details were sent out in several directions from the Confederate camp across Chickamauga Creek. Thomas went out with a half dozen men eastward into Georgia, just south of the Tennessee border.

As they were riding on their third day out on patrol, suddenly they heard a whoop from Travis Durkin. They looked and saw him spurring his horse ahead. The rest of their small detail hurried after him. They saw that he had spotted a small group of slave girls picking berries.

"Hey look, boys," yelled Durkin behind him, "we found us some nigger girls!"

"Yeah, but ugly as sin," said Cardiff riding up to join him. "I can tell even from this far."

"They's girls, Max," added Durkin with an evil grin. "They got all the equipment I need. Let's go!"

The four girls saw the soldiers almost the same moment. Immediately they realized they had wandered too far from the farmhouse. They dropped their buckets as the riders galloped toward them and ran for their lives.

Like dogs enlivened by the chase, the riders whooped and shouted and spurred their horses on. Though the terrain was uneven and uncultivated, with scattered trees and one stream to negotiate, and with a denser wood five or six hundred yards beyond, the pursuers quickly closed the distance, excited to yet greater heights by the shrieks reaching their ears.

Lagging behind his companions, Thomas feared what might be the outcome if they overtook the terrified girls. He had seen enough during the past two years to know what was on the minds of Travis Durkin and Max Cardiff. Like many rowdy youths unpossessed of the backbone of character, once out from under parental authority, they gave full vent to their untamed nature. To such half-men, casting off the restraints of conscience validated what they perceived as their dawning manhood. They were in fact but boys now occupying the bodies of men who had never learned that the first sign of maturity is the capacity to discipline oneself, and to curb the lusts of the flesh.

Though the perceived constraints of his own parental covering had grown oppressive, out on his own in a world where sin ruled, the younger son of Richmond and Carolyn Davidson was slowly recognizing that he was not like other young men, and that their ways disgusted him. He was more the son of his father than he yet realized. He did not exactly define the struggle taking place within him as resulting from his being a *Christian*. Had he paused to reflect upon it, he might have confessed uncertainty about his beliefs. A time would come for him to wrestle through matters of *faith*, but that time was not yet. He only knew that in matters of *behavior* he was set apart from most of those around them. He could not drink like them, swear like them, kill like them . . . and did not view women like they did—as objects of pleasure. Till now he had been a silent, unwilling, uncomfortable, and sometimes conscience-burdened observer. But a crossroads of courage for Thomas Davidson was nearly at hand.

Suddenly fifty yards in front of them, one of the girls tripped and fell to the ground with a cry. Thinking she would jump back up, the other girls hurried on. But she had twisted her ankle and was slow to her feet. Travis Durkin was the first to reach her and reined in. She struggled up to her knees and glanced toward him paralyzed with fright.

"Look here, boys," he called back. "We got one of them . . . didn't even have to run her down. And you's wrong, Max—she's mighty fetching, this one is."

The girl stood and tried to hobble away.

"Hey, where you think you're going, pretty nigger girl!" yelled Durkin, urging his horse forward again. He cantered past her and turned back to block her way. "You ain't trying to run from Travis, are you? You and me's got some getting acquainted to do."

In terrified despair, again the girl attempted to get around him. By now the others had caught up and formed a circle with their horses to block her way and prevent her taking more than a step or two in any direction. Slowly Durkin dismounted.

"Please, massa," the girl pleaded. "Please don't hurt me . . . please just let me go."

"I ain't going to do you no harm, nigger girl," said Durkin, walking toward her. "You and me's going to have a little fun together, then I'll let you go like you say."

"It's my turn after you!" laughed Cardiff where he sat on his horse.

"Go get your own!" laughed Durkin, tossing his head back in the direction of the wood. "This one's mine. There's plenty for the rest of you."

"They're already gone," said Cardiff, glancing over his shoulder where the other girls were disappearing among the trees. "Besides, that's just about the prettiest nigger girl I ever saw."

The girl cowered back, trembling, her eyes wide with terror as Durkin took off his gray jacket. He now unbuttoned his shirt and tossed it to the ground, glancing around at his companions with a wink and grin whose meaning was unmistakable. He took hold of the girl's arm and began pulling her away through the ring of horses.

"All right, boys," he said, "me and this pretty little thing want to be alone for a spell. What you do about the others is up to you, but you just give me ten minutes or so."

He half dragged the girl toward a thicket of wild shrubbery thirty or forty yards away. She cast an imploring look back. But no help would come from Durkin's friends. They sat and watched, laughing and coaxing their leader with lewd remarks and shouts.

But before the two were out of sight, suddenly one of the horses jumped into motion and galloped away from the group. In less than three seconds Durkin saw its huge side blocking his own way.

"Let her go, Durkin," said the last voice he would have expected to oppose him.

Durkin looked up, shocked to find himself staring down the barrel of a Confederate-issue rifle.

"What do you think you're doing, Davidson?" he said.

"I told you to let her go."

"Or what . . . you'll shoot me?"

"I hope we don't have to find out."

"Come on, Davidson—what's she to you?"

"Nothing. But I'm not going to stand by while you rape her."

"You think you can stop me?"

"You once called me a sissy. Well, maybe I am and maybe I'm not. But I know how to use this gun."

"You intend to kill me over a nigger girl? You'd hang for it."

"Maybe. But that wouldn't do you any good. You'd still be dead."

"You don't have the guts!" spat Durkin.

"Can you take that chance?"

Durkin hesitated momentarily. A quick glance at Thomas's quivering hand and then into his eyes revealed as much fear as determination. Durkin saw that one false step could easily make the gun go off and blow a hole in his head.

Sensing her opportunity, the girl yanked her arm free. Durkin glanced toward her and started to react. But the end of the gun was still less than three feet away and he dared not make another move in her direction.

"Run, miss!" said Thomas. "Get out of here. He won't hurt you now."

The girl hesitated only another second, cast one look full of silent emotion up at Thomas where he sat holding his rifle, then dashed away, not quite as fast as she had been running before but with surprising speed on her weak ankle.

Durkin looked back up at Thomas with hate in his eyes.

"You're a fool, Davidson," he said. "You're a complete coward in battle, afraid of your own shadow. You're about the most worthless soldier I ever seen. Then you pull an idiotic thing like this. What now? You gonna shoot me? She's gone. What you gonna do now?"

Thomas waited another few seconds to give the girl more time, then slowly withdrew his rifle. As he did he glanced after her.

Durkin sprang toward him with uncanny speed, grabbed his booted foot from its stirrup and thrust it upward. The next second Thomas thudded onto his back, his rifle bouncing to the ground five feet away.

"Come on, boys—get him!" cried Durkin. Before Thomas could recover his wind from the fall, Durkin fell on him in a rage and began pummeling him with his fists and knees.

Relishing nothing more than an uneven fight with a helpless victim, the four others galloped to the scene and leapt off their horses to join the fray. They were weaklings and followers, motivated not by reason, not by decision, not by conscience, not by right, but only by that great societal evil by which sin is perpetuated through the ages—*going along* with the cruelest bully of a crowd. None would have dared oppose Travis Durkin. In their fear of nonconformity, each sacrificed his own individuality on the altar of cowardice. Only one among them had taken strides toward manhood that day, and he soon lay unconscious at their feet.

The girl whose purity Thomas had defended heard the vicious attack behind her and glanced back. Seeing that no one was chasing her, or even looking in her direction now that their lust had given way to hatred, and knowing that she could never hope to outrun their horses, she quickly looked about for a place to hide. And thus it was that from beneath a fallen log in a damp ditch surrounded by scratching brambles and thick green shrubbery, she listened in horror to the terrible sounds of the beating.

It did not take long. The thud of boots into Thomas's stomach and side and back, the relentless whack of fists against his face and chin and head quickly silenced his groans into oblivion.

Gradually the onslaught ceased. The small mob stood back, panting and sweating as they looked down on Thomas's broken form and bleeding face. No one said a word, a pang or two now first suggesting itself to their dull consciences that they might have gone too far.

"Is he dayed?" asked a sixteen-year-old Mississippi boy in a thick timid drawl after a few seconds, the youngest of the group, doing his best to hide the quaver in his voice.

"No, he ain't dead, Shorty," said Durkin, trying to sound more confident than he felt himself. "He's just banged up a little. The fool just got what was coming to him—he should have known better."

Again the small group was silent. Most of them had liked Thomas and hadn't known why Travis Durkin had had it out for him from the beginning. But when the moment of truth had come, they had collectively taken their stand with the bully.

"What we gonna do with him, Travis?" asked Cardiff. "Can't just leave him here like this."

Durkin thought a minute. "No, I don't reckon we can," he said scratching his chin. "First we gotta get our story straight. You all saw what happened—he pulled his rifle on me and threatened to kill me. It was self-defense. I was just protecting myself and you all was helping me. He went crazy—and we done what we had to."

A few nods went around the group. It was more or less what had happened. No consciences dared speak.

"All right, then . . . somebody go get his horse. Let's lug him over his saddle and get back to camp."

"Captain ain't gonna like it," said young Mississippi, "us brangin' hiyum in like thayat."

"Shut up, Shorty!" snapped Durkin. "You just mind your own business and keep your mouth shut and make sure you don't end up the same way."

"What if he talks?" asked Cardiff.

"Course he'll talk!" rejoined Durkin testily. "Who they gonna believe—him or the rest of us? What's he gonna say, that he stuck up for a nigger girl and threatened to kill me? Now, Max, go get his horse . . . we gotta get going."

Five minutes later, Thomas's form draped over the saddle with his head and arms dangling from one side, legs from the other, the small band of soldiers began riding back in the direction where the rest of their regiment was encamped.

"Hey, look . . . here comes Sergeant Beaumont. He ain't gonna like this neither."

Cameron Beaumont rode up and surveyed the scene.

"Who's that?" he asked, nodding to the horse with the unconscious form draped over it.

"Private Davidson, Sergeant," replied Durkin.

"What happened?"

"He went a little crazy . . . pulled a gun on me."

Cameron took the information in but said nothing further. He reined his mount around and rode back toward the camp with the others.

From the hollow where she had been watching and listening, and obeying an inner compulsion she could neither ignore nor explain, the form of a young black woman crept out from under the fallen log of her hiding place, and, keeping well behind and out of sight, stealthily followed the six horses.

When Thomas began to come to himself, the first sensation he was aware of was a dull ache in the vicinity of his chest. He was hardly aware at first of the bandages covering half his face and one eye. As consciousness gradually returned, he tried to roll over and sit up. Sharp pain exploded from his three or four broken ribs. He winced softly and lay back down.

It was dark. A campfire burned twenty feet away. Everyone was asleep except the sentry on guard. He drew in two or three breaths, almost as painful as trying to sit up. Slowly the events of the day returned to him. With consciousness returned his memory and he instinctively realized it would be best to keep silent and not call attention to himself. He did his best not to make a sound.

For the rest of the night he lay in agony, dozing occasionally, but in too much pain to sleep. He was dreadfully thirsty but did not see his canteen anywhere and dared not speak up or try to move. Morning finally came, though with it came no relief to his aching body. Someone brought him some coffee and breakfast but mostly the rest of the regiment ignored him. Travis Durkin had obviously been talking.

Midway through the morning, Captain Young approached. Thomas looked up.

"You got yourself hurt pretty good, Davidson," he said.

"Yes, sir," replied Thomas solemnly.

"Want to tell me what happened?"

"Just a little ruckus with Durkin, sir. He obviously got the best of it."

"He says you pulled your gun on him. That true?"

"I suppose it is, sir."

"He says there were some niggers causing them trouble and you took the niggers' side. That how you see it?"

"No, sir."

"But you don't want to tell me about it."

"Travis and the others'd just say I was lying, Captain. I don't want to cause any more trouble. I got beat up for what I did, and if it's all the same to you I'd just rather try to forget about it."

"I've been talking to Sergeant Beaumont. He says he knows you from home. He says you were always a troublemaker . . . that you come from a family of troublemakers."

A surge of anger almost brought an unwise reply to Thomas's lips, but he managed to swallow it.

The captain drew in a breath and thought a moment. "We'll be pulling out of here tomorrow. A Yankee unit's been spotted in the hills west of here. We don't know if it's been sent out from Chattanooga or is part of Grant's advance. We're going to swing south and try to surprise them. You're lucky to have a day to recuperate. But you'll have to mount a saddle in the morning and keep up with the rest of us. I can't keep a cripple on. You be able to handle your gun?"

"I'll manage, sir."

"And pointed toward the enemy, not your own regiment?"

"Yes, sir."

"All right, then, Davidson, you get rested up—I don't want any more trouble or I'll bring charges against you myself if Durkin doesn't. I can't have a bad apple spoiling discipline in my unit."

Thomas closed his eyes and laid his head back down with a sigh. How did he get himself into such a mess? Why did he volunteer for this idiotic war anyway? Now all of a sudden he was in trouble, and hated by everyone in his unit for the same reason everyone hated his father—for standing up for Negroes.

For years he had despised his father for his idealistic values. Now look at him—he was in the same boat! His comrades walked by but kept their distance, glancing his way with mocking stares and whispered comments. Travis Durkin had managed to poison the entire unit against him.

Minute by minute, the hours crept by and the day slowly passed.

Thomas talked to no one, the pain in his ribs and shoulders and head worsened. He began to wonder if he actually could mount a horse like he'd said. The idea of bouncing along in a saddle was too excruciating to think about. His ribs would never heal in the saddle. But if he didn't ride, the captain would probably put him in one of the wagons with the sick and wounded, or, like he had said, bring charges against him and have him court-martialed.

The afternoon gave way to evening, the evening to night. Wood was added to the several campfires around the encampment. Slowly the regiment settled into small groups talking quietly around them, most of the men sipping from a tin cup of coffee and a few from bottles they had managed to smuggle in among their things.

The night advanced. Still worried what the morning would bring, gradually Thomas drifted into a fitful sleep.

Eighteen

*T*wo young men's voices were speaking in low tones across the dying embers of a campfire.

". . . trouble ever since I've known him," said one.

"What do you want me to do?" asked the other. "Are you saying you'd be willing to look the other way if I finished what I started out there?"

". . . can't be that obvious . . . better way of taking care of this kind . . ."

"You got a plan?"

". . . just say it won't go too well for him next time we run into the Yankees."

Neither of the two knew that they were not as alone as they thought, or that in the stillness of the night their voices could be heard at the edge of the woods next to the camp only a short distance away.

Thomas awoke abruptly. Something had disturbed him. The sky was pitch black and silent. But smoldering embers remained in the few fires scattered throughout the camp.

He lay still and listened. He sensed a presence close by him . . . a presence of something . . . someone.

Suddenly warm breath disturbed the back of his neck. Almost the same instant warm lips pressed against one of his ears. He started up in fright, but a hand on his shoulder restrained him.

"Massa," whispered a girl's voice so soft he could barely hear it, "you've got to get away."

He tried to turn his head, but again a firm but gentle hand kept him motionless. "Massa," said the girl, "you're in danger. They're going to kill you—tomorrow, they said. I heard them myself. Please, massa, try to get up . . . you've got to get away."

By now Thomas was wide awake. He knew well enough who was speaking into his ear. The girl's speech was unmistakable. But he had no leisure to wonder about it. The important question was what she was doing here! If someone woke up and found a slave girl in the middle of the camp, they would kill her without hesitation. *She* was the one in danger, not him!

He managed to roll partway onto his uninjured side and turn his head. The sentry on duty was nowhere nearby, and thankfully no one was sleeping near him. He peered out of his one unbandaged eye. He could just barely make out the outline of the girl's form against the glow of the dying fire.

"You've got to get out of here!" he whispered frantically. "I don't know what you think you're doing, but if anyone sees you, they'll kill you. What are you doing here?"

"I followed you, massa. After what they did, I was afraid you were hurt or dead. I had to try to help."

"But why . . . why me?"

"Because you saved me, massa," said the girl. "You kept that man from hurting me. I had to help you."

"You're in the middle of a Confederate camp," insisted Thomas. "If they find you, it will be worse than it was out there—for both of us. Go away . . . you've got to go away."

"Not without you, massa. I can't let them kill you, not after what you did for me."

Thomas sighed inaudibly and thought a few seconds. The girl may have been pretty, as he saw again even in the dim light, but she was a stubborn one! He had to get her out of here! They were both in too much danger.

With great effort, and careful not to groan, he struggled from under his blanket and to his knees, then slowly inched away from the fire and his sleeping comrades. He had had to go off to the woods a couple times during the previous day. Hopefully if the sentry happened along and saw his blanket empty he would assume that he was obeying nature's summons and wouldn't go looking for him.

He crept along slowly on his hands and knees for two or three minutes. The ribs on the left side of his chest screamed in pain with the pressure from his hand on the ground. He knew the girl was following beside him, but he heard not a sound. Her step was as stealthy as an Indian's.

When he judged himself far enough away, he stopped and tried to stand. Immediately two hands grasped his and helped gently ease him to his feet.

Thomas turned to face the girl, though he could see nothing of her features.

"Now please, miss," he said, still in a low whisper, "I am grateful for your concern. But I must insist that you get away from here. If they find you, they will do bad things to you, just like they were going to before."

Instead of answering, she merely took one of Thomas's hands and pulled, leading him again away from the camp.

"Come, massa," she said. "Please . . . just a little farther."

Once on his feet, Thomas found that his legs felt fine—better than his head and ribs! Reluctantly he followed. After four or five minutes, again he stopped.

"All right, miss," he said, feeling more determined as he felt himself gradually regain strength, "I will not move another step until you explain what you think you are trying to do."

Still clutching his hand, Thomas could feel the girl begin to relax.

"I followed you, massa," she began. "After I ran away from that man

who tried to hurt me I saw what he did to you. I knew you were hurt
real bad, so I followed. I couldn't stand it when I saw them put you
on that horse and your body slumping over it like you were dead. I
was so afraid they'd killed you because of me. So I followed to see if I
could help you. I watched all that night, and today, and tonight, after
you were asleep—that's when I heard the others talking about you, the
bad man that kicked and beat you. He was talking to one of the others
that was there. I heard them say they were going to kill you. So I had
to get you away."

"What did they say?" asked Thomas, at last sobered by the girl's story.

"They said if they didn't do something, you were sure to cause them
trouble again. They said that the next time there was a battle that they
would look for a chance, when there was fighting everywhere and
nobody saw them, to shoot you and make it look like the Yankees did
it. Then the man who rode up later, somebody they called *sergeant,* he
told him not to worry—that he would make sure you didn't get out of
the battle alive."

Thomas sighed. Cameron Beaumont! Remembering Seth's horror
as he told the family of the terrible night Cameron and Wyatt hung
a runaway, and then shot him, returned vividly to him. He knew
Cameron would have no qualms whatsoever about ordering him
straight into the line of fire . . . or shooting him himself.

Thomas let out another long sigh. He knew Cameron and Travis
Durkin well enough to realize the girl was probably telling the truth.
Who could make up such a story? And *why* would she make it up?

He also knew that after what had happened, he hadn't a single
friend in the whole unit. Captain Young wouldn't believe him or back
him up if he said anything about what he had just heard. Besides,
what could he say—that a slave girl had come to him in the night
telling him of a plot by Travis Durkin and Sergeant Beaumont to kill
him? The captain would laugh in his face.

Even though he had been in several terrible battles, until this
moment he had not faced how close death really might be. Suddenly
the fact was stark and clear—his life was in grave danger.

It did not take long before Thomas began to realize that his options were severely limited—stay where he was and be looking over his shoulder every minute until a bullet found his head . . . or try to escape like the girl said.

"How long have you been watching our camp?" he asked as he tried to think what to do.

"Ever since they brought you back, massa."

"What about your home? Don't you belong somewhere?"

"Master Smith's plantation is where I've been. But I don't belong there."

"What about those other girls you were with out there?"

"They're slaves too, just like me. The mistress sent us out to pick berries. I've only been there a year since I was captured and sold to him."

"Captured . . . what do you mean? Had you run away?"

"Yes, massa. My family ran away, but I got separated from them and captured. Then they sold me. But Master Smith doesn't like me. He's mean to me."

"You are a slave though?"

"Yes, massa. But I'm not supposed to be. My family used to be free, but we got captured and sold."

"And you've been watching our camp all this time?" he said again, "—since the day before yesterday. Have you had anything to eat?"

"No, massa."

"We'll have to get you something. We can't have you fainting this close to camp."

"You're a kind man, massa. Why are you so kind to one like me?"

"Why shouldn't I be? You risked your life for me."

"You risked yours for me first. What made you do that, massa? You're white, I'm a Negro. What did you care what those men did to me?"

"You're a person. They had no right to take advantage of you."

"But now you're in danger."

Thomas nodded. "Yeah, I suppose I am," he said thoughtfully. "Maybe you're right and I need to get out of here . . . but where can

I go? If I'm in danger now, I'd *really* be in for it if I left. What would I do . . . where would I go?"

"I can help you, massa. I can hide you until they're gone."

"Where are you going to hide me? At that plantation you came from?"

"No, not there, massa. Master Smith, he'd shoot you too if he knew you ran away and I was trying to hide you. He's got a son in the army. I only saw him once, but he's like that man that beat you up. He's always looking at girls with those eyes that make you know what he's thinking. Master Smith wouldn't like you one bit. We've got to get north, massa."

"Yeah . . . I suppose you're right," said Thomas. "Why do you call me *massa*?" he added. "I'm not your master."

"I don't know what else to call a white man."

"I'm not a man either. I'm just a kid who went off to fight in this war and is now wondering why. I'm only twenty-one. I suppose some folk would figure I'm a man at twenty-one, but I don't feel much like one right now. Just call me Thomas. That's my name."

"You want me to call you by your Christian name, massa?"

"Of course."

"But you're white."

"That's right, I'm white and my name's Thomas. What's yours?"

"Deanna. I'm eighteen."

"Well, Deanna," said Thomas with a sigh of resignation, "if we're going to get out of here, I had better go back and get some of my things, and my gun and maybe the blanket, and try to get a horse from the corral."

"No, massa Thomas. They'd know you ran away. If you don't take anything, and if your blanket and gun are still there and no horses missing, maybe they'll think you went out into the woods and then got lost or something."

Again Thomas thought for a minute.

"Hmm . . . I see what you mean," he said. "That's good thinking. If I was trying to escape, they'd figure me to take *something*, especially my gun. Maybe I should even leave my hat, though I ought to get my jacket. And you've got to have something to eat. You wait here, I'll sneak back and get what we need."

"No, massa Thomas, please—why can't we just go now?"

"Don't worry, Deanna, I'll be quiet and careful. You've convinced me. I'll come back. You just wait here."

Thomas turned and began making his way back through the trees, his one eye by now sufficiently accustomed to the darkness to keep from making too much noise. Slowly the faint glow of the campfires neared, along with the sounds of snoring and horses in the distance. With great care he found his things, knelt down and felt about for his jacket, leaving everything else as it was. After a few seconds, again he stood and glanced about. If only he could get to the cook's wagon and scoop out a cup of last night's cold beans from the pot. But he couldn't risk it.

With one last look around, hardly pausing to contemplate what a crossroads moment of life these few seconds of decision truly were, again he turned and crept on his toes as noiselessly as he was able away from the camp, this time not to return. He hardly knew whether he was going in exactly the same direction as he had come from, but he knew that Deanna was probably keeping track of his movements and would find *him* again, even if he couldn't find her.

He was not wrong. After three or four minutes, he heard a step and felt a hand reaching for him in the darkness.

"Are you feeling all right, massa Thomas?" whispered the girl's familiar voice. "You ready to get away now?"

"I'm feeling as good as I can expect with broken ribs and bruises all over my face," replied Thomas. "But my legs are okay. Here, I brought you something. It's not much, only a cold biscuit I had left over from last night. But it should keep you from being too famished until we can find some apples or something."

"You're a kind man, massa Thomas," she said, taking the biscuit from his hand. "But we have to get away from here before light."

The two deserters from regiment and plantation, one white, one black, an unlikely partnership in the struggle to stay alive and not get caught, had covered probably two hilly forested miles, though not as the crow flies, before Thomas's regiment began to stir in the light of a damp, chilly dawn. Thomas had known roughly in what direction his regiment would be moving, and though in the darkness his orientation was not entirely to be trusted, he and his young Negro guardian nevertheless bore in more or less an opposite easterly direction. But they had to take great care. Wearing the Confederate gray, encountering a Union regiment would be just as dangerous as if Travis Durkin found them.

"Do you know where we are?" asked Thomas, stopping and looking about.

"Not exactly, massa Thomas," replied Deanna. "But if we can just get to the top of that hill yonder, I think I might be able to tell. Somewhere about here's where the conductor meets folks. At least that's what I picked up from listening when some runaways were caught one time, before they took them away."

Thomas knew well enough what the term *conductor* meant from the clandestine activities at his own home.

"Let's go, then," he said. "It shouldn't take us more than another twenty or thirty minutes. Then we can decide what to do."

The sun was just cresting the eastern hills when they reached the top of the hill, and from its direction and the layout of the hills and valleys around them, they could at last get their bearings.

"That's Master Smith's plantation down there," said Deanna, pointing to the south.

Along the same valley, Thomas saw the thin smoke from two campfires which he took to be the encampment of his regiment. To the west, opposite the valley out of which they had come, lay the range of foothills where he assumed they would be moving next.

"Well," he said, drawing in a deep breath and looking all about, "we didn't make it very far. If they spot us they'll catch us in no time. But at least we know which direction *not* to go. And . . . there's north up that way," he added, glancing over his shoulder. "We're in the Blue Ridge Mountains in northern Georgia or Tennessee or eastern North Carolina somewhere. I'm not sure quite how far we've moved east of Chattanooga. I don't want to go any further south. But I won't be welcome in the North in this uniform either. But that's the only place you will be safe, so I suppose that's the direction we have to go."

"We've got to get back onto that railroad for runaways," said Deanna. "*You* won't be safe otherwise. We can't try to go north all alone. We're sure to be seen and caught. There's bad people everywhere. But there's folks called Friends who help people like us. The conductor would help us find them. Please, massa, let me show you where to go."

Even as she spoke, a wave of lightheadedness and fatigue swept through Thomas's body. He sat down on the ground and tried to recover himself. He was exhausted from the sleepless night's walk and the pain from his chest and head.

"Right now I'm too beat to argue with you," he said with a weary smile. "Let me just rest for a minute or two. Then if you think you can find a safe place for us to stay, you lead the way."

"Not now, massa Thomas. We can't go in the daytime. The Negro railroad sleeps in the day. We've got to find a stream with water to drink and a place to rest. You need sleep, and something to eat. Your face is pale. Then at night we'll keep going and try to get to a station."

Thomas sighed. "You're right," he said. "Suddenly I am so tired I don't know if I can take another step."

⟨⌒⟩

Captain Young did not know that one of his men was missing as they broke camp the following morning. But as they were mounting up, Travis Durkin galloped toward him and reined in.

"What is it, Corporal?" asked Young, returning his salute.

"It's Davidson, Captain," replied Durkin, "—he's gone."

"What do you mean . . . gone?"

"He's not here, sir. His bedroll looks slept in, his horse was with the others, his saddle and gun and hat is lying there beside the blanket. But nobody's seen him."

"Boots?"

"Uh . . . no, his boots ain't there neither."

"Well go find him then. He's probably just out doing his business."

"We combed the woods, sir. I sent out several men. They found a trail for a hundred yards or so, but there weren't no sign of him."

Captain Young thought a minute.

"Have you talked to Sergeant Beaumont?"

"No, sir."

"Look, Corporal," he said at length, "that kid's already caused us enough problems. He's a troublemaker and I do not want him left behind. Now you talk to the sergeant, then take what men you need and you find him. He's out there somewhere. I don't care if you have to drag him back. Just get him. Follow his steps again and don't give up until you know where he went. He can't have got far. He could hardly walk yesterday. He could be hiding somewhere. He was hurt pretty bad and he hasn't eaten much. He may have passed out. You know the direction we're headed. We ought to intercept that unit of Yanks by tomorrow. That'll give you time to catch back up to us. And I want Davidson with you. I just might have him lead the attack tomorrow."

"He ain't gonna be no good with a gun, Captain," said Durkin.

"Then things won't go too well for him, will they? Just get him back here."

"Yes, sir. Uh . . . Captain?"

"Yes, Corporal?"

"You want him alive?"

"I'll leave that up to you, Corporal."

Durkin wheeled his mount around and rode off. Thirty minutes later the regiment pulled out with Thomas Davidson's empty horse. Travis Durkin and four others rode off in the opposite direction.

Nineteen

Veronica Fitzpatrick and Cecil Hirsch returned to Washington from Chicago with Veronica in high spirits. She had more packages than would fit in one buggy!

True, it was a little difficult to settle back into the humdrum of life in the capital. But after all that had happened, she was actually relieved that Richard was away, and would not be back from England for some time. It would give her time to settle on her story about her new wardrobe.

She hardly had time to be bored. Cecil had taken to calling almost every day. The evening they did not dine together was a rarity. Probably people were talking. But she didn't care. Life had not been so full of zest and interest since her marriage. She would settle down again as soon as Richard came home from Europe. She still had no intention of being untrue to him, it just felt so good to *live* again!

She was in Washington to welcome Richard back from Europe. Veronica sensed a difference beween them immediately, but did not recognize that it was because of changes in her not Richard. She did not want him aware of her secret life with Cecil, but had not realized how difficult it would be to keep it from him. Going out of town on a moment's notice was suddenly not so easy anymore.

Richard began to suspect that something was going on, but still had no glimmer of the truth.

Veronica made several more trips to Richmond for Mr. Garabaldi, two with Cecil, and usually brought back a bottle of wine for him. By now she could hardly be unaware that she was delivering more than mere personal greetings, but she did not summon the mental courage to inquire too deeply into the thing. Nor did she read the papers or keep track of the war with sufficient interest to realize that both her activities and Cecil's bore uncanny parallels to places involved in later war activity.

She made three trips down to Fredericksburg in March and April for Mr. Garabaldi, and only connected the nearby battle in Chancellorsville in May with a vague sense of concern that the fighting was taking place so close to Dove's Landing and her former home.

Vicksburg was so far away she hardly took note of it. She had no idea who Ulysses S. Grant might be, though she had heard of Robert E. Lee. Her father had mentioned him once, she thought.

Cecil never spoke of the war. Every two or three weeks he just said he would be gone for a few days. He never told her where he was going or why.

Veronica knew about the terrible fighting in Gettysburg in July. Everybody in Washington was talking about Lee's invasion of the North and whether the war was about to end. As for the dreadful casualties, they struck no more deeply into her than the vague news that circulated after every battle. But later, during a brief visit home in August, when she heard that Brad McClellan and Sally O'Flarity's brother Jack had been killed, something birthed in her heart that she could not get rid of. The very word *Gettysburg* caused her to ache in a way she was unfamiliar with on the high personal cost of this war, and that real people were actually dying. A germ of compassion had been born within her. Only time would tell whether she would nurture it, or allow its faint flicker of life to be extinguished by more pressing concerns.

But as the stakes of Veronica's clandestine activity continued to increase, more than once she thought she was being followed. When she told Cecil about it, he merely laughed it off and said it was part of the game.

What game, Veronica wanted to know.

Cecil brushed off her comment as he had the first, with more laughter and vagueries. The next time she met with Garabaldi, after a delivery, she found $300 in the envelope he had waiting for her rather than her customary payment of $200. The message was clear—she was being renumerated well enough to put up with a few unpleasantries and unanswered questions.

By the time fall came, Veronica was more than a little uncomfortable. She knew she had been followed twice more, and didn't like it.

Denton Beaumont, seeing Veronica upon occasion when she had business with Wyler, by now had his own suspicions. But as long as the Confederacy benefited, he saw no reason to worry anyone about it, though he was concerned for Fitzpatrick, whom he liked. He was not anxious to see Veronica ruin her marriage. But he had problems of his own to worry about.

The Confederate Congress was in shambles. They quarreled amongst themselves, met in secret because they were so unpopular with the people of Richmond, and disliked one another almost as much as they despised Jefferson Davis. There were reports of personal attacks—with every conceivable weapon from inkstand to bowie knife, from umbrella to handgun. The journal clerk of the Confederate House shot and killed the chief clerk. The continual disorder, dissension, and strife prevented any reasonable progress toward democratic nationhood. Though Davis had obvious faults, the task before him was daunting—trying to win a war and at the same time forge a nation out of eleven suspicious, bickering states where the tiniest move toward compromise was seen as paying homage to that holy grail of the Confederacy—states' rights. Money was printed almost randomly until the simplest things cost hundreds of dollars, with prices doubling weekly. And then, because Confederate money was so valueless, farmers and plantation owners were taxed one tenth of their produce to sustain the war effort. Looting and rioting was beginning to break out in some Southern cities for lack of food.

It was hardly any wonder Denton Beaumont had other things on his mind than his daughter.

Twenty

*W*hen Thomas Davidson awoke, the sun was high in the sky and he was alone.

He came to himself gradually, remembered what had happened, then sat up and looked around. He was sitting at the trunk of a large oak twenty or thirty feet up the bank from a small stream. He was still trying to orient himself to his surroundings when he heard a sound behind him.

He turned and saw Deanna hurrying toward him from up the hill.

"Here's some apples, massa Thomas," she said, kneeling and opening a fold in her dress she had been using as a pocket. A dozen or more green and yellow apples tumbled onto the ground.

"Where did you get these?" exclaimed Thomas, grabbing one, wiping it off briefly, and biting off a juicy chunk.

"From the plantation. I know it's not much of a breakfast for you, but it's something to put in your stomach."

"You went back to your own plantation . . . in the middle of the day! What if they'd seen you?"

"I was careful," replied Deanna. "I was worried about the dogs getting a whiff of me. But I know where they store the apples and I kept downwind."

"What about you—come on, have some," said Thomas, tossing away the core of one apple and grabbing another. "You're hungrier than me."

"I ate four or five when I was there so I could carry more for you. And look—I found us a chunk of dried venison from the smokehouse."

She now took a long thin slab of brown meat from somewhere else in her dress and handed it to Thomas.

"It's a feast!" exclaimed Thomas, chomping down on one end and gnawing off a sizeable piece. "Good for you, Deanna! Here, you have some too."

She took it from him and bit off a more modest portion. They sat a few moments in silence as they munched on the tough deer meat.

"What now?" said Thomas. "I feel better already. Are you ready to get moving to wherever we're going?"

"You were so exhausted a couple hours ago you could hardly stand up," replied Deanna. "I think you need to rest. And we're still so close to the plantation, I don't want to take any chances of being seen."

"Will your master go looking for you?"

"I don't know, but if he knew I was so close, he'd try to get his hands on me, if only to give me a good whipping."

Thomas looked at her with a strange expression. "Do they really whip girls like you?" he asked.

"Every chance they get," answered Deanna. "I watched my papa almost killed from a whipping once. What kind of a question is that, massa Thomas? You're from the South. Have you never seen slaves whipped before? They must have had slaves where you came from."

Thomas's lips formed a thin pensive smile. "I came from an unusual kind of place, I suppose you'd say," he said.

"I just hope we can find a conductor and then follow the railroad to the place with the wind in the horse's head—that's what they sometimes call the stations."

Again, Deanna's words jolted into Thomas's ears with unexpected familiarity.

"Uh . . . where did runaways meet this . . . the conductor?" he asked.

"Beneath a bridge over a river," replied Deanna. "I don't know where it is, but that's what I heard. I know there's a river somewhere around here because I've heard the people at the plantation talk about it."

"We marched across a good-sized bridge several days ago," nodded Thomas. "I think I could find it again. But how does a conductor know when to meet slaves that are on the run?"

"I don't know. Somehow they know when folks are coming."

"They won't know *we're* coming," said Thomas.

"All we can do is find that bridge and then see what comes next. My daddy always says that when you don't know what to do, you've got to take the next step the Lord shows you before he can show you the step you're supposed to take after that. He says the Lord always works one thing at a time, not five things at a time."

It was just like something *his* dad would say, thought Thomas. A surge of nostalgic fondness swept through him.

He did not have time to reflect on it. Suddenly the sound of horses' hooves broke the stillness of late morning. By the sound of it, whoever the riders were, they were a hundred or hundred and fifty yards away, and coming toward them!

Thomas and Deanna glanced at each other. Deanna jumped to her feet. Thomas struggled to get up. Forgetting his wounds, he winced in pain. Deanna reached down, took his two hands, and helped him to his feet.

"This way, massa Thomas," she said. "We can hide on the other side of the stream."

He hurried after her, clutching her hand for support. They splashed through the water, up the opposite bank, through some brush, until suddenly Deanna knelt down, pulling Thomas after her.

"How'd you know where to hide?" said Thomas.

"I looked around before, when you were asleep. That's something we always did when my daddy was leading us—we always kept our eyes out for places to hide, just in case something happened. He taught us always to plan ahead . . . but shush! They're coming! Get down and keep real still."

Already they could hear several voices now along with the horses.

In another few seconds the riders reined in, by the sound of it not far from the oak where they had just been sitting.

"Look, here's some apples," said a voice Thomas recognized instantly. "You was right, Travis—he's making for that plantation down yonder, likely where that nigger girl is."

"Yeah, I thought as much," said Durkin. "Where else he gonna go? He probably figures she'll help him."

"Must have been following the stream," said another voice. "These apples are fresh. We can't be far behind him."

"What if he's not going to the plantation, Travis? Maybe he's going the other way."

It was silent as Durkin thought a minute.

"Yeah . . . all right, we better split up," he said. "Max, you and Shorty follow the stream up a ways further. Me and Clint, we'll go have us a talk with the farmer, see if he's seen him and make sure he knows to keep an eye out. Maybe we'll get some of his dogs to help us. If you don't see nothing after a mile, then come back and we'll meet somewhere along the stream or between here and the plantation. If you find him, give a shot in the air. But don't hurt him, you hear. I got a slug in my gun that's meant for him. I don't want no one spoiling my fun. Okay, let's go."

The horses galloped off in both directions. After a few minutes again they were left in silence.

"How did they get on our trail so fast?" sighed Thomas.

"We haven't gone that far, massa Thomas. They've got horses too. If they bring some of massa Smith's hounds, they'll sniff us out for sure. We've got to go, massa Thomas. We've got to move fast, and we've got to find that river. Even hound dogs can't follow us across a river."

She jumped to her feet and again helped Thomas up.

"Nothing else we can do but follow the stream down the hill and hope it leads us to the river."

"That's toward the plantation," said Thomas.

"How else are we going to find the river?"

"Let's keep climbing," suggested Thomas. Harper's Peak had

suddenly come to his mind. "If we get high enough, in this sunlight, we'll be able to see the river somewhere, with the sun glistening off it. I'm sure it's to the north."

"All right, massa Thomas. But let's get going. . . . I'm afraid of massa Smith's dogs."

By the time Thomas and Deanna reached the Hiwasee River midway through the afternoon, the lack of food, as well as fatigue from the pain of his wounds, were taking their toll on Thomas's energy. His face was pale and Deanna knew he could not keep up the pace much longer. But the unmistakable baying of dogs in the distance behind them kept urging them on.

Deanna ran the final few yards down the gently sloping bank, half dragging Thomas behind her, then stopped at the water's edge. She glanced up and down the flowing current with a sinking feeling of despair. It was not a rapid river, but was wide and moving steadily. She wasn't sure whether she could swim to the opposite bank herself. But in his weakened condition and without the full strength of his arms, she knew Thomas could not make it even halfway across.

She could not prevent a groan of hopelessness as she glanced for the twentieth time behind them. There could be no mistake—the dogs were louder than they had been only a few minutes before. They were obviously on the scent.

"Come, massa Thomas," she implored, though Thomas hardly heard her. "We've got to keep moving. We'll go along at the edge in the water—maybe that will throw them off."

"Effen you's tryin' ter git away from dem dere dogs," suddenly said a voice from the bank above them, "you ain't gwine do hit like dat."

Deanna spun around and looked toward it. Above them, as if he had been watching calmly for some time, stood a lanky black man who appeared to be in his mid-forties. She stared up at him with a blank expression, so surprised that for a moment she could not find her voice.

"Wiff you stirrin' up dat mud like dat," the man went on, beginning to chuckle, "hit don't take no houn' dog ter foller yo track. Laws almighty, a blin' man cud foller you!"

"Well what would you do if you were us?" snapped Deanna, a little annoyed at his manner. "We know we're in trouble and you standing there laughing at us doesn't do us any good."

"What kind er trubble you in?"

"Those hound dogs are chasing us, what do you think! We're runaways, and those men back there are trying to catch us."

"Den wha'chu doin' talkin' like er white girl? An' why's you wiff a white soldier? Dis look like sum kind er unushul situashun ter me."

"Well maybe it is, but you're not doing anything for us—do you know where the bridge is? We've got to get to the bridge."

"You's neber make da bridge. Dem dogs'll interecep' you long before dat."

"Then we'll just have to keep running. Come on, massa Thomas," said Deanna, again urging Thomas forward along the bank through the shallow water. "We have to go. We've got to find that conductor before those dogs find us."

On the bank, the man watched as they struggled to continue, slowly shaking his head. He was more convinced than ever that they would never make it alone. He had been watching them for the last ten minutes, trying to figure out just who they were and what they were up to. He was still not entirely sure. They were in trouble, that was clear enough. But to help a Confederate soldier, even if he was a runaway, went against everything the railroad stood for.

He continued to watch, thinking hard. If he made the wrong decision, it would put many people in danger. If he did nothing, they were sure to be caught. He sighed and shook his head. Sometimes you had to go with your instinct and trust that things would turn out for the best.

Finally he hurried down the bank toward the river after the two fugitives.

"Wait . . . jest hol' up dere a minute," he called after them.

Deanna stopped and turned, though she was in no mood for more small talk.

"What is it now?" she said.

"Jes' what I tol' you before—you'll never make it dat way. Dey'll cotch you. If you want ter git ter da bridge, dere's only one way. You gots ter swim for it. Can you swim, girl?"

"I can swim."

"Den foller me. You get on one side ob dis boy an' I'll take da other, an' we'll git him right on across."

He took Thomas's hand, though his grip was weak, and led him straight into the current.

"Come on, we can do it," he said. "I knows dis river like da back ob my han'. Dere's nuhin' ter be feared ob—we'll jes' flow wif da current. Even if dey see us dere won't be nuthin' dey can do, cause we'll be long gone in a few minutes."

Hardly knowing what to think of the strange man, but offering no objection, Deanna held on to Thomas's other arm as they eased their way forward and slowly gave themselves to the current. The black man proved to be a powerful swimmer. He moved them straight out into the middle, working his way across even as he allowed the current to take them along with it. Within minutes they were moving rapidly.

It took twenty minutes to navigate the crossing. Even as they felt the water begin to slow and the opposite bank draw near, Deanna looked up to see that they were approaching a bridge spanning the river they had just swum across.

"Dere it is," said the black man. "Now you two keep floatin' right on down till you're directly under it, den carefully git out, makin' as little mess on the bank as you can, an' sneak up underneath an' wait dere."

"Wait for what?"

"For who you's expectin'—your conductor."

"How do you know about our conductor?"

"I know a lot ob things, miss."

"Who are you, anyway?"

"I'm da conductor on dis side. But don't worry, you'll be met. Someone'll come fer you under da bridge. An' dere's some other folks dere too. I jes' lef' dem off an hour ago. Dat's when I ran into you. You'll have ter explain 'bout da soldier boy. Dey'll be afraid when dey sees him. But tell dem I said dey could trus' you. An' you stay real quiet. I've got ter git back now where dey'll be able ter see me directly across when dey get ter da river an' make a mess an' a fuss an' give dose men who were after you somebody ter follow. Dey'll still likely use da bridge, so if you hear dem keep real still. If I don't lead dem off someplace else dey's sure ter come over ter dis side tryin' ter pick up da trail. Don't worry, I'll lead dem where dey'll never see you two again."

Still bewildered at the sudden turn of events, Deanna watched the black man climb out of the water and up the bank and upriver.

"Thank you, mister," she called after him.

The water of the river had somewhat revived him, but Thomas was still weak and could hardly keep to his feet as they struggled out of the water under the bridge.

"Who was that man?" he asked.

"I don't know," replied Deanna. "A black man from the other side of the river. He said he was a conductor. Come, massa Thomas," she said, tugging Thomas behind her up the bank. Their water-soaked clothes made it all the more difficult to move. As they made their way, Deanna glanced up and saw two figures seated in the shadows. As they drew closer, she saw that two men were watching them—an older man about forty and a young man perhaps half that.

They collapsed on the sloping grass beneath where the timbers of the bridge met the ground. Thomas groaned in pain.

"Wha'chu doin' comin' here?" said the older man. "An' who dat white boy!"

"Look, Papa," said the younger. "He's a soldier!"

"Laws, girl—you tryin' ter git us all caught an' killed?"

"We're just trying to get away, same as you," said Deanna. "The same conductor man that brought you here just met us up the river and told us where to come."

"What 'bout him?" said the man, looking at Thomas.

"It's him they're looking for," replied Deanna.

"Den let dem have him! Leastways den dey wudn't find us."

"I'm not going to do that," said Deanna. "He's hurt bad and I'm not about to let them get their hands on him."

Within minutes, in spite of the wet, Thomas was to all appearances sound asleep. The rest of the small group fell silent and waited. The man and his son continued to eye the newcomers with suspicion.

It was not much longer before they again heard the dogs and shouts and horses' hooves.

"Look wha'chu dun!" exclaimed the man. "You brung dem right to us! Now we's all dun for."

Deanna did not reply but held her breath and put a finger to her lips as she heard their pursuers coming closer and closer. A minute or two later, the four soldiers from Thomas's unit thundered over the bridge overhead, followed by the dogs and several men from the Smith plantation. In their haste to hurry back upriver and pick up the trail at the point where they had seen the black man climbing up the bank opposite them, they did not stop to search the area around the bridge. The dogs, too, went howling straight over the top of them, so intent to keep pace with the four horses and so excited by the chase and with the multitude of smells from the river in their noses that they did not so much as slow down.

As quickly as they had come, the sounds of the chase soon died away in the distance and the four unlikely fugitives were left alone beneath the bridge.

The hours passed slowly under the bridge. Thomas dozed fitfully. Deanna tried to make him as comfortable as possible though on the uneven ground and in wet clothes, and with nothing to eat, there was little she could do. Wherever the black man had led their pursuers, they heard nothing from them again.

As evening began to descend, suddenly a voice sounded above them.

"Dere be any travelers down under dere dat's needin' ter be gettin' on ter da nex' stashun?"

Deanna looked up to see a black face leaning over the side of the bridge.

"Dat dere is," said the man. "You be da conductor sent fer us?"

"Dat I is. How many ob you is dere?"

"Dere's suppozed ter be two, but dere's four," said the man. "We got us a Confederate soldier boy here dat don' belong on da railroad nohow."

The conductor now walked down the slope and around to where three of his passengers stood waiting. Behind them he saw Thomas lying on the ground.

"What dis all about?" he asked.

"He's with me," said Deanna. "We were trying to get away and a man met us who said he was the conductor on the other side. He told us where to come and said to tell you that you could trust us."

The man eyed her a moment.

"You hab a strange tongue," he said. "Where you from, girl?"

"My family and I were slaves in North Carolina. But before that we came from up north. We got captured and sold to a man in North Carolina. We were escaping a year ago but I fell off my horse and got captured and was sold again."

The man took in Deanna's story and nodded slowly. "What 'bout dis here white boy?"

"He saved me from some bad white men, and then they were going to kill him. They beat him and hurt him real bad, so I helped him get away. Please, Mister Conductor, he's a good boy, but I'm afraid for him. He needs help."

The man thought a moment more, then drew in a deep breath.

"All right, den, all ob you—let's go. Foller me. Help da boy to his feet, miss," he said to Deanna. "You's gwine hab ter make sure he keeps up 'cause we gots a long way ter go."

The long night passed like a blur to Deanna. For Thomas it was like a waking dream of which he could remember nothing. When he finally staggered into the dry barn of their destination two or three hours before dawn, it was all he could do to make it to the pile of straw across the floor before collapsing unconscious in a heap. Deanna lay down next to him while the father and son made themselves comfortable some yards away. The conductor disappeared.

Five minutes later, the creaking hinges of a door opened again. A tall white woman walked in holding a lantern. She was followed by a girl of twelve or thirteen who carried a tray laden with food and cups of water. Deanna wasted no time emptying one of the cups and attacking the bread and cheese with ravenous hunger. Then as the women took the tray to the father and son, she knelt at Thomas's side, placed an arm under his shoulder and tried to raise him and put a cup to his lips. But she could hardly succeed in getting him to come to himself enough even to sip at it.

"You poor dear," said the woman. "How long has it been since you've eaten?"

"We had some apples yesterday," replied Deanna, "and before that it was a day or two. This tastes better than anything I've eaten in my life! Thank you, ma'am. But I'm worried about massa Thomas. He's so weak and hurt—I can't even get him to drink this cup of water."

The woman knelt down on Thomas's other side. Now that she looked at him more closely she saw how pale his face was. She reached a hand to his forehead.

"Lord have mercy!" she exclaimed. "The lad's burning with fever."

She stood. "I'll be back in a minute or two with a wet washrag," she said. "We'll try to cool him down. We have to get some water into him, and get him out of those wet clothes."

While the father and son ate and drank in silence, Deanna continued to try to get something into Thomas's mouth.

"Please, massa Thomas," she said, "you've got to drink this water so you don't get sick. We're safe now. We got to the station and there's a nice lady who's going to help us. But you've got to drink, massa Thomas. You're too hot. You've got to drink."

A feeble smile broke over Thomas's parched lips. He reached up and touched Deanna's hand holding the cup and eased it to his lips. He managed to take two or three swallows before falling back again on the straw, too weak to sit.

⁓

When Travis Durkin and his three comrades caught back up with their regiment, Durkin went immediately to find Captain Young.

"We lost him, Captain," said Durkin, riding up alongside.

"What happened?"

"We got onto his trail, and we was close. He crossed the river and we followed him up the other side. We had dogs from one of the plantations and thought they was closing in. But them stupid mutts lost the trail. Before we knew it those fools was leading us back across the river, upstream across a narrow ford. We figured Davidson had crossed back. By then all we was doing was going around in circles. There weren't nothing to do but give up. I don't know where he got to, Captain, unless he's hiding out in one of the farms round about. You want us to start searching them tomorrow?"

Young thought a moment.

"No," he said at length. "I need you with the regiment. Besides, Davidson's not worth it. We haven't lost much. But I don't want a deserter on my record. So you tell your boys to spread it around that you found him fallen off a cliff in the woods and you buried him right there. He went out in the night for his business, and with his wounds he stumbled and fell in the darkness and that was that. You got that, Corporal?"

"Yes, sir, Captain. I'll tell the boys."

Durkin wheeled his mount around and went back to join the others.

Twenty-One

The last letter to arrive at Greenwood from Thomas had been so full of despair that Carolyn was almost afraid to open the one that arrived midway through the month of October, 1863. She longed daily for some word from her son. Yet her mother's heart ached with grief for the loneliness she knew he felt.

She stared at the envelope for some time until it gradually dawned on her that the handwriting on it was not Thomas's. Nor had Thomas ever addressed a letter with the impersonal inscription: "Mr. and Mrs. Davidson."

A premonition seized her. She hesitated no longer but tore the envelope apart. With trembling fingers, she yanked out the single sheet inside and unfolded it.

Dear Mr. and Mrs. Davidson, she read,
> *I don't know whether Thomas told you or not, but he and I have both been serving in the same regiment of Gen. Bragg's army in Tennessee. Thomas was wounded pretty bad after the battle at Chickamauga last month. And during his recuperation, I regret to have to inform you, that he suffered a bad fall near where we were camped and did not recover. I speak for our captain, Capt. Young,*

and for the entire regiment, when I tell you that we are sorry for your loss. I told the captain that I knew you and would write to inform you of Thomas's death.

I am,

Sincerely yours,
 Sgt. Cameron Beaumont.

Twenty-Two

*D*uring the week between November 19–25 of 1863, two events took place at opposite ends of the Union and the Confederacy. The one seemed so significant, the other insignificant even in the eyes and ears of those who witnessed it.

At Chattanooga, with Ulysses Grant now in charge of federal forces, the Union reversed their loss at Chickamauga, and in another great victory for Grant, the Union now controlled the entire Tennessee and Mississippi river valleys. Atlanta was now in reach as Union forces in the West began inexorably to extend their control of the Confederacy eastward.

Of far less note that week in the eyes of the nation was President Lincoln's trip to Gettysburg to speak a few words. He was billed as the second on the ticket to featured speaker Edward Everett, former governor of Massachusetts, at the dedication of a new Union cemetery at the scene of the horrific battle from five months earlier.

Everett spoke for two hours. At last Lincoln rose.

"Fourscore and seven years ago," he began, "our fathers brought forth on this continent a new nation, conceived in liberty, and dedicated to the proposition that all men are created equal.

"Now we are engaged in a great civil war, testing whether that nation, or any nation so conceived and so dedicated, can long endure. We are met on a great battlefield of that war. We have come to dedicate a portion of that field as a final resting place for those who here gave their lives that that nation might live. It is altogether fitting and proper than we should do this.

"But in a larger sense, we can not dedicate—we can not consecrate—we can not hallow—this ground. The brave men, living and dead, who struggled here, have consecrated it, far above our poor power to add or detract. The world will little note, nor long remember, what we say here, but it can never forget what they did here. It is for us the living, rather, to be dedicated here to the unfinished work which they who fought here have thus far so nobly advanced. It is rather for us to be here dedicated to the great task remaining before us—that from these honored dead we take increased devotion to that cause for which they gave the last full measure of devotion—that we here highly resolve that these dead shall not have died in vain—that this nation, under God, shall have a new birth of freedom—and that the government of the people, by the people, for the people, shall not perish from the earth."

PART FOUR

BEGINNING OF HEALING
January-September, 1864

Twenty-Three

$\mathcal{S}$eth Davidson was no soldier. The captain of the regiment to which he had been assigned had tried to give him a gun to carry but he had refused it. He would rather be killed than kill.

Neither was he a medic. The sight of blood sickened him as much as the thought of carrying a gun.

But he could take photographs. He had learned his craft and was good at it. His editor, who sponsored and paid for his efforts, the *Boston Herald*'s Adrian McClarin, and the photographer who had trained him, Mr. Phillips, both said that he had a "cameraman's eye" and knew how to capture on film the undefined essence that made this new medium unique. He was both artist and reporter. A *silent* reporter. He told stories without words. He had to point his camera in such a way that it could tell the story within the story, bringing out the emotion and pathos and heartache of the war. He wanted people to *feel* something when they looked at his photographs. Thus, photography had become for him far more than merely capturing images on film. He sought to capture the *meaning* those images had to convey.

Seth began setting up his tripod as he had hundreds of times before. The fighting in and around the strategic Southern city of Chattanooga was in its second day. What everyone in the South had expected to be a turning point for the Confederacy was on its way to becoming yet one more victory for Union General Ulysses Grant.

Seth could just see the general in the distance astride his horse
about half a mile away. It was not his habit to photograph action.
He had learned from experience that the movement was too rapid
for his lens to stop sufficiently to get a decent picture. But he didn't
think there had yet been a photograph of Grant in battle. If he could
preserve this moment on film, it would be historic.

At last everything was ready. Seth lifted the black cloth hood and
ducked under to make his final adjustments. Yes . . . Grant was still
there . . . and not moving too fast. If he could just—

The deafening explosion of an artillery shell sounded close beside
him.

He cried out as the blast threw him sprawling backward on the
ground several feet away. Thinking at first he had been wounded, Seth
struggled to his knees and felt about his legs and arms.

He seemed to be all in one piece. He felt no pain. Then he remembered his equipment!

He looked back to where he had been standing. The tripod and
hood and camera were strewn all over the ground. But a second blast
knocked him flat again. This time when he picked himself up and
looked about through the dull haze of smoke and several nearby fires,
he heard yelling and men crying out for help.

He struggled again to his knees. Medics were running toward the
scene from the medical wagons back behind the fighting where he had
his own supplies.

Seth managed to stand. He walked toward what was left of his
camera. Thirty feet beyond a man lay moaning. Seth tried to walk,
then, as his strength returned, ran toward him and stooped down.

"Where are you hurt?" he said.

"Are you kidding!" groaned the man. "I feel like my leg's blown off!"

"You've still got them both," said Seth. "Come on, let's get you out
of here."

He slipped his hands under the man's shoulders and legs and lifted
him off the ground.

With the man in his arms, Seth staggered back the way he had come, but had only managed to take a few steps when the whine of another shell screamed past them. He heard a thud almost at the very spot where the man had been lying.

"Run, kid!" cried the man. "Run before it goes!"

Seth stumbled on. But the man was heavy and his own legs were still wobbly.

He managed to get back to where he had been standing before the shell suddenly exploded behind them, throwing both again to the ground. When the echo died away, once more Seth picked himself up and hurried back to the soldier. He slipped as he went and fell in a wet patch, again picked himself off the ground then lifted the wounded man once again and struggled toward the medical wagons, stepping over bodies as he went, artillery exploding and whining through the air everywhere. When they were out of the range of fire, at last he set the man down beside one of the wagons.

A medic thanked him and took charge of the man.

"Guess I'll get this mud cleaned off, then go see about my camera," said Seth.

"What mud?" said the medic. "What you slipped in back there wasn't mud."

Seth glanced down. The entire front of his shirt and trousers were covered with blood.

"I wouldn't go back for that camera of yours just yet," added the medic. "Not until the fighting shifts. But you saved this man's life. That's pretty good work for one day, even if you got no photographs."

Seth stumbled away, repulsed to see the blood of another man all over him.

After Chattanooga, though there was little fighting throughout the winter, McClarin had wanted him to travel through the western states where Grant had subdued the western armies of the Confederacy, and down the Mississippi. Seth visited and photographed Shiloh, then Memphis and Vicksburg and then traveled down to New Orleans. He would much rather have gone home. But for now, McClarin was his boss.

All this would not last forever, he told himself. As the first few months of 1864 passed, he hoped that maybe this would finally be the year it would all come to an end.

As much as he loved photography and was grateful to Mr. McClarin, he hated this war.

Twenty-Four

One fine afternoon in March of 1864, Carolyn Davidson bounced along the road to Dove's Landing in a solitary buggy. Cynthia and Cherity had both offered to accompany her, but she needed some time alone. Since the arrival of Cameron's letter, the entire Greenwood community had grieved, each in his own way. But no matter what happened, the women looked to her and the men looked to Richmond for strength. Right now, however, she didn't want to be strong. She wanted to be weak, vulnerable, confused, angry, hurt. She didn't want anyone watching her. No, she didn't want to have to be strong, because she *wasn't* strong.

Still . . . life continued on.

It always did. The best—indeed, the only—way to move beyond grief, was simply to continue on. To do what God set before you to do.

Though several months had passed, the grief continued to come and go in unexpected waves. A good week or two . . . then more tears and heartache. How long would it be before she got used to it?

The needs of the household did not stop, even for a tragedy. Just yesterday Nancy brought word that one of the black women in town was sick.

As Carolyn rode into Dove's Landing, she carried a list for supplies, and a basket of provisions for Mrs. Thomkins. She intended to call on

the invalid first, drop off a jug of soup and loaf of fresh bread, then
continue to Baker's Mercantile to pick up what they needed from
Mrs. Baker. It was a relief to get away. And a relief to know that Mrs.
Thomkins knew nothing about Thomas.

The day was warm and pleasant. By the time she reached the
Thomkins's shack at the edge of town, Carolyn had managed to push
away at least some of the sorrow of the last few days and summon a
smile to her lips.

After a brief visit with Mrs. Thomkins, Carolyn climbed back in the
buggy and continued into town. But Delaware Thomkins's words still
rang in her ears.

"Dis be a turrible, turrible war," the old woman had said. "How
long it gwine last? How much mo' bloodshed duz dere hab ter be?
It's a turrible war! Too many boys dyin' . . . too many boys!"

A tear fell down Carolyn's cheek. So many days, so many long
nights she had prayed and cried and worried over Seth and Thomas.
Now her youngest was gone.

"Why, Lord?" she whispered silently.

She rode up to Mrs. Baker's store, climbed down from the buggy,
and walked inside. As she greeted Mrs. Baker and began to fill her list
from about the shop, she thought she detected a cool response from
the shopkeeper. Finally Mrs. Baker walked toward her with an embarrassed look on her face.

"Mrs., uh . . . Mrs. Davidson," she said timidly.

"Yes, Mrs. Baker," replied Carolyn.

"I . . . uh, do not want to have to . . . but, well—it is just that . . .
I hope you understand, but I simply cannot extend you further credit,
without some payment on the Greenwood account."

"Oh . . . oh, I see," said Carolyn in surprise. "Yes . . . I realize we are
somewhat behind in our payments. I am sorry, Mrs. Baker. You know
how it is through the winter."

"Yes, of course, Mrs. Davidson, but . . . the account is higher than
usual."

"Why don't you give me the balance, Mrs. Baker."

"I happen to have checked on it when you came in. It . . . amounts to $163, Mrs. Davidson."

"Goodness, that high! I am sorry—I had no idea. I will talk to Richmond this afternoon and see what we can to do settle the account."

"I couldn't help overhearing, Mrs. Davidson," said another woman in the shop, now walking up to Carolyn.

"Oh . . . hello, Mrs. Stretton," said Carolyn.

"Things are bad everywhere," the lady went on. "I heard that half the McClellans' slaves are gone."

"They are not the only ones," said another woman, walking over to join them, Mrs. Perkins, wife of the bank manager. "Dozens of loans all around town are behind . . . but you heard nothing from me!"

"It is a shame what this war has done to Virginia," added Mrs. Stretton.

"It will be over soon," Mrs. Perkins went on. "Then everything will return to normal."

"Will it?" said Carolyn with a sad smile. "I don't know, Mrs. Perkins . . . I hope you are right."

"Of course it will. Once the men are home they will put the Negroes in their place. When do you expect your boys home, Mrs. Davidson?"

The abrupt question took Carolyn surprise.

"I, uh . . . I am not certain," she said. "But . . . Thomas will not be coming home."

She burst into tears and ran from the store, leaving the three women staring after her.

Two days later, the blacks of the community came to Greenwood for Sunday service as was their custom. Since the war they had taken to meeting in the largest of Greenwood's barns and no longer tried to keep the unofficial church secret. Everything was changed. No one was worried about being arrested for teaching or preaching to blacks, or holding public gatherings with slaves, or *former* slaves, depending on one's point of view. If anyone wanted to arrest her, Carolyn said, let them. She still regularly urged Richmond to take over leadership of the small black congregation. But he continued to insist that it was a unique ministry to the women that God had given to her, not him.

After several hymns, Carolyn stood to face the fifteen or eighteen women and handful of men. On this particular Sunday, Richmond, Cynthia, and Cherity had gone into Dove's Landing for the services there.

"Good morning, ladies and you men who have come," she said, trying to put on a smile and remind herself that all of these dear ones had suffered loss too. Nancy Shaw had lost a husband. To have been a slave in this country meant you lost loved ones. Her loss of a son was no more tragic than the great tragedy of slavery, or of this terrible war. Tens of thousands of mothers just like her were weeping for the sons they would never see again.

"This is a day," Carolyn went on, Bible in her hand, "when it may be difficult for some of us to remind ourselves of all the Lord has done for us. But to help us remember that even in the darkest hours of life, God is always beside us and watching over us, I want to read to you the story of the Israelites and about something that happened to them in the desert when—"

She stopped and turned away. Hot tears stung her eyes. Again a great wave of fresh unplanned grief suddenly poured over her. She tried to regain her composure, but it was no use. The tears would not stop.

She sat down on the nearest bale of straw and buried her face in her hands.

The barn grew silent

After thirty or forty seconds, Nancy Shaw rose and walked forward. Old Mary got up and followed her.

Carolyn felt a gentle hand on her shoulder, then another. Gradually the two black women were followed by others who gathered around her. She was no longer white and they black. She was no longer the wife of their former master. She was no longer their unofficial pastor.

She was a woman, as they were women. They were all women together. When one of their hearts ached, they ached as one.

"Miz Dab'son," said Nancy, "it's gwine be all right. Dat's what you's always tellin' us, dat da Lord's good, dat he takes care er his chilluns."

At last Carolyn looked up. She saw six or eight black faces in a circle around her. She wiped her eyes and forced a smile.

"I know," she said softly. "You're right, Nancy."

"Dat's gotta be good fo' you too, jes' like fo' us," now said Mary. "He's got massa Thomas in his heart too."

She paused a moment, then Carolyn was surprised to hear her break out in prayer.

"Dear Lawd," prayed Mary, "we's ax dat you'd comfort our dear Miz Dab'son an' her man an' da res' ob dere family at dis time er grief an' tribulashun. She's taught us all 'bout you an' how you takes care ob folks like us, an' now it's her dat's needin' sum takin' care ob."

"Amen!" said several of the ladies.

"So, Lawd," Mary went on, "ef you's dat good Father like she tells us, den she's needin' fo' you ter show her sum ob dat compashun right now, 'cause dis be sum sore trial an' dey needs you mo' den eber afore."

Carolyn looked up into Mary's face.

"Oh, Mary, thank you for that lovely prayer!" she said. "I know God is good. But it hurts to lose a son!"

"Ain't no mo' den what God dun," rejoined Mary. "He los' a son too."

When Richmond returned from town he found Carolyn facedown on their bed. He sat beside her and laid a gentle hand on her back. She wept again for a minute or two, then turned toward him. She drew in a deep sigh, then told him what had taken place earlier.

"Mary, the dear!" said Carolyn. "The dear woman! Everything I've been trying to teach these humble folk all these years about God's goodness . . . and they prayed for me! More has been getting through than I realized."

Again Carolyn let out a long sigh.

"Oh . . . but, Richmond, it is hard to practice what you preach!" she said. "Our poor blacks have suffered in life far more than we can imagine. And I tell them that God is good. Now it is my turn to find out whether I believe it or not."

"And do you?"

"Of course. But even God's goodness doesn't make the pain go away. It just means that there is a goodness in the universe that lies deeper than the world's pain."

"And sometimes it is suffering that enables us to see the goodness."

"If we know where to look," added Carolyn with a sigh. "Perhaps I need to look a little harder."

The next letter to arrive at Greenwood was more welcome than the last they had received from the battlefront. Though its news was not so shattering, it yet brought tears to the eyes of its Greenwood readers.

Dear Mother, Father, Cherity, and Cynthia, Seth began.

As is often the case, I sit down to write as a way to forget the dreadful sights with which my days are filled. In this small way I can be with you for a while in the midst of my aloneness. Not a moment goes by that I do not think of you. Yet sometimes writing is so painful it increases the loneliness all the more. The mere act of sitting down to a blank page can be almost too overwhelming. I miss you all so much that it is easier not even to try. This war wears me down every day. All I can do at day's end is lie down in a cot in a tent or perhaps, if I am lucky, occasionally in a real bed, and try to sleep. Sleep is the only remedy for the horror.

The battles are indescribable to one who has not been there. How much more terrifying to be in the very midst of it, with gunfire and confusion and yelling and explosions all around. At least I am able to sit on a hill somewhat removed from it all and watch from a distance. But once the smoke and gunfire die away, it is we photographers, along with the medics and nurses, who see the horrors of what is left behind—the bodies strewn everywhere, creeks and streams running red with blood, overturned wagons and carts, horses bloating because there are too many human casualties to worry about the animals. The one thing the camera lens cannot capture is the horrible stench of death after days of battle.

I was at Gettysburg and when it was over there were so many bodies that I could hardly walk ten paces without having to step over a dead boy no older than myself, bodies leaning against fences or on the slope of a hill, gray pale faces leering in grotesque silence at any who passed by. I always think that they are all boys like me, with families who probably do not even yet know that they are dead, families who will forever feel the pain of a loss that seems to me so senseless. The longer this war goes on, rather than grow in significance, it means less and less. Does anyone in the Confederacy actually still think it is worth it?

I have photographed a boy with no arms, a man with no legs, a prisoner of war so malnourished he more resembled a skeleton. Many are the times I have turned away from my camera and wept inside, sometimes shedding tears, for the sights I have seen. They are images that will never leave my mind. Though every day I long to forget what I have seen, I also hope I will not forget. No one should ever forget the terrible cost in human suffering of war.

Yesterday I visited a field hospital. As I made my way through the rows of wounded, visiting some of the men, asking where they were from, suddenly the most horrifying shriek erupted, though the men lying nearby hardly flinched. What was that, I asked. Just another leg being amputated, someone told me. That kind of screaming goes on all day. It's the lucky ones who have whatever they're going to lose blown off in battle. That way it's over quickly. That's what the man told me. And he was one to know—he was lying there in bed without an arm, cut off, he told me, by a doctor with a saw two inches above the elbow.

I do not always observe the battles from a detached distance for

*I am often pressed into service with the medics. The sheer volume
of injury and bloodshed is so great that they need all the help they
can get. The nurses who follow the armies from battle to battle are
the most amazing people I have ever met. Clara Barton is one of the
most well known, but there are thousands like her. Their selflessness
and compassion are some of the only bright spots of this war.*

*McClarin is grateful for my work and is exhibiting it in Boston as
well as at the Brady exhibit in New York. But being the one to take
the photographs is sometimes more than my stomach is able to bear.
Simply keeping food down is a greater problem than you might think.*

*Being a photographer is not without its dangers. We are, as a class,
lumped together as journalists, who enjoy a certain level of protection and freedom to move about more than a soldier in uniform. I
can ride a train or walk through a Southern town or even, when I
am lucky, stay in a hotel or boardinghouse. But when they learn that
I work for a Boston paper, instantly they are suspicious. In the South
journalists are almost despised, every one suspected of being a spy for
the Union. They assume that journalists are listening and taking
notes as they move here and there, and then running off to the nearest telegraph office to dispatch their news back to their paper. In the
imaginations of many, all the dark secrets, by this means, find their
way into the hands of the Union generals. Many journalists have
been beaten, even shot.*

*My big news is that President Lincoln has named Gen. Grant
commander of all the Union armies. And Mr. McClarin has secured
an invitation in March for me to attend a reception at the White
House to be held upon his arrival to receive his new commission
from the president himself. We are hopeful that I will have the
opportunity to photograph him! Now that he is coming east perhaps
the war will not last too much longer.*

What do you hear from Thomas? I hope and pray he is safe.

Carolyn broke into tears at Seth's question and handed the letter to
Cherity. She and Richmond left the house hand in hand.

"I will have to write and tell him," said Richmond.

"I wish we did not have to tell him at all," said Carolyn through her tears. "He has too much death around him as it is. But I know we cannot keep it from him."

Twenty-Five

The war years had not been particularly kind to Harland Davidson, attorney at law, in Richmond, Virginia. The citizens of the Confederate capital had been too consumed of late with trying to keep the Union army at bay to require the services of a lawyer to draw up deeds, contracts, or depositions.

Things were not going well all through the South. For the first time in his life, Harland found himself envying Stuart living in Philadelphia. He wondered what things were like up there.

He set aside the newspaper in his hand and sat back in his chair thinking about what he had just read. Stuart had predicted it last Christmas, and now this news that Grant had been appointed Union commander and was coming east . . . it did not bode well for the Confederacy. He probably would have to get out of Richmond, as Stuart had said.

He thought back to Christmas when the four of them had been together at Pamela's. When the conversation had turned to their cousin, as it invariably did, it came out that Harland and Stuart had received their end-of-the-year payments on time, but the two girls hadn't.

"How far behind is he?" Harland had asked.

"I haven't heard from him in two months," replied Margaret. "Last quarter's draft was a month late, and now this quarter's hasn't come at all."

"And you, Pamela?"

"It's been about the same, I think."

"Neither of you has received a check?"

Both girls shook their heads.

"Then we've got him!" Harland had exclaimed. "That is so like Richmond, paying *us* on time while he defaults with the two of you so that Stuart and I won't get suspicious—it's nothing but outright deceit."

"But what can you do?" asked Pamela.

"File proceedings against him, of course," replied Harland. "It's what we've been waiting for all along."

"But, Harland . . . do we really even want Greenwood now . . . I mean with the war and everything?" said Stuart. "Especially if it's failing. I'm certainly not going down there. The way I hear it, Grant is going to ravage the whole area this spring and make an assault on Richmond that Jefferson Davis will not soon forget. You need to get out of there. And with all that going on, do we really want Greenwood? None of the rest of us want it—do you?"

"Probably not . . . though who can tell?" replied Harland. "Perhaps one day I might return there, after the war, of course. I was always fond of the place."

"You're not going to live there, Harland. Let's be realistic—so what if the money is a little late? It is still the most practical way for us to get our portion out of Aunt Ruth's estate."

"The point isn't about any of us living there or actually operating it as a day-to-day enterprise. Of course I don't mean that. All I want to do is knock Richmond down off his holier-than-thou perch, and for us to get what is rightfully ours. I assume, once we have Richmond out of there, that we will sell it, perhaps break it into smaller parcels, have those huge oaks and other trees cut and milled into lumber. We stand to make a good deal of money—more than $225 a quarter. There are already opportunists from the North coming down looking for property to snatch up. All we have to do is provide it for them."

"And you actually think you can pull it off?" asked Stuart.

"I am an attorney, Stuart. We can do anything!" he laughed. "To answer your question—yes, I've been saving a few cards up my sleeve for just such an occasion as this."

"Will you file immediately?" asked Margaret.

"I think it will be best to wait until he reneges on payment to all four of us. So, Margaret . . . Pam," he said glancing back and forth between the two women, "you have to let us know if you fail to receive another payment. I will get to work on the papers, and once he has missed a payment to all of us, or two payments in succession to either of you, I will file them."

He raised the glass of eggnog in his hand. A cunning smile spread over his lips.

"To the future Davidson heirs," he said.

"Hear, hear!" added Stuart, lifting his own glass to his cousin.

And now, in March, thought Harland, they just had to await developments . . . and hope Grant did not overrun the city.

Twenty-Six

$\mathcal{G}$reenwood's workforce and financial outlook continued to decline as the weather warmed and the planting season approached. By then Richmond knew he had no alternative but to ask his cousins for extensions on their loan payments. With no money in the bank, what else could he do? It wasn't even a matter of *asking* for extensions. He would simply have to tell them he couldn't pay them for a while.

Their aid to blacks fleeing the South had in some ways changed dramatically, yet in other ways was much the same. Since Abraham Lincoln's Emancipation Proclamation of a year and a half earlier, all slaves were supposed to be free. There was no more slavery.

Yet technically, too, in its own eyes, the eleven states of the Confederacy were no longer part of the United States of America at all. Abraham Lincoln wasn't *their* president. His proclamations meant nothing. So plantation owners throughout the South, many more war-ravaged than Greenwood, tried to go on as usual, telling their slaves nothing and treating them as always, secure in the belief that the old Southern ways would go on forever. For the great majority of blacks in the South, therefore, slavery indeed continued as before.

But the Underground Railroad had by then established such an intricate system of stealthy communication that word of Lincoln's proclamation spread through the slave shanties of the South like a silent, invisible brushfire. While their masters and overseers pretended that nothing had changed, the vast slave population of the South began, one man and one woman at a time, to look around and say, "Maybe we don't hab ter live like dis no mo'."

And thus the slow black exodus from the South grew. As it did, so also grew the anger of white slave owners and bounty hunters. They no longer had the Fugitive Slave Law to back up their efforts with the law of the land. If a slave now made it to the North, he had no fear of being returned. But in the South something even more powerful than the Fugitive Slave Law had taken hold—hatred.

Before the war, though slavery was the curse of every Southern Negro, slavery had also been their protection. Their owners may have looked down on their slaves, whipped them, even despised them. But they did not hate them. Slaves weren't worth hating.

But now freedom brought with it hatred to the South. A new kind of hatred. Slaves had always been beaten. But *former* slaves were now being hung. Revenge now replaced restitution as a motive for capturing runaways.

No one of black skin wanted to go back to how it had been before. Freedom was better than anything. But how free would the emancipated slaves be if hatred and prejudice created an invisible bondage as deep as that once enforced by the slave-chains of their white masters?

Thus the efforts of the thousands who had been helping slaves for years, most notably Quakers, continued, and brought with it even more complexities. For with a war on, and with chaos everywhere as the Confederacy gradually disintegrated, the danger to those trying to get out of the South was in some ways even greater than before.

Considering how he had felt through most of the winter months, Thomas Davidson might just as well have been dead as his captain had tried to pretend. There were times he thought he *was* dead!

Had it not been for the kind ministrations of their Quaker hosts and his rescuing black angel, he would surely have made Cameron Beaumont's letter to his parents a prophetic one. The strain of the escape, the cold, the exhaustion, along with the inflammation of his broken ribs, all combined with a fever to enter his lungs. The resulting pneumonia had indeed put his life in danger. Many a long night after their arrival at the safe house, Deanna sat gently wiping his burning face and forehead and arms and praying desperately that he would live for one more day . . . and one day after that.

By the time his fever and delirium began to subside, Thomas was so weak and had lost so much weight that no one imagined that he would be able to travel anytime soon. Under the best of conditions, broken ribs take months to heal. And in its state, Thomas's body was slow to recover. The winter set in and still he lay in bed too weak even to stand.

Thomas's months as an invalid gave fertile opportunity for many long talks with Deanna at his bedside. They learned much about one another, without realizing the full extent of the similarities between their two upbringings. Thomas found it easier to tell *facts* about his family than to dwell on the spiritual foundations of his parents' lives. Though Deanna was obviously proud of the Quaker faith of her parents, and shared it herself, and looked upon her father as nothing less than a hero for what he had done, Thomas felt far more conflicting emotions. Thus, even in such a setting as where he found himself—in a Quaker home, in a station on the railroad—and learning of Deanna's similar spiritual background, he said nothing about the activities or faith of his parents.

But such things were occupying his thoughts. And he found himself in no little turmoil over them.

These people who had opened their home to them were just like his parents. He had come into their home as a complete stranger. Yet here he was staying in one of their bedrooms like he was part of the family, and Deanna in another room of the house even though she was black. What made them care so much about helping people? It was exactly what his parents would have done.

"Do you mind if I ask you a question?" said Thomas from his bed one day.

"Of course not," said Deanna.

"What actually are Quakers?" asked Thomas. "I've heard about them, of course, but what do Quakers believe?"

"I don't know . . . we believe in God, that Jesus was God's son and died for our sins."

"Everybody believes that. What is different about what Quakers believe?"

"I don't know. It's just how I grew up."

"And you believe everything your parents taught you?"

"I suppose I do."

"Did it never bother you to have your parents try to make you believe like them?"

"No, of course not. They didn't *make* me. They just taught us what was true and what wasn't. That's what parents are supposed to do, isn't it? Why would that bother me?"

"I don't know. It bothered me about my parents."

"Why?" asked Deanna.

"Actually . . . I don't know," replied Thomas. "Maybe it seemed like they were trying to force it on me or something."

"Do you think they were really doing that?"

"I don't know. Maybe I just thought they were. I guess I'll have to think about that some more."

"I always admired my father and mother for their convictions. Even if they had tried to make me believe like you say, I don't think I would have minded because they are a good man and woman."

That night Thomas thought about Deanna's words. Why had he not been able to admire *his* father and mother? Seth had. Deanna admired her parents. Why had their beliefs and convictions bothered him? Now that he thought about it, it didn't make much sense.

Gradually Thomas was able to get out of bed, and then began to venture outside. He and Deanna were walking and talking outside near the house on a snowy afternoon in February.

"What comes to mind when you think of your parents?" he asked. "Are they happy thoughts?"

"Of course. They are so happy that—"

Deanna turned away and began to cry. "I miss them so much!" she said. "They are happy *and* sad. What about you?"

"I don't know," smiled Thomas thoughtfully. "Yeah . . . I guess mine are happy and sad too."

As winter relaxed its grip and spring set in, Thomas slowly regained his strength. Though his ribs were still painful if he turned wrong or tried to lift something, he was nearly well enough to travel.

"Now that I am better," he said to Deanna one day, "we need to think about moving on, getting north, and getting you home. What part of New Jersey are you from again?"

"I'm not sure exactly," replied Deanna. "I was so young, but I think it's somewhere near Philadelphia. The town is called Mount Holly. That's one thing my father told us never to forget."

"Then we need to start making plans to get back on the railroad and get you there."

Twenty-Seven

$\mathcal{S}$ome awakenings of conscience explode like a thunderbolt from a clear untroubled moral sky. Others begin so invisibly their gentle naggings in the region of the soul slowly cause but a faint new sensation—the undefined sense of being ill at ease. The reasons may be nebulous at first. But gradually they coalesce around two stark and unmistakable realizations: *I am not the person I ought to be*, and *I have done wrong*.

The first is the fundamental truth upon which all spiritual development, and all true human growth, is based. But it is too enormous a realization for many to take in. It lies utterly outside the realm of previous conscious thought. The idea of becoming other than one *is*, of attempting by whatever means to make oneself *better*, is neither taught nor recognized as the primary objective of the human race. Individual growth toward *betterment* is scarcely acknowledged as a possibility, still less an imperative and eternal necessity, by the larger percentage of humanity. How should the individuals of that humanity, then, be capable of recognizing that they are less than what they must one day become?

The second realization, however, is a tangible truth that circumstances may make undeniable. It is therefore a wonderful starting point for the waking of conscience. And when *I have done wrong* leads to repentance rather than self-justification, and therefore to the greater realization, *I am not the person I ought to be,* then at last does God get a foothold in the soul. Real growth and change at once begin to be possible.

All human activity affects character—every choice, every friendship, every deed, every word. Especially do our associations affect what we are in the process of making ourselves. Relationships change us. Associations with men and women of truth pay dividends of light, kindness, wholesomeness, and goodness. Associations with those whose motives are self-interest and personal gain exact an opposite tribute, taking their toll by pulling one down into the darkness of greed, ambition, selfishness, and untruth.

For all his appeal and personality, Cecil Hirsch had spent a lifetime seeking his own gain, and using people to get what he wanted. So too had Veronica.

But Veronica Beaumont Fitzpatrick was slowly beginning to sense that possibly something was amiss within her. She had ignored the first naggings of her conscience by trying to convince herself that she was not *really* being untrue to Richard, only trying to bring some interest into her life.

And yet . . . gradually she began to have regrets. She began to suspect that she was living a lie—a lie against Richard, a lie against truth, a lie against right.

In short, she was at last coming face to face with the unfamiliar and unpleasant realization that, just possibly, she had done and was doing *wrong.*

Why had the pangs of conscience begun to stir in her heart? What is that invisible distinction within human beings that at some crossroads of life causes one to reflect personally on right and wrong, while another continues thoughtlessly on the well-trod path where self-interest is the only guide to action, attitude, and response?

The Spirit of Truth is constantly attempting to enliven and quicken toward humble self-reflection. Some hear, some do not. Who could have foreseen, knowing her as a child or a youth or a scheming young woman, that Veronica would be capable of becoming such a Spirit-listener? As yet she was hearing but faintly, for her spiritual ears were plugged with a lifetime of disuse. But that a few strains of self-reflective truth were penetrating her heart, that she was allowing them to get through without dismissing them, and that she was heeding them, would speed her capacity to hear more and greater truth when it came.

Veronica was to meet Cecil at one of the obscure Washington parks. As she approached she saw him sitting on a bench waiting. He was holding a large leather packet. She walked toward him. He stood, kissed her, then handed her the packet along with a sheet of further instructions.

"Cecil," she said, "do you mind if I ask you a question?"

"Of course not," he said.

Veronica hesitated and looked away. She did not speak for several long seconds. At last she drew in a breath and sighed.

"What is this all about?" she said.

"All of what?" laughed Cecil.

"Everything—Mr. Garabaldi and all the people we meet in strange places? . . . What about Congressman Wyler? . . . What about—there was a lady I met once coming out of Mr. Wyler's office . . . what was her name?—Mrs. Greenhow, I think. What about her? Do you know her too? Does she do the same thing that I do?"

Cecil seemed perturbed. It was clear that he was not interested in talking about it further. Veronica asked no more questions. But his manner at mention of the woman's name made Veronica all the more curious.

That evening at home she summoned her courage to ask Richard about her, though she didn't dare tell him about the packet she had hidden upstairs with her things. She was already having enough trouble accounting for her trips out of town and knew he was suspicious.

"Have you ever heard of a Mrs. Greenhow?" Veronica asked as they were finishing their dinner.

"You mean Rose Greenhow?" said Richard, glancing up and lowering his eyebrows slightly.

"I don't know her first name."

"What about her?"

"I heard her name today. I was just curious who she was."

"Rose Greenhow was in prison in the Old Capitol prison in '62. She was a Confederate spy."

"A *spy!*" exclaimed Veronica as her face went pale.

"They deported her to Richmond after a year or so in jail," Richard went on. "That was a couple years ago, I seem to recall. She was greeted in the South as a hero. And why wouldn't she be—she had betrayed our country . . . the Union I mean. There is nothing lower than a spy. They deserve to be hung."

Suddenly Veronica felt faint. She was going to be sick!

Twenty-Eight

$\mathcal{H}$arland Davidson did not have to wait long for his schemes to come to fruition.

In early spring the letter he had been anticipating arrived from Pamela. The brief note in her own hand was far less interesting to him than the letter she had enclosed from Greenwood. It was nearly identical to the one he had himself received only a week earlier.

Dear Pamela, it read.

> *It is with deep regret that I am writing to beg your forgiveness for not being able to enclose the payment for the past two quarters on your note. The war has unfortunately intruded upon us more closely than is comfortable. Though we remain grateful to God for our health and safety, our workforce and crop yields have so declined that finances are rather more difficult than we had anticipated. We look forward to better times ahead, however, and of course will resume payments as soon as we are able. Thanking you in advance for your patience and understanding, and wishing you and yours all the best,*
>
> *I am,*
> *Your cousin Richmond Davidson.*

A telegraph to Stuart, and Stuart's prompt reply, confirmed that his first quarter's payment, too, had not been made.

Though Richmond did not necessarily expect cordial greetings when he saw the thick envelope arriving from the law offices of Harland Davidson, nothing could have prepared him for what he saw when his eyes fell on the top page of the series of documents inside.

He found Carolyn in her sewing room with Cynthia and Cherity. One look at his face told all three that something serious had arisen. Carolyn had seen the envelope when it arrived, and she suspected it as the cause of her husband's expression. She rose and they left the house together. They walked slowly toward the arbor and Richmond explained the gist of the sudden developments.

"But how can he do that?" said Carolyn. Every other time Richmond's cousins brought out their requests and threats, she had reacted angrily. But now concern was evident in her voice. For the first time she realized just how deeply serious this was.

"There was a clause in the loan that I did not give enough thought to," answered Richmond. "I thought striking out the guarantee clause gave us protection enough. I was wrong."

"What kind of clause?"

"It states that upon delinquency of any payment, the balance of the loan becomes immediately due and payable in full. It's not really so unusual . . . actually quite common. I simply did not anticipate the difficulties we would face. So Harland is now calling for full payment of all four loan balances."

"I cannot believe he could be so callous! Why would he do that? Isn't he satisfied to get what you've already given which he had no right to anyway? I just don't understand it!"

"Not everybody in this world thinks according to the principles of the kingdom of God," said Richmond softly. "Not that we do to the extent I hope we learn to before this life is over. But for some, self-motive is the only foundation for action they know. I am afraid my poor cousin Harland is such a one. He has never learned to think about others. But he will learn the lesson one day, even if it takes the fire of God to teach him what he was too stubborn to learn without it. Until then we must submit to look like, and be treated like fools in his eyes."

"You know I hate this, Richmond."

He smiled tenderly. "My dear, dear wife—you don't hate it as much as you think," he said. "You know as well as I do that we are under different orders than my mammon-blinded cousin. You teach your women the very same thing."

"Maybe you are right. But the unfairness of this grates on me."

"He has anticipated our failure to comply with notice that after ninety days proceedings will begin against our assets. That means Greenwood."

"Oh, Richmond!"

"Harland cites a Virginia law saying that even in a case where there is no specific guarantee of collateral or assets, if two or more defaults are made by the same debtor in excess of five hundred dollars, then assets can be attached and seized to enforce payment. He quotes something about a double breach of contract enforcing seizure of collateral."

"I've never heard of such a thing!"

"Nor have I."

"Do you think Harland knew about it all along?"

"I would assume so," sighed Richmond. "Though I refused to comply with his attempt to guarantee the loans with Greenwood, he must have known that this obscure law would be an effective backup remedy in the event we ran into trouble. It is no doubt why he drew up the settlement as four separate transactions, so that if anything happened he could be able to prove, as defined by this law, multiple breach of contract against us."

"Why don't we make the back payments to them all now and get caught up?"

"We would probably still be legally liable," replied Richmond, "though I doubt any judge would issue foreclosure proceedings against Greenwood if we did so. There is only one thing wrong with your suggestion, Carolyn."

"What's that?

"Harland knows if we haven't been able to make the payments that
there is no way in the world we can pay off the loans. We don't have
the money to make the back payments. We're already a thousand
dollars behind. We simply don't have it. We are barely going to make
it till fall when we can begin selling a few things before our bank
account runs completely dry. To tell you the truth, my dear, I am not
completely sanguine about our catching back up."

"Oh . . . I am sorry, Richmond, but I wish you had never agreed
to this!"

"I did what I thought was right at the time, and as I thought God
was leading me. I don't intend to begin doubting that now because we
find ourselves in a tight situation. God's promises to take care of our
needs are not predicated on times of ease and comfort."

Tears filled Carolyn's eyes. Richmond stretched his arm around
her. Carolyn wept quietly for two or three minutes, after which they
continued to sit in thoughtful silence.

"Are we going to lose everything, Richmond?" sighed Carolyn at
length.

"I don't know . . . we may. Don't get me wrong, it would break my
heart, but God will take care of us."

"It would kill me to have to move. I love Greenwood. And what of
all our people, what of the railroad? What will become of it all?"

"God will have to see to them too. If he closes one door, he will
open another. Besides, these things take time. Even if Harland and
the others eventually force us out, nothing will happen for sixty or
ninety days, and then another two or three months for all the legalities
involved."

"But, Richmond . . . are you saying . . . that means we could have
to move out by this fall!"

"I'm sure by then the war will be over and much will have changed.
Perhaps we will be ready for a move."

"Oh, Richmond, don't say such a thing!"

Twenty-Nine

Seth quickly wrote back in response to his father's letter that had been sent to him in care of the *Boston Herald*.

> *Dear Father, Mother, Cherity, and Cynthia,*
> *I was saddened beyond words at receipt of your letter, Dad, telling me about Thomas. I still cannot believe it. I wept at the news. The worst of it was having to weep alone. I have never felt so lonely in my life as throughout the night after I received your letter. I cannot imagine the grief this must be causing you and Mother. To lose a brother is heartbreaking, but to lose a son must be far more excruciating. I am so sorry. Though I hurt for myself, I think perhaps I hurt even more for you two whom I love with all my heart.*
> *I told you of the reception at the White House. It went well, and though I did not actually meet the president, I saw him and that was an experience in itself. But it was Gen. Grant who stole the show. What a contrast between the two men! Gen. Grant scarcely came up to Mr. Lincoln's shoulders. But what a stir he caused in the city. When Mr. Lincoln saw him, he was nearly beside himself with enthusiasm and praise, though Gen. Grant looked uncomfortable and embarrassed by it all. I had the feeling that he was anxious to get back to his army. He had come to the capital to receive from the president the specially created rank of lieutenant general, which no*

one since George Washington has held. He is now in command of half a million men in all the armies of the United States.

By the time this letter reaches you, Grant may have already begun his march toward Richmond. I hope his army does not take a path through Dove's Landing! Everyone here has the utmost confidence that he will be able to accomplish what no other Union general has, defeat our friend Robert E. Lee and end this terrible conflict. How different this war might have been had Mr. Lee followed his spiritual conscience rather than his political conscience. I know he is your friend, Father, but that is how I see it. To have placed his loyalty to Virginia, as much as I love our state too, above the conviction that slavery is wrong, in my opinion, was not an act of courage as most in the South see it. How many thousands of lives could he have saved if he had said, I will not go to war against my nation or my president. I am sorry, Father, but as I see it, our dear Gen. Lee has prolonged the war. He is the one, probably the only man who could have ended it long ago, and this he did not do. How many more young men will have to die because of his determination to fight to the bitter end? The handwriting has been on the wall a long time. The Confederacy has already lost. Why do its generals fight on when their cause is hopeless? Only so that thousands more will die? The South has so lost its reason and its humanity that, rather than exchange black Union prisoners for their own, they simply shoot them en masse. And this represents some ideal Southern way of life, as they call it. I am sorry to speak so bluntly. I have seen too much death to honor those Southern leaders who took this nation into this horrible and unnecessary war. Their bravery is undisputed. Their moral judgment, however, will go down in history, in my opinion, as a great travesty.

My apologies for such a cynical note!

My big news of this letter is for you, Cherity. Do you remember my telling you about the occasional hospitality I have enjoyed? I had reason to stay at a boardinghouse in Louisville for several days about a year ago. There I met the nicest man and woman who keep horses, as we do there at home. One of their mares had given birth about a year before to the loveliest white and brown foal, but then died the next day. They have taken great care to raise the colt with their other horses but knew that he needed extra special care. I fell in love with the yearling immediately and asked if I could buy him. They agreed, but we decided it would be best for him to remain where he was for another year, until he was strong and ready for training. I returned recently on my way back to Boston and made arrangements for him to be sent by rail to you. I knew when I first saw him that you and he were meant for each other. He is an Arabian quarter horse, and is now just over two years of age. He is of gentle temperament though is not yet trained. You and Alexander will be able to see to that, and he will be able to determine when he is strong enough for you to ride him. I would think that time might be now, but he will know best. I cannot wait to see you on him!

With all my love to each of you,
  Seth.

Richmond set the letter down and looked across the table at Carolyn.

"Our Seth is becoming a bold and independent thinker!" he said.

"I have never heard him speak his mind so forcefully," smiled Carolyn. "What do you think of his comments?"

"I am not sure what to think," mused Richmond. "He makes some strong points. He is certainly closer to the war than we are. Perhaps some of his emotion is a reaction from the news about Thomas. To be honest, however, I had felt some of the same questions. On those rare occasions when we have had the chance to visit, Robert speaks of his dislike of slavery. Yet it does seem to be as Seth said, that his loyalty to Virginia and the South is greater. I think it is clear what Mount Holly's tailor would have done if facing a decision between his colonial New Jersey and what his conscience told him of right and wrong. I know what Robert was thinking, that he could not fight against his own state. But the honorable thing to have done, it seems to me, is what Seth did, say you will fight for *neither* side."

"But General Lee is a military man," said Carolyn. "*Could* he have realistically done that?"

"It is often not easy or convenient to follow one's convictions. But what was to stop him doing what Seth did? He could have resigned his commission and refused to take up arms against his state or against his president, by which I mean President Lincoln. In honoring his state, he has dishonored his nation and its president. Where is the virtue in that? I believe Seth is right. How many lives might have been saved had more conscientious men on both sides simply refused to fight against their brother Americans? Living out one's Christian faith in a world of conflict is never easy. But if men and women of conviction simply go along with the trends and responses of those around them, how can they expect to change the world for the cause of Christ? I confess, I do not see how Robert's loyalty to the South has furthered the cause of Christ in the world."

"Would you tell him that?" asked Carolyn.

"Only if he asked me specifically. Until then, his conscience is *his*, my conscience is *mine*. The world God has given me to change is not the world of Robert Lee, but the world of Richmond Davidson."

Thirty

Veronica scarcely slept for days. She could think of nothing but Richard's words, She was a Confederate spy. . . . *There is nothing lower than a spy. They deserve to be hung.*

Suddenly the curiosity to know what was inside the packet Cecil had given her became overpowering.

As soon as Richard left home the following morning, she got out the packet. With trembling fingers she broke the seal, then opened the packet and slowly removed the contents.

As she began looking through the papers inside, Veronica's eyes widened in shock.

She was holding maps, diagrams, planned Union troop movements, and communications between several Union generals, including a letter from Abraham Lincoln himself to General Sherman about the upcoming campaign against Atlanta.

These were top secret papers about Union army plans!

The papers fell from Veronica's hands as her brain spun with wild fantasies about what would happen if her own role in Cecil's schemes was discovered. She had to put a stop to this! She had to get out of this horrible nightmare!

She took a deep breath as if to summon her resolve, then picked up the papers and stuffed them back into the packet. Ten minutes later she set out for the middle of the city.

Holding the packet Cecil had given her, Veronica walked into the lobby of the Bradford Hotel and glanced around, as if hoping to see him standing waiting for her. But he was nowhere to be seen. She went to the counter.

"I would like to see Mr. Hirsch," she said.

The man behind the counter returned her question with a blank expression.

"Who?" he said after a moment.

"Mr. Hirsch," repeated Veronica. "Cecil Hirsch."

"I'm sorry, we have no guest by that name."

"Perhaps he is not a guest, but he stays here," said Veronica, doing her best to sound confident. "You must have seen me with him—I've met him here a dozen times. He told me to come here . . . now please tell me what room he is in."

By this time the hotel manager remembered Veronica's face, not an easy one to forget. He hesitated another moment, then nodded.

"Yes, of course," he said. "Mr. Hirsch has given strict orders not to be disturbed. But as it is you . . . I will send someone up to tell him you are here."

Veronica turned away. She was too agitated to sit down. Instead she walked back and forth in the lobby until she heard footsteps descending the stair. She turned and saw Cecil reach the ground floor and walk toward her. He was clearly not pleased to have *her* summon *him*.

"What are you doing here?" he said with a cloudy expression, leading her to a corner where they would not be overheard.

"I had to see you," replied Veronica.

"We have no business together until you come back from Atlanta."

"That's what I want to talk to you about—Atlanta. I can't go."

"What do you mean you can't go? You have to go."

"I can't . . . I won't go."

Veronica hesitated and glanced away.

"Cecil, I know you are going to be angry with me," she added after a moment. "But I opened the packet."

"You what!" he exclaimed, his eyes flaming. Veronica had never seen Cecil Hirsch truly angry in her life. He was clearly angry now.

"I opened the packet," she repeated. "I had to know what was going on."

"McFee will never take it with the seal broken. How could you have done such an idiotic thing?"

Cecil strode back and forth shaking his head.

"You have put us in a terrible fix," he said. "I *have* to get that information to Atlanta."

"But it is—"

"I know well enough what it is!" snapped Cecil. "Keep your voice down. Look, Veronica, we can talk about your future later. For right now, you have to take that train to Atlanta and deliver that packet. I'll include a note explaining what happened and hope McFee buys it."

"Cecil . . . I don't want to do this anymore."

Cecil laughed, though not with humor.

"You're in too deep, Veronica. You can't get out now. Besides, the war will be over soon. You will be rich."

"I don't care about being rich. You can have all the money back. I just want—"

Veronica stopped and glanced away. She had begun to cry.

"I just want out," she whimpered, "and I . . . I don't want to do it anymore."

An expression came over Cecil's face that she had never seen.

"Tears, my dear Veronica?" he said sarcastically. "Do you really think playing the injured woman will sway me? Veronica . . . Veronica!" he laughed, "save your acting for someone else. Ha, ha, ha. It is really too hilarious to see you trying your games on me."

"I'm not playing a game, Cecil. I'm afraid. I had no idea what we were—"

"Oh, come, Veronica! What did you think they were paying us so much money for?"

"But it's wrong."

"Veronica! There is a war on. Information is wealth. I've always told you that. There is no right and wrong, no good and bad. Everyone is out for themselves, including the North and the South. War is a business and I am in the business of information. I've never made any secret of that. If you didn't know what was going on, you should have."

"But I didn't, Cecil. Please—"

"Look, Veronica," said Cecil, "it's not only that you can't get out, I don't want you out. I have too much to lose too. I'm not about to hang because of your conscience. You and I are in this together all the way. Now you either go to Atlanta and deliver that packet, or I will arrange for certain information to come to light about Mrs. Richard Fitzpatrick, Washington socialite, revealing that she has been stealing secrets from her husband and selling them to the South."

"You wouldn't . . . would you really do that, Cecil?" she said, looking into his face with disbelief.

"I hope it will not come to that, Veronica. Don't try me."

Thirty-One

*C*herity stood on the platform of the Dove's Landing station as the train pulled in, hardly able to contain her excitement. They had received word by telegram yesterday that her new horse would be arriving today. She and Alexender had been waiting already for an hour.

As the man led the two-year-old colt down the ramp ten minutes later, the sight took Cherity's breath away.

He was the most beautiful horse she had ever seen!

"Oh, Seth!" she said under her breath. "How can I ever thank you? He's gorgeous!"

Ten minutes later, Alexander and Cherity were on their way back to Greenwood with the young brown colt cantering along behind the buggy.

"You decided what you's gwine call him, Miz Cherity?"

"I've been thinking a lot about it, Alexander," answered Cherity. "I think I am going to name him Cadence."

"Dat's a right pretty soundin' name, an' jes' perfect for a horse."

"How long do you think it will be until I can ride him?"

"Well, he seems ter me ter be well formed an' strong, an' you ain't exactly as big as Mister Dab'son. An' he didn't flinch none when we touched an' stroked him, so as likely as not he's had plenty er luvin' care. So I reckon you could ride him 'most any time, soon's we git him trained an' used ter da saddle. You jes' talk ter him an' pet him an' stroke him as much as you can an' let him git used ter yo' voice an' yo' smell. Horses is like people, dey git attachments an' likes an' dislikes jes' like we duz. An' we want him luvin' you like you's gwine luv him. Dat way he knows he kin trust you, an' you kin trust him."

Cadence proved as cooperative and as rapid a learner as he was beautiful. Within two weeks Cherity was able to sit on his back, as Alexander led him gently about the corral. Gradually Cherity saddled him and mounted him herself and took him into the near pasture. Within a month she was ready to venture out into the lower hills beyond and her first ride away from Greenwood.

She walked to the stable and whistled her greeting. Then she waited for the reply from Cadence. There it was—the low, soft nicker greeting her in return. She entered his stall, slipped the halter over his head, talking softly into his ear, and then led him out into the barn. She brushed him down briefly, affectionately scratching those little itchy spots she had come to know, then threw the saddle pad up high over his back. When she had it just right, she took the familiar old black saddle Seth had given her and, with what was still a great effort because of her height, threw it up atop the pad and centered it just right on Cadence's wide back. After fastening the girth and breast collar, she checked his legs to make sure nothing was pinched, then gave the girth its final tightening and led him to the corral outside.

She led Cadence round in several circles. Once she was satisfied that he was well warmed up and ready for a ride, she lifted her left foot up into the stirrup and swung herself up into the saddle.

Cherity led the way out of the corral and across the pasture in a leisurely walk up the incline toward the woods and the ridge beyond. A few patches of snow still lingered in the shadows of the woods and at the top of the ridge. The ground was a little soggy from a recent rain. But the sun was out and the fresh earthy scents of springtime filled the air. Cherity's heart swelled with gratitude to God for the beauties and pleasures of his world. Her life was filled with uncertainty. She was anxious for Seth's safety. But God was *good*. No matter what they faced, Richmond and Carolyn always returned to that great truth of the universe. As simple as it seemed, it was the truth around which revolved all the other truths of life. God really was good!

They went further than she had yet taken Cadence, even further than she had expected to go. But she could tell that Cadence too felt invigorated by the new sights and sounds and smells of the Virginia hillside, snorting occasionally with pleasure.

They came to the high meadow, empty now, spring grasses and wildflowers bursting out of the earth in profusion. Cherity reined in and looked all about her. Everything was still and quiet and at peace. It was hard to imagine that a war was being waged so close, and that soldiers had been camped at this very spot such a short time ago.

She sat contentedly on Cadence's back absorbing every ray of warm sunlight, every sight, smell, and sound of God's beauty in his creation. Nothing was to be heard but the gentle rhythmic breathing of the great horse lungs beneath her and the birds in the nearby woods. It was a lovely peaceful silence. The ground, still wet, seemed covered with a blanket of sparkling diamonds that seemed silently to say, "We come from above where the glory far surpasses the beauties of this world."

Cherity drew in a great breath of the fragrant afternoon. The cold, crisp air enlivened her lungs with its purifying chill and a sense of peace. It was a peace that said, everything will turn out good in the end.

By now the sun was lowering in the sky above. A few puffy clouds wandered in front of it, sending a sudden shadow over the meadow. It reminded Cherity that she did not want to be gone too long, or tax Cadence beyond what was comfortable on this first ride. She glanced up at the cloud. Its edge was illuminated with a rim of light from the sun behind it.

"All right, Cadence," she said, bending low against his brown neck, "you have done well today. But it is time to go home. Good boy," she added with a loving pat on his neck.

A gentle snort sounded from the big fleshy lips as Cherity gently turned him and began to return to Greenwood the way they had come.

Thirty-Two

Veronica Fitzpatrick sat on the train returning from Atlanta with a pit in her stomach that would not go away. After all this time doing Cecil's bidding . . . suddenly she was terrified.

She needed help! But where could she turn?

If Richard found out what she had done . . . would her marriage survive?

How could he possibly understand? Especially if he had actually been the source of information she had unknowingly passed on. Cecil was always asking questions, and she had not been guarded in her answers.

It was too awful! How could she not have seen his duplicity? He had just been using her like he used everyone!

She took out a book she had brought along. But trying to keep her mind on a story was impossible. She set the book aside with a sigh and took out the newspaper she had picked up and absently began thumbing through it.

Her eyes came to rest on a small article titled: PHOTOGRAPHY CHANGES FACE OF WAR.

New developments in photographic reproduction, she read, *have brought this present war between the North and the South, for the first time in the history of wartime, into the lives of average citizens on both sides. No longer is it possible to gloss over the horrors of the conflict. The*

*accurate images brought from the battlefield by photographic reproduction
are at once breathtaking and horrifying in their realistic detail.*

　　*All around the country, displays and exhibitions of war photographers
are drawing huge crowds. The images by such brave men as Matthew
Brady, Alexander Gardner, Timothy O'Sullivan, and Seth Davidson of
the* Boston Herald—

　　A gasp of astonishment sounded from Veronica's lips.

　　Seth!

　　A hundred childhood memories flooded through her. With them
the image of a face rose in her mind's eye—the face of a friend, one
of the few *true* friends she had ever had . . . Seth Davidson—a young
man true enough to tell her he did not love her.

　　Slowly tears rose in Veronica's eyes at the thought of her neighbor
and friend. She loved Richard, but Seth would always hold a special
place in her heart. She had been fond of him, even thought she loved
him. But she had been too selfish back then to love anyone but herself.
If she was not quite yet aware of that truth, the reminder of Seth
was even more special now that she had begun to realize that she was
perhaps not all she ought to be.

　　She had been angry at him. Yet even before this moment she had
come to recognize that what he had done had taken courage. Suddenly
a new sensation arose within her—a newfound respect for Seth . . .
respect for him even for rejecting her.

　　Where was Seth now? she wondered.

　　She stared down at the article again, reading its words over and
over. Her eyes flew over the articles and pictures and advertisements
until suddenly another caption caught her eye, this time as the heading of a small article: JEFFERSON DAVIS TO APPEAR BEFORE CAMERAS.

　　Quickly Veronica read what followed.

　　*Confederacy President Jefferson Davis is set to speak in Raleigh, North
Carolina next month, at which event photographers from several major newspapers are scheduled to be on hand to take photographs of the president that
will be seen in both North and South for the first time by many Americans.*

　　Veronica set down the paper, her brain spinning.

With a new set of civilian clothes provided by their winter's Quaker hosts, Thomas and Deanna at last set out again for the North, joining a group of four fugitives who had arrived two days before. Thomas still stood out like a sore thumb. But at least he was no longer wearing a Confederate uniform. Thus far he had not seen another single white person on the Underground Railroad, as why should he? It was a secret network for escapees. Whites had nothing to escape from, unless they too were runaways . . . like him.

The first few nights and days passed wearily but without danger. Thomas and Deanna accompanied the others northeast through the Great Smoky Mountains along the border between Tennessee and North Carolina. When their companions turned north, bound for a series of stations that led toward Ohio, they left them. For two nights they walked alone, then were taken by a conductor, not to a lonely farmhouse as usual, but into a town where he led them through a succession of back alleyways and deserted streets. Wondering if the man planned to turn them in, Thomas was about to object, when their guide stopped in a deserted part of town where they were surrounded by old dilapidated brick warehouses. He turned toward them.

"Dere's gwine be an ol' man comin' along here by'm by," he said. "He's be pullin' an ol' rickety wagon full er crates an' barrels an' boxes. He ain't gwine slow down or look fo' nobody, but when he cums, you jes' jump up an' get in dem containers. He'll take you where you's goin'."

With that the man hurried off and disappeared.

Thomas and Deanna scarcely had time to look at each other with questioning glances when behind them they heard a wagon clattering slowly toward them along a side street. Before it reached them, suddenly from the surrounding buildings what appeared to be a dozen blacks of all ages poured out and swarmed toward the wagon. Thomas and Deanna ran to join them, scrambling up in the confusion. Thomas helped Deanna into a large empty barrel and set the lid down on top of her, then himself squeezed into a big wood crate along with a teenage black boy who was not pleased to have to share his hiding place with a white. Neither said a word and the wagon continued to rumble along.

Gradually they heard the sound of voices and machinery and iron train wheels grinding slowly along their tracks and could tell they were approaching a rail yard.

The wagon stopped. The heavy footsteps of several men approached and they felt themselves being lifted onto a flatbed train car. Not a word was spoken. Outside they heard what sounded like the arrival of army troops, who also loaded into the train.

Twenty or thirty minutes later, slowly the train began to pull out of the station.

For what seemed like hours they clattered along, so cramped that arms and legs and everything else went numb.

"Where are you going?" Thomas finally said to his crate companion.

"Anywhere, massa . . . jes' norf. What 'bout you?"

"Me too."

"What's a w'ite man doin' on dis nigger railroad?"

"I ran away from the army," said Thomas. "I was afraid they were going to kill me, so I ran away."

Thomas tried to shift his position for the fiftieth time. Would he ever be able to stretch his legs again! On and on the rhythmic clickity-clack of the wheels hummed along. The boy's question sent his mind drifting back over the terrible sights he had seen . . . men strewn across muddy trenches . . . bodies without legs . . . and the ceaseless roar of artillery in his ears. And the face of the boy he had encountered in the woods and later found dead on the battlefield.

Slowly he fell into a trancelike sleep . . . woke . . . slept again . . . and woke again. Still the train clattered on. He felt nothing. His whole body was numb.

Then came a slowing. How long had they been moving . . . six hours . . . twelve . . . a hundred?

Gradually the train came to a stop. All was silent. There were no sounds of town or station.

Thomas heard someone jump onto the flatbed and begin rapping gently on the sides of the containers.

"Effen der be any passengers boun' fo' liberty here," said a voice, speaking softly, "dis here train's cum ter da end er da line an' I's passin' out tickets fo' da nex' station. Come on, git out. Time ter go. Hit's a water stop, but hit won't las' long."

A great scurrying followed. Lids came up and one by one dark faces and white eyes peered out of their cramped quarters. It was night. All was black. The train stood in the middle of open countryside, steam puffing from its engine and water pouring into the huge tanks of the water car up ahead of them.

Struggling to stretch out their limbs and stand, bodies began jumping off the side of the flatcar and running into the blackness. Almost as soon as the commotion had begun, all fell silent again. Thomas had barely climbed out and to his feet when he found himself standing alone. For all he could tell, there never had been anyone else. Everyone had vanished into the night.

"Deanna," he said softly. "Deanna . . . ?"

He walked amongst the barrels and crates, but all were empty.

"Deanna!" he said a little louder.

Thomas turned about, squinting into the darkness. Beneath him the train jerked into motion.

"Thomas . . . Thomas, where are you?" he heard a voice call from out in the field.

He jumped to the ground and ran toward it.

"Deanna . . . I'm here," he called. "Deanna!"

Suddenly he felt arms around him.

"Thomas!" panted Deanna out of breath, "I couldn't find you and was afraid—"

Suddenly she stepped back, realizing what she had done.

"Where did everyone go?" asked Thomas.

"I don't know," she said. "They ran off so fast."

Behind them the train clattered away. The lights from its two passenger coaches slowly disappeared in the distance, and they were left alone in the night.

Thirty-Three

Though summer on the calendar was still a couple weeks away, the glory of a Virginia summer had come to Greenwood with the color and greenery and fragrance that distinguishes the summer of June from the high summer of a hot dry August. Roses were in bloom. Indeed flowers of infinite variety, both cultivated and wild, were springing out of the ground everywhere.

A more perfect day could not be imagined as Richmond and Carolyn walked together in the arbor. But these were not happy times. Carolyn's heart especially was heavy.

Only a month before, the war had come very close as the Union army led by General Ulysses Grant slashed down through the wilderness of central Virginia. A great battle had been fought less than thirty miles away at Spotsylvania. Richmond and Sydney and many men from Dove's Landing had gone with wagons to help transport wounded to homes and hospitals in Fredericksburg and Chancellorsville, both cities still suffering from their own battles. Grant, meanwhile, had pushed on and was, even now, at the very threshold of the Confederate capital. Though the fighting thus far between the two titans, Grant and Lee, had proved inconclusive, it seemed that at last Robert Lee had met his match. It was doubtful how much longer the Confederacy could hold together with Grant now at the helm of the Union army.

But more pressing and personal concerns were on their minds. Both knew that they might well be enjoying their final months at their beloved Greenwood.

"I was just reading Woolman's words this morning," said Richmond. "Do you remember when he speaks of not being easy in his mind with what he calls 'cumbering affairs,' and his being able to be content with few possessions and a simple way of life?"

"You have read it to me before. It is one of the striking passages."

"I earnestly hope and pray that we have been able to live to some degree by the same principle," said Richmond. "Yet, Carolyn, even with our present troubles, there is no denying that we have much in the way of this world's goods. It strikes me that perhaps a time is coming when the Lord would have us less encumbered by them, as it did for Woolman when he closed his shop. I think that we must be prepared to let go of Greenwood."

"I know you are right," said Carolyn sadly. "We have always tried to keep in the forefront of our prayers whether there exists anything in our lives we cannot let go of. Oh, but how I love this place. It would be very difficult for me to say good-bye."

"If you knew the Lord was requiring of us to lay Greenwood on the altar," said Richmond, "you would do it in a moment, and with a heart of gratitude."

"But that is just it, Richmond—it isn't the *Lord* requiring it, but your conniving cousins!"

Richmond chuckled. "Of course," he said. "But you know as well as I do that God usually works through circumstance, and often through people whose ways may *not* be committed to him, in order to accomplish his will in *our* lives."

They heard a horse galloping in the distance, and glanced toward the sound. Cherity and Cadence were just coming into the pasture after a long ride.

"She is absolutely in love with that young stallion," said Carolyn. "How did Seth know he would be so perfect for her?"

"Men know things about the women they love, my dear," said Richmond.

"And by the same principle, I think Cherity knows something is wrong with us. She has noticed our quiet talks together. We cannot keep Harland's action from everyone too much longer, especially not from Cynthia, Cherity, Sydney, and Chigua. We have to tell them soon."

"I suppose you are right," sighed Richmond. "But I have not had clarity about when or how to do so."

Cherity found Richmond and Carolyn ten or fifteen minutes later seated on one of the benches in the garden. Cherity knew her spiritual mother well enough by this time to recognize that she had been crying.

"I know I really don't have the right to ask," she said approaching, "but . . . is something the matter?"

Carolyn stood and embraced her.

"Oh, Cherity, dear—you have every right to ask!" said Carolyn. Even as she spoke she began crying again.

"Oh, Carolyn," said Cherity in a voice full of tender sympathy, "what *is* it?"

Carolyn led her back to the bench where Richmond still sat. Cherity sat down between them.

"Do you remember when your father was here," said Richmond, "when we were having some difficulty with one of my cousins?"

"Vaguely," answered Cherity. "Though I was never quite sure what it was all about."

"Those troubles have escalated to a rather more serious level recently. They have now issued proceedings against us, which, if carried as far as is possible, might mean that we could lose Greenwood altogether."

"What! No . . . that's awful! But why?"

"I'm afraid we have fallen behind in our payments on several loans resulting from my father and mother's estate. Our finances have been something of a struggle since the war began, and . . . the long and the short of it is that they are threatening to take the house and land if we do not pay off the notes in full. Unfortunately, it amounts to something over twelve thousand dollars and we have nowhere near that kind of reserves. Actually," he added with a sardonic laugh, "our reserves, if you could call them that, are completely gone."

"Oh, Mr. Davidson, I am so sorry!" said Cherity. "I wish there was something I could do to help."

"Have no worry," smiled Richmond. "It will sort itself out in time."

"How imminent is all this?"

"It may actually not be that far away. We may be packing our bags by late summer or early fall."

"My goodness! You mean . . . just two months from now!"

"We hope it will not come to that."

Thirty-Four

$\mathcal{A}$s Jefferson Davis wound down his remarks, the crowd applauded, then began to disperse. Seth, however, worked against the tide, moving toward the platform.

A small crowd of reporters was clustering about the president. The other half dozen or so photographers were also climbing up onto the platform and beginning to set up their tripods and cameras for the long-awaited session to photograph the Confederate president.

A remnant of the crowd stayed to watch, curious about the new technology; one stood for another reason, patiently—and a little nervously—waiting for the session to be completed.

At last, the president stepped away, then walked down the steps and off the platform. Seth and the other photographers gathered and disassembled their equipment and began packing their things in several waiting carriages.

Some instinct caused Seth to turn and look down. Two familiar eyes were staring straight into his. A momentary disbelief froze him in his tracks.

"Veronica!" exclaimed Seth.

She smiled, a little timidly. It was an expression he had never before seen on her face. Clearly some change had taken place within her.

"But . . . what are you doing here?" he said, now breaking into a great smile. He set down his things and bounded off the platform and rushed toward her.

Whatever Veronica had been expecting, it was not for Seth to greet her so exuberantly. He came toward her, gave her a warm hug, then stood back looking her over, still smiling broadly.

"I can't believe it . . . I can't believe it's really you!" he said. "You look great."

"So do you, Seth," she said, at last finding her voice.

"It is so good to see you again!"

"And you. As for what I am doing here . . . I came hoping to find you."

"*Me* . . . how could you possibly have known I would be here?"

"I didn't. I just hoped you would, when I heard there were going to be photographers present. I saw a small article about the event in the paper."

"But why did you think I would be here?"

"I read an article about war photographs in the newspaper. Your name was mentioned. That's how I knew you were a photographer. I could hardly believe my eyes. And then when I saw the article about this speech, I thought maybe you would be here. I . . . I needed to talk to you."

"Sure—let me get my things."

The childhood friends and onetime fiancés from Dove's Landing sat in the restaurant of the Raleigh Arms Hotel sipping tea and catching up on their lives since they had last seen one another. But how different was the exchange than any they had had previously. Seth was now mature and self-assured, while Veronica was obviously embarrassed at the circumstances that had brought her here. They had until now mostly been catching up on news about each other and their respective families.

"Have you seen Wyatt and Cameron since the war began?" Seth had just asked.

"No. Richard and I left for Luxembourg after we were married. By the time we came back they were off fighting. And Thomas . . . and your family?"

A pained look came over Seth's face and he took in a deep breath.

"Thomas was killed," he said after a moment.

Veronica gasped. "Oh, Seth . . . I am so sorry."

"Actually, he and Cameron were in the same unit. My father and mother received a nice letter from Cameron afterward. He was the one who notified them about Thomas."

A melancholy several seconds followed.

"But tell me about going to Europe after you were married," said Seth at length. "Was it exciting?"

"I don't know . . . not really. I didn't know anyone. It was a relief to come back, though Washington wasn't much better. That's . . ."

Veronica paused and glanced down.

"Do you think people can change, Seth?" she said after a moment. "I mean . . . really change?"

"How do you mean?"

"I mean can someone who has been selfish all her life, someone like *me* . . . do you think I can ever be a nice person . . . nice—like you?"

"Aren't you being a little hard on yourself, Veronica?"

"You know it's true. I'm not a nice person."

"Well, I don't know about that. But to answer your question—of course people can change. We would all be in trouble if they couldn't. I've changed too. Everyone does."

"I hope you're right. I don't want to be selfish anymore."

"I still think you're being a little hard on yourself."

Veronica looked away, then drew in a deep breath.

"I am in trouble, Seth," she said after a moment. "I have nowhere to turn."

"I can tell," he smiled kindly. "I can see it in your face."

"Seth," Veronica went on, looking at him earnestly across the table, "you are a *friend*. I know I can trust you. No matter what I tell you, I know you will be fair to me. I am not sure I can say that even about Richard . . . what I have done is so . . . so horrible. I honestly don't know what he would say. As for my father, because of his position, I am not sure he could help."

"How can I help?"

"I don't know . . . maybe you can't. Maybe no one can. But I have to tell someone. I have no one to turn to but you, Seth."

Veronica looked away. Seth realized that she had begun to cry. This was certainly a different Veronica than he had previously known. He waited patiently.

Veronica dabbed her eyes and nose with her handkerchief and forced a smile.

"Do you remember my eighteenth birthday party at Oakbriar?" she asked.

"How could I forget?" laughed Seth. "It seems like a long time ago now."

"There was a man there . . . a young man, a few years older than you and me," Veronica went on. "He passed himself off as a journalist, though I am not really sure what he was. His name was Cecil Hirsch. He ingratiated himself first to my mother, and then I later met him when we went to Washington. . . ."

Veronica went on to tell Seth everything that had happened, up to her recent trip to Atlanta and what the packet she had delivered had contained. By the time Veronica was finished, her eyes were red and she was so contrite that the tears had again begun to flow.

"I don't know what to do, Seth . . . I'm afraid. How could I have been so blind? Whatever I might think about Cecil, I wasn't very nice for a long time either. I certainly wasn't nice to you."

"Oh, it wasn't so bad."

"You're being nice, Seth. You were always nice. But I was dreadful to you."

"That was a long time ago. We were young. All is forgiven."

Veronica looked at Seth with a thoughtful expression.

"But what am I going to do?" she said again. "I don't want to go to jail, Seth. Maybe I deserve it, I don't know. But I still don't want to. Is that wrong of me?"

"I don't know, but let's don't worry about jail just yet."

Seth thought a moment.

"From everything you've said, it sounds to me as if Hirsch is playing both sides of the fence," he said at length.

"What do you mean?" asked Veronica.

"Spying for both the North and the South. That would explain both the money you say he has, and that envelopes and information are apparently going in both directions. There is good money in passing information—the better the information the more people will pay for it."

"Cecil says things like that too."

"Stories of double spies have been circulating ever since the war started."

"If what you say is true, what can I do, Seth?"

"We'll have to give it more thought," answered Seth. "Somehow we'll have to get something on Hirsch that will prevent him turning you in."

"What do you mean, get something on him?"

"I don't know exactly, somehow put him in a position where he *can't* expose you without implicating himself. If he is playing both sides of the fence, threatening to reveal him to both his Northern *and* Southern contacts might be a powerful weapon to use against him."

"Why would he be afraid of that?"

"Because exposing his game to both would make *neither* side trust him again. He would be finished."

"I still don't see how I could ever do something like that."

"To be honest, neither do I. I'll have to think about it further. If you don't mind, I will talk to a few people I know at the paper who may know more about the espionage end of the war than I do. It may help us figure out what to do."

"So . . . do you mean . . . will you really help me?"

"I'll try, Veronica."

"What should I do?"

"Go home and do nothing. I'll try to get in touch with you before Hirsch gives you another assignment."

"But what about the war and your job and everything?"

"My editor is an understanding man. Once I tell him what is going on, he won't mind. This is potentially a better story than anything else I could give him. Write down your address in Washington for me so that I can contact you. If I call, introduce me as an old friend from home, which I am. If Hirsch contacts you again before I do, telegraph me at the *Boston Herald*. Oh, I just had a thought . . . if there is any way for you to find out the people Hirsch works for, like the restaurant fellow . . . what was his name?"

"Mr. Garabaldi."

"Oh, right . . . and maybe someone even higher up than him, and anyone like that in the South other than the contact people you have seen only once. If we could learn the names of his main contacts, the real source of the money and information, they would be the people we could threaten Hirsch with. If there is any way you can find out more about the people involved above Hirsch, that's what we really need to know."

"I will try. Oh, Seth, I cannot thank you enough!"

"I haven't done anything yet!" laughed Seth.

"Just knowing that you are going to try gives me hope. I feel much better already."

Seth turned serious again and nodded. It was no laughing matter and he knew it.

Thirty-Five

*R*unning . . . running . . . someone was chasing him. He was running toward Harper's Peak.

He glanced back in terror. A great black horse, with wide flaming nostrils, was bearing down on him. He could not hope to escape! On its back, a rider whipped the huge beast into a frenzy . . . a gun was in his hand . . . he saw a flash of fire explode from the barrel, but there was no sound.

More silent gunfire . . . he turned and ran . . . bullets spraying the ground all about his feet. He tripped and sprawled on his face. The horse thundered toward him, but the great hooves jumped in the air to leap over him . . . the rider fell off beside him.

He struggled to get up . . . more gunfire . . . where was it coming from?

He looked down. It was Cameron! He lay flat on his back, eyes leering up at him, blood pouring out of his chest.

Suddenly in shock, he looked at his own hand . . . *he* was holding the pistol . . . its barrel smoking! He opened his mouth to scream, but from his lips came only silence.

He threw the gun from his hand and tried to run. He stumbled over Cameron's dead body and toppled onto him, silently screaming in horror at the blood—

Thomas suddenly started awake.

The night was black. He was sweating and breathing hard. Soft voices from across the barn were whispering in the darkness.

"All we hab ter do is fin' da win' in da horse's head," someone was saying. "Den we'll be safe."

A chill went through him at the words.

"Wha'chu mean?" asked another.

"Dere's a place we's tryin' ter get, it ain't far now. Dey say hundreds ob runaways hab gone an' dey's always safe. Dey say dere's angels watchin' ober dat place on account er da white folks who live dere. I don't know 'bout dat, but dat's where we's boun'. Dey say no one has eber been captured from dere."

Thomas listened in silence.

"Where is it?" asked one of the voices in the darkness.

"I don't know. But hit ain't far now."

Thomas was fully awake now. Could they be . . . actually talking about . . . Greenwood!

Had he really been so blind to all that God was doing in the lives of so many people through his parents? Thomas thought back to the many runaways who had come through that his parents had helped get to freedom. Now he was in the same plight—on the run. Suddenly things looked very different.

Why had his father's spirituality grated on him so as he had grown into his teen years? It made no sense. With all the bad people in the world, why would his father's desire to live an upright life with God annoy him? Why hadn't he been proud of his father's convictions?

Thomas had no answers to the many *whys* now facing him.

But the first step toward growth and wholeness is the turning of the searchlight of truth inward. And this, during his long weeks of convalescence, Thomas had begun to do. Now that he was strong and thinking clearly again, much was changing inside him.

Slowly and invisibly a radical new thought began to take shape: What if the problem lay with *him* not his father? What if his father had merely been a mirror to reflect back upon him, his *own* unrightness, his *own* sourness of spirit?

It was not a pleasant question to face. But his weakened physical condition had heightened his moral and spiritual sensitivities. And he now found himself more introspective than he had ever been in his life. Death had come uncomfortably close. He had seen it all around him.

Though he did not exactly relate his predicament to the swine stalls or fleshpots of Scripture, his brain had begun tentatively probing the uncomfortable realization that the story of the prodigal was not altogether alien from his own spiritual condition. His problems at home had been because of what was inside *him*. He hadn't been what a son was meant to be.

What if he were to die? What if the illness that had so weakened him over the winter had been more serious than it was? What if someone walked in right now and told him he had only a week to live?

The thought sobered him as he lay in the darkness. He felt a tear rise in his eye. The one thing he would want to do before that week was over . . . was see his father and mother again . . . and tell them how much he loved them.

By now tears filled his eyes. Thomas blinked hard. He realized that he was lonely. He missed his home and family. He wanted to be with his parents again.

He heard Deanna's soft breathing where she slept beside him. Almost as if in response to his thoughts, she sighed in her sleep, rolled toward him, snuggled a little closer as her arm stretched out across his chest. She sighed contentedly and once again fell into the steady breathing of a contented sleep.

Tenderly Thomas wrapped his arm around Deanna's shoulder, closed his eyes, and gradually drifted again to sleep.

Thirty-Six

Perhaps it is the quiet stillness that night brings, or the sense that everyone more or less shares at such times of being completely alone. Perhaps it is that darkness of itself stimulates a keener awareness of primal fears and aspirations, and with them forces humanity into more elemental regions of spiritual attentiveness. But for whatever reason, out of the depths of blackness, voices from above, below, and within probe with more penetrating intensity than is possible during the noise and bustle of the day. Thus it is that the Spirit of God often carries out its most vital contact with the human species in the hours between midnight and the crow of the cock at first morning's light.

Cherity Waters had not been actively engaged with her heavenly Father for long years. Still there was much for her to discover. And she continued to ask many questions about the new outlook she had recently discovered of attempting to live as God's daughter.

It was not immediately, therefore, that it occurred to her that she had been awakened for one of the holiest of all life's exchanges—a prayer dialog with her Father-Creator. She only knew that suddenly she was wide awake. It was very, very quiet and the night was very, very black.

Something strange was in the air . . . a sense of life . . . a sense of presence.

She did not know the story of young Samuel. Yet she had the sense—how could it be!—that, like the young prophet of old, someone had just called her name out of the night. It was as though some unknown silent summons had brought her instantly awake.

She reached for the lantern beside her bed, turned it up, then looked at her small watch on the nightstand. It showed thirty-seven minutes past two.

Sleep was out of the question. Her brain was too full. The events of the day rushed back upon her . . . the conversation with Carolyn and Richmond in the garden . . . the dreadful news that they might lose Greenwood.

Then her own statement returned forcefully to her memory: *I wish there was something I could do to help.*

Almost instantly three words seemed to speak themselves out of the night with such clarity that she thought she had actually *heard* them:

"You help them."

Unconsciously Cherity glanced about. The night was as quiet and empty as before. But something was in the air . . . something meant for her.

Then first it occurred to her that who else could be with her than God himself?

"God," she whispered, "are you speaking to me?"

Twice more came the strange injunction—You help them . . . *you* help them.

"But, Lord," she prayed, "what could I possibly—"

Suddenly Cherity's eyes shot open.

She jumped from the bed and ran across the floor to the desk and bureau where she kept her things. She sat down and pulled out the top drawer and removed the envelope that had come to her several months before from Mr. Glennie, her father's attorney in Boston. She had scarcely thought about it since. She took out the paper inside and unfolded it.

Dear Miss Waters, she read again.

    Enclosed please find a current statement of your third of your father's investment assets. Your sisters have moved their accounts elsewhere according to their needs, and I want to reiterate again that if I can be of assistance in advising you in the matter of your investments, or should you need to liquidate any portion of them for your own needs, please do not hesitate to contact me. Until I hear from you to the contrary, be assured that your funds are secure and growing at a reasonable rate given these uncertain and troubled times.

With regard to the disposition of the house, previously your father's, at 17 Constitution Hill, I have the pleasure to inform you that all legalities of probate are finalized and title to the house is now fully in your name. Until hearing from you otherwise, I have the deed to the property, in your name, here safely with your other financial records. Should you wish me to attempt to sell the house on your behalf, or should the time come when you will again take possession of it personally, I am at your service. Until then, it is being cared for and watched over pending further instructions from you.

I am,

Sincerely yours,
R. Glennie, Paul Revere Court, Boston.

The letter slipped from Cherity's hand as her brain spun excitedly with possibilities.

The next morning at breakfast she announced her intentions, though not the reason for her decision.

"I need to go to Boston," she said. "There are some things regarding my father's house, as well as some other matters, that I need to attend to."

"Isn't this rather sudden?" said Carolyn. "You've not mentioned a word of it before now."

"I received a letter from my father's attorney some months ago. I've delayed a reply for too long. In the middle of the night I woke up thinking about it and suddenly realized that I wanted to get it taken care of. Is it safe to travel, Mr. Davidson?" she asked, turning to Richmond.

"Things remain a little dangerous in Virginia," he replied. "But most civilian trains are moving through pretty well. I think I would want to accompany you as far as Washington just to be on the safe side, if you would not find that an imposition."

"Of course not!"

"Once you are back in the Union, you should have no difficulty the rest of the way to Boston. Isn't one of your sisters in Norfolk?"

"Mary and her husband went back to New York when the war started. That's where her husband is from. I will spend the night with her on my way to Boston and back."

Thirty-Seven

~⌒

Thomas had known for several days that they were getting close to Greenwood. He could smell it in the air. He could see it in the terrain.

He *sensed* it.

He had known for some time that the place he had heard his fellow pilgrims talking about was his own home, and that the angels were his own father and mother.

So many feelings filled his brain and heart as they moved closer and closer. He was excited, afraid, nervous. What would he tell his parents about what he had done? How would they react? Would his father be angry with him for deserting his unit?

So many confusing thoughts swirled within him that he had not yet even told Deanna that one of their next stations was his own home.

Then came the day when Thomas began to recognize specific sights. He knew *exactly* where they were! He and Seth had ridden these same hills. He had helped rescue runaways coming on this same route! He could lead them the rest of the way himself!

They spent the next two days hiding out, before moving on again as darkness fell. Thomas became more nervous. How would he explain himself? But he could not turn back now!

Yet one final time they walked all night. When they lay down to rest in a cave as the sun was coming up, and were told that someone would be along for them that day, Thomas knew where that someone would be from, and where he would be taking them!

He had hardly noticed Deanna hesitate, as they approached the cave, looking with a curious expression at a large boulder standing to one side of the cave's mouth, before following the others inside.

Late in the morning as they dozed in one of the caves that Thomas had grown up thinking was haunted by the ghosts of dead Indians, they heard a voice outside.

"Any railroad trab'lers in dere who's waitin' fo' a stashun break?"

Thomas sat up and crept to the back of the group. Everyone stood as Isaac Shaw ducked and walked into the cool darkness. "All right, I see dere is," he said. "Come wiff me. We gots a meal waitin' fo' you."

He turned and walked back out into the sunshine and the group of runaways followed. Thomas hung back. Deanna waited, glancing toward him with a confused expression. At last Thomas came out of the cave behind the rest of the group.

They followed Isaac down the hill toward Greenwood. It was not until they had been walking for ten or twelve minutes that Isaac turned around to say something to the man in the lead. Behind the others his gaze fell on a white boy who looked about his own age. Suddenly his eyes shot open wide as two saucers and he stopped in his tracks.

"Laws!" he exclaimed. "Dat be . . . Laws almighty . . . Thomas! Dat really be you?"

At last Thomas came forward, a sheepish grin on his lips. "Hello, Isaac," he said. "Yes . . . it's really me."

The next instant he found himself crushed in a bear hug reminiscent of Isaac's father Malachi. The others watched in amazement. They had always sensed something a little peculiar about Thomas. Now here he was being greeted by a black boy like he was his own brother!

"I don't know what you's doin' here, or how you got here," said Isaac, "but dis is gwine cause da biggest uproar eber seen at Greenwood!"

"What are you talking about?" laughed Thomas. "I just came home, that's all."

"Dat ain't hardly all dere is to it!"

"What do you mean?"

"You don't know?"

"Know what?"

"You really don't know?" asked Isaac again.

"No, Isaac!" laughed Thomas. "What are you talking about?"

"Den I'm not sayin' a word! I's jes' gonna stan' by an' watch da commotion when you walks in! I got me a heap er questions, but dey kin keep. Dere's gonna be more folks den me wiff questions, an' dat's a fact!"

Isaac turned, and continued down the hill, chuckling to himself.

"What is he talking about, Thomas?" said Deanna. "Why do you know each other?"

"I've been trying to find a way to tell you," replied Thomas. "But . . . this station we're going to—it's my home."

Isaac made no attempt to follow the usual paths that kept out of sight. He walked onto the road that led straight to the main house.

While they were still far off, Richmond, who was working outside, saw the group approaching. Among them he saw a white face that he knew and recognized instantly, even from a distance.

Without pausing to ask himself how it could be, his heart swelled with the fullness of a father's love. He dropped the shovel in his hand and broke into a run.

Thomas saw him. His heart began to pound. He stood watching a moment, then left the others and ran toward his father.

They met in the road and embraced. Richmond was weeping like a baby and stroking the hair on Thomas's head as he once had when he was a child. Thomas allowed himself for the first time in years to be comforted by his father's arms.

"Dad," said Thomas in a shaky voice, tears pouring from his eyes. "I am sorry for everything. I was so full of resentment that I had no right to feel. You were such a good father and I could not see it. I am so sorry. I know I don't deserve it, but I hope you can forgive me."

Richmond's heart was bursting in an agony of joy. "Oh, Thomas . . . Thomas, you were always forgiven! I love you more than you can know."

They stood for several moments in one another's arms. Thomas's fellow travelers walked slowly toward them, shy to get too close. They did not understand what was going on, but they could tell this was a holy moment.

Some premonition led Carolyn out the front door. She saw the small crowd gathered some fifty yards from the house. Though she could not see Thomas's face, an inkling of the truth swelled in her mother's breast.

She gasped as a rush of heat swept through her, and she started to run. With every step she was more and more certain of what she thought she had seen. Before she was halfway to them, tears were streaming down her cheeks and she was babbling in confused but ecstatic thanksgiving.

Richmond stepped back and she ran straight into Thomas's arms, sobbing without restraint on his chest where he stood now several inches taller than she.

"Isaac!" called Richmond behind them, "go get Sydney. Tell him that Thomas has come home! Our son who was dead is alive . . . he was lost and now is found! Tell him to butcher the calf. All Greenwood will feast tonight!"

Word spread through Greenwood like a wind rushing down out of the mountains. While the black railroad passengers still stood in bewilderment, and as Richmond and Carolyn cried and laughed and overwhelmed Thomas with happy questions, men and women and boys and girls began pouring out of the big house and the black houses and running toward the scene—Cynthia and Sydney and Chigua and Nancy and Aaron Shaw and the other former slaves who had known Thomas all their lives.

Gradually Thomas began to put two and two together and realize what the fuss was all about. Cynthia and Cherity embraced him weeping. Thomas, who for years had unconsciously felt overshadowed by his older brother realized perhaps for the first time in his life just how greatly he was loved. For no matter how much love is poured out upon son or daughter, unless that love is *received,* its full effect cannot be accomplished in the heart. At last Thomas was capable of receiving the love that had always existed toward him. It entered deeply into him, and continued the healing in his soul that he had allowed to begin some months before.

Nancy eventually led the newcomers away to take charge of them and see to their accommodations. One of them, however, a black girl of eighteen or nineteen, hung back, still watching Thomas where he and his family stood talking excitedly.

Out of the corner of his eye, Thomas saw her standing alone. He turned toward her.

"Oh, but you have to meet the girl who saved my life!" he said. "Deanna . . . Deanna, come over here! I want you to meet my family!"

At the name, Richmond and Carolyn glanced at one another.

Shyly Deanna walked slowly toward the excited group. Thomas ran a few steps, took her hand, and pulled her toward the others.

"This is Deanna!" he said, and his voice was obviously filled with pride. "I *would* be dead now if it wasn't for her! Deanna, this is my father and mother and my sister, and my brother's . . . I mean our friend Cherity Waters. And this is Sydney . . . and his wife Chigua."

"Welcome to Greenwood," said Carolyn, taking both Deanna's hands in hers. "I am Carolyn Davidson. And your name again is—" she said, then hesitated.

"Deanna," replied Deanna, "—Deanna Steddings."

Carolyn drew in a sharp breath and her face went pale. The next instant Deanna found herself swallowed in the embrace of this white lady who was perhaps an angel, but who until a few seconds ago had been a perfect stranger.

"Did you say . . . *Steddings?*" exclaimed Richmond.

"Yes," laughed Deanna. "Deanna Steddings. Why . . . do you know the name from somewhere?"

"I should say I do! I cannot believe my ears! Your father's and mother's names would not by chance be Aaron and Zaphorah?"

Now it was Deanna's turn to gasp in astonishment as she slowly nodded.

Again Carolyn burst into sobs. "Oh, Richmond!"

"They have been very worried about you!" said Richmond.

"You know my parents!" now exclaimed Deanna.

"They were here," said Carolyn, weeping with yet more disbelieving joy. "They came to Greenwood just like you did! They told us about you. We have been praying for you!"

"Where are they?" asked Deanna.

"Home . . . in Mount Holly."

Now the tears of disbelief and thanksgiving poured out all over again. The homecoming of those who had been lost and now were found became the blessing of a double homecoming! Suddenly it was Thomas who was full of questions.

They all began making their way to the house, everyone talking and clustered about and asking questions at once.

Never had Greenwood witnessed such a joyous occasion.

Thirty-Eight

The rest of the day of the homecoming passed like an excited blur. Simply being in his father's presence again removed every burden from Thomas's mind. He and Richmond talked and laughed like old friends, as indeed they had always been. How could he have forgotten how much fun his father was! Not a word of judgment or condemnation was spoken all day, only acceptance, love, and free-flowing good times between father and son. He should have known there was nothing to worry about. His father and Seth were the two best friends he had in the world. How could he have forgotten?

About an hour after his arrival, Thomas saw Nancy Shaw leading Deanna down toward the black houses. He went to find his mother.

"Mom," he said, "where is Nancy taking Deanna?"

"Down to find her a place to stay with the others, I think," answered Carolyn.

"But, Mom . . . I thought . . . ," began Thomas.

Suddenly he realized that he was embarrassed.

"But, she's . . . I mean," he went on, "but she's with me, Mom, not with them. She's . . . you know, like one of the family."

"I think I understand," she said. "I'm sorry, Thomas. With everything happening, I didn't think of it. Nancy was just trying to help. I'll go down and talk to her. We'll put her in the room next to Cherity."

"Thanks, Mom."

Two mornings later, after breakfast, Thomas and Richmond walked together outside talking man to man in a way they had never done before.

"I meant what I said when I came," said Thomas. "I don't know why I was so angry about so many things. I really am sorry. You were the best father a son could have had."

"We all have to grow up in our own way," said Richmond. "I faced some things when I was young too. I didn't handle everything as I wish I had. But we grow even through our immaturities."

Richmond went on to share some of the heartaches of his own past, much as he had on a previous occasion with Seth.

"Thanks, Dad," said Thomas. "I guess I understand some of your struggles better now. I was nervous about coming home. I didn't know what you would say. Now that I'm here, I realize I had nothing to worry about. But . . . there is one thing I need to say . . . that I *want* to say."

Thomas paused and drew in a breath of resolve. This was hard!

"I just want to say, Dad," he continued after a few seconds, "that I love you. I have always loved you, and I'm sorry I didn't show it."

Richmond blinked hard as tears welled up in his eyes.

"Thank you, Thomas," he said softly. "Your words mean more than I can tell you. I love you too."

He threw his arm around Thomas's shoulders and the two walked on. For the first time in years, Thomas realized that it felt good to have his father's arm around him. It felt good to be loved. It felt good to be loved by a *father*, his father.

It did not take long for Cherity and Deanna to hit it off. Though Cherity was several years older, they were close enough in age that they were drawn toward one another. And the fact that both stood in unique relationships with the two Davidson brothers may also have contributed to the friendship that quickly sprung up between them.

And, too, they shared a love of horses, though Deanna did not have a fraction of Cherity's experience. She had not ridden during her slave years, and the last time she had been on the back of a horse had ended with her falling off and being separated from her family. Nevertheless, she was excited when Cherity suggested a ride.

They walked into the stables to pick out two mounts.

"This is a new young stallion Thomas's brother had shipped to me," said Cherity. "He is gentle and shies at nothing. You can ride him. You will be safe and comfortable. I will ride Patches."

Twenty minutes later they were heading slowly away from Greenwood up the incline toward the ridge. Within no time Deanna seemed as comfortable on Cadence's back as if she had been riding every day for years.

⟨⎯⎯⟩

"Dad," said Thomas hesitantly,, "I . . . uh, I need to ask your advice about something."

"Sure, Thomas . . . what is it?"

"Well . . . you know, what I did—leaving like I did, running away from my unit. It doesn't seem right, and I don't know what to do about it. I mean, it isn't that I have thought seriously about going back. I told you what happened and what Deanna overheard them saying. In one way, I suppose I had no choice. But in another way . . . deserting your unit is something they used to hang people for, isn't it? You know, duty to one's country and treason and all that."

"Maybe at one time they did," said Richmond seriously. "Tell me, Thomas, do you feel that you did wrong?"

"How do you mean?"

"Leaving aside for a minute that your life was in danger, do you feel that it was wrong to run away from the war?"

Thomas thought a minute.

"I don't know," he said at length. "I guess I really don't. I have come to believe that this war itself is wrong, that the South was wrong to have started it, and that I was wrong to join in a fight that should never have taken place at all. The wrong I feel is not my leaving, but my joining the army in the first place. I mean . . . I know that desertion is wrong in ordinary circumstances. An army can't just have people leaving when they decide they don't like a war. Sometimes duty to one's country *is* higher than one's own life. If Mr. Lincoln walked into Greenwood right now and said, 'Thomas, I want you to go fight for me, for the good of the country,' I think I would do it. At least I hope I would. But I don't think the Confederacy is a legitimate nation with a legitimate claim to my allegiance. The Confederate army is not a legitimate army at all because it is in rebellion against its true president."

Richmond nodded. "I see," he said. "Then perhaps your leaving as you did—putting aside again for the moment that your life was in danger—was your way, not to desert your principles but actually to stand up for your convictions in a way you hadn't done before. Is that perhaps how you see it?"

"In a way . . . yes, that's exactly it, Dad. But I don't want to make myself sound too heroic. That's how I've been thinking of it in the months since it happened. But at the time, I was just trying to stay alive. Maybe I was being cowardly and I am just making excuses for myself."

"Is the guilt you feel perhaps not so much for what you did, but from the stigma associated with desertion?"

"I suppose so."

"It is a difficult dilemma, Son. I would not for a moment advocate your going back. I think the war is about over anyway. Yet you may still have a duty to fulfill, as you say. I trust that the Lord will show you if he does indeed have some alternate way for you to faithfully obey that duty to your country."

Cherity and Deanna rode through the woodland that was part of the Brown tract, talking freely as they went. Cherity was explaining about the Brown house and the caves and legends associated with

them. Deanna was telling Cherity about her family and how they
had escaped and everything that had happened with Thomas on the
Underground Railroad.

"You know how fond of you Thomas is?" said Cherity.

Deanna felt the heat rise on the back of her neck. She glanced away.

"What do you mean?" she said.

"He worships you, Deanna. Anyone can see that from the way he
looks at you."

"It's just because I helped him. He's just being nice to me."

"It's more than that. I can tell."

"But . . . I'm black and he's white."

"Do you think that makes any difference around here!" laughed
Cherity. "I don't think anyone at Greenwood even knows what skin
color is! Believe me, that is the last thing Thomas is thinking about."

They reached the Brown house.

"What is this?" said Deanna as they stopped.

"This is the house where the Indian Mr. Brown lived. I like to
come up here whenever I can. I'm certain there is some mystery
about this place I am going to discover eventually. Maybe it's silly,
but whenever I come up here I feel like I am in a story whose ending
I don't know yet. There's something . . . I don't know . . . spooky and
yet exciting about it."

Deanna laughed. "You're braver than I am," she said. "I would
never come out here alone!"

"Let me show you something—come look at the carvings on this
tree."

They dismounted, tied the horses, and Cherity led the way to the
tree where she had seen the strange markings.

"What do you think it is?" asked Deanna.

"I don't know, but doesn't it look like some secret code or
something?"

"I think I saw something like that carved on a rock outside the cave
where we stayed when we got here."

"You did?" exclaimed Cherity. "Let's go—I want to see it!"

They ran back to their horses, and were soon off in the direction of the cave, which was about half a mile from the Brown house.

They reached it and again dismounted.

"Look, it's right over here," said Deanna excitedly. She led Cherity to the boulder beside the entrance to the cave. On one side of the rock they could faintly make out what looked to be lines and dots that had been hammered or scraped onto it. Cherity could not imagine that she had never noticed them before. As she knelt down to look at the markings more carefully, all at once she heard Deanna cry out.

She glanced up just in time to see her disappear inside the cave.

"Deanna . . . ," she called.

"Cherity . . . Cherity, help!" screamed Deanna, her voice echoing from inside the cave. "A man's got me!"

A chill swept through Cherity as she jumped to her feet. *Elias Slade!*

Suspecting the worst, she pulled the pistol from the holster strapped to her waist, and, her knees trembling, crept toward the mouth of the cave. From inside she heard sounds of scuffling and more muffled cries for help.

In the few seconds she had to prepare herself, a hundred things flashed through her mind. If it was Elias Slade, there was little doubt he could overpower and rape them both easily. The only way she had escaped his clutches before was by surprising him. But if he had been watching them from the cave, she would not be able to surprise him now. How could she, at barely more than five feet and a hundred pounds, get Deanna away from him?

All this raced through her brain in a second or two. She had to act fast. From the sounds of the scuffling, whoever it was had been dragging Deanna inside. He would expect her to peer in cautiously and slowly. So she would do the opposite!

Cherity dashed into the darkness, glancing frantically about as she ran.

"Cherity!" shrieked Deanna.

Cherity saw two sets of eyes glistening toward her from the depths of the blackness reflecting the light of the cave's mouth. She ran inside as far as she dared, then quickly hugged the cave wall as far from Slade and Deanna as she could get. Sight of their eyes glimmering in the dark gave her an idea. She closed her own eyes tight, and tried silently to catch her breath.

With her eyes closed, hopefully Slade could not see her. She waited as long as she dared, allowing her eyes to accustom themselves to the darkness, then opened them a slit. She could just barely make out two forms on the opposite side and about ten feet deeper into the interior of the cave. Again she shut her eyes.

If she could just work her way behind them!

Carefully Cherity set the gun down on the ground and pulled off one boot, then the other. Retrieving the gun with her right hand, and feeling about with her left so that she wouldn't clunk her head on the roof of the cave, and opening her eyes just a slit to get her bearings, she crept on her toes back deeper and deeper into the darkness.

"Where you be, w'ite girl?" called Slade. His voice was so close she nearly leapt into the air in fright. "Tell me where you is an' I won't hurt dis girl."

Cherity remained silent. She crept a few more steps. She was behind them now. She could see their outlines against the light of the cave opening in the distance.

"Don't git me angry, w'ite girl! Or else I's gwine hab—"

"I am right next to you," said Cherity, jabbing the pistol hard into his huge back. "And this is Mr. Davidson's gun. I'm not very good with it, so you probably shouldn't frighten me or I might pull the trigger. Now let her go."

Slade could hardly believe that the little girl would have a gun. But it did feel like steel in his back and he couldn't take any chances. He relaxed his grip. Deanna wriggled free.

"Run, Deanna!" cried Cherity, "Get out of here!"

The instant his hands were free, Slade swung behind him with a mighty blow intended to whack Cherity to the ground. But she ducked and was shorter than he had anticipated. His powerful arm came crashing against the jagged rocks of the cave wall.

He exploded in a fury of pain, swore violently, then grappled furiously in the darkness for Cherity whom he now intended to kill not rape.

But the instant he made his move, she ducked past him and bolted after Deanna for the cave mouth, pausing only long enough to turn and fire three or four quick shots inside, aiming low and intending only to slow Slade up if he tried to follow them. Another great roar echoing from inside made her wonder if she had accidently hit him. But the charging sound of footsteps assured her that at least he was still alive.

They raced to their horses, Cherity in her stocking feet, and were soon on their way back to Greenwood as quickly as Deanna was ready to ride.

The moment Richmond heard of the incident, he went to his office, sat down at his desk, and wrote a brief note addressed to his neighbor:

> *Dear Denton,*
>   *There has been another dangerous incident involving your*
> *man Elias Slade. I am sorry, but this is no longer a request. I am*
> *graciously demanding that you get rid of him or I will take action.*
>
>   *Richmond Davidson.*

Richard Fitzpatrick was away from home when Cecil Hirsch came to see Veronica with a new assignment. Trying to remain calm, she listened and nodded quietly. Cecil could tell some change had taken place in her, but could not quite put his finger on it.

Ten minutes after he was gone, Veronica left for the telegraph office to notify Seth.

She heard back from him that same day when to expect him.

Seth arrived in the nation's capital, checked into a hotel, then sought a hansom cab to take him to the address Veronica had given him. Veronica was anxiously waiting for him.

"Oh, Seth, I am so glad you're here!" she said. "Cecil will be back tomorrow. I am supposed to leave for Columbia two days after that. What should I do?"

Seth sat down at the kitchen table while Veronica prepared a pot of tea.

"Have you managed to find out the names of any of Hirsch's contacts?" asked Seth.

"Not yet. I asked him who he worked for but he looked at me a little angrily and asked why I wanted to know."

Seth nodded. "My editor has a plan," he said, "that might get you out of trouble and break up Hirsch's spy network. It might be frightening for you. If Hirsch finds out what we're up to he will probably disappear. Then for all we know he might turn *you* in. It will also mean a trip to Boston."

"Boston . . . why?"

"Mr. McClarin wants to see the documents you are supposed to deliver."

"But I am supposed to take them to Columbia. If the seal is broken—"

"Don't worry, he can take care of that. But we will have to act fast. McClarin wants us to leave for Boston as soon as possible after you get the documents from Hirsch. He will arrange to replace the documents with fake ones so that no important information will be passed to the Confederacy. Then you will deliver the fake documents. We will keep the real ones to use as evidence against Hirsch, along with anything you are to bring back to him."

Thirty-Nine

*P*rowling Bear's son Black Wolf listened to all his father told him, and vowed to complete what was left undone.

At twelve, he had gone out into the hills alone and, in a ceremony meaningless to any but himself, had taken a knife and cut a slit in the third finger of his left hand until his blood dripped onto the earth. He looked to the heavens, shouted a bloodcurdling cry, and in that moment vowed never to forget the Cherokee blood law. He himself would hunt out the traitors who sold their lands, even from long ago, and spill their blood on this dry evil ground as his own had been this day. If Stand Watie, Boudinot's brother, still lived when he reached his own manhood, Black Wolf promised himself that he would kill him, just as his father had killed his brother. He would root out others as well—anyone who had participated in the treachery . . . man, woman, child, son, daughter, or even grandson or granddaughter—*anyone* who, even if but by blood, had participated.

Besides the Watie brothers and the Ridges, he had heard his father speak also of one of his own cousins from many years before, a son of Nakey Canoe, daughter of the great warrior Dragging Canoe, who had also sold his birthright. His house had been burned and his family killed. But there were others, his father said, even some living among them, whose treachery had been forgotten, those who had taken the white man's money and hid it for their own gain. There were still others who had taken the gold of the Cherokee and abandoned the tribe, to live in luxury among the white man. Some had returned in secret, their betrayal hidden from view.

The influence from all these forms of betrayal was that now the whole tribe looked like whites, acted like whites, talked like whites. It rested with those such as himself to bring back the former glory of their proud nation. Both leaders, John Ross and Stand Watie, in the mind of Black Wolf, were but weak agents of white culture. They dressed like white men and spoke the white man's tongue. They had done nothing to reestablish the birthright of the Cherokee.

"Tell me again of the old times, Papa," said the eager young Black Wolf over and over in the years of his boyhood. The question and his father's answers were always in the Cherokee tongue, for his father refused to speak any other. On each occasion a different recollection added fuel to nurture the smoldering embers of generational hatred in the boy's soul.

"It was a dark night," replied his father to the question one night as he stared into the fire and his mind drifted back even more distantly into his past than usual, all the way back to his own youth when he himself was a young man. "Rumors had been spreading for days that blood money had changed hands with the white man. The elders of the tribe did not at first know who was the latest to commit the treachery. Then suddenly on this night my father burst into our hut with passion in his voice. *It is Nakey Canoe's own son!* he cried. *The traitor is of my own clan. But he will not live to see the sun!* My father grabbed a few things and again disappeared. My soul was in turmoil," Prowling Bear went on. "I was seized with fear at the sound of my father's voice with the threat of death in his tone. I ran after him and followed into the night. I saw bright flames rising in the sky. I knew what it meant, that the blood law had been avenged. Even those of one's own clan could not escape it. Then I saw a figure running through the darkness. I waited as the runner passed close to me. It was a boy . . . my own younger cousin fleeing for his life! Some impulse made me follow him. What I later heard I dared not tell my father for fear of what might happen to me for allowing him, even though but a boy, to escape. I kept the words of that night buried in my soul, terrified to speak them . . . until now."

"What did you hear, Papa?" asked Black Wolf, his eyes wide with fearful curiosity.

"I heard the man tell my cousin, 'Come, Swift Horse, we must flee . . . we must flee in the night, not to return until our posterity can right the evil of this terrible deed. They of our own tribe have turned against us. . . .'"

Prowling Bear fell silent, staring into the embers of the fire. His next words plunged deep into the heart of his son:

"'The next generation depends on us,' the man said. 'We must take what we have been given . . . take it away and hide it and protect it for those who come after.'

"They took it . . . stole it that night . . . stole it to hide it, for they knew they had betrayed Cherokee law."

Black Wolf knew that his father spoke of the blood money from the treacherous sale of sacred lands. And as his father never forgot, Black Wolf never forgot.

"My father thought the whole family killed," Prowling Bear went on after several minutes. "He always said that none must escape the vengeance of the blood law. But Swift Horse *had* escaped the vengeance that fell upon his father. Only I knew it. Only I had seen him running from the fire through the night."

Who the man was whom he had heard in the shadows, Prowling Bear never knew. As he grew, he suspected another of Swift Water's clan of helping them, for he had seen the two talking together as the house burned.

"And I knew," he went on, "that if my father had been unafraid to punish one of his own clan for betrayal, neither could I fear to exact the same punishment on the son. Only I knew that the vengeance of that night was not complete. I knew I must wait and watch. And when they returned, what they had stolen must be returned and retribution exacted upon them."

With many such stories Prowling Bear filled Black Wolf's impressionable boy's mind—mingling legend and hearsay with fact and exaggeration and outright untruth. By the time Black Wolf was ten, the requirement of the blood law had deeply penetrated as an obsession into his consciousness. It was not only the white man who was his enemy but those of his own tribe, even his own clan, who were traitors against their heritage, those who had sold their land and had given themselves to the white man's ways.

Throughout the rest of his life, fiery images of retribution and violence filled the soul of Black Wolf son of Prowling Bear and turned his heart toward darkness. Nor did he forget the rumors of those who had escaped, cowards fleeing in the night, fleeing with gold gained from selling their lands, and later gold stolen from the Cherokee caves. Whenever and wherever a son or even grandson or granddaughter of such a traitor was discovered, one who possessed what belonged to the tribe, he would himself carry out the duty of the ancients which now rested on him.

As his father had said, he too waited and watched . . . waited for the moment when vengeance for the past would be demanded.

His anxiety now redoubled concerning Elias Slade, Richmond at last forbade further rides away from Greenwood until he had the chance to attempt to deal with the matter satisfactorily. The very afternoon he drafted a brief note to Denton Beaumont, it was followed by a more formal letter to the authorities in Richmond.

Cherity had intended to leave for Boston before now. Her plans, however, had been preempted by Thomas's sudden appearance. Deanna, however, was anxious to get home, and Cherity knew she could not delay her own plans indefinitely. Time was ticking away, and Greenwood's future was in jeopardy.

"Why don't we go north together?" Cherity suggested to Deanna, "at least as far as Philadelphia. Then you can go home and I will continue on to Boston."

Unknown to either of the girls, Richmond and Carolyn had also been talking about accompanying Deanna back to Mount Holly, to ensure her safety but also as an excuse to see her parents again. That would be a reunion, like theirs with Thomas, they did not want to miss!

And Thomas, when he heard of the plans, was not about to be left behind!

Thus it was that Richmond, Carolyn, and Cherity, along with Thomas and Deanna, boarded the train together in Dove's Landing, bound for Washington, then Philadelphia. From there Cherity would continue north, and the three Davidsons would take Deanna the rest of the way to Mount Holly.

When Cecil Hirsch presented himself at 37 Myrtlebriar Court, Washington D.C. and asked to see Mrs. Fitzpatrick he was met by the housekeeper.

"Are you Mr. Hirsch?" she said.

"I am," he replied.

"Mrs. Fitzpatrick is expecting you," said the woman. "She is not here but she left something for you. If you will just wait a moment."

The woman disappeared inside the house leaving Cecil waiting, a little perturbed, at the door. He did not like surprises, unless he was himself the author of them.

The housekeeper returned and handed him a letter. He took it brusquely, and began walking away from the house, then unfolded it.

> *Dear Cecil,*
> *I thought it best not to meet at the house. I was afraid Mrs. Notting might be growing suspicious. I will wait for you at Garabaldi's instead.*
>
> *Veronica*

Still annoyed, Hirsch mounted his carriage, flicked the reins, and hastened into the city. The thing made sense, but he still didn't like Veronica calling the shots.

He walked into Garabaldi's Restaurant thirty minutes later and glanced around for Veronica. She was seated in a corner at the far end. Some commotion was under way at one of the tables nearby that appeared to be a wedding party. He noticed a man standing with some contraption on a three-legged device giving directions to the people at the table. *One of these new photographers*, he thought to himself. But he strode past whatever the festivities and sat down opposite Veronica.

"What do you mean telling me to come here like this?" he said. "We could just as well have—"

"I didn't want to meet at the house," said Veronica. "I explained that in the note. Besides, I was in the mood for a nice lunch."

Before Hirsch could object further, he glanced up to see the owner of the restaurant approaching.

"Garabaldi . . . ," nodded Hirsch, betraying a tone of inquiry.

"Hello, Hirsch," said Garabaldi, taking a seat beside Hirsch. "What did you want to see me about, Mrs. Fitzpatrick?" he asked.

But Veronica did not answer him. Instead she turned and addressed Cecil.

"Is that the next packet you have for me?" she said, reaching for the thick envelope in Hirsch's hand. Almost before he realized what she was doing, she grabbed it from him. "Oh, look!" she exclaimed. "There's a man taking a—"

The two men glanced in the direction of Veronica's gaze. At the same moment a blinding flash illuminated the interior of the restaurant along with the light explosion of a brief *poof.*

"What in blazes!" exclaimed Garabaldi.

"It's a man photographing those newlyweds," said Veronica. "How sweet."

"Not in my restaurant," said Garabaldi, rising. "I'll get rid of him."

But already the photographer was hastily gathering up his things.

He required little persuasion by the angry restaurant owner before he was on his way and gone, and the small wedding party behind him.

Ruffled but relieved, Garabaldi returned to the table. "I apologize for that incident," he said.

"No harm done," said Hirsch.

"Now, Mrs. Fitzpatrick . . . ," said Garabaldi.

"I wanted to speak with you both," said Veronica. "It is simply this. I have finally figured out what you are doing. I should have sooner, but I did not stop to think about it. You see, Mr. Garabaldi, I have seen the contents of one of Mr. Hirsch's mysterious packets which I have been delivering. So now I know that you are using me to pass information to the South."

"Keep your voice down!" whispered Garabaldi, who glanced at Hirsch with a dark expression.

"Now Cecil has threatened to turn me in as a spy," Veronica went on, looking back and forth between the two men. Both wore serious and angry expressions.

"But I can do the same," said Veronica. "Maybe no one will believe me and that is a chance I have to take. But I am willing to take it. I do not like being used as you have used me. So I am telling you that if you intend to continue using me to deliver your information, I want to meet whoever this information is coming from . . . and I want more money for my part in all this. I will take this packet to Columbia. But when I return I want to meet whoever else is involved and I want a third of whatever you receive. Otherwise I will go to the authorities and tell them what I know and take my chances with whatever you might tell them."

She looked back and forth between the two men who sat looking at her stunned and furious, but for the moment speechless.

"Well, Mrs. Fitzpatrick," said Garabaldi calmly at last, for he did not want to cause a scene in his own establishment. "It would seem that you have taken us both by surprise. I presume you will give us time to think over your, ah . . . your demands?"

"You have until I return from Columbia," replied Veronica. "Now,

Cecil," she said, turning toward Hirsch, "what do you want me to do when I get there?"

Veronica breathed a great sigh of relief as she took a cab from Garabaldi's back to her house. She was shaking and perspiring, but she had done it just as she and Seth had planned. He came to call later that same afternoon, and they boarded a train for New York. There they booked two rooms and spent the night, then caught the early morning train to Boston.

Forty

The departure farewell at the Philadelphia station between Cherity and Deanna was filled with tears and promises of letters and future visits. In the short time they had known one another, their hearts had been knit together in much the same way Carolyn's had with Deanna's mother.

Cherity felt very lonely waving through the window to the four standing on the platform as her train pulled out of the station.

As for Richmond, Carolyn, Thomas, and Deanna, the moment Cherity's train was out of sight, they dashed for the next platform to board their train for Burlington, scheduled to leave in twenty minutes. This would be one of the most exciting rides of Deanna's life!

They knew that after the Steddings' return to Mount Holly, Aaron and Zaphorah had stayed with the Bortons. As Richmond guided their rented carriage along the road beside Rancocas Creek, however, he realized that after a year Deanna's family might no longer be with Aaron's former employer. Carolyn's last letter from Zaphorah had been three months earlier. But as long as they could find the Borton farm, if they had moved since then, they would surely be able to locate them.

Along the way, Richmond recalled Aaron's explaining to him the close connections between the Borton and Woolman families, of the marriage that had taken place in 1684 on New Jersey soil between John Woolman and young Elizabeth Borton, and that his employer, John Borton, a Quaker minister in the tradition of his fathers and grandfathers, and his wife, Martha Woolman, had again linked the two families in marriage five generations later.

As they bounced along, Carolyn turned around to where Deanna sat quietly at Thomas's side.

"Do you recognize anything?" she asked with a smile.

"I don't know," replied Deanna. "I can't really tell. The memories are hazy and distant. The trees and bushes have grown."

The carriage slowed. A sign beside the road read "John Borton." Richmond pulled into the drive.

"This must be it," he said.

A minute later they slowly pulled up to the house.

No one was in sight. Then a tall black man strode slowly out of the blacksmith's shop a hundred feet away.

Deanna gasped. "*Papa!*" she whispered.

Carolyn and Thomas helped her down out of the carriage, and Deanna dashed toward him.

As they watched, Carolyn heard the door of the house open. She turned toward the sound. Zaphorah walked onto the porch and saw the buggy in front of the house with three people standing in front of it.

"Carolyn . . . ," she said in disbelief as she came down the steps and hurried forward.

But then her eyes were drawn to the sight of Aaron in front of his workshop holding someone tight in his arms.

She caught her breath and her hand went to her mouth.

"Oh . . . oh . . . ," she began, then broke into a run.

Carolyn seemed to be crying a lot lately. She could not help it again as she saw mother and father and daughter wrapped in each other's arms. Nor was she alone. Both Thomas and Richmond were wiping at their eyes as well.

John Borton was in town with his brother Pemberton. When they returned they saw an unfamiliar buggy standing in the drive. John walked into the house and heard the talk and laughter of familiar voices coming from the kitchen.

Aaron rose when he entered.

"Mr. Borton," said Aaron, "we have guests! I want thee to meet the dear brother and sister in the Lord who brought our daughter home."

"Richmond," he said, beckoning Richmond forward, "this is the man I told thee of, Mr. John Borton."

"Mr. Borton, it is an honor to meet you," said Richmond, shaking the older man's hand. "I am Richmond Davidson."

"Mr. Davidson."

"And may I present my wife, Carolyn."

"Mrs. Davidson," said Borton, shaking Carolyn's hand. "And please meet my brother Pemberton," he added. More handshakes went around the room.

"And look," said Zaphorah excitedly.

Both Bortons glanced around the room and saw four black young people rather than three, along with Borton's own three children: Rebecca eighteen, John fourteen, and James twelve. With them also sat a young man who bore a striking resemblance to Richmond.

"Would this be . . . ?" began John, looking toward Deanna.

"It's Deanna, Mr. Borton!" exclaimed young Suzane Steddings. "Deanna's come home!"

"I see that!" laughed Borton. "How does she come to be here . . . and with thee, Mr. Davidson?"

"It is quite a story!" laughed Richmond. "But I hope you will call me Richmond. And I would like you to meet our son Thomas."

Thomas stood.

"Thomas, this is John Borton . . . and Mr. Pemberton Borton."

"I am pleased to meet you both," said Thomas, firmly shaking the hands of the two men.

"Thomas and Deanna wound up on the Underground Railroad," said Zaphorah. "Isn't it wonderful how God works?"

"It surely is indeed!"

"And Aaron tells us he is buying several acres from you," said Richmond, "and plans to build."

"That is right," replied Borton. "He had his heart set on five acres that were for sale years ago before they left. Feeling responsible for what happened—after all, he was on an errand as a favor to us at the time—we felt the least we could do was to help him reach his dream."

The three Davidsons remained at Mount Holly four days. Aaron proudly gave Richmond a tour of nearly every inch of his five-acre parcel. Richmond and Thomas helped with the clearing of the land that was then in progress in preparation for what Aaron hoped would be the site holding a completed house by the end of that year.

Though he had not met John Woolman himself, in the venerable John Borton, fifteen years his elder, Richmond Davidson felt that he had connected with the very roots of Quaker faith in America. From a line of six generations of Quaker ministers, the name Borton was as linked as that of Woolman to the foundation of the Society of Friends back to the days of George Fox in England. Within minutes of their arrival Borton offered his home to them for as long as they wanted to stay.

Richmond was full of questions. He learned not only much about the history of the Society of Friends, but also of the founding of the New Jersey and Pennsylvania colonies. Borton, on his part, was eager to learn about the Davidson experiment, for by now he had learned from Aaron of the freeing of the Davidson slaves some years before. The parallel between Richmond Davidson and the famous Quaker from Mount Holly did not escape him. To be compared with Woolman would have drawn immediate objection from Richmond. But to the rest of those gathered under the Borton roof, the similarities between the two men were not hard to observe. It was no wonder, they thought, that Richmond felt such an affinity with Woolman's writings—the two men were cut out of the same spiritual cloth.

The Davidsons accompanied the Bortons and Steddings to the following Sunday's Meeting in Mount Holly, a new experience in group worship for Richmond and Carolyn.

In the following days, Richmond and Carolyn, sometimes alone, sometimes accompanied by one or more of their new friends, rode or walked through the town and countryside, walking past John Woolman's former apple orchard, through the streets where he had his shop, and through the peaceful countryside along Rancocas Creek. For both it was a time of reflection and prayer and spiritual renewal, as if, though they were not Quakers themselves, they were touching their own deep spiritual foundations.

The evening before they were to leave, Thomas found Deanna and, as difficult as it was with so many other curious and pestering young people about, managed to get her away from the throng. They walked away from the house and then along the creek, which at this time of the year was more like a river.

"I picked these for you," said Thomas, handing Deanna a small bouquet of wildflowers. "Probably half are weeds, but it's all I could find."

"They're beautiful!" said Deanna, who had immediately fallen into the speech of her childhood when reunited with her parents. "I thank thee."

They walked on in silence.

"I, uh . . . I just want to thank you again for all you did for me," said Thomas. "I wouldn't be alive if it weren't for you."

"Who knows what would have happened to me if it weren't for thee," smiled Deanna. "I wouldn't be home now if it weren't for thee and thy family. I have much to thank thee for too."

"Yeah . . . well, I guess we both have quite a bit to be thankful to God for."

This time the silence lasted for several minutes as they walked slowly along in the twilight. The crickets in the trees along the stream had come out and the water of the stream was splashing along beside them.

"I, uh . . . hope it's all right . . . that is, if you don't mind," said Thomas at length, "if maybe I came to see you again sometime."

Deanna could hardly believe her ears! Had Cherity been right?

"Of course," she said softly. "I would like that very much."

"And maybe . . . wrote to you?"

Deanna nodded, then ventured a glance up at Thomas with a smile. He was looking straight into her eyes. She glanced shyly away.

Thomas hesitated another moment, then turned toward her, slowly took Deanna in his arms, and brought her close. Deanna returned his embrace, and they stood a moment in contented silence.

After several seconds, her eyes filling with tears and her heart exploding within her as they pulled away, Deanna turned and ran for the house.

Forty-One

That same night, the six adults gathered to break bread together in the name of the Lord.

The night was late. Suzane was in bed. Rebecca and Mary lay in bed talking in Rebecca's room. Moses and John and James were talking in the room of the two Borton boys. And Thomas and Deanna were wide awake in their beds with thoughts of one another.

The aging Borton brothers, John and Pemberton, sat down with Aaron and Zaphorah and their Davidson guests in the parlor of the Borton home.

"Thee will be leaving us tomorrow," said John, looking at Carolyn and Richmond. "Our lives are enriched from knowing thee and we desire to share wine and bread with thee and pray that the Lord will go with thee and bless thee."

"Thank you," nodded Richmond. "We cannot adequately express our gratitude for your hospitality. You will go with us in our hearts. I came here hoping in some way to touch the spirit of John Woolman and his legacy. What I discovered to be even greater is the *living* faith represented by each of you. Faith that is alive is more to be honored than reverence for the dead, though I am certain that too has its place. However worthy old John Woolman, and such I consider him, in each of you I have found the true unity of the brotherhood. This unity I cherish above much of what passes for spirituality in today's churches."

"The unity we represent may be greater than you think," smiled Pemberton Borton. "I am now a Baptist."

"You don't say! And your brother still speaks to you?"

John laughed. "We have discussed the relative merits of our doctrinal differences at some length," he said, "as you might imagine! But we are both committed to unity as the bond cementing together Christ's church rather than doctrinal sameness. We have learned to take pleasure in our differences rather than allow them to divide us."

"A most uncommon point of view," said Richmond. "And one with which I heartily concur."

"To be honest," added John, "I am not in disagreement with many of the concerns that my brother has felt about our Society that at length led him to the change he felt necessary. All movements, in time, stray from their founding principles, and the Society of Friends is no exception. For all George Fox's talk of not wanting to start a church or a denomination, we *are* a church. We have become the very thing he spoke against. For all Quaker talk of religious tolerance, when some of our number broke away for doctrinal reasons, even before Woolman's time, they were brought up on charges of sedition. So much for tolerance, even within the Society of Friends! The ideals of Quakerism have not always been faithfully lived by its adherents."

"The same would be said of all movements of faith," nodded Richmond.

"To be sure. And in our time, many Quakers hardly even consider themselves Christians. Quakerism is in many places drifting toward a sort of secular mysticism that I find most disturbing—a slap in the face of our founders and our faithful men such as John Woolman. But I have determined to remain where I am and to try to use my influence to do what I can to slow these trends."

"It is not that I have lost my affection for my Quaker roots," added Pemberton. "But with secularism literally running rampant, and with so many in our Meeting no different than Unitarians and Universalists, I simply felt my faith would be better served in another environment. Of course I still treasure my Quaker heritage. It is a rich legacy even though I am not optimistic about the direction it is moving. But I have made no attempt to change my dress or my speech or my way of life."

"In a spirit of brotherhood, then," said John, "we would like to partake of wine and bread with thee. Our Society does not look to such sacraments as necessary rites of the church. We view all fellowship of believers as fulfilling the communion of which Christ spoke. In that spirit, and in respect of my brother who is now in a church where such observances occupy a more important role, we pass the cup and share the bread in remembrance of the Lord's sacrifice, and in recognition of the bonds of brotherhood and unity between all those believing sons and daughters of his family."

"Amen," said Aaron.

A silence fell in the room. Nothing more was spoken. John Borton took the plate upon which sat a small brown loaf of bread. He broke it in half, then passed the plate to Zaphorah Steddings. She took one of the chunks, broke off a portion, then turned to Carolyn at her side, broke the piece in her hand in two and handed one to Carolyn with a smile. Carolyn took it and they ate together. Zaphorah then passed the plate to Aaron, who shared his portion with Richmond. As they ate, the two Borton brothers divided another portion and shared the pieces with one another.

Then John took the cup of wine. In the same manner, each serving another rather than himself, he offered the cup to Carolyn, who drank, then he drank himself. Borton then handed the goblet to Richmond. He offered it to Zaphorah, who drank, then Richmond drank. He handed it to Aaron, who offered it to Pemberton, who drank, followed finally by Aaron, who drank and set the cup back again on the table next to the bread.

Each of the six then sat in reverent stillness, praying within the quietness of their own hearts. The Quaker spirit of silence descended upon them as a holy blanket of peace.

After thirty or forty minutes, the voice of Pemberton Borton broke the hush. "Our Father," he prayed, "we thank thee for watching over

the daughter of dear Aaron and Zaphorah, thy own daughter. She is
in thy sight and thy heart even now. We thank thee for bringing her
safely through this time of trial and restoring her to her home. Amen."

"Amen," said Carolyn

"Amen," whispered Zaphorah.

Again it was silent for ten minutes.

"Bring this dreadful war to an end, Lord," prayed Richmond. "Heal
our nation. May the blood that has been shed not be spilled in vain.
And protect our nation's sons."

"Amen," said Carolyn and John Borton at once.

Another twenty minutes of silent communion and prayer went by.
John Borton's prayer now broke the silence.

"Oh, Lord," he prayed in a soft voice, "we thank thee for the
precious heritage of our faith, that of our Society of Friends and of all
the diverse expressions of Christianity upon which this country was
founded. In these days when so many are drifting away from thee, the
true Light of truth, and are losing sight of our founding principles,
renew and restore the roots that made our ancestors strong in thee.
Bring all thy wandering children back to their anchor in thee."

For another thirty minutes they sat communing silently with God.
By then it was late.

At last Pemberton rose. With a smile he extended his hand to
Richmond, who stood and shook it. He did the same to Carolyn. Still
without speaking, he turned and took his leave. Next his brother also
rose and with a nod and a smile and the hand of fellowship, also bade
them good night.

At last Aaron, Zaphorah, Carolyn, and Richmond were left
together.

"We are going to miss the two of you," said Richmond.

At his words, Carolyn burst into tears and took Zaphorah in her
arms. Richmond and Aaron shook hands, gazing long and earnestly
each into the other's face.

At last the four departed for the night.

Richmond was up at daybreak walking the following morning. His spirit was quiet and peaceful and he drank in the beauty and peacefulness of the morning.

As he completed a long final walk through the Borton and Woolman woods and was making his way back to the home of their hosts, he saw Carolyn and Zaphorah together walking toward him.

They approached and stopped.

"Well, my dear," said Richmond, "are we about ready?"

"It is a sad farewell," replied Carolyn, "but we have promised one another that this is but the beginning of a long friendship."

"Aaron is hitching the buggy now," said Zaphorah. "We will both ride into Burlington with you and see you off at the station."

Forty-Two

$\mathcal{A}$s Cherity Waters stepped off the train onto the station platform in Boston, many thoughts and emotions from the past crowded in upon her, memories of her childhood, of her youthful dreams of the West . . . and of her dear father.

Her mood quieted all the more as she rode in the buggy of a single horse-drawn cab to the familiar house where she had spent the early years of her life. The cab driver drew up in front and reined in.

"Here you are, miss," he said.

"Thank you," said Cherity. "I will just be a few minutes. I want to have a look around, then I need to go into the city. Would you mind waiting?"

"Certainly, miss."

The man helped Cherity to the ground. Slowly she opened the gate and walked up the short path to the two-story white house. Everything looked exactly as she remembered it. Yet somehow the house seemed smaller. Surely she had not grown that much. She doubted she had grown at all since she had last been here!

She drew in a deep breath, took from her handbag the key she still had, and walked up the steps to the front door. She inserted it into the lock, opened the door, then tentatively walked inside.

A thousand sensations rushed upon her at once . . . long forgotten smells . . . reminders of her father . . . even the sound of her own

laughter as a child. Slowly she made her way about, looking at all
the furniture and rugs and paintings and vases and chairs. The house
was cold, yet everything was remarkably well preserved, just as she
remembered it . . . though the *life* of the place was gone. She felt
no sense of her father's presence, only happy but now melancholy
memories of her years with him—so fleeting they seemed now that
they were gone.

Tears slowly filled her eyes and she did not discourage them. It felt
good to cry, though the tears only increased the heartache of remembering the man she had loved as a girl and whose memory grew daily
all the more dear to her as a young woman.

She wandered through each of the upstairs rooms one by one, reliving memories and crying afresh in each, pausing to linger over the
bed where she had exchanged her final holy moments with her father
before his passing into the life beyond.

With thoughts of her father came into her heart many reminders
also of Seth, for it was here that she had first learned that he loved her.
Such memories also brought pain. It had been a long time since she
had heard from him. She had no way of knowing when she would see
him again. She could not help worrying. Young men were dying every
day, not all of them soldiers.

From her own former room she gazed down upon the garden at the
back of the house. It was a little overgrown and unkempt, though, like
the house, in tolerable condition. Such a place of wonder it had been
when she was a girl. She always thought it so huge. She could hardly
believe how small it really was now to her grown-up eyes.

She turned from the window and continued to wander slowly about
the house. Gradually the reason for her coming here began to coalesce
into the single specific question: Could she sell this house that was so
deeply a part of who she was?

In its wake came the series of related questions she must answer
first: Did she *want* to sell it? Was she *supposed* to sell it? And perhaps
most important of all, would she ever live here again?

Being reminded of Seth could not help but turn her thoughts

toward the future. She had her dreams. How could she not? But even if the war somehow changed Seth, and changed his feelings for her, she could not envision coming back to live in Boston. Now that she had had a taste of country life, she knew she would never again live in the city, any city. She needed space around her, space to walk and ride and explore . . . space to think.

But it had not been thoughts of living here again that had brought her north, but her dear friends' need. *Their* need now was greater than whatever *her* future might hold.

Cherity drew in a deep breath, glanced about one more time, then walked toward the stairs and back down to the front door.

She was ready to do what she had come here to do.

Cherity sat in Mr. Glennie's office in a chair opposite the lawyer's desk. Her father's attorney had been going over her share of her father's bank accounts and investments, which amounted to some twenty-four hundred dollars.

"In your letter, Miss Waters," said Glennie, "you asked about selling the house. I realize of course that I was the one who broached the subject in my letter of some months ago. However, I would be remiss in my responsibility were I not to point out the advantages to one such as yourself in maintaining high-quality real property as an integral component of any investment portfolio."

"To tell you the truth, Mr. Glennie, I am not really interested in an investment portfolio," said Cherity. "I need a sizeable amount of money as soon as possible. It seems that selling the house is the easiest and best way to get it."

"But think of your future, Miss Waters. Your father left you enough assets to—"

"I realize that there is probably enough for me to live comfortably for many years, Mr. Glennie," interrupted Cherity. "I am grateful to him, and also to you for your faithfulness in seeing to his wishes and looking out for mine. I know this may be difficult for you to understand, and I know I am young in your eyes, but I am reasonably sure I know what I am doing. Right now my own future is not so much on my mind as is that of the people I am living with. I owe them my life, Mr. Glennie. They took me in after Father died and I cannot stand by and watch them lose what they have worked for their whole lives Now . . . what is your estimate of the worth of my father's house?"

"I am not a real property broker in any official capacity, of course," replied Glennie, "but I would estimate it to be in the neighborhood of eight or nine, possibly nine and a half thousand dollars. It is in rather an exclusive Boston neighborhood. I would think it should command a very attractive price."

"And how long would you anticipate it requiring to sell?"

"That is hard to say, Miss Waters. Anywhere from a month . . . up to, well . . . up to however long it takes to find the right buyer. The more quickly you want to sell, of course, the lower might be the price you will have to take. But are you absolutely certain that you—?"

"Yes, Mr. Glennie, I am certain."

Cherity left the lawyer's office an hour later. All the necessary papers had been signed to place the house on the market and to fully authorize Mr. Glennie to act as Cherity's agent in all matters concerning a potential sale. The attorney remained somewhat reluctant, requesting that Cherity return prior to her departure to confirm that, indeed, after another day or two, she was still in earnest about parting with it. Cherity agreed. She intended to spend the rest of the day, and whatever additional time was necessary, going through everything to determine what to have sent either to Greenwood or to her sisters Anne and Mary, and what to let be sold along with the house.

It was with the relieved sense of having an important decision behind her, yet with a return of the inevitable sadness that could not help but accompany such a difficult decision, that she

walked out to the street and began looking for a cab to take her
back home.

She drew in a deep breath of resolve. She felt good about her decision. Yet she knew that the hardest part of the process lay ahead—
going through the house and saying her final good-byes to all that
represented her past. It wouldn't be easy. But it had to be done and
she would not shrink from it.

Cherity did not return to the house immediately. She needed to let
her decision settle before undertaking the necessary but difficult job
ahead.

She spent the next several hours reacquainting herself with Boston,
having lunch near the harbor, and taking a ride out to see her mother's former church which had been so deeply a part—even though
it had turned her away from God for a time—of her own spiritual
development.

She sent telegrams to Mary and Anne telling them of her arrangements with Mr. Glennie, asking what they might want from the
house. She had discussed her plans at length with Mary on her way
north and had at the time notified Anne concerning her intentions.
Cherity then returned to Constitution Hill.

The rest of the afternoon and evening passed leisurely, full of
nostalgic melancholy. Cherity slowly made her way through the
house, designating for shipment whatever items of furniture or
other of her father's belongings she thought the Davidsons would
be able to use, boxing up small personal items from drawers and
cabinets, as well as what clothes she had left behind, in the empty
trunks and cases from the storage room. Her father's clothes,
which she hadn't had the heart to go through after his death, she
also boxed up for shipment to Greenwood. Somebody would be
able to use them, perhaps one of the blacks on their way north.
A smile crossed her lips at the thought. Her father would surely
approve of such a use of the garments that had once housed his
earthly frame.

She went out again for a light supper, then returned and went to

bed. The night passed more quickly than she had anticipated. She
slept soundly and awoke at first light.

⟨⟩

With the new day, rather than doubts, came a strengthening of Cherity's
resolve. She resumed her tasks with yet greater vigor. Telegrams arrived
midway through the morning from each of her sisters, Mary again
endorsing her decision and Anne offering similar encouragement
though adding a few specific requests. Both her sisters were considerably
older than she and had been married for years. Neither could think of
much remaining in Boston they needed or would want.

Cherity went again to see Mr. Glennie, gave him final instructions
regarding disposition of the contents of the house, then visited a ship-
ping agent to arrange for the furniture and trunks that were to be sent
to Greenwood, along with one box and a small chest of drawers for
Anne. By late afternoon she began to breathe easily, feeling that most
of what she had come to do was at last behind her.

She would leave for New York by train the following morning, and
after a day or two with Mary return again to Greenwood.

One more errand remained. She wanted to visit Mr. McClarin at
the *Herald* and give him her regards and thank him again for his kindness to her father and to her in the days following his death.

⟨⟩

The afternoon sun was waning and most of the newspaper's work
of the day put to bed when Cherity stepped down from the cab
that had brought her again into the middle of the city, and began
walking toward the building where her father had worked for so
many years.

Her thoughts were filled with the man who had given her life.
Memories flooded her of the thousands of stories he had worked on
and articles he had written. She had taken so much for granted when
she was young. But now she realized what a wonderful profession it

was to which her father had dedicated his life—a truly noble calling. She realized further how proud she was of the seriousness and integrity with which he had been faithful to that dedication.

It was not difficult for her thoughts to turn to Seth. He was never far from her in her heart and mind. And now, because of her father, he too was what her father had always so proudly called himself—a *newspaperman*. He actually worked for the same paper.

The reminder that her father had arranged for Seth's first job here filled her with a happy feeling.

Forty-Three

$\mathcal{S}$eth and Veronica arrived in Boston in late afternoon.

They immediately set out to see Seth's editor, stopping briefly by the exhibit of Seth's photographs on the way, then walking the final two blocks on foot.

As they made their way toward the offices of the *Boston Herald*, Veronica held the envelope Cecil had given her. Seth could tell she was nervous.

As Cherity approached the offices of the *Boston Herald*, her thoughts dwelt on Seth as much as they did her father. Where was Seth now? she wondered. Was he safe? Was he lonely, cold . . . did he have to sleep outside on the ground with the soldiers? How close to the actual fighting did he—?

Suddenly Cherity froze in her tracks.

Was she dreaming? This was too wonderful to imagine!

She could hardly believe her eyes, but . . . was that actually Seth across the street?

Yes!

Seth . . . how could it be? . . . What was he possibly doing here? But why not? He worked for the *Herald*. Of course!

He was coming toward her!

Her heart pounding and a great smile on her face, Cherity broke
into a run and began to cross the street. She opened her mouth to call
his name—

Suddenly her steps slowed and she stopped dead in her tracks.

⟨⟩

Half a block from the building, Veronica paused.

"Oh, Seth," said Veronica, "I'm sorry . . . I can't help it—I'm afraid."

"I know you're nervous," said Seth. "But I promise, there's nothing
to worry about—Mr. McClarin is completely trustworthy. He won't
do anything you are uncomfortable with."

"I know . . . but I can't help it. I feel so foolish for letting myself get
duped like this. I should have known better."

Seth paused, smiled tenderly, and put a hand on Veronica's
shoulder.

"We all do things we look back on and are ashamed of," he said.
"I was ashamed of myself several years ago for not being more honest
with you."

⟨⟩

Cherity gasped and her face went ashen. Who was that young woman
with Seth? She felt herself going faint. She could not believe her eyes!
She would know that face anywhere.

Veronica!

Standing like a statue, her eyes wide, her mouth gaping open,
Cherity watched in horror as Seth gazed into Veronica's eyes. They
stood a moment together on the walkway. His hand went to her
shoulder. Veronica smiled, then put her arms around him and hugged
him. Seth returned the embrace.

⟨⟩

"What happened between us back then—that was my fault, Seth . . .
not yours," said Veronica as she stepped back.

"Maybe we were both to blame," rejoined Seth. "We were young and that probably explains most of it. But the point is that I am embarrassed when I think of it, but that is part of growing up. Now you've done something you feel foolish about. But we are going to turn it into something you can be proud of in the end."

Veronica smiled and nodded appreciatively.

"I'll try to believe that," she said. "All I can do is trust that what you say is true. Thank you, Seth. You've been such a good friend—it's more than I deserve."

She gave him another quick hug, then drew in a deep breath.

"Then let's go see your editor," Veronica added, "before I change my mind."

In stunned shock, her eyes stinging with hot tears of confusion and anguish, Cherity spun around and fled. She ran and ran, heedless of direction, having no idea where she was going, only knowing that she had to get as far away as possible.

Seth and Veronica walked into Mr. McClarin's office. Seth introduced his editor to his childhood neighbor and friend, and the daughter of one of the Confederacy's outspoken senators.

"Well, Mrs. Fitzpatrick," said McClarin, "Seth has told me about your predicament. We'll see what we can do both to get you out of it as well as put a stop to this flow of information. Is that envelope you're holding what you've been given to take to your Confederate contact?"

Veronica nodded.

"Why don't you let me take a look at it?"

With one last glance of hesitation in Seth's direction, Veronica handed the editor the envelope.

"Don't worry," said McClarin. "When you take this to your contact, it will look exactly the same. He will never know we have substituted different documents for the real ones."

McClarin hesitated a moment.

"Come to think of it, Seth," he said, "we should record this. Why don't you get your equipment set up and we'll photograph Mrs. Fitzpatrick handing me the envelope, and then me looking at the documents."

"Right," said Seth, rising and leaving the room. He returned a minute later and began setting up his camera and tripod. When everything was ready, Veronica and McClarin stood behind the editor's desk, with Veronica handing the editor the packet.

With a flash, the moment was preserved on film. Seth pulled his head out from under his black cloth-hood as McClarin immediately sat down at his desk. He broke the seal on the envelope and removed the documents. He looked them over briefly then gave a low whistle.

"This is dynamite," he said. "If the Confederacy gets its hands on this, it could mean disaster for Grant's Richmond campaign. We'll need to continue to document everything we are doing with photographs. We have got to have an irrefutable photographic trail showing the travels of this envelope and its contents. When we go to the authorities, we have to have solid proof both of the spy operation as well as Mrs. Fitzpatrick's full cooperation. Okay . . . well, it looks like we have some work to do."

When Cherity came to herself, with no notion how much time had passed but realizing she was getting cold, she found herself seated on a bench in a small park.

Again came the tears. She made no attempt to choke them back, but sobbed in bewildered and uncontrollable grief.

The morning following their meeting with McClarin, Seth and Veronica again sat in the editor's office. He returned the envelope to Veronica. It looked exactly as it had the previous day when she had given it to him.

"Here you are," he said, "complete with fake documents. Seth, make sure you get evidence of the transfer, then bring whatever they may give you back to me and we will again photograph the contents."

"Good . . . I think we're ready, then," said Seth. "We've got a train to catch."

Forty-Four

Cherity's final night in Boston, the train ride to New York, and her visit with Mary, comprised the most miserable days she had ever experienced in her life.

All the way south she sat staring out the window expressionless . . . unthinking . . . unfeeling . . . dead to everything around her. After two days with Mary and her family, her natural exuberance—never to be kept down for long—again began to stir into life. It did not, however, in its customary fashion, bring a cheery smile and laughter to her lips. She began to wake again, it is true, but she awoke as a very different person, as if something had died inside her that would never come to life again.

As her brain again began to function with something of its previous energy, a host of new questions now presented themselves that she had not encountered before. Till that fateful, horrible, shattering moment in Boston outside the *Herald* offices, Cherity had hardly distinguished her responses to Seth, to his parents, to Greenwood, and to God. It was because of all three of the Davidsons, as well as Greenwood and what it represented in her life, that she had come to a belief in God in the first place. Even her love for Seth could not be separated from God and his parents. It was a complete response of belief and love.

All at once everything had changed.

If Seth could be duplicitous, so unlike what she thought him . . . what about the others? What about his parents? What about God?

If Seth's words of affection on Harper's Peak were lies . . . was it *all* a lie? Was everything she thought Greenwood and the Davidsons represented—truth, goodness, integrity, honesty, sincerity . . . had it *all* been a sham?

Where did that leave her new faith? She had so believed in Carolyn and Richmond, and by extension in Seth, that . . . if *they* were not true . . . what did that say of their God?

Doubts began to flood Cherity's mind, doubts not only about the foundations of her own faith, but about what she had just done in Boston. God now seemed very, very far away.

Everything seemed far away.

Suddenly came the dreadful thought: What if her future in Virginia was not as secure as she had assumed? If she and Seth had no future together . . . what did that say about her future at Greenwood? She was certainly not going to stay under the same roof with the future Mrs. Seth Davidson, if that Mrs. turned out to be Veronica Beaumont! Could Greenwood ever be home to her again?

She would need someplace to live when Seth returned from the war. If her future at Greenwood was in doubt . . . perhaps she *shouldn't* sell her father's Boston house.

Question followed question, doubt followed doubt, until Cherity's brain became a quagmire of confusing dilemmas.

The train trip from New York back to Washington, then Dove's Landing, resolved nothing. By the time she reached Greenwood and Carolyn came forward to greet her with a warm hug, all Cherity could do was burst into tears. But she could not tell Carolyn why.

She fled to her room, but it offered no comfort now. It was as cold and dreary and unfriendly as had been her former room in Boston. She looked out her window at the hills and fields and pasturelands, and the high bluff in the distance, once the very land of her dreams. But the life had gone out of them, because the love in her heart had gone out of them.

Everyone at Greenwood recognized that there had been a change. Cherity was different. Everyone assumed it had to do with the house and estate and fresh grief over the loss of her father. None suspected the real cause.

It was with enormous difficulty that Cherity went through the motions of life without telling Carolyn, to whom she had previously confided everything, about the stone of ice that lay in her heart. She was not very good at pretending, though Carolyn did not pry or push.

Long walks and rides were part of every day. To say that Cherity *prayed* as she went would convey more direct conversation with God in her mind and heart than was really the case. Prayer, however, is more complex than those suspect who would define it by rigid ways and means and words and expressions. Men and women cry out to God in a thousand subtle ways that they would never define by the word. What is *prayer* but the lifting up of the total human consciousness, and subconsciousness, to the Creator and Maker of our humanity. Even the honest atheist, though he would be the last to admit it, engages in prayer, in those quiet moments of aloneness deep in his heart when he humbly *wonders* about the truthfulness of his creed.

Cherity thought, she wondered, she questioned, she cried . . . and altogether, therefore, her heart found itself in almost constant prayer. But the words, *Please, dear God, help me and show me what to do,* did not yet form specifically on her lips. Had she been asked during this time of sojourn through the valley of the shadow whether she still believed in God, her answer would have been a tearful, "I don't know . . . I'm not sure of anything anymore . . . I don't know what I believe."

Nevertheless, her Father in heaven had not forgotten her. As her heart wept and her confused brain cried out, he was closer than she imagined, beside her, within her, whispering gently unheard words of comfort that would blossom within her in time like fragrant healing flowers. He cared for his hurting daughter as would the gentlest and tenderest of fathers. He would not allow her suffering to exceed what she was able to bear, nor allow her to suffer in ways that would not work to the ultimate strengthening and deepening of her character and faith. All his ways, indeed, everything in life, if we have eyes to see it, combine to work toward his ultimate purpose—which is the perfecting unto Christlikeness of his sons and daughters to the salvation of all the world. Thus, all would be well, for all would work together for good in the life of this precious one of God's own.

At last a day of insight and revelation came. Cherity was returning from a long, solitary, thoughtful ride with Cadence. She had been pondering whether to notify Mr. Glennie to delay sale of the house until such time as she had resolved within herself what she ought to do. She came out of the woods on a rise that looked down a long slope at the house and barn and other buildings of Greenwood, with the oak wood and wonderful garden spread out to one side. She reined in and sat looking at the panorama before her.

How she loved this place!

Suddenly the horrifying image came into her mind of Greenwood and all it represented passing into the hands of Richmond Davidson's grasping cousins. Richmond and Carolyn would be displaced and forced to move. All the good they were doing in so many lives would come to an end. Probably all the workers who lived here would be sent away . . . no doubt sent away with nothing.

Suddenly she realized that it didn't matter about Seth and Veronica. It didn't even matter whether she still believed in God. She still loved this place, and she loved Richmond and Carolyn! Nothing could take that away. Alongside all that Greenwood was, even her own future didn't matter. She could go elsewhere. She could live with one of her sisters.

But she *had* to do her part to save Greenwood!

What came after that . . . she would worry about when the time came.

"Let's go, Cadence," she said, then dug her heels in and galloped down the sloping hill toward the house.

In the vegetable garden, Carolyn looked up to see Cherity dismount and run toward her. Suddenly she found herself nearly knocked off balance by a great embrace as Cherity burst into tears.

"Carolyn, I'm so sorry," faltered Cherity, sobbing on Carolyn's breast. "I know I've . . . I haven't been . . . I'm sorry . . . I just haven't known what to do . . . but I think . . . I don't even know what I'm saying . . . but I love you and . . ."

Just as suddenly, Cherity turned and ran off again, leaving Carolyn more perplexed than ever.

Forty-Five

$\mathcal{F}$ive days later, Veronica left her Columbia hotel room after a brief conference with Seth, who had a room just down the hall. Leaving the packet from Cecil Hirsch containing the replaced documents in her room, she walked to the address, an office building only a few blocks away, where she was to meet a certain Mr. Smythe.

"I have come to ask about the weather in New Orleans," she said when the door opened to her knock.

"Fitful with rain expected," replied the man inside.

"I have come from Washington."

"You are two days late," said Smythe, looking Veronica over without expression.

"The war makes the train schedules not as reliable as one might wish," said Veronica.

"You're here now, that's the important thing. . . . Where is the information?"

"In my hotel room," said Veronica, desperately trying to keep her voice from trembling. "Are you ready to come with me now?"

"What are you talking about!" exclaimed Smythe. "You didn't bring it with you?"

"I didn't want to carry it through the streets. I thought you would pick it up there."

"That is never the arrangement. You were to bring it to me here!"

"I am sorry. I must have misunderstood. Shall I go back and get it?"

"No, too much time has already gone by," he replied irritably. "Let me get my hat and coat."

The man called Smythe turned into his office and came back out a moment later. He and Veronica walked to the stairs and outside to the street in silence. Veronica led the way back to the hotel.

"My room is on the third floor," she said as they entered.

"Just lead the way and let's get this done," snapped Smythe.

Veronica walked to the stairs, with Smythe at her side, and up to the third floor. They emerged into the corridor. As they went, Smythe glanced ahead of them and saw a man fumbling with a black apparatus standing on a three-legged stand of some kind. Before he had a chance to wonder what it was, Veronica stopped and pulled out the key to her room.

"You will have to wait here, Mr. Smythe," she said. "I refuse to have a man come into my room. I am sorry, but it is a matter of principle. I will bring the packet to you here."

Shaking his head in yet greater annoyance, Smythe waited while Veronica disappeared inside. When she returned she was holding the envelope from Hirsch, via Boston, in her hand.

She handed the packet toward him but did not let go of it. Instead she turned to face the end of the hall. Momentarily confused, Smythe turned also.

A sudden flash of light and faint explosion sounded from ten feet away where the man and his strange contraption stood.

"What was that?" exclaimed Smythe, now grabbing the envelope out of Veronica's hand.

"Hello, sir . . . madam," said Seth, coming out from behind his camera and walking forward with a bright smile. "I am a photographer taking photos of tourists to our fair city. For only five dollars—"

"I am no tourist, you imbecile!" exclaimed Smythe. "Keep your photographs to yourself. Get out of here and leave us alone!"

Seth returned to his camera, where he hurriedly set one more charge of powder and quickly changed plates.

"I understood, Mr. Smythe," said Veronica, "that you would also be giving me something to take back to Mr. Garabaldi."

"Keep your voice down!" said Smythe in a low whisper, handing her another envelope. "We don't use names. Did they tell you nothing!"

Again a *poof* and flash of light came from the end of the corridor. Smythe spun around and stormed toward Seth.

"I thought I told you to get out of here!" he cried. "If you aren't out of here in seconds, I will destroy that thing!"

"I'm very sorry," said Seth, quickly grabbing his camera and tripod in both arms. "It won't happen again."

He hurried past Smythe and down the hall and was soon out of sight.

Smythe returned in a huff to where Veronica stood.

"All right," he said, "we each have what we came for. Tell Roberts next time to send someone who knows what they're doing."

"What about the money, Mr. Smythe?"

"Good heavens! It's in the envelope—what did you think?"

He turned and strode away. Veronica watched him until he turned around a corridor and disappeared from sight, then breathed a sigh of relief and went into her room to sit down and wait for Seth.

Forty-Six

*A*ny decision, and the subsequent doing of one's duty in the common exchanges of life as that decision is put into daily action, is the most direct way out of any mental or emotional desert. Doing one's duty, no matter how seemingly insignificant the activity, because of duty's other name, *obedience*, is the surest antidote to gloom.

No sooner, therefore, had Cherity decided to proceed as planned with the sale of the house than her spirits began to brighten. The next morning she was down again at the black cabins—greeted by shouts of rejoicing by some of the children and becoming acquainted with a few new arrivals—telling stories and making herself helpful in whatever ways presented themselves with the needs of the underground community.

Almost as if in response to her brighter outlook, a telegram arrived four days later from Mr. Glennie with surprising news:

UNEXPECTED RESPONSE SHOWING INTEREST YOUR
HOUSE. PRELIMINARY OFFER NEIGHBORHOOD
EIGHT THOUSAND FIVE HUNDRED. WITH CASH AND
INVESTMENTS, NOT SUFFICIENT ACHIEVE STATED
NEED TWELVE THOUSAND. PLEASE ADVISE PROCEED
OR HOLD OUT HIGHER OFFER.
R. GLENNIE.
BOSTON.

Cherity let out a long sigh as she read the message a second time. It was really happening. And far more quickly than she had thought possible. But if, as Mr. Glennie said, it wasn't enough, would it do any good? And how urgent was the Davidsons' need? Should she take this price or hope to get more? Eight thousand dollars seemed like a fortune, but it was not near the twelve thousand they said they needed.

It took a day or two for Cherity to find Sydney alone.

"I need to talk to you about something, Sydney," she said. "Something serious."

"Of course, Cherity," replied Sydney, "what is it?"

"I don't know if I should tell you this or not, but . . . I don't know what else to do. Maybe Mr. Davidson has told you all this, but . . . do you . . . are you aware of Greenwood's financial problems?"

"Indirectly, I suppose," answered Sydney. "I mean, Richmond and I have been struggling to find workers, and the crops aren't bringing in as much as they should. I know he's concerned. Beyond that . . . what exactly do you mean?"

"Sydney . . . they are about to lose Greenwood," Cherity blurted out.

"Lose . . . what do you mean?"

"Lose it, Sydney—the house, the land, everything."

"But why . . . how?"

"They are behind on the payment of some loans. That's all I know. Papers came about a month ago from a lawyer cousin of Mr. Davidson's. Sydney, we can't let it happen . . . not after all they have done for so many."

Sydney let out a long sigh, obviously stunned by what Cherity had told him.

"Sydney," added Cherity, "do you have any money?"

"Not much," replied Sydney, shaking his head, "only what Richmond has paid me since I've been here. We arrived at Greenwood penniless. I've probably saved fifty dollars. But it is theirs if they need it. Do you know how much they need?"

"Not exactly. But it's over twelve thousand dollars."

A low whistle sounded from Sydney's lips. "That's a fortune! Where would any of us come up with money like that?"

"I think I can help with most of it," said Cherity. "But do you think there is any way to find, say, a thousand dollars?"

"I don't know," sighed Sydney again. "I know Richmond pays all the other workers. I can talk to them. Whether they have saved anything, or would be willing to pitch in . . . I don't know . . . but . . . a thousand dollars!"

"A little bit at a time . . . Who can tell? Maybe we need to ask God to turn what I have and your fifty dollars into twelve thousand."

"If you say so," laughed Sydney. "So you pray, and I'll talk to some of the others."

Cherity did pray.

And because her thoughts were now focused away from her own confusion about Seth and Veronica and toward helping others, faith came in to bolster her prayers. As it bolstered her prayers it also bolstered her spirits. And as faith to believe on behalf of her friends blossomed within her, so too did her faith in her own faith. She began to realize afresh that she *did* believe. She did not believe in God because of Seth or even because of Richmond and Carolyn Davidson. They had been instrumental, of course, in helping her see things in new ways. But she believed in God because *she* believed in him—because she had come to know him, and knew that he was good and loving, knew that he cared about her and all men and women, and knew that he was a good Father and that she was created in his image to learn to be a good and trusting and obedient daughter.

She believed because God was real and true. She believed because he was the Creator of the universe and was the Father of Jesus Christ who told man about him and taught mankind what it means to obey him and be his children.

In truth, there is only one reason to believe, and Cherity was now discovering it anew.

She believed because God was true!

Again the sun of faith, which is a reflection into our lives of the great warmth of the overspreading Fatherhood-Sun of the universe, began to dawn into Cherity's countenance.

And as Cherity prayed, Sydney talked to others . . . quietly, confidentially. He divulged nothing specific, only that Greenwood had fallen upon some hard times, and that those who loved them were collecting donations for Richmond and Carolyn Davidson in appreciation for their generosity through the years. And, he always added emphatically, no one must utter a peep about it.

Most of the transient blacks hadn't a penny to their name any more than had Sydney and Chigua upon their arrival. But those who had been with the Davidsons for years and who had benefited from their generosity were all, to a man and woman, ready to turn over every scrap they possessed, all of which had come from the Davidsons in the first place.

Most enthusiastic was Nancy Shaw. Though she had only twenty-nine dollars of her own saved beneath the mattress of her bed, she immediately embarked upon a one-woman mission to all the blacks who were left on the various plantations surrounding Dove's Landing, quietly spreading the word that even half a dollar here, half a dollar there would be greatly appreciated by the man and woman who had sacrificed so much for the blacks of the community by keeping their little church congregation alive.

Meanwhile, Cherity wrote back to Mr. Glennie.

INTERESTED IN SALE. WILL AGREE TO $8,750 PLUS
$100 FOR FURNISHINGS. PLEASE NOTIFY RESPONSE
SOONEST POSSIBLE.
CHERITY WATERS.

It didn't take like long, with Nancy Shaw curiously devising more errands into town and to several of the neighboring plantations than she had been on in five years, to create a stir and hubbub in the black community among those who wanted to help. All around Greenwood for several miles in every direction, unknown to either Richmond or Carolyn Davidson or any of the white community, pennies and nickels and dimes, even with here and there a silver dollar, began to be shaken and broken out of jars and dislodged from hiding places in beds and under boards and from a multitude of secret stashes that dozens of the region's blacks had been hoarding away like squirrels their acorns in hopes of someday buying their freedom and starting a new life. Nancy told them all that they would be notified when the day was at hand.

Meanwhile, during a brief conversation with Quaker Brannon after a transfer of runaways, Sydney chanced to mention the Davidsons' need and their attempt to raise what money they could. Brannon listened seriously, then nodded and said that, if they would allow them, he and his wife would like to help. He thought they could likely raise two hundred dollars, and said he would talk to his cousin Mueller in Hanover, Pennsylvania and see that the word spread there too among what blacks they were able to contact who owed their freedom, in some measure, to a railroad layover at Greenwood. Overjoyed as he rode back to Greenwood, for the first time Sydney began to think that their wild scheme just might succeed after all.

Now came the hardest part of all . . . the wait.

Cherity heard back, in a more detailed letter from Mr. Glennie, that the party interested in her house had agreed to her terms.

Forty-Seven

Seth and Veronica returned to Boston where McClarin excitedly opened the envelope Veronica had received, with Seth photographically recording the event.

Again the editor looked over papers she was to deliver to Cecil Hirsch and shook his head with amazement.

"I can hardly believe they have been able to pass this level of information back and forth without being caught," he said. "This fellow Smythe and your man Hirsch are definitely playing both sides of the fence without scruples. When are you supposed to meet Hirsch again?"

"I was supposed to meet him today," replied Veronica. "He will be angry when I am not there. But it can't be helped."

"If you can put up with it just a little while longer, with the photographs from Garabaldi's and the evidence from the transaction in Columbia, you should have enough to turn the tables on him for good."

When Veronica walked to where Cecil Hirsh was waiting for her after her return from Columbia, she could tell even from a distance that he was upset. Seth was already in place across the street to capture the final exchange of documents. The day was sunny and bright and required no artificial light. He was confident Hirsch would never know he was being caught on film.

"You were supposed to have been here three days ago," said Cecil angrily as Veronica approached. "Where have you been? I called at your house three times and your housekeeper said she hadn't seen you in a week."

"It is a long way to Columbia and back," replied Veronica.

"Not that long. I know the train schedules. What's going on, Veronica?"

"Nothing's going on. I met your man Mr. Smythe. Here's what he gave me for you," she added, handing him the envelope. "He said the money was inside. And remember, a third of it is mine."

"I never agreed to that."

"It was understood."

"Maybe by you, but not by me."

"Cecil," said Veronica determinedly, at last voicing the words she had been practicing for days, "I told you, I want a third. Otherwise I am out of this for good and you can find someone else to do your dirty work for you."

Hirsch laughed with derision. He had for so long looked down on Veronica as intellectually empty-headed that her sudden display of backbone struck him as humorously ridiculous. But his laughter was short-lived. Quickly he became serious again.

"I told you, Veronica," he said, "that you're in it too deep. You'll get out when I say you're out, and not before. Here is your payment—two hundred as always." He handed her a small envelope.

Veronica took it but did not reply immediately. She returned his gaze with an expression Cecil could not quite understand. She stared straight into his eyes with a bold look of confidence that was every bit the equal of his own. He found himself momentarily nonplussed. He did not exactly know how to respond. This was a side of Veronica he had never encountered before.

"If I refuse to continue?" she said at length.

"Come, Veronica," rejoined Cecil, "why be difficult? Don't force my hand. I told you that if you try something like that, I would have no choice . . ."

He let his voice trail away, making his meaning clear.

"No choice but to turn me in? Is that what you are thinking? Have you never stopped to think, Cecil, that perhaps two can play that game?"

"Veronica!" laughed Hirsch. "Do you honestly think I have left myself so vulnerable as that? If you so much as hint to anyone that I am involved, it will all fall on your head faster than it did Rose Greenhow's. Remember what happened to her—she was thrown in prison."

"Maybe that is a chance I am willing to take," said Veronica. "Maybe I have a few cards up my own sleeve, Cecil."

"Veronica!" laughed Cecil. "I have known you too long!"

"Have it your way," she replied. "But I am telling you that I am through. If you try to implicate me in any way, you may find it more unpleasant than you anticipated."

She rose and walked away, shaking a little but feeling better than she had in a long time.

Hirsch watched Veronica go, chuckling to himself at what he considered her empty threats, yet with a qualm or two in his stomach.

She sounded confident in herself . . . too confident. He was going to have to think about all this, and let her cool her heels for a while. He would handle the next couple of deliveries himself before bringing her into it again.

Forty-Eight

$\mathcal{A}$s no additional payments on any of the loans to his four cousins were forthcoming by Richmond Davidson, additional documentation continued periodically to arrive, furthering step by inevitable step the legal procedures against Greenwood. Together Richmond and Carolyn prayed—what else could they do but pray, for they saw no way out of the legal morass other than that Harland and Stuart and Margaret and Pamela drop the proceedings. Thin though they considered that possibility, it was eliminated altogether from their considerations when Harland himself appeared one day at Greenwood.

They greeted him with attempted cordiality which he received with the aloof air of a man who is all business, even with one of his closest relatives, and asked that a room be prepared for him. He would be staying a few days, he said, to look things over and decide what was to be done with the place once it was his.

"Oh, and I thought it best to serve you these papers in person," he added, handing his cousin a brown envelope. "A court date has been set for a hearing on the case. You will find everything in here and in order—that is, of course, unless you have in recent weeks come up with some means to comply with our demand for full payment."

"No . . . no, there has been no change," said Richmond. "We are unable to meet the demand."

"Yes, well . . . right, then—I suppose we shall see you in court, then, and have the matter settled there."

He glanced to Richmond's side to where Carolyn stood, her eyes swimming in tears of crushing disbelief to see her beloved Greenwood slowly slipping away.

"I reiterate again," said Harland, "how deeply I regret this unfortunate turn of events. If there was only some other way . . . but, sadly, you see, as things stand, my hands are tied. The other three insist on their rightful due from the estate, and . . . well, there you are. I really have no choice but to go along. Of course, none of us want to see you destitute. We are not without compassion. We will make certain that you are left with ample provision to see that there is a roof over your heads . . . perhaps some small house in the town here. Now, if you don't mind, I would like to go to my room and be left alone to go over these papers and double-check the legal descriptions. What time would dinner be served?"

"Six-thirty," replied Carolyn in a choking voice.

"Ah, yes . . . right. Good . . . I will see you then."

The following days were excruciating for Carolyn, quietly humiliating for Richmond. Slowly word spread throughout the Greenwood family that the haughty visitor who was snooping about and poking his head in everywhere uninvited, was Mr. Davidson's cousin who was likely to soon be the new owner of Greenwood, after which time none of them would have a place to live. Smoke blew out of Nancy Shaw's ears to see her beloved master spoken to in such a degrading manner and treated as a common servant as the two men walked about, and she redoubled her efforts to forestall what now seemed to be the inevitable. If for lack of a nail a war could be lost, she would not see *her* private war on behalf of her master and mistress lost for lack of so much as a single copper penny.

Harland Davidson left.

Papers and packets continued to arrive.

The day approached when they would have to leave for the Southern capital and face the court of judgment. Through Cynthia to

Cherity, from Cherity to Sydney and Chigua, and thence to Nancy and the rest, it became known that ten days hence Mr. and Mrs. Davidson would leave and be gone for two or three days, after which time no one could predict what the future would hold for Greenwood. In her own heart, though they never suspected a thing, the hours of waiting hung just as heavy for Cherity as they did for Richmond and Carolyn. Time was running out for everyone.

The ten days became eight . . . then five.

The next day the mail arrived. Along with the rest was an envelope for Cherity. Carolyn took it to her.

"Cherity, dear," she said, "you have a letter from Boston."

Trying to hide her agitation, Cherity took it, closed the door, and with trembling fingers tore open the envelope. Moments later, overjoyed beyond belief, she was dashing out of the house in search of Sydney and Nancy.

Forty-Nine

*W*hen Nancy Shaw appeared at the big house to see Carolyn, with all that had been on her mind lately, Nancy's request was altogether unexpected.

"Does you hab anything speshul planned fo' services dis Lord's day, Miz Carolyn?" asked Nancy.

"No, I don't suppose so, Nancy," replied Carolyn. "To tell you the truth, I had hardly thought about it. I am not sure I'm going to be much good to do anything," she added with a weary smile. "Mr. Davidson and I have to leave on Tuesday for a few days and my mind has been occupied with that. Why—did you have something in mind?"

"No, Miz Carolyn, only jus' dat I been tellin' folks dey oughta be comin' ter services. I'm thinkin' we's maybe gwine hab a heap er folks on Sunday."

"That sounds wonderful," said Carolyn, thinking it appropriate if it was to be one of the final such services to be held at Greenwood. "We will look forward to it."

Sunday came and dawned bright. Still not quite understanding why Nancy would expect an influx of visitors on this particular day, Richmond and Sydney and some of the Negro men were out early moving carriages and buggies out of the barn to make room for thirty or forty people, which they considered more than ample.

Nancy's predictions were indeed prophetic. By midmorning blacks from around the neighborhood began arriving in ones and twos and threes. Nancy and Sydney were on hand to greet them and lead them into the barn, but until Carolyn chanced to glance out her upstairs window she had no idea of the magnitude of the crowd gathering outside.

"My goodness!" she exclaimed. "Richmond . . . Richmond, come here—you have to see this!"

"What in the world is going on!" said Richmond as he joined her. "Is something afoot I didn't know about?"

"I know nothing about it either. Nancy told me she had invited a few people, but I certainly expected nothing like this. I don't know if the barn will hold everyone! Look at them—there must be fifty people milling around down there!"

"Well, wife, we had better get ready and get down there. Your congregation awaits!"

"This is hardly my doing! I want you standing beside me—I am used to sharing my heart with women, not speaking to a crowd!"

Their astonishment had only begun. As they walked outside together, they saw a large carriage just rounding into sight.

"If I am not mistaken . . . ," began Richmond gazing at it making its approach, then as it slowed and stopped in front of them.

"It is Mr. and Mrs. Brannon!" he exclaimed, walking forward with outstretched hand to greet his Quaker neighbor from over the hills. "What a surprise, this is delightful!"

"You remember my cousin Mueller," said Brannon as they shook hands. He gestured back toward the carriage where the rest of Brannon's passengers were climbing to the ground. But Carolyn's eyes had suddenly recognized the Negro man and woman who had come with the two Quaker couples.

A gasp sounded from her mouth.

"Lucindy!" she exclaimed, dashing forward and swallowing the black mother in her arms. "And Caleb!" she added to her husband beside her. "I can't imagine . . . Whatever are you doing here?"

"We heard dere wuz gwine be a speshul church service dis mornin'," replied Caleb with a wide grin. "So Mister and Missus Mueller an' us, we figgered dat wuz somethin' we didn't want ter miss."

"Well I am delighted! I don't know that it is going to be anything special. Good heavens—oh, it is *so* good to see you both!"

Richmond and Carolyn walked with their friends, still greeting and talking with them enthusiastically, toward the barn whose doors stood wide open. The sight as they walked inside took their breath away. The barn was nearly filled to overflowing, mostly with blacks, from Greenwood and Oakbriar and the McClellan and other plantations, as well as from Dove's Landing.

A hush descended as they walked in, every eye in the place upon them, for all knew why they were there . . . everyone but Richmond and Carolyn Davidson in whose honor and out of respect and admiration for whom they had come, in some cases great distances. There were easily more than a hundred faces staring back at them as the two Davidsons entered, paused, and looked around dumbfounded in the dim light. At first they could see only the whites of a multitude of eyes and white teeth. But as their eyes became accustomed to the shadows of the barn, they looked about to see people on all sides of them, spread out seated on the ground and bales of hay, crowded into every corner, some clustered together on what equipment remained in the place, and rising like a wave of humanity upward into the hayloft, where a few of the more adventurous of the men were crowded together with their legs dangling over the massive crossbeams of the roof.

From somewhere, a woman's low voice began to sing. They recognized it instantly as Nancy's.

Nearer, my God, to Thee . . .
Nearer to Thee!

Within seconds she was joined by the great spontaneous choir all around her, and the barn filled with more complex and rapturous harmonies than could have been imagined this side of glory.

E'en though it be a cross
That raiseth me.
Still all my song shall be,
Nearer, my God, to Thee.
Nearer, my God, to Thee,
Nearer to Thee.

Richmond and Carolyn, along with the Muellers, Brannons, Eatons, and the few others who were still wandering in, found places in the center of the floor which had been kept for them. As the hymn continued, a sense of quiet worship descended upon them all, such that by the time the final strains of the last verse died away, Carolyn had sufficiently collected herself to stand and attempt to speak.

"My goodness," she said with a great smile, "that was so beautiful! I don't think I have ever heard anything like it. Or *seen* anything like this! What a joy to see you all! Thank you so much for being here as we pray and give God thanks together."

She paused, looking around in amazement all over again. "In fact, that was so wonderful, let us sing a few more hymns and give God thanks in our hearts for his goodness to us. Nancy, we will follow you."

Without hesitation, again Nancy began to sing. She was instantly again joined by the great congregation surrounding her.

Rock of ages, cleft for me,
Let me hide myself in Thee.
Let the water and the blood,
From Thy wounded side which flowed,
Be of sin the double cure,
Save from wrath and make me pure.

After three more hymns, Carolyn again stood.

"I have to admit," she began, "that for certain personal reasons the last few weeks have been particularly difficult for me. I have lost sight of God's goodness at times. Even as I said the words a few minutes ago about thanking God in our hearts for his goodness, I realized that I was speaking to myself most of all. But seeing all of you here today has reminded me that love is larger than our own difficulties and—"

She stopped and glanced down, tears flooding her eyes.

"What I am trying to say . . . is that . . . just seeing you . . . it means so very much—"

Again she stopped, struggling not to break down altogether. "I'm sorry, I—"

Richmond stood up beside her and put his arm around her shoulder.

"I think what Carolyn is trying to say is that we are both more grateful for your presence here with us today than you can know. It means so very much during what, as she told you, has been a difficult time for us. We are reminded of what the church really is, after all— not a building or fancy choirs and clothes and robes or pretty windows . . . but *people*, just ordinary people coming together in Jesus' name, people who love one another and share life together. I cannot think of a more fitting place for God's *church* to gather than in a barn, since it was in a stable that Jesus was born. Is this not what the church, God's true church, means—people coming together in love to sustain and build one another up? And it is you who have sustained us today. We thank you from the bottom of our hearts."

Richmond glanced toward Carolyn.

"Is that something like what you were trying to say, my dear?" he said.

"Yes!" smiled Carolyn through her tears. "That is exactly it."

Both were surprised now to see Cherity stand where she had been sitting between Thomas and Cynthia midway toward the back of the barn. She smiled down one last time at Thomas and his sister, who were also in on the scheme. Slowly she walked forward and turned to face the crowd as she stood between Carolyn and Richmond.

"Would you mind if I said a little something?" she asked.

"No . . . no, of course not," nodded Richmond.

"Sydney and I were talking the other day," Cherity began. "And I thought of Jesus' feeding of the five thousand and the four thousand. I decided to read the stories over again. So last night I got out the Bible Carolyn and Mr. Davidson gave me and I did. What I noticed about both stories when I read them again, was what ordinary men the disciples were. They were just like you and me. If Jesus happened to appear today, even here and if he walked right into this barn and looked around at all of us, he might pick any of us to be his present-day disciples. Well," she added, "maybe he wouldn't pick any of us *women*, I don't know about that! But he might. It was clear that there were many women among his followers. But for sure he certainly might pick any of you men. Rich or poor, white or black . . . those kinds of things didn't matter to Jesus. He might pick one of you men who used to be a slave. Or he might pick a landowner like Mr. Davidson or Mr. Brannon. Jesus liked ordinary, down-to-earth people.

"But what I wanted to say was that the disciples were so ordinary, they didn't really have very much faith. You and I probably wouldn't have either if we were looking out at five thousand hungry people and then Jesus said to us, *Give them something to eat.* No wonder they looked around at each other, wondering if they'd heard him right, and then started asking questions about how they were supposed to do it.

"But Jesus was always so practical. He knew they didn't have very much faith. He knew that the need seemed huge and overwhelming, and their resources and their faith seemed far too small.

"So Jesus just gave his disciples something practical to do, and then told them to do it, and then waited for a miracle to take place in their hands. I noticed that too when I was reading last night. Jesus is the one who made the miracle of the bread and the fish take place, but the miracle actually happened in the *disciples'* hands. When they did what he told them, no matter how small a thing it might have seemed, he made a miracle happen."

Cherity paused briefly, glanced with a smile toward Carolyn and Richmond, then continued.

"We often find ourselves in exactly the same situation," she went on. "Our resources seem so small, and our need seems so huge and overwhelming. And yet . . . God knows how to take care of us. And he does, just like he took care of all those hungry people . . . and just like he has taken care of me.

"After my father died, I felt so alone and didn't know what would become of me. My need felt so big and overwhelming. But God had bread and fish to give me, and he gave them to me through you two dear people here. You all know them, and you have all received life and love from them too. They gave me a new home, and they loved me, and they taught me about God, which is the greatest thing they could have given me at all.

"I know this may not be my place," Cherity said, pausing briefly and turning to Carolyn, "but I hope you will forgive me. Something I have noticed about your services that are different than the few others I attended before coming here, is that you never take a collection. I thought all churches took offerings."

"Well, I suppose most do," said Carolyn slowly, not understanding why Cherity would be thinking about passing a collection plate at a time like this. "But . . . I never saw a need for one. And who would have had anything to put into it?" she added, laughing and looking around.

"Up until now maybe that has been true," said Cherity, smiling and glancing about. "But perhaps people have more to contribute now than before."

Laughter spread about the barn. Every face wore a big smile in anticipation of what was coming.

"So I thought it would be nice today, just this once, if we took a collection, so that all of us could show our appreciation to you and Mr. Davidson for all you have done for us."

Sporadic clapping broke out, along with a dozen or more enthusiastic *Yeses* and *Amens*.

"Really, my dear, that is hardly necessary," faltered Carolyn, embarrassed by the suggestion of their taking money from all these Negro men and women who had so little.

"But if we all want to," persisted Cherity, "truly *want* to, you wouldn't refuse us that . . . would you?"

"I . . . I don't—," began Carolyn, looking around helplessly at Richmond.

"We understand that the two of you are going to Richmond for a few days," Cherity continued, "on some kind of business. We thought perhaps we might gather something to help with your trip. Sydney, do you have the bowl?"

Sydney stood from where he sat on the floor and walked forward holding a dented metal milking pail.

"I thought we might need to have a little more faith than just a bowl's worth," he said. "So I brought this instead. Don't worry, it is cleaned and washed!"

"Then shall we pass it around?" said Cherity, by now grinning excitedly.

Richmond and Carolyn watched in astonishment, as a great shuffling and moving transformed the barn into a beehive of activity, people whispering and stirring and reaching into pockets and handbags and inside vest pockets. Soon the bucket was making the rounds, with a clinking and clattering and chinking of coins as they fell into it.

Nancy Shaw sat beaming in pride. When the bucket came to her, she looked forward toward Carolyn, tears filling her eyes in spite of her smile, then deposited her twenty-nine dollars and passed the bucket along. And so it was with every set of hands the bucket passed through. Every contribution, whether it was a single penny or, like Nancy's, an entire lifetime of savings, was placed inside as a gift of love into a humble vessel of sacrifice. And as it was passed from one to another, the weight of the tabernacle of blessing steadily grew.

Richmond and Carolyn watched in speechless amazement. They saw Lucindy and Caleb Eaton take from their pockets what appeared to be a handful of paper bills, as did Mueller and Brannon. And still the dull clinking of hundreds of copper and silver coins from small to large poured in.

After its journey the length and breadth of the barn, and its detour up to the loft and back down, at last the bucket returned to Sydney. He held it to his wife. Chigua placed something inside that no one could see. Then Sydney walked forward and held the bucket in front of Cherity. She placed a folded piece of paper inside it. Then Sydney walked toward where Carolyn and Richmond stood staring in wonder. Richmond was shaking his head in disbelief, Carolyn was by now quietly weeping.

Sydney held the bucket with both hands toward them. The entire gathering stilled and grew absolutely quiet.

"This is for the two of you," he said, "from all of us to whom you mean so much. We want you to take it as a love gift, from our hearts to yours, in appreciation for the freedom, the life, and the love you have given to so many. We want you to use it to keep Greenwood flourishing and full of life."

"We . . . I don't know what to say," said Richmond. "All we can say . . . is thank you. We love you all so very much."

He glanced at Carolyn. "Is there anything you want to say?"

Carolyn shook her head, then could contain herself no longer. She burst into tears, then spun around and ran from the barn sobbing.

Richmond took the bucket from Sydney's two outstretched hands. Unprepared for its weight, he nearly dropped it on the hard-packed dirt floor. The sight of what sat inside nearly took his breath away. Coins and bills of every denomination nearly filled the bucket, with Cherity's folded paper on top, and a gold ring beside it which he knew to be Chigua's.

He stood shaking his head, still speechless, still not suspecting the whole truth of what was in his hands. Not a man given to frequent tears, they rose unbidden now.

"I . . . I think I had better go see how Carolyn is doing," he said in a husky voice.

He turned and, holding the holy receptacle of love, followed Carolyn through the door.

Cherity, Chigua, Cynthia, Sydney, Thomas, and Nancy found their two beloved friends some minutes later where they knew they would be, on their favorite bench in the garden. Almost timidly the six approached. Richmond glanced up and smiled in humble gratitude. Carolyn again burst into tears.

"You have each given us . . . everything you had," said Richmond softly, his voice barely more that a whisper. "*Everything*. Chigua . . . your ring! We cannot possibly take it—we would never sell such a treasure! But what your gesture means to us. And Nancy, you dear, dear lady. I saw what you put in and I know it was all you had."

Finally he glanced to Cherity. All he could do was smile and shake his head. He was still holding the check from Mr. Glennie in his hand, made out to her in the amount of eleven thousand eight hundred and fifty-seven dollars.

"What can I say? You know we cannot possibly—"

"Mr. Davidson," said Cherity, "it is already done. The house is sold. Greenwood has to be saved, and I realized this is more home now to me than Boston. Why should I not sell a place that is no longer my home for the sake of what now *is* my home? If you try to give the check back to me, I will go to that lawyer and give it to him myself. I hope you will forgive me for telling the others that you had a need and inviting them to come share with you."

Richmond bowed his head. He had no words. Carolyn still wept in thanksgiving to have been given such true and loving family and friends.

Several minutes went by. No one spoke. At last Carolyn drew in a steadying breath or two and began to remember her responsibility, that this was Sunday, and that all those people back in the barn had come expecting a church service.

"Oh, my!" she said, wiping at her eyes and standing up as she forced a smile. "We cannot leave everyone like this! What will they think?"

"Don't worry, Mother," said Cynthia, placing a hand on Carolyn's arm. "The sermon is now in progress. We cannot go back in and interrupt it."

"Sermon . . . what do you mean?"

"When you and Father left, Nancy led two more hymns, then Mr. Brannon stood up. Even though Quakers don't usually preach, he rose to the occasion and took charge. That is when the rest of us slipped out."

"The dear man!" smiled Carolyn, wiping at her eyes again. "But perhaps we should be ready to go back in when he is through. Oh, I wish we had known about all this, we could have planned a meal. It seems that we ought to—"

"It's all been seen to, Miz Dab'son," said Nancy. "We tol' folks ter bring what dey cud, an' Miz Cherity an' Miz Cynthia an' me, we been bakin' fo' two days. We gots enuf food down in da cabins—tryin' ter keep everythin' out er you an' Mister Dab'son's sight—ter feed Mister Lincoln's whole army. Ain't nobody gwine ter be hungry roun' here today!"

And so it was that something less than five thousand visitors to Greenwood ate their fill that afternoon, and had so much left over that it just might have filled twelve baskets. But the fellowship and bonds of many friendships that were renewed and deepened throughout the day were more precious even than the offering that had been given on behalf of the man and woman who had done so much for them all.

Fifty

Richmond and Carolyn departed for Richmond two days later taking with them the milk pail exactly as Sydney had handed it to them, with only Chigua's gold ring removed. By then Grant's army had moved south of the city and, though evidence of the Union siege of the Confederate capital could be seen, they were able to make it into the city safely and without incident.

Getting into the courtroom with the bucket proved something of a challenge. But they managed to get it on the floor between them, unobserved by Richmond's cousin where he sat across the room.

When he was ready, the judge called Richmond forward.

"You are Richmond Davidson, the defendant?" he asked.

"I am," answered Richmond.

"Do you have counsel, Mr. Davidson?"

"No, sir. I am here on my own behalf."

"What defense do you have to make? You are delinquent on the loans in question, are you not?"

"I am, your honor. I have no defense. Our plantation has not generated sufficient income lately and I simply have not been able to pay what I owe. But I would like to do so now."

"Do what, Mr. Davidson?"

"Comply with the demand for payment that was issued to us."

"Comply . . . you mean, with *full* payment . . . of all *four* notes?"

"Yes, sir—at least I think there will be enough to do so. I apologize for only doing so now, and in such a fashion. I know that technically we may still be liable for some penalty for not complying sooner, and again I apologize for the seeming theatrics of this. However, we only came into these funds two days ago, and therefore we brought them straight here just as they came to us."

Richmond turned back to where Carolyn sat.

"My dear," he said, "would you please bring up the, uh . . . the container?"

Carolyn rose, stooped and lifted the pail from the floor, and carried it forward with both hands and handed it to Richmond. With obvious effort Richmond lifted it onto the judge's desk, where it echoed heavily down with a thud.

"I believe this should cover the amount in question," he said.

"This is highly irregular . . . ," began the judge, as he peered into the bucket. "For the love of—what is this, Mr. Davidson? A bucket of loose coin . . . although I do see a few notes scattered here and there . . . but this is hardly sufficient to clear off your responsibilities."

"If you will just look at that check there on top, your honor," said Richmond. "You will see that it has been signed over to me. I think, along with the rest, it may just be sufficient to meet the case."

The judge reached in and withdrew Cherity's check and unfolded it.

"Ah . . . yes, I see what you mean," he said. "Well, this changes things considerably. Well . . . it will have to be counted, of course. But for the present we will assume everything is in order as you say."

He turned to Harland Davidson where he sat in fuming disbelief at the ridiculous display.

"I must say, Mr. Davidson," said the judge, speaking to the attorney, "that having thoroughly reviewed the facts of this case, all the way back to the decease of Grantham and Ruth Davidson and the disposition of their estate, and up through all the efforts made by the defendant to be far more fair to you and his other three cousins than any of you deserve or should have felt entitled to by any standard, legal or otherwise . . . I found your suit to be nothing short of a mockery to the justice system, and even more a mockery to the system of fairness itself. The law compels me to hear such cases, and the law might even have compelled me to decide in your favor. But I find your suit an embarrassment against right and truth. It gives me great pleasure to say that this case is dismissed, and to tell *you*, Mr. Davidson, to get out of my court. Furthermore, it is my judgment, and I hereby order that the defendant be awarded damages in the sum of one thousand dollars for legal fees and disruption to the work of their plantation, to be paid by plaintiffs. All matters pertaining to the estate of Grantham and Ruth Davidson and the property known as Greenwood, are hereby and forever closed. Good day, gentlemen and ladies."

Richmond and Carolyn returned to Dove's Landing feeling, not exactly triumphant for the victory had not been theirs, but relieved beyond measure and gratefully humbled by the experience. With the six hundred dollars contributed by the Muellers and Brannons, the total inside the milk pail was determined to be $12,117.89, which, with the interest that had accumulated, turned out to be $93.13 in excess of what was due on all four notes. The judge ordered that the thousand dollars in damages be paid then and there, with the result that, instead of returning to Greenwood penniless, they still had the milk pail, and it contained $1,093.13.

Richmond immediately gave all his own people immediate raises and without the quarterly burden of the payments to his cousins was able to offer better pay to blacks coming through, such that by the following spring, Greenwood again had enough workers to prepare, plough, and plant what they hoped would result in a bumper harvest and at last right the wobbly ship of Greenwood's bank account. Richmond would not keep the local blacks' widows' mites in the face of Greenwood's bounty but would return it pressed down, overflowing, and shaken. God had done his work, to increase the faith of them all. Now it was time again to give, out of their blessing, to those for whom the little they had given represented a small fortune. Most took the gifts with gratitude, and even more convinced than ever that Richmond Davidson was no ordinary man.

But when he made the same attempt to his friends Brannon and Mueller, they would have nothing of it.

"What," said Brannon, "would you deprive me of the blessing that comes to those who give? Surely you, Richmond, of all men, understand the principle of the centurion when applied to giving and receiving, that we are called upon both to give *and* receive graciously and with humility. It is a great privilege to give. Allow me to reap the fruit of my gift as you use it and spread the leaven of giving in the lives of others."

Humbled anew, and knowing his friend was right, Richmond smiled and nodded in appreciative gratitude.

No more words were spoken. The two men embraced. Then Richmond, blinking hard, turned and mounted his horse to begin a quiet and prayerful ride back to Greenwood.

The events of the service and the collection and the paying of Greenwood's debts had overshadowed for a time Cherity's own personal troubles. But the moment Richmond and Carolyn departed for Richmond, the dreadful memory of what she had witnessed in Boston returned in full force upon her. It was as if she had awakened from a nightmare to discover that—horror of horrors!—the bad dream had been true after all.

Yet by now enough time had passed that she found herself beginning to doubt what she was certain at the time that her eyes had seen. She relived the few moments over and over in her brain. The two individuals she had seen were some distance away, and on the opposite side of the street . . . and it had been years since she had seen Veronica. Nor could it be denied that, in having to deal with the matter of the house, her mind had been almost completely absorbed and preoccupied with the past, with her father . . . and with Seth and the time he had spent with them in Boston.

Surely . . . of course, that was it!—her brain had been playing tricks on her. She had only imagined it to be Seth and Veronica.

It couldn't *really* have been them. Hadn't she heard that Veronica and her husband were off in Europe somewhere?

And Seth . . . he wouldn't have been anywhere within several hundred miles of Boston. He was off with the army somewhere.

How silly of her!

If only she hadn't been so impulsive and started crying and run off, she might have stood and watched until the two people had come closer. To have seen their faces close up and known beyond any doubt that they *weren't* Seth and Veronica . . . she could so easily have avoided all this heartache.

Slowly Cherity began to breathe more easily. It was not a matter of immediately erasing the image from her mind—that wasn't easy . . . she had been so sure! Yet by degrees as the days passed she managed to convince herself that all was well, and that she had *not* seen what she *thought* she had seen.

Fifty-One

More than a month passed before Cecil Hirsch again contacted Veronica. Their last interview had unnerved, and also angered him. But eventually the time came when he could not get by without her services. It was finally time to put Veronica's determination to the test. He sent her a message to meet him. He had another assignment for her.

Wanting Seth to remain on hand until the thing played itself out, McClarin had Seth photographing sites around Washington and planned to run a series showing readers their first realistic images of the capital city. Seth's photos were gaining popularity in Boston. Mr. McClarin was now setting up a second display in the *Herald* offices as advertisement for the paper. Seth and Veronica saw each other frequently and Veronica invited him to the house at least once a week for dinner. During that time Seth and Richard struck up a friendship, though as yet Veronica had not divulged to Richard her problems with Cecil Hirsch.

Hirsch found Veronica already seated inside Garabaldi's when he walked in. He approached and sat down opposite her holding a thick packet.

"I need you to go to Atlanta," he said. "The city is in shambles and virtually deserted, but something big is in the works. I may even give you the third you wanted for this one."

"Is that the delivery?" she asked.

"It is."

Casually Veronica reached across the table and slowly drew it toward her.

"But then, as I told you, Cecil," said Veronica calmly, "I will be through. This will be the last delivery I will make for you."

"Come, come, Veronica," said Hirsch. "I assumed that by now you would have come to your senses. Have you forgotten what I said I would do?"

"Of course not. But I don't think you will try to expose me."

Hirsch smiled. "Can you take that chance, Veronica?"

"I am willing to."

"Look, Veronica, if you refuse me, I will go straight to the *Post*. I will tell them that I have information implicating the wife of Richard Fitzpatrick in passing information to the Confederacy. The public is always more than ready to believe that their governmental officials are corrupt. And the beautiful wife of a diplomat—it is too juicy for words. They will believe it in a minute. So don't push me too far. Now here are your reservations," he added, taking a small envelope out of his pocket and handing it to her. "Wait at the hotel until you are contacted. The same password as before. When you return, you be ready for your next assignment. There will be no more talk of your getting out until I am ready."

Hirsch rose to go. As he turned toward the door, however, he saw a young man approaching who looked vaguely familiar.

"Sit down, Mr. Hirsch," said Seth, walking up and staring straight into his eyes. "You and I have something to discuss."

"Who are you?" asked Hirsch irritably, the smile vanishing from his face.

"My name is Seth Davidson."

"I have never heard of you, and have nothing to discuss with you."

"But I have heard of you, Mr. Hirsch. Veronica has told me a great deal about you. I know all about your activities."

Cecil spun around and glared at Veronica. As he did, Veronica quickly handed the packet to Seth.

"Hey, give me that!" cried Hirsch.

But Seth took a step or two back. Hirsch saw that he was at a disadvantage and would likely not be capable of overpowering the fellow by force.

"I think you might want to listen to what he has to say, Cecil," said Veronica. "You threaten to go to the newspaper about me . . . well this man is *from* the newspaper. Perhaps you would like to tell your story to him. Of course, I already have. He knows everything, Cecil."

Flustered momentarily even in the midst of his anger, Cecil glanced back and forth between the two, then slowly sat back down. Seth took a chair and sat where he could see both the others. Now for the first time Cecil noticed a second thick envelope in his hand. Seth set it down on the table in between them.

"I am a photographer, Mr. Hirsch," he said. "I am also a friend of Veronica's. She and I have known one another for years—far longer than your acquaintance with her family. I work for the *Boston Herald*, mostly photographing the war. More recently I have been photographing a very interesting series of transactions between you and she, and between Veronica and a certain Mr. Smythe of Columbia."

By now Hirsch's face was red with wrath.

"Therefore, before you make any attempt to implicate Veronica," Seth went on, "you should give careful consideration to your own prospects. What I have here," he said, laying his hand on the envelope, "is incontrovertible proof that you have been engaged in spying against the Union, *and* against the Confederacy. You have been playing both sides, Mr. Hirsch. I understand it has been quite lucrative for you. There is probably nothing we can do about that. But this, along with the envelope you just gave Veronica, are enough to put an end to it."

"A few photographs . . . what do they prove?" said Hirsch smugly. "You've got nothing on me!"

"I'm afraid you're wrong, Mr. Hirsch," said Seth. "You see, it is also possible to photograph documents."

The word dropped around the table like a bombshell.

As Hirsch absorbed the implications of Seth's statement, he looked toward Veronica shaking with passion.

"You . . . you opened the packet!" he seethed. "How dare . . . why you slut—"

"Careful, Hirsch," said Seth, reaching out and laying hold of Cecil's arm. His grip was tight and the command in his voice unmistakable. "Another word like that and you will have to answer to me. What Veronica has done took courage, far more courage than the slinking about of a coward who would profit from deceit."

"You dare call me a coward?" spat Hirsch.

"You *are* a coward, Hirsch," returned Seth. "You prey upon women in their weakness. You lie and deceive for your own gain. Yes, you are a coward. Veronica has shown more courage than I think you are even capable of."

"You are a fool if you think anyone will believe her! I have contacts in high places."

"Your contacts will mean nothing alongside what is in these envelopes. The documents in your recent transactions were completely photographed and are part of the evidence that will be used against you along with this," he added, patting the envelope he still clutched under his arm that Hirsch had just brought, "if you make any move against Veronica."

"Don't make me laugh!" chided Hirsch. "You will never get away with it."

"I think you are wrong. It might also interest you to know further that, as those documents would have proven damaging to the war effort, they were replaced with documents which we had falsified and which Veronica then passed on to your contact, Mr. Smythe. I am certain, they have already discovered the information to be useless and are assuming you to have double-crossed them."

"How dare you—" began Hirsch.

"You are finished, Hirsch," interrupted Seth. "Your contacts on both sides will think you have played them false. No one on either side will trust you again."

Hirsch jumped to his feet in a rage.

"You think you are clever," he cried. "You think this is the end of it. But you have not heard the last of me."

He turned to Veronica, shaking his head contemptuously.

"I could have done so much for you, Veronica," he said. "Look at all I have already done, and now this. I will ruin you, Veronica. What do you think your devoted husband will say when he learns what I have to tell him? You will pay for this folly!"

He turned and stormed out of the restaurant. Seth and Veronica sat a few moments in silence.

"He's right," said Seth at length, "he could make it very unpleasant for you."

"I know," smiled Veronica a little sadly. "I intend to talk to Richard and tell him everything. But Cecil has to be stopped, and I have to get free from his clutches."

"What do you want to do?" asked Seth.

Veronica drew in a deep breath. "Take me to the authorities," she said. "I am ready to make a full statement. Then I think Mr. McClarin should run the story in your paper."

"I will telegraph him this afternoon."

"But please . . . you won't say anything to anyone until this is over. I need time to tell Richard in my own way."

"Of course, I promise."

"Unless it is your father. I don't mind what you tell him."

Again it was silent.

"Once the story does break, Washington might be uncomfortable for you," said Seth.

Again Veronica smiled, a little sadly.

"I have thought of that," she said. "If they don't put me in jail, I think I will go back to Oakbriar for a while—just to put all this behind me. My mother is there most of the time now. It is peaceful. It will give me the chance to think about everything that has happened. What about you?"

"I will see what Mr. McClarin wants. He thinks the war may be coming to an end before long. He wants me in the thick of it."

"Oh, Seth, it frightens me to hear you talk so. You will be careful?"

"Always."

"Do you have to leave . . . immediately?" asked Veronica.

"I don't know, why?"

"I'm still afraid, Seth. I am afraid of Cecil, I am afraid of them all. I know it is a great deal to ask, after all you've already done, but, after I've made my statement and all this is behind me . . . would you take me home—to Oakbriar I mean?"

"Talk to Richard first. If he thinks that is best, I will tell McClarin I need a few more days."

Fifty-Two

*H*er trip to Boston had been emotionally draining for so many reasons. But at last Cherity put it behind her and began to breathe more normally again. The sunshine of her natural optimism returned and she once more radiated the sparkle of a happy countenance.

The passage of time always helps send away the doldrums. The most important factor in Cherity's new outlook, however, was the simple realization how foolish had been her worries and fears. She had let her silly girl's imagination run away with her.

It had been some time since she had taken a long ride just for the sheer enjoyment of it. Her mind had been so weighed down since Boston that even the few rides she had taken were sad and thoughtful. Now she decided to go out and ride and ride and ride until she could ride no more, and just enjoy being alive in the midst of God's creation.

She set out about eleven o'clock on a bright early September morning. Though this particular morning had dawned chilly, by the time of her departure it was warm enough to ride without a jacket or coat.

Instead of riding immediately east and upward into the hill country as was her normal custom, Cherity set out in a westerly direction along the river, then wound her way through the open pastureland and expansive valley that stretched out south for miles, gradually completing a huge arc slowly back eastward into the gently rising foothills. She stopped several times to drink from one of the many

streams she encountered, and to allow Cadence to drink and graze. By
the time she found herself clomping slowly along the ridge of Harper's
Peak from the far side on her way back to Greenwood several hours
later, she was weary with the glow of a peacefully tiring day.

Thinking of Seth, as she usually did up here, hoping he was safe,
and upbraiding herself yet again for her impetuous reaction in Boston
to a complete stranger, she climbed to the summit, then stopped and
gazed all about her. It was just like she remembered it the first time she
and Seth had ridden here together—the town of Dove's Landing in
the distance to her right, the Beaumont plantation at the base of the
ridge in front of her.

She recalled their suspicion that it had been Denton Beaumont
snooping around the Brown house when Chigua was there. She was
glad the senator was gone. Even though she had never met him, from
what she had heard, she didn't trust him.

From the direction of town, the movement of a small buggy in the
distance caught Cherity's eyes. It was pulled by a single horse and,
unless she was mistaken, was bound in the direction of Oakbriar.

A premonition swept through her. She had heard the far-off whistle
of the train on its way into town ten or fifteen minutes before. The
sound was so familiar she had hardly taken notice of it. Why would
she think that perhaps Denton Beaumont had returned home? If he
was back, Mr. Davidson ought to know it before his neighbor did
any more snooping around looking for things that were none of his
business.

She dug her heels into the horse's flanks and galloped off the ridge
and down in the direction of Oakbriar.

Keeping to the woods, and watching for any of the Beaumont
workers, especially Elias Slade, she covered the ground rapidly and
was just coming out onto level ground when she again spotted the
buggy about half a mile away. She had been right—it was on its way
to Oakbriar!

She didn't really care whether Denton Beaumont saw her or not. Yet
it would be a little awkward trying to explain herself. And her presence

here would probably reflect badly on Mr. and Mrs. Davidson, so she should keep out of sight. She slowed her pace, guided Cadence back amongst the trees, then took a course similar to that of the road in the direction of the Beaumont plantation. The buggy was not moving fast. If she stayed ahead of it, she ought to be able to get a good look at its occupant where the road wound briefly through the woods.

Reaching the spot, she quickly dismounted, tied her reins to a branch, and ran toward the road and took a position behind a tree large enough to shield herself from sight. Three minutes later, she heard the approaching *clomp, clomp, clomp* of the horse's hooves and the rhythmic clatter of the buggy along the road. She took off her cowboy hat and set it down behind her so it wouldn't give her away poking out behind the tree, then peered around the trunk.

The sounds grew louder. Around a bend about a hundred yards away she saw the horse, then the buggy, come into view.

It looked like there were *two* people seated side by side. Of course, she thought . . . Mrs. Beaumont probably went into town to pick him up at the station.

On the buggy came. Unconsciously Cherity shrunk a step back to keep from being seen. She heard them reach a point only about fifteen yards from her where the road veered away out of the woods. Slowly she inched her head around the tree again.

A horrified gasp escaped her lips. Paralyzing chills seized her whole body even as her eyes flooded hot with liquid agony.

There was no mistaking it this time! She had seen both their faces as clearly as it was possible to see them.

It was Seth and Veronica!

Quickly the buggy rounded the curve and moved away. Cherity's knees nearly buckled in stunned shock. She staggered from behind the tree. Arms hanging limp at her side, her mouth drooping open, eyes red and blinking hard, she watched numbly as the blond hair of the man she thought she had loved, and the silky black hair of the woman to whom he had once been engaged, both blowing happy and carefree in the wind, slowly disappeared from her sight along the road.

Senseless of all thought and feeling, somehow Cherity found her horse and remounted. Instead of retreating to the safety and oblivion of Harper's Peak, or the comfort of Greenwood and her own room and bed where she could cry and cry until she decided what to do, almost without thinking she found herself prodding Cadence on, she hardly knew why, toward Oakbriar.

Was she, even now, desperate to find some logical explanation, some way to excuse what she had seen? Or was she drawn by the terrifying yet irresistible lure of still worse that might yet be revealed?

She did not stop to think. She did not analyze her motives. She was merely compelled to know more, to know *all* . . . though to know more of what she feared would surely destroy her, and make her incapable of ever loving again.

She rode without haste. What was there to make haste about? She no longer even tried to hide, but sought the road, and then turned and rode, slowly and methodically, along the entry drive toward the magnificent plantation house of Oakbriar. Fleeting thoughts of Elias Slade reminded her of the gun on her hip. If this were some Greek tragedy, or even a dime novel of love and betrayal, she might gallop up, run into the house, and shoot the two lovers dead and then herself face the hangman's noose of justice, tearfully and stoically defiant to the end.

Such morbid thoughts did not last long. She saw the house in the distance. The buggy stood in front . . . empty.

Several seconds later the door opened. She reined in and stopped. Seth stepped out onto the porch. A moment later Veronica followed him through the door. Veronica stepped forward and embraced Seth affectionately.

Cherity saw nor heard nothing more. By the time Seth turned to descend the porch and walk back to the buggy, she was galloping in full retreat away from the plantation.

Seth heard the thunder of hooves on the road. He glanced up and saw a small cloud of dust in the distance. It looked to be a rider, and moving fast.

But he had not the slightest suspicion who it might be, and did not recognize the horse that had been his own gift to the young woman who occupied his heart.

In an oblivion of tumultuous anguish, Cherity pushed poor Cadence onward and upward through the woods and again up to the ridge of Harper's Peak from where she had just come, then westward into the yet higher hills, galloping as fast as was possible for horse and rider to go. As long as she was moving, in the sheer motion and exercise of flight, she could keep at bay the torrent of tears that must eventually come. But neither she nor Cadence could sustain it indefinitely. At last she sensed his legs slowing under the strain.

She let up on the reins and allowed him to slow to a canter, then a walk. She jumped from the saddle, hit the ground, then ran herself . . . ran and ran and ran, she knew not where. By now she was miles from Greenwood.

At length, in sheer exhaustion, both mental and physical, she collapsed in a heap on a grassy clearing in the midst of thick forest. The moment her motion finally ceased, the pent-up flood burst forth and she sobbed bitterly, sobbed until the merciful balm of sleep overcame her.

Seth's approach up the drive to Greenwood in a buggy from the livery in town was greeted with great rejoicing even before he reached the house. Aaron Shaw saw him first and ran shouting toward him, joined by Isaac and a few other of Seth's lifelong black friends. He came up to the house with a small crowd yelling and shouting on all sides of him.

Carolyn ran outside to see what was the cause of all the commotion and erupted in tears of joy. By the time Richmond and Sydney arrived, the celebration of Seth's surprise homecoming had brought a halt to every activity from the big house to the black village. Cynthia and Seth embraced warmly as his sister followed his mother from the house. Then Seth saw Thomas.

"Thomas!" he exclaimed, running toward him.

As the two brothers embraced as men for the first time, Richmond shook his head with disbelieving joy and Carolyn wept again. For the first time since the war, their whole family was together again!

"I cannot tell you how good it is to see you again," said Seth. "And alive!"

Thomas smiled. "You and I have to have a long talk, Seth," he said. "There are some things I need to tell you."

Seth now glanced all around the happy welcoming throng. "Where's Cherity?" he asked.

No one had been paying much attention, but now as a few heads glanced about, they realized that Cherity was not among them. It grew quiet as everyone looked about.

"She said she was going on a long ride," said Cynthia.

"That was hours ago," said Carolyn.

"She said she felt like the longest ride she had ever been on in her life and said not to expect her back until supper."

"I can't wait to see her face when she sees you!" laughed Cynthia. "She is going to be positively beside herself!"

Fifty-Three

Cherity was awakened from the slumber brought on by her tears and her exhaustion by Cadence's long wet tongue licking the dried salt from around her eyes.

She raised her head and looked about with a shiver. She drew in a shaky breath, as if she had just finished crying only moments ago. The jerky motion of her lungs brought the horrible reminder of what she had seen rushing back upon her and she broke down weeping all over again.

But this time her tears did not last long. She realized she was cold. It was obvious that the sun was setting. The shadows of the trees around her were lengthening by the minute.

She stood and looked around. She had no idea where she was. But wherever it was, she couldn't stay here all night. This high up in the hills, it would get very cold before morning.

Trying to remember which direction she had come from, slowly she climbed back into the saddle. She must have been riding up the incline. That way seemed a little familiar, and she took it. As she rode, all the events of the afternoon came back into her mind. Instead of bringing tears, they now brought a cold sense of resolve.

She and Seth were obviously through. She had been naïve to think he loved her. He had made no promises. He had never spoken definitely about their marriage. She had assumed far too much.

She would have to leave Greenwood, of course. If he had come back to Dove's Landing merely for a visit, then she would be in no hurry about making a decision. She still loved Carolyn and Richmond. They had been good to her. She would write to Mary and Anne about living with one of them until . . .

Well . . . until she didn't know what. Until she decided what to do with her life . . . until she could figure out what was to become of her.

If Seth had come back to stay, however, she would have to leave immediately . . . tomorrow at the latest.

She couldn't possibly stay with him here. For all she knew, Veronica had come back from Europe and divorced her husband. Seth had found out. Somehow they had met . . . and now Seth realized he was ready for what he hadn't been ready for before. He had gone away to war and had grown up, and now realized that he had loved Veronica all along.

That must have been what they were doing in Boston. He had taken her to meet Mr. McClarin, who was now his boss, and then told him he was quitting his job at the paper to return to Virginia and marry her.

What must he think of *her*? Cherity wondered with chagrin. No doubt she had become an embarrassment to him.

Oh, it was too horrible to think about!

Seth was probably right now trying to think of some way to be rid of her! What an inconvenience that she was living with his parents. Now he was faced with the problem of what to do about the orphan waif his parents had taken in, that he had tried to pretend he had loved after his failed engagement with Veronica.

Again hot tears stung at Cherity's eyes at the mortification of it all.

If only she had some of her things with her, and a little money, she would go away and never go back to Greenwood at all. Where she didn't pause in her thoughts to consider . . . just *away*. As far away from Seth as she could get. She would have to sneak into her room, and then somehow slip away tomorrow without being seen.

She *couldn't* lay eyes on him again. She just couldn't bear the humiliation!

Dusk fell over Greenwood. The celebration was in full swing and Richmond and Carolyn had turned the event into a reunion party for all three of their now-grown children.

But an invisible cloud had descended over the festivities. Cherity had still not returned and inwardly they were all worried. The one person Seth had most looked forward to seeing was nowhere to be found. He had to leave in the morning. McClarin wanted photographs of Sherman's devastation of Atlanta. Union forces would be leaving the city within the week and McClarin wanted him traveling with Sherman's army documenting their movements. He had to get to Atlanta without delay.

Richmond had quietly slipped out of the house already two or three times and gone wandering, lantern in hand, through the barn and stables and then out toward the pasture and hills in the directions he knew Cherity usually rode . . . peering into the dim light of descending darkness . . . listening for any sound that might tell him something.

But the night was still, and the crickets were making too much noise to hear anything in the distance.

After his third such venture outside, he walked back into the house. Carolyn caught his eye and he could read the anxiety in her face.

Seth, too, was worried. He knew as well as his mother and father that this was not like Cherity. He did not know quite all that his father had to worry about, nor that Cherity had taken to riding with a gun. Twenty minutes later, when there was still no sign of Cherity, Seth went to his father.

"Dad, why don't Thomas and I go out and look for her?" he said. "We'll be careful. We'll take the two dogs and stay within earshot of each other. We know every inch of the hills for miles. If she's out there, we'll find her."

Richmond thought a minute. "I suppose you're right," he said, letting out a long sigh. "We've got to find her before the night gets away from us. The temperature is going to drop fast before long. Why don't you go out and start saddling three horses . . . I'll go with you."

Seth nodded, grabbed a lantern, and hurried out to the stables. What he saw there, however, instantly changed his plans. There was his old worn black saddle sitting over the rail where he had always kept it. It hadn't been there earlier. He walked to it and laid his hand gently on the seat. The leather was still warm.

He glanced excitedly around. There was the young brown stallion he had bought for her munching on the oats in his trough like he hadn't eaten all day. He reached through the railing and stroked his neck. He too was warm!

"Hey, fella," he said softly. "Do you remember me? I'm glad you seem happy in your new home."

How could he have missed seeing her? Seth thought as he turned and ran for the house.

He met Thomas and his father walking out into the night air.

"Where is she?" he said excitedly.

"What do you mean . . . aren't we going to look for her?" said Richmond.

"She's back! Her saddle and horse are inside. You didn't see her?"

"No, nothing."

Seth ran past them into the house and bolted up the stairs two at a time. He dashed down the corridor until he came to a stop in front of Cherity's room. The door was closed.

"Cherity, Cherity!" he cried, pounding on the door. "Are you in there! We've been so worried—we didn't know where you were. Cherity, it's me . . . it's Seth! I'm home for a day."

Only silence met his ear behind the door.

"Cherity . . . Cherity, it's—"

Finally Cherity's voice interrupted him.

"I know who you are. Go away!"

Shocked at what he heard, Seth persisted.

"Cherity, please . . . open the door. I've been dying to see you all day."

"Well I don't want to see you. I told you to go away."

"What are you talking about?" laughed Seth. "Cherity, is this a joke? I don't know why you're—"

Suddenly the door flew open. There stood Cherity with a steely expression like he had never seen on her face before. Her look was hard and set, her red eyes piercing straight through him.

She was obviously angry.

"Cherity," he said, overjoyed to see her, but utterly bewildered by her expression.

"Is that what I am to you," she said coldly, "—a joke?"

"Of course not . . . what are you talking about? Are you all right? Did something happen?"

"As if you don't know! Please, just leave, Seth. I don't want to talk about it."

"Talk about what? What is going on? I don't have any idea what—"

"Seth, don't lie to me anymore," said Cherity icily.

"But, Cherity, please . . . I have to leave in the morning for Atlanta—"

He stopped abruptly. "I wasn't supposed to say anything about that. Our movements are secret. I gave my word. Please don't tell anyone. But I do have to leave tomorrow and I want—"

"Oh, believe me, I won't say a thing. Your *word* is safe with me. Ha!"

The bitter sarcasm in her voice was obvious.

"Cherity, what are you talking about?"

"I've had enough of your lies, Seth," she shot back. "I finally know them for what they are."

Stunned, Seth stared back, gaping in bewilderment. The next instant the door slammed in his face. Its echo was followed by a key locking the bolt from inside.

Shaking his head in disbelief, Seth tried desperately to make sense out of Cherity's obvious anger. He still wondered if it was some kind of weird joke. He had never seen anything like this from her before.

"Cherity, please," he said through the door, "—honestly, I have no idea what you mean. If you'll tell me when you think I lied to you . . . please, just tell me what this is about."

"I saw you, Seth," yelled Cherity from inside. "You told me things you had no right to say as long as you still loved Veronica!"

"Veronica! What does she have to do with it?"

"She has everything to do with it! You love her and you lied to me about it."

"I don't still love her. I *never* loved her. I told you that."

"I know what you told me. But I saw you, Seth. . . . I saw you and Veronica in Boston . . . I saw you today at her house. I saw her in your arms, Seth. Can you imagine what a fool I feel like . . . all this time thinking you and I . . . when you and she were—"

Cherity's voice faltered.

Stunned into silence Seth's mouth went dry and he swallowed hard. He listened through the locked door. All he could hear were the choking sobs of a heart he now realized that he himself had broken.

Speechless, a terrible lump rising in his throat, he turned and walked softly back down the corridor.

Fifty-Four

Seth Davidson sat alone in his room, heartbroken and grief stricken at what had taken place in the hallway outside Cherity's room. He hoped no one from downstairs had heard Cherity yelling through the door.

He was so stunned he didn't know what to do. It would be useless to try to explain things to her now, not in her present state. Should he tell her at all? *Could* he tell her? What about his promise to Veronica? Certainly she would understand . . . yet he *had* promised.

This was awful!

How could she possibly have seen them in Boston?

Lethargically he pulled himself to his feet. He couldn't stay up here. He had come to see his family . . . and Cherity of course, but if she was going to lock herself in her room, he at least could visit with everyone else.

He left his room and walked downstairs and back into the parlor. He did his best to put on a happy smile.

"Where is Cherity . . . is she coming down?" said Carolyn.

"I don't think so, Mom," replied Seth. "She's . . . uh, pretty tired."

"Oh . . . that's too bad. But you talked to her?"

"Yeah . . . we saw each other."

"Maybe I should take something up to her."

"I think she is going to bed."

"Oh . . . well, I suppose if she gets hungry she'll come down," said Carolyn, still puzzled.

"Hey, Seth," said Thomas walking up to his brother, "is Cherity okay?"

"Yeah, she's . . . uh, fine," replied Seth. "Just had a long ride, I guess."

"Surprised to see you, I bet!"

"Yeah," laughed Seth, "—yeah . . . she sure was!"

"She'll probably be coming down pretty soon. . . . Would it be all right if I talked to you first. I know you've got to leave tomorrow and I want the chance to tell you what happened with me."

They went out to the porch and sat down. Seth listened with interest as Thomas told his story, recognizing many of the same questions and issues he had struggled with in arriving at his own decision regarding possible enlistment when the war had broken out.

By the time the evening had grown cold and forced them back inside, the two brothers had shared more deeply and personally on issues that touched them both than ever before. In one evening they had taken giant strides toward becoming what it is hoped all brothers become when they grow into manhood—lifelong friends of the heart.

The next morning Seth was up early, walking outside around the familiar grounds, passing back and forth several times beneath Cherity's window in hopes that, seeing him, she would come out to join him.

But he saw no sign of movement inside, and eventually came in, by now thoroughly depressed, to join his family at the breakfast table. Though being together again with his family was cause for thanksgiving and they all made a pretense of happy conversation, by now the others sensed from Seth's mood and Cherity's absence that something unpleasant had taken place between them. Seth did not quite fill in all the gaps in his recent itinerary—making no mention of his involvement with Veronica and her problems, which rendered whatever was going on with Cherity, to all but him, utterly mystifying.

"Do you really have to go on *today's* train?" said Carolyn at length. "Why couldn't you just stay a few days more?"

"I've been away far too long already," replied Seth. "I'm behind schedule already. McClarin gave me just two days extra and then said I had to get back."

"Why have you been away so long?" asked Richmond.

"I was working on a special assignment for the paper."

"What about?" asked Thomas.

"Something that came up that took me away from my unit for a while. It involved the war effort, but . . . well, it is still I suppose what you would call confidential. I can't talk about it yet, until the story breaks. Not that any of you would say anything," he added. "That's not what I mean. But I gave my word and I have to honor that. Sometimes journalists have to keep what they are working on to themselves—even just lowly photographers."

"Now you've got us curious, Seth!" laughed Richmond. "When will this mysterious story *break*, as you say?"

"I don't know . . . probably in another week, maybe two."

"Can you give us a hint what it is about?" pleaded Carolyn.

"Sorry, Mom."

"And from here you're going to . . . ?" said Richmond.

"Sorry, Dad," replied Seth, "I'm not supposed to say. I know you wouldn't tell anyone, but I promised. All I can say is that from here I'll take the train to Petersburg, then catch the southbound to Columbia and then west. Beyond that . . . all I can do is let you know when I've arrived and am safe."

"Isn't it dangerous traveling on a train with so much fighting everywhere?" asked Cynthia.

"There are always a few soldiers," replied Seth, "sometimes wounded men going home or others on their way back to their units. But there aren't enough on board that either side would try to capture a train. So, no . . . it's fine. But on the battlefield," he added, shaking his head with a sigh, "that's a different story. It's awful. I hope and pray I never have to live through anything like it again."

"I can't help it, Seth," said Carolyn. "I hope you don't think me too motherly, but I worry about you constantly. I worried about you both," she added, glancing toward Thomas, "until you came home, Thomas."

"We don't mind, Mom—do we, Seth?" said Thomas, smiling warmly at Carolyn, then glancing toward his brother.

"Of course not. That's what mothers are for."

"I am glad to hear that," smiled Carolyn, though it was a smile tinged with sadness. "Because I will probably cry when you leave again, and will cry many times when I think of you, and will probably keep crying until this war is over and you are back safe and sound for good."

Mention of the end of the war and Seth's eventual return to Greenwood, subconsciously turned Carolyn's thoughts toward the one who was missing. Involuntarily she glanced about. "I can't imagine why Cherity isn't down yet," she said.

"Maybe I ought to go up and talk to her," suggested Cynthia, rising from the table.

Changing the subject quickly, Seth turned to Richmond. "Dad, could I talk to you?" he asked.

"Yes, of course," replied Richmond, rising from the table.

Richmond and Seth left the house together. As soon as they were alone, Seth grew quiet. Richmond suspected that it had to do with Cherity. He waited patiently.

They walked away from the house toward the pasture where half a dozen horses were grazing.

"Dad," said Seth at length, "has Cherity been to Boston recently?"

"Yes, a little over a month ago. She had some business concerning her father's estate. She went north to sell her father's house."

"Sell the house . . . why?"

"It's a long story, Seth, my boy. Actually, we have been having some difficult financial troubles here at home."

"Dad, why didn't you tell me? Maybe I could have helped. I make a good wage from the paper."

"I doubt that would have been enough to help with the thousands we needed. It wasn't something I wanted to burden you about. Now that he is back, Thomas knew, of course. The fact is, we came very close to losing Greenwood altogether. Cherity found out about it and sold her Boston house without our knowing anything about it, then gave us the money she received from it."

"Wow!"

"It was pretty astonishing," nodded Richmond, "—and humbling. God has his way of making provision, sometimes unexpected. Anyway, to answer your question in a roundabout way . . . yes, Cherity made a trip up to Boston. Why do you ask?"

Seth let out a long sigh.

"Remember that mess I got myself into with Veronica, Dad?" he said at length.

"How could I forget!"

"Well . . . as hard as it is to believe—I thought I was through with these kinds of things!—it looks like I'm in over my head again, this time with both Veronica *and* Cherity."

"What do they have to do with each other?"

"Cherity thinks I'm still in love with Veronica."

"Surely she can't think such a thing," said Richmond. "She's never even mentioned Veronica."

"Believe me, Dad, she really thinks so. That's why she didn't come downstairs and won't see me. Dad, she is furious with me. She thinks I've been lying to her this whole time."

"How could she possibly think so?"

"It's a little complicated, Dad."

Seth paused and sighed again. "The fact is . . . she saw me in Boston . . . with Veronica."

Richmond's eyes clouded slightly, but he waited patiently.

"That's not all," Seth went on, shaking his head as if trying to forget a bad dream. "She saw us together again . . . yesterday, over at Oakbriar. That's what I'm doing here, Dad—I brought Veronica home from Washington. We didn't think it was safe for her to travel alone. She's going to be staying with her mother for a while."

If Richmond was experiencing sudden doubts about his son's moral character, he kept them to himself for the present. His own difficult and ambiguous past had made him more than commonly tolerant of the failings of others. He was reluctant to rush to judgment until he knew the whole of any story.

"Is there . . . trouble in Veronica's marriage?" he asked, fearing, yet not for a moment entertaining the thought, that Seth himself might be the cause of it.

"No, it's nothing like that, Dad. Richard's a good man. Veronica knows how lucky she is. Honestly," he added with a light laugh, "the way Veronica used to be, I don't know how she found a man of his caliber! She was . . . well, she was something! Richard is the one who asked me to bring Veronica home."

"Are you saying she has changed?" asked Richmond, breathing an inward sigh of relief at what he had just heard.

"She's changed a lot, Dad. You would hardly know her. What she's been through has humbled her, if you can believe it. It's remarkable to say it, but I almost . . . I think I *like* her now."

"You still haven't told me what happened."

"Veronica got herself into trouble," said Seth. "She came to me for help."

"What kind of trouble?" asked his father. "Not . . . marital?"

"No, nothing like that. She got involved with a man who was using her. He drew her into some questionable things—more than just questionable, dangerous and even illegal things. He lured her with money and excitement. Veronica was alone and bored, Richard was away, and . . . she got swept in over her head."

"Were you able to help?"

"I think so . . . I hope so. Anyway, she came to me and I didn't feel I could turn her away. So I tried to help and that's what we were doing in Boston. The paper got involved and McClarin wanted to meet her, and I guess that's when Cherity saw us."

"So you didn't see Cherity?"

"No . . . I had no idea, until last night when she hit the roof."

It was silent a few minutes. Both father and son were thinking.

"Did you tell Cherity all this?" asked Richmond at length. "I'm sure she would understand."

"I didn't have the chance. She wouldn't listen. And . . . it's complicated, like I said. I made a promise to Veronica that I wouldn't divulge her trouble. So I *can't* tell Cherity everything. Veronica still may be in danger too. That's why she's here, not exactly in hiding, but out of the way until it all blows over."

"It sounds mysterious."

"It is, I suppose. Even if I was able to tell Cherity, the way she's feeling about me right now, she would probably just laugh it off."

"I doubt that."

"But it sounds more than a little implausible, you have to admit."

"Maybe. But she will come to her senses. Women always do eventually. She will realize that you are telling the truth."

"If I had the time. But I don't. I have to leave today, Dad. I'm not going to force her to listen to me. That's just not something I can do. What would I do—yell at her through the locked door?"

"Do you want me to talk to her?"

"Thanks, Dad," replied Seth. "But not yet. I guess I want her to trust me . . . trust me enough to know that I would never lie to her, and to know that Veronica means nothing to me in the same way that Cherity means everything to me. Veronica is a friend, like a sister. But I love Cherity. There's all the difference in the world."

"I still don't understand why it is so secretive. What does your paper have to do with it?"

Seth thought a minute before answering.

"That's the reason I've been vague, Dad, and why I still can't tell everything until the story comes out," he said at length. "But I will tell you what I feel I can without breaking confidence. Then you can handle it as you think best . . . with Cherity and everyone else. There's no reason even for Mom to know, unless you think she should."

"I have to admit," said Richmond, "you are making this sound more and more mysterious all the time."

"Dad . . . it's about spying," said Seth.

Richmond's face went instantly serious. "Spying?" he said, almost as if he had mistaken what he thought he had heard.

Seth nodded. "Veronica got herself mixed up in a spy ring with connections on both sides," he said. "They were people who had the power to change the course of the war. They are very powerful. When I say that she is in danger, I mean her life is truly in danger, as mine might be as well for all I know. The stakes are high, Dad. That's all I can say."

Richmond exhaled a low whistle and nodded intently.

"I see," he said. "At last I begin to understand your concern."

"That's what the story is about. But until it appears in print and the people involved are either arrested or put out of business, we have to be very careful."

"Right . . . it is indeed complicated as you say."

"I wish I could tell Cherity everything. Right now I just don't feel I can."

"When is the article scheduled to appear?" asked Richmond.

"Literally any day. It may already have run in the *Herald*. If so, it will make it into the Southern papers any moment. Then the people involved will be out of business and you can tell Cherity what I've told you. I'll write when I'm back with my unit and I'll explain the whole thing in detail."

Seth and his father returned to the house an hour later, having spoken of many things. Still no one had seen Cherity.

For the remainder of the morning, Richmond, Seth, Thomas, and Sydney worked together, laughing and talking as if Seth's presence were nothing out of the ordinary. Yet each of the other three were aware of Seth's frequent glances toward the house, and knew that he was hoping for a glimpse of Cherity coming toward them. But steadily the hour of Seth's afternoon departure approached, and still there was no sign of her.

At last the time came. Seth cleaned up from the work, then said his last good-byes to home, friends, and family.

Carolyn had not the slightest idea what was going on between Seth and Cherity, but ached for them. All her mother's instincts told her to go upstairs, pull Cherity out of her room and take her to Seth, and tell them to talk it out.

But she had seen the looks and expressions on her son's and husband's faces after their talk that morning. She knew both well enough to recognize that whatever was going on, they had discussed it. It was therefore not her place to speak up. She would not interfere in the holy order of things with her own womanly two cents' worth.

As she had predicted, Carolyn cried when Seth embraced her.

"You be sure to write us," she said, smiling through her tears.

"I will telegraph the moment I am back with my unit to let you know I arrived safely, and follow that with a letter."

Seth and Richmond shook hands and gazed into one another's eyes.

"Handle it as you think best, Dad," said Seth, forcing a smile.

"And you be careful until this is all over," said Richmond.

Thinking it a curious exchange, but assuming Richmond to be referring to the war, Carolyn said nothing further.

Seth got into the buggy and, in one of the loneliest rides he had ever taken in his life, returned to Dove's Landing and the train.

PART FIVE

MISSING
October, 1864 - April, 1865

Fifty-Five

From her window, Cherity saw the buggy bearing Seth away from Greenwood. She cried two or three more times, unable to distinguish the remnants of her anger from her grief.

Once he was gone, she did her best to put on a presentable face, then crept downstairs. She heard Cynthia and Maribel in the parlor but was able to get to the kitchen unseen. She found something to eat and drink, for she was famished and thirsty, and snuck outside by the back door. By the time Seth stood on the platform waiting for the train, she was again galloping up the hill away from Greenwood on Cadence's back. She again remained away until nearly dusk, having by then all but resolved to leave Greenwood at the earliest convenient opportunity.

Far to the north in Boston, meanwhile, Adrian McClarin of the *Herald* had put everything connected with the spy story on a rush timetable, such that, as Seth had anticipated, the article was on the presses even before he reached home.

After his departure, Seth spent the night in Richmond before catching the next morning's train to Columbia. Picking up a copy of the Richmond *Gazette*, it was while seated on the train that he saw a reprint of the article that had appeared the day before in the *Herald*.

The same paper found its way to the breakfast table at Greenwood a few days later.

"Did you hear that Veronica is back home for a while," Carolyn was saying. "I heard several women talking about her when I was at Baker's in town."

"What is she doing here?" asked Cynthia.

"I don't know," answered her mother. "The old gossips were talking about marital troubles and other things I won't mention. But knowing who it was, I doubt any of it is true."

Richmond, who had been silent till now, engrossed in the newspaper, set it down long enough to put the rumor to rest.

"I can tell you on good authority," he said, "that Veronica's marriage is absolutely sound. She is at home for other reasons altogether."

Carolyn looked at her husband with surprise. Expecting him to go on, she waited. Gradually it became obvious he intended to say no more.

"You knew Veronica was home?" she said.

"I did," he answered.

"How?"

"I have my sources."

"Do you also know *why* she is here?"

"I do."

"Are you going to tell us?"

"Soon," said Richmond, then returned to the paper to finish the article.

Carolyn continued to eye him, then finally let sound a good-natured *humph*. She turned back toward Cynthia.

"I really ought to go pay a visit to Lady Daphne," she said. "Even if I weren't curious about Veronica. Would you ladies like to join me?" she added, glancing also in Cherity's direction.

"I would, Mother," replied Cynthia. "I haven't seen Veronica since we were both married."

Cherity kept her head down and said nothing. Veronica was the *last* person she wanted to see.

"I wonder what Veronica is doing at home," said Cynthia.

"I think I might at last be able to answer that," said Richmond, setting down the paper he had been reading. "In fact . . . I have just been reading about her."

"Reading about whom?"

"Veronica."

"In the newspaper!" exclaimed Cynthia.

Richmond nodded. "Seth is here too, though his role remains mostly invisible."

"What—Seth . . . in the paper?" exclaimed Carolyn.

"Only behind the scenes. He told me all about it, so I am able to read between the lines."

"He told you *what*? What did he tell you that he didn't tell *us*?"

"There were things going on that Seth was not at liberty to talk about openly," said Richmond, glancing briefly toward Cherity across the table. "Things . . . ," he added, "involving Veronica. As a matter of fact," he went on, choosing his words carefully, "did you know that it was Seth who brought Veronica home from Washington? They traveled down together on the train from the capital. The day he arrived here he had just returned from seeing her safely home to Oakbriar."

"I can't believe it," said Carolyn. "Surely he would have told us."

"There were reasons he couldn't," rejoined Richmond. "But he told me some of it and said that I could tell the rest of you at the appropriate time."

"I'm not sure I like the sound of it," said Carolyn. "That's what the ladies in Baker's were talking about, though I didn't want to say. Mrs. Peterson saw the two of them getting off the train together."

Richmond laughed. "Are you going to pay any attention to what a couple of busybodies say? It was all perfectly aboveboard. Richard, Veronica's husband, *asked* Seth to bring Veronica home. She was in danger and had turned to Seth as an old friend she could trust. Seth had been helping her. Once it was over, they decided that it would be best for Veronica to come back here for a while."

Cherity sat listening intently, but still said nothing. It had slowly begun to dawn on her that she may have misread the entire incident, though Seth's father had said nothing yet to explain what his son and Veronica had been doing together in Boston.

"Danger . . . what kind of danger?" asked Carolyn.

"It's all in this article," explained Richmond.

"Read it to us! I'm dying to know what's been going on."

Richmond picked up the paper.

"'In one of the most dramatic non-battlefield episodes of the war thus far,'" he began, "'the *Boston Herald* has gained exclusive evidence of a major underground spy ring, operating on both sides of the conflict. From information gained by the *Herald*'s undercover reporter—'"

Richmond paused briefly and glanced at the other three.

"That is Seth, by the way," he said.

"The undercover reporter!" exclaimed Carolyn.

Richmond nodded. "'—the *Herald*'s undercover reporter, working closely with an eyewitness source privy to firsthand knowledge of the passage of information by courier—'"

"And that," Richmond said, "is Veronica. She is the eyewitness source."

"Goodness!" said Carolyn. "I don't understand . . . why was she involved?"

"I don't know the specifics," replied Richmond. "All I know is that she got drawn into this thing, and after she realized she was in over her head she turned to Seth to try to help get her out."

"Keep reading!" said Cynthia.

"'—the passage of information by courier to and from contacts on both sides. Chief among those implicated in the affair is one Cecil Hirsch, known under various aliases, who passed information in both directions between the Union and the Confederacy using a variety of accomplices and couriers. Hirsch remains at large and is being sought by Union authorities. Also involved are Enrico Garabaldi and Congressman Stanley Roberts. Photographs of transactions were taken to authorities in Washington D.C. that demonstrated incontrovertible evidence of the flow of information. It is thought that Hirsch's and

Garabaldi's activities are connected to the former spy ring involving Rose Greenhow earlier in the war, and—'"

Suddenly in the middle of the article, Cherity stood up and quickly hurried from the room, trying desperately to keep back her tears until she was alone. She ran from the house moments later, bursting into sobs as she went.

The next afternoon Carolyn planned a visit to Oakbriar. Cynthia accompanied her but Cherity, who had been quiet and had kept to herself ever since Seth's visit, declined.

They found Lady Daphne almost beside herself with pleasure to have her daughter home again. She said her husband would be home in a week or two as well. As had Seth, they found Veronica much changed, more subdued, almost introspective. They left Oakbriar an hour and a half later both thinking that they ought to visit more often.

Several days went by. The life and routine of Greenwood gradually resumed its former patterns.

"Don't I remember Seth saying he would write the moment he was safely back with his unit?" said Carolyn one day after Richmond returned from town with the mail.

"He did," replied Richmond. "He said he would telegraph as soon as he arrived."

"It's been a week."

"I'm sure he's been busy. I doubt there's anything to worry about. It can't be an easy life living in a tent and traveling around all the time."

"Not to mention being in the middle of battles and fighting!" added Carolyn. "But I do worry, Richmond. I can't help it."

Cherity continued to be embarrassed about her behavior during Seth's visit. But she could not bring herself to mention it to either Carolyn or Richmond. As transparent as she had been with Carolyn about most things, in matters of the heart, especially given the fact that she was Seth's mother, she was hesitant to be as free with her thoughts and feelings. On the surface she returned to normal and her characteristic exuberant nature again spread light all about her. She resumed her story times with the visiting black children, all of whom loved her. But deep inside she ached for the rift that her untrusting heart had allowed to come between herself and Seth. She yearned for the moment when she could apologize to him and make it all right again. Her walks and rides were more melancholy and thoughtful than before. Until it *was* right again between she and Seth, a cloud of unsettledness hung invisibly over her spirit.

Carolyn sensed the change and intuitively guessed the reasons for it, though neither did she bring it up.

More often than not, now, when Cherity and Carolyn saw one another, they smiled or gave the other an affectionate embrace, often silently, with an expression that said they were both missing their Seth.

Fifty-Six

Out riding one day, again Cherity saw the Beaumont plantation in the distance below her. Ever since Seth's visit she had known that eventually she must confront Veronica face to face and hear from her own mouth exactly where things stood with Seth. She had not planned such a visit for today. Yet almost before she realized it, she found herself once again pursuing a course that led her down from the ridge and ultimately again straight toward the plantation house. This time there was no buggy in sight as she walked Cadence slowly up the drive.

As she neared one of the outbuildings, the huge form of Elias Slade leaning on a crutch came limping into sight around the corner of the wall on his way to the barn. He hesitated, eyed her briefly without revealing any change to his expression, then continued on. Cherity shuddered involuntarily, then made her way to the front of the house, where she dismounted, took off her hat and gun and hung them from her saddle horn, then walked up the steps to the front door. She drew in a breath, then reached for the heavy brass knocker. Jarvis answered the sound almost before its echo had died away.

"I am here to see Miss Beau—" began Cherity, smiling somewhat nervously. "Oh . . . I'm sorry," she added, "I forgot she is married . . . but I am afraid I don't know her married name."

"If you'd be meanin' Miss Veronica, ma'am—"

"Yes . . . Veronica," smiled Cherity. "Is she at home?"

"Yes, ma'am. I'll jes' fetch her fo' you."

The black man disappeared inside.

Cherity waited on the porch, becoming now aware of her clothes and remembering her first meeting with Veronica in Dove's Landing. Perhaps this had been a mistake, she thought. She should have planned this ahead of time, worn a dress, and—

She glanced back at her horse where he was tied at the rail, thinking fleetingly of making a run for it. Almost the next instant she heard footsteps behind her. She turned back and through the partially open door saw Veronica descending the stairway toward her.

Veronica paused. The eyes of the two young women met. In the merest fractions of seconds, like two cats seeing one another for the first time and each sizing the other up, a hundred undefined thoughts and emotions raced through each of their brains. As quickly as it had come, the spell was broken. Veronica smiled and continued down, went to the open door and extended her hand in welcome. She was even more stunning than Cherity remembered her, and so graceful. All Cherity's fears and anxieties rushed back upon her. Suddenly she felt very self-conscious about being dressed like such a bumpkin. Veronica probably had no idea who she even was!

"I'm sorry," said Veronica, "I have forgotten your name."

"It's Cherity . . . Cherity Waters," replied Cherity, trying to return her smile.

"That's right," rejoined Veronica. "I remember seeing you once in town with Seth, but . . . that was a long time ago."

"A very long time ago!" laughed Cherity nervously. "I was hardly more than a girl."

"You are certainly more than that now," said Veronica in a complimentary tone without a hint of the edge that might have once accompanied such a comment, "though I recognized you immediately. Would you like to come in and have some tea?"

"I'm afraid I'm not dressed very presentably," said Cherity, glancing down at her worn dungarees and men's boots, fresh from the saddle. "I was just out for a ride and thought I would come by."

"You look fine," said Veronica. "Please . . . do come in."

"All right, thank you," said Cherity, following as Veronica led the way into the house. "I suppose I did come to see you, although now that I am here . . . I'm not exactly sure why. I probably should have sent word ahead."

"No, it's perfectly all right. I am glad you came."

Veronica led Cherity into the parlor, where she pulled a cord on the wall. A bell rang faintly. Several seconds later Jarvis reappeared.

"Jarvis, would you please bring us a pot of tea?" said Veronica.

"Yes, Miss Veronica."

"Thank you. Please," she added to Cherity, "sit down wherever you're comfortable."

"Are you sure?" said Cherity, hesitating. "I've been out riding. My clothes are—"

"My daddy comes in here all the time in his boots and riding things. Sit anywhere you like."

Cherity smiled and sat down on a high-backed oak chair with an embroidered cushion.

"Are you visiting the Davidsons again?" asked Veronica, sitting down opposite her. "It was years ago when I first saw you. You were here with your father, weren't you, from somewhere up north, wasn't it?"

"Yes, from Boston," replied Cherity.

"Oh . . . Boston. Seth works for a newspaper in Boston."

"Yes, my father worked there for years too. He's the one who introduced Seth to the editor at the paper."

"Yes, I remember Seth mentioning your father."

"That's how Seth got started in photography. Actually, my father died a few years ago."

"Oh, I am sorry. I didn't know."

"Thank you," smiled Cherity. This was more pleasant than she had anticipated. She hadn't expected Veronica to be so gracious.

"And you are down visiting again?" asked Veronica.

"Actually . . . I've been living with the Davidsons since my father's death," answered Cherity.

"Oh . . . really."

"My mother died when I was born, you see, and when he was gone I was left alone. I have two older sisters, but they both have their own families. Mr. and Mrs. Davidson offered to let me come stay with them. They have been extremely kind to me."

"Yes, they are . . . well, they are very nice people."

Just then Jarvis entered with a tray of cups and saucers. He set it down on the table.

"And you just recently returned home too, I understand," said Cherity.

Veronica nodded. "I got myself mixed up with some bad people. Richard—that's my husband—thought I should get away from Washington for a while. I hope you don't mind . . . I mean, I don't know how it is exactly with you and Seth—but Richard asked Seth to bring me home, so he came with me on the train. He thought it would be a good chance to visit home at the same time."

"Yes, I . . . uh, I knew that," said Cherity. "But I—"

She paused and glanced away.

"I'm sorry, I hope you won't think it terribly forward of me," she said, embarrassed, "but would you mind telling me . . . if you could just help me understand . . . what you and Seth were doing in Boston together."

"You knew we were in Boston? Did . . . did Seth tell you that?"

"No. Actually, I was there at the same time. I had some business to attend to and . . . I saw you and he together."

"Ah, I see. And . . . but you didn't think—"

At last Veronica recognized the expression on Cherity's face and saw that she was terrified for what might be coming.

"Oh . . . I hope you didn't think there was something—I am so sorry . . . it was nothing like that."

"I . . . I didn't know . . . I had to—"

"You poor dear," said Veronica. "I see what you must have been going through. I am sorry."

Cherity looked away and tried to collect herself, then drew in a deep breath.

"Then . . . would you mind explaining to me . . . what is going on, and why you and Seth were together," she said. "I'm afraid I did misunderstand, and I behaved very badly to Seth because of it. I feel terrible. . . . I just want to understand."

Jarvis brought in the pot of tea and poured out two cups, then left again.

"As concerns Seth and me," said Veronica when they were again alone and each had cups in their hands, "there is nothing other than that Seth has once again proved himself a good friend. You can set your mind completely at ease. Believe me, you have nothing to worry about. I love my husband, and, if you are in love with Seth, you have truly found an admirable young man. Seth is a brother to me, and always will be. I once thought I loved him. Maybe I did, maybe I didn't. I don't really know. But he didn't love me, and that was the most important thing we both had to realize. And this recent situation has shown me what a true friend he has always been."

She went on to tell Cherity everything in detail about what had happened, how she had contacted Seth, and how he and Mr. McClarin had devised a plan to get her out of the clutches of Cecil Hirsch. By the time she was through, Cherity was in tears.

"What is it?" asked Veronica, worried that she had said something to offend or worry her.

"I'm sorry," smiled Cherity, wiping her eyes. "I am just feeling very, very foolish all over again for how I behaved to Seth. I acted like a little schoolgirl!"

"We have all done that at times," said Veronica. "When I think how I used to be, it positively makes me cringe."

"You really are very beautiful," said Cherity. "I couldn't help worrying. What man wouldn't find you attractive?"

"Oh, don't say such things! You are very pretty too. I suppose the way someone looks affects people differently. I can't tell you how jealous I was of you the first time I saw you with Seth. You looked so lively and spunky and energetic and with *such* a wonderful smile. I think it's energy that makes people attractive, don't you? . . . More than just looks, I mean. I had never seen a girl in boots and dungarees before. I was so angry with Seth!"

Cherity laughed. "I can hardly believe it to hear you say all that. I was jealous of you too. I knew that you and Seth were engaged, and then for a long time after my father and I returned to Boston, I thought you and he were married."

"It was a good thing Seth had the courage to break off our engagement," said Veronica almost introspectively. "It would never have worked. I was dreadfully angry about it at the time. But he was right to do what he did. I have him to thank that I eventually met Richard. Are you and Seth . . . ?"

Veronica let her words trail off, hoping that Cherity would supply the rest.

"I don't know," sighed Cherity. "I thought I loved him, and maybe I do. But sometimes it's not easy to tell what is really love and what might be something else. And I think Seth—maybe because of what went on between you and him—is cautious to commit himself. He has said some wonderful things to me that I treasure in my heart. But beyond that . . . I just have to wait and see what the end of the war brings."

"Well my advice to you is to give him time. He is a man worth waiting for. I can assure you in every way, both before and more recently, that he has always behaved toward me as a perfect gentleman. He is a Davidson."

It fell silent for several moments.

"Well . . . perhaps it is time for me to be going," said Cherity, shifting in her chair.

"Do you have to?" said Veronica. "At least stay long enough to come upstairs. I want you to meet my mother."

She rose. Cherity stood also.

"Now that all this is behind us," said Veronica, "maybe you could come back again . . . just for a visit, you know, and . . ."

She hesitated and a strange, almost sheepish look came over her face. It was one of the few times in her life that Veronica had felt embarrassment.

"Would you mind if I asked you a favor?" she said.

"Of course not," replied Cherity, unable to imagine anything *she* could do for someone like Veronica.

"Would you . . . I know this probably sounds silly, but . . . would you teach me to ride?"

Cherity stared back not sure she had understood.

"You want me . . . to teach you to ride? A horse, you mean?"

Veronica nodded. "Seth loved horses so much. I always hated the very thought of saddles and sweat and manure and all of it. But Richard loves to ride too. I think I am finally ready to learn."

"Of course," said Cherity enthusiastically. "But . . . there's really nothing to do but just get on."

"I'm sure it seems simple, but the whole thing terrifies me. I don't know the first thing about how to get up and how to make them go and stop and turn, and what you do with those leather things—"

"The reins."

"Yes . . . whatever they're called. And I don't even know what to wear."

"Do you have any riding clothes?"

"Do you mean men's dungarees—good heavens, I've never worn a pair in my life. I do have a riding habit for riding sidesaddle, but—" she laughed—"I've never worn it."

"Well, that would be fine. But it is so much more comfortable in dungarees."

"Would you come back tomorrow and go into town with me and help me get what else I need?"

"That would be fun! Sure, I would love to."

"Maybe I will even get a men's hat! You look so wonderful in yours. Mrs. Baker will have a fit. I can't wait to see the look on her face!"

Cherity returned to Oakbriar the following afternoon. Veronica had asked Leon Riggs to hitch the buggy for her. It stood ready in front of the house and Veronica was proud to be able to drive them into town with at least a small degree of confidence. They returned from Dove's Landing two hours later. Veronica changed into her new riding clothes and, to her mother's surprise, told Lady Daphne that she and Cherity were going for a ride. After selecting the tamest horse at Oakbriar, again with the help of the Beaumont overseer, Cherity showed her how to saddle him, then helped Veronica into the saddle and jumped up into her own.

Even before they set out, Mrs. Baker had hurried to tell Mrs. Peterson about her two customers, and Mrs. Peterson had proceeded to set the rest of the of the town's women abuzz with the news.

The next day Veronica was a little more comfortable in the saddle, and the two girls set off together into the hills, Cherity chose gentle terrain, and by the end of the afternoon had shown Veronica the basics of a gentle canter. Veronica was not quite brave enough to try it for herself yet. But her initial fears were subsiding rapidly enough that Cherity was confident she would be galloping alongside her within a week or two.

Fifty-Seven

Though she continued to carry Richmond Davidson's gun whenever she rode alone, Cherity did not again encounter Elias Slade. By then, hearing that he was still at Oakbriar, Richmond notified the authorities, outlining everything he knew about the man.

Cherity did, however, have another unexpected encounter that proved destined to change all their lives in ways no one at either Greenwood or Oakbriar could have foreseen.

It was a warm day some three weeks after Seth's departure and the day seemed perfect for a long ride to take her mind off her growing anxiety about their not having heard from him. She set off after lunch, rode toward Harper's Peak the long way around, through the high meadow where some of their horses were grazing, and up to the ridge where she rode the length of it twice, before starting down through the Brown tract.

Ever since her discovery of the carved symbols on the tree matching the design on the skin painting that Chigua had restored, she was convinced that some mystery concerning the enigmatic Mr. Brown was just waiting to be discovered . . . and that it was up to her to discover it.

Why she was drawn to the place, Cherity could not say. The mystery of the Cherokee man had possessed her since that first day she and

Seth had ridden here together when she was a mere girl. Now she was a young woman with a woman's heart filled with a woman's love. Chigua's talk of the caves of North Carolina where the Cherokee had hidden the gold prior to the Trail of Tears had infected Cherity with the certainty that Brown had done the same thing prior to his strange disappearance from Virginia. There was no factual basis for such an idea. Yet in her heart of hearts . . . she was sure of it. The caves of the region had filled her with awe since she and Seth had explored the very first one together all those years ago. But in all her rides and investigations since, she had found nothing beyond the markings on the pine trunk near the house. And after the incident with Elias Slade, she had not ventured inside any of the caves again.

Denton Beaumont had been back to Oakbriar half a dozen times since he had rushed away excitedly, planning to return within the hour. But he had always been too distracted and busy to devote an afternoon to the more thorough search of the Brown place he had intended. But at last came an afternoon when he had time on his hands. He went to his office and closed the door, the events of a time long past running through his mind again.

It was with trembling hand that he opened the safe in his office, fumbled through its contents, and withdrew the envelope in which for thirty years he had kept the small faded scrap of paper hoping that someday its strange secrets would reveal themselves. He placed it carefully in his pocket, then hurried outside to saddle his horse.

The day he had long anticipated was finally at hand!

Cherity's ride had been longer than usual and the afternoon had grown yet warmer and more sultry as she went, such that by the time her way led her past Mr. Brown's house, she was weary and growing a little sleepy.

Not wanting to take any chances of being seen, she tied her horse behind the house out of sight, then walked inside.

She lit a lantern and made her way slowly through all the rooms, her eyes resting on all the same familiar items they had seen so many times before, especially now the beautiful skin painting that Chigua had restored where it hung above the fireplace. At length she blew out the lantern and set it on the table, and wandered toward one of the bedrooms, the weariness of the ride returning upon her.

Denton Beaumont rode up to the Brown house, reined in, and dismounted. Even in his eagerness, he walked toward it with slowing steps. He opened the door cautiously, almost timidly, knowing no one else was within miles, yet somehow unwilling to make any unnecessary noise.

He caught a whiff—or did he only imagine it?—of the faint smell of heat. He reached toward the lantern sitting on the table. Was its glass warm? A chill went through him. The place was utterly silent. Had someone been here before him? Or was his brain again playing tricks on him?

He would have scoffed at any suggestion that he was being watched by the spirit of the dead. He was far too much a materialist for such mumbo jumbo. Yet some impulse urged silence upon him, as if the mere echo of his steps across the floor might wake the slumber of the departed to shout to the world the dread secret he had managed to conceal for so long.

Cherity had not intended to fall asleep. She had only lain down to rest briefly before continuing her ride. But she was more fatigued than she realized. Within three minutes she was sound asleep and dreaming of Indian legends and gold rings and weird geometric designs carved on trees and rocks and on the flanks of white deer racing through the forest trying to keep from being seen by the eyes of men.

Suddenly she started awake!

Cherity's eyes shot open. She lay still, not daring to move a muscle. A sound had disturbed her sleep. Someone was in the next room!

She was sweating freely from the hot day and the sudden rush of adrenaline through her system. For several moments she lay still, breathing heavily and trying to gather her wits back inside her brain. It might be a runaway who had stumbled upon the place. But she couldn't afford to take any chances.

With extreme care, Cherity sat up, then slowly rose to her feet. With thoughts of Elias Slade reverberating in her mind, her hand went to her side and she drew the pistol from its holster.

Denton Beaumont was engrossed with his search of the stones of the fireplace, which he had been tapping at to dislodge any that might be loose. The sudden sounds of steps behind him made him nearly leap out of his skin.

He spun around. Across the room stood a little girl with a gun in her hand pointed straight at him.

"What are you doing here?" he exclaimed. "And put that thing down—who are you anyway?"

"What are *you* doing here?" returned Cherity.

"That is none of your affair!" retorted Beaumont, recovering from his temporary fright.

Strange as it may seem, though she had been at Greenwood for several years, and though his name came up often enough, Cherity had never before laid eyes on the Davidsons' neighbor. Nor had he seen her before this moment. They were complete strangers to one another, and both were utterly perplexed to find someone else in the Brown house who appeared perfectly at home in the place.

Now that he had heard the girl's voice, however, Beaumont did not think her crazy enough to shoot him. His natural abusive nature returned quickly to the surface. "Now get out of here and leave me alone. I don't know who you are or what you are doing, but I have business here. Put that gun away, I tell you! And I asked you who you were."

Cherity, too, was by now wide awake and fully recovered from the shock of seeing a man she did not know rummaging about and disturbing the place she considered almost sacred. She walked slowly forward as she holstered the pistol. She noticed that the skin painting was gone from the wall. She glanced about and saw it lying on the table. On top of it rested a small torn piece of yellowed paper.

"What are you doing with Mr. Brown's painting?" she asked. "And why did you take it down?"

"What do you know of Brown?" snapped Beaumont.

"That this was his house, and that it now belongs to Mr. Davidson," said Cherity.

"For now, perhaps."

"I want to know what are you looking for." insisted Cherity. She did not like this man and was growing irritated. "Why did you take the painting down?"

"Look, little girl, I don't have time for your questions. What is your name?"

"My name is none of your affair," retorted Cherity, getting angry now too. "If you don't tell me what you are doing here, I will go get Mr. Davidson immediately."

"Go get him, see if I care. I will be gone before he gets here anyway."

Cherity's eyes drifted again to the table and the torn piece of paper that lay on top of the skin. She had never seen it before. It must belong to the man in front of her. On it were drawn a series of lines, a few sketches of what might be trees and the contour of a hillside, and a squiggly line that could represent a stream.

And there was the same pattern of lines and dots as were on the painting and on the tree outside!

Whoever this man was, he must be looking for the same thing she was!

But he was right. Even if she galloped all the way, she could not possibly get back here with Richmond for thirty or forty minutes. It did not take her long to assess her options.

Suddenly she leapt forward, grabbed the torn paper in one hand, and darted for the door.

But Beaumont had been watching her carefully. His cunning eyes had seen her examining the torn bit of map. He hoped she would think nothing of it. Obviously he was mistaken.

He was nearly as quick as she, and his legs were longer. With two swift strides he caught her in front of the door and his hand closed tightly on her wrist.

"Ouch . . . that hurts!" Cherity yelled. "Let me go!"

"Let go of that paper," he demanded.

"This house belongs to Mr. Davidson. Whatever you are up to, I am going to tell him."

"You are going to do no such thing. Drop it."

Beaumont's hand twisted Cherity's arm backward until she screamed in pain.

"I can break your arm in a second, little girl," he said, staring into her eyes with an expression that indicated clearly enough that he was serious. "Now let go of that paper."

Cherity kicked Beaumont's leg as hard as she could. The shock of Cherity's sudden attack caused him to release his grip. Cherity dashed for the door, and within seconds was outside and sprinting for her horse behind the house.

Cursing his foul luck to have been seen, Beaumont hurriedly resumed his search. When he left the place twenty minutes later, the painting that Chigua had so meticulously restored, already torn in several spots from his rough treatment, was rolled up under his arm and on its way to Oakbriar.

Fifty-Eight

Cherity went straight to Richmond with news of her encounter and to give him the piece of paper she had taken from Beaumont. Richmond looked at it with obvious interest, thanked her, said he would handle it and suggested she divulge nothing about it until he decided what was to be done.

All thought of Denton Beaumont, however, faded into the background of Cherity's mind the next day. Richmond returned from town holding a newspaper. Cherity was in the kitchen as he perused it and mentioned this and that as he read.

"Hmm . . . there was a train accident a couple weeks ago," he said, "an explosion set on the tracks near Atlanta, just outside Jonesborough."

"What happened?" asked Carolyn.

"The train derailed. From the sound of it, it was pretty serious. A number of people were killed, and many more wounded. They've had to turn half the farmhouses along the route into makeshift sickrooms. There was heavy fighting in the region too, compounding the problem of what to do with the wounded."

"Will this war never end?" sighed Carolyn.

As they went on to talk about other things, Cherity's throat went dry. The words *near Atlanta* rang in her ears. It was just where Seth had said he was going. And they had heard nothing from him since!

Was it possible . . . ? She couldn't bear to think of what it might mean!

Quietly she got up and left the room.

⌒

A pall settled over Cherity's spirits. But what could she do until more news came . . . *any* news. Until they heard from Seth, she could do nothing but wait . . . and hope . . . and pray.

Yet another week of silence went by.

At last a day came when all Cherity's pent-up anxiety broke as they sat around the breakfast table.

"I can't stand it anymore," she said. "We've got to find out what's happened to him!"

She left the house, with the others staring after her wondering what she meant.

Cherity walked away from the house, her eyes stinging and her brain spinning. She couldn't just sit and wait any longer. She had to *do* something. Foolish as it might be, she *had* to go look for him. She couldn't bear the uncertainty a moment longer.

When she returned an hour later her mind was made up. She went to her room and began packing into her carpetbag a change of clothes, a warm coat and a blanket, and what few other things she could think that she might need. She returned downstairs a few minutes later.

"Where are you off to?" asked Richmond as he saw her bag in hand.

"I . . . I am going, uh . . . I have been thinking about going to visit my sister," replied Cherity in a tone of determination.

"This is rather sudden, is it not?"

"I've been thinking about it for several days. I just need to get away for a while."

"All right, then, but you be careful, young lady. We have grown to love you as if you were our own daughter. So you mustn't think ill of us for being protective."

"I don't," smiled Cherity.

"Remember what I told you in connection with Elias Slade. The world is not always a trustworthy place. You watch yourself. If you get into any danger, don't be afraid to ask for help. There are bad people in the world. But it is my belief that there are more good people than bad, and that most people will help when asked."

Cherity smiled again. "I will remember what you say, Mr. Davidson. And thank you . . . thank you for everything. I love you both . . . very much."

Carolyn walked over and embraced Cherity tightly, then stepped back, wiping nose and eyes with her handkerchief.

Cherity turned to Richmond. He now took her in his arms as well. Her small frame was nearly swallowed up in his giant embrace.

"Would it be asking too much . . . ?" said Cherity as she stepped back. "I would appreciate a ride to the station."

"Not at all. Of course," nodded Richmond. "I will go hitch up the buggy."

Fifty-Nine

Cherity had not wanted to mislead Richmond and Carolyn about her unknown destination. But she couldn't betray Seth again by revealing his destination after what he had said. And she didn't want to worry his parents with her own fears. She would tell them everything when she returned.

She took the train first to Richmond where she spent the night in a boardinghouse near the station. The next day she continued on to Columbia where she changed trains for Atlanta, following the route Seth had spoken of to his father without revealing Atlanta as his final objective. All along the way she asked conductors and station attendants about the accident, whether there had been official reports released of the dead and injured, and where she would be likely to learn more. No one knew other than what sketchy information had been passed along the line. They told her to check the station bulletin along the way for possible news, and for lists of the dead and wounded.

Gradually she learned that most of the wounded from the accident had been taken to makeshift wards in the towns of Bend and Jefferson's Crossing. There had also been several skirmishes in the area whose wounded were also being put up wherever there was space between Jonesborough and Atlanta. As for the young man she was looking for, most of them said, her chances of finding him were one in a thousand. Sherman's Union forces had moved on toward Savannah.

⟨⎯⎯⟩

Denton Beaumont had been in a foul mood ever since his return to
Dove's Landing.

The Confederate Senate had spent the last several days discussing
what was now almost surely an impending defeat for the South, and
how the terms of a surrender should be handled and the government
dissolved. Grant was closing in. It was time to pack their bags and get
out. With a few handshakes and well-wishes, the once optimistic senators of a fledgling nation had hurried out of town before the Union
army stormed in.

It was a bitter pill to swallow to realize that his brief career in
politics was all but over and that he had bet his future on the wrong
horse. Of course even after the war things might resume their former
patterns. Virginia would become incorporated into the Union again
and would need congressmen and senators just as before. He might
again run for office. But he was not optimistic about the chances of
any of those who had gone down with the defeat of the Confederacy.

Meanwhile, he had to get his plantation back to normal, which,
without slaves, would be no easy task. It galled him all the more
to realize that his neighbor had been right about that too. Slavery
was over and he had to figure out a way to get crops in and make a
profit with a paid workforce. Notwithstanding his previous visit to
Greenwood, the last thing he was about to do was ask for Richmond
Davidson's help. He would let Oakbriar sink into bankruptcy first!

⟨⎯⎯⟩

Richmond Davidson's thoughts were occupied with his neighbor as
well. He sat in his study, the torn portion of map that Cherity had taken
from the Brown house in his hand. The moment he had seen it, though
he had never laid eyes on it in his life, he had known what it was, for
he had heard about it from his father. It had not taken long for him
to begin to piece together its full significance. He kept his thoughts to
himself. But slowly they grew into a terrible weight upon his mind.

There was only one way Denton could have come by it. He had not wanted to actually voice his suspicions. But as he reflected on it, the more the suspicion grew into certainty. It was a bitter way for a friendship between neighbors to end, he thought.

What should he do? The torn paper held the key to the truth. Yet without the rest—and how many other similar portions had been torn off?—how could he know for certain what these markings and strange designs were trying to tell him?

His thoughts strayed to the safe against the far wall, and he glanced toward it. In that very safe his father had placed this bit of paper. It had inexplicably disappeared and its fate had been an ongoing mystery . . . until Cherity had seen it in Denton Beaumont's possession at the Brown house. In that safe now was also a sealed brown packet Seth had given him to safeguard for Cherity until some future time, which he did not specify. Even Cherity herself did not know of its existence. James had given it to Seth on his deathbed, for Seth to give to his daughter when he judged the time right.

What secrets that safe held, thought Richmond. His father's secrets, his brother's secrets, and now James Waters' secrets.

Richmond drew in a deep sigh and closed his eyes. At such times as these, the *Not my will* prayer of relinquishment upon which he attempted to order his life's path did not come to his lips in the specific words of his Lord and Master. Rather it was a silent prayer expressed by the inarticulate heavings of his spirit as it lifted and sank on the eternal tides of life.

Though he had not voiced it to Carolyn, nor would he, he knew that he must prayerfully keep in the forefront of his mind that his older son was still right in the middle of the war. Bad things happened. News could come to them any day that Seth had been wounded or killed. War brought tragedy in its wake, and no family touched by this terrible conflict was immune. He must remain strong. He must be capable of affirming God's love and goodness in grief no less than in joy. Nearly every one of the hundreds of blacks whom God had purposed to send their way during the last half dozen years had faced tragedy up close. He had faced it when they thought Thomas was dead. If more tragedy befell their family, he must demonstrate that the words of solace and comfort he gave others were more than mere words, but were life and truth and strength that could stand even in the face of death.

He drew in a deep sigh. *God help me*, he breathed. *Give me courage to be your man even in the darkest hour of human suffering—the loss of a child.*

Richmond sat several more minutes in silent inner contemplation.

His thoughts turned toward Cherity. What was his duty toward her?

Slowly Richmond rose, walked across the room to the safe, turned the dial to the right and left, opened it, pulled out the brown packet James had given to Seth, then returned to his desk and sat down again. He stared at the envelope, which obviously contained a few papers and some lumpy object that felt as though it might be wrapped in cloth.

He began to open it when an inner impulse stopped him. His hand paused as the words sounded inaudibly in his mind, "Do not fear, only believe."

Confused, the prayer arose, "What are you saying, Lord . . . what fear?"

Almost immediately came the reply: "Respect the charge given your son. Its revelation is his to make. *Do not fear, only believe.*"

Richmond's eyes fell again on the bit of torn paper on his desk beside the packet with what appeared the partial markings of a map. Perhaps it was time for the disclosure of the one, not the other.

He rose, returned James Waters' packet to his safe, then, careful to protect it, he placed the torn fragment in an envelope and left his study.

If Richmond had been keeping his own deepest prayers from his wife, he needn't have been concerned to shield her. Carolyn's own thoughts were bent in the same direction. Though they had no reason to share

Cherity's fears with regard to the train accident, Cherity's departure and Seth's silence had begun to weigh heavily upon both elder Davidsons.

Even as Richmond sat pondering and praying in his study, the quiet urging of God's Spirit had drawn Carolyn to the garden, where, like him, she was thinking of Seth, wondering when she would again feel her mother's arms around the manly shoulders of this son she loved so much. War is hard on everyone, but hardest of all on mothers.

While her husband's prayer as he thought with heavy heart of his son was the Lord's *Not my will,* the prayerful expression of the ache in her own soul took the form of the Lord's mother's, *Be it unto me according to your word.* In truth, they were the same prayer—the prayer of self-abjuring submission into the great loving Father-will of the universe. It is a prayer prayed daily, with words and without them, in a million different ways by those whose motives have been self-circumcised to God's purpose rather than their own. It is a prayer that acts as a shuttle between the threads of choice and circumstance to interweave their invisible tapestry of character in the deep invisible regions of the heart.

Even as Mary prayed the magnificent prayer for which she would be known through all time, the life of *Not my will* sonship and saviorhood was already birthed within her. Prompted by the same life-originating Holy Spirit, Mary declared by different words the very prayer her son would one day pray in the garden of his own severest trial. Surely in her own submissive obedience, Mary's lifetime countenance of *Be it unto me* was a visible example to the boy Jesus as he grew in wisdom and in stature and in favor with God and man, strengthening him unto the hour when the ultimate *Not my will* would be required of him.

And as Carolyn walked alone on this day in the paths of the garden and arbor of Greenwood, Mary's example was near and precious to her. Sometimes in life, mothers are called upon to lose sons. They have the opportunity to do so with tearful dignity, following the lonely path of heartache trod by the mother of God's son. For Mary too lost a son. She was *privileged* to lose her son, who was unlike other sons. And though Carolyn felt no joy on this day as she prayed *Be it unto me according to your word,* she yet felt the warmth of the Father's arms enclosing her in his love in this, the hour of her own lonely garden sojourn.

Sixty

The lady at the boardinghouse in Bend knew more about the accident than anyone Cherity had yet spoken with, and knew every place where they had taken those who had been hurt. She said there had been three railway cars that overturned, mostly full of civilian passengers which probably didn't amount to more than fifty or sixty people and that half of them were back on their feet and gone within several days or a week. But then two battles nearby had produced several hundred casualties, and hearing about the makeshift quarters in the region that had been set up for the accident, wagons full of wounded soldiers had begun arriving in Bend and Jefferson's Crossing, and kept coming and coming until beds and cots were full and men and women with any experience or supplies, or simply extra space, found themselves trying to care for them. A few army doctors and nurses and surgeons, from both sides, had come to do what they could, but the situation remained difficult and all the wards were desperately short-handed.

Cherity left after breakfast with instructions how to find three farmhouses and the school in Bend where wounded were being cared for. She packed her carpetbag and set off for the first. She found it without difficulty. Her knock was answered by a small girl of eight or nine.

"Mama's in with the sick men," she said, then turned and went back inside, leaving the door open.

Assuming she was meant to follow, Cherity did so. The girl led her
to a huge room that must have once been a dining room for a large
staff of plantation workers, but where now a dozen or fifteen men
were laid out on cots, some on blankets on the floor. The smell as she
walked in nearly caused Cherity to swoon—the stench of bodies and
sickness and disinfectant and coffee and eggs all mixed sickeningly
together. She stood and stared aghast.

A woman was working her way among the men with a tray in
her hand, apparently taking them breakfast. She glanced up and saw
Cherity standing in the doorway.

"I see you're finally here," she said. "They told us you'd be here last
night. Well, no matter . . . you can get started helping with the breakfast. Missy," she called to the girl, "show her to the kitchen. There's a
tray all set out on the table. You can bring it in and then start by feeding that man on the end there," she said with a toss of her head. "He
lost one of his arms and the other's in a sling."

Cherity stood speechless. Before she had a chance even to think
what to say, the little girl had taken her by the hand and led her to the
kitchen. A minute later she had donned an apron and was on her way
back into the makeshift ward with a second tray of lukewarm scrambled eggs and biscuits.

The woman glanced up again without expression. "Missy," she
called, "take this tray back to the kitchen."

The girl reappeared. Her mother handed her the empty tray,
took the tray from Cherity, then nodded toward the man she had
mentioned before who lay to all appearances dead.

"Here's a plate," she said, dishing out a few eggs and tossing a
biscuit beside them. "You'll have to help him sit up, then get what
food into him you can. Not that it matters, he's likely to die anyway,
but . . . just see what you can do."

Bewildered and numbed by it all, Cherity took the plate from her
hand and walked to the end of the row of wounded men, wincing as
she approached the broken and bandaged man at the end. Slowly she
stooped down beside him.

"Would you . . . would you like something to eat?" she said in a trembling voice.

The man's eyes opened like two thin slits. He saw Cherity's face and attempted to smile though his lips were cracked and parched.

"Thank you, miss," he whispered in the weakest voice Cherity thought she had ever heard. "Do you think you might get me some of that coffee? That's about the best thing I've ever smelled in my life."

"I think I could," said Cherity.

She set the plate beside him, then stood and looked around. Thinking better of asking the grumpy woman whom she assumed was the woman of the house, she left the sickroom again and returned to the kitchen where she found a tin cup and a pot of coffee. She poured out a cup and returned.

This time as she approached and stooped down beside him, the man's eyes opened a little wider.

Cherity reached behind his neck and shoulders and gently pulled him to a sitting position, glad for the bandages and blankets that covered his wounds, especially over the right side of his body. She could see well enough that his arm was missing. She did not think she could bear the sight of the bloody bandaged stump of its end which looked like it had been either amputated or shot off between his shoulder and elbow.

She reached the cup to his lips and gently tilted it toward him. The coffee was not very hot, and after a few sips, as she continued to lift the cup, the man drank the entire contents down. Finally he closed his eyes with a sigh of satisfaction.

"Thank you, miss," he said. "That was as good as anything I've tasted since I left home."

Cherity set the cup aside. "Would you like some eggs and a biscuit?" she asked.

"If you don't mind feeding me," he replied. "You can see I can't do much for myself."

Again Cherity helped him to sit partway up and leaned a pillow behind him. Slowly and carefully she fed him from the plate in her hand.

"I could sure use another cup of that coffee, miss," he said after several mouthfuls.

"I'll go refill your cup," smiled Cherity.

She rose and returned to the kitchen. The woman glanced at her as she passed with the cup in her hands.

"Get on with it," she said. "We got too many here for you to spend all your time with one man. The others have got to be fed too, then we've got to change the bandages and get them all up and to the outhouse. So don't take all day with that one there."

The rest of the morning passed like a blur. It was after noon before she had a chance to tell the woman that, whoever she had been expecting, it wasn't her. Rather than expressing gratitude for her help, the lady was clearly annoyed as Cherity made preparations to move on to the next ward to continue her search in the town school.

Cherity put on her coat and got her carpetbag, then thought again of the first man she had fed. She set down her bag and went back into the ward and again to the far end where he lay. He was awake and smiled faintly as she approached.

"I'm leaving now," she said. "I just wanted to say good-bye. I will be praying that you will get better soon."

"Thank you, miss. That's right kind of you."

He paused and a peculiar look came over his face.

"You mind if I ask you something?" he said.

"Of course not," replied Cherity.

"I got no arms left, least that's what they tell me. Or . . . I think I've got one that doesn't work and the doctor had to cut the other one off. But the funny thing is I can still feel them like they was both there. But when I want to move them, I just lay here and nothing happens. I know it's taking a terrible liberty—I probably look a sight to a pretty young lady like you, and I know I smell pretty bad too. But the inside part of me's just the same as it always was and that's the real me, isn't it, not this broken body that's laying here."

"Yes, it certainly is," nodded Cherity.

"Like I said, I know it's asking more than I got a right to, but would you give me a hug, miss? I want to feel a woman's arms around me one more time in case I don't pull through this."

"Do you have a wife?" asked Cherity.

"Yes, ma'am. Her name's Anne. She's nearly as pretty as you."

"Do you and Anne have children?"

"No, ma'am. We only been married three years. Most of that I've been gone on account of this war."

"Well then, I shall give you a hug for your Anne," said Cherity.

She leaned down, stretched her arms around the poor man's shoulders and pulled him to her and embraced him tight for several long seconds. Then she relaxed and eased him back down onto his pillow. As she leaned away Cherity saw tears in his eyes.

"Thank you, miss," he said. "That was real nice. I almost felt like an angel was taking hold of me and was just going to carry me right away and up to heaven."

Struggling to keep back her own tears, Cherity left the house a few minutes later. She stood outside the door and took a deep, but shaky breath, then let it out slowly and walked in the direction where she had been told she would find the school.

Cherity's afternoon passed considerably less traumatically than had her morning. Within three hours she was ready to move on to the next town and walked back to the station. An hour later, after a ride of only about twenty minutes, she was the only passenger to step down onto the platform at Jefferson's Crossing just as the sun was sinking behind the hills to the west. She looked about, her thoughts momentarily interrupted by the shriek of the whistle behind her as the great iron locomotive puffed its way out of the station.

Grasping her slim carpetbag, she walked wearily across the wooden platform to the ticket office. The long day was catching up with her and she was tired. She hardly noticed the grime and few splotches of dried blood on her dress. The last train gone, a lanky youth who hardly appeared much past his teens was just closing the window for the evening.

"Excuse me," said Cherity, "I'm looking for someone I think was injured in the train accident. Can you tell me where they've put them up in town?"

The young man shifted a wad of tobacco from one cheek to the other.

"Well, there's a few here and a few there," he said in a thick drawl. "Dick Garr's been tending most of 'em, though he ain't no doctor but he seems to know more about it than anybody else in town. Powerful lot of 'em dying, though, especially those they brung in from the battle just north of here."

"Where are they staying?" asked Cherity.

"Like I said, here and there. Rev. Wilcott's church has a lot of folks in it. Then there's the Walton farm further on."

"Where is the church?" asked Cherity.

"Yonder down the street," he said, pointing behind him, "back of the dry goods store."

"And one more question, if you don't mind . . . can you tell me if there's a good boardinghouse in town?"

"Don't know if it's any good, ma'am," he replied. "I ain't never had occasion to stay there. But Mrs. Butterfield advertises the finest of rooms for affordable prices. Course it's also the only place in town. It's just down the street yonder too, and then first street to your left."

Cherity left the station and followed his directions.

Several hours later, she found herself turning over on a lumpy mattress for the dozenth time. The night was cold and she was wearing every piece of clothing out of her carpetbag under the one thin blanket, as well as the blanket she'd brought with her. This finest of rooms had a colony of mice living behind the wainscoting. A few hours after dark they had started up what sounded like a boisterous game of hide-and-seek. And now that what little moon there was had drifted behind thick clouds and turned her room almost totally black, their tiny clawed feet had taken to scampering across her floor. Somewhere outside a dog howled. Never had she felt so lonely in her life. The dog's mournful wail reminded her of the wounded men she had seen throughout the day. She thought of the men out there lying on the ground trying to sleep in the cold—sometimes in the rain. What if Seth was lying in some such miserable sick ward? She could hardly bear the thought!

Gradually she drifted back into an uneasy and fitful sleep, dreaming of mice desperately trying to scratch at the walls but without hands with no claws, and somewhere Seth calling her name but she could not hear him because he had lost his tongue in battle.

When Cherity awoke, the gray morning seemed almost as lonely as the night. It was too early to get up and Cherity lay for another hour until at last she heard stirring below. If it was possible, she felt more exhausted than when she had gone to bed.

She tossed back the blankets and dragged herself to her feet, splashed her face with cold water from the basin on the chest of drawers, then dressed and went downstairs.

After breakfast, as she had done in Bend, and getting a few more directions from Mrs. Butterfield, she set out to explore Jefferson's Crossing and see what she could learn. She walked out from the boardinghouse and turned onto the boardwalk of the main street. Carts and wagons rumbled down the road in both directions, raising clouds of dust behind them. Spotting the dry-goods store, she darted across the street between two slow-moving wagons. A terrible stench suddenly filled her nostrils. She glanced toward one of the wagons whose open bed was clearly visible from where she stood.

He stomach lurched and her knees weakened. It was filled with eight or ten corpses . . . men without arms . . . without legs . . . amputated limbs thrown in on top of the bodies.

Faint-headed and dizzy, Cherity stumbled across the street and slumped against a hitching rail. She gagged once, twice, then lurched and lost her entire breakfast on the dirt street at her feet.

While she still stood hunched over and breathing heavily trying to recover, a shadow darkened the street beside her.

"Takes a little getting used to, doesn't it?" said a man's voice.

Cherity stood and turned toward it, covering her mouth with her handkerchief. A man with a compassionate expression was gazing down at her.

"Mrs. Butterfield told me you were here," he said. "I'm Dick Garr . . . the man who wrote for you."

"I'm sorry . . . I don't . . . What do you mean?" said Cherity, still struggling to get control of her stomach and her head.

"You are one of Miss Barton's nurses?"

"I'm sorry . . . no," said Cherity, shaking her head and trying to smile.

The man called Dick Garr sighed and glanced toward the wagon disappearing along the street.

"Those poor fellows didn't make it through the night," he sighed. "I expect we'll have more tomorrow. We hardly have time to give them a proper burial anymore, the ones we can't identify. The men take them out to the cemetery, say a brief prayer, and bury them without even a name on their marker. Are you alone in town, miss?" he asked.

"Yes," replied Cherity, at last standing up and forcing a smile. "I arrived on yesterday afternoon's train. I'm trying to find a young man named Seth Davidson."

"Can't say I've heard of him. Sure hope he's not like one of those that just went by. He a Confederate or a Yank?"

"He's not a soldier," replied Cherity. "He takes pictures of the war for a newspaper. The last we knew he was on his way to Atlanta. I thought he might have been injured on the railway accident near here?"

"I wish I could help you, but we've had hundreds through here. Why don't you come with me. You can take a look yourself. You never know, maybe you'll find him."

Cherity followed the man's long stride as he led along a street at right angles to the main street, then stopped in front of a simple wooden church building and entered. Men's groans filled Cherity's ears. The sights that met her eyes brought her stomach again into her throat . . . men lying row upon row on dirty pallets . . . some without arms and legs, nearly all with bloody bandages over their faces, chests, and stomachs.

She gagged again at the sight and hesitated. She drew in a breath and slowly followed Garr into the large room.

"Nurse . . . nurse," said one of the men, his face beaded in sweat, clutching at her as she passed. "Can you get me some water?"

Cherity turned toward him and glanced down. The dressing on his chest was drenched with yellow pus and the red of oozing blood. The nausea of a few minutes before returned like a swelling tide. She stumbled away and leaned for a moment against the wall. Already the man she had come with had moved on down the row. She tried to catch her breath, but the stench of infection and the reek of chloroform filled the air. She clamped her hand over nose and mouth and gradually began to breathe more easily.

She looked around the large room. A pail and dipper stood in one corner near the pulpit. She walked over to it, scooped out a dipper of water and brought it to the young man who had spoken to her. She knelt beside him and held it to his mouth. He sipped, choked a little, then sipped again and finally lay back and closed his eyes.

"Thank you, nurse," he mumbled.

"I . . . I hope you get better soon," said Cherity.

"I will," he said, opening his eyes again. "Nothing much wrong with me except my foot. Well, and this chest wound, but they say it ain't too bad. But my foot hurts something terrible—got three toes blowed off."

Cherity winced and stood and took the dipper back to the pail. She walked slowly along from bed to bed, both relieved and disappointed to see Seth nowhere among the wounded. She began to realize that she didn't know whether she wanted to find him or not. To find him lying unconscious or wounded or mutilated would break her heart.

Dick Garr had already disappeared into a little room off to one side of the pulpit. He now reappeared with a woman wearing a bloodstained apron whom he introduced as Nurse Beech. She was mostly interested in whether the newcomer, queasy stomach and all, had come to help. Before Cherity knew it, once again the morning passed like that of the previous day.

About noon, when it seemed they could get along without her, Cherity left the church for the Walton farmhouse on the outskirts of town, only to discover that they were even more shorthanded than at the church. At least there she found several people who had been on the train and were able to tell her in horrifying detail about the accident. None of them remembered anyone like Seth.

When Cherity realized that the sun was beginning to set, she told the farmer's wife, who was considerably friendlier and more appreciative than the woman at her first stop on the previous day, that she had to get back and tell Mrs. Butterfield to expect her for a second night.

"You handle yourself with the men like a trained nurse," said Mrs. Walton. "I know you're just looking for your young man, but if you'll help me out for another day, it would be an enormous boost for me. I've got plenty of room upstairs where you can sleep, and a hot supper to go along with a bed. A softer bed than you'll find at Mrs. Butterfield's!"

"What about mice?" asked Cherity with a smile.

"I'll put a cat in your room, no extra charge," rejoined Mrs. Walton with a kindly smile of humor. "What do you say?"

Cherity smiled and nodded. "All right, then," she said. "But I really must move on tomorrow."

"Have you been to the accident site?" asked Mrs. Walton.

"No, where is it?"

"Couple miles up the line toward Jonesborough. Not that you'd find anything there either . . . just thought you might be interested. Lot of folks been going out there to see what they could find, even some of the injured when they were up and could travel again, picking up whatever was left. With the war being so close like it is, and most of the men gone, nobody's had time to clean it up. The railroad just patched the rails to get the trains back on schedule. But the overturned coaches are still laying there, broken and turned on their sides where they fell down the bank, with stuff strewn about everywhere. Least that's what they tell me. I haven't been out myself. First I knew of the accident was a rider galloping into town yelling everywhere he went asking folks to come out to the site to help and others to make places for the wounded. Then wagons full of them started creaking and rumbling in an hour later. Lots of folks were out helping load them up and doing what they could there. It was hard to find space to put them all. It was bad. You'll never get me on a train after what I've seen. And then as we were getting some of them back on their feet and the dead either buried or the families contacted—Rev. Wilcott mostly saw to that—then came the battle at Jonesborough and we were flooded with wounded soldiers and it hasn't stopped yet."

"Well," said Cherity, "maybe I will go out to the accident site like you say. You wouldn't have a horse I could borrow to ride up there tomorrow?"

"I just might. Can you ride—some of the terrain's a little rough between here and there?"

Cherity smiled. "I'll be able to manage it," she said.

The sound of a cannon exploding in the distance interrupted them. The woman shook her head. "Sounds like the fighting's getting closer again," she said. "Will it ever end? I hate this war."

"Do you have anyone close in the army?" Cherity asked.

"Not anymore," answered Mrs. Walton, her characteristic smile fading. "I did," she added, "but I lost my son at Shiloh."

Sixty-One

*W*hile the newspaper article about Veronica's involvement with the Union and Confederate spy ring occupied most of the attention of those at Greenwood, Chigua LeFleure found an altogether unexpected reaction springing up within her. It was, however, as a result of a different article on page three of the same issue of the *Boston Herald* that went largely unnoticed by most of the others.

Where she stood listening behind him, she had seen its headline as Richmond had opened the paper to finish his reading of the lead story. The words FORMER CHEROKEE CHIEF PROMOTED TO GENERAL IN CONFEDERATE ARMY jumped off the page at her. When Richmond and the others were through with it, Chigua picked up the newspaper from the table and opened it again and read the article from beginning to end.

> *Principal chief of the Confederate Cherokees, Stand Watie, was promoted on May 6, 1864 by General Samuel Bell Maxey, to the rank of brigadier general in the Confederate army. At the same time Watie was given command of the two regiments of mounted rifles and three battalions of Cherokee, Osage, and Seminole infantry.*
>
> *He is the first officer of Indian descent in either North or South to attain such a high rank.*

At the outbreak of hostilities, siding with the Confederacy,
Watie raised his own private regiment of Cherokees to fight against
the Union. He was later offered a commission as a colonel in the
Confederate army.

Watie, great-grandson of legendary chief Attacullaculla, is of
ancient Cherokee lineage. With his brother Buck Watie and cousin
John Ridge, son of controversial Cherokee leader Major Ridge,
Watie represented a movement of young Cherokee intellectu-
als in the 1820s who helped lead the Cherokee nation toward a
new emphasis on education and literacy. The discovery of gold on
Cherokee lands in Georgia and the Carolinas, however, turned
the attention of a greedy nation toward the Cherokee holdings
of millions of acres and resulted in their removal from the area,
culminating twenty-five years ago in what became known as the
Trail of Tears. Rumors persist to this day of hidden caches of gold
through the East.

A schism developed within the Cherokee Nation which persists
to this day between those calling themselves the Ridge group and the
Ross group. The dispute became violent among the Cherokee immediately after the completion of the Trail of Tears. Three months after
the arrival of the weary wagons from the East, a council of Cherokee
leaders attempted a formal union of the two groups. Though reviled
by many of the recent arrivals, Major and John Ridge, and both
Watie brothers attended, hoping to heal the wounds of recent years.
But their presence so angered some that a secret council was convened
to seek retribution against them. The Cherokee blood law from
ancient times indicated death as the penalty for selling tribal lands.
The secret gathering unanimously condemned Major Ridge, John
Ridge, Elias Boudinot, and Stand Watie to death.

The executions began the next morning when John Ridge, Major
Ridge, and Elias Boudiinot were all brutally murdered. The only
one of the four to escape was Boudinot's brother Stand Watie, who
had been traveling and escaped the vendetta.

More assassinations followed, though Watie himself managed to

escape the fate of his brother and cousin. With his comrades gone,
Stand Watie gradually became the leader and primary spokesman for
the treaty party—a divisive split which created a rivalry for leader-
ship between himself and Cherokee chief John Ross that lasted for the
next twenty years.

With the outbreak of war in 1861, Watie sided with the South
and raised a following called the Cherokee Regiment of Mounted
Rifles. Cherokee chief John Ross temporarily also agreed and sided
with the South. But he was at heart a Union supporter. When Ross
later left Indian Territory for Philadelphia in 1862, Watie became
Principal Chief of the Confederate Cherokee Nation.

Throughout the war Watie continued to distinguish himself.
After his promotion to general last spring, the two regiments and
three battalions under his command have been based south of the
Canadian River.

Sydney found Chigua sitting on the back porch of the house several
days later, staring thoughtfully into the distance.

"You've been quiet all day," he said sitting down on the wide porch
seat beside her. "What are you thinking about?"

Chigua smiled . . . a far-off, melancholy smile.

"My people," she replied softly.

Sydney looked deep into her eyes. It was not that he was ever
capable of forgetting his wife's Indian ancestry, or his own French and
Jamaican roots. Yet in the melting pot of ethnic mixes that Greenwood
had become, it was easy to overlook skin color and racial backgrounds
to such an extent that they almost ceased to exist. But now he beheld
in Chigua's features and expression and skin and in the distant gaze of
her eyes, a heritage that was uniquely native to this American main-
land to which he had been brought as a youth.

"Perhaps I am feeling my Cherokee blood more than usual,"
Chigua went on after a moment. "There are times when I feel, I don't
know how to explain it . . . isolated, cut off from my heritage—like

a stranger in the white man's world . . . perhaps that a part of me belongs elsewhere."

She smiled. "Does that sound silly?"

"Of course not," said Sydney. "But this is not really the white man's world at all. It is the land of *your* people."

"Perhaps," rejoined Chigua. "Yet we are now surrounded by the white culture. My people no longer possess their ancient lands. In the same way that the Cherokee were taken from their lands, I was taken from my people at such a young age that my memories grow dim. I cannot remember what it was like to be a Cherokee, living with Cherokee, on lands that had belonged to the Cherokee for generation upon generation."

As he listened, Sydney heard a longing in Chigua's voice that he had never heard before.

"I find," she went on thoughtfully, "that it makes me sad. I do not want to lose touch with my roots and my heritage. As an Indian, I am alone. My Cherokee past becomes more and more faint. But I do not want to forget. And yet," she added, again smiling as she looked deep into Sydney's face, "it is no different with you and your ancestry."

Sydney nodded. "That may be true," he said. "Yet you were taken away from your family at a younger age than I. You lost an entire culture that was ripped from you in a single moment."

"It is not that I am ungrateful for Richmond and Carolyn and this wonderful place. Yet I am aware that it is not *my* world. And," Chigua added, "I almost tremble to think what might have become of me without you. I hope you do not think that I wish my life were other than it is. I love you and our family. Yet . . . part of me longs to know what it means to be a Cherokee."

Sydney nodded. "I understand," he said. "I sometimes feel similar yearnings. I think all people who have been torn from their families or homelands do. Being uprooted from the only life I knew, having to adjust to the life of a slave, and now being treated by Richmond as an equal though my skin is tan—sometimes I lie awake at night beside you wondering who I *really* am. Deep down I am the same person I always was. Even when I was a slave all those years, pretending to be something I wasn't, I was still me—Sydney LeFleure. Yet I wonder if the man other people see is the same *me* that I am inside. Perhaps we of darker skin will always wonder such things."

"But why only those of darker skin? White people have come from other places too."

"I had not thought of that," said Sydney. "Your people are the only true natives. But most whites have come here freely by choice—to find the freedom of a new life. No one can fault them for that, but it is much different than the historical legacy of the Negro who was brought here against his will, and not for freedom but as a race of slaves."

"And my people have always been here. We have not been enslaved, just displaced and our lands taken from us."

"Your people are the only true rightful possessors of this land. Yet it is an enormous land, rich in possibilities for many rather than the sole possession of a single race. Times change. People and races move and mix and adapt and flow together and have throughout time. All lands over all the years of our history have been shared. So will this one be. But they must be shared in mutual respect. It is not for we blacks and your Indian people to be angry for past evils but to find good and sincere people like Richmond and Carolyn and share life with them."

It was silent for several minutes as they pondered the things Sydney had said.

"There was an article in the same newspaper Richmond was reading from the other morning," said Chigua. "Another article—about the Cherokee chief Stand Watie. It is what prompted my thoughts toward wanting again to know more of my heritage. I want to connect again with that past. I think I remember my grandfather speaking of the man in the article. Cherokee blood flows in my veins. All at once I long to know what that means. Suddenly I find so many unanswered questions stirred up in my heart."

Chigua paused, glancing away as she struggled to find the words to express what she felt.

"I realize how illogical it sounds," she went on, "but I almost feel guilty that I was taken from the Trail of Removal when so many died along the way. Reading that article stirred up many things. It probably sounds funny, but I want to *complete* the Trail . . . or perhaps I *need* to complete it. I know it would be symbolic. But I feel it is something I need to do for myself, as a pilgrimage to discover who I am."

"But *where* would you go?"

"Where the rest of the Cherokee are now, to the Indian Territory of Oklahoma."

"You mean . . . you want to go all the way . . . back *there?*"

Chigua nodded. "It is where my people are," she said. "I must have relatives there. I never knew what happened to my sister. I had many cousins on the trail too, aunts and uncles. Now that we no longer have to fear slavery, I want to find them—perhaps when the war is over. I must know if any of my own people are left. And the ring—"

She paused and drew in a deep breath, thinking as she spoke.

"I think," she continued slowly, "I think I realize that I must no longer keep such a precious treasure to myself."

"What are you saying?" asked Sydney.

"Whatever the ring's history and significance, it seems that it should be in the hands of a chief, perhaps this Stand Watie. I must know about the ring, and then decide what is to be done with it."

"Maybe it will be knowing the history of the ring," said Sydney, "that will also help you discover what being a Cherokee means."

Sixty-Two

After helping Mrs. Walton feed and wash the men in her care, Cherity saddled a horse from her stable, where there were only two to choose from, and rode out of town west alongside the track of the rail line. She had found herself wondering whether she would know the site when she came to it. But it would have been impossible to miss. As she came around a bend in the line, suddenly there spread out before her a scene she could only describe as one of devastation. Beside the track was a deep crater where the explosion had obviously occurred. Gnarled and twisted rails lay off to the side of the new track that had been laid. Down the embankment to the right lay the three shattered and twisted passenger cars that had been derailed and sent toppling off the track. Two lay on their sides, badly broken, the third was actually split in two pieces and was blackened from fire. How anyone could have survived was a miracle. All around the ground for a hundred or more yards were strewn bits of the wreckage—paper and torn bits of clothing, hats, carpetbags some still with belongings and clothes spilling out of them, a few books and newspapers and shoes and tools and bits of wood and metal . . . everything wet from being out in the weather and blown about in the wind.

Cherity pulled up on the horse and sat gazing out over the scene. Again, as seemed to be happening frequently these days, her eyes filled. A terrible knot formed in her stomach.

"Oh, Seth . . . Seth!" she whispered and began to cry.

Slowly she dismounted and began to walk down the slope, stepping between bits of the wreckage of human life. Everything here had once belonged to someone. Now it was just out here being swallowed up by the earth and the elements. She was almost afraid to look about, afraid that she might see an overlooked dead body or a hand or foot or finger. After the horrifying sights she had seen in the last two days, nothing would surprise her.

Everything filled her with an overwhelming sense of empty sadness. She was never going to find Seth. It was a hopeless search. It had been hopeless from the beginning. She had done what she came here to do. But it was no use. Seth was not in Bend or Jefferson's Crossing.

He was nowhere.

Slowly she continued to walk around, stepping over a torn piece of a man's shirt, then around an open carpetbag with a mud-splattered woman's dress spilling out of it . . . a baby doll . . . some letters and papers, a bit of lace, a boy's cap. Thankfully she saw nothing that looked like what Seth had been wearing when she had seen him last.

She stooped down and gently picked up a sheet of paper whose ink was splattered and faint.

Dear Harriet, she read in the splotched page, *I am sitting in the train on my way to Memphis to visit George. He is in the hospital there after being wounded in the fighting. I have not seen him since he left three years . . .*

She could make out no more of the blurred hand.

The poignant words broke her heart. Was George still lying in a bed somewhere waiting for his mother or father or grandmother or aunt or whoever was the author of this letter, wondering what had happened to them?

She let it fall back to the ground and continued her way about, stepping gingerly over the remnants of so many lives whose suddenly shattered stories would never be known. It was so quiet. All was silence, as if even the birds and squirrels and rabbits did not want to disturb this place where life had been suddenly interrupted . . .

and where some lives had been snuffed out before their appointed time.

On she went down to the bottom of the embankment. Timidly she looked inside one of the overturned wooden coaches through a huge hole gashed in its roof. She almost feared to see what might be inside, but it was just more of the same, broken and overturned benches and seats, some luggage, papers, clothes, hats . . .

As she turned away, a shrill train whistle shrieked behind her. Nearly jumping out of her boots, she spun around as the thunder of a great locomotive clattered around the bend on the repaired rails above, followed by a coal car and three coaches. Her heart in her throat from the sudden sound, she watched as it rounded the curve and slowly disappeared. Gradually again quiet descended upon the woods.

More dejected than ever, Cherity began to climb back up the hill to the tree where she had tied Mrs. Walton's horse.

She trudged up the hill toward the track. The sun angling down glinted off the shiny new lengths of iron rail. She squinted briefly and looked away. As she did her gaze was arrested by a shiny object on the ground about ten feet from her reflecting the ray of sunlight piercing through the treetops. She followed the sight and drew in a sharp breath, then ran forward and stooped down.

Half buried in the dirt, a third of it protruding out, lay a metal-encased photographic plate. She recognized it immediately as similar to what Seth had used when taking their photographs at Greenwood before leaving for the war.

With heart pounding, she fell to her knees, pulled it out of the ground, and scraped off the dirt caked over it. It was now worthless. Yet it suddenly became the most precious thing in all the world.

Frantically Cherity glanced around her. What else might be here . . . other pieces of his equipment . . . maybe part of a camera?

She crawled around in a circle, desperate to find anything else that might offer a link, however slight, to Seth and what had happened to him. Heedless of the mud and dirt on her boots and dress, she made her way about on hands and knees, clawing as if the dirt itself was filled with gold and diamonds and precious gems.

Her hand felt something . . . it was long and thin and hard. She dug at the earth like a dog searching for a bone, then grasped and pulled . . . a pen . . . the end of a pen! She couldn't be sure . . . but it *might* be Seth's!

Energized to a frenzy of excitement, she scraped and clawed and looked about feverishly to her right and left . . . and there was what looked like a ripped portion of a leather writing folder!

She grabbed it and yanked it from the ground and wiped at it with her grimy palm. It was but a piece of stiff leather, perhaps six inches by three or four, but . . . was that a faint monogram? . . . She squinted and rubbed frantically, trying to clean it off enough to read . . . she could barely make out a few letters . . . *The Bos— Hera—*

Seth *had* been here!

Sweating almost in a fever of hopeful panic, she crawled about until suddenly . . . was that a corner of a wad of folded paper? . . . just beneath where she had found the torn bit of leather satchel!

Her hand closed on it and she tugged gently with one hand as she dug out around it with the other, taking care not to rip the damp and fragile paper. A few seconds later she gently pulled out two crumpled sheets of writing stationery, bits of dirt caked to them, that had somehow clung together and been partially protected by the piece of leather. With heart beating louder than the locomotive that had just passed, slowly she unfolded the crumpled, damp, dirt-stained pages.

Dear Cherity, she read in the familiar hand, the words blurred and running together.

It was enough. She broke into tears, able to read no more until she could gain control of her wild emotions.

It took a minute or minute and a half. Gradually she settled herself enough, then wiped her eyes as dry as she could get them, and tried to continue.

> *Dear Cherity,*
> *It has been three days since I saw your face at the door of your room. I have thought of nothing else since, and your look of anger*

has haunted me day and night. I am so dreadfully sorry for hurting
you as I obviously have. I know that perhaps I have not earned your
trust, but I hope you will trust me enough to listen to an explanation
that I pray will set your mind at ease. Believe me when I tell you
that I love you with all my heart, and I—

By now Cherity was fighting a losing battle against the flood of
tears.

—I would never intentionally do anything . . .

The writing stopped. With a choking sob, Cherity turned the sheet
over, then scanned the second sheet of paper in vain. But there was no
more. Seth's words ended in midsentence. The explosion must have
thrown satchel, letter, pen, and Seth, from the train the next instant.
Whatever else he had intended to write, she would have to keep as a
hoped-for treasure in her heart.

Cherity sat back and slumped to the ground, the pen and wet fragment of letter clutched in her hand, and wept.

How long she sat it was hard to say. When she next became aware
of herself she was on the other side of the overturned cars still clawing
and digging searching for even the tiniest something that might have
been Seth's. Her knees and fingers were raw and her whole body shiv-
ering from the cold. She had been back and forth over every inch of
ground, but other than a muddy boot that *might* have been Seth's, or
just as well might have belonged to a complete stranger, the rest of her
day's search yielded nothing.

Slowly she realized that she could do no more. Mentally and physically exhausted at last, she stood. Lugging the boot, the pen, the scrap
of letter, the bit of leather, and the photographic plate back up the hill,
and managing to mount the horse and keep them in her lap, she set
out again for Jefferson's Crossing.

Forty minutes later, Cherity rode slowly back into the yard of Mrs.
Walton's farm, slumping in the saddle, a more dejected and defeated
sight than could be imagined.

She walked into the house in a stupor. Mrs. Walton saw her, dirt all over her dress and arms and face, at first thinking she must have fallen from the horse. She approached with a look of compassion. Cherity said nothing. She just fell into the older woman's arms and sobbed.

"I . . . I found some of his things," she choked after a minute. "But . . . oh, Mrs. Walton . . . I'm so afraid!"

Mrs. Walton held her a few minutes until Cherity's outburst had subsided.

"I'll tell you what I am going to do," she said. "I think I will boil some water and draw you a nice warm bath."

Cherity tried to smile.

"But . . . but don't you need help with the men?" she asked. "I can get changed myself and—"

"Nonsense. The men can keep and I've got the stew for their supper on the stove. You have your bath and we will clean you up and get you into a clean dry dress and then decide what to do."

Cherity nodded gratefully.

Suddenly all she could think was that she wanted to be home.

Sixty-Three

*C*arolyn had again been praying in the arbor. She glanced up and saw Richmond coming toward her along the walkway.

"Where are you off to?" asked Carolyn.

"I have an errand to attend to that has waited many years," Richmond replied. "I have decided that I must ignore its inevitability no longer."

Richmond rode into the precincts of Oakbriar with a heavy yet determined heart. This would be one of the most difficult things he had ever done. But the truth must prevail. Light had to shine. Whether that truth must be shouted from the housetops, he wasn't sure. But it must at least be brought to light.

Even had he not been following news of the war and the Union march toward the city of Richmond, which every Virginian was well enough aware of since they were again caught in the crosshairs of the conflict, he knew that Denton Beaumont was at home. There were few secrets in a small community like that surrounding Dove's Landing. Word about everyone traveled fast. On this day, however, Richmond approached Oakbriar in hopes of bringing one of its longest-lasting and darkest secrets at last into the light.

He dismounted and walked to the door.

"Hello, Jarvis," he said when Jarvis answered his knock.

"Mister Dab'son," returned the black man respectfully.

"I am here to see Mr. Beaumont."

"I will tell him you's here, Mister Dab'son."

A minute later Beaumont's heavy step descended the stairs. He approached his visitor without benefit of a smile or offered hand.

"I would like to talk to you, Denton," said Richmond. "In private if you don't mind."

Beaumont eyed him skeptically.

"What about?"

"Mr. Brown and his house, his land," replied Richmond. "And possibly the secrets he took with him when he disappeared."

Beaumont hesitated another moment. "All right, then," he said. "Come upstairs to my office."

He led the way inside and up the stairs. When the door to Beaumont's private sanctuary was closed behind them, both men took chairs.

"I don't like the way you went behind my back about Elias Slade," Beaumont began.

"I am sorry," replied Richmond. "But I asked you to deal with him earlier, and after a second attack, I could wait no longer. Is he finally gone?"

"I told him a warrant had been issued but that I did not want to be involved. I told him to get out and never show his face around here again. Yes, he is gone."

"I am glad to hear it. But I came to see you about other matters."

"Ah, the Brown land," nodded Beaumont. "So . . . have you finally decided to sell that worthless tract? If so, I cannot guarantee that I could possibly pay as much as I once offered you. You should have taken it when you had the chance, Richmond."

"That is not why I am here. The Brown land is still not for sale."

"Why are you here then?" snapped Beaumont irritably.

"I want to speak with you seriously about some things that

happened many years ago. What do you know about the disappearance of Mr. Brown?"

"Nothing! Why should I know anything about it?"

"I have reason to believe that you may have been the last one to see him around here."

"What are you talking about!"

"My father had great respect for Mr. Brown. I want to get to the bottom of what happened and why."

"But why? As you said, it was a long time ago. The man is gone, what does it matter?"

"It matters to me."

"He was just an Indian, for heaven's sake! Why would you care about such an inferior people?"

"Guard your tongue, Denton. That is an outrageous thing to say."

"Bah! You and your notions! It's perfectly true and everyone knows it."

"The Cherokee are a noble people."

"Just like, I suppose you'll be telling me next, the darkies are!"

"They too are a noble race."

"Listen to yourself, man! What have you sunk to talking like that? They're not the same as whites."

"So is it true that you regard the life of a white man more highly than that of a red or a black man?"

"Of course. All enlightened people do."

"There are many who think the compass of enlightenment swings around in exactly the opposite direction. But your point of view raises another question," added Richmond. "My brother was neither Indian nor Negro. Did you show his life equal respect with your own?"

Beaumont sat staring straight ahead, momentarily stunned into silence.

"What does Clifford have to do with Brown and . . . and anything else?" he asked after a moment, his tone slightly subdued.

"He may have everything to do with it, Denton. I think you and he may have been together when, as I say, you were the last to see Mr. Brown before his disappearance."

"What are you accusing me of?" Beaumont shot back.

"I am accusing you of nothing. I only said that I think you and Clifford may have been the last to see Mr. Brown."

Soothing his ruffled feathers, Beaumont gradually calmed.

"I believe you know this portion of map," said Richmond, pulling the envelope from his pocket and withdrawing the torn paper from it.

"Yes, it's mine. That girl who is staying with you stole it from me. I'm glad to see you had the good sense to return it."

He reached out for the paper, but Richmond withdrew it.

Beaumont's eyes flashed with fire.

"I didn't bring it here to return it to you, Denton. I am not altogether sure it rightfully belongs to you at all."

"Now you're calling me a liar!" exploded Beaumont.

"I think you heard me, Denton, and I said nothing of the sort. I only said that I am not sure this paper is rightfully yours. Where, may I ask, did you come by it?"

"That is none of your business."

"It may be both of our business, Denton."

"What is that supposed to mean?"

"Just this—that this piece of paper once belonged to my father. He told me that it had been given to him by Mr. Brown. Then suddenly it disappeared. I would like to know how it came into your possession."

"Your brother gave it to me. What of it? How he came by it I didn't ask."

"What was his purpose in giving it to you?"

"He said he thought Brown had buried something and this was the map to it."

"So naturally you and he considered stealing it your prerogative . . . since he was an Indian?"

"He and I were young, for God's sake! What of it? We smelled adventure and thought we would dig up buried treasure. All boys have such dreams. By heaven, I'll warrant you've had them too! It's hardly worth making such a fuss over."

"You and Clifford were hardly boys at the time."

"So, what of it! The man was an old fool of an Indian. We were just having a little fun. Why shouldn't we have looked for whatever it was?"

"Did you and Clifford look for the treasure . . . together?" asked Richmond pointedly.

"I told you we did!"

"You looked for it *together* . . . using this map? I thought you said Clifford gave it to you. Why did he give it to you to keep if you were searching together and if it wasn't yours?" Richmond's early legal training and logical mind were still keen.

Beaumont began to squirm slightly. He realized that Richmond was by degrees drawing the noose closer around his neck and that he must be a little more guarded with his words.

"That's . . . that's a good question," he said slowly. "Perhaps I should have asked him. Unfortunately, it did not occur to me at the time. And it is too late to go back and ask him now."

"So he gave you the piece of map, you went searching for what you thought was Brown's buried treasure together, then you kept the map and went home, and . . . what then? Did you ever see my brother again?"

"No. You know as well as I do that he was found after he fell off his horse."

"What do you suppose he was doing back out there?"

"How the devil should I know! Maybe he went back to search again. Maybe he was trying to cut me out."

"But by then he didn't have the bit of map to search from."

"How should I know what he was thinking!"

"Strange, doesn't it seem, if he planned to continue his search, that he would give you the piece of map?"

"I can't read his mind! I always maintained that Brown had something to do with it. I've said so publicly. I have no idea what happened."

Richmond sat a moment quietly thinking.

"All right then, Denton," he said. "Thank you for your time. You've been very patient with my questions. I think I have a clearer understanding of things now."

He glanced across Beaumont's desk where lay a rolled leather skin. "You, uh . . . won't mind," he added, pointing toward it, "my taking that skin painting that you borrowed from the Brown house?"

Taken by surprise at the directness of the accusation, Beaumont erupted in anger.

"Go to the devil!" he shouted.

"I hope to avoid such a contingency," replied Richmond calmly. "I would, however, like to restore Mr. Brown's painting above his mantel where he left it."

"Take it then and be off with you!"

Richmond rose, picked up the rolled skin from Beaumont's desk, then left the office and showed himself downstairs and out of the house.

Sixty-Four

The night after her visit to the site of the crash, Cherity lay awake in Mrs. Walton's bed, clean and finally warm again and reliving the events of the day. Even before she drifted off to sleep, her mind was made up.

She told Mrs. Walton of her decision the next morning as they were dishing bacon and porridge and biscuits onto tin plates to serve the wounded men lying in Mrs. Walton's parlor.

"I've decided to go home," she said. "I've looked everywhere. There's no place else. I feel so helpless. I have a dreadful feeling that Seth is dead. I don't think I can bear to be alone when I find out for sure."

Mrs. Walton opened her arms and gave Cherity a hug.

"I hope you find him, dear. You're too young to have to face the kind of tragedy I have. Thank you for your help."

"Oh, thank you, Mrs. Walton. You've helped me feel at home while I've been away."

"When will you go?"

"Today."

"I think I will miss you, Cherity," said the woman kindly. "Some of these poor men will too. I know you came to find your own young man, but in these two days you've given them a ray of sunlight and a reason to hope."

Cherity smiled. "When does the eastbound train come through for Augusta?"

"Both east and west come through about two o'clock," replied Mrs. Walton. "There's two lines that run for several miles so the trains can pass."

Cherity nodded. "Then I suppose two o'clock it is."

An expression came over Mrs. Walton's face, as if she had something more to say but wasn't sure whether to say it.

"Have you spoken with Reverend Wilcott?" she asked at length.

"Only briefly," replied Cherity.

"I haven't wanted to mention it, dear, but . . . well, he's kept a list of all the dead whose families he's tried to contact. You might . . ."

She did not finish.

Cherity understood her meaning well enough.

"I will talk to him on my way to the station," she said.

When Richard and Veronica Fitzpatrick had walked into what had been Garabaldi's Restaurant in Washington over a month earlier, Richard knew from Veronica's demeanor that something serious was on her mind. She had given all the money from her private bank account to Union authorities to be used for the care of war wounded, keeping back five dollars to take Richard to dinner and try to explain everything that had happened.

"You know my friend from back home, Seth Davidson," began Veronica when they were seated with a bottle of wine on the table between them, "and that man Mr. Hirsch whom I don't think you liked too well?"

Richard nodded.

"Well, it all began on my eighteenth birthday when my parents threw me a huge party. At the time I thought I loved Seth, but he had the good sense to realize that he didn't love me. And somehow Cecil Hirsch had managed to wrangle himself an invitation. . . ."

The story she unfolded was as incredible for the change it had wrought in Veronica as for the events themselves. She was humbled, contrite, embarrassed, and apologetic, and Richard could hardly find it in his heart to be angry with her.

"I am so sorry, Richard," said Veronica, with even a few tears spilling out of her eyes. "I cannot believe how foolish and stupid I was. Please forgive me."

Richard smiled and reached across the table and took her hand. "You did the right thing in the end," he said. "I think I need to offer you an apology too."

"*You* . . . what for?"

"I allowed myself to become far too busy. I was away too much and did not stop to consider the effect on you of suddenly being in a strange environment and being alone. So I too ask your forgiveness."

"Oh, Richard, you were just doing your job, but . . . thank you." Veronica was thoughtful a moment.

"I want to make up for what I have done somehow," she said. "I have been thinking of volunteering in the hospitals and clinics, wherever I might be useful with the wounded. What would you think?"

"I think that is a fine idea," replied Richard. "But . . . that sort of thing has not exactly been your forte . . . could you do it?"

"I don't know, but I would like to try. I've changed, Richard. Or at least I want to change. The old Veronica couldn't have worked with the wounded but I hope the new Veronica will have the courage and good sense to put the needs of others ahead of her own."

Veronica returned again to Oakbriar during Cherity's time away, this time accompanied by Richard. When he returned to Washington Veronica went instead to Richmond where she served on and off throughout the rest of the war in the city's hospitals.

Meanwhile, Cecil Hirsch remained at large and Union authorities had not been able to lay their hands on him.

However, a man in a white suit and a wide-brimmed straw hat, sporting an outsized mustache and speaking in a thick Southern drawl, had been seen stepping off a train in St. Louis answering to the name Cyrus Hunt.

He had gone by many names in his time, but that for which he was most widely known he would probably never be able to use again.

Sixty-Five

*C*herity had been away from Greenwood now for a week. It was with a heavy heart that she said her final good-byes several hours later and, again with carpetbag in hand, walked from Mrs. Walton's farmhouse back into town and to Rev. Wilcott's church. Neither Nurse Beech nor Dick Garr were anywhere to be seen.

"You're the young lady who's been helping out with the wounded?" said the minister as she walked in.

"Yes, sir," she answered. "I've been looking for a young man I have reason to think might have been involved in the train accident. But I've searched all the wards in Bend and Jefferson's Crossing and there is no trace of him. I . . . uh, Mrs. Walton told me that you've been writing to the families of those who were killed. . . ."

"Those I could locate."

"She said you've kept a list of the dead."

"That's right," nodded Rev. Wilcott.

"I wondered . . . I mean, may I look at your list?"

"Of course."

He disappeared into his office and returned a few moments later holding two sheets of paper.

Cherity took a deep breath, then took them from him. Fearfully and with heart pounding, she began scanning the list of names. The minister waited patiently, half expecting for one of the callings of his office soon to be required of him—consoling the bereaved.

He was relieved when he saw Cherity reach the end of the second page of names and exhale a sigh of relief. She looked up, smiled weakly, and handed the papers back to him.

"I take it his name is not here?" said Rev. Wilcott.

"No," replied Cherity. "I am desperate to find any news of him, but I'm glad I found nothing here. I suppose, then, that it's time for me to go home."

"Have you been to the hospital?" asked the minister.

"Uh . . . what hospital?" said Cherity.

"Further east . . . in Jonesborough. It's where they sent the worst of the cases."

"The . . . *worst*. There were worse than I've seen here?"

"Oh, much worse. Some needed operations . . . gangrene, infection . . . cases where we thought amputation was needed. . . . Dick Garr had his hands full as things were. He wasn't equipped for the most severely wounded . . . brain injuries when men didn't know who they were. You can imagine how impossible it was to notify families when a wounded man didn't even know his own name. And," he added grimly, "there were many we knew we couldn't save no matter what we did."

Cherity gulped. "How . . . this hospital," she asked, "how far is it?"

"Eight or ten miles east . . . it's in Jonesborough, next stop along the line west."

Cherity sighed. "It is the last thing I want to do . . . but maybe I should take one more day and look there too. I won't be able to rest if there's someplace I haven't been."

"Prepare yourself, miss," said Rev. Wilcott. "It's no place for the faint of heart. It can be a terrible shock if you've never seen such sights before."

With a sinking feeling, Cherity walked out of the church building and made her way again through town to the train station where she had arrived three days before.

All the way as she went the minister's words sounded in her brain, *It's where they sent the worst of the cases . . . terrible shock if you've never seen such sights before . . . men didn't know who they were . . . many we knew we couldn't save no matter what we did.*

After what she had already seen, she could not imagine how much worse it could be! She wasn't sure she had the courage to face the truth if Seth were among them.

Why not just go home as she had planned? Get a ticket east for Columbia and go home! But . . . what if Seth was one of those who couldn't remember who he was? She *had* to find out if he was there.

Cherity walked to the ticket window. There stood the tall thin boy she had seen when she arrived.

"Where to, miss?" he said, glancing up at her.

"When does the eastbound for Augusta and Columbia arrive?"

"'Bout an hour . . . just before the west."

Cherity thought a moment longer.

"Give me a ticket . . ." she began, then hesitated again, "—a ticket to Jonesborough."

"That's the westbound, miss. I thought you said you was heading east."

"I changed my mind."

"All right, if you say so . . . that'll be four bits."

Cherity paid him, took her ticket, then turned and walked out onto the platform. As she waited, doubts again assaulted her. A terrible sense of foreboding came over her that maybe the hospital in Jonesborough might indeed contain the answers she had come to find. But did she really want to know?

Was she brave enough to discover the truth?

A whistle sounded in the distance. She glanced along the line and saw a few puffs of white smoke amongst the trees from the approaching train.

The station boy walked out onto the platform and glanced eastward, then down at his watch.

"Hmm . . . that's some peculiar," he mumbled. "Here comes the

westbound, miss," he said. "That's your train. Looks like the eastbound's late. You might have to wait a spell after you board till it gets
here so's the trains can pass."

A few minutes later the train came into the station, slowed, and
came to a screeching stop amid a great blast of steam from under the
wheels. Two or three passengers got off, then Cherity boarded the last
of three cars. She walked in and set her things on an empty seat and
sat down to wait.

After about five minutes a whistle sounded from the opposite direction. The eastbound was finally pulling in. With a few final lingering
doubts that she should have taken the other train, Cherity sat waiting.
But it was too late now. Her fate, at least for what was left of this day
and tomorrow, lay at the hospital in Jonesborough.

A few seconds later she felt the wheels jerk into motion beneath her.
She looked out the window again as slowly the train began to inch its
way out of the station, then stood and walked to the back of the car.
She opened the door and went outside and stood beside the rail looking out at the town she was leaving.

Her gaze went to the spire of Rev. Wilcott's church in the distance.
Then on the adjacent track, the two trains met. The engines passed.
A few seconds later Cherity's gaze was interrupted by the movement
close beside her. First the engine rumbled slowly by, then one by one
the passenger coaches.

As brakes ground the incoming locomotive to a stop, her own eastbound gradually accelerated out of the station. Absently Cherity stared
into the windows of the train slowing next to her, vaguely seeing
people seated inside but hardly able to focus on them.

She turned her gaze again out toward Jefferson's Crossing. Though
it had only been three days, she felt like she was leaving a piece of
her behind in this place. If she found nothing in Jonesborough and
returned in the opposite direction through here tomorrow or the next
day, would she stop or just stay aboard the train and travel through?

Clattering along now, she drew even with the last car of the eastbound, as it screeched to a final stop.

A lone figure stood at the railing on the back rail just like she stood . . . he looking out in one direction, she in the other.

Her eyes unconsciously flitted toward him. He was a young man, like so many others she had seen, arm and shoulder bandaged, leg bound and wrapped, leaning on a single crutch. Her eyes drifted up to the wounded man's face and his blond hair. It seemed like he was trying to say something, but the train on the tracks beneath her were too loud for her to hear him.

And why was he suddenly waving his hand so frantically? Someone must be meeting him at the station.

Absently she smiled to herself. Her brain was playing tricks on her . . . it almost looked like—

A sudden gasp sent Cherity's brain spinning. She opened her mouth . . . she tried to shout . . . nothing came out. She was breathing hysterically . . . her mouth was dry . . . she began to feel faint.

The man was waving his good arm and shouting . . . he was shouting at *her*!

Cherity . . . Cherity! But they were unreal dream words. They sounded far off . . . mingled with the clanging of iron upon iron beneath her.

Her brain swam in light. A dream . . . only a dream. Her head swirled in dizzying confusion.

Cherity stood paralyzed. She could not move nor speak. Slowly the dreamy frantically waving figure spinning in light grew smaller and smaller in the distance.

But then suddenly she woke from her stupor. She turned and hurried back into the coach. She grabbed her carpetbag from the seat and dashed back out the rear door. The station of Jefferson's Crossing had disappeared from her sight.

She stood for a moment again at the rail.

"Oh . . . oh, God . . . help me!" she stammered in a frenzy of confusion.

Not pausing to think, she unlatched the bar across the platform. She stepped down the two stairs where the tracks were speeding beneath her, then threw her bag from her. Mightily summoning more courage than she thought possible, Cherity drew in a deep breath, closed her eyes, and leapt.

She hit the ground hard to the side of the rails, rolled over several times, hardly feeling the pain shooting knives up from her ankle, then crawled to her feet and looked around for her bag.

Twenty seconds later she had it in her hand and stood in the middle of the tracks. A faint metallic echo from the rails was all she heard of the train she had left as it receded in the distance.

She stood a moment bewildered and in shock from the vision she had seen and then her sudden jump and fall. Had she imagined what she thought she had seen? She was delirious from the days looking at wounded men. By now they all looked the same.

A whistle blew from the direction of town. Its sound brought everything back in a rush of fearful panic.

She had to get back to Jefferson's Crossing before the train left the station! She couldn't let it leave . . . she had to know what she'd seen.

She picked up one edge of her dress and tried to run. But her ankle hurt from the fall.

The whistle sounded again. She crested a slight rise. There was the steeple in the distance. She kept on and the station came into sight.

The train began slowly to inch away. "No!" she cried. "Stop . . . wait!"

In desperation she hurried on. But the engine continued to chug into motion and the giant wheels slowly turned and gained speed. She could never get there in time.

"Wait, please . . . stop!" She yelled again. "You can't—"

Suddenly Cherity froze.

Descending from the platform and now hobbling awkwardly toward her as fast as he was able on a single crutch across the railroad ties, was definitely no illusion nor mirage.

"Oh . . . oh!" she cried, gasping for breath. "Oh, no . . . how can . . . oh, no . . . oh, Seth . . . Seth!"

Cherity's carpetbag dropped from her hand. She ran, babbling, tripping and stumbling, all the rest of the way until she fell into Seth's arms, a mass of tears and hair and kisses smothering his face.

"Oh, Seth, Seth . . . what are you doing here? . . . How did you . . . ? But I was so worried . . . I knew something had happened. . . . I thought you were dead . . . I . . . I didn't know what—"

At last the moment overcame her and she broke down in heaving sobs, completely collapsing in his embrace.

Seth had managed to keep hold of his crutch more than Cherity her carpetbag. Steadying himself by it with his right hand, he held Cherity tight with his left, her head buried on his chest weeping, until the tempest of her emotion began to subside.

"It seems that it is me who should ask you what *you* are doing here," said Seth at last, speaking into her hair, flying about in the breeze over his face as her head lay against his shoulder and neck.

The sound of his voice so close in her ear was the final proof that she was not dreaming. Cherity burst into a fresh round of sobs.

A minute later she eased herself back, then smiled and wiped at her eyes.

"I can't believe it's you!" she said, shaking her head and beginning to laugh and cry all at once. "I can't believe . . . What were you doing on that . . . and how did you know . . . did you know it was me? Why did you get off . . . you weren't going to Jefferson's Crossing!"

"Which of your questions do you want me to answer first?" laughed Seth.

"All of them! Oh, Seth . . . I can't believe it. I am so happy to see you!"

"You couldn't possibly be any happier than I am to see you!"

"Don't be too sure! But what are you doing here?"

"I am on my way home . . . at least I was until I jumped off the train at that station there just as it was starting to move. No, I wasn't on my way to this town—what did you call it?"

"Jefferson's Crossing."

"Well, whatever it is, I was on my way home. But the instant I saw you I knew I couldn't just keep going. So I hopped off. Then the train left and there I was all alone and I realized maybe I'd been stupid. But how did you get off *that* train up there?" he said, pointing along the line behind Cherity.

"I jumped!" giggled Cherity. "That reminds me, my ankle hurts!"

"Jumped! Are you crazy?"

"I did go a little crazy when I saw you. I thought you were a dream. You *are* really Seth Davidson . . . aren't you?"

Seth leaned down and kissed her gently on the lips.

"I guess you are," she smiled. "No dream can do that!"

"So . . . what are we going to do?" said Seth, looking about. "We're out here in the middle of nowhere."

"Oh, that's easy—I know lots of people here. There's a boarding-house with lumpy beds and mice. There's Mrs. Walton's farmhouse where we could stay."

"What are you talking about?" laughed Seth. "You sound like you live here! What *are* you doing here? How long have you been here?"

Cherity laughed with delight at Seth's bewilderment.

"I came looking for you," she said. "When we didn't hear from you I thought you'd been hurt in the railway accident. So I came here and have been searching all the wards where they took people. I looked everywhere and was about to give up and go home. Oh, Seth . . . I was so afraid!"

"But home is in the other direction. That's where I was going."

"I was going see if you were in the hospital at Jonesborough. *Then* I planned to go home."

"Well, if I'd have waited another day to leave, you'd have found me. That's where I was. I was banged up pretty good, broke my leg and two ribs. But I was lucky. Quite a few didn't pull through at all."

"But why did they take you to the hospital? I thought it was only for the severe cases."

"I don't know. It was all mixed up and confusing after the acci-dent—people coming and going and yelling and some trying to help and others injured and others dead. Once the people from the towns came to help, they just put us wherever there was space and I wound up at the hospital. They did think at first that my leg might have to be cut off."

"Oh, Seth . . . I can't bear the thought!"

"But a surgeon there splinted and set it and said he'd keep an eye on it and see how bad the infection got. After a couple weeks, he said he thought it was going to heal and that I could keep my leg after all. Then yesterday he finally said I could start walking on it with a crutch. I was on my way on the very next train."

"What about your equipment?"

"It was all destroyed. I've got to talk to McClarin and see what he wants me to do. And this war may be over soon. Who knows, McClarin may be through with me anyway."

"Why didn't you write us and tell us what had happened and that you were all right?"

"I did. You didn't get my letter?"

"No. We heard nothing."

"Oh . . . now it begins to make sense. No wonder you were worried. But what are we going to do now? We need to get home. How often do the trains come through here anyway?"

"Once a day," answered Cherity. "We'll have to wait until tomorrow. Oh, but I can't wait to tell Mrs. Walton! You can meet her for yourself!"

Suddenly Cherity remembered their last meeting, and became serious.

"Seth . . . ," she began, "I hardly know what to say . . . I am so sorry for the way I was back at Greenwood. I should have trusted you. Can you ever forgive me?"

"After what we've both been through, it hardly seems important anymore. But yes . . . of course I forgive you."

"Your father explained to me . . . and we saw the article about you and Veronica in the newspaper. I am so sorry."

"I feel awkward to ask," said Seth sheepishly, "but . . . with the article and all, do you know . . . is Veronica all right?"

Cherity smiled. "You don't need to worry—it's all right if you talk about her," she said. "Actually, I went over to visit her and . . . believe it or not, she and I have become quite good friends."

"You and Veronica!" exclaimed Seth in astonishment.

Cherity nodded.

"That's . . . that's unbelievable. But I think it's terrific. How in the world did it happen?"

"I went to visit her, after the article . . . she explained everything to me about how you helped her. She asked me to teach her to ride."

"Veronica!" laughed Seth.

"We rode all around together. I think I'm actually going to miss her."

After the happiest evening imaginable together at Mrs. Walton's farmhouse and a morning spent joyfully helping her again with her wounded, Seth and Cherity made their way together again to the Jefferson's Crossing station. This time, adding all the more to the bewilderment of the station boy, they purchased *two* tickets east to Columbia, South Carolina.

Never had the jostling of the train clattering along beneath them felt so good to Cherity as when they pulled out of the Jefferson's Crossing station and began to gain speed. To be sitting with Seth at her side, on her way back to Greenwood, on her way *home*, was just about the best feeling in all the world.

As the train slowed into Bend, Cherity rose and went in search of the conductor.

"How long is the stop here?" she asked.

"Just a few minutes, ma'am," he answered. "Sort of depends on if the mail's got to the station or not. Sometimes we gotta wait five or ten minutes. But as soon as it's here, we're off again."

The moment the train was stopped, Cherity jumped out. Seth followed her from the car. The mail pouch had not yet arrived.

"I'll be back in less than five minutes," Cherity said to the conductor. "Please wait for me."

She turned to Seth. "There's one of the wounded men I want to say good-bye to, and tell him I found you. I'll just be a few minutes. *Don't* you go anyplace without me!"

She dashed off the platform, through the station, and into Bend. It seemed so long ago that she was here, when in fact it had been a mere few days. She ran all the way to the farmhouse where she had first encountered the horrors of the train accident and the war firsthand and where her search for Seth began.

She knocked on the door but did not even wait for an answer and walked right in.

"Hello, Missy!" she said to the sad-faced girl who was on her way to answer her knock. "I came to see your mother again."

Without a word, Missy reached up and took her hand and led her back into the sick ward. Cherity walked in. Nothing had changed other than her own increased capacity to cope with the sights and smells that had overwhelmed her on that first day.

"Oh, come back to help after running out on me, I see," said Missy's mother irritably. "Well, get a towel and some hot rags—you know what to do."

"I'm sorry," said Cherity, trying to smile. "I'm not here to stay. I'm on my way home. I just came by to see the man again . . . down there at the end," she added, glancing along the row of invalids, though at first glance she did not see him. "Uh, you remember . . . the man with no arm."

"Oh, him . . . he's dead. Didn't make it another two days after you was gone. He asked about you, though, if that's makes you feel any better . . . something about telling you when I saw you again that the angels was coming, but I couldn't make out half of what he was talking about."

Cherity turned and tripped her way out of the house, holding back her tears until she was alone. She then broke into sobs as she walked in a daze back to the station. She hardly heard the urgent whistle of the train, nor Seth's shouts when he saw her.

She stumbled into the station where Seth was waiting.

"Oh, Seth . . . he's dead," she whimpered as he nearly scooped her up with his one good arm and hurried her to the waiting train. "And I realized after I left," Cherity went on, "I realized . . . that I . . . I didn't even know his name."

Sixty-Six

Seth and Cherity arrived back at Dove's Landing two days later to great rejoicing. Seeing him wounded and hobbling on a crutch, Seth's family was more bewildered than anxious and was full of questions. Cherity now came clean about her misleading them about a visit to her sister, which, she said, she still did want to make, after Seth was better. Then followed the complete story of Seth's accident and Cherity's search.

There was no question of Seth's returning to work anytime soon. Never was such a happy convalescence endured by so happy an invalid. He telegraphed Mr. McClarin saying a detailed letter, which he began that same day, would follow.

The tumultuous events which consumed Greenwood during the final months of 1864 completely overshadowed the November elections north of the Pennsylvania border. As the year drew to a close the momentum of the war lay all on the side of the Union. The Confederacy had not won a battle of significance since the summer. Even then their only victories had been in forestalling Grant's juggernaut around the city of Richmond. And Sherman's taking of Atlanta and march across South Carolina to the sea in the late fall of the year, as hated as it made him throughout the South, so buoyed optimism in the North that Lincoln was easily reelected in November.

The cause of the Confederacy was lost. Yet still Lee fought on against Grant around Richmond, the two armies encamped for months within but a few miles of the city.

The two Davidson brothers, now grown men of twenty-four and twenty-two, spent many long hours discussing the relative merits of the war and its causes, and grew yet more angry at their father's friend and his fellow Confederate generals for their stubbornness in prolonging the war in the face of inevitable defeat.

Though Seth was recovering and was on his way back to full strength, he was not anxious to leave Greenwood. He wanted to be with his family and with Cherity and was weary of following the war about with a camera. Whether Mr. McClarin sympathized or not, Seth wasn't altogether sure. But since Seth was firm in his decision, and was also by now recognized as one of the best photographers in the country, the editor did not raise too many objections. He did send him replacement camera equipment in hopes that when Seth was feeling better he would change his mind.

Thomas, however, was more involved in the war effort than ever, though in a way he would never have foreseen.

They were all surprised to see Veronica appear at Greenwood one day. Her husband had just left for New York for two weeks and Veronica had come south. Her visit was welcomed joyfully for she had become a family friend to all. She was greeted with hugs all around as if they hadn't seen her in years. After a brief visit, however, they were surprised to learn that Veronica had actually come to see Thomas.

As a way to fulfill his duty to state and country, Thomas had dedicated himself, for as long as the war lasted, to caring for wounded and helping blacks to escape oppression, whether at Greenwood or elsewhere. He and Veronica had both become increasingly active in medical work in recent months. They had been in touch by telegraph and had made plans to go into Richmond together to work at one of the large hospitals for war wounded. Hearing of their plans, and after her own experience on the outskirts of Atlanta looking for Seth, Cherity asked if she could join them.

Veronica returned to Washington after two weeks, continuing

her volunteer efforts there, while Cherity and Thomas remained in Richmond another month. Richmond, Seth, Sydney, and the two Shaw boys, meanwhile, planted far more acreage during the spring months than Greenwood had been able to sustain since the start of the year.

And still . . . Robert Lee refused to give in.

Defeat followed defeat until his army was finally driven away from Richmond into south central Virginia. Grant pursued him with his entire army, finally surrounding what was left of the Confederate force near the small town of Appomattox.

Hearing that surrender was imminent, Seth hurriedly packed up the new equipment and left overland by horseback, with Thomas, who had by then returned from Richmond, as his assistant. They reached the scene in time to photograph the historic encounter between Lee and Grant at Appomattox Court House on April 9, as 28,000 young Southerners like themselves laid down their arms, and Robert E. Lee signed documents of surrender to Ulysses S. Grant.

They had only just returned home when on the 16ᵗʰ of April came shocking news—sweeping through the North and South by telegraph: Abraham Lincoln had been assassinated the night before by a Confederate sympathizer named John Wilkes Booth. Though some in the South rejoiced, unwilling even at the end to concede the extraordinary virtue of the man who had suddenly become a martyr, all in the Union mourned, and most within the dying Confederacy were stunned and sobered by the news.

A week and a half later, General Johnstone surrendered his Confederate army to the Union's General Sherman at Bennett Place outside Raleigh. Though one last Confederate general had not yet surrendered, the war was finally over!

Two months later, as a lasting legacy to Abraham Lincoln, Congress added to what it had begun in February with the 13ᵗʰ Amendment to the Constitution prohibiting slavery, by passing the 14ᵗʰ Amendment which guaranteed to freed slaves the right of citizenship in the United States of America.

Cynthia returned to Jeffrey who was stationed again in New Haven. Tears were shed on all sides, both mother and daughter especially were grateful for the opportunity, given to few, to be together again as adults for an extended period of time. They knew it must end eventually, and therefore when the time came Carolyn's and Cynthia's gratitude overshadowed their sadness of parting.

Shortly after Cynthia's departure, there arrived at Greenwood a letter from McClarin in Boston.

Dear Seth, it read.

I appreciated the Appomatox photos. That was a nice surprise.

Not knowing your postwar plans, I have a proposal I would like to set before you.

I realize that with the war over your vocational interests may now change. I know that photography provided a means for you to fulfill your duty to country without joining sides in the fighting. I consider it an honor to have worked with you. You did your job well and demonstrated great skill, as well as courage, in carrying it out. I sincerely believe that you have an aptitude for photography, and, should it fit in with your plans I would like to offer you a permanent position with the Herald, *at a significant increase in salary, which would also include a further upgrading of your equipment with the latest that is available.*

It is clear now that photography will stand at the vanguard of the future when it comes to the representation of the news to the public. It is a field that grows more exciting by the day. It is my sincere hope that you will want to be part of it. I do not think it will be long before we are capable of reproducing photographs in printed newspapers.

It would be more convenient of course if you were to relocate to Boston. But if that is not possible or does not fit in with your plans, I think we might be able to make it work, as we have for the last four years, by courier and rail if you choose to remain based at your home in Virginia.

Please give my best to Mrs. Fitzpatrick, and to Miss Waters.

I hope that you will use this opportunity to consider the benefits of a future in the Herald's employ.

I am,

Sincerely yours,
A. McClarin, Boston Herald.

Sixty-Seven

The next afternoon Cherity saw Chigua walking alone outside. Cherity had noticed that she had been unusually sober and quiet since Cherity and Seth had returned. Something seemed heavy upon her mind.

Cherity left the house and walked out toward the woman who, along with Carolyn and Cynthia, had become her dear friend.

Chigua heard her coming and turned.

"You seem . . . preoccupied," said Cherity. "What is it?"

Chigua smiled. "Does it really show?"

"Something is on your mind. I am afraid you cannot hide it. Are you sad about something?"

"No, not sad . . . just thoughtful."

"I have two willing ears," said Cherity.

They walked a minute or two in silence.

"I have been thinking recently about my Indian heritage," said Chigua at length. "I have—"

She stopped and looked down.

"It is too unrealistic an idea even to speak aloud," she said. "Though I have told Sydney."

"What is it?" asked Cherity. "You needn't tell me if you do not want to. But if you do, I am interested."

"What I was about to say," Chigua went on a little sheepishly, "is that I have been harboring a dream, ever since reading about the Cherokee chief Stand Watie."

"A dream?"

Chigua nodded. "I want . . . to visit the Indian Territory . . . to see if I might find some of my own people."

"Oh," exclaimed Cherity, "I think that is a wonderful idea!"

"You do?"

"Of course. What could be more exciting than discovering your heritage? It is something I have wanted to do too."

"But . . . do you not know all about your family?"

"I know next to nothing," said Cherity shaking her head. "I never knew my mother—she died when I was born. My father is now gone and I know nothing about his past. He never spoke of it when I was young. I did not even think to be curious. Once he was gone, I realized how much had died with him. I have two sisters of course, and everyone here and all the Davidsons are wonderful to me. But deep inside I sometimes feel very alone. I also wonder where I came from."

"And your sisters know nothing of your father's people?"

"They know as little as I."

"I suppose in that way we are very much alike," said Chigua. "I knew my family when I was young. But that was so long ago that I find it hard now to remember. My parents died and it was my grandfather who took care of my sister and me."

"I wish I could go with you, but such a long trip hardly seems realistic for two women like us."

"And me with a family," nodded Chigua. "Have you ever been to the West?"

"Once, with my father. I was only eleven—we went by stagecoach most of the way."

"The train goes all the way to Memphis now, I think. That's almost to Kansas. I wouldn't be afraid if you went with me. You're so confident about everything"

Cherity laughed. "My father did instill confidence in me—that

I could do anything. Maybe that's why I went off looking for Seth. I *knew* I could find him . . . although I almost didn't!"

"But you did. And the way you use that gun Mr. Davidson makes you carry! I think you really could do anything you set your mind to!"

As he recovered, Seth too became quiet and reflective. The letter from his editor had prompted his own thoughts about the future. And also his lengthy deathbed talk with James Waters lay heavily upon his heart, along with the promise he had made to Cherity's father.

The discussions between Chigua and Cherity had not escaped his notice. Seth knew that Cherity's roots were not nearly so deeply buried as she supposed.

When to tell her what he knew was the question plaguing him. When was the right time? It was a question that had been on his mind throughout the entire course of the war. Perhaps the time for revelation was nearly at hand.

At last he went to his father.

"Dad," said Seth. "Remember that packet I gave you for safekeeping?"

"Of course," nodded Richmond. "It's in the safe."

"I think the time has finally come when I need to take some action on it."

"I'll get it for you."

Father and son walked upstairs to Richmond's study. Richmond opened his safe, withdrew the packet, and handed it to Seth. "I almost opened it myself not long ago," he said.

Seth glanced at him with a curious expression.

"I wondered, whatever this was about, if it would fall to me by default."

"I'm sure you would have handled it . . . no doubt better than I will be able to," smiled Seth. "But as it was given to me to do, I have to try to do it as best I can."

Richmond nodded. "I understand."

They turned to go and Seth paused.

"Dad, do you mind if I ask you a question?" he said.

"No, of course not."

"How do you . . . I mean, how can you tell when something is *right*—when you're supposed to do something? I mean, how can you be . . . *sure?*"

"An age-old question," smiled Richmond. "And one for which there is no simple answer. The biggest problem with that question is that so few people ask it at all. Just asking what's right and trying to do what is right—that's half the battle right there. They say Davy Crockett's motto used to be, 'Be sure you're right, then go ahead.' But it is easier said than done!"

"What about knowing *when* you're to do something?" asked Seth. "I'm pretty sure I know *what* I'm to do with regard to this packet . . . but not *when.*"

"It never hurts to wait. God is rarely in a hurry. Not knowing the situation, I would simply say that you have to wait until the sense comes—*This* is God's time."

"It's hard, Dad. It's not easy trying to walk in God's will."

Richmond nodded. "It's also how spiritual maturity grows. If it wasn't hard it wouldn't produce depth of character."

PART SIX

ROOTS
Spring - Fall, 1865

Sixty-Eight

*W*hen civil war had broken out in 1861, Black Wolf son of Prowling Bear was twenty-four. He joined and fought haphazardly with a regiment of loyal Cherokee, not to advance the Union cause, or any cause other than his own. The white man's fight was not his fight. He joined mainly to oppose Stand Watie, "the traitor," as he had grown up hearing his father call him. To kill Stand Watie was his passion, along with raising the Indian nations against the continued advance of the white man. It was his plan to rise as chief of his people and for the Cherokee to lead a great federation of tribes to retake their land. But he was still a young man. Both objectives had to be accomplished at the right time and in the right way in order to succeed toward the higher hope of Indian supremacy in the West.

The war gave Black Wolf the chance to test his mettle in the heat of battle. He hoped more than anything for the opportunity to face Stand Watie warrior to warrior. As a Union soldier he carried a rifle, but in his belt he carried a far more personal weapon. He dreamed of plunging his father's tomahawk, the very same that had killed Watie's brother, deep into the hated forehead, with Watie's eyes looking straight at him, knowing by whose hand his death had come.

While far away in Pennsylvania armies struggled away from the blood-soaked fields of Gettsyburg, a smaller and little-known skirmish took place between Indian troops in the heart of Cherokee territory.

Those who rode under Colonel Stand Watie and Brigadier General Cooper prepared for a surprise attack on Fort Gibson held by the Union. But federal troops caught wind of the rumor and prepared a surprise of their own.

Among the soldiers quartered at Fort Gibson was a long-haired warrior by the name of Black Wolf. When he heard the orders, the Cherokee warrior glanced down at the gleaming tomahawk in his left hand and sharpened it several times more against the stone in his right. At last, perhaps his long-awaited chance had come! He would find Watie on the battlefield, ride him down, and then cut out the old man's tongue and send it to Watie's widow.

The Battle at Honey Springs quickly became a rout against the badly outnumbered Confederate forces. As Watie realized their danger, he wheeled his horse around and shouted for retreat. But there sat a mounted young Cherokee wearing the Union blue blocking his way.

Something in the young warrior's eyes looked evil as they bored straight into his own. Watie knew instantly that this was no mere battlefield encounter but something far more personal.

With a fearful cry, his tribesman suddenly galloped forward, pulling from his belt a tomahawk and raising it above his head. Watie raised his rifle and aimed. But he could not pull the trigger. He had killed many times before. Yet some impulse prevented him taking the life of this crazed soldier who was trying to end his.

His hesitation might have cost him his life. In two seconds the young man was on him.

Watie had but a moment to react. He yanked the reins of his mount sideways with his right hand, and with all his strength swung his rifle in a wide arc with his left. He heard rather than saw the swish of the blade that had killed his own brother miss his ear by inches, just as the barrel of his gun whacked his attacker above one ear and toppled him to the ground. He dug in his heels and galloped away, turning back only long enough to see the young warrior climb to his feet and shriek after him with fist high in the air, "You will die, Watie . . . you will die!"

Both knew they would meet another day.

When the war ended, Stand Watie's notoriety in the Cherokee nation continued to rise. Proudly mounted on his wall was a statement of commendation from the Confederate Congress, signed by President Davis himself. The defeat of the South caused him to treasure it no less.

Those vowing revenge on Watie kept their hopes to themselves until after the general's historic final surrender in June of 1865, going down in history as the last Confederate general to surrender.

By then Black Wolf, son of Prowling Bear, was a twenty-eight-year-old Cherokee who had already begun to attract notice and gain a following among some of the younger and more radical of the tribe.

Sixty-Nine

The youths of Dove's Landing were slowly returning to their homes and families. But not all homecomings were filled with joy nor every home with happiness.

Brad McClellan would not be returning home at all. He now lay buried with the rest of the dead at Gettysburg. His younger brother Jeremy was one of the lucky ones to come home unscathed. No one had heard from Scully Riggs in three years. Even his father had no idea where he was or if he was even still alive. Wyatt Beaumont returned quieter and moodier than before, limping from a leg wound. Though he did not broadcast it about, word gradually got around that his brother Cameron had become involved with a group of desperadoes calling themselves Bilsby's Marauders. No one knew where he was. Wyatt kept to himself that Cameron was wanted by the law.

The interview with Stand Watie that appeared in the paper was read with great interest around the table at Greenwood, especially by Chigua who had been thinking much of late about her Cherokee heritage. Seth, too, listened with more interest than he allowed himself to show. His thoughts were on Cherity and her father and what he should tell Cherity of what he knew of her past . . . and when.

I caught up with Stand Watie, the interviewer wrote, *outside the small town of Vian near Salisaw far to the south in the Indian Territory of Oklahoma. Having been drawn to him because of his singular role in the recent War Between the States, I also hoped to learn more about the division within the Cherokee tribe, which had led to half the Cherokee siding with the Confederacy and the other half with the Union.*

As we spoke of the ongoing dispute, Watie mentioned a mysterious elder of the tribe, his own distant cousin through Dragging Canoe, son of the great chief Attacullaculla.

"Though he descends from the Canoe line," said Watie, "known for Dragging Canoe, the warlike son of the great chief, the man I speak of carries within him the spirit of the white feather of Attacullaculla himself."

"The white feather . . . what does that signify?"

"In ancient times, the Cherokee had multiple chiefs. The chief of the red feather led during war, the chief of the white feather led during times of peace. The white feather thus came to symbolize peace."

"Who is this elder you speak of?"

"He is called The Man Who Wears the White Feather."

"Is that actually his name?"

"It is how he is known," replied Watie a little cryptically. "Most simply call him the Wise One. He has been a tireless voice for peace among the two factions. Both sides would sway him if they could— even I have tried. But he will endorse neither. He is respected by and yet occasionally angers those on both sides. He took no position on the recent war and nothing would make him change his neutral stance. He is one of the few still alive from the old times, who knows much of the story of the Cherokee people."

"How can there still be such tension between the two groups?"

"It is worse now than it has been for twenty years," Watie answered. "My life may even now be in danger. It is a dangerous time. There is at least one young renegade who has vowed to kill me."

"What is the essence of the dispute?" I asked.

"The roots go back to the Ridge-Ross conflict of the 1830s," replied Watie. "It is no longer about whether to relocate or remain in the East. Some now call it a dispute between the Full Blood party and the Mixed Blood party. When the war broke out, some sided with the North and others, like myself, were on the side of the Confederacy. Those differences intensified the old feelings on both sides and brought everything to the surface again. The Cherokee have long memories. Indian bitterness dies hard. Healing will take longer among the Cherokee. There has not been healing in thirty years, and I see no end to the breach in sight."

"That is hardly the civilized approach to conflict."

"It is the Indian way," rejoined Watie. "Wrongs of the past are never forgotten. Forgiveness is not spoken of, only vengeance. And how civilized was the recent war between the so-called civilized whites of the North and South? It is hardly appropriate for such to condemn the Cherokee."

"Perhaps. But would it not be for the good of all the Cherokee to lay it to rest?"

"The ancient Cherokee blood law cannot be forgotten. Many are still alive who vow never to forget the retribution required by the blood law. They will never forgive those of us who agreed to the treaty in 1835 and who sold our lands. Vengeance passes through generations. We are still seen as traitors in their eyes."

"And the old man you spoke of—the man who wears the white feather—he can do nothing to resolve the dispute?"

Watie shook his head. "He is held in high respect by most, but not all. There are some who despise him for his talk of peace. There can be no peace, they say, until all the traitors are rooted out, no matter how long it takes, generation upon generation. From such as these, my life and even the life of the wise man are in danger. They murdered my brother and uncle and cousin twenty-five years ago. There are some who yet consider the duty of that massacre incomplete."

"And so the hostility continues."

Watie nodded. "I do not forget the night they were murdered. To avenge them is my duty as well."

I sat and listened as Watie drew in a thoughtful breath and his forehead wrinkled slightly.

"I told you of the young man who has vowed to take my life," he went on. *"He has gained a sizeable following. If the spirit of the white feather lives on in the old wise man of whom I spoke, in this outlaw renegade lives the spirit of the warrior Dragging Canoe. There are those who suspect his mother of Comanche and Kiowa blood. He is stirring up much havoc among some youth who are easily swayed. The rumors surrounding the old man only make it worse for such hotheads."*

"What rumors?"

"That he knows where gold is buried. But he has not confided everything he knows even to me. We have known one another all our lives, but he knows that I will never be neutral as he is. I remain a warrior and fighter. He has put the white feather on the back of his head. This difference will always exist between us."

Richmond continued to read aloud and finished the article. It fell silent in the Greenwood kitchen as they pondered the solemn content of the interview and Stand Watie's words. More than he had been able to before, Seth was at last coming to understand James Waters' concerns about Cherity's safety.

The letter that arrived at the home of John Borton, Mount Holly, New Jersey addressed to Deanna Steddings, was met with a shriek the moment Deanna saw the envelope.

She ran outside to be alone, then ripped the envelope open and pulled out the two white sheets inside. In the distance she heard the faint sound of her father's hammer pounding on the roof of their new house, where he and her mother and Moses were working at the far corner of the former Borton homestead.

Dear Deanna, she read,

> *I have been going back and forth to Richmond, not quite as frequently as in the final months of the war, but enough to feel that I am doing some good. It is so satisfying to see the wounded men gradually getting back on their feet and going home. For the first time since the war, some of the wards and hospitals are actually beginning to have a few empty beds.*
>
> *I have been thinking a great deal about what I will do now. I never really thought about such things when I was young. But after what happened during the war, I have become introspective and prayerful about what life means and what we are put on this earth for. I have realized that I really am very fortunate—God has given me so much. I have a wonderful family and friends—like you!— and I realize that I want to use what God has given me to help those who haven't been so fortunate. So I have been thinking about going to school to become a doctor. I have talked to my father about it and he is completely in favor of it and said he would help with the cost of schooling. I haven't decided for certain yet, but I am thinking seriously about it.*
>
> *For now, especially with Seth not back to full strength from his injuries, I am helping my father with the work around Greenwood. It is good working alongside him as a man instead of a boy—I think the war made us all men. My father is a good man! I don't know why it took me so long to see it. I really enjoy being with him. . . .*

When Deanna finished the letter a few minutes later, she immediately went back into the house, ran upstairs to the room she shared with Mary, Suzane, and Rebecca Borton, and sat down at the writing table to begin a return letter of her own.

Far to the west in the Cherokee Territory of Oklahoma, the man who, even if indirectly, had been the subject of the recent newspaper interview was out walking in the small village which for years had been his home.

The end of the war had sent him into a period of deep reflection. The years had crept up on him with surprising haste. He had always hoped that a time would come when he would be shown clearly what to do about the old times . . . and the new. But the recent war, far from clarifying his vision for the future of his people, had obscured it all the more. And new pressures, and with them new dangers, were upon them.

He grieved for the ongoing conflict.

Yet what could he do? He was but one man, and an aging one. Youth did not respect antiquity as it once had. What could his words accomplish now, one lone voice amid winds of change?

He knew that his days among his people were slowly drawing to an end. The time when he would be gathered to his fathers was approaching like a slow dusk settling down upon his earthly life.

He had concluded a portion of his duty. Yet it still remained for him to pass on the heritage that had been given into his possession. He was old and getting older. As the great chief Attacullaculla and the Ghigua before him, he must now seek worthy young Cherokee who valued and honored the old ways.

And perhaps . . .

It had been so many years. But was a time of returning, even at his age, also at hand?

How else to complete the sacred circle of beginnings and endings? How else to secure the heritage . . . and pass it on to those destined to follow him?

Seventy

Stand Watie knew that he was in danger. Not only him, but his friend of the white feather. Black Wolf would not rest until he saw them both dead. Whatever their differences, that chilling fact now united them. He must warn his friend. Hopefully he could persuade him to leave the territory for a season, as he had done many years before.

Once his own family was safe, Watie set out for the north of the territory—a ride of two or two and a half days. As he went, he was welcomed into prominent Indian homes each night of his journey.

Unknown to him, however, his every step was watched by allies of Black Wolf.

Before the end of the first day word was being sent to Black Wolf's followers to meet at dawn in Cherry Tree. The assassination of Watie with his father's tomahawk would signal the beginning of the uprising. The old wise man would be next. Their scalps would ensure Black Wolf's claim to the chieftainship of the nation.

But Stand Watie also had his supporters. Getting wind of the attack, and fearing the worst, Watie saddled his fastest mount and before dawn of the second day set out. On the way he sent word to his own allies that he feared violence, and with instructions to gather at Bull Hollow.

With the war over, Richard Fitzpatrick was no longer traveling as much as he had been. Both he and Veronica had committed themselves anew to one another, and to being home together most evenings, now riding together and spending as much time with one another as possible. If they had traveling to do in the future, they would do it together.

But Veronica had changed. How much of her self-centeredness was due to the lack of integrity and character of her parents would never be known, but her recent troubles had forced her to look inside herself and she began to find a new source of strength. She had always been a strong personality but now that strength had a purpose. She could no longer content herself with sitting around the house all day, nor to looking forward to this or that social function. The looks and smiles and expressions of appreciation from the many wounded men she had ministered to, mostly in Richmond but in the wards and hospitals of Washington as well, had helped her overcome her initial squeamishness with the whole idea of being around pain and blood and death. Gradually she found rising within herself genuine compassion for the men who she realized were lonely in the midst of their suffering. And she felt a remorse, a responsibility toward them. How many of them might be here wounded because of her foolishness?

She now, therefore, was keeping as busy a daytime schedule as Richard. She had learned enough from her practical experience over the course of the year to be a genuine help to the doctors and nurses who came to depend on her as one of their regular staff.

Midway through one morning, as she was walking through the ward which had been set up at St. Joseph's Catholic school in the nation's capital, having just changed the dressings on an arm that had been amputated a month before, she was surprised to hear her name.

"Miss Veronica . . . is that you?" said a weak man's voice from somewhere in the row of beds.

Veronica stopped and turned, her eyes quickly scanning the faces, half of which had been watching her as she walked by. She saw no one she recognized.

"It's me, Miss Veronica . . . over here," said a wounded man several beds away.

Still Veronica stood with a puzzled look on her face. The man who had spoken looked to be about twenty-five or twenty-six, though the long thick, reddish beard made it difficult to tell. He looked like a mountain man from the West somewhere. There was, however, something in his voice that sounded familiar.

"It's *me*, Miss Veronica!"

Veronica approached, staring intently down into his face.

She caught her breath. "Scully . . . ?" she said questioningly. "Is that really you behind that beard?"

The smile and laugh that met her ears in reply removed all remaining doubt. "It's me, all right!"

"Scully Riggs . . . I cannot believe it!" exclaimed Veronica. "How do you come to be here? Oh, I can't believe it. It is good to see you again!" She looked around and then lowered her voice. "But . . . weren't you fighting for the South?"

She sat down on the edge of his bed, such a gracious and forgiving and compassionate smile on her face as was capable of melting all the former barriers of division between them as all barriers, one might presume, even between those from whom we are most estranged and distanced, will instantly dissolve when we greet them on the other side. Then will the venom of humanity evaporate in the sun of righteousness. Even those we despised here will in a moment become our most cherished brothers and sisters. Such it was now between Veronica and Scully. They talked and chatted as if they had been the closest of friends.

"I got through most of the war all right," said Scully. "I even got made a sergeant."

"Scully—good for you!"

"But then I got hit pretty good at Cedar Creek just last year. I was put up for a while near there somewheres, but I didn't heal up too good, so they brung me here when the war was over."

"Well I am so glad they did! I shall come and see you every day and get you back on your feet!"

"What about you, Miss Veronica?"

"I'm married," replied Veronica. "I am Veronica Fitzpatrick now."

"I heard something about that a while back. You ever go home anymore—to Dove's Landing, I mean?"

"Occasionally, though not too often."

"My dad still working at your place?"

"Yes . . . yes he is."

"Next time you see him, maybe you could tell him you seen me and that I'm okay. I never was much for letter writing."

"I will be happy to, Scully. I'm sure he will be relieved to know that you are well."

"Tell him I'll be back soon as I'm on my feet."

"Of course. Well, I had better get back to work," said Veronica, standing again. "But I will see you every day, and make sure you have whatever you need. And I will write to your father this week."

She hesitated a moment, smiled again and bent down and kissed Scully on the forehead, then continued on her way feeling strangely warmed and at peace by the encounter.

The dreadful screams in the night would surely have brought an entire village to their defense. But William Thundercloud's farm sat by itself, two miles outside Oak Hill. By the time he reached his window to look out, his barn was already aflame and the shrieks from the guesthouse where several single workers lodged had been silenced.

Thundercloud's rifle was in his hand the next instant and he bolted for the stairs, leaving his wife trembling in terror behind him. He met his twenty-three-year-old son, also with gun in hand, on the landing.

Father and son dashed down the stairs in the darkness and the older Thundercloud threw open the front door. The ghastly sight that met his eyes momentarily turned his stomach. A rider bore down upon them, flaming torch in one hand and in the other a woman's scalp still dripping with blood. Enraged fury exploded within him. His rifle was to his shoulder in an instant. Three rapid shots toppled the rider from his pony. But they were his last.

As his son followed him through the door, the silent swish of an arrow sent a razor-tipped flint thudding four inches into Thundercloud's chest. His rifle clattered to the porch as he crumpled dead at his son's feet. Two or three more shots aimed wildly at the charging war party were all the boy could get off before blood splattered from his own forehead and he fell in a heap over his father's body.

Everyone in the guesthouse was already dead. A bare-chested warrior ran forward, stepped over the two bodies, and ran into the main house. He found the widow Thundercloud, her daughter-in-law, and five-year-old grandson in their rooms screaming for mercy.

All three were lying in their own blood within a minute, and what little jewelry the two women possessed clutched within the bloody hand of their murderer.

Stand Watie had lain down to sleep exhausted on the second night of his journey at the home of a friend in Bull Hollow. In the middle of the night sudden shouts awakened him. The yelling from outside and downstairs portended danger.

While Watie struggled to come awake, his Cherokee host burst into his room. Leaping from bed in pitch blackness to defend himself, Watie realized that the man intended him no harm.

"Come . . . come quickly!" he said in Cherokee. "You must be away . . . quickly, quickly!"

When Watie hurried out into the corridor moments later, the entire household was astir. People were running everywhere and shouting. Torches lit the yard outside and the whinnying of many horses added to the tumult. Some danger was obviously upon them.

Clomping steps pounded up the stairs. Watie recognized the silhouette of two of his own men in the thin light from below.

"You must come!" said one. "Our lives are in imminent danger.

There was a bloody attack in Oak Hill. Eight people were murdered, including two women in their bedclothes and one small child."

Warrior that he was, even Watie went faint at the news.

"They thought we were there. The women's fingers were chopped off to get at their rings. Two of the men and another woman were scalped. Already Black Wolf knows his mistake. We must flee. Our horses are waiting outside."

Seventy-One

$\mathcal{F}$or days Seth Davidson had been thinking of James Waters.

Cherity's father had given him a charge to protect his daughter. In agreeing to do so, he had given James his solemn promise that he would not tell Cherity of her Cherokee past until the right time.

But would there ever be a *right* time? What if something were to happen to him? It almost had. What if he hadn't survived the train accident? Then he would have waited too long. It was true that the war was over. But life was not dependable. The entire war, climaxed by the train accident, made him aware of his own vulnerability and mortality.

Cherity was old enough to know of her heritage. Might it now be time, Seth thought, to fulfill James' wish by doing the very thing James had himself feared to do?

Should he speak with his father again? Five minutes of his father's wisdom would be a treasure indeed.

But no, this was his *own* decision to make. He must try to think what his father would say, and what counsel he would give, and then act accordingly. He must decide for himself what right in this situation truly was.

He knew what his father would say anyway: Ask God for guidance, submit your way to him, and then do what seemed the right and obedient thing to do.

All day, Seth revolved these things in his mind and prayed. The feeling grew upon him that he must talk to Cherity. Whatever hesitations and precautions her father had had about her Indian roots, Cherity was now a grown woman. She deserved to know. James had entrusted that knowledge to him. Now it seemed a time was at hand when it was no longer fair to keep her past from her.

That night after supper, Seth led Cherity outside. The warm quiet evening drew down upon them. Crickets sounded from the trees. They made their way toward the pasture where Greenwood's horses were grazing and preparing for the night.

They climbed onto the top rail of the fence, not far from the place where they had had their first conversation together many years ago.

"I told you inside that I need to have a serious talk with you," said Seth as they sat astride the fence.

"You have me worried," said Cherity.

They sat in silence for a minute or two. Seth's obviously changed demeanor began to concern Cherity all the more.

"Do you remember," Seth began slowly, "before your father died . . . when he asked to see me alone?"

Cherity nodded.

"He had some things he wanted to tell me," Seth went on, "that for reasons of his own he did not want to tell you at that time. Though he knew he was dying, there was information that . . . that he did not think would be safe for you to know."

"Safe?"

Seth nodded. "He was concerned about possible danger to you—and your sisters as well."

"What kind of danger could I possibly have been in?" asked Cherity. "What could my father have been worried about?"

"The very kind of danger that newspaper article spoke of," replied Seth. "Danger in the Cherokee nation."

Again Cherity looked at him with a puzzled expression.

"What could that possibly have to do with *me*?" she asked.

"Your father told me about his past," Seth went on. "It was a past that he kept from you and your sisters because he feared reprisals should his true identity become known to the wrong people."

"Seth, you are frightening me! What do you mean, his *true* identity? He was James Waters. Who else would he be? I mean . . . wasn't he?"

"Actually," sighed Seth, realizing he could not beat around the bush forever, "your father was *not* born as James Waters."

"What!"

"And . . . do you know *your* full name?"

"What do you mean, my full name? Of course . . . it's Cherity Michel Waters."

"Actually . . . ," said Seth slowly, "your given name is *Cherokee* Michel Waters. That's why Cherity is spelled the way it is—it is short for Cherokee."

A short gasp sounded from Cherity's mouth.

"It was your father's way," Seth continued, "of passing on a piece of his heritage to you—a heritage he feared to tell you about for exactly the reasons the man called Stand Watie told that interviewer about— the vendetta between the two factions of the Cherokee people."

"I . . . I don't understand any of this. What heritage? What could the vendetta possibly have to do with *me*?"

"You inherited it," said Seth. "At least that was your father's greatest fear. You inherited the vendetta from him. Come," said Seth, climbing down off the fence. Cherity followed. "Let's walk," said Seth, "and I will tell you everything he told me the day he died. But first I want to give you something your father gave to me for safekeeping." He pulled from his pocket a ring.

"What are you doing with Chigua's ring?"

"It isn't Chigua's—it belonged to your father."

Cherity looked even more confused.

They walked out into the evening. When they returned an hour later, walking slowly hand in hand in the darkness that had now fallen, tears were spilling down Cherity's face and her heart was full of the memory of her father and what she now knew about him. On the middle finger of her right hand she wore a solid gold signet ring of ancient kingly design.

They walked inside. Cherity immediately went to find Chigua. Without a word she embraced her.

"What is this?" asked Chigua as they fell apart and she saw Cherity's eyes, swimming in tears, gazing deeply into her own with an expression whose meaning she did not comprehend.

"I think," said Seth where he stood behind Cherity, "that she has realized that she may just have found a distant cousin."

Cherity was awake long before daybreak and out walking through the fields surrounding her beloved Greenwood.

She remained quiet all morning. Her whole life had been turned upside down by what Seth had told her. What she had always thought meant by the words *Cherity Waters* was no more. Everything was new. The old Cherity Waters had passed away, to be replaced by someone she had yet to come to know . . . someone called *Cherokee* Waters, and, from what Seth had said, maybe not even *Waters*.

The thought of the change was both exciting and fearsome. So much suddenly made sense . . . so many questions remained unanswered. And what did this ring she now wore on her finger mean for her future?

What did it *all* mean?

Every time she thought of Chigua, with her brown skin, strange new feelings of kinship swelled in her heart, not merely for Chigua herself but for an entire race of people. It was a kinship she realized she had always felt even without knowing why, from her love of horses to her fascination with the West.

Now for the first time it was truly part of her . . . or she was part of it.

Seventy-Two

Stand Watie arrived in the small village of Bluejacket without incident midway through the afternoon. He led his small party through the cluster of houses, then reined in and dismounted in front of one of the smaller among them. He waved a hand to his men and they continued around to the barn and stables behind.

He dismounted, approached the building, then ducked low and entered through the small door of the wood frame house. The very air inside was filled with solemnity. In the dim light of a fire in the hearth and one small window, only the outline of a man seated on the floor was visible in front of him. Slowly one thing, then another, came faintly into view—several skins on the floor, colored blankets hung upon the walls, spears and a bow and quiver of arrows leaning against one corner.

Watie sat down on a light tan skin, presumably deer. "It has been some time since we saw one another face to face," he said.

"I have been expecting you, my cousin," said the old man in a low and solemn voice. "A change is coming. I have sensed it."

"I only wish the circumstances were less urgent."

"The times are perilous. The end of the war has not brought resolution to the strife of the Cherokee."

"The times are more perilous than you realize. We are both in grave danger. I have come to warn you, and to urge you, if I can, to leave the

territory for a season. You must gather what you need. My men will
accompany you safely to the border. Where you go after that, it is best
I do not know."

The hint of a smile came to the old man's wrinkled lips in the dim
light.

"It is as I foresaw," he said. "The wait is over. My return is at hand."

Even as they spoke, the distant thunder of many horses could gradually be heard galloping toward them.

Stand Watie jumped up, ran to the door, and peered out. What
looked to be thirty riders were coming hard amid billowing dust and
the faint shouts of war cries.

"The danger was closer than I knew!" he said, turning hurriedly
back into the house. "They have followed us!"

"How many men do you have?" asked the old man, now also rising.

"Only four," said Watie. "We will be no match for them. Quickly—
gather what you will need and hurry to my men. They are waiting at
the stables. They will get you into the hills and away. I will go out and
keep them away as long as I can."

Watie raced outside, rifle in hand, and ran on foot toward the
approaching war party. The renowned general of the Confederacy was
about to face the most dangerous challenge of his life . . . and face it
alone. Inside the house, the old man, however, after gathering a few
things for a journey, did not, as Watie had supposed, run out to his
waiting men. Instead, he took down from the peg where he kept it an
ancient chieftain's robe of white.

Seventy-Three

*W*ith the courage of his race, Stand Watie hurried from the village, well knowing that he could be running straight into the jaws of his own death. He met the approach some hundred and fifty yards from the outer houses.

Black Wolf rode in front of the others, bare from the waist up, chest and cheeks streaked in red war paint. Watie knew immediately who he was. He had long anticipated the day they would meet again, and had silently cursed himself a dozen times for not putting a bullet between his eyes when he'd had the chance.

The young warrior reined in as dust flew about him from more than a hundred hooves, then cantered the final few yards alone, looking down upon the old chief with undisguised disdain. He pulled his horse to a stop.

"I am here for one called the wise man," he said in a commanding voice. "He is brother to the traitor Swift Water. I demand him by tribal law. His blood is forfeit for his treachery against the Cherokee nation."

"The blood for that grievance was spilled long ago, Black Wolf," said Watie calmly, addressing the young warrior by name though he knew him only by reputation.

"Not all of it!" spat Black Wolf. "There was one who fled like the coward he is. My father saw him with his own eyes. Now I demand

him in satisfaction of the ancient decree. I will show with his scalp
that the blood law must be satisfied."

"You will not lay a hand on him, Black Wolf."

"Who will stop me? I intend to kill you along with him!"

He turned to the warriors behind him. "Take him!" he commanded.

Two of them burst into a gallop, jumped from their ponies, and
grabbed Watie viciously by both arms.

By now Watie's four men, hearing the commotion, came running
from around the house. Seeing the standoff, they hurried toward the
scene, guns poised, and waited for Watie to give the order. Every one
of the four had followed him into battle wearing the Confederate gray,
on a few occasions facing worse odds than these. They would not hesitate to give their lives defending him.

But their blood would not be spilled on this day.

Before the standoff could reach its seemingly inevitable climax,
Black Wolf's eyes were diverted beyond Watie to a lone figure
approaching slowly on foot. The walker spoke briefly to Watie's men
as he passed. As he then continued on, they ran back to the stables,
mounted their horses, and then galloped back again toward the scene
of confrontation.

Black Wolf was clearly taken by surprise by their boldness. Before
he could act, Watie's men snatched their general away from his two
captors and whisked him away.

Sitting on his pony bewildered by the sudden move, Black Wolf
came to himself to see the hooves of Watie's small band disappearing
through the village into the hills beyond to the east. Some hundred
yards away, the Wise Man of the White Feather was walking alone
straight toward him. He wore the deerskin robe that had been passed
down to him, adorned with the feathers of eagles, a six-foot chieftain's
spear grasped firmly in his right hand.

Black Wolf let out a piercing shriek, and dug his heels into the flanks
of his mount. His war party followed. Within seconds more than thirty
horses bore down upon the living legacy of the Cherokee, who now
stopped and calmly held his ground as they flew toward him.

In a fury at having let Watie slip through his fingers, Black Wolf's first impulse was to send an arrow into the old fool's heart and to pound the feet of his horse straight over the top of his body.

But even as he reached for an arrow, he was restrained by an unseen hand. A silent thunder, as of many voices rising up out of antiquity, seemed to settle over the scene like an invisible cloud. But within Black Wolf son of Prowling Bear dwelt the spirit of Dragging Canoe, not that of Attacullaculla. Unnerved, therefore, but not humbled by the plea of his dead fathers, he continued to charge hard, straight toward the figure standing in his path.

At the last instant, the old man raised his spear into the air toward the charging warrior. His feet did not flinch. Black Wolf's horse shied sideways to miss him. Seconds later the following riders splintered apart and thundered past on both sides of him.

Black Wolf wheeled around to face, as he supposed, his adversary.

"Where have they gone, old man?" he yelled.

"Where you will not follow them," returned the Wise Man in a voice that echoed with quiet power.

"Tell me or you die!"

The old man's eyes bored into those of the young warrior with the commanding gaze of the Chief of the White Feather.

"You shall not leave this place in pursuit of them," he said slowly. There was no mistaking that his words were those of command. "It is time for you to lay this vendetta down."

"It will only end when you and the other traitors are dead. We represent the old ways, and we will fight to the death to preserve them."

"You know nothing of the old ways!" the Wise Man shot back, his anger rising at the presumption of one so young. You are young and foolish and see only what the rebellion in your heart wants to see. The ways of Moytoy and Attacullaculla are the old ways of peace among brothers. In the old days the red feather and white feather walked together as brothers. And so they will walk again."

He turned and gazed out upon Black Wolf's men who were slowly riding toward him in twos and threes after wheeling their mounts around. "You young warriors," he called out, "you do no honor to the Cherokee nation by following this man who would destroy all that our heritage represents. Return to your homes," he added deliberately. "Your business here is finished. There will be no killing today."

Slowly again he lifted his spear above his head toward them, whether in benediction or threat could not be said.

"Where I go, you will not follow. Now go!"

He turned and returned the way he had come. Black Wolf's men shuffled about on their horses, uncertain. Black Wolf himself sat staring at the slowly retreating figure as if in a stupor.

Gradually his men began to disband and ride off. By the time Black Wolf came to himself and succeeded in rounding up eight or ten of them to accompany him in pursuit, the old man had disappeared into the hills after Stand Watie and his small band of faithful followers.

For all his pride as a warrior, Black Wolf was a child in the ancient Indian art of tracking. By the time Watie and his cousin had rejoined and were on their way east, the small group had split apart, doubled back, laid down false tracks, reconnected and split again so many times that Black Wolf was no more successful in following them than a kitten chasing its tail. Once again he had seriously underestimated the wisdom of his Cherokee elders.

When they were safely out of Black Wolf's reach, Watie sent his men away to further obscure their trail.

"Two of you go north to the border of the territory," he said, "and two south. Hopefully they will pick up your trail and follow you. But do not let them get too close. Black Wolf remains dangerous. Then make your way back to Salisaw. I will meet you there."

Watie's four men galloped off. The rest of the way, the Confederate general and the Wise Man of the White Feather rode alone. Exactly what route they followed would have been difficult to pinpoint even with a map. Through woods and streams, up steep hills and down, backtracking, through dry riverbeds, here and there through a small canyon or ravine, up more hills and through more forests they went until finally they arrived at a farmhouse where dwelt a Watie supporter. All the way they spoke together of the old chiefs and the hopes and disappointments of their tribe.

The famous general's final tactical maneuver to get his kinsman out of Indian territory had been successfully waged.

After a few final words of farewell, Watie left the way he had come, to leave clues and markings that, if he should be followed, would lead Black Wolf on a wild goose chase back in the direction of Salisaw and the south.

Meanwhile, the old man continued his journey alone. He had much to ponder.

He crossed the border into Missouri the following day, put away the robe of the ancients in favor of the garb of the white man, and disappeared from sight.

Seventy-Four

$\mathcal{R}$ichmond Davidson left the house with a tall glass of lemonade in his hand.

The day had been a hot one. The air was still warm and sultry after seven o'clock. He and Thomas and Seth and Sydney and Isaac and Aaron and their other hired men had been at work since sunup harvesting a big crop of early summer wheat. They were all exhausted. But it felt good to bring in a crop again! And the rest of the fields were ripening well under the June sun and he had high hopes for what autumn would bring. This was one of the most pleasant times in the perpetual seasons of farming—the planting done, the crops growing, the early fields cut and in and the hope of a good harvest ahead— when Richmond took stock of his life and awaited what would come next.

God had been so good to them!

He entered the arbor, walked through the beloved pathways, and sat down on one of his favorite benches. He set the glass down beside him and drew in a long and contented sigh. He loved this season of the year when the earth produced of its bounty.

"Thank you, Lord," he whispered. "You are such a good Father to your children."

He had brought John Woolman's *Journal* with him on this quiet evening. How prophetic the old Quaker had been about slavery! How true it was that it was the slave owner himself upon which the burden of slavery fell with equal weight as upon his slaves. How he grieved for the soul of his neighbor and friend Denton Beaumont—a man at peace neither with himself nor his family, not with God nor with his place in the order of things. Ironic as he would have considered such an observation, it was Denton who was the slave. And the refusal of men such as Denton to face that terrible burden of soul, as well as to face the cruelty of owning another human being, had led to this horrible war and the division in the country.

Would the nation ever heal completely? Richmond wondered. How long would such healing take?

His thoughts turned toward Thomas who, with the summer wheat now in, planned to leave tomorrow for Mount Holly to visit Deanna and her family. He had seen a change in Thomas when they had taken Deanna home, almost from the moment they crossed into Pennsylvania. The burden of his desertion, though he had come to terms with it, never entirely left him. The mere fact of being in the South seemed to keep the memory alive. But he had sensed that his younger son was at peace in the North in a way perhaps he never could be here again.

If only the rebel Confederacy could do what the rebel Thomas Davidson had done, thought Richmond—repented and gone home and sought ways to work toward healing. Yet he feared that the Confederacy, though surrendering its arms, had not laid down its attitude of rebellion. And therefore, like in his poor neighbor, the root causes of the strife still lay beneath the surface. How long would that root of rebellion against equality fester? he wondered. And how much longer would the nation's blacks have to suffer as a result?

All through man's history, he thought, Christians had differed in the responses of their consciences to the conflicts of their times. His two sons had chosen different responses to the war, and yet had at length come to similar conclusions in the end.

He took a sip from his glass, then opened the book and fell to reading a passage in which Woolman reflected on much the same principle.

"Orders came at night to the military officers in our county," Richmond read, "directing them to draft the militia, and prepare a number of men to go off as soldiers, to the relief of the English at Fort William Henry; orders were sent to the men so chosen, amongst whom were a considerable number of our Society. My mind being affected herewith, I had fresh opportunity to see and consider the advantage of living in the real substance of religion, where practice doth harmonize with principle.

"I have been informed that Thomas à Kempis lived and died in the profession of the Roman Catholic religion; and, in reading his writings, I have believed him to be a man of true Christian spirit. All true Christians are of the same spirit, but their gifts are diverse, Jesus Christ appointing to each one his peculiar office, agreeably to his infinite wisdom.

"John Huss contended against the errors which had crept into the church. At length, rather than act contrary to that which he believed the Lord required of him, he chose to suffer death by fire. Thomas à Kempis, without disputing against the articles then generally agreed to, appears to have labored, by a pious example as well as by preaching and writing, to promote virtue and the inward spiritual religion; and I believe they were both sincere-hearted followers of Christ. True charity is an excellent virtue; and sincerely to labor for their good, whose belief in all points doth not agree with ours, is a happy state.'"

---

* From John Woolman's *Journal*, Chapter V.

Seventy-Five

*E*verything had changed for Cherity Waters. She could not fully enter into this wonderful season of harvest with the joyful abandon she once had when she had come to Greenwood with her father so long ago. Her mind and heart were too full of strange new sensations. While the others of the Greenwood family were happily talking about the day's work, her thoughts were far away. Early in the morning while the others slept, she was out walking alone. Late in the descending dusk of the summer evenings, while Seth and Sydney and the others relaxed on the porch and Richmond read his Woolman in the arbor, she often mounted Cadence and set out into the quiet hills alone.

Seth watched it all with loving patience, having some faint idea what she was going through, though knowing he could never fully enter into it with her.

When she needed him, or wanted to talk, she would tell him. Until then, he would wait.

It was early one Sunday afternoon when Cherity walked down to the LeFleure house. The work of the harvest was stilled for the day. A calm quiet lay over Greenwood. She found Sydney outside with Milos.

"Hello, Cherity," said Sydney, looking up with a smile.

"Hi, Sydney. Do you mind if I borrow Chigua for a couple of hours?"

"Not at all. She's inside with Laylie."

Cherity walked into the house. Chigua greeted her warmly.

"Would you feel like a ride today, Chigua?" asked Cherity.

"Yes, certainly."

"We need to have a long talk," said Cherity. "I want to know everything you remember—as a girl, you know, before you were taken away—as much as you can tell me of what it was like back then, what the people were like, before the Trail of Tears, and during it."

"That was so long ago," said Chigua. "My memories are distant and faint."

"I know. But I am hungry to know anything. Your memories may be the only link I have left to my father."

Chigua saw the look of entreaty on Cherity's face, then smiled. "Of course," she said. "I will tell you whatever I can . . . everything I remember. Where do you want to go?"

"There is only one place where it seems fitting to talk about the old times."

Chigua nodded. "I'll meet you up at the stables in . . . ten minutes?"

"Thank you," said Cherity. "I'll go start saddling the horses."

As Cherity walked back toward the main house, she saw Seth in the distance with Alexander where the two were training a year-old colt with a rope and halter. She hesitated a moment, then turned toward them. It was because of Seth that she knew what little she did of her heritage. If it was possible for her to learn more, she wanted him with her when she did.

The journey from the West had not been difficult in spite of his age. He had never ridden a train before and found the experience exhilarating. He had always been able to blend into his surroundings when he needed to, and he hardly attracted a second look.

Now that he was here, the past rushed back upon him like it was yesterday. He tied his horse in the rear and dismounted. What he had anticipated, he wasn't sure . . . that the house would be occupied, even perhaps torn down? But he had not expected it to be so unchanged, in such good repair, so clean. Hardly a chair or table had been moved. Yet inexplicably . . . the painting above the mantel was now bright and vivid. What could account for it?

But sacred business had brought him here. He must not tarry. He had no idea who might be the rightful owner of the place now. The passage of years and the recent war had surely changed much. Whether he would recognize the young man who had survived that fateful night so long ago was doubtful. But of one thing he was certain—if the young man was still here, and had he not found what was hidden with such care, he would not hesitate to kill to lay his hands upon it now. He had already killed once for it.

But what this traveler had come to do, he would not do in disguise, but in the dress of his people whose legacy he had come here to preserve. Dangerous though this final earthly mission might be, he would not let fear rule his steps.

He opened the carpetbag which contained his few earthly possessions of value, then slowly unbuttoned and removed the white man's shirt from his chest.

⟋⟍

As Cherity and Chigua and Seth rode up in front of the familiar house and dismounted, they had no inkling that they were not alone. They had not spoken much on the ride into the hills from Greenwood. Both Chigua and Seth sensed the solemnity of Cherity's mood.

Cherity sat a moment longer in the saddle than the others, looking about quietly, almost reverently, then climbed to the ground, tied Cadence's reins to the hitching rail, and slowly walked toward the door. Seth and Chigua followed.

Seventy-Six

Cherity stopped in her tracks before she had taken three steps inside, Seth at her side, Chigua just behind.

The unexpected stranger turned to face them. Their eyes met momentarily. He revealed nothing by his expression, only glancing down momentarily at Cherity's hand and the ring that glistened on her finger. He then looked back and forth between the three, his eyes—indeed, his entire expression—full of mystery. His gaze penetrated their very depths. As they became accustomed to the thin light inside the house, they were able to observe his features.

His dark face, wrinkled with years, bore the characteristics of leather, hardened and cracked in the sun. It was a strong, expressive face, with high prominent cheekbones, piercing black eyes, a straight nose, slightly wide in the nostrils but well shaped above a wide mouth. His lips remained closed, revealing little, though were downturned at the ends reflecting the sadness he felt for the fate of his once proud nation. Despite his years, his hair was plentiful with the hue of a rich brownish gray. Two thick braids fell across the front of his ears down below his shoulders to his chest. A small cluster of short fine white feathers adorned the back of his head. A tight beaded necklace circled his neck, from which hung two claws of what must once have been a giant eagle. He was clad in a brown leather tunic, fringed at the sleeves and neck. The mere sight of the man, though simple and of a world and time fading into the bygone mists of history, was august and imposing.

Cherity was the first to find her voice.

"Who are . . . what are you doing here?" she asked in surprise.

"I did not know who might now be the owner of this place," the old man replied. His voice, though gravelly with age, was firm with calm authority. "The door was unlocked and I entered."

Now Seth spoke.

"This house belonged to a friend of my grandfather's," he said.

"Who was this . . . friend?" asked the man.

"I did not know him, sir. He disappeared many years ago. Not knowing his true name, my grandfather had no way to make inquiries. My father has been keeping the house and its land for him ever since. That is the reason it is not locked."

"Why does he keep it?" asked the stranger.

"Because he did not feel it rightfully his," replied Seth. "My grandfather retained it unchanged, as has my father, in hopes that some claim would one day be made upon it by the man's posterity."

The faintest hint of a smile crept to the man's lips. "It is no more than I should have expected. You remind me of your grandfather."

"I'm sorry . . . ," began Seth, "I am afraid I don't understand."

"And you, young lady," said the man, turning toward Cherity, "you possess your father's eyes. They are the eyes, as we would say, of a beloved woman among our people."

Cherity stared back as perplexed as Seth. Then the old man looked deeply at the face of Chigua. "You carry the sorrow of our people in your spirit," he said.

"I am still confused," said Seth. "What are you doing in Mr. Brown's house?"

Once more silence followed. Then again the man spoke.

"Young Davidson . . . I *am* Brown."

Seth and Cherity and Chigua gasped in a single breath. Their eyes widened in speechless astonishment.

"And in fact," the old man went on. "Brown *is* my true surname. At birth I was given the name Long Canoe by my mother Nakey Canoe, daughter of Dragging Canoe, son of the great chief of our people, the Chief of the White Feather Attacullaculla, who is my great-grandfather. My mother married a white man called Alexander Brown. I am, therefore, Long Canoe Brown."

Seth's brain was spinning. He could not believe what he was hearing!

The old man looked toward Cherity. "Though you do not know me, young lady," he said, "the moment I laid eyes on you, I knew you. Unless I mistake, you are the daughter of a certain man from Boston known as James Waters."

Cherity nodded.

"Your father was my nephew," the old Cherokee went on to Cherity. "How much of your father's history you may be familiar with, I do not know. His given name was Swift Horse Brown, son of my brother Swift Water Brown and your grandmother Rose Blossom."

"I had a grandmother called . . . *Rose Blossom?*" said Cherity with awe in her voice.

"Indeed you did. When my brother was killed in the treacherous conflicts that consumed our people early in this century, I escaped with his son, my nephew, your father, and left North Carolina in order to protect our lives and, I hoped, the heritage we represented. The year was 1819. Young Swift Horse was twelve. We fled north, I to Virginia where I purchased this land and built this house and went by the name Brown. I enrolled Swift Horse in a boarding school in Boston where I listed his family name as Water after his father, and called him *James*. Somehow the family name became *Waters*. You are my great-niece. You too are in the line of your great-great-great-grandfather, Chief Attacullaculla. Nakey Canoe was your great-grandmother."

Cherity found her way to a chair and sat in stunned silence. She had still only begun to absorb what Seth had told her a few days ago. Now this wise man was telling her that she was in the line of a chief!

Seth beckoned Chigua forward. "This is our friend Chigua," he said. "She also is Cherokee. She and her family found their way to us on the Underground Railroad and have been at Greenwood ever since. She was on the Removal Trail but was captured by Seminoles on the way."

"Ah, I am sorry, my daughter. You must tell me all. Of what family do you come?"

"My grandfather was Eaglefeather," replied Chigua softly, as awed by the man's presence as was Cherity.

"Eaglefeather! Then you are from the Kingfisher and Harlan line."

He paused and stared at Chigua intently. "I remember you," he said slowly, "though you have changed from the little girl of my memory."

"You were on the Trail?" said Chigua in a voice of astonishment.

"I was," nodded Brown. A look of pain passed over his features. Then he motioned for them to sit.

Seth and Chigua joined Cherity and took chairs beside her in Brown's former home.

"Cherity only recently learned of her Cherokee roots," said Seth to Brown. "We came here today, to your house, to learn more, if we could, from Chigua about her past and the removal from the East. But they . . . all of us, would be eager to learn whatever *you* might want to tell us."

"I see. But, if you could answer me one question, young Davidson . . . my friend, your grandfather, you say, Grantham Davidson, had two sons. One left for England and the other, the elder who remained, died . . . I believe, an untimely death. He had no sons I do not think. How do *you* then come to be here?"

"My father is Richmond Davidson," Seth replied. "He returned to Virginia from England after my uncle's death."

"Ah," said Brown, nodding, then turned toward Cherity. "How much did your father explain to you?" he asked.

"Nothing at all, Mr. Brown," she replied. "He died four years ago, almost exactly as the war was breaking out."

"Ah, I am deeply sorry to hear of it. I had hoped that someday it might be possible to see him again. I am truly sorry."

"I knew nothing about my Cherokee roots," Cherity went on. "What little I know he told Seth, who only told me recently. My father was concerned for my safety."

"As he well should have been."

The house fell silent. At last Brown also sat down. The four remained in deep contemplation for several minutes.

"Then let me tell you . . . both of you young women," said Brown at length, looking first to Cherity, then to Chigua, "about the Ani-Yunwiya—the people who are your people."

He paused. His eyes narrowed slightly and seemed to gaze far into the distant past.

"The story of our people began," he went on, "with the ancient great man of the Great Telliquo in the region of the waters of the Tannassy. His name was Moytoy and his woman's name was Quatsy. From their seed you both have sprung. . . ."

As they listened, Cherity and Chigua were transported back, not mere years, but generations, indeed centuries, to a time and place and culture that existed before the eyes of any white man beheld the wonders of a land that had been the birthright of the Ani-Yunwiya already longer than memory.

An hour went by, then two, as if they had been mere moments. They sat listening to the voice as of wisdom itself tell of the ancient times and then of the coming of the Spaniards and the English and the French, and of the great Chief of the White Feather and of Nanye'hi Ward, the Ghigua from whom Chigua had derived her name, and then of his own forebears of the Canoe line.

"Then came a day," he went on, "when a child was born to Nakey Canoe. The moment she saw him, aging Nanye'hi Ward knew that it would be through him that she would fulfill her pledge to Chief Attacullaculla. She kept the secret of his legacy in her heart, and the secret of the rings in an ancient hiding place of the Cherokee, high on the sacred mountain where she was certain they would not be found. The words the great Attacullaculla had spoken on the mountain had long remained with her: 'You must pass on the legacy as I am passing it on to you . . . to one who will preserve the heritage and will treasure the unity of our people.'

"Ever since that day, Nanye'hi listened to the young boy's every

word as he grew into manhood. Much had changed among our
people. His brother Swift Water took Rose Blossom as his wife and
became one of those who urged our kinsmen to sell their land while
there was still time to profit by it. But speaking out placed him in
great danger with those who intended to stop westward migration.

"Secretly Swift Water confided to me his intention to take his wife and
son, Swift Horse, your father," he added, turning to Cherity, "to Arkansas
when the time was right. I tried to dissuade him, knowing of the blood
law and that there could be reprisals. But his mind was made up.

"A day arrived when aging Nanye'hi appeared at our home in her
finest deerskin robe and the same feathers in her hair she had worn on
the similar sacred occasion so many years ago. She gazed at me as if
piercing my very soul with her deep black eyes and said she must talk
to me . . . alone . . . on the mountain.

"We left the town together on horseback. The eyes of our friends
and neighbors followed us with curiosity. Nanye'hi led the way up
the familiar trail to the top of Ooneekawy Mountain. Not a word was
spoken between us. We stopped at the summit of the sacred mountain, and dismounted from our horses.

"'I too was brought to this place, though I was older than you
are now,' Nanye'hi told me. 'I was brought here by the great chief
Attacullaculla, your own great-grandfather, and told many things about
the heritage of our people. That is why I have brought you here, because
I have chosen you to pass on what was given to me. I have chosen you,
Long Canoe, to preserve a sacred and secret legacy of our people.'

"'What legacy, Nanye'hi?' I asked.

"'This legacy,' she replied, holding up her thumb.

"'Your ring?'

"'It is not merely a ring—it is one of the sacred council rings that
came from the king across the water, a lasting symbol of peace and the
unity of our people. Now come, there is more I have to show you.'

"She led the way to a great oak about three hundred yards from the
summit.

"'You see this mark where the bark has swollen around the cut of the knife. I enscribed my own sign here thirty-eight years ago as a marker. You know the secret of the triangles. This oak is the first of the three corners. To find the location of the secret, you must find the other two corners, then, with the midpoints of each line joining them, locate the center. That is where I will take you now.'

"She led the way a little further pausing often to glance at the tree trunks around them. I followed, noting carefully the signs carved on the trees.

"Within minutes we approached the center. The roar of a waterfall became audible and I saw the falls. The cascade poured over the lip of the rock and fell twenty feet before descending to the valley. A cave was hidden in the rock behind the falls. We entered from behind a pile of boulders which would have been impossible to find without knowing the center of the triangle. We crouched low as we went, and finally Nanye'hi stopped and handed the torch to me. She removed one large rock from the wall, and thrust her hand into a cavity in the wall. When she removed her hand she held a small deerskin pouch.

"She turned to me, took one of my hands, then opened the pouch and into it poured five rings of pure gold.

"'The council rings!' I exclaimed. 'I thought they were a legend.'

"Nanye'hi's eyes grew even more serious. 'You must learn to understand what the rings mean, Long Canoe,' she said. 'You must protect what they symbolize, and, as I have done, when your own time comes, pass them on so that the legacy will be preserved. When you are old, it will be you who will preserve the legacy of the rings, and who will preserve the heritage of our people.'

"Not long thereafter, Swift Water came to me late one night to tell me that he had sold his house and was preparing to move west. But the retribution fell swiftly upon him. Only three nights later I awoke suddenly. Terrible sounds had disturbed my sleep. I jumped from bed and rushed into the night. In the distance flames leapt high into the blackness. I knew it was my brother's home. I ran toward it. Halfway there, I suddenly stopped. A voice was calling me.

"'Uncle . . . Uncle!'

"I ran to the edge of the wood. There stood twelve-year-old Swift Horse, trembling in terror.

"'You know my house, Swift Horse,' I said. 'Run to it . . . run now. The door is open. You will be safe there until I return. Go . . . go now. I will see to your father and mother.'

"The boy dashed off through the night. I continued toward the blaze, fearing the worst.

"By the time I reached it, the house was engulfed in flame, surrounded by a band of six warriors.

"'Is this your idea of justice!' I cried angrily.

"'He sold the house to the white man,' replied the leader of the group. 'He was a traitor. This is the penalty as demanded by ancient law.'

"'You are murderers!' I cried tears rising in my eyes at the horror before me.

"I felt hands on my shoulders. It was my friend Eaglefeather," he added, glancing at Chigua. "He was gently pulling me away from the fray, for he knew my efforts were no use.

"'Come, Long Canoe,' he said. 'You must leave this place. This battle is lost. We must win peace in another way. My family is not involved, but now you are. You will never be safe here again. You must disappear.'

"I clasped my friend one last time arm in arm, then turned and ran away to my own house. I had no time to waste. My first thought was for the safety of my nephew, and also of my sacred vow to the Ghigua. I knew I must protect our heritage, and protect my suddenly orphaned nephew. Who could tell what might be his destiny one day, or that of one of his offspring. He must be protected from those who would kill him as Swift Water's son.

"Two hours later, while darkness still covered the land, the man and boy, my nephew and I, made our way on horseback away from the land our people had possessed for more generations than any of their wisest men now remembered.

"I knew we must travel far beyond the borders of the Cherokee and keep our identity hidden. Surely the assassins would not soon forget either the son or the brother of Swift Water, or, as it now turns out, even his posterity.

"I knew your grandfather well, my child," he said, looking at Chigua. "He was a fine man and grieved the rest of his life for you. I recall vividly the day you and your sisters were taken and your grandfather's bitter tears. We all mourned with him."

A deep silence fell and lasted several minutes.

"When years after my escape with Swift Horse," Brown resumed at length, "the conflicts of the 1830s consumed our people, I knew I could stay away no longer. I had a good life in Virginia, among people I considered friends, most of all your grandfather Davidson," he said, turning toward Seth. "But to me had been entrusted the five rings from Nanye'hi, the Beloved Woman of the Cherokee. And when our lands were taken and our people were doomed to be removed from what land remained, the spirit of the white feather filled me. I knew I must return to my people and be a voice for peace, as Chief Attacullaculla and Nanye'hi would have wanted. For such they entrusted me with this ring."

He pulled from somewhere in the folds of his tunic a ring identical to Cherity's that hung from a chain around his neck that they had hardly noticed before, a chain of pure gold.

He glanced toward Cherity, then Chigua.

"The ring you are wearing is of the seven, Miss Waters, from your father which I gave to him. And you, young daughter of Eaglefeather, is it too much to hope that you may once also have been in possession of a similar ring—the one I have not been able to account for all this time, that of the Ghigua herself, passed through her daughter Cata'quin Harlan?"

Chigua pulled out a ring identical to the other two which had been hanging from a leather strip around her own neck. For the first time they saw the Cherokee Wise Man register unconcealed surprise as he gasped in astonishment.

"However were you able to conceal it during the years of your captivity?" he exclaimed.

"You must meet my husband," smiled Chigua. "Were it not for him, both the ring and I am sure my very life, would have been lost."

"Then the Cherokee owe him a great deal."

"As do I."

"The sacred trust we three share is thus greater even than I suspected—three of the rings together again at last, and worn by their rightful descendents. Surely this is a fortuitous time for our people."

Again Brown paused briefly, then continued with his story, turning toward Cherity.

"When I knew that I must return to my people, I first sojourned north to see your father one last time. I left him a letter detailing much of what I have told you today," he added, glancing with question toward Cherity as if to ask if she knew whether it had survived her father's death.

Cherity shook her head. "He did not show such a letter to me," she said. "I know nothing of it."

"He gave me the letter," interjected Seth, glancing between Brown and Cherity. "It is in my father's safe," he added, glancing toward Cherity with a smile. "I have been waiting for the right time to give it to you."

"From Boston," Brown went on, "I returned briefly through Virginia and back to my people in North Carolina. I put a white feather in my hair on that day and have not ceased to wear it since. I knew it was time to fulfill that which Nanye'hi had spoken of to me.

"I could not, however, identify myself as Long Canoe Brown without raising many questions and endangering others besides myself. It was best that my identity remain unknown until the times of danger were past. I had hoped such a time would have come long before now. It was my wish to have seen your father again, daughter of Swift Horse. I have thought of him nearly every day of my life. Yet it appears that for all my efforts toward peace and reconciliation, the animosity within the tribe remains as great as ever. Therefore, as your father's identity was kept secret, so too has mine these many years. My appearance again in North Carolina as a man already gaining in years caused more than a few questions. But I took care not to settle among my own kinsmen and kept mostly to myself. People gradually assumed me to be a widower from some other part of the tribe. The only one who knew my true identity was Degodoga, he known as Stand Watie."

"Why did you not come back until now?" asked Seth.

"That is a question even I cannot answer," said Brown thoughtfully. "The time was not right. Persecution and treachery were rampant. Nor was travel as easy then as it is today. No trains connected the territory with the East. The Removal Trail was a gruesome ordeal and thousands starved to death before my eyes. I was not anxious to make such a journey again. Gradually the years crept up behind me.

"Even during my years in Virginia, I suspected that my movements might have been known. Long after arriving in the Indian Territory I heard rumors, through those I was in contact with, that told me that others knew that Swift Horse was still alive and had offspring who would, with him, inherit the vengeance of the blood law. Your life," he added, glancing toward Cherity, "was in danger more than your father realized. That is another reason I did not return. I did not want to run the risk of bringing that danger upon others. What can you tell me of your mother and sisters?"

"My mother died when I was born," answered Cherity. "My two sisters are both married and have families. But why would someone like me be in danger?" she asked.

"Probably because of me," answered Brown. "Rumors have circulated for years about wealth stolen from the tribe. Those rumors came to be associated with your father, when in fact they were a mingling of many rumors, with a germ of truth at its center that had more to do with me than him. For indeed when I lived here I did possess a certain amount of gold that had been taken from our lands."

Cherity drew in a sharp breath and glanced at Seth with an expression that said, *I told you so!*

"Does this have anything to do with it?" said Seth. From a pocket

in his coat he pulled out a piece of a torn map that he had brought
with him.

Brown smiled. Another long silence followed.

"It is a portion of a map in my own hand," he said at length. "I drew
it prior to leaving this place. It is in the old Cherokee triangle code. I
presume it is the portion I gave to your grandfather many years ago."

"Actually . . . no," said Seth with a confused expression. "This
is from what Cherity's father gave me for safekeeping. I planned to
show it to Cherity here today. I never knew anything about my father
having something like this."

"But he does!" exclaimed Cherity. "Or at least he does now!"

"What do you mean?" asked Seth.

"Mr. Beaumont had it," she said. "I found him with it here at the
Brown house." She looked toward Mr. Brown, suddenly realizing how
different it now sounded to call it that. "But I grabbed it and took it
to your father. He said he would keep it safe until more was known,
but that we should keep quiet about it. I assumed he told you about it.
And all along you had a piece too, from *my* father!"

Brown's brow clouded as he listened. "And this one you call
Beaumont, he would be the son of my former neighbor, Giles
Beaumont?"

Seth nodded.

"I remember him as a lad," said Brown. "Your father had an older
brother . . . and the two were inseparable friends."

"Yes, my uncle Clifford. He was killed almost exactly the same time
you disappeared—thrown from a horse it was assumed. It is a mystery
that has remained unsolved all these years, along with your disappearance . . . until now. At least one of them is cleared up. I cannot wait to
tell my father about you. He will be so anxious to see you!"

"And I him. I have much to thank him for."

Brown was pensive and thoughtful for several seconds.

"How did this man Beaumont get the piece of map you found him
with, Miss Waters," he mused, "when I gave it to your grandfather,
unless . . ." his voice trailed off.

"Well, he doesn't have it now!" said Cherity. "I made sure of that."

Brown listened with interest, then rose, went to his carpetbag, and produced another bit of yellowed paper with similar lines and markings.

"As you no doubt realized," said Brown, "these were pieces from a larger, more complete map. By it I meant to hide much that had been entrusted to me. I drew the map, then went to see your grandfather. I gave him a third and took a third to Swift Horse in Boston. That was before you were born, Miss Waters, but I did know of your two sisters. I kept this third portion of the map myself. It was my way to ensure that what I had hidden would never be found unless there was a coming together of all three. Even then, as we now see, rumors somehow got out about what I possessed."

"But what is it?" asked Cherity. "What is it that you hid?"

"What do you know of the Cherokee gold?" asked Brown.

Cherity again glanced at Seth.

"Only that gold was discovered on Cherokee lands in 1828, I think it was," he said, "and that much of what the Cherokee had unearthed and mined of it was hidden in caves before the removal to the West to keep it from being stolen."

Brown nodded. "You are very well informed."

"Much was explained to me by Cherity's father," answered Seth.

"Some felt," Brown went on, "that the gold would provide the opportunity to build our nation again, *if* it could be preserved. Of course I had been long away from North Carolina when the main reserves of gold were discovered."

He paused thoughtfully, again allowing his mind to drift back through time.

"Then came a night, here in this very house, when it was clear that our people would be removed from the lands of our posterity. It was 1833. Four leaders of our tribe came to see me in secret—the only four who knew of my identity and whereabouts. Degodoga and his brother Kilakeena and Kahnungdatlegeh and his son Shahtlelohskee. They told me of their decision to form a new Treaty party among the

Cherokee, as well as to discuss my hiding what gold and other tribal treasures they might safely manage to get to me.

"Throughout the following year there were more visits. Much gold indeed was brought here for safekeeping. Yet as I said, soon I knew that I must return to my people for the times were troublesome. Even then I suspected that I was being watched. I hid the gold and recorded my movements with an extensive map which I tore in thirds, knowing that the gold would rest forever unfound until either I returned for it myself, or until all three portions of the map were brought together again by those I would entrust with them.

"Then I left it to fate and both the Davidson and Waters posterity to discover that which could only be discovered should a divine hand drive events toward a common center. It would seem that such a time has indeed come."

On the floor before them, Brown now set the two torn portions of the paper he had drawn over thirty years before them side by side. "If indeed your father possesses the final third, young Davidson, I think you will discover that it completes the drawing precisely."

"Oh, oh—just look!" exclaimed Cherity. "The markings are just like on the skin painting over the mantel. And—"

Suddenly she glanced toward Chigua whose eyes were also riveted on the two pieces of paper.

"We have seen these marks before!" said both women in unison.

"Where?" said Seth.

"There is one on a tree," replied Cherity.

"And another on a rock beside the opening to a cave!" added Chigua.

Even stoic Long Canoe Brown now began to chuckle at their enthusiasm. "Perhaps you will not need my map," he said, "and did not need me to return at all, to find what was hidden. Yet I suspect that you may need it in the end."

"Let's go get the third piece from Mr. Davidson!" said Cherity, excitedly jumping up.

"Don't forget, Cherity," said Seth, "the house and this land, and everything on and in it, belong again to Mr. Brown. They are his treasures to decide what to do with."

"Of course, I'm sorry," said Cherity, turning to Mr. Brown. "I was just excited."

Again Brown laughed. "Think nothing of it, my child," he said. "I am delighted at your enthusiasm. But my thoughts remain on the man Beaumont. I know something about him that gives me cause for grave concern. Before anything more is done, we must seek other wise counsel. It is time I met with your father, young Davidson."

Seventy-Seven

When Richmond Davidson, who happened to be outside, saw
the slow approach of the four riders descending out of the woods
toward Greenwood, whether he suspected the full truth or not, he was
certainly arrested in midstride by the imposing sight. Beside his son
rode a man of many years, of darkened and weathered skin, in the full
garb of an Indian. It was to see a phantom-dream come to life before
his very eyes. He stood and waited, mesmerized.

By the time the riders had drawn within a hundred yards, he recognized the man with Seth well enough. The enigmatic Cherokee had
seemed old to Richmond as a young man, and after both of them had
left Dove's Landing he had never allowed himself to imagine that he
would see him again in this life.

A sharp intake of breath was the only sign of his momentary amazement, then a great smile spread across his face and he strode out to
meet them.

"It's Mr. Brown, Dad!" called Seth. "Mr. Brown has come back!"

It would be impossible to say which of the two venerable men was
most moved by the encounter. The four horses drew in. Brown sat
a moment simply gazing down at the son of his friend Grantham
Davidson, now a man himself. A solitary tear stole down his cheek
and he climbed wearily down from the back of the horse.

The two wise men, each revered with greatness in their respective cultures by those capable of perceiving true greatness, stood for a moment simply gazing upon one another with full hearts, then slowly embraced.

"On behalf of my father, who loved you like a brother," said Richmond softly, "and for myself and my whole family . . . welcome back to Greenwood. We have longed for this day."

"Thank you, young Davidson," said Brown in a husky voice more full of emotion than is customary for a Cherokee to show. "You *are* your father . . . as your son is you. I see more clearly than ever that I did not mistake many years ago in leaving all in his hands."

They fell apart, gazed into one another's eyes a moment longer, then Richmond turned back toward the house.

"Come," he said, placing a hand on Brown's shoulder. "I want you to meet my wife and Seth's brother. Then I want to hear all—all that you are at liberty to tell me."

A blanket of solemnity and antiquity hung over Greenwood. Everything seemed to grow quiet out of respect for their honored visitor. The muscles and machinery of work stilled. Even the animals, the birds, the very air itself grew calm.

Richmond was most interested in Brown *the man,* and in the aging Cherokee's relationship with his father and what he could reveal about Greenwood during the critical years of his own absence in England. The two men walked and talked late into their first night together. It being well after midnight before they began to think of retiring, Brown consented to spending the night in one of the guest rooms at Greenwood. The next day resumed according to much the same pattern. After breakfast the two were out walking in the arbor together, and so it continued. As Brown began to speak of returning to his own former home for the duration of his visit, however, Richmond's countenance darkened and he sought to dissuade him.

"You can see that we have ample room for many guests," he said. "Your presence here has been a great boon to everyone's spirits. And to be entirely candid, there are other reasons that I would prefer you not to stay up there alone. I have cause to be concerned for your safety."

Brown nodded seriously. Then followed a lengthy discussion about much that Richmond had long suspected concerning events surrounding Brown's abrupt disappearance from Virginia many years before.

But Richmond did not occupy *all* of Brown's waking hours. The young women who represented the posterity of two of the four major Cherokee lineages, and Cherity as the daughter of his own nephew with whom he had fled North Carolina, were much on the old man's heart. It did not take long for deep bonds of filial affection to develop between the two girls and he who became for them a beloved grandfather. Between Brown and Chigua, possibly because she had been part of the removal and for so many years known no blood family at all and because he had known her grandfather, the connection became like one of true family.

Cherity, however, as intrigued and curious as she was about her Cherokee roots, was nearly beside herself wondering when Richmond and Mr. Brown would get around to the missing portion of the map!

At long last Richmond and Brown began to discuss one of the primary reasons for Brown's return, the retrieval of those Cherokee artifacts and treasures that had been removed from North Carolina for safekeeping prior to what was now called the Trail of Tears. One of the factors in Brown's hesitation was the simple fact, given the ongoing conflict within the tribe, that he did not yet know what was best to be done to preserve that legacy for the future.

"Uncle Long Canoe," said Cherity one evening, her patience at last overflowing, "could we go up and look for what is hidden on your land—Seth and Chigua and I? I remember what you said, but we have two thirds of the map."

A thin smile creased the lips of the wise old Cherokee.

"You could never find it without the entire map," he said. "The triangle drawings with their dots and lines cannot be interpreted unless you know what you are looking for. You will need the final third."

"Is it all right if we *try?*"

"To find the center of the triangle, as Nanye'hi did behind the water-fall on the top of Ooneekawy, requires all three points. They may each be marked such that the unseeing eye never recognizes them at all. And do not forget," he added with the hint of a humorous grin, "I devised their locations myself just so that people like you would *not* find them."

He saw disappointment begin to creep over Cherity's normally cheery face.

"But I understand your eagerness," he went on. "I too was once young. So perhaps it is indeed time to place all three portions of the map together again and see what you can do with it."

An excited walk to Richmond's office followed. A few minutes later, for the first time since the night he had bade farewell to Richmond's father in 1834, all three portions of the map he had drawn that day again were placed together on Richmond's desk.

A lengthy explanation then took place, Brown showing them place after place on the reassembled paper that they recognized from his descriptions, telling them what to look for. As Cherity listened, she looked up at Chigua—they knew where two of the triangle's three corners were located.

The next morning, Seth and Cherity were out early saddling their horses.

"Where are you two off to?" asked Carolyn when they came in for an early breakfast before setting out.

"Up to the Brown tract!" replied Seth. "Now that we know where to look, we want to see if we can decipher Mr. Brown's markings."

"I'll run down to Sydney and Chigua's," said Cherity. "Chigua is coming with us."

An hour later the three adventurers, along with Thomas, were on their way up the ridge. Brown and Richmond watched them go, Brown with an indulgent fatherly smile at their determination to make the attempt without him.

"How long will you allow them to search without coming to their aid?" asked Richmond.

"They will find the opening," replied Brown. "If they are patient, I do not think I will need to assist them at all. I have given them all the information they need."

Thirty minutes later, with the three segments of the completed map laid out before them on the table of Long Canoe Brown's house, the two young Davidsons and the two Cherokee women were confident that at last the remaining mysteries of Mr. Brown's tenure in Virginia decades before were about to be solved.

Excitedly Cherity and Chigua showed Seth and Thomas the tree Cherity had discovered with the markings carved in its bark, and the stone near the cave mouth that Deanna had seen, both of which they had been puzzling over ever since. Now that they knew what they were looking for, they were clearly visible on two of the three portions of the torn map, and corresponded exactly to Brown's description. But the third set of symbols they would never have guessed, even with the map, had Brown not told them where to look.

The location of the third point of the triangle, as the basis for the cleverly devised Cherokee map, was inside the very house that had always been at the center of the mystery. For years they had been carved on the wall above the fireplace behind the skin painting.

With the completed map before them and knowing all three points of the triangle—the tree, the rock at the cave mouth, and the hearth inside the house—according to Brown's instructions they set about carefully walking off and measuring a straight line between each of the three. It was difficult to do over hilly and sloping terrain, in a wood full of trees, and with half a mile between points. They then had to accurately calculate the midpoint of each line. From these three points, the three lines to the opposite corners should precisely intersect at the exact center of the triangle. There, Brown said, if they had done everything correctly, they would find a small and unremarkable pile of stones, no doubt long grown over with moss and grass and leaves and brush. Those stones, he said, were but the top of a great many stones that had taken him a year to carry to the site as he had filled in and buried from view a small opening about two feet in diameter—an opening that was in fact one end of a small tunnel into a much larger cave in the side of the hill. The opening was so small that it could only be entered by crawling on one's hands and knees and belly, but, inside, it gradually opened wider. He had always suspected, Brown said, that it connected with other caves along the ridge, but he had not ventured all the way to the end of each of its labyrinth of tunnels. The large room near the opening he had discovered had suit his purpose and he had been satisfied with it. There he had hidden the relics of his people before blocking up the entry with hundreds of heavy stones, which he then covered over with dirt. It would never be found without knowing the precise place to look, which would be impossible to find without knowing the three corners of the cunningly conceived triangle.

Seventy-Eight

$\mathcal{A}$fter the four treasure hunters rode up the hill toward the Brown tract, and leaving Brown himself in conversation with Carolyn and Sydney, Richmond Davidson rode out of Greenwood in another direction.

His errand on this day, perhaps even more unpleasant than his previous visit to his neighbor, would again take him to Oakbriar. He had been praying for months for guidance how to handle what he had surmised and now knew about the events of that fateful night of so many years before. Mr. Brown's disclosure gave the final confirmation that his suspicions had been correct.

Richmond was a man who neither sought nor shrunk from confrontation. Believing in unity as one of the highest principles in the universe, he was intrinsically always looking for points of commonality and brotherhood in every human relationship and endeavor. Yet the commonality he sought was a brotherhood based in truth. And compromise of truth he hated almost as much as disunity within God's true family of believers. So when he felt he must stand for truth, and against untruth, he would stand.

What to do in this present case had caused him no little uncertainty. Was his a wider obligation than to the truth alone? Or did he have a civic responsibility to discharge in the matter?

In the end, he had decided that he must only stand with God and with truth, and attempt to awaken something in the man's conscience, but that accountability beyond that lay in God's hands to attend to, not his. If the kingdom of his master was not of this world, then he would seek no retribution according to the world's laws. God would have an eternity to see to what needed seeing to. He would only hope to open a few inner doors in the direction of that eternal healing in the here and now.

Richmond rode up to Oakbriar with a calm and determined heart. He well knew that this might be his final exchange with a man he had known all his life. That possibility made him mindful of how fleeting life truly is, and how rapidly it sped by. He prayed this might be the beginning of a season of renewal between them. Veronica's changed character was nothing short of miraculous. Why not also her father? Yet Richmond's expectations were realistic. He could only do what God had shown him to do, and leave the rest to the Spirit who quickens the hearts of men toward their heavenly Father.

He was shown by Jarvis upstairs into Denton Beaumont's study. The cloud on his neighbor's face did not bode well.

"Good morning, Denton," said Richmond cheerfully, extending his hand. "Thank you for seeing me."

"I should have thought after our last conversation that you would not have been eager to show yourself here again anytime soon."

"We are neighbors, Denton. How are things going this season?"

"Wyatt is back and helping some, though I remain short of men."

"Any word from Cameron? I understand he has still not returned."

"No, nothing."

"Well, we are all planted and have harvested one field of early wheat. If I could send a crew of men over to help you with anything, I would be happy to do so . . . with no obligation, of course."

Beaumont nodded but offered no reply.

"What I came to talk with you about," Richmond went on in a serious tone, "was to ask if you had given more thought to our previous discussion, and whether you have any further response?"

"I have thought about it," answered Beaumont, "and am more

convinced than ever that you have no right to interfere in my affairs. Do you actually have the gall to do so again?"

"I believe they are equally my affairs as yours . . . or if not mine, then God's."

"Bah! There you go again with your holier-than-thou claptrap! If they are God's, then they are none of yours!"

"Then let me simply put it to you calmly and directly, Denton," said Richmond. "I ask not only for myself, but on behalf of God too, whose children we are—did you kill my brother Clifford?"

The sudden directness of the question took Beaumont momentarily off guard. But only momentarily.

"How dare you make such an accusation!" he said angrily.

"I make no accusation, Denton, I merely pose it as a question."

"I take it your mind is already made up," rejoined Beaumont. "What good would it do for me to deny it?"

"Probably none."

"There, you see!" retorted Beaumont. "You are prejudiced against me before even giving me the chance to defend myself!"

"There was a witness, Denton. I have it on his words. I only want to hear it from your own lips."

"What witness, for God's sake?" exploded Beaumont. "There was no one within—"

He stopped abruptly, realizing what he had done.

"Who is this so-called witness?" he shot back. "I don't believe you for an instant. These are just more of your lies."

"I have never told you a lie in my life, Denton."

"Yes, and you are our resident saint, no doubt! I ask you again, who is the witness?"

"Mr. Brown."

"He wasn't anywhere near here. Everyone knows he had disappeared long before."

"He came back, that same night."

"How do you know all this? The old fool hasn't been seen or heard from in years."

"Until recently," replied Richmond." He just returned from the Oklahoma Territory. He and I have had a long talk about many things."

The news seemed to sober Beaumont. But only briefly.

"And what of it?" he said after a moment. "Everyone knows the Indians are liars. He always had it out for me."

"Denton, listen to yourself!" implored Richmond sadly. "He had no reason to have it out for you, and no reason to lie about what he saw and heard."

"Then why would he make up such a preposterous story!"

"Why indeed? The logical explanation is that he did not make it up."

"It is obvious that you believe him. Why should I try to defend myself? You would not believe me anyway. So what do you intend to do—press charges, turn me in . . . you will never prove a thing against me, Richmond."

"I have no desire to turn you in. Proving anything against you is not my intent, Denton."

"Then why in God's name are you here?" roared Beaumont, rising from his chair in a fury.

"I am here in God's name, as you say, Denton, to implore you to make a clean breast of it, to repent and cry out to your Father in heaven to forgive you. I beseech you to make yourself right with God, Denton, for your own sake, not for mine . . . not because anyone is going to turn you in, not for any reason but that you have sinned against God, and against one of his own, a precious one of his children, your own dear friend. How long must this go on, Denton? When will you make it right and ask your Father to make you clean and whole, that you might become his son?"

"Sinned, Richmond! You sound like a puritanical hellfire preacher! Would you turn my study into an altar? Repent . . . by God! Get out and do your worst! Take your story to the authorities if you want, but I will listen to no more of it. I will see the flames of hell lapping around me before I will repent on your orders! Get out, Richmond— I never want to see your face here again!"

With a depth of sadness such as he had never known, Richmond closed his eyes for a moment, then rose and left. No more words were ever spoken between the two men.

Beaumont sat down at his desk, trembling passionately, his face red with wrath, poured out a full glass of scotch and drank it down in two quick swallows.

Richmond stopped halfway back to Greenwood, led his mount off the road and rode a short distance out into the quiet countryside to a place of solitude, and there sat for some time and wept for his neighbor.

Seventy-Nine

*W*hen Richmond arrived back at Greenwood, Seth, Thomas, Cherity, and Chigua were just returning from Mr. Brown's. They were excited and all talking at once, though had no progress to report toward locating the small pile of stones Mr. Brown had spoken of. But they remained optimistic.

To their flurry of questions, Brown himself only returned a knowing, but silent smile. He knew, even from their uncertainties, that they would be successful in the end. He did not want to spoil the enthusiasm of discovery by giving them more information than absolutely necessary.

"How did you measure the halfway distance between the parts of the triangle?" Richmond asked.

"By pacing them off," replied Seth.

"Not the most accurate of methods, over such uneven terrain."

"What else could we do?" asked Thomas.

"Perhaps you need to measure hundred-foot lengths of rope and try to get a more precise measurement. Failing that, we might have to get some surveying equipment."

"I think we could do it by means of rope, Dad," rejoined Seth. "What we really need to do is stretch a straight line between the points of the triangle, to make sure we do indeed have a straight line. If we are even a foot or two off, we might never find those stones. But that would take a half mile of rope!"

It took several more visits to the Brown tract with all the rope they could tie together—and by now Sydney and Richmond were involved and had summoned the full strength of their deductive and engineering powers—to run straight lines between the points of the triangle at the hearth, the stone, and the tree, and to compute the midpoints and again to run straight lines from them to the opposite corners of the triangle. After three days, they were convinced they were close. Brown himself was now accompanying them and enjoying the adventure immensely, though continued to keep his own counsel.

They had narrowed their search to a thirty-by thirty-foot section of a pine wood some three eighths of a mile up the hill from Mr. Brown's former home. However, no pile of stones was to be seen amid the grass and moss and accumulated humus of many years, and no amount of entreaty would induce Brown to give so much as a hint by word or gesture whether they were on the right track. Eventually they took everyone to the site with them—Carolyn and the Shaws and the rest of the LeFleures. The entire company stretched out together hand in hand across the clearing, then sunk to their hands and knees and began creeping across the forest floor, feeling and probing and digging with hands and fingers as they went over every inch of the ground. As he watched, Brown could hardly contain himself with surpressed merriment.

At last it was thirteen-year-old Laylie LeFleure who shouted, "Here's some rocks under the grass!"

They all swarmed around, and as they helped her frantically clear away the vegetation, more stones became visible. The more they pulled off the pile, the more were revealed below.

All afternoon the men worked, hauling away the stones as they found themselves going steadily deeper on a slant into the side of the hill. There could be no doubt that they had at last discovered the tunnel leading to Mr. Brown's secret cave.

When at last an opening was cleared and the rocks from inside, some sizeable, removed, Seth and Thomas and Cherity were all beside themselves with eagerness to be the first to crawl in. The Southern gentlemanly spirit—though reluctantly!—prevailed. Cherity got down on her stomach and wriggled out of sight, followed by Thomas, then Seth. To the onlookers it was indeed a strange sight, but certain confirmation that they had indeed discovered something incredible, for within seconds all three sets of legs disappeared and all they could hear were muffled sounds coming from the black hole they had excavated.

Twenty or more seconds passed. Richmond, Carolyn, Sydney, Chigua, Aaron, Isaac, and Sydney's two sons Milos and Darel and daughter Laylie all knelt listening at the opening.

"It's pitch black!" at last came Seth's voice echoing back toward them. "We can't see a thing! Get a lantern from the house!"

Ten minutes later, a lit lantern was being shoved into the hole.

"In you go, Isaac!" said Richmond.

Now Isaac scooted inside, followed by his brother along with Darel and Milos. Richmond and Carolyn, and Sydney and Chigua and Laylie were at last left alone outside on either side of Mr. Brown.

When Isaac's face became visible where Cherity, Seth, and Thomas sat in the dark, shoving the lantern in ahead of him, the sight that the flickering flame illuminated was nothing short of spectacular. They all gazed around with silent awe at the cave which had opened to a room of seven or eight feet high and probably twelve feet across.

Curious but willing to wait rather than go in themselves, Richmond and Sydney sat listening to the far-off muffled echoes from inside. Finally they heard movement, and a few seconds later Seth's head appeared as he crawled back out to join them.

"Look at this, Dad!" he said, shoving a small but heavy metal box in front of him as he came. It was about six inches by four inches and some three inches in height and appeared to be made of some non-corrosive material, mostly brass judging from the green stains, though some of the fittings looked to be of silver. Richmond knelt down but could hardly pick it up. He left it on the ground and lifted the lid. The box was full of gold nuggets of varying size, from tiny pebbles up to some an inch in diameter.

"Amazing!" exclaimed Richmond. He turned toward Brown, who was smiling broadly, at his side. "So there really is Cherokee gold!"

Brown only nodded, still smiling, too full of emotion to find words by which to respond.

"There must be fifteen or more boxes just like this one," said Seth, "as well as a dozen or more leather bags filled with gold powder. There is a *lot* of gold. Some of the leather isn't in very good shape, but the bags are still intact. And there are other things—containers of shells and flints and bone necklaces and stones—some of them look like jewelry but I only looked hurriedly. There are feathers, a few old leather vests and jackets, quite a few woven baskets and blankets that don't appear to be in great condition, as well as ornaments and bracelets and necklaces. What should we do now?"

Seth glanced back and forth between his father and Mr. Brown. Richmond looked toward their venerable friend.

"Now that the young people have had their fun and made their discovery," he said, "you must give us your instructions of what you want done. Do you . . . ?"

"Want to go inside myself?" said Brown, chuckling as he completed the sentence himself. "Only if you will join me! But speaking for myself, I do not think it would be possible to do now what I did with such ease thirty years ago. No, if you and your friends can remove everything with care, young Davidson," he said to Seth, "I am happy to observe from here."

"You and the others must handle everything with extreme caution," said Richmond.

"Cherity is standing guard!" laughed Seth.

"One of the first things we need to do," said Richmond, "is get the gold down to the house—today. Word about this will spread— it always does. No matter what precautions we take to secrecy, word will get out. The very trees have ears! Once the gold is safe, you will want to go through the relics," he said, turning again to Brown, "and pack them up and preserve them for transport back to Oklahoma."

"Most should still be packed in blankets and leather skins," nodded Brown, "as it was brought to me from the South."

As he spoke, Brown's expression became thoughtful and serious. "Although now that this long-awaited moment has finally come," he said, "what ought to be the final disposition of these treasures of our people is a question I must consider with great care."

Eighty

That same evening, after they had bathed and cleaned up from their exploration of the cave, Seth and Cherity walked out into the warm twilight spreading over Greenwood. A large full moon was just rising above the horizon. It was difficult to contain their enthusiasm over the events of the day.

"How I wish my father could have been part of this!" said Cherity. "But then," she added a little sadly, "perhaps it is better this way. He was not altogether at peace with his Cherokee roots because of how his parents were killed, and also his concern for me and my sisters."

Seth took Cherity's hand as they went, feeling at the gold ring on her middle finger. "Your father's ring is swimming around on your finger!" he laughed.

"It is far too big for me," smiled Cherity. "But I want to wear it for my father's sake. I should probably hang it around my neck like Chigua does hers."

They walked for a minute or two in silence, enjoying the quiet evening, but both enjoying most of all simply being in the other's presence.

"It is still hard for me to understand why my father did not eventually tell me everything himself," said Cherity at length.

"Even after what Mr. Brown explained happened in Oklahoma?"

"That man called Black Wolf would hardly have harmed me in Boston."

"But your father knew the danger was still real."

"I know."

"He did what he thought best. And . . ."

Seth hesitated.

"And what?"

"There is one part of that last conversation I had with your father that I did not tell you," said Seth.

"About my Cherokee past?" asked Cherity.

"No . . . about you and me. He also—," began Seth, then hesitated again.

"He, uh . . . had a favor to ask of me," he added.

"A . . . favor?"

"I don't know how this will sound to you, but . . . he asked me to promise to take care of you after he was gone—"

A rush of warmth surged into Cherity face.

"I have tried to do that," Seth went on, fumbling for words, "but then the war came and I was gone and we were apart those three and a half years. But . . . I think it is now time, and with all this behind us . . . and Mr. Brown and everything sort of setting the past to rest . . . the time now seems right, and . . . I want to take care of you even more completely than I have up till now. What I am trying to say, Cherity, is that I love you. I don't want us ever to be apart again."

Cherity sighed and leaned against Seth's side as they walked. He slipped his hand out of hers and stretched his arm around her shoulders and they continued on into the dusk.

From inside the house, Carolyn stood watching as her son and the young woman she loved as her own walked away from the house.

She heard Richmond approach behind her. They stood in silence a moment.

"Well, wife," he said in a playful tone, "what is that brain of yours pondering?"

"I am wondering if we are soon to have two new daughters, one black and one half Cherokee."

"Do you know something about Thomas and Deanna that I don't?" smiled Richmond.

"Only that I have seen a look on his face when letters come from her that is unmistakable. You must have seen the love in her eyes when she was here. She was obviously devoted to him. And I think the feeling is mutual. Cherity insists Thomas is in love with Deanna too."

"You and Cherity talk about whether Thomas and Deanna are in love with each other!" laughed Richmond.

"Richmond, surely you know that women always talk about such things!"

"Then do you also talk about whether Seth and Cherity are in love?"

Carolyn smiled. "Cherity is quieter and more reserved about her feelings toward Seth. But of course they are in love. Everyone knows it, the two of them most of all. They are just waiting for the right time. Now that the war is over and Mr. Brown has come back and all the mysteries of the past are laid to rest, I have the feeling that time may not be too far away."

"We are indeed blessed that our sons have both chosen so wisely."

"Cherity and Deanna are remarkable young women. I have come to love Cherity as a daughter. I think in time we will feel the same way about Deanna. I could not imagine our good fortune to have Aaron and Zaphorah's daughter actually in our family, if it indeed comes to that. What a dream come true!"

"I still say we may be getting a little ahead of ourselves!" laughed Richmond again.

"Didn't you say Thomas was planning another trip to Mount Holly next week?"

"I think so."

"And Seth said something about Thomas visiting the jeweler the last time they were in town. Seth just laughed about it, but I have my suspicions!"

Eighty-One

*W*ith the gold and other relics retrieved from their crypt and safely in storage at Greenwood, and after Richmond's tense encounter with Denton Beaumont, both Richmond and Brown now considered any potential danger from that quarter minimal. Supplied with every necessity by Carolyn, and brought more food than one man could possibly consume once or twice a day by the loving ministrations of Carolyn, Cherity, and Chigua, Brown, therefore, removed himself again to his former abode. There, he said, it was time for him to complete and bring to a close what had been a happy chapter in his long life.

Everyone at Greenwood urged him to remain with them indefinite-ly, for the rest of his life if it were possible. Here, the women especially felt, he might be cared for and loved through his old age and beyond.

But in their hearts of hearts, they all realized that his present tarry-ing in Virginia was destined like his last to be but a temporary season in the ever-changing life of the Cherokee Wise Man, for whom no earthly place would ever quite fully be home. He was a sojourner of the Ani-Yunwiya . . . a people of ever-changing paths and byways under an unchanging sky.

Brown remained with them though the summer. Occasionally they saw him daily, occasionally a week would pass without contact. He helped with the harvest and the animals, borrowed horses for long rides into the hills, and he and Richmond continued to have lengthy talks about many things. But as the morning air began to take on a crisper chill, and as a few yellowing leaves began to fall on flurries that portended stronger gusts to follow, Richmond saw that a change was coming. He knew he would not be with them much longer.

A day came when Brown appeared at Greenwood bearing an envelope containing a single sheet. He left it at the door with Moses without word or explanation. It was an invitation, for the next day, to a traditional Cherokee meal at his former home. It was addressed to Richmond and Carolyn, Seth and Cherity, Thomas, and Sydney and Chigua. The moment they saw it, all knew this was his way of saying good-bye.

They entered the house the following evening in a spirit of solemn expectation tinged with sad expectation of what was to follow. The simple meal was set out on cloth mats on the floor. There were no chairs. Attired again in the full regalia of his ancestors, with the white feather prominent, Brown greeted each of his guests with a kiss on the cheek, then bade them sit on the floor in a circle.

"I came among you," he said as they slowly ate, "not knowing what I would find. My chief mission was to retrieve those things I had hidden many years before. Yet as I came, on my mind also was the future, and what should be done with them for the good of our people. The events which drove me from the Indian Territory spoke of evil times which are not yet resolved. As I journeyed, therefore, my heart was torn. It has remained torn for the conflicts among us which refuse to die.

"When I arrived here I discovered, if possible, new friends that mean as much, if not more, than the friends of past generations I left behind."

He gazed slowly around the circle, allowing his eyes to linger upon each one in his or her turn. To both Cherity and Chigua he gave a smile of such love that melted both their hearts and brought tears flowing from their eyes.

"And thus, while here among you," he went on, "and because of the continuing heritage of the Cherokee that I know will live on here after I am gone, I have at last reached my decision. With that decision, I am at peace and can now return to my people, where it is my destiny not long hence to be gathered to my fathers."

At the words, a stifled cry sounded from Cherity. She looked away and did her best to stop the tears, which had become a flood, with her handkerchief.

"My decision is this," Brown went on after a brief pause. "The gold is to remain here."

"But surely . . . it belongs to your people," said Seth.

"What you say is true, young Davidson," rejoined Brown. "But it would only divide our nation further. Even to attempt to do good with it, as I always intended, would result in greed and conflict and lead to further bloodshed. Though it breaks my heart to say it, we are not a nation yet ready for unity. It would be unsafe to take it back, even now. This is perhaps more than anything the answer you put to me earlier, why I did not return for it before now. The time was not right."

Brown gazed deep into the eyes of each of the seven.

"It is no accident that you are all now here," he said softly, almost reverently. "Fate and the higher powers of Providence have brought us together at this moment and ordained that we should meet. As there were once seven rings, there are now seven of you, which I believe has been guided by forces higher than any of us. Whether it be the Christian God of the white man or the Great Spirit of the Indian, it was He who guided our steps to this moment."

Again he turned one at a time to Cherity and then to Chigua.

"You two young ladies bear two of the rings and represent two of Attacullaculla's four lines, the Canoe line and the Kingfisher line of the Ghigua. To you history has entrusted what I stored away long ago for our people. Therefore, I desire for *you*, and these witnesses who are with you, to use it in whatever ways you determine that will benefit the legacy of the Cherokee nation."

Cherity and Chigua sat silently pondering his words.

"This, therefore, is my decree," Brown went on. "All the relics will be returned to the tribe. We will together determine how to transport them and I will have to take steps to ensure their preservation. As for the gold . . . both of you young ladies were separated from your families and your Indian heritage. Yet Providence has shone its light upon you favorably and has protected you in the midst of much adversity. I believe you were both *chosen* to inherit the rings of your forebears. And . . . perhaps you were also chosen to step into the destiny of your people in other ways as well.

"Therefore, half of the gold that I put away is to be split equally between you three families—the Waters, the family of Eaglefeather, and also the Davidsons, for to you the Cherokee owe a great debt. You will split this half between the three families. It is yours to use. The remaining half I entrust to you seven together on behalf of the Cherokee nation, to purchase land for our people—either in the Indian Territory or in the East where a few settlers remain. Wherever you are best able to do good for our people, use this legacy I bestow upon you to do that good."

None of the seven had words suitable to reply. The voice of Long Canoe had spoken. They knew they could only receive his words with quiet gratitude, and then faithfully obey.

Eighty-Two

*B*rown left Virginia four days later. This time he would not return.

The parting on the Dove's Landing platform was tearful. He and Richmond held one another's gaze for long silent seconds of mutual respect and affection.

"The land and the house are yours," said Brown at length, "as I arranged with your father. I shall not set foot upon or within them again. You were faithful in awaiting my return, but that debt is now fully discharged. Do with both as you will."

Brown then embraced Carolyn, shook Thomas's and Sydney's hands, then turned to Seth and Cherity where they stood.

"Young Davidson," he said, "care for this treasure of yours."

Seth nodded.

"To you and her is entrusted much. You must protect yourselves that you may carry out that trust. May God go with you."

He looked at Seth, took two steps forward and clasped him by both arms, then added a few words that none of the others heard.

Brown then turned to Chigua and took her two hands in his.

"Granddaughter of Eaglefeather," he said, "may the spirit of our people be your constant companion, guide, and strength. Wear the ring proudly, and pass on to your children the story of our people, and the legacy of peace that accompanies the ring."

Chigua smiled, wiping at her eyes as she stepped back.

Finally Brown turned toward Cherity and smiled, a deep, sad, tender smile that was full of love.

"And you, daughter of Swift Horse—"

Cherity burst into tears and rushed forward to embrace the old man whom in a short time she had grown to love. Gently he stretched his long arms around her and held her close for several long silent seconds. Tenderly he stroked her hair and whispered his blessing into her ear, as Cherity quietly wept against his chest.

At last she stood back and drew in a deep breath, her eyes swimming but a smile on her face.

"Thank you," she said. "Thank you for taking care of my father. . . . Thank you for everything."

The sound of the train whistle interrupted them.

"I must be away, my child," said Brown, his voice husky with suppressed Indian emotion.

"Thank you . . . again," said Cherity.

"Carry your father's legacy proudly, daughter of Swift Horse."

"I will, Uncle Long Canoe . . . I promise. I will never forget you."

Richmond now stepped forward and walked with Brown, dressed for the journey not unlike any aging tan-faced farmer of Virginia, the final few steps to the waiting train door. Brown took one last glance around, then stepped up and inside.

With a final wave a minute later, and with tears spilling from Cherity's and Carolyn's and Chigua's eyes, they followed the train out of the station until it was out of sight.

As they rode in silence back to Greenwood Cherity realized that her entire sense of being had been altered in the two months her great-uncle had been with them. So much was now clear. Her spirit was quiet as she tried to absorb the change. Feelings she had had since childhood but had never been able to identify now made sense.

The greatest change of all was getting accustomed to two new names. She was now *Cherokee* Michel Waters *Brown*.

After his arrival back in the Cherokee Territory of Oklahoma, Long Canoe Brown entered upon a period of deep reflection.

Now that he had passed on his legacy to worthy descendents, he knew that his days among his people were slowly drawing to an end. The time when he would be gathered to his fathers was approaching like a slow dusk settling down upon his earthly life.

He had concluded a portion of his duty. It now remained for him to pass on the other four rings in his possession. He was old and getting older. As the great chief Attacullaculla and the Ghigua before him, he must now seek worthy young Cherokee who valued and honored the old ways.

He took to long walks and traveling throughout the territory, thinking, watching, listening, and especially speaking with many young people about the old times, as well as about the future of the Cherokee people. He met with John Ross when he returned west and continued to exercise what influence he possessed to work toward a reconciliation between the chief and Stand Watie, his longtime friend.

When he was laid to rest three years later, his own and the other three rings were in the hands of four young Cherokee, three men and one woman, to whom he had entrusted their legacy.

As the six rings were passed on, however, the seventh was never found. And division remained in the Cherokee nation awaiting a future time when the spirit of the red feather would be buried forever and unity would reign within the hearts of the Cherokee people.

Eighty-Three

Seth and Cherity were married in October of 1865 at Greenwood. The Steddings family came to Virginia for the wedding. Rarely had guests to Greenwood been received with more rejoicing.

After his year-long hiatus, Seth realized that he missed photography. With Cherity's encouragement, he wrote to Mr. McClarin to ask if his offer still stood. Receiving an enthusiastic reply, he and Cherity traveled to Boston and for the next several years spent a good deal of time in Massachusetts and traveling throughout the country under the auspices of the *Herald*, photographing the continued growth of the country.

Thomas and Deanna were married in Mount Holly the following spring of the year 1866. The entire Greenwood family of Shaws, LeFleures, and Davidsons took the train north for the festive occasion which took place at the newly built home of Aaron and Zaphorah Steddings.

The newlyweds located for a time at Greenwood, where, with Seth and Cherity gone much of the time, Thomas worked with Sydney and his father. Within two or three years the plantation was as prosperous as ever, and able to offer good paying jobs to most Negroes who wanted them, whether from the area or traveling through. Though the Underground Railroad was no longer in operation, Greenwood's reputation had spread so wide, with so many blacks having spent a night or two there on their travels, that for many years thereafter, transient blacks continued to appear, often hoping simply for a night's lodging, sometimes asking for food, and occasionally hoping to find work. It was one of the greatest blessings of Richmond and Carolyn's later years that they never had to turn anyone away, and were always able to offer work to the willing.

Thomas too had felt what Richmond had noticed, that he was more at peace with himself in the North. He knew that wherever they went, as a white man with a black wife, they were sure to face prejudice and condemnation. It was obvious from looks cast their way whenever they went into Dove's Landing. But it would likely be less in the North, and it would be there that they would be most able to live a normal life.

Thomas continued to contemplate and pray about his dream. After more discussion with his father, he enrolled in the Philadelphia College of Physicians. By the time of his graduation three years later, he and Deanna had a daughter, with another child on the way. They settled in Mount Holly, where, before many more years, Dr. Thomas Davidson was known and loved by everyone for miles around. No longer under his brother's or his father's shadow, whenever his family came to visit, they had only to identify themselves as Dr. Davidson's brother, or Dr. Davidson's father or Dr. Davidson's mother, and instantly smiles and welcoming greetings spread across the faces of perfect strangers. It warmed Carolyn's heart to see how respected and loved her youngest son had become in the Quaker community.

Thomas's decision to relocate to Mount Holly, along with the realization that they were gradually tiring of travel, eventually brought Seth and Cherity back to Greenwood. By now with a considerable reputation following him, Seth retired from professional photography, though kept up on the latest developments and continued as an amateur photographer for the rest of his life. Much to Carolyn's delight over the next seven years, two sons and two daughters were born to them.

Seth and Cherity had visited Veronica and Richard every time their travels took them to Washington, and continued to keep in touch. Veronica became a nurse and was greatly loved everywhere her caring hands ministered to the sick. She and Richard had two daughters.

Thomas and Deanna eventually became father and mother to seven children to carry on the two proud family lines.

Mr. Brown's gold was distributed according to his wishes. In 1866 when land in Kansas was opened for sale, Seth and Cherity and Sydney and Chigua traveled to Kansas together, fulfilling Cherity's own dream of returning to the place of her girlhood fancies, as well as Chigua's to connect again with her ancestry. There they purchased five thousand acres in southern Kansas which they gave to the Cherokee tribe. After extensive searching in the area in and around Bluejacket, Chigua found several cousins, as well as one uncle and two aunts who had known her grandfather.

Word eventually came that Cameron Beaumont had been shot and killed while attempting a bank robbery in Missouri.

Denton Beaumont died a few years later of unknown causes.

After his father's death, Wyatt Beaumont attempted to run operations at Oakbriar for a time though he did not enjoy the work. Less and less of Oakbriar's land was cultivated and the place gradually ran down. Eventually Wyatt gave up the plantation for politics. He ran for Congress representing Virginia and in time became one of the state's leading democratic politicians, while secretly also rising in the leadership of the Ku Klux Klan. With Washington as the center of his activities, and facing desperate financial pressure at Oakbriar, he finally offered the property for sale.

Seth and Cherity and Chigua had been keeping the rest of their portion of the Brown money for some purpose. They now put it to use to fulfill an idea they hoped he would approve of and be proud of. They bought Oakbriar for the purpose of establishing a home and school for displaced black and native Indian children. They also hoped to turn the plantation around into a profit-making venture again where, as at Greenwood, any man or woman willing to work could find a job. It was an ambitious dream. But with the LeFleures and

Shaws initially overseeing the operation, word began to spread about
their work, and people brought children in need to them, and they
slowly began to reclaim the fields and bring the plantation back to
life. Leon Riggs was hired as the man who knew more about Oakbriar
than anyone, and he and Sydney became close friends.

And now, as third owners of a large Virginia plantation with
land they could pass on to their children, Chigua and Sydney had
indeed risen high from the days of their affliction. The stately son of
a Jamaican plantation owner was a landowner again. He had always
walked tall and proud since escaping the bonds of slavery. All who
knew him recognized, like Joseph of old, sold into foreign chains by
his brothers, that he was a man in whom the mettle of character had
grown strong in the furnace of suffering, preparing him for a higher
destiny than his captors could ever have imagined.

Scully Riggs returned to Dove's Landing with a Washington D.C.
nurse as his bride. He bought the lumberyard near the train station,
where he had worked for years.

Though still a young man, Richard Fitzpatrick retired from government work. He and Veronica had been discussing the advantages to
their daughters of a slower paced country environment, now regretting
that Oakbriar had passed out of the family. Lady Daphne, who had
lived with them in Washington since the death of Veronica's father,
as much as she had once longed for the city life, could not think of
anything she would rather do than return to Virginia.

Richmond and Carolyn heard of their wish to return to the country
and immediately set their minds revolving on possibilities. The one
drawback to the project at Oakbriar had till then been finding capable
teachers and staff. They set the matter before Richard and Veronica,
whether Veronica would consider being the matron of the orphan-
age, and whether Richard would want to assume partial oversight
of Oakbriar's farming operations with Sydney, and in time, if they
chose, also to buy into the ownership of the cooperative venture. They
would be free to live at Oakbriar without cost as if it were theirs, and
share in the profits of what was produced. Within a year Veronica and

Lady Daphne were back in their old home. Richard took quickly to plantation work, and the joint operation of the two adjacent plantations, with what was still called the Brown tract between them, under the oversight of Richmond, Seth, Sydney, Richard, and Leon Riggs became the envy of central Virginia. Isaac and Aaron Shaw remained, both married, and eventually became foremen for the two plantations. Veronica's two daughters became avid horsewomen and often went riding with Seth and Cherity's girls.

It was clear that Lady Daphne found it trying to have dark-skinned children underfoot everywhere in the once proud old Southern plantation house. And the commotion was often a little too much for her. But the *life* of the place did her good. If she were not yet color-blind, the fact that the children were did her soul good in the end. There are those to whom only a single talent is given, and from them, perhaps, less is expected.

Veronica, on the other hand, thrived. She took the children to her heart and to them she became the mother many of them had lost. Though Nancy was on hand as a black mother, and Chigua was at Oakbriar most days as a Cherokee mother, Veronica remained the favorite of most, for it was she who tucked the younger ones in most nights and came to soothe away their nightmares in the darkness with soft lullabies at their bedside. She was one of those rare souls, so dear to the Father's heart, who truly *change* and grow toward life's good, who perhaps had only been given two talents, but who in the end gave him back four in return. She and Cherity remained dear friends, and, when their involved schedules would permit, were often seen riding out in the hills together.

Eighty-Four

$\mathcal{A}$ black lady appeared one day at Greenwood, alone and having apparently walked all the way from town. As she trudged up to the front of the house carrying a single carpetbag, the sweat on her face might have been from a much longer walk. She had taken a journey similar to that which many in years past had traveled on foot. She, however, had come most of the way by train.

She walked onto the porch, dropped her bag, and knocked on the door. It was Cherity who answered it.

"Dis be da place dey call Greenwood?" said their strange visitor.

"Yes it is," answered Cherity, now thirty-one.

The lady let out a long sigh of relief. "Dat's da bes' news I heard all day!" she said. "I cum a long way an' I's too old ter be trab'lin' so far. I don' reckon you git many railroad visitors dese days, but duz you maybe hab room for an' old black woman wif no place else ter go who remembers dat railroad dat took a heap er folks ter freedom?"

"Of course!" smiled Cherity. "We always have room. Won't you come in and—"

Just then Carolyn joined them from inside the house. Her hair was graying, for she had recently turned sixty, but her smile was more radiant than ever.

"Carolyn!" said Cherity excitedly. "The railroad is back in business! We have a visitor."

Carolyn stepped forward and held out her hand. "Welcome to Greenwood," she said. "I am Carolyn Davidson. You may stay as long as you need to. Where are you going?"

"Well, I sent so many people through here when I wuz a stashun mistress, I figgered it wuz time fo' me ter git on dat railroad an' ter my sister's in da Norf afore everyone forgot an' I had no more places ter stay."

"Surely you did not walk all this way!" said Carolyn in surprise.

"I cum by train moster da way. But I knew where da stashuns wuz, an' I speshully knew 'bout dis place here on account er lots er folks dat cum back tol' me 'bout it. An' dere's one young lady I wants ter see agin an' I's hopin' you kin tell me where she got to. Her name's Lucindy."

"Lucindy!" exclaimed Carolyn. "Of course we can! It's not much farther from here. How do you know Lucindy?"

"She cum from da plantashun where I wuz. I's Amaritta . . . Amaritta Beacham."

"Well, Amaritta, you just come in and rest," said Carolyn, taking her hand as Cherity picked up her carpetbag. "We have a room that is just waiting for you."

It happened that Thomas and Deanna and their first daughter were visiting Greenwood at the time.

Five days later, Amaritta was sitting on Greenwood's front porch, fanning herself in the heat and gradually feeling rested from her long trip, but in no hurry to leave this idyllic setting. She had already come to realize why she kept hearing about the place called Greenwood through the years, and why they said angels watched over it.

A little three-year-old girl ran out of the house, saw her sitting there, turned and ran toward her, then scampered up into her lap.

"Tell me yo' name agin, honey chile?" asked Amaritta.

"I'm Hannah Steddings," she replied. "Would you tell me a story, Grandma Amaritta?"

"I's reckon I cud do dat."

Little Hannah snuggled down in the huge lap and waited.

"It wuz a long, long time ago," Amaritta began. "Dis big land wuz as fresh as spring. It wuz a mighty big land wif green mountains an' clean ribers an' everythin' good dat you cud ermagine. An' dere were people who lived here too. Dey wuz called Indians. But da good Lord saw dat dey needed frien's. So he put it inter da hearts er people ober da sea, kings an' common folk, dat here wuz a land where all people cud live together, whatever da color er dere skin. So folks started ter cum, dey did—w'ite folks an' black folks, sons an' daughters er kings. An' dey wuz kings wif black skin an' w'ite skin an' brown skin like yours. An' dey came from da lan' er ribers, ter dis lan' dat had even bigger ribers runnin' wiff clean clear water. Duz you know what da water in dose ribers wuz called, chile?"

"No, what, Grandma Amaritta?"

"Dey wuz called da waters er freedom, chile."

From an open upstairs window, Carolyn Davidson stood listening with tears in her eyes as Amaritta told the story of America so simply that her own little granddaughter could understand it.

Behind her, two young women saw her and approached quietly. They also heard Amaritta's voice from below and did not want to disturb the story. Carolyn heard them walking softly up behind her. She glanced back, smiled, and stretched out her arms and pulled both of her sons' wives to her, the one a Cherokee, the other a Negro.

How blessed they were, Carolyn thought, to be able to know such love between the races in a single family. She prayed that her grandchildren never noticed that they were of different colors.

Cherity and Deanna leaned their heads against the shoulders of this wonderful woman they loved so much and listened to the story from the porch below.

"Well, folks came, an' dey lived wiff dose Indians dat wuz here before," Amaritta continued to Deanna's little daughter. "But sum er dose folks forgot 'bout dose waters er freedom, an' dey did terrible things ter dere brothers an' sisters. But everybody didn't forgit dat dream er freedom, folks like dese folks dat live here—dey didn't forgit, an' so finally dat dream cum true when folks cud be free an' all live together like it is here. Now, chile, it ain't like dis everywhere, no sir! Dere's still folks dat habn't taken a good drink er dose waters yet. But one day, dis whole country'll be like it is here, an' den maybe one day da whole worl'. Least dat's what God's got in mind, I reckon. Dat's God's dream an' effen he's dreamin' it, den it's gwine happen one day. But till den, we's jes' all gotter do our part ter live dat freedom dream where he puts us. Dat's what I tried ter do where I wuz. An' it seems ter me dat he put you in a right good an' happy place, 'cause da waters from dose ol' ribers—they's jes' springin' up all ober roun' here!"

The American Dreams Series

Best-selling author Michael Phillips brings
readers an epic series of love and sacrifice leading
up to the turbulent Civil War.

CP0001

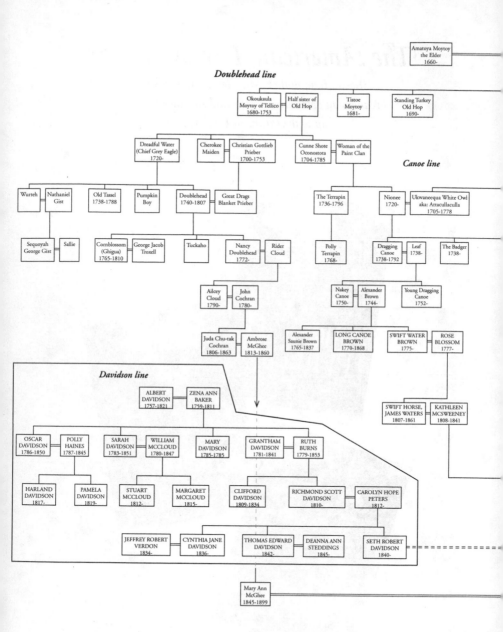

All capitalized names are fictional characters

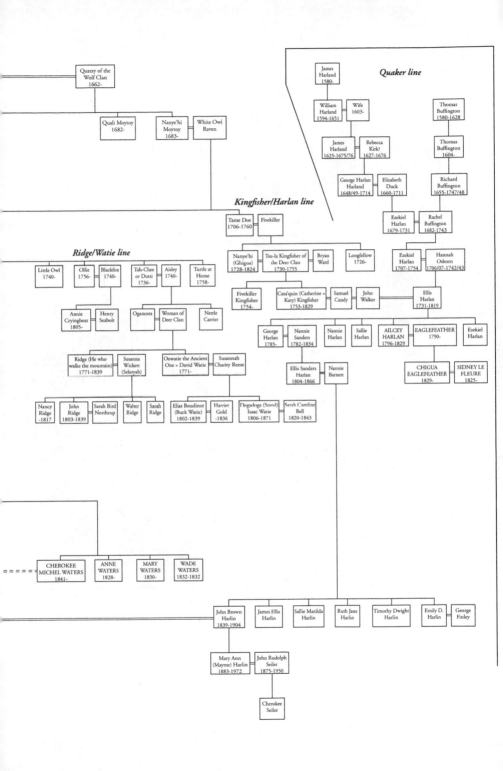

Quaker line

Kingfisher/Harlan line

Ridge/Watie line

Quatsy of the Wolf Clan 1662-

Quali Moytoy 1682-

Nanye'hi Moytoy 1683-

White Owl Raven

James Harland 1580-

William Harland 1594-1651 — Wife 1603-

James Harland 1625-1675/76 — Rebecca Kirk? 1627-1676

George Harlan Harland 1648/49-1714 — Elizabeth Duck 1660-1711

Thomas Buffington 1580-1628

Thomas Buffington 1604-

Richard Buffington 1655-1747/48

Ezekiel Harlan 1679-1731 — Rachel Buffington 1682-1743

Tame Doe 1706-1760 — Fivekiller

Nanye'hi (Ghigua) 1728-1824 — Tsu-la Kingfisher of the Deer Clan 1730-1755 — Bryan Ward

Longfellow 1726-

Ezekiel Harlan 1707-1754 — Hannah Osborn 1706/07-1742/43

Little Owl 1740-

Ollie 1756-

Blackfox 1740-

Tah-Chee or Dutsi 1736-

Aisley 1740-

Turtle at Home 1758-

Fivekiller Kingfisher 1754-

Cata'quin (Catherine = Katy) Kingfisher 1753-1829 — Samuel Candy — John Walker

Ellis Harlan 1731-1819

Annie Cryingbear 1805- — Henry Seabolt

Oganosta

Woman of Deer Clan

Nettle Carrier

George Harlan 1785-

Nannie Sanders 1782-1834

Nannie Harlan

Sallie Harlan

AILCEY HARLAN 1796-1829

EAGLEFEATHER 1790-

Ezekiel Harlan

Ridge (He who walks the mountain) 1771-1839 — Susanna Wickett (Sehoyah)

Oowatie the Ancient One = David Watie 1771- — Susannah Charity Reese

Ellis Sanders Harlan 1804-1866 — Nannie Barnett

CHIGUA EAGLEFEATHER 1829-

SIDNEY LE FLEURE 1825-

Nancy Ridge -1817

John Ridge 1803-1839

Sarah Bird Northrup

Walter Ridge

Sarah Ridge

Elias Boudinot (Buck Watie) 1802-1839 — Harriet Gold -1836

Degadoga (Stand) Isaac Watie 1806-1871 — Sarah Caroline Bell 1820-1843

= = = = = CHEROKEE MICHEL WATERS 1841-

ANNE WATERS 1828-

MARY WATERS 1830-

WADE WATERS 1832-1832

John Brown Harlin 1839-1904

James Ellis Harlin

Sallie Matilda Harlin

Ruth Jane Harlin

Timothy Dwight Harlin

Emily D. Harlin — George Finley

Mary Ann (Mayme) Harlin 1883-1972 — John Rudolph Seiler 1875-1950

Cherokee Seiler

TAKE A SECOND LOOK!

FIND OUT WHAT THOUSANDS OF
READERS HAVE ALREADY DISCOVERED!

CP0017

If you have enjoyed the

American Dreams series,

you will also enjoy the author's other best-selling series:

THE SECRET OF THE ROSE

SHENANDOAH SISTERS

CAROLINA COUSINS

THE JOURNALS OF CORRIE BELLE HOLLISTER

THE TRILOGY AND LEGACY OF STONEWYCKE

THE SECRETS OF HEATHERSLEIGH HALL

RIFT IN TIME AND HIDDEN IN TIME

CALEDONIA

Information on all Michael Phillips' titles, his work to expand awareness of and increase the availability of the books of nineteenth century Scotsman George MacDonald, as well as details concerning the publication of *Leben*, a magazine dedicated to bold thinking Christianity, the spiritual vision of Michael Phillips, and the legacy of George MacDonald, may be found at www.macdonaldphillips.com or by writing to the author c/o:

P.O. Box 7003
Eureka, CA 95502
U.S.A.

have you visited tyndalefiction.com lately?

Only there can you find:

→ books hot off the press
→ first chapter excerpts
→ inside scoops on your favorite authors
→ author interviews
→ contests
→ fun facts
→ and much more!

Sign up for your **free** newsletter!

Visit us today at: **tyndalefiction.com**

Tyndale fiction does more than entertain.

→ *It touches the heart.*
→ *It stirs the soul.*
→ *It changes lives.*

That's why Tyndale is so committed to being first in fiction!

TYNDALE FICTION

CP0021